CommunicationCounts

Getting It Right in College and Life

David Worley
Indiana State University

Debra Worley
Indiana State University

Laura Soldner
Northern Michigan University

PEARSON

Boston   New York   San Francisco
Mexico City   Montreal   Toronto   London   Madrid   Munich   Paris
Hong Kong   Singapore   Tokyo   Cape Town   Sydney

Editor-in-Chief: Karon Bowers

Assistant Editor: Jenny Lupica

Editorial Assistant: Jessica Cabana

Marketing Manager: Suzan Czajkowski

Production Editor: Claudine Bellanton

Editorial Production Service: Progressive Publishing Alternatives

Composition Buyer: Linda Cox

Manufacturing Buyer: JoAnne Sweeney

Electronic Composition: Progressive Publishing Alternatives

Interior Design: Gina Hagen

Photo Researcher: Naomi Rudov

Cover Administrator: Linda Knowles

Cover Designer: Susan Paradise

For related titles and support materials,
visit our online catalog at www.ablongman.com

Between the time website information is gathered and then published, it is not
unusual for some sites to have closed. Also, the transcription of URLs can result in
typographical errors. The publisher would appreciate notification where these
errors occur so that they may be corrected in subsequent editions.

Library of Congress Cataloging-in-Publication Data
Worley, David.
    Communication counts: getting it right in college and life / David Worley,
Debra Worley, Laura Soldner.
        p. cm.
    Includes bibliographical references and index.
    ISBN-13:   978-0-205-56468-2 (pbk.)
    ISBN-10:   0-205-56468-2 (pbk.)
  1. Communication in education.   2. Interpersonal communication.
  3. Universities and colleges. I. Worley, Debra. II. Soldner, Laura. III. Title.

  LB1033.5.W665 2007
  370.1'4--dc22

                                                                2007027307
Printed in the United States of America

10 9 8 7 6 5 4 3 2 1 RRD-OH 11 10 09 08 07
Credits appear on page 331, which constitutes an extension of the copyright page.

BriefContents

UNIT ONE   Essential Communication Elements

1   Appreciating and Understanding
    Human Communication   1

2   Communicating Ethically and Competently   24

3   Perception: Self, Others, and Communication   43

4   Effective Listening   65

5   Verbal Communication/Language   87

6   Nonverbal Communication   107

UNIT TWO   Interpersonal Communication

7   Understanding Interpersonal
    Communication   127

8   Applying Interpersonal Communication:
    Principles and Practice   154

UNIT THREE   Public Communication

9   Public Speaking: Process, Purposes, Topics,
    and Audiences   172

10 Organization, Development, and Support   203

11 Delivery and Visual Aids   230

UNIT FOUR   Groups, Organizations, and Mass
               Communication

12 Groups in Discussion   253

13 Communication in Organizations   279

14 Technology and Mass Communication   305

Contents

Preface   xiv
Acknowledgments   xxii
About the Authors   xxiii

UNIT ONE   Essential Communication Elements

Chapter 1   Appreciating and Understanding Human Communication   1

Knowledge Checklist   2
Thinking About Communication, College, and Career   2
Communication and College Experience   2
Campus Links: Transitioning   3
Community Links: Service Learning   4
Communication and Life After College   6
Career Links: Effective Communication   7
Descriptions of Human Communication   7
Examining a Descriptive Phrase   8
Components of Communication   9
Computer Links: Computer-Mediated Communication (CMC)   10
Cultural Links: Culture to Communication   11
Communication Links: Concentration   12
Communication Links: Willingness to Communicate   14
Models of Communication   16
Characteristics of Human Communication   18
Some Clarifications about Communication: Addressing Misconceptions   20
Communicating in College and Life   21
Summary ◎ Questions for Discussion ◎ Exercises ◎ Key Terms
   ◎ References   21

Chapter 2   Communicating Ethically and Competently   24

Knowledge Checklist   25
Ethical Communication   25
Understanding Ethics and Communication   25
Communication Links: The National Communication Association Credo for
   Ethical Communication   27
Sources of Ethical Guidelines   27
Cultural Links: Understanding Differing Values   28
Campus Links: Understanding Moral Growth   29
Ethical Principles   30
Career Links: Honesty in the Workplace   31
Campus Links: Truthfulness and Romance   33
An Ethical Orientation   33
Community Links: Consequences of Silence   34
Moral Theories   35
Goals of Studying Communication Ethics   37

Ethical Communication as Competent Communication   37
    Computer Links: Ethics on "the Net"   38
Ethics, Responsibility, and College Student Life   39
Summary ◎ Questions for Discussion ◎ Exercises ◎ Key Terms
    ◎ References   40

Chapter 3   Perception: Self, Others, and Communication   43

Knowledge Checklist   44
The Process of Perception   44
    Attention and Selection   44
    Organization   45
    Campus Links: Student Perceptions of Teachers   45
    Interpretation and Evaluation   46
Problems with Perception   46
    Prior Experience   46
    Stereotypes   47
    Selectivity   47
    Cognitive Orientation   48
    *Computer Links: Using the World Wide Web to Discover
    Yourself*   48
Perception and Communication: A Reciprocal Relationship   50
    Perception, Self, Identity, and Communication   50
    Career Links: Using the Self-Fulfilling Prophecy   51
    Self and Others   53
    Social Comparison   53
    Reflected Appraisal   53
    Self and Communication   53
    Perception of Others and Communication   55
    Perception and Communication with Others   56
    Cultural Links: The Influence of Culture on Perception   57
Improving Perception   57
    Guard against Perceptual Error   57
    Gather Additional Information   58
    *Communication Links: Communicating with People with
    Disabilities (PWD)*   58
    Use Perception Checking   59
    Adjust Your Perceptions   59
    Practice Empathy   60
Perception in College and Career   60
    Perception, Self-Concept, and Academic Success   60
    Perception and the Workplace   60
*Summary ◎ Questions for Discussion ◎ Exercises ◎ Key Terms
    ◎ References*   61

Chapter 4   Effective Listening   65

Knowledge Checklist   66
The Reluctance to Listen   66
   Cultural Links: Silence as Responding   66
   Problems in Listening   68
   Career Links: The Costs of Poor Listening on the Job   69
   Computer Links: Listening and Computer-Mediated Communication
     (CMC)   71
   Poor Listening   74
The Requirements for Listening   75
   Pleasurable Listening   75
   Informational Listening   75
   Campus Links: Use a Recall/Cue System of Note-Taking   76
   Relational Listening   77
   Communication Links: Rhetorical Sensitivity   78
   Evaluative Listening   79
The Rewards of Listening   80
   Increased Enjoyment   80
   Improved Understanding   80
   Enhanced Empathy   80
   Heightened Civility   81
   Community Links: Community Listening Sessions   81
The Role of Listening and the College Experience   82
   The Role of Listening in Learning   82
   Listening on Campus   83
   Communication Links: Are You Listening?   83
The Role of Listening in College and Career Relationships   84
Summary ◎ Questions for Discussion ◎ Exercises ◎ Key Terms
   ◎ References   84

Chapter 5   Verbal Communication/Language   87

Knowledge Checklist   88
Understanding Language   88
Properties of Language   88
   Symbolic   88
   Triangle of Meaning   89
   Denotation and Connotation   90
Power of Language   91
   Language Shapes Culture   92
   Language Creates Meaning   92
   Language Confuses Meaning   93
   Language Classifies People   93
   Communication Links: Gender Labels   94
   Career Links: Creating Nonsexist Environments   95
   Language Clarifies Meaning   95
Gendered Language   96
   Cultural Links: Transmission of Culture to Children   98
Language and Culture   98
   Computer Links: Hate Speech and Indecent Speech   100
Guidelines for Competent and Ethical Use of Language   101
   Adapting to One's Audience   101
   Attending to Context   101
   Employing Rhetorical Sensitivity   102
   Community Links: Who's in the News?   103

Learning and Using "College Language"   103
  Understanding Typical College Language   103
    Campus Links: Combating Hate Speech on Campus   104
*Summary ◎ Questions for Discussion ◎ Exercises ◎ Key Terms
  ◎ References*   105

Chapter 6   Nonverbal Communication   107

Knowledge Checklist   108
Understanding Nonverbal Behavior   108
Fundamentals of Nonverbal Communication   109
  *Cultural Links: Nonverbal Communication between Asian and Western
    Cultures*   109
The Functions of Nonverbal Communication   110
  Modifies Verbal Communication   110
    Communication Links: How Can You Tell if Someone Is Lying?   110
  Expresses Feelings   111
    Computer Links: Nonverbal Communication on the Internet   111
  Regulates Interaction   112
    *Campus Links: Noverbal Communication in "Casual" and "Involved"
    Dating*   113
Types of Nonverbal Communication   113
  Body Movement (Kinesics)   113
  Physical Characteristics   114
  Touch (Haptics)   115
  Paralanguage   115
  Proxemics   116
  Artifacts   117
  Chronemics   117
Gendered Nonverbal Communication   118
  *Career Links: Gender and Nonverbal Communication in the
    Workplace*   118
  Gendered Space and Territory   119
  Gendered Fashion   119
  Gendered Touch   119
  Gendered Eye Contact   120
Nonverbal Communication and Culture   120
Competent and Ethical Nonverbal Communication   121
  Self-Presentation   121
  Mindfulness and Respect   121
  Accuracy and Immediacy   122
Nonverbal Communication in College and Life   122
  *Community Links: The Role of Ceremony and Ritual in Building
    Community*   123
*Summary ◎ Questions for Discussion ◎ Exercises ◎ Key Terms
  ◎ References*   124

UNIT TWO   Interpersonal Communication

Chapter 7   Understanding Interpersonal Communication   127

Knowledge Checklist   128
Impersonal vs. Interpersonal Relationships   128
The Key Concept of Intimacy   129
  Intimacy and Attraction   129
  Intimacy and Need Fulfillment   130
  Campus Links: Physiological Needs and Self-Care   131
Intimacy and the Stages of Relationship Development   134
  Initiating   134
  Computer Links: Dating and Relationship Development Online   135
  Experimenting   136
  Intensifying   136
  Integrating   136
  Bonding   136
Interpersonal Communication Dialectics   136
  Communication Links: The Spiritual Child   137
Intimacy and Stages of Relationship Dissolution   139
  Stages of Relationship Dissolution   139
  Relational Dissolution Model   140
Relationship Development between Professors and Students   141
Intimacy and Conflict   142
  Campus Links: Five Ways to Say "I"   143
Gender and Culture in Relationships   144
  Communication between Women and Men   144
  Communicating across Cultures   144
  Cultural Links: Intercultural Romantic Relationships   145
Competence and Ethics in Interpersonal Communication   146
  Community Links: Interpersonal Relationships and Community   146
Interpersonal Communication in College and Life   147
  Communication Links: Important Characteristics of a Possible Mentor-Professor   148
  Career Links: Feedback: Essential to Interpersonal Communication in the Workplace   150
Summary ◎ Questions for Discussion ◎ Exercises ◎ Key Terms ◎ References   151

Chapter 8   Applying Interpersonal Communication: Principles and Practice   154

Knowledge Checklist   155
The "Reality" of Relationships   155
Interpersonal Dialectics and Families   155
Interpersonal Dialectics and Friendships   156
Interpersonal Dialectics and College   157
  Cultural Links: Intercultural Relationships on Campus   158
  Computer Links: Expanding Your Knowledge of Cultures   158
  Communication Links: So, What Do You Call Your Professor?   159
  Campus Links: Choosing an Academic Advisor   160
Interpersonal Dialectics and Communities   161
  Community Links: Teaching Tolerance   162
Conflict Management in Interpersonal Relationships   163
  The Value of Conflict   163
  Pseudo-, Destructive, Constructive Conflict   163
  Career Links: 5 Steps to Reduce Conflict at Work   164
  Conflict-Management Styles   165

Rhetorically Sensitive Interpersonal Communication in College and
Life 167
Summary ◎ *Questions for Discussion* ◎ *Exercises* ◎ *Key Terms*
◎ *References* 170

UNIT THREE Public Communication

Chapter *9* Public Speaking: Process, Purposes, Topics, and Audiences 172
Knowledge Checklist 173
Why Study Public Speaking? 173
 Career Links: Public Speaking as Marketing Strategy 174
 Community Links: Public Speaking and Community 174
Communication Apprehension 176
 Communication Links: Dealing with Communication
 Apprehension 176
The Process of Public Speaking 178
Public Speaking Purposes 180
 General Purposes 180
 Specific Purposes 181
How to Select a Subject 182
 Brainstorming 182
 Perspectives to Consider in Choosing Your Subject 183
 Cultural Links: Rhetorical Traditions 185
 Communication Links: Using Multiple Intelligence Theory in Public
 Speaking 188
How to Select a Topic 191
 Computer Links: Computer Help in Finding a Topic 192
How to Relate a Topic to Purposes 192
How to Write a Thesis Statement 192
Celebratory, Informative, and Persuasive Speeches 193
 Celebratory Speeches 193
 Informative Speeches 193
 Campus Links: Approaching Lectures as Informative Speeches 195
 Persuasive Speeches 196
Connecting College and Public Speaking 198
 The College Classroom as a "Real" Audience 198
 Relevance of Celebratory, Informative, and Persuasive Speaking to the
 College Experience 199
Summary ◎ *Questions for Discussion* ◎ *Exercises* ◎ *Key Terms*
 ◎ *References* 200

Chapter *10* Organization, Development, and Support 203

Knowledge Checklist 204
Organizing Your Speech 204
   Principles for Effective Organization 204
   Communication Links: Clarifying Terms 205
   Understanding the Parts of a Presentation 207
   Patterns of Organization 212
Supporting Your Presentation 214
   Finding Supporting Materials 214
   Cultural Links: Culture and Evidence 215
   Campus Links: Doing Research 215
   Evaluating Materials 216
   *Community Links: Community Resources and Supporting
      Materials* 217
   Types of Supporting Material 217
   Using Supporting Material Effectively 219
   Career Links: Critical Skills in an Information Age 220
   Citing Sources 221
Outlining 221
   Planning, Preparation, and Presentation Outlines 221
   Alternatives to Outlining 225
   Computer Links: Software for Speakers 226
**The Importance of Organizational Skills for College Learning
   and Life** 227
*Summary ◎ Questions for Discussion ◎ Exercises ◎ Key Terms
   ◎ References* 228

Chapter *11* Delivery and Visual Aids 230

Knowledge Checklist 231
Types of Delivery 231
   Career Links: Job Interviews as Impromptu Speaking 232
Elements of Effective Delivery 233
   Using Your Voice Effectively 233
   *Communication Links: Proper Breathing in Public
      Speaking* 233
   Cultural Links: Dialects and Accents 237
   Using Your Face Effectively 238
   Using Your Body Effectively 238
Using Visual Aids to Enhance Delivery 239
   Types of Visual Aids 239
   Guidelines for Using Visual Aids 241
   Integrating Visual Aids with Delivery 242
   *Computer Links: The Problem with PowerPoint as a Visual
      Aid* 243
Preparing for Effective Delivery 244
   Guidelines for Effective Preparation 244
   How to Practice for Effectiveness 245
   Community Links: Labs for Ongoing Practice 246
   Campus Links: Time Management 247
Effective Delivery for Differing Contexts 249
   Common Core Principles 249
   College and Public Speaking 249
   The Workplace and Speaking 250
   The Public and Speaking 251
*Summary ◎ Questions for Discussion ◎ Exercises ◎ Key Terms
   ◎ References* 251

UNIT FOUR   Groups, Organizations, and Mass Communication

Chapter *12* Groups in Discussion   253

Knowledge Checklist   254
Characteristics of Groups   254
  Group Size   254
  Interaction for a Purpose   255
  Mutual Influence   255
  Interdependence   255
  Career Links: Dependence, Independence, Interdependence   255
  Group Norms   256
  Collective Identity   257
  Communication Links: Group Contracts   257
  Group Cohesion   258
  Commitment to the Group   258
Goals in Groups   259
  Individual and Group Goals   259
  Learning, Therapy, Problem-Solving, and Social Groups   259
  Groups vs. Individuals   260
  Computer Links: Online Support Groups   260
Roles in Groups   261
Leadership in Groups   262
Stages of Group Development   263
  Forming Stage   264
  Norming Stage   264
  Storming Stage   264
  Performing Stage   264
Culture, Values, and Gender in Groups   264
Group Climate, Conflict, and Problem Solving   266
  Supportive and Defensive Climates   266
  Types of Conflict   266
  Cultural Links: Cultural Differences among Group Members   267
  Styles of Conflict Resolution   269
Making Quality Decisions in Groups   270
  The Reflective-Thinking Approach   270
  Brainstorming: Creativity Is the Key   271
  Groupthink and Decision Making   272
Making Groups Work in College, Community, and Career   274
  Campus Links: How to Engage Classroom Discussion   274
  Community Links: Contribution and Reward   275
Summary ◎ Questions for Discussion ◎ Exercises ◎ Key Terms
  ◎ References   276

Chapter *13* Communication in Organizations   279

Knowledge Checklist   280
The Importance of Communication in Organizations   280
Organizational Cultures   281
  Language   281
  Cultural Links: Organizational Cultures and Mission Statements   281
  Stories   282
  Rites and Rituals   282
  Structure   283
  Roles   283
  Rules and Policies   283
  Communication Links: Uncertainty Reduction Theory   284
Organizational Systems: The Systems Model   284
  Wholeness   285
  Interdependence and Synergy   285
  Openness   285
  Adaptability through Feedback   286
  Equifinality   287
  Communication in the System   287
Communication Contexts in Organizations   287
  Superior-Subordinate Communication   287
  Communication and Career Links: Key Principles for Successful
    Organizational Relationships   288
  Communication with Peers   290
  Using Networks and Channels Effectively   290
  Communicating Outside the Organization   291
  Computer Links: Communicating Social Responsibility through a
    Website   291
Challenges in Contemporary Organizations   292
  The Diverse Organization   292
  Personal Relationships in Organizations   293
  Motivation in Diverse Organizations   293
Understanding and Avoiding Sexual Harassment   294
Technology in Organizations   295
Effective Organizational Communication Beyond College   295
  The Job Search Process   295
  Interviewing   297
  Types of Interviews   297
  How to Be Interviewed   298
  Avoiding Common Mistakes in the Interview   298
  Following up the Interview   298
  Campus Links: Should I Work While Attending College?   299
Effective Organizational Communication in College   300
  Campus Links: Using Campus Services   301
Summary ◎ Questions for Discussion ◎ Exercises ◎ Key Terms
  ◎ References   303

Chapter *14* Technology and Mass Communication   305

Knowledge Checklist   306
Definition and Characteristics of Mediated Mass Communication   306
  Computer and Communication Links: Are You Computer Savvy?   306
  Mediated Mass Communication Defined   307
  Characteristics of Mediated Mass Communication   307
  Cultural Links: Children's Access to Computers and the Internet   308
  Career Links: Technology and Job Hunting   311
Effects of Mass Communication   312
  Communication and Cultural Links: Cultural Imperialism   312
  Media Affects Cultures   313
  Media Affects Individuals   314
  Community Links: Mediated Violence   316
Being a Critical Consumer of Media   317
  Critical Analysis of the Message   317
  Critical Analysis of the Channel   317
  Critical Analysis of Senders   318
  Critical Analysis of Receivers and Context   319
  Critical Analysis of Noise and Our Feedback   319
Mass Communication in College and Life   320
  *Campus Links: Web-Based, Web-Enhanced, or Face-to-Face
    Courses?*   320
  *Summary ◎ Questions for Discussion ◎ Exercises ◎ Key Terms
    ◎ References*   322

Glossary   324
Photo Credits   331
Index   332

Preface

OUR VISION

We believe that communication truly matters; communication counts. Research and life experience confirm that the need for competent communicators has never been greater. With this understanding, we offer this book, which is the result of years of thought, practice, and interest in helping students develop communication knowledge and skills. We are all teachers at heart and we see this book as an extension of our passion for teaching. Therefore, students are the primary audience for our work; we wrote this book for students. We have worked to make this material relevant to students. However, we also believe this book will appeal to both beginning and veteran teachers who seek to make the basic communication course relevant to students' lives.

Conceptually, we seek to integrate essential content for the hybrid basic communication course with college students' lived experiences. Specifically, we focus on how communication principles and practices can assist students in their college years and later in their personal and professional lives; thus, the title: *Communication Counts: Getting It Right in College and Life*. Practically, we seek to blend theory and skill building, so that students develop fundamental communication knowledge and skills and work toward communication competence as a life-long goal.

TO STUDENTS

How many times have you thought about or sat in a college class and wondered, "What has this got do with my major or for that matter my life?" You may be asking the same question about *this* course and this textbook. You need to know, however, that we, your authors, have worked hard to provide you with a textbook that answers this question. Within these pages we offer you the essential knowledge critical to developing a fundamental grasp of communication principles and practice. Whether you are a recent graduate of high school or an adult returning to school while juggling multiple responsibilities, we wrote this text with *you* in mind because we want you to see the significant role communication plays in your everyday life as a college student. This text focuses on how you can use communication in your college life as you move from learning experiences in the classroom into your home or residence hall conversations, campus organizational meetings, community placements for service learning and internships, and eventually, professional life in the working world. Of course, this text will only help you if you read it and use it! So, we encourage you to make the most of this resource and this course to enhance your success in college, work, and everyday life.

TO OUR COLLEAGUES

*T*ogether, we have invested decades of our professional lives learning, teaching, reading, writing, and researching to produce this book. Foremost, however, this book is the fruit of our classroom teaching in basic communication courses, our long-term association with first-year initiatives, and our ongoing interactions with the growing population of mature learners returning to college. With the help of our publisher, editors, and reviewers, we have produced what we hope you will find to be a well-written, useful text that will help *you* help students find their voices and engage their various learning environments, while also thinking ahead to their future lives when they complete their studies.

You may well be asking, "*why* publish yet another hybrid, basic course textbook, given the excellent options that already exist?" This is a fair question; one we have asked ourselves numerous times in the rigorous process of producing this text and in assessing the numerous well-crafted books that already exist. In answer, let us explain our view of this text. In our text, we assert that students' college experience is an authentic context, not a "waiting room" for real life after college. Therefore, the illustrations and applications we offer draw on the actual world of college students; we demonstrate how communication principles are relevant here and now for college students. However, we also identify how the communication concepts and skills learned in college transfer to social and professional spheres after graduation. Not surprisingly, much of the content you will find in these pages is similar to the content you will find in many other basic, hybrid course textbooks. The difference is not in the concepts and skills, but in the illustrations and applications. In other words, this text helps students see the relevance of the basic oral communication course to their everyday lives. In particular, the types of text boxes we offer stress this connection.

We also wish to emphasize that, while we have incorporated concepts and strategies from first-year programming initiatives, this text is *not* a substitute for college success texts or courses. We are not asking you to absorb another course or to attempt to replace the work of your colleagues who are dedicated to helping college students succeed. This book is not about competing with college success texts and teachers, but about cooperating with them by confirming the significance of their work and applying what we have learned from them through illustration and integration. We have worked diligently to relate communication knowledge and skills with college success principles in order to stress the relevance between the two. Given the numerous learning community initiatives springing up on campuses across the United States, we believe this text offers a strategic pedagogical tool to link college success courses and basic communication courses, as we have been doing in our pedagogical practice for a number of years, without compromising the unique content of either. Therefore, the four units in this text, described briefly below, introduce fundamental communication concepts and skills and answer the questions many students ask when taking a basic oral communication course: "So, what? What has this got to do with my life right now?" Ultimately, *you* decide if this text successfully accomplishes our intention. We trust that you will find our text to be a good pedagogical tool to further the goals of your course. Further, we trust that your students will discover that the material covered in this text has everything to do with their lives, now and in the future.

ORGANIZATION

*T*his book takes a contextual approach, beginning with basic communication concepts and, for the most part, moving concentrically to increasingly larger contexts. Therefore, after reviewing important communication concepts, we move from a discussion of interpersonal communication to public speaking and then to small group, organizational, and mass communication. However, the book is written so that teachers do not need to move through the book as it is organized, but can easily assign the sections in the order that best fits their pedagogical purposes.

This book is organized into four major sections.

Unit I: Essential Communication Elements This unit offers an overview of basic communication theory, including descriptions of communication, communication competence and ethics, self and perception in communication, listening, and verbal and nonverbal communication.

Unit II: Interpersonal Communication This unit considers essential interpersonal communication concepts to help students understand interpersonal communication conceptually and practically.

Unit III: Public Communication This unit provides an overview of the essential aspects of public speaking by focusing on the process of developing, supporting, organizing, and delivering informative, persuasive, and special occasions speeches. We have purposefully abbreviated this section to provide fundamental principles without overwhelming students given that the hybrid course incorporates a range of principles and practices, including public speaking.

Unit IV: Groups, Organizations and Mass Communication This unit incorporates fundamental information about the theory and practice of effective communication in groups, organizations, and in mass communication.

UNIQUE FEATURES

This text offers a variety of distinctive features, some of which are found in each chapter and others in individual chapters.

Features Common to All Chapters

Campus Links

Transitioning

Transitioning
According the American Heritage Dictionary, a *transition* is the "passage from one form, state, style, or place to another." Whether you are a third-year student who hasn't declared a major, you are in a state of transition and will continue to be throughout your lifetime. Certainly, you have undergone many changes in your life, and this development has led you to pursue a college education. Understanding the stages of transition you are undergoing, as well as the role of communication in these stages, may help you to feel more at ease and help make the most of the transforming experiences you encounter in college.

Stages of Transition
According to Dr. Vincent Tinto (1993), professor of sociology and education at Syracuse University and expert on college student retention, there are three distinct phases or stages of transition that college students undergo: separation, transition, and incorporation. Tinto bases his stages on Dr. Arnold Van Gennep's study of rites of passage. Van Gennep, a Dutch anthropologist, observed how people and societies grow and change and then developed theories about mechanisms that promoted social stability in times of transition.

Stage One: Separation
For many of you, the first phase of your college career involves separating or disconnecting yourself from old friends, former schools, and immediate family. Indeed, some of you may have already made many of these transitions before taking this course; however, many of you may be currently undergoing this "breaking away" process. According to Tinto (1993), students in the separation stage feel isolated and may be under a great deal of stress. Even if you are presently attending a community or two-year college, you may be going through some aspects of separation, because college involves new sets of norms or behaviors and new types of expectations. During the separation phase, students often feel like quitting school, going back home, or withdrawing from others; these feelings are completely normal.

Stage Two: Transition
This is the stage of trying to "fit in." How well you weather this phase of college adjustment depends, in large part, on how much changing you need to do. For example, if your college environment is similar to the one from which you came (in terms of student population, size, geographic region, etc.), you might need to make fewer changes and accommodations. On the other hand, if your college environment is substantially different than the one you came from, you may experience more challenges as you make the transition

Content
- Each chapter provides connections with students' lived experiences, particularly emphasizing issues of concern for both traditional and nontraditional students as they navigate their college and career experiences.
- Each chapter has a series of text boxes that address significant issues for students by providing "links" to campus, computers, career, culture, and communication
- Each chapter emphasizes the connection between culture and communication, thereby integrating issues of diversity throughout the textbook.

Pedagogy
- Each chapter begins with clear learning objectives and a graphic depiction of the content in order to facilitate student learning.
- Each chapter provides relevant, engaging examples, as well as visual materials, such as photos, tables, and figures, to help emphasize and illustrate important information.
- Each chapter defines key terms in the margins, lists them at the end of the chapter, and defines them in a glossary at the end of the book.
- Each chapter concludes with a bulleted summary to help students identify key points.
- Each chapter offers discussion questions and exercises to assist students and teachers in applying the information.

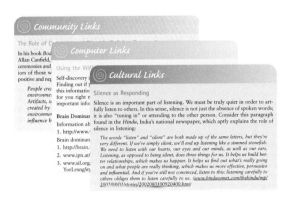

Features in Individual Chapters

- Chapter 1 provides a fresh description of human communication that emphasizes communication as a uniquely creative, human enterprise.
- Chapter 2 emphasizes the centrality of ethics in communication and offers an extended discussion that links theory with practice.
- Chapter 3 stresses the reciprocal relationship between perception and communication and integrates typical interpersonal communication concepts in a fresh manner to emphasize this vital linkage.
- Chapter 7 uses the concept of intimacy to integrate essential interpersonal communication principles, which helps to provide a focus for various concepts.
- Chapters 9 through 11 provide essential information about public speaking in an integrated fashion given the time constraints in teaching a hybrid course.
- Chapter 12 focuses on groups in discussion, thereby providing a specific context for understanding group concepts and practices, especially as they apply to college and university life.

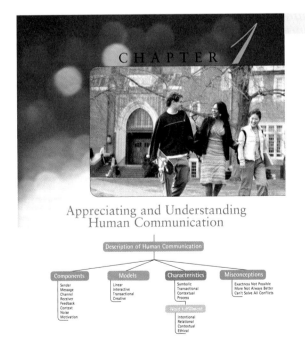

- Chapter 13 discusses organizational communication, which is a unique feature in a hybrid text. However, this chapter helps students recognize the importance of navigating organizations, including colleges and universities, in order to succeed. This chapter also includes information on interviewing and situates interviewing in an organizational communication framework.

- Chapter 14 addresses technology and mass communication, given its increasing importance in human communication and in students' everyday experience.

INSTRUCTOR'S RESOURCES

Print Supplements

Instructor's Manual and Test Bank, by David Worley, Indiana State University and Jennifer Lee Walton, Ohio Northern University. This *Instructor's Manual* provides a sample syllabus and assignments, along with worksheets, templates, and grading rubrics. Additionally, the *Instructor's Manual* contains chapter-by-chapter resources, including chapter objectives and outlines, discussion topics and questions, as well as classroom activities to enhance active learning. The Test Bank contains multiple choice, true/false, and essay questions.

A&B Public Speaking Transparency Package, Version II. One hundred full-color transparencies created with PowerPoint™ software provide visual support for classroom lectures and discussions.

The Blockbuster Approach: Teaching Interpersonal Communication with Video, 3/e, by Thomas Jewell, Bergen Community College. This guide provides lists and descriptions of commercial videos that can be used in the classroom to illustrate interpersonal concepts and complex interpersonal relationships. Sample activities are also included.

Great Ideas for Teaching Speech (GIFTS), 3/e by Raymond Zeuschner, California Polytechnic State University. This instructional booklet provides descriptions of and guidelines for assignments successfully used by experienced public speaking instructors in their classrooms.

A Guide for New Teachers of Introduction to Communication, 2/e, by Susanna G. Porter, Kennesaw State University. This instructor's guide is designed to help new teachers effectively teach the introductory communication course. Topics such as choosing a text, structuring your course, effectively using group work, dealing with classroom challenges, and giving feedback are included, as well as a number of sample materials in the appendix.

Electronic Supplements

MyCommunicationLab is a place where students learn to communicate with confidence! As an interactive and instructive online solution designed to be used as a supplement to a traditional lecture course or completely administered as an online course, MyCommunicationLab combines multimedia, video, communication activities, research support, tests, and quizzes to make teaching and learning more relevant and enjoyable. Students benefit from a wealth of video clips that include student and professional speeches, small group scenarios, and interpersonal interactions—some with running commentary and critical questions—all geared to help students learn to communicate with confidence. Go to http://www.mycommunicationlab.com (access code required).

TestGen EQ: Computerized Test Bank. The user-friendly interface enables instructors to view, edit, and add questions, transfer questions into tests, and print tests in a variety of fonts. Search and sort features allow instructors to locate questions quickly and arrange them in preferred order. Available on CD-ROM or via download through our Instructor's Resource Center at www.ablongman.com/irc (access code required).

PowerPoint Presentation Package, by Jennifer Lee Walton, Ohio Northern University. This text-specific package consists of a collection of lecture outlines and graphic images keyed to every chapter in the text. Available on the Web at www.ablongman.com/irc (access code required).

Communication Digital Media Archive, Version 3.0. The Digital Media Archive CD-ROM contains electronic images of charts, graphs, maps, tables, and figures, along with media elements such as video, audio clips, and related web links. These media assets are fully customizable to use with our pre-formatted PowerPoint™ outlines or to import into an instructor's own lectures. Available in Windows and Mac formats.

VideoWorkshop for Introduction to Communication, Version 2.0, by Kathryn Dindia, University of Wisconsin. *VideoWorkshop for Introduction to Communication* is a new way to bring video into your course for maximized learning. This total teaching and learning system includes quality video footage on an easy-to-use CD-ROM, plus a Student Learning Guide and an Instructor's Teaching Guide. The result? A program that brings textbook concepts to life with an ease that helps your students understand, analyze, and apply the objectives of the course. *VideoWorkshop* is available for your students as a value-pack option with this textbook.

Lecture Questions for Clickers, by Keri Moe, El Paso Community College. An assortment of questions and activities covering a multitude of communication topics are presented in PowerPoint. These slides will help liven up your lectures and can be used along with the Personal Response System to get students more involved in the material. Available on the Web at www.ablongman.com/irc (access code required).

A&B Contemporary Classic Speeches DVD. This exciting supplement includes over 120 minutes of video footage in an easy-to-use DVD format. Each speech is accompanied by a biographical and historical summary that helps students understand the context and motivation behind each speech. Speakers featured include Martin Luther King Jr., Barbara Jordan, John F. Kennedy, Richard Nixon, the Dalai Lama, and Christopher Reeve.

Allyn & Bacon's Interpersonal Communication Video Library contains a range of videos from which adopters can choose. Each of the videos features a variety of scenarios that illustrate interpersonal concepts and relationships, including topics such as nonverbal communication, perception, conflict, and listening. Please contact your Allyn & Bacon representative for details and a complete list of videos and their contents to choose which would be most useful in your class. Some restrictions apply.

Allyn & Bacon's Public Speaking Video Library. Allyn & Bacon's Public Speaking Video Library contains a range of videos from which adopters can choose. The videos feature different types of speeches delivered on a multitude of different topics, allowing you to choose the speeches best suited for your students. Please contact your Allyn & Bacon representative for details and a complete list of videos and their contents to choose which would be most useful to in your class. Some restrictions apply.

A&B Small Group Communication Library. This small group communication collection presents video case studies of groups working in diverse contexts and highlights key concepts of communication including group problem-solving, leadership roles, diversity, power, conflict, virtual group communication, and more. Please contact your Allyn & Bacon representative for details and a complete list of videos and their contents to choose which would be most useful to in your class. Some restrictions apply.

STUDENT RESOURCES

Print Supplements

Multicultural Activities Workbook, by Marlene C. Cohen and Susan L. Richardson, both of Prince George's Community College, Maryland. This workbook is filled with hands-on activities that help broaden the content of speech classes to reflect the diverse cultural backgrounds of the class and society. The book includes checklists, surveys, and writing assignments that all help students succeed in speech communication by offering experiences that address a variety of learning styles.

Public Speaking in the Multicultural Environment, 2/e, by Devorah Lieberman, Portland State University. This two-chapter essay focuses on speaking and listening to a culturally diverse audience and emphasizes preparation, delivery, and how speeches are perceived.

Preparing Visual Aids for Presentations, 4/e, by Dan Cavanaugh. This brief booklet provides a host of ideas for using today's multimedia tools to improve presentations, including suggestions for how to plan a presentation, guidelines for designing visual aids and storyboarding, and a walkthrough that shows how to prepare a visual display using PowerPoint.

Research Navigator.com Guide: Speech Communication. This updated booklet, by Steven L. Epstein, Suffolk County Community College, includes tips, resources, and URLs to aid students conducting research on Pearson Education's research website, www.researchnavigator.com. The guide contains a student access code for the Research Navigator database, offering students unlimited access to a collection of more than 25,000 discipline-specific articles from top-tier academic publications and peer-reviewed journals, as well as the *New York Times* and popular news publications. The guide introduces students to the basics of the Internet and the World Wide Web and includes tips for searching for articles on the site as well as a list of journals useful for research in their discipline. Also included are hundreds of web resources for the discipline and information on how to correctly cite research.

The Speech Preparation Workbook, by Suzanne Osborn, University of Memphis. This student supplement contains forms to help students prepare a self-introductory speech, analyze the audience, select a topic, conduct research, organize supporting materials and outline speeches.

Speech Preparation Workbook, by Jennifer Dreyer and Gregory H. Patton, both of San Diego State University. This workbook takes students through the stages of speech creation—from audience analysis to writing the speech—and includes guidelines, tips, and easy to fill-in pages.

The Speech Outline: Outlining to Plan, Organize, and Deliver a Speech: Activities and Exercises, by Reeze L. Hanson and Sharon Condon, both of Haskell Indian Nations University. This brief workbook includes activities, exercises, and answers to help students develop and master the critical skill of outlining.

Study Card for Introduction to Speech Communication. Colorful, affordable, and packed with useful information, Allyn & Bacon's Study Cards make studying easier, more efficient, and more enjoyable. Course information is distilled down to the basics, helping you quickly master the fundamentals, review a subject for understanding, or prepare for an exam. Because they're laminated for durability, you can keep these Study Cards for years to come and pull them out whenever you need a quick review.

Electronic Supplements

MyCommunicationLab is a place where students learn to communicate with confidence! As an interactive and instructive online solution designed to be used as a supplement to a traditional lecture course or completely administered as an online course, MyCommunicationLab combines multimedia, video, communication activities, research support, tests, and quizzes to make teaching and learning more relevant and enjoyable. Students benefit from a wealth of video clips that include student and professional speeches, small group scenarios, and interpersonal interactions—some with running commentary and critical questions—all geared to help students learn to communicate with confidence. Go to: http://www.mycommunicationlab.com (access code required).

Communication Studies Website, by Terrence Doyle, Northern Virginia Community College, and Tim Borchers, Minnesota State University at Moorhead. This site includes modules on interpersonal communication, small-group communication, and public speaking, and includes web links, enrichment materials, and interactive activities to enhance students' understanding of key concepts. Access this site at www.ablongman.com/commstudies.

Introduction to Communication Study Site, accessed at www.abintrocommunication .com. This website features communication study materials for students, including flashcards and a complete set of practice tests for interpersonal communication, group communication, and public speaking. Students also will find web links to valuable sites for further exploration of major topics.

News Resources for Speech Communication Access Code Card. News Resources for Speech Communication with Research Navigator is one-stop access to keep you abreast of the latest news events and for all of your research needs. Highlighted by an hourly feed of the latest news in the discipline from the *New York Times*, students will stay on the forefront of currency throughout the semester. In addition, Pearson's Research Navigator™ is the easiest way for students to start a research assignment or research paper. Complete with extensive help on the research process and four exclusive databases of credible and reliable source material including the EBSCO Academic Journal and Abstract Database, *New York Times* Search by Subject Archive, and *Financial Times* Article Archive and Company Financials, Research Navigator helps students quickly and efficiently make the most of their research time.

ResearchNavigator.com Guide: Speech Communication. This updated booklet, by Steven L. Epstein Suffolk County Community College, includes tips, resources, and URLs to aid students conducting research on Pearson Education's research website, www.researchnavigator.com. The guide contains a student access code for the Research Navigator database, offering students unlimited access to a collection of more than 25,000 discipline-specific articles from top-tier academic publications and peer-reviewed journals, as well as the *New York Times* and popular news publications. The guide introduces students to the basics of the Internet and the World Wide Web, and includes tips for searching for articles on the site, and a list of journals useful for research in their discipline. Also included are hundreds of web resources for the discipline, as well as information on how to correctly cite research.

Speech Writer's Workshop CD-ROM, Version 2.0. This speechwriting software includes a Speech Handbook with tips for researching and preparing speeches, a Speech Workshop that guides students step-by-step through the speech writing process, a Topics Dictionary that gives students hundreds of ideas for speeches, and the Documentor citation database that helps them to format bibliographic entries in either MLA or APA style.

VideoLab CD-ROM. This interactive study tool for students can be used independently or in class. It provides digital video of student speeches that can be viewed in conjunction with corresponding outlines, manuscripts, notecards, and instructor critiques. A series of drills to help students analyze content and delivery follows each speech.

VideoWorkshop for Introduction to Communication, **Version 2.0,** by Kathryn Dindia, University of Wisconsin. *VideoWorkshop for Introduction to Communication* is a new way to bring video into your course for maximized learning. This total teaching and learning system includes quality video footage on an easy-to-use CD-ROM, plus a Student Learning Guide and an Instructor's Teaching Guide. The result? A program that brings textbook concepts to life with ease that helps your students understand, analyze, and apply the objectives of the course.

Acknowledgments

This book is the result of the labor and investment of many individuals. We are grateful to all who have contributed to its development. First, we wish to thank the students who have shared classroom life with us and have taught us as we have worked to teach them. We are equally grateful to the many teachers and professors who invested their knowledge and pedagogical expertise in us during our years of education; their contributions live on in us and through us in our students. More specifically, we thank our families, friends, and colleagues who have supported us in this endeavor. Dr. Jennifer Walton, a former graduate student and teaching assistant at Indiana State University, is due a special word of thanks for her excellent work on many of the instructor's supplements. Thank you, Jenny! We are especially grateful to the excellent staff at Allyn & Bacon, including Karon Bowers, Editor-in-Chief; Jenny Lupica, Associate Development Editor; Jessica Cabana, Editorial Assistant; Claudine Bellanton, Production Editor; Jeff Houck, project manager at Progressive Publishing Alternatives; and designer Gina Hagen.

We also want to thank all of those reviewers who read through and offered excellent suggestions for improving various drafts of our manuscript. Our sincere thanks to the following:

Mark Buckholz, New Mexico State University at Carlsbad
Melissa Crawford, University of Central Arkansas
Teresa M. Hayes, DeVry University
Jeffrey S. Hillard, College of Mount St. Joseph
Susan A. Holton, Bridgewater State College
Emily Holler, Kennesaw State University
Mary E. Hurley, St. Louis Community College at Forest Park
Charles J. Korn, George Mason University
Shirley Maase, Chesapeake College
Jim Parker, Vanderbilt University
Ané Pearman, ECPI College of Technology
Jeff Pierson, Bridgewater State College
Darci Slaten, University of Arizona
John T. Warren, Bowling Green State University

About The Authors

Dr. David W. Worley is Professor and Chairperson in the Department of Communication at Indiana State University in Terre Haute, Indiana. He also serves as Director of Communication 101, a hybrid basic oral communication course required of all graduates at Indiana State University. He received his Ph.D. from Southern Illinois University at Carbondale with a concentration in communication education. Dr. Worley is the recipient of the Central States Communication Association Outstanding New Teacher Award, the Caleb Mills Distinguished Teaching Award at Indiana State University, the Excellence in Education Teaching Award from the College of Arts and Sciences at Indiana State University, and the Federation Prize from the Central States Communication Association. He teaches courses in communication education, research methods, and cross-cultural communication. His research interests include disability and communication, communication education, and instructional communication. He has published in *Communication Education, Communication Studies, Communication Quarterly, Review of Communication, Journal of the Association for Communication Administration,* the *Basic Communication Course Annual,* and the *Iowa Journal of Communication.* He is a regular contributor at the National Communication Association and the Central States Communication Association Annual Conventions.

Dr. Debra Worley is Associate Professor of Communication at Indiana State University, where she has taught since 1999. She received her doctorate from Wayne State University. Dr. Worley is the recipient of the Caleb Mills Distinguished Teaching Award and the Excellence in Education award from Indiana State University, as well as the Federation Prize from Central States Communication Association. She teaches courses in small group communication, organizational communication, public relations, and communication ethics. Dr. Worley has presented lectures on communication in the workplace, and has published articles in *Communication Studies, Public Relations Review, The Journal of Business Ethics,* the *Basic Communication Course Annual* and serves on the editorial boards of *Communication Teacher* and the *Journal of Applied Communication Research.*

Professor Laura Soldner is a Full Professor in the Department of English at Northern Michigan University where she serves as Director of Composition as well as Learning and Study Skills Specialist. Professor Soldner graduated from the University of Wisconsin—Madison and has spent two decades teaching incoming students through graduate students. She was awarded NMU's Excellence in Teaching Award in 2006; served as the Director of NMU's First-Year Experience Program, a nationally recognized freshmen transition program; received the Executive Director's Advisor of the Year Award from the national freshmen honor society, Alpha Lambda Delta (ALD); and was a semi-finalist for the National Outstanding First-Year Advocate Award. Professor Soldner has also published over a dozen articles and given 27 presentations in national and international venues.

CHAPTER 1

Appreciating and Understanding Human Communication

Description of Human Communication

Components
- Sender
- Message
- Channel
- Receiver
- Feedback
- Context
- Noise
- Motivation

Models
- Linear
- Interactive
- Transactional
- Creative

Characteristics
- Symbolic
- Transactional
- Contextual
- Process

Need fulfillment
- Intentional
- Relational
- Contextual
- Ethical

Misconceptions
- Exactness Not Possible
- More Not Always Better
- Can't Solve All Conflicts

Knowledge Checklist

✓ To understand and appreciate the importance of communication for college life and life after college

✓ To appreciate the uniqueness of human communication

✓ To understand a fundamental description of human communication

✓ To identify the essential components of human communication

✓ To explore four different models of human communication

✓ To understand five core characteristics of human communication

✓ To clarify common misunderstandings of human communication

THINKING ABOUT COMMUNICATION, COLLEGE, AND CAREER

As you begin your experience as a college student, you are learning "how to do college." Perhaps you have already faced some challenges this term as you learn to manage your academic, financial, family, and personal responsibilities as a college student. Although not all of the problems you face are communication related, many of them are, as Johnson, Staton, and Jorgensen-Earp (1995) report in their study of first-year students. As we will see later in this chapter, human communication is a complex and multidimensional activity. Miscommunications and misunderstandings are inevitable, but learning more about the components of communication and about different models of how humans communicate may help to ease some of these problems. Moreover, understanding the characteristics of communication and clarifying some misconceptions may also help you to become a better communicator in your college and personal life and in your professional career. Before we begin our investigation of some fundamental communication concepts, let's discuss the relationships between communication, your college experiences, and your life outside the classroom.

Communication and College Experience

You are in an exciting and challenging time in your life: You are in college. Whether you are a first-year student, a mature learner, or a returning student who "knows how to do school," college presents opportunities to experience invigorating intellectual, social, and personal growth. At the same time, you also face numerous challenges. (See the box "Campus Links: Transitioning"). You must develop the essential academic skills necessary to learn, and you must identify, set, and achieve personal and career goals. You will want to develop meaningful relationships with your peers, professors, and other important people on campus, including staff and administrators. There will be many opportunities to become involved in campus life, which means you must choose if, how, and where to become involved. In addition, you must decide how to finance your education and make choices about your behaviors and their consequences. Whether you are a recent high school graduate or an adult learner, you will face these issues and more.

Although it is much too simplistic to assert that communication is the key to dealing with all of the situations you are likely to encounter, certainly communication plays a key role in adapting to and navigating through the college experience. When reading this text, you will see the value of becoming a creative, competent communicator as you engage the college experience.

For example, as a student-learner, you are required to employ a wide range of communication skills. We use the term *student-learner* because being enrolled as a student doesn't necessarily mean you are a learner. Some people believe that if a student is in college long enough, he or she will eventually graduate. But this is not always the case; there is no social promotion in college. At least two issues impact whether you become a student-learner or just a student.

First, remaining in college is a challenge. According to the National Center for Education Statistics, in 1994, 37 percent of students who began college as first-year students were either no longer enrolled or did not graduate. The National Center for Education Statistics' *Digest of Education Statistics* also notes that students in two-year institutions are more likely to fall short of obtaining a degree than students at four-year institutions, usually due to work demands or low grades. Noel, Levitz, and Saluri (1985) suggest that students decide during the first six weeks of college whether they will stay or leave. Gardner and Jewler (2003) report that 40 percent of the students in four-year institutions do not complete their degrees.

You may also be faced with homesickness, separation from long-time friends, new living environments, and changes in diet. In addition to this, you must decide how to spend free time, manage money, go to class, and meet academic expectations unlike any you have ever faced. As a result, some first-year students are in danger of never assuming their role as a student-learner because they are tempted to drop out of college before having to make the difficult transition. When you grow discouraged, remember that college can affect your earning potential. According to the National Center for Education Statistics *Outcomes of Education* report, in 2002, men with a bachelor's degree earned more than $22,000 more per year than men with only high school diplomas, while women earned more than $15,000 more per year with a bachelor's degree.

Campus Links

Transitioning

Transitioning
According the American Heritage Dictionary, a *transition* is the "passage from one form, state, style, or place to another." Whether you are a third-year student majoring in the sciences or a first-year student who hasn't declared a major, you are in a state of transition and will continue to be throughout your lifetime. Certainly, you have undergone many changes in your life, and this development has led you to pursue a college education. Understanding the stages of transition you are undergoing, as well as the role of communication in these stages, may help you to feel more at ease and help make the most of the transforming experiences you encounter in college.

Stages of Transition
According to Dr. Vincent Tinto (1993), professor of sociology and education at Syracuse University and expert on college student retention, there are three distinct phases or stages of transition that college students undergo: separation, transition, and incorporation. Tinto bases his stages on Dr. Arnold Van Gennep's study of rites of passage. Van Gennep, a Dutch anthropologist, observed how people and societies grow and change and then developed theories about mechanisms that promoted social stability in times of transition.

Stage One: Separation
For many of you, the first phase of your college career involves separating or disconnecting yourself from old friends, former schools, and immediate family. Indeed, some of you may have already made many of these transitions before taking this course; however, many of you may be currently undergoing this "breaking away" process. According to Tinto (1993), students in the separation stage feel isolated and may be under a great deal of stress. Even if you are presently attending a community or two-year college, you may be going through some aspects of separation, because college involves new sets of norms or behaviors and new types of expectations. During the separation phase, students often feel like quitting school, going back home, or withdrawing from others; these feelings are completely normal.

Stage Two: Transition
This is the stage of trying to "fit in." How well you weather this phase of college adjustment depends, in large part, on how much changing you need to do. For example, if your college environment is similar to the one from which you came (in terms of student population, size, geographic region, etc.), you might need to make fewer changes and accommodations. On the other hand, if your college environment is substantially different than the one you came from, you may experience more challenges as you make the transition

from one school and community to another. According to Tinto (1993), nearly all college students have some difficulty in making the transition to college; therefore, if you are having or have had challenges adjusting to college life, just remember that your experiences are very similar to those of most students in higher education throughout the country.

Stage Three: Incorporation

Incorporation or integration is the third stage of college adjustment. The root of the word *incorporation* is *corp*, which comes from the Latin root of *corpus*, meaning "body." After students have passed through the stages of separation and transition, they must work to become part of the student "body" of the campus, to become actively involved in student life.

The following is a brief list of possible ways for residential and commuter students to become and stay involved. These activities include but are not limited to

- intramural sports;
- interest groups and clubs;
- service organizations;
- residence hall associations or governments;
- fraternities and sororities;
- on-campus movies or events.

Another important way for students to become "incorporated" into college life is to make connections with people on campus: fellow students, faculty members, support staff, residence-hall advisors, work-study employers, and so on. Daily communication with people who become enmeshed in the fabric of your college life makes you feel like you "belong" in college and assists in making a smooth transition to college.

In sum, transitioning is an integral part of your college experience that is not limited to your freshman year. Understanding Tinto's stages of transition may help you identify which stage or stages you are in and may offer you ideas on how to make the most of your college experience.

Communication and Transitioning

All of these transition phases require communication skills. Johnson, Staton, and Jorgensen-Earp (1995) note that communication plays an important role in the transition of first-year students into college because regardless of whether you live in campus housing, in a Greek house, or commute, you face communication challenges in building and maintaining relationships with others. Interpersonal communication skills are, therefore, especially important in order to link with new friends while maintaining connections with hometown friends and family. In other words, as you separate from one context and transition into a new one, you must be able to effectively communicate with others to fit in. According to Johnson et al., communication with other students provides you with a cadre of friends who offer support, provide important information about college, help you study, and add to your social life, regardless of where you reside. This text and course will offer you opportunities to explore the communication knowledge and skills to help you chart the transition to college.

Second, those who stay in college must engage learning. This means you must attend class regularly; complete required homework; learn to use the library; use a variety of technologies; and develop your listening, writing, and speaking skills. Moreover, you need to become involved in campus life (Astin 1985), navigate the financial-aid maze, and develop supportive relationships with other student-learners and faculty (Terenzini et al. 1996). We also suggest that you look for opportunities to engage your local communities. There are many ways to do this, including service learning. (See the box "Community Links: Service Learning"). As you move ahead in becoming a student-learner, you must learn and use several new skills. Communicating effectively with others is essential to learning these skills.

Community Links

Service Learning

You can learn a great deal about service learning from many outlets. The National Service-Learning Clearinghouse (NSLC) provides a great deal of useful information at www.servicelearning.org/. Campus Compact (www. compact.org) also offers a great deal of information. However, information is not a substitute for involvement, which is the ultimate goal of service learning. As you pursue your college education, you will likely find courses that either encourage or require you to engage in some form of service learning. While these courses may have different emphases or learning objectives, clearly understanding and actively responding to these opportunities will enhance your college experience. Below, we provide you with some basic information to help you engage service learning as you study communication and other courses.

Definition of Service Learning

Although there are many different specific definitions of service learning, the NSLC provides this definition, which offers the core ideas of service learning:

> Service-learning combines service objectives with learning objectives with the intent that the activity changes both the recipient and the provider of the service. This is accomplished by combining service tasks with structured opportunities that link the task to self-reflection, self-discovery, and the acquisition and comprehension of values, skills, and knowledge content. (www.servicelearning.org/)

To illustrate, when you and your peers from your health class volunteer with an after-school program to help provide physical educational activities for children, this constitutes service. However, when you then draw on this service to learn about and analyze the level of physical activity of children in this specific program and the resulting health consequences, you are learning *and* serving. In some cases, service learning may emphasize *service* more than learning or emphasize *learning* more than service. In other instances, service and learning may be balanced. Whatever the configuration or course, linking service and learning is an important initiative on many campuses and one you will likely have an opportunity to engage.

Linking Service Learning and Communication

You can't truly serve or learn without developing and using appropriate and effective communication skills. As you work with others in order to be of service, you must learn to listen, empathize, and respond appropriately to those who may be very different from you. As you link service to learning, you must be able to think, speak, and write about your experiences. For example, in this course, you will probably deliver at least one speech. If you are engaged in service learning, you have a ready-made speech topic about which you can inform your peers (i.e., what you are learning from your service work). If you are delivering a persuasive speech, you may want to encourage your peers to volunteer their time and energy to help improve the lives of others. Regardless of whether you use your service-learning experiences for speech topics, learning the foundational principles of communication will help you serve and learn.

Although mature learners do not necessarily face the same specific challenges as recent high school graduates, you face equally difficult obstacles. These often include managing your time in order to meet work and family responsibilities while setting aside sufficient time to study. Managing money also presents challenges, especially if you have taken a leave of absence or quit your job in order to complete your degree. You may also feel a considerable amount of fear if you can truly succeed in the college environment (Brown 1996). Many of you are likely experiencing other significant personal changes as you begin college, which may include dealing with a divorce, becoming a single parent, changing your career, or facing an "empty nest" when your children have moved out (Aslanian 1996). While you may truly want to learn, distractions abound.

As you can see from these brief descriptions, the transition to college is demanding. As we noted earlier, many of the challenges and opportunities you face

Mature learners face challenges in college.

as a student-learner are linked, to a greater or lesser degree, with communication. This list summarizes some of the communication issues you face:

- Listening to professors explain concepts you need to know
- Engaging class discussions
- Establishing friendships with other students with whom you can socialize, study, or complete group projects
- Developing a comfortable working relationship with your academic advisor
- Posing questions to and talking with professors, staff, and administrators
- Expressing your opinions and insights clearly in class discussions
- Negotiating your relationships with significant others and family members
- Addressing relevant campus and community issues that concern you

Even though this list is not comprehensive, it represents the central role communication plays in college. Research also confirms the importance of communication in college given that college students spend 69 percent of their time engaged in speaking and listening (Barker, Edwards, Gaines, Gladney, & Holley 1980). Whether you are analyzing your self-talk; taking notes from a lecture; engaging a small group project; talking with your friends, family, or partners; posing a question in class; planning next semester's courses with your advisor; or articulating your position on an issue of concern on campus, oral communication is fundamentally important. Therefore, appreciating the role communication plays in the college experience and developing your oral communication skills will help you make the most of the experience. We sincerely hope this text will help you understand and apply important principles of communication here and now.

Communication and Life After College

Although college ends, learning does not. We continue to learn throughout our entire lives. Likewise, we also continue to rely upon communication in our personal, professional, and public lives.

Relationships with other people are often our greatest sources of joy and our greatest sources of pain. Later in this book, we will talk more about personal relationships and the important role communication plays in them. At this point, however, it is sufficient to note that both during and after college, healthy relationships with romantic partners, friends, family, and coworkers require effective, appropriate, and creative communication. For example, what *do* you say when your female partner, friend, or family member asks you, "Do you think I look fat in this dress?" This is a loaded question, and how you answer it may decide whether or not it backfires. More importantly, the very fact that the question is posed and the way you respond reveals important dimensions of your relationship as constructed and maintained through communication. In short, communication plays a central role in relationship development and maintenance.

Communication plays an equally important role in our professional lives. Surveys confirm that competent communication skills, including speaking, listening, and writing, are among the top skills required by employers. Listening in particular improves opportunities for advancing at work (Sypher, Bostrom, & Seibert 1989) and is identified as an important skill by Fortune 500 companies (Wolvin & Coakley 1991). Although you may think that your chosen career does not entail using communication skills on a regular basis, we encourage you to talk with a seasoned professional in your field of interest in order to check the validity of your belief. In all probability, you will find that every career path calls for effective, creative communication skills (see box "Career Links: Effective Communication: The Key to Getting and Keeping a Job") in order to interview well for a job; make presentations to clients, customers, or colleagues; and work with a team to complete a project. For example, the *Scientist* (Richman 2002) reports that communication skills are crucial to obtaining a job in science-related fields. Gardner and Jewler (2003) note that "regardless of which career you choose, people are likely to judge your effectiveness—at least in part—by your speaking skills" (p. 137).

Competent communication skills, including speaking, listening, and writing, are among the top skills required by employees.

Effective Communication: The Key to Getting and Keeping a Job

You may be saying, "Okay, I get it. I need to communicate well to get and keep a job. I've heard this over and over." But perhaps you've heard it so often because it is fundamentally true. In a report from North Carolina State University entitled "Communication in the Workplace: What Can NCSU Students Expect?" employers from a variety of businesses all confirm that oral communication plays an important role in recruitment, job success, and promotion. This survey, summarized in the chart below, indicates that 95 percent of employer respondents perceived oral communication as *very important* and *important* for promotion and for job success, and the figure for recruitment was 87 percent. In other words, if you want to get, keep, and progress in a job, according to these employers, you need to have strong oral communication skills.

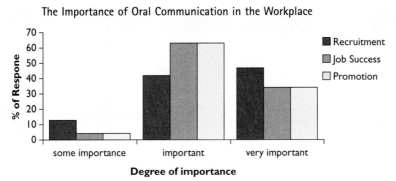

The Importance of Oral Communication in the Workplace

Importance of oral communication for job success, promotion, and recruitment.

Source: "The Importance of Oral Communication in the Workplace" from *English for Specific Purposes,* Vol. 21, 2002, pp. 41–57 (48). Reprinted by permission of Elsevier.

Although your personal and professional lives are important, you also share in the public life of your communities, states, and nations. As U.S. citizens, in order to participate in the privileges and responsibilities of a democracy, you must communicate. For example, listening carefully to candidates' positions on issues of critical importance allows you to obtain vital information that helps you choose how to vote. Or, you may be motivated to speak to a local school board about an issue that impacts public education in your community, especially since adults in the United States give public education a grade of C (2.08 on a 4.0 scale; National Center for Education Statistics, Outcomes of Education). These and numerous other situations of public concern will likely prompt you to engage the communication process as a result of your role as citizen.

Now that we have considered the importance of communication to our lives in college and in future careers, let's get a better understanding of some of the basic, yet vital information about human communication. We will start with thinking about the nature of human communication.

DESCRIPTIONS OF HUMAN COMMUNICATION

*D*efinitions of *communication* abound. Dance and Larson (1976) identify over one hundred definitions of communication. The sheer number of definitions suggests the difficulty of defining the term. Furthermore, when we define any term, by the very nature of the act, we specify, and thereby limit, the concept. This is useful and necessary in many instances, but human communication is flexible and situational by nature and, therefore, difficult to define. Consequently, it may be better to say that we can *describe* human communication in a variety of ways in order to assist our understanding. In this chapter, we describe communication by examining a descriptive phrase, identifying important components of communication, reviewing models of communication, explaining characteristics of communication,

Human communication is the process of negotiating symbolic meaning.

and clarifying popular misconceptions about communication. We hope this variety of approaches will help you to develop an understanding of the complexity, creativity, and challenge of human communication.

Examining a Descriptive Phrase

human communication negotiating symbolic meaning

Human communication may be described as "negotiating symbolic meaning." This statement identifies important ideas for us to consider. First, this book focuses on *human* communication. Perhaps, like many pet lovers, you insist that your pet communicates with you in a variety of ways. Wanting to enter a career in professional communication because you are "really excellent at working with people" is not a strong reason, because a career in communication calls for multiple skills. As one of your authors comments, "Some dogs are excellent at relating to and working with people, but that doesn't qualify them for a communication career."

symbolic using words, vocal utterances, or body movement to represent a host of referents

Second, communication is **symbolic**. This means that humans use words (verbal communication), vocal utterances (oral communication), or body movement (nonverbal communication) to represent a host of referents (that to which one refers). For example, verbal communication uses words like *chair*. The spelling, sound, and definition of this symbol is arbitrary because there is no firm reason why the word *chair* should not be spelled *chare* or the first two letters pronounced as a "sh" rather than a "ch," or even used to refer to a completely different object than a piece of furniture upon which one sits. Because we have agreed upon the conventions of language or the rules that guide language, we use verbal symbols in order to communicate.

Oral communication or vocal utterances may also act as symbols. Consider, for example, the sound we make when we gasp. A gasp is actually a sharp intake of air that creates a whispery sound using our mouth, lips, and vocal cords. A gasp is not a word, so it is not verbal communication; however, a noise or an utterance can be classified as oral communication. When you hear a gasp or respond with a gasp, what does this communicate? Usually it implies or denotes surprise or shock. Therefore, when a novelist writes, "She gasped at the sight before her," we understand the behavior, and this cues us to expect the writer to describe the shocking scene the character observes.

paralanguage (or vocalics) the vocal sounds we make such as pitch, volume, emphasis, or other similar sounds

Nonverbal communication is also symbolic and includes oral communication because vocal utterances, such as the gasp, typically fall within the area of nonverbal communication called *paralanguage* or *vocalics*. **Paralanguage** or **vocalics** refers to the vocal sounds we make such as pitch, volume, emphasis, or other similar sounds. However, we usually think of nonverbal communication as facial or bodily movement.

Facial movements like frowns, smiles, or grimaces communicate feelings. Gestures represent words, give directions, or express feelings. Although we will further discuss nonverbal communication later, it is important at this point to understand that non-verbal communication is symbolic—that is, nonverbal communication represents or accompanies a word, a feeling, an object, or some other referent. For example, the simple act of pointing is symbolic because we use it to give others directions, to focus others' attention, or perhaps to express our displeasure toward someone else, such as when we give a thumbs-up or a thumbs-down.

All of these symbols are significant to communication because we use them to construct *meaning*. These symbols help us create a shared understanding with one another. However, this meaning is not always clear! Imagine that your professor says to your class, "We will have a quiz at the first of next week." After reviewing important information for the quiz, he or she went on to teach the class and, as planned, the next week administered the quiz. One of your classmates exclaims, "I thought this was supposed to be a quiz. This is an exam!" What makes the difference between a quiz and an exam? The difference is not arbitrary; it is a matter of the meaning we attach to the symbols. In the student's mind, a quiz was a short, relatively easy, focused assessment. In your professor's mind, it was also a shorter, focused assessment, but not as short, focused, or easy as the student expected! Different meanings for the same symbol, therefore, created miscommunication. The point is this: Symbols carry meaning, but *we* create the meaning as a result of our prior experience and expectations. We will add more information about verbal communication later in this book, but for now, consider this important idea: *People, not symbols, create meaning.*

Because human communication rests on symbols that carry a variety of personal meanings, it must be negotiated. In other words, when we communicate with one another, we seek to create shared understanding. This does not mean that we have exactly the same definitions for every verbal, oral, and nonverbal symbol, but we find a common ground that allows us to share greater clarity, or **fidelity**. As you likely know from your own experience with others, this is not always easily done. Myers and Myers' (1992) humorous summary makes the point well: "I know you believe you understand what you think I said, but I am not sure you realize that what you heard is not what I meant!" How many times have you felt this way? We must consciously work at creating shared meaning. There are numerous strategies we can employ to enhance shared meaning, which we will discuss in the remainder of this text, but it is important to realize early that *when we communicate with one another, we are negotiating meaning.*

fidelity greater clarity

Components of Communication

In order to better understand this process of symbolic negotiation, we should consider the various components of communication. These include a sender, a message, a channel, a receiver, feedback, contexts, noise, and motivation.

A **sender** is the originator of a message, whereas a **receiver** is the target or recipient of the message. The sender is also referred to as the **encoder,** because he or she creates a message by using a system of symbols the receiver will understand, such as a shared language. The receiver, on the other hand, is referred to as the **decoder,** because he or she interprets the message. To put it another way, the sender and receiver constitute the *who* in the communication process.

The **message** is twofold (Watzlawick, Beavin, & Jackson 1967). First, the message constitutes the content one person seeks to share with another; it is the topic or substance of communication. The message is the *what* of the communication process. Second, the message reflects the relationship that exists between the people communicating. For instance, although both your romantic partner and your mother may tell you, "I love you," there is an obvious difference in the meaning because of the nature of the relationship.

As Schramm (1955) emphasized, when people communicate, they respond to one another. This response, whether verbal or nonverbal, constitutes **feedback.**

sender the originator of a message

receiver the target or recipient of the message

encoder the person who creates a message by using a system of symbols the receiver will understand; the sender

decoder the person who interprets the message; the receiver

message the content one person seeks to share with another; the topic or substance of communication

feedback a verbal or nonverbal response to communication

channel the means by which a message is delivered from the sender to the receiver; the medium by which the message travels

Feedback, therefore, is also a message, although it is typically a responsive message the receiver provides to the sender. Consequently, feedback may also be thought of as a part of the *what* in the communication process.

The **channel** is the medium by which the message travels from the sender to the receiver. When people communicate with one another face-to-face, the air carries the messages they send and receive. However, additional channels have emerged over time. Handwritten letters once acted as the primary channel for people to share messages at a distance. Later, the invention of the telegraph and telephone created additional channels. Today, video conferencing, e-mail, instant messaging (IM), and other emerging computer-mediated communication tools provide new channels that require us to reconsider our views of communication. (See the box "Computer Links: CMC".) The channel, then, is the *how* of communication.

Computer Links

Computer-Mediated Communication (CMC)

The computer has dramatically impacted human communication by providing new channels. Chat rooms, e-mail, Listserves, and instant messaging have replaced many of the former modes of communication in practically every field of work and in personal relationships. The proliferation of computer-mediated communication (CMC) research is but one indicator of the growth of this new channel; another is the number of e-mails you receive each day. For example, we often hear colleagues and professionals in the workplace bemoan the number of e-mails they receive daily. In short, human communication has and will continue to dramatically change with advancing technology. As computers become more affordable, smaller, and efficient, we can expect greater reliance on CMC.

This dramatic shift to computer-mediated communication is not without its challenges and problems, however. For example, some feel our reliance on computers is making us lose our "human touch." Others express concern over the degree of access to technology experienced by people in the United States and in other nations. The proverbial economic distinction of the "haves" and "have-nots" equally applies to technological access. For example, your authors teach on two different campuses. In the United States, some institutions issue every student a laptop computer for which he or she pays a semester fee; this ensures every student at those schools has immediate, personal access to a computer. In contrast, at other institutions, students may or may not have their own computers and may pay a technology fee for access to university-supported computer labs. Even greater differences than these exist globally, which has given rise to such terms as *digital divide* and *cybersegregation*. As a way to personalize the issue, consider keeping a log for one week on your use of CMC. For example, consider keeping a chart of the number of e-mails you receive and send, how long you spend sending and receiving instant messages, and how many Listserves you belong to. This simple assessment is likely to reveal that you, like many others, are truly reliant on CMC as a primary channel of communication.

context a specific environment that includes a number of situational factors including physical, cultural, linguistic, social, temporal, and personal aspects.

People do not communicate in a vacuum. All communication occurs in a **context** or a specific environment that involves several situational factors, including physical, cultural, linguistic, social, temporal, and personal aspects. (See the box on Cultural Links.) Consider how students communicate differently in the library and in the commons. What are some of the differences? Why do these differences exist? How does the physical arrangement, the cultural expectations, the social significance, or the time of day impact communication in these two very different spaces? Are you likely to hear different types of language used in these locations? Why? By reflecting on these questions, you can see that *where* and *when* communication takes place directly impact the nature of the communication.

◎ *Cultural Links*

Culture ◀━━▶ Communication

This simple diagram makes an important point: Culture and communication share a reciprocal relationship. Culture, then, is an essential and primary context of communication. It surrounds and infuses human communication; in turn, communication reinforces culture. Although a variety of definitions of culture exist, Martin and Nakayama (2001) offer this helpful definition: "The learned patterns of perception, values, and behaviors, shared by a group of people that is also dynamic and heterogeneous" (p. 23). Given this definition, consider the reciprocal relationship shared by culture and communication by reviewing two simple statements:

1. **Culture influences communication.** Most obvious, the language we speak and the nonverbal communication we employ are culturally determined. However, less-obvious cultural influences affect our communication. For example, our culture determines whether certain topics or terms are appropriate for casual or intimate conversation or even whether we should speak or remain silent. In other words, our culture "programs" us to communicate according to particular patterns that are imbued with unconscious ideas and ideals. Some cultures such as New Zealand, for instance, have a lower power differential and seek to de-emphasize hierarchy and differences in status, preferring a more egalitarian approach to human interaction, even in situations where a power difference due to rank or authority exists. On the other hand, countries such as Mexico and India tend to emphasize a large power distance and therefore rely on hierarchical, formalized decision making and sharper distinctions between, for example, bosses and subordinates. Even though these patterns provide points of reference to understand cultural differences, it is important to remember that not every individual from a given culture will necessarily communicate according to the stereotypical patterns. Martin and Nakayama emphasize this by noting that culture is dynamic (it changes) and heterogeneous (diversity exists within a given culture). Nevertheless, these patterns provide us with a way to compare and contrast culture and its impact on communication.

2. **Communication influences culture.** Culture is learned, expressed, and shared. In other words, we constitute culture through communication. For example, everyday greeting behaviors differ among cultures. These communication patterns reinforce the cultural values and behaviors of a given group of people. To illustrate, in many Asian cultures, bowing still remains an important social rule of greeting, while in Western cultures, shaking hands prevails as the primary form of greeting. These simple, everyday behaviors reinforce cultural expectations, and when examined closely, reflect even deeper differences among cultures. For example, when one of your authors was in Guatemala, he discovered two different types of handshakes. Some people shook hands with him in the typical "American" manner—they gripped his hand as he gripped theirs. However, others gripped his elbow, so that his entire forearm touched their forearm. Upon inquiry, he discovered that this second type of handshake constituted a "warmer welcome" than the traditional form; it was a way for the greeter to express a hearty welcome. Although this difference may seem like a peculiarity, it actually reflects a cultural difference: Some cultures are contact cultures (touching is welcomed and expected), whereas others are noncontact (touching is restricted and not expected). The "Guatemalan handshake," then, does more than express warmth—it also reflects and reinforces cultural values and expectations.

noise any interference that occurs as
people communicate

Noise is yet another component of communication and refers to any interference that occurs as we communicate. This interference may be external or internal. For example, consider an early morning summer class where the groundskeeper was mowing the grass outside. Suddenly, a riding mower became the object of interest for a number of students! The external noise of the mower interfered with the communication in the classroom. Internal distractions such as being preoccupied with a problem or excited about an upcoming event also interfere with communication. How many times have you sat in class worried, bored, sleepy, or hungry and suddenly realized that you had missed an important lecture point? In this instance, you were experiencing internal interference or noise. (See the box "Communication Links: Concentration".)

Communication Links

Concentration

Can't concentrate?
Lose your train of thought?
Find your mind wandering all the time?
Can't remember what you've been reading or studying?

These are all examples of mental noise that interferes with learning. How do you deal with this noise in order to more effectively engage your learning in college? To start, you can learn to improve your concentration; this can reduce frustration and earn you better grades. But improving your concentration requires developing methods of monitoring your attention span and redirecting your focus. Eliminating or minimizing distractions is a good place to start.

Reducing External and Internal Noise

External noise comes from things like sounds (phones ringing, TVs blaring, fans blowing), others (children, pets, roommates), or external situations (noisy cafeterias, high-traffic study areas, glaring overhead lights). *Internal noise*, on the other hand, comes from worries or emotions you are experiencing. For example, you may be concerned about money, guilty over not spending time with family members, or angry over a recent argument. Internal distractions are the "mental conversations" that you have with yourself.

You can often control external distractions by changing locations or arranging set study times. Internal distractions, however, are much more difficult to control because they interfere with your concentration and focus. To combat both types of distractions, try employing one or more of the following suggestions.

Combating External Noise

Establish a "Distraction-Free" Study Area Find a study location away from your dormitory room, apartment, or home. Find a location on campus, in the community, or in your building that you find conducive for studying. After trial and error, you might find that the laundry room, the back booth in the student union, an out-of-the-way study room of the public library, or some other quiet, well-lit location works well. Think of your study time as your "part-time" job. Go there and put in your hours.

Take Care of Your Physical Needs Overlooking your needs for rest, nutrition, exercise, and relaxation can cause concentration problems. Shortcutting your sleep or overdoing it with caffeine negatively affects your ability to concentrate. Make sure that you are taking care of your body's needs so that your mind can do its work.

Institute Regular Study Times   Start paying attention to your level of concentration throughout the day and in various settings. Are you able to concentrate better in the early morning or later in the afternoon? Do you accomplish more in a shorter amount of time working at a back table in the student union or at a study desk in the library? Determining when and where you are at your peak levels of concentration will help you to set regular study times throughout the week.

Be Honest with Those Who Are Important to You   Let roommates, spouses, children, parents, and others involved in your life know that you need privacy and quiet to get your studies done. Involve them in deciding how you'll use your study and free time. Use family or down time as rewards and incentives to keep you on track while you study.

Fighting Internal Noise

You can change locations or reason with those around you, but it is much more difficult to control what is happening in your mind. In order to make the most of your study time, it is imperative that you find ways to fight internal distractions. Here are some things you can try.

Develop a "Purge" List   In order to get worries off your mind, begin your study session by jotting down on a piece of paper everything that's on your mind (i.e., needing milk and bread from the store, paying your telephone bill, worrying about your aunt's surgery). Keep this paper nearby while you study; when you find yourself getting distracted, you can "unload" these distractions and concentrate on your studies. Later, after you finish studying, you can look at your list of distractions, create to-do lists, or determine what things are interfering with your concentration.

Pay Attention to Concentration   When you begin to study or read, jot down the time you begin in the margin of your text or notes (i.e., 4:12 P.M.). Begin studying. Note when your attention begins to wander and write down that time (4:19 P.M.). Repeat the process when you begin again. Caution: When you first begin comparing your attention times, you may get discouraged because it may seem you aren't getting very far. However, some students report that this technique of "paying attention to paying attention" works because it forces them to think about what they are doing and to gradually increase the amount of time they can stay focused on their task.

   In sum, improving your concentration can help you accomplish more work in less time, reduce your levels of frustration and anxiety, and prepare you to function more effectively in your chosen field. Unfortunately, noise is more likely to increase as you take on additional responsibilities, so finding ways to enhance your attention span now will help you in college and will assist you in your profession. ◎

Motivation is the final component of communication. Up to this point, our discussion of the components of communication sounds mechanistic: A sender inputs a message through a prescribed channel with a resulting output that is picked up by the receiver. This is hardly the case, because human communication, as we have already suggested, is creative. We must never forget that communication is a *human* endeavor that arises from a variety of motives. Sometimes we communicate to achieve practical ends; we refer to this as **instrumental** or **functional communication.** When you ask a classmate, "Can I copy your notes from the last class I missed?" you are engaged in instrumental communication. Other times, we communicate to express our emotions, strengthen bonds with others, or secure a sense of belonging; we refer to this as **relational communication.** For example, hanging out with your friends may include small talk, jokes, or serious conversations that help to express how you feel about one another, while also reinforcing your ties to

motivation the reason or *why* of communication

instrumental (or functional) communication communication that achieves practical ends

relational communication communication that expresses emotions, strengthens bonds with others, or secures a sense of belonging

one another. Whatever the reason we communicate, there *is* a motive. This constitutes the *why* of communication, yet another important component of the communication process. The Communication Links box provides more information about how willing you are to communicate in different situations.

Willingness to Communicate

You may be someone who talks frequently in almost any situation, while your roommate, spouse, or best friend may be inclined to speak only in situations where he or she is more comfortable or knows others better. Although situations may also impact the degree to which you are willing to speak, this personality difference has been labeled *willingness to communicate* (McCroskey & Richmond 1990).

Willingness to communicate (WTC) can be thought of as varying degrees in communication motivation. Someone who is more willing to speak generally possesses a higher degree of motivation to communicate, whereas someone who is more reluctant to speak is less motivated. It is important to note that while the degree of motivation may shift depending on circumstances, WTC is a fairly constant personality trait. Complete the scale below to discover your own level of WTC in various situations and with various types of communication partners. After you complete the scale, consider the questions that follow.

Willingness to Communicate Scale

Directions: Below are twenty situations in which a person may or may not choose to communicate. On the line at the left, indicate the percentage of time you would choose to communicate in each situation. Using 0 for never and 100 for always, rank each situation.

_____1. Talk with a service station attendant.*
_____2. Talk with a physician.*
_____3. Present a talk to a group of strangers.
_____4. Talk with an acquaintance while standing in line.
_____5. Talk with a salesperson in a store.*
_____6. Talk in a large meeting of friends.
_____7. Talk with a police officer.*
_____8. Talk in a small group of strangers.
_____9. Talk with a friend while standing in line.
_____10. Talk with a waitperson in a restaurant.*
_____11. Talk in a large meeting of acquaintances.
_____12. Talk with a stranger while standing in line.
_____13. Talk with a secretary.*
_____14. Present a talk to a group of friends.
_____15. Talk in a small group of acquaintances.
_____16. Talk with a garbage collector.*
_____17. Talk in a large meeting of strangers.
_____18. Talk with a significant other.*
_____19. Talk in a small group of friends.
_____20. Present a talk to a group of acquaintances.

---

* A filler item that you will not use in completing your scores.

Scoring: To compute the subscores, add the percentages for the items indicated and divide the total by the number indicated below.

Setting	Questions on Survey	What to Divide By	Your Score
Public	3 + 14 + 20	3	
Meeting	6 + 11 + 17	3	
Group	8 + 15 + 19	3	
Dyad	4 + 9 + 11	3	
Stranger	3 + 8 + 12 + 17	4	
Acquaintance	4 + 11 + 15 + 20	4	
Friend	6 + 9 + 14 + 19	4	

Total WTC = Stranger + Acquaintance + Friend

Questions for Reflection

1. Given the following average scores drawn from research, how willing are you to communicate, comparatively?
   - Willing to communicate with friends—85.5 percent
   - Willing to communicate with acquaintances—75 percent
   - Willingness to communicate with strangers—41.3 percent
   - Willingness to communicate in dyads (twos)—79.5 percent
   - Willingness to communicate in groups—73.4 percent
   - Willingness to communicate in meetings—60 percent
   - Willingness to communicate in public—56 percent
2. McCroskey and Richmond (1990) assert that people generally prefer to communicate with a small rather than large group. They also state that individuals are less willing to communicate with others with whom they have a more distant relationship than with people with whom they are closer. Do you agree with these observations? Why? Why not?
3. What impact may willingness to communicate have on your college experience? Your future career? Read the research summary at http://www.jamescmccroskey.com/publications/138.pdf. After reading this summary, what is your opinion of the possible impact of WTC on your college and career success?
4. Why are we interested in learning about willingness to communicate? What difference does it make? What values or beliefs does our interest in this topic suggest?
5. Do you think willingness to communicate shifts between cultures? Why? Consider the information at http://www.jamescmccroskey.com/publications/152.pdf. What insight does this research offer that may help answer this question?
6. In general, do you think men or women are more willing to communicate? On what do you base your opinion?

Source: "Willingness to Communicate Scale" from "Willingness to Communicate: A Cognitive View" by J. C. McCroskey and V. P. Richmond in *Journal of Social Behavior and Personality*, 1990, pp. 19–37. Reprinted by permission of James C. McCroskey.

These components of communication help us analyze most human communication and are summarized in Table 1.1. The following question helps summarize the components while providing us with a way to carefully observe almost any communication situation: *Who* (sender/receiver) is talking, listening, or responding to *whom* (receiver/sender), about *what* (content), *where* (context), *when* (context), *how* (channel), and *why* (motivation)?

■ **Table 1.1**   **Components of Communication**

WHO	Sender (Encoder)	Creates messages using symbols
	Receiver (Decoder)	Interprets symbols and assigns meanings
WHAT	Message	The content or the topic
		Indicates the relationship between sender and receiver
	Feedback	Responsive message
HOW	Channel	Means by which the message is delivered
		Examples: e-mail, letters, IM, videotape
WHERE	Context	The situation where communication occurs
WHEN	Context	The time of the communication
WHEN/WHERE	Noise	Interferences with communication
WHY	Motivation	Instrumental or functional—practical reasons Relational—connecting to others

Models of Communication

In order to see the relationships between these various components of communication, let's look at three models of communication, summarized in Figure 1.1 (Worley & Worley 2000). Note that each model is named, diagrammed, assigned a symbol, and compared with a sport or physical skill. Each model also includes several of the components of communication we identified in the previous section, namely, the sender (S), the message (M), the channel (C), and the receiver (R). The two arrows and the two-way arrow represent feedback in the interactive and transactional models. The check mark represents noise, and the brackets in the last two models represent the contexts that directly impact communication. Let's consider each of these models in turn, and then we will examine a way to further adapt one of the models.

Laswell (1948) first diagrammed communication using the **transmission** or **linear model.** Later, Shannon and Weaver (1949) added noise as a component of this

transmission (or linear) model depicts communication as a straight line where communication flows in only one direction—from sender to receiver

FIGURE 1.1   Three Models of Communication

Name of Model	Transmission	Interactive	Transactional
Diagram of Model	$S \rightarrow \sqrt{} M \rightarrow C \rightarrow R$	$[S \rightarrow \sqrt{} M \rightarrow C \rightarrow R$ $\leftarrow \ \leftarrow \ \leftarrow$ Feedback	$[R/S \leftrightarrow \sqrt{} M \leftrightarrow$ $C \leftrightarrow R/S]$
Symbol	$\rightarrow$	$\rightarrow$ $\leftarrow$	∞
Metaphor for Model	Archery	Tennis	Juggling

Source: "Three Models of Communication" by D. W. Worley and D. A. Worley from "Explaining, Envisioning and Embodying Basic Communication Models" in L. & B. Hugenberg (Eds.) *Teaching Ideas for the Basic Course,* pp. 17–22. Reprinted by permission of Kendall/Hunt.

model. Notice how this model depicts communication as a straight line (this is why it is called a *linear model*) where communication flows in only one direction, from sender to receiver. A single arrow represents this model; it is likened to archery because the sender "shoots" a message to the receiver or target of the message. Therefore, in this model, communication occurs when the sender has successfully delivered his or her message. After you did not comprehend a message, perhaps someone has said to you, "But I *told* you that yesterday!" Or maybe you have said the same thing to a friend, partner, or parent. Whenever we use this statement, we are assuming that by sending a message, we successfully delivered the message and that our intended target has received it. In reality, we know that this is not how we communicate with one another; communication is not like transmitting a signal and is seldom one-dimensional.

The second model, the **interactive model,** draws on the work of Schramm (1955), who emphasized the role of feedback in human communication. In this model, there is still a sender, message, channel, receiver, and noise, but the receiver responds to the sender. This view of communication is much like playing tennis: The sender lobs a message to the receiver who, in turn, fires back a message. Therefore, two arrows depict this model, because both the sender and receiver are actively engaged in the communication process. The interactive model stresses turn-taking.

> **interactive model** emphasizes the role of feedback in human communication; communication flows from the sender to the receiver and back

Communication, however, can most often be depicted in the third model, the **transactional model** (Wood 2001). If you observe people talking with one another, it soon becomes apparent that while we do take turns, sometimes we talk simultaneously or we may even interrupt or talk over one another. Even if we are not speaking at the same time, we still send nonverbal messages while we communicate. In other words, there is no time lapse in sending and receiving messages, as suggested by the interactive model. We send and receive messages simultaneously and therefore act as senders *and* receivers at the same time, as depicted in the transactional model. In order to demonstrate this simultaneous process, we use two-way arrows and an infinity symbol. Juggling acts as a metaphor for communication, because people are actively engaging in sending and receiving messages at the same time. In a sense, we could say that communication is always "up in the air," because it is ongoing.

> **transactional model** depicts communication in which people act simultaneously as senders and receivers

Communication theorists identify context as the key difference between an interactive and a transmission view of communication, although context is an equally important consideration in transactional communication. As Wood (2001) explains, these contexts or systems impact the kinds of meanings people create, especially if the communicators share similar or have very different personal experiences. For example, think of the challenges international students encounter in studying at universities in the United States. They face many strange contexts because their prior experiences include different native languages, climates, foods, holidays, values, and beliefs. Because of so many contextual changes, international students face **culture shock,** which Martin and Nakayama (2002) define as "a relatively short-term feeling of disorientation, or discomfort due to the unfamiliarity of surroundings and the lack of familiar cues in the environment" (p. 89). An international student recently described her experience of studying in the United States by saying, "I feel invisible," while another said, "Learning in English is like trying to see through a gauzy cloth; everything was there but nothing was clear. Over time, it was like the cloth was being removed so that I could see what was going on around me." These students express the overwhelming challenges in understanding the context for communication in English, which is a significant factor in communication, as depicted by the transactional model.

> **cultural shock** a relatively short-term feeling of disorientation or discomfort due to the unfamiliarity of surroundings and the lack of familiar cues in the environment

Both of these examples illustrate the importance of context in the transactional model. As the model indicates, the communication context surrounds the entire process of communication and therefore influences every aspect of the process.

In addition to these three models, we propose a fourth model—the **creative communication model** (Worley & Worley 2000). This model, depicted in Figure 1.2, has all the elements of the transactional model but stresses two important differences. First, pictures of two *people* replace the *roles* of sender and receiver. As we

> **creative communication model** contains all the elements of the transactional model, but emphasizes communication as a creative process and a uniquely human activity

International students face unique challenges studying in the United States.

emphasized earlier in this chapter, communication is a unique *human* activity. In fact, Burke (1961) defines *humans* as "symbol users." In other words, our ability to communicate is essential to our humanness. The creative communication model emphasizes this important fact. Second, as people, with all our thoughts, motivations, and behaviors, we work together to create and share meanings with one another as we simultaneously send and receive messages. This is, indeed, a creative process that requires us to draw on a range of abilities unique to our species. Through our use of words, voice, face, and body, we can share information and emotion or seek to persuade others to our viewpoint. As one ancient writer phrased it, "A word fitly spoken is like apples of gold in pictures of silver" (Proverbs 25:11, KJV). In other words, the right word at the right time can leave a legacy of beauty. At some point in your life, someone has probably said something to you that moved you so much that it lingers in your memory to this day. This demonstrates how people make meaning through creative communication.

FIGURE 1.2   Creative Model of Communication

These four models, then, help us relate the components of communication to one another, while also identifying some important characteristics of communication. However, there are additional characteristics that will further clarify our understanding of communication, which we consider next.

Characteristics of Human Communication

We have already identified communication as symbolic, transactional, and contextual. These constitute the first three important characteristics of communication. Let's consider the remaining characteristics. As the linked loop ∞ in the transactional model suggests, communication is a **process**. In order to think carefully about

process an ongoing activity

communication, we divide and diagram the process into components. However, in reality, communication is not a series of separate acts but is ongoing; it is not like a series of single frames examined one at a time, but more like a movie in which the frames flow together. To illustrate, before coming to college, you probably spent a great deal of time thinking about which college to attend, what college life would be like, and how your life might change. Your thinking was probably influenced quite heavily by your life experiences and by the people with whom you spent a lot of your time. In other words, the communication you experienced before coming to college impacts your expectations and behaviors now when you are attending college; it also influences how you communicate with others about your college experience both now and in the future.

To take another example, if you have a best friend, you probably share a special communication code you have created as a result of prior communication with each other. Therefore, the two of you enjoy verbal or nonverbal shorthand: a word, phrase, or name holds special significance for both of you and creates a predictable reaction, even if you have not seen each other for a long period of time. This demonstrates that communication is indeed a process, because what you have shared before continues to influence your communication in the present and in the future.

Communication is also **complex.** Given what we have already discovered about the nature of human communication, this may seem apparent. As one student commented, "I never realized communication was so complicated!" To make the point even clearer, let's briefly review and then consider some additional information. Communication is complex because it requires people with possibly very different backgrounds and experiences to use ambiguous symbols to co-create meaning in an environment that may be very noisy. Additionally, human communication is complex because it is **intentional, relational, contextual,** and **ethical.**

Communication Is Intentional

Intention refers to what we plan or propose to do. The word suggests that we make choices and then act upon them. Consider this question: Do we communicate even when we don't intend to do so? Watzlawick, Beavin, and Jackson (1967) contend that "one cannot *not* communicate." They believe that we communicate regardless of whether we choose to do so. Other communication theorists distinguish communication from communicative behavior. These scholars contend that communication is, by definition, always intentional or purposeful behavior. This may at first seem like a senseless debate, but this debate serves to emphasize the complexity that attends both the study and the practice of communication. Have you ever been totally misunderstood and you did not know why? Think about what happened. In all likelihood, something you said or did was misinterpreted. To put it in terms we introduced earlier, the receiver of your message attached an intended meaning to your words or behavior that was, in fact, not your intention at all.

Many of your previous experiences may help you understand the complexity of communication. One day an elementary school student sat in his music class listening to a group of students (of which he was not a part) sing a particular phrase from a song they were practicing for an upcoming spring concert. As the group sang, the student rubbed his nose with his right hand. The teacher stopped the class and verbally rebuked him for the behavior. The young boy was astonished; he scratched his nose because it itched, but the teacher interpreted the behavior to mean that the student thought the group's singing "stunk." This example illustrates communication that is unintentional. It also illustrates that communication is a process, because this event continued to influence the student's communication with his teacher during and after elementary school.

Communication Is Relational and Contextual

As we explained earlier, communication is also complex because it includes both content and relational dimensions. We communicate information or a request, and we indicate how we feel about others in the manner in which we share the information or present the request. Although we may not be aware of it, we tell others how we view our

complex incorporating intention, relation, context, and ethics

intentional purposeful

content the information or request in a message

relational indicative of the relationship between the sender and receiver

ethics the right or best way to communicate in a given situation

relationships with them when we communicate. If a faculty member asks students to complete an assignment and invites questions and offers help, he or she is demonstrating that he or she recognizes the interpersonal quality of a teacher-student relationship. However, if a faculty member gives an assignment and does not allow an opportunity for questions, tells students to work problems out for themselves, or threatens to lower the students' grades if they pose questions or ask for help, the instructor communicates a very different view of his or her relationship with students by emphasizing the superior-subordinate roles of teacher and student.

In order to be successful in college, you must learn how to read these cues and respond accordingly from semester to semester as you meet new teachers. Even though this may at first seem relatively simple, learning to read relational messages is actually quite complicated. It becomes even more complicated given that people have days when they do not feel well or may be frustrated or overwhelmed and, as a result, act out of character. For example, a teacher who has been helpful and approachable all term may one day, in a stressful moment, become irritable and speak more firmly with students. No doubt his or her students ask, "What happened? I thought the teacher liked us! What did we do wrong?" Suddenly, the relational message shifts and communication becomes even more complex!

Communication Is Ethical   When we are faced with asking what is the *right* way or the *best* way to communicate in a given situation, we are dealing with the ethics of communication. If we seek to escape or ignore these questions, we have made a clear ethical choice. Consider these important questions about communication ethics: Is it ever appropriate to lie to someone? Should you confront a speaker in a public setting if you know his or her argument relies on false or misused information? Is it wise to tell your best friend that his partner is cheating on him? Should your campus allow all groups, even hate groups, to speak freely on campus? What is the best way to respond to a university employee who becomes verbally abusive when you ask to speak to her manager? Making these and other decisions about what is the right or appropriate communication in a given situation requires considerable wisdom and skill and makes communication even more complex! We will discuss ethical communication further in Chapter 2.

Some Clarifications about Communication: Addressing Misconceptions

We have examined a descriptive phrase, considered models of communication, and identified components of communication. Now let's consider some common misconceptions about communication.

Misconception #1: Communication Is Exact   Exactness in communication is impossible. As we have stressed throughout this chapter, communication requires creative negotiation, not transmission or translation. Because of our unique backgrounds and experiences, the limitations of symbols, and the nature of meaning, we can never avoid miscommunication or the hard work required to negotiate meaning. It is unrealistic to think that we can attain perfect precision with our communication skills. Although we can certainly improve our skills and learn how to reduce miscommunication and enhance fidelity, or greater clarity, we can never achieve exactness.

Misconception #2: More Communication Is Better Communication   Even though communication is fundamentally important to every part of our lives, we should not assume that increasing the *amount* of communication results in greater benefit. More is not always better, because communication is governed by the law of diminishing returns—that is, increasing the quantity of the communication may actually compromise its quality. For instance, some of you may have wrestled with whether you should have enrolled in college this semester. You may have talked about it repeatedly and still not made a decision until almost the beginning of the

Sometimes increasing the quantity of communication diminishes its quality.

term. As a result, when you decided to enroll in college, you found that you had *talked* about the decision rather than made the decision and therefore had a more difficult time registering for the classes you wanted because they were already full. In this case, less talk and more action would have helped. Therefore, *more* communication does not always equal *better* communication.

Misconception #3: Communication Solves All Conflicts Communication does not solve all conflicts. Often people speak of communication as a cure for all ills. You have likely heard the following assertions. People would have better health if they just communicated their feelings more. Relationships would be stronger and more satisfying if parents, partners, and friends opened up to one another. International tensions would be reduced if representatives from the affected nations engaged in peaceful negotiation. Even though all of these assertions have some degree of validity, they are not absolutely true. Communication does not necessarily cure health or relational and national conflicts. Communication may help people and nations to identify difficulties and discover ways to address conflicts, but it is not a magic elixir that will cure all problems. To believe otherwise is to misunderstand communication.

COMMUNICATING IN COLLEGE AND LIFE

As we noted at the beginning of this chapter, developing effective communication skills is vital to your college experience and to your future after you complete your education. Consider the story of Mike, an engineer who designs computer chips used in wildlife tracking equipment. Mike spends much of his day sitting at a computer and manipulating technical programs. It may seem as if he does not need to rely on communication with others; however, he also interacts with customers and makes presentations at scientific conferences and trade shows. He also regularly teaches classes at his church and voices his opinions about political issues that concern him. At one point, Mike observed, "I would never have developed the confidence and ability to organize and express my thoughts if I had not taken a basic speech course in college. What I learned there has helped me think, write, and speak as nothing else ever has. I used these skills while I was in college, and I continue to use them in my life and work every day." While you may not share his exact experience and while the course you are enrolled in is but one introductory course to human communication, remember that this course and future courses in communication can help you navigate college with greater ease and assist you in developing skills that will aid you for a lifetime, especially if you begin applying them now. We encourage you, then, to begin working on your communication skills today to enhance your success in college and later.

SUMMARY

In this chapter we introduced the important role communication plays in our college environment and in our personal, professional, and public lives. Rather than define human communication, we have offered various ways to describe it. As a result, we have established that human communication is a creative negotiated process. The following list highlights the major ideas in this chapter:

- Human communication includes senders, receivers, messages, channels, contexts, feedback, noise, and motivation.

- There are four models of communication: transmission, interactive, transactional, and creative.
- Communication is a complex, intentional, ethical process that includes both relational and content messages.
- There are numerous misconceptions about communication.

Questions for Discussion

1. In what ways have you used oral communication to enhance your learning as a college student?
2. Provide personal examples that illustrate this phrase: "*When we communicate with one another, we are negotiating meaning.*"
3. How might a different channel influence how a message is understood? Give examples of messages that might have different interpretations depending on the channel used to send and receive the message.

EXERCISES

1. Think of a time when you have been misunderstood. Using at least two of the concepts from this chapter, write a brief paragraph that explains why this misunderstanding took place.
2. You have had considerable experience with a variety of teachers during your twelve-plus years of education. Without naming any teacher, identify one of your teachers who you believe was an effective communicator and one who was not as effective. Using the communication models provided in this chapter, analyze these two teachers. To which model of communication do you believe the effective and the less effective teacher subscribed? Why? Write a one-page essay explaining your analysis.
3. Assume that you want to break up with a romantic partner whom you have been dating for several months. Analyze this communication situation drawing on the information you have read in this chapter. How will you do this? What kinds of messages will you develop? What channels will you use? Where will you explain your decision? What ethical issues will you need to consider?

KEY TERMS

Human Communication
Symbolic
Paralanguage or vocalics
Fidelity
Sender
Receiver
Encoder
Decoder
Message

Feedback
Channel
Context
Noise
Motivation
Instrumental/functional communication
Relational communication
Transmission/linear model

Interactive model
Transactional model
Culture shock
Creative communication model
Process
Complex
Intentionality
Content/relational dimensions
Ethical dimension

REFERENCES

Aslanian, C. B. 1996. *Adult learning in America: Why and how adults go back to school.* Washington, DC: Office of Adult Learning Services, the College Board.

Astin, A. W. 1985. *Achieving educational excellence.* San Francisco: Jossey-Bass.

Barker, L., Edwards, B. R., Gaines, C., Gladney, K., and Holley, F. 1980. An investigation of the proportional time spent in various communication activities by college students. *Journal of Applied Communication Research* 8:101–110.

Brown, A. C. 1996. Older & better: Back to the classroom (Minneapolis-St. Paul) *Star Tribune.* Online (www.startribune.com/mcu/projects/learning/content/story2.html).

Burke, K. 1961. *The rhetoric of religion.* San Francisco: University of California Press.

Dance, F. X. E., and Larson, C. E. 1976. *The functions of human communication: A theoretical approach.* New York: Holt, Rinehart and Winston.

Gardner, J. N., and Jewler, A. J. 2003. *Your college experience: Strategies for success.* 5th ed. Belmont, CA: Wadsworth.

Johnson, G. M., Staton, A. Q., and Jorgensen-Earp, C. R. 1995. An ecological perspective on the transition of new university freshmen. *Communication Education* 44:336–352.

Laswell, H. D. 1948. The structure and function of communication in society. In *The communication of ideas*, ed. L. Bryson. New York: Harper & Row.

Martin, J. N., and Nakayama, T. K. 2001. *Experiencing intercultural communication: An introduction.* Mountain View, CA: Mayfield.

McCroskey, J. C., and Richmond, V. P. 1990. Willingness to communicate: A cognitive view. *Journal of Social Behavior and Personality* 5:19–37.

Miller, C. R., Larsen, J., and Gaitens, J. October 1996. Communication in the workplace: What can NCSU students expect? North Carolina State University Center for Communication in Science, Technology, and Management, Publication Series Number 2.

Myers, G. E., and Myers, M. T. 1992. *The dynamics of human communication: A laboratory approach.* 6th ed. Boston: McGraw-Hill.

National Center for Education Statistics. (n.d.). *Digest of education statistics for 2002: All levels of education.* Retrieved January 26, 2004, from http://nces.ed.gov/programs/digest/d02/dt022.asp.

National Center for Education Statistics. (n.d.). *Digest of education statistics for 2002: Outcomes of education.* Retrieved January 26, 2004, from http://nces.ed.gov/programs/digest/d02/dt381.asp.

Noel, L., Levitz, R., and Saluri, D., eds. 1985. A study of first-generation college students and their families. *American Journal of Education* X:144–170.

Richman, J. 2002. The news journal of the life scientist. *Scientist* 16(18):42.

Schramm, W. 1955. *The process and effects of mass communication.* Urbana: University of Illinois Press.

Shannon, C., and Weaver, W. 1949. *The mathematical theory of communication.* Urbana: University of Illinois Press.

Sypher, B. D., Bostrom, R. N., and Seibert, J. H. 1989. Listening communication abilities and success at work. *Journal of Business Communication* 25:293–303.

Terenzini, P. T., Rendon, L. I., Millar, S. B., Upcraft, M. L., Gregg, P. L., Jamolo, R. Jr., and Allison, K. W. 1996. Making transition to college. In *Teaching on solid ground: Using scholarship to improve practice*, eds. R. J. Menges, M. Weimer, and associates, 43–73. San Francisco: Jossey-Bass.

Tinto, V. 1993. *Leaving college: Rethinking the causes and cures of student attrition.* Chicago: University of Chicago Press.

Van Gennep, A. 1960. *The rites of passage.* Trans M. Vizedon, and G. Caffee. Chicago: University of Chicago Press. Originally published as *Les rites de passage.* Paris: Nourry, 1909.

Watzlawick, P., Beavin, J., and Jackson, D. D. 1967. *Pragmatics of human communication.* New York: Norton.

Wolvin, A. D., and Coakley, C. G. 1991. A survey of the status of listening and training in some Fortune 500 companies. *Communication Education* 40:52–164.

Wood, J. T. 2001. *Communication mosaics: An introduction to the field of communication.* Belmont, CA: Wadsworth.

Worley, D. W., and Worley, D. A. 2000. Explaining, envisioning, and embodying basic communication models. In *Teaching ideas for the basic course IV*, eds. L. Hugenberg and B. Hugenberg, 17–22. Dubuque, IA: Kendall/Hunt.

CHAPTER 2

Communicating Ethically and Competently

Ethical Communication

Sources
- Family
- Religion
- Culture

Principles
- Honesty / Truthfulness
- Fidelity
- Confidentiality
- Fairness
- Significant Choice

Orientation

Approaches

Consequentialist
- Principle of Veracity

Nonconsequentialist

Goals
- Stimulate Moral Imagination
- Recognize Ethical Issues
- Develop Analytic Skills
- Tolerate Disagreement

Guidelines
- Knowledge
- Sensitivity
- Understanding

Knowledge Checklist

✓ To understand the ethical component of every communication situation
✓ To understand a number of sources of ethical guidelines
✓ To recognize the goals of studying communication ethics
✓ To develop a broader set of ethical guidelines for analyzing communication

ETHICAL COMMUNICATION

*W*hen you hear the word *ethics*, what do you think of? Do you think of news headlines that describe yet another example of misconduct by a government official, or of another faulty product sold to unsuspecting consumers? If this is what immediately comes to mind, you may not have a complete picture of ethics. Although we see examples of unethical behavior every day in newspapers, television, and other media, most of us never make the headlines. Yet in our daily lives, we are faced with decisions that have ethical dimensions. In any situation where you think about a decision in terms of right and wrong or good and bad, or when you consider what the consequences of your decision might be to yourself, friends, or family, you have begun to touch on the ethical dimension of your communication.

Understanding Ethics and Communication

What do ethics have to do with communication? Professor Richard Johannesen (2002) suggests, "Ethical issues may arise in human behavior whenever that behavior could have significant impact on other persons, when the behavior involves conscious choice of means and ends, and when the behavior can be judged by standards of right and wrong" (p. 1). Thus, if there is little possibility of significant, immediate, or long-term impact, ethical considerations are minimized. If we have little or no choice in our decision or are compelled to a decision, ethics is minimally relevant to our actions. But, Johannesen writes, "whether a communicator seeks to present information, increase someone's level of understanding, facilitate independent decision in another person, persuade about important values, demonstrate the existence and relevance of a societal problem, advocate a solution or program of action, or stimulate conflict-potential, ethical issues are inherent in the communicator's symbolic efforts. Such is the case for most human communication whether it is between two people, in small groups, in the rhetoric of a social movement, in communication from government to citizen, or in an advertising, public relations or a political campaign" (p. 2). Communication clearly possesses an ethical dimension, even though it may be more apparent in some cases than in others.

According to ethics professor Thomas Nilsen (1966), "As a subject of study, ethics deals with questions about the meaning of 'good' and 'bad,' 'right' and 'wrong,' and 'moral obligation.' Without any formal study of ethics, we can describe many acts that we would unhesitatingly call 'wrong,' and others that we would call 'right.' Further, we feel there are some things we *ought* to do, such as help someone in need or keep our promises, and some things we *ought not* to do, such as be cruel or cheat at cards. We feel we ought to do what is right and ought not to do what is wrong" (p. 1). Sometimes these decisions are simple and clear, but we should reflect carefully before making this conclusion. Another ethics professor, Dr. J. Vernon Jensen (1997), defines ethics "as the moral responsibility to choose, intentionally and voluntarily, oughtness in values like rightness, goodness, truthfulness, justice, and virtue, which may, in a communicative transaction,

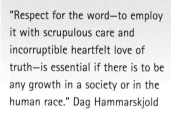

"Respect for the word—to employ it with scrupulous care and incorruptible heartfelt love of truth—is essential if there is to be any growth in a society or in the human race." Dag Hammarskjold

significantly affect ourselves and others" (p. 4). These definitions share one important insight: They both indicate that communicators who are not coerced into a communication situation must understand and accept responsibility for the outcome of their communication interaction.

Instead of taking for granted that we "know" how others will react to our communication and that we "know" they won't be "harmed," we should think critically about our communication before we act. For example, is it wrong to tell a lie in order to spare someone's feelings? Should we tell the "whole" truth in all situations? If not, then under what circumstances is it acceptable to lie? What is a "lie" anyway? Are we lying when we let someone draw erroneous conclusions from something we said without attempting to clarify their misunderstanding? These questions are basic to any understanding of the role ethics plays in our communication. Ethics is fundamental to communication because any time our communication affects another, we are responsible for the outcome. In our daily interactions, we directly and sometimes dramatically affect others through our explanations, instructions, endearments, approval, rebuke, courtesy, and so on.

All of our communication has consequences for ourselves, for others in the communication interaction, and for the larger society in which we reside. Former secretary-general of the United Nations Dag Hammarskjold once wrote, "Respect for the word is the first commandment in the discipline by which a [human] can be educated to maturity—intellectual, emotional, and moral. Respect for the word— to employ it with scrupulous care and incorruptible heartfelt love of truth—is essential if there is to be any growth in a society or in the human race. To misuse the word is to show contempt for [humanity]. It undermines the bridges and poisons the wells. It causes [humans] to regress down the long path of evolution" (cited in Nilsen 1966, p. 1). What Hammarskjold means by "respect for the word" is, in part, to speak truthfully, without intentionally deceiving someone; we should consider the outcome or consequences of our communication when we try to make a "good" decision.

How do we analyze a situation in order to make a "good" decision? First we examine our basic beliefs and values. These become the principles that provide a foundation for what is important to us and are derived from a wide variety of sources in our lives: family, church, school, friendships, media, organizations, and so on.

Communication Links

The National Communication Association Credo
for Ethical Communication

The statement that follows is from the National Communication Association and outlines ethical communication (see www.natcom.org/policies/External/ EthicalComm.htm). How well do you think this statement captures the ethics of communication? How might this statement inform or influence your communication practices?

Questions of right and wrong arise whenever people communicate. Ethical communication is fundamental to responsible thinking, decision making, and the development of relationships and communities within and across contexts, cultures, channels, and media. Moreover, ethical communication enhances human worth and dignity by fostering truthfulness, fairness, responsibility, personal integrity, and respect for self and others. We believe that unethical communication threatens the quality of all communication and consequently the well-being of individuals and the society in which we live. Therefore we, the members of the National Communication Association, endorse and are committed to practicing the following principles of ethical communication:

- We advocate truthfulness, accuracy, honesty, and reason as essential to the integrity of communication.
- We endorse freedom of expression, diversity of perspective, and tolerance of dissent to achieve the informed and responsible decision making fundamental to a civil society.
- We strive to understand and respect other communicators before evaluating and responding to their messages.
- We promote access to communication resources and opportunities as necessary to fulfill human potential and contribute to the well-being of families, communities, and society.
- We promote communication climates of caring and mutual understanding that respect the unique needs and characteristics of individual communicators.
- We condemn communication that degrades individuals and humanity through distortion, intimidation, coercion, and violence, and through the expression of intolerance and hatred.
- We are committed to the courageous expression of personal convictions in pursuit of fairness and justice.
- We advocate sharing information, opinions, and feelings when facing significant choices while also respecting privacy and confidentiality.
- We accept responsibility for the short- and long-term consequences for our own communication and expect the same of others.

Source: The National Communication Association Credo for Ethical Communication. Reprinted by permission of the National Communication Association.

Sources of Ethical Guidelines

For most of us, our family is the first source that helped us develop our beliefs and values. We learn our basic sense of right and wrong from our family environment, where our behaviors are either encouraged or discouraged. Many of us probably received more instructions on what *not* to do rather than on what to do. Our parents discouraged behavior that affected our health or safety (i.e., look both ways before crossing the street), that disturbed others (i.e., don't interrupt when someone

Cultural values are often communicated through television.

else is speaking), or that differed from "accepted" conduct (i.e., don't use profanity). Some behavior was forbidden because our parents believed it was sinful or violated an important precept of our religious teaching.

Our religious background or church affiliation also provides us with a definitive source of ethics. If your family did not attend a church or identify with a specific religion, perhaps other types of authority (police, politicians, etc.) became a significant source of the "do nots" in your life. Teachers are some of the most significant authority figures who impact our sense of right and wrong. Can you identify a teacher who had a significant impact on you? How did he or she treat you? Was this person concerned about you as an individual? In addition to your teachers, the school you attended was most likely full of "rules of conduct" that provided stability and consistency throughout your childhood (even if you didn't think all the rules were necessary). (Consider the National Communication Association Credo for Ethical Communication in the Communication Links box on the previous page for additional insight about ethical communication). Whatever the source of authority that helped develop your belief and value system, you began to develop a sense of right and wrong.

Another source of ethical guidelines or values comes through the larger culture of which we are a part. The box Cultural Links: Understanding Differing Values provides more information about the links between culture and communication. For most of us, culture comes through mediated channels—radio, television, the Internet, and so on. We learn what individuals and groups outside of our geographic areas, religious training, cultural background, or educational upbringing believe should guide ethical reflection. Think about your favorite television program. How does this show portray values regarding relationships? Would you define these values as "good"? The view of our larger culture often provides us with a dramatically different understanding of right and wrong or provides us with differences of opinion on what is right and wrong. We may learn that some of our early sources of morality (i.e., family) were not always right. We also learn that what may be considered right at one time may be wrong at another; right and wrong are not fixed categories. Laws and rules vary from place to place and from person to person, and they are often adapted to new circumstances. Think about issues such as slavery, segregation, or women's right to vote. In each of these cases, the "right" or "ethical" position within our culture has changed substantially over time. To illustrate, religious institutions may modify their moral prescriptions from generation to generation in order to respond to changing social conditions—for example, many religions that were male dominated now accept women as ministers.

◎ Cultural Links

Understanding Differing Values

Should people live their lives focused on spiritual matters, career aspirations, or family expectations? Should people use the natural world as they see fit, actively protect the natural world, or seek to strike a balance? The answers to these and like queries are valuable because they reveal what you believe the world should be like. Answers also differ depending on the background from which you originate. Consider these five important questions created from research by Kluckhohn and Strodtbeck (1961):

1. What is human nature?
2. What is the relationship between humans and nature?
3. What is the relationship between humans?
4. What is the preferred form of activity?
5. What is the orientation toward time?

The following chart shows the range of cultural answers to these questions, according to these authors' research. As you read this chart, where do you place yourself? Can you think of people from different cultures whose answers are likely to be different from yours? Why might the answers differ?

Question	Alternatives		
#1	**Evil:** People are basically evil; evil must be controlled	**Mixed:** People are both good and bad when born	**Good:** People are basically good
#2	**Controlled by nature:** People have little control over nature; nature decides your life	**Harmony with nature:** People are one with nature; nature is one's partner in life	**Humans control nature:** Humans dominate nature and should use it for their own purposes
#3	**Authoritarian:** Clear lines of authority are followed and dominate relationships (e.g., patriarchy)	**Group-oriented:** Individual goals and wishes are less important than group goals and wishes	**Individualism:** Individual goals and wishes are more important than group goals and wishes
#4	**Being:** Emphasizes who you are and encourages free expression of emotion and desires	**Growing:** Emphasizes becoming who you are through growth; encourages self-expression along with self-control	**Doing:** Emphasizes action; emphasizes self-expression measured by external criteria, not by self
#5	**Past:** Traditions and customs matter most; they should be carefully followed	**Present:** What matters is here and now; yesterday is gone; tomorrow is not here yet	**Future:** Think about tomorrow and plan for it; be prepared for what is ahead

Source: Kluckhohn, F. K. & Strodtbeck, F. L. from *Variations in Value Orientations.* Evanston, IL: Row, Peterson, 1961.

Because the sources of our beliefs and values change as we mature, we may face internal conflict as we utilize a wider variety of sources to make critical, ethical decisions—that is, given the influences in our lives, we may question what we once believed to be right or wrong, or may change our opinions. (The box Campus Links: Understanding Moral Growth provides more information about how we grow morally and ethically.) One of the most difficult issues for many college students is how to respond to the broader range of values and beliefs they are exposed to in college classes, civic organizations, campus media, and so on. Is it "ethical" to maintain your previously established beliefs and values under all circumstances? Or is it more "ethical" to adapt your beliefs and values to new situations, such as when meeting new people and learning new concepts and skills? These are not easy or simple questions. Evaluating one's ethics is difficult and often confusing. It may also been seen as threatening to others who may not approve of changes in our thought processes or actions. Despite these obstacles, one of the steps in becoming an adult is establishing one's own value system; whether you are aware of it or not, you are likely in the midst of this process now.

To help you develop ethical communication skills, there are several generally agreed upon principles.

 **Campus Links**

Understanding Moral Growth

As you further your education, you will encounter a variety of ideas, opinions, and perspectives that are very different from those you have been taught. Consequently, you are likely to become confused and perhaps even troubled by the challenge of charting your own moral path. In the end, however, you are responsible for your personal ethical standards. While you may "borrow" ethics from your family, religion, or other sources, you must make these principles your own through the hard work of personal reflection and choice. Even if you evade this process, you cannot escape personal choices and their consequences. For example, if you declare, "I don't have any ethical standards," you have just made an ethical declaration! Understanding how moral growth occurs may help you embrace rather than avoid the process.

Perry's Four Stages of Ethical Growth

William G. Perry Jr. (1970) theorized that ethical growth occurs in four stages. While there are a variety of opinions about this scheme, it is worthwhile to consider Perry's work, because his research focused on what happens during the college years.

Stage One: Dualism

In dualism, students believe simply and firmly that things are right and wrong; they have no room for middle ground. Students in the dualism stage want direct, complete, and certain answers, or they may believe they already have such answers from their prior training. Therefore, dualistic students will make statements such as, "It is always wrong to steal."

Stage Two: Individual Relativism

In the second stage, students realize there are multiple answers to ethical questions coming from a variety of sources and understand there are no certain, clear, complete answers to these questions. Therefore, students in the individual relativism stage may believe that the best they can do is listen to their individual, inner voices and do whatever they think is the best, since there is no one right answer. At this stage, a student might state, "It's okay to steal if you think it's okay."

Stage Three: Contextual Relativism

This stage of moral development is also relativistic (i.e., there are no certain, complete, clear ethical answers). However, students using contextual relativism rely on the situation and context, rather than on individual opinion, to make ethical decisions. In this stage, students are apt to say, "It's okay to steal if, for example, your children are hungry and you don't have any way to feed them."

Stage Four: Commitment in Relativism

Students committed to relativism also recognize that there are many ethical positions. However, after reflection, consideration of others' views, and personal choice, students in this stage stake out a moral position that they recognize has consequences and accept the personal responsibility it carries. Students in this stage may say, "It's wrong to steal, except in circumstances that require one to steal for life, health, safety, or well-being." While this may sound very similar to contextual relativism, the difference is that in this stage, students commit to a broader principle rather than to situational decision making.

Ethical Principles

honesty and truthfulness the first two principles of ethical communication

Perhaps the two primary principles that each of us will utilize when making decisions concern **honesty** and **truthfulness**. (The ethical principles discussed in this section are summarized in Table 2.1). Ethicist Sissela Bok (1978) explains, "There is great risk [in discussing truth and truthfulness] of not seeing the crucial differences

Table 2.1	Ethical Principles in Communication	
Principle	**Definition**	**Example**
Honesty & Truthfulness	Telling the truth and not withholding the truth	Not lying to or misleading friends
Fidelity	Keeping promises and acting faithfully	Completing your share of group work which you agreed to do
Confidentiality	Keeping secrets and confidences when requested	Guarding friends' private information
Fairness	Appropriate treatment for everyone	A professor offering *all* students extra credit opportunities
Significant Choice	Sufficient information to make good choices	Knowing enough about college policies so that you can make an effective decision

between two domains: the *moral* domain of intended truthfulness and deception, and the much vaster domain of truth and falsity in general. The moral question of whether you are lying or not is not *settled* by establishing the truth or falsity of what you say. In order to settle this question, we must know whether you *intend your statement to mislead*" (p. 6). In other words, to lie is to intentionally mislead another—by telling someone something that you know to be untrue or by withholding information that would change another's interpretation of the information. Whenever we intentionally manipulate information, we lie. Bok suggests, "A false person is not one merely wrong or mistaken or incorrect; it is one who is intentionally deceitful or treacherous or disloyal" (p. 8).

Though people who adhere to the principles of honesty or truthfulness may occasionally lie while still valuing *truthfulness* as the "norm," most of us cannot imagine a society in which *lying* is the norm. In order to function in our society, we must trust to some degree that what others say is true. For example, on the first day of your communication class, did you presume that your instructor would tell you the truth regarding the course's requirements? When you filled out your application for college, did you presume that the individuals reading that application would believe you were telling the truth? In the beginning stages of relationship development, we need to balance our expectations of "truthfulness" with our knowledge that some individuals, in some circumstances, do lie. Without some degree of trust, however, we would never be able to develop relationships of any significance. Additionally, as the box Career Links: Honesty in the Workplace points out, honestly is also important at work. Thus, in order to survive, individuals in society must generally regard truthfulness as a central virtue.

Following the principles of honesty and truthfulness are the related principles of **fidelity** (keeping promises and acting faithfully) and **confidentiality** (keeping secrets and confidences when requested). We learn early in our lives that keeping a promise or a secret is fundamental to successful relationships. Think about the individuals in your life to whom you act faithfully and whose promises you keep. The common denominator in each of these relationships is the degree of established trust between you and them. In turn, trust ensures fidelity and confidentiality.

We learn early in our lives that keeping a promise or secret is fundamental to successful relationships.

fidelity keeping promises and acting faithfully

confidentiality keeping secrets and confidences when requested

Honesty in the Workplace

Consider this piece, and ponder whether you agree with Mr. Barada's advice. Why? Can you think of a situation when lying might be a viable alternative in securing a job?

Honesty Is Still the Best Policy

by Paul W. Barada
Monster Salary and Negotiation Expert

As archaic and obvious as it may sound, when it comes to getting the job you want, honesty is still the best policy. During the 20-plus years I've been in the reference checking business, dishonesty is still one of the most common reasons people don't get the job they want. The most valuable piece of advice I could ever offer any job seeker, therefore, is to tell the truth—on the application, on the resume and during the job interview. Being

less than honest when applying for a job is the quickest way to end up standing in the unemployment line.

Lying about academic credentials is probably one of the most frequent deceptions, while embellishing some aspect of past job performance ranks a close second. Most job applications contain some sort of statement that provides for immediate termination for falsifying any information requested. As more and more companies thoroughly check references and credentials, taking the chance that an embellishment or falsehood won't be uncovered is foolish—and career threatening.

Falsifying academic credentials, for instance, is not only dishonest, [but it's also] a dumb thing to do because they're so easy to verify. I'm reminded of the candidate who was being considered for a very well-paying position with a petrochemical company. He had over two decades of solid performance, but he hadn't completed the degree in geology he claimed he had. As a result, he didn't get the job. Here's why: The prospective employer told him his years of experience would have more than offset not completing the degree, if he had only been honest with them about it, but they didn't want to start a relationship having caught him in a lie. Not a smart career move at all.

I recall another instance worth mentioning. A large Midwestern hospital was having problems with their new director of physical therapy. We were retained to verify his credentials. To make a long story short, he produced a diploma from a college in Wales in Britain. We sent a copy to them. The reply came back, "First of all, if this had been a diploma from our university it would have been written in Latin, not in English."

The guy had created a completely phony diploma! He was fired. Another frequent deception is putting down a phony response to the "reason for leaving" question. I wish I had a dollar for all the candidates who put down a response like "by mutual agreement" when, in fact, they were terminated. It's far better to be honest about the reason for leaving than to have a prospective employer discover the deception during a background check—that's a sure way to be dropped from further consideration.

Not every job is made in heaven. Sometimes the match simply isn't right. Sometimes personalities clash. Sometimes the reality of the job doesn't match the expectation. That stuff is normal. The key is being prepared during the job interview to candidly and honestly explain your perception of what happened. The real question to be answered is what you learned from the experience! Even if you were fired, it's far better to admit it and explain what you learned from the experience, than it is to lie about it and run the risk of getting caught. People make mistakes, especially during the early years of a career. We learn and grow as a result of those experiences. Employers can understand that far more readily than they can ever understand or tolerate dishonesty.

As my great-aunt Nell used to say, if you tell the truth, you don't have to worry about remembering what you said.

fairness takes many forms; used in making effective and ethical decisions

Also related to the principles of honesty and truthfulness is that of **fairness**. Fairness takes many forms. We may say something is fair if every person receives similar treatment. We may believe a situation is fair if the reward is commensurate with the effort or if the "punishment fits the crime." We may also believe that fairness means those who have more resources should help provide for those less fortunate. Regardless of your personal conception of fairness, we utilize this principle in making effective and ethical decisions. Think about what you believe is a "fair" grade for a course. Should fairness be decided only by doing assignments "correctly," or should other considerations such as completing work on time, neatness, and research weigh in the grade? Should special consideration be given those with certain circumstances such as illness, personal problems, or other coursework? These are ethical questions both you and your instructors will consider at some point during your college experience.

significant choice having sufficient information about a situation to make a "good" decision

Finally, **significant choice** is a principle central to our democratic process. *Significant choice* refers to having sufficient information about a situation to make a "good" decision. It also refers to our ability to make choices for ourselves. Our democracy requires that individuals become involved in the political and social processes that ground our society. Most of us consider significant choice a right. We may become angry, frustrated, and hostile when we perceive that others are keeping secrets from us or are withholding information critical to our ability to make good decisions. Significant choice is based upon respect for individuals. Providing information in order to make rational, effective decisions means we value people as decision makers. If information is withheld, our autonomy (self-determination) is in jeopardy. When our autonomy is jeopardized, we resent the lack of respect this represents.

While significant choice is fundamental to our democracy, it is also fundamental to our intimate, interpersonal relationships. In good faith, we ground our closest relationships on exchanging truthful, complete information. When we discover that we can no longer trust someone we confided in, our whole world seems out of alignment. In order to develop healthy personalities and self-concepts, we need to believe that those important to us are providing us with complete and truthful

Campus Links

Truthfulness and Romance

Many of you, especially those of you who do not have a life partner, are likely excited about the prospects of dating and romance during your college years. However, have you thought about what you expect from a college romance? Research regarding romantic relationships suggests that being able to trust your partner is vitally important and that intentional deception brings a number of results, including "(1) a strong effect on beliefs about the honesty of the other in the relationship, (2) negative emotional responses, (3) communication patterns of either avoidance or engagement, and (4) consequences for relationships, such as terminating or continuing them" (Jang, Smith, & Levine 2002, p. 236).

Although college romances may not endure, working toward honest, open relationships is important. All of your authors have talked with students who have been devastated by broken relationships. However, in our experience, when a partner has been deceived in some manner, the hurt is multiplied. We have seen students lose focus, become depressed, and even quit school because they have been so deeply hurt by a relationship that ended due to deception. Moreover, these students often find it difficult to trust others again and, understandably, become very self-protective. So, how can you enjoy dating and interacting with potential partners and still maintain honesty? Here are some suggested communication strategies for you to consider:

1. **Be honest with yourself.** Before you can be truthful with others, you must be honest with yourself about the kind of relationship you want. This may differ depending on your personality, your other life commitments, your age, or other factors. However, it is important that you have a clear sense of where you are in your own life and how much energy you wish to place in a relationship at this point. In other words, you need to have clear communication with yourself.

2. **Share your intentions.** If you're interested in having a good time and getting to know someone but not interested in a romantic commitment, make this clear from the outset. Don't let a dating partner assume your intentions; make them known in an appropriate way.

3. **Communicate courageously and kindly.** At some point, you may have to break up with someone. Whatever the reason, if you are no longer interested in dating someone or continuing a relationship, have the courage to say so as kindly as you can.

4. **Ask for forgiveness.** People make mistakes, and sometimes we may lie or break a trust. If this happens, you can continue trying to deceive or you can admit your wrongdoing, ask for forgiveness, work toward repairing the relationship, or end the relationship. All in all, people are human, and many of life's most important lessons are learned painfully as we grow.

information. Thus, it is in these close, interpersonal relationships that a special sensitivity to ethical communication must be exercised. The box Campus Links: Truthfulness and Romance, for example, discusses the importance of ethics in romantic relationships.

An Ethical Orientation

How do we go about developing ethical communication? To this question, Dr. Nilsen (1966) replies, "Whatever develops, enlarges, enhances human personalities is good; whatever restricts, degrades, or injures human personalities is bad" (p. 9). Developing and enhancing humanity means we develop a climate of care. This includes concern, warmth, acceptance, support, and trust. We communicate these behaviors because human beings have value. An ethical orientation also means that we seek to morally justify an action or decision by seeking good reasons to support it. We need to separate "liking" people from our belief that they have value as human beings. We can care for individuals and still disagree with them. We can care for people even if they anger and frustrate us. As the box Community Links: Consequences of Silence points out, caring for others means be willing to speak up rather than maintain silence.

We communicate concern, warmth, acceptance, support, and trust because human beings have value.

Community Links

Consequences of Silence

At various points in our lives, each of us belongs to a number of "communities." Sometimes these communities are small, such as our extended family; others are midsized, such as our college community; and still others are quite large, like the town, city, state, or country we reside in. We might also believe that a particular group we belong to is our "community"—such as a religious organization, a sports team, a work group, or an ethnic enclave. As a member of any community, one of our ethical obligations is to know when to respond to and stand up for an injustice. Whether we speak up or remain silent, our communication has an ethical dimension. Silence as a communication strategy does communicate to others. In our culture, silence is usually perceived as "implicit consent." For example, have you ever been at a family gathering where a family member told a joke that was racist, sexist, or sexually inappropriate? Did you speak up and confront the joke-teller about the inappropriateness of the joke? Most of us do not. But what we often fail to realize is that our silence tells the joke-teller we think these types of jokes are "okay."

We can probably think of several situations in which a friend, coworker, or fellow church member said or did something that we believed was inappropriate, but we went along with it for fear of "rocking the boat." What about situations where an individual requests assistance and we don't respond because "someone else will do it"? Have you ignored requests for help because you didn't want others to think differently or badly of you?

The following poem, which has several forms and about which there remains some controversy, refers to one situation in history during which the "consequences of silence" were devastating.

First They Came for the Jews
First they came for the Jews
and I did not speak out
because I was not a Jew.

*Then they came for the Communists
and I did not speak out
because I was not a Communist.
Then they came for the trade unionists
and I did not speak out
because I was not a trade unionist.
Then they came for me
and there was no one left
to speak out for me.*

Pastor Martin Niemöller

An important consideration in terms of ethical responsibilities as part of a community is the concept of *social justice*. According to the Center for Economic and Social Justice (www.cesj.org/thirdway/economicjustice-defined.htm), "Social justice encompasses economic justice. Social justice is the virtue which guides us in creating those organized human interactions we call institutions. In turn, social institutions, when justly organized, provide us with access to what is good for the person, both individually and in our associations with others. Social justice also imposes on each of us a personal responsibility to work with others to design and continually perfect our institutions as tools for personal and social development."

Moral Theories

When we disagree with someone, we must communicate honestly and appropriately about why we disagree and why we are angry. In other words, we need to justify our actions. Several moral theories can assist us in working through the justification process. One type of moral theory utilizes a **consequentialist approach**, which insists good consequences are the measure of decision making. At one end of the spectrum is the egotistic approach, which focuses only on the consequences of a decision for oneself. At the opposite end are the utilitarians, who believe that good decisions promote the greatest good for the greatest number.

> **consequentialist approach** the idea that good consequences are the measure of decision making

The Consequentialist Approach and the Principle of Veracity

Ethicist Sissela Bok (1978) provides us with a process that may help determine the consequences of a decision. Fundamental to her process is what she calls the **principle of veracity**, which holds that a negative weight is attached to any lie. At the outset, the liar bears the burden of proof that his or her lie is necessary as a last resort. Bok insists that acceptable alternatives to lying that accomplish the same ends are always to be sought and chosen first. In order to justify a lie, according to Bok, the individual must utilize a process that must be capable of being made public. Any moral principle worth considering, she believes, must be capable of public statement and defense. She combines the concept of *publicity* with the view of justification in ethics being *directed to reasonable persons*.

> **principle of veracity** the idea that a negative weight is attached to any lie

Bok's justification process utilizes three levels, all of which are critical to sound, ethical decision making. First, an individual must look to his or her own conscience for a good decision. However, Bok suggests that this level of justification is incomplete because each of us is likely to look at the consequences of a decision from an egotistic point of view. Therefore, a second level of justification is to look to friends, colleagues, family members, or those with special knowledge of our situation. We are likely to find a somewhat more objective point of view in these discussions. However, again this level is not completely sufficient since we are likely to go first to others who think and act as we do. Many historically disastrous decisions can be laid at the feet of like-minded individuals who believed they were making a "good" decision.

In order to sufficiently justify a decision, Bok believes a third level of justification is required: "At this level, persons of all allegiances must be consulted, or at least not excluded or bypassed" (p. 103). In other words, we should consult individuals who might be affected by our decision or who can provide a more objective point of view. The process should be open to public scrutiny, and the more complex the decision, the more consultation is necessary. Bok concludes, "The test of publicity is not always needed; where needed it cannot always be implemented; if implemented it does not always bring forth solutions to moral quandaries. Given these limitations, it can nevertheless reduce the discrepancy of perspectives, shed light on moral reasoning, and facilitate moral choice" (p. 108).

Here is a dilemma that might help to clarify Bok's test: You have been given a take-home exam and have procrastinated and avoided working on it until the night before it is due. Your roommate has a friend who took this course the prior semester who is familiar with the exam and received a good grade. Should you ask that individual to help you write the exam or submit his exam as your own? For some of you, the first level of justification would be enough to say no. For many of you, basic values of honesty, fairness, and fidelity would prevent you from using another's work. But what if other considerations are important as well? If you have never used someone else's work before, is it okay to do it "just this one time"? If you know that others in the class have also plagiarized, is it acceptable for you to as well? For some of you, this second level of justification would support the "rightness" of using another's work.

But what happens when we go to the third level of justification? A representative group would have to include anyone who might be affected by this decision. Therefore, it would include your instructor for the course, other students in the class (both those who completed their own work and those who plagiarized), and other instructors on campus (who might use similar types of exams or potentially have you as a student in their classes). This group would also need to include your family (who has an interest in your success in college) as well as potential employers (who would want to know whether they were hiring an honest employee). Can you think of others who should be part of this representative group? Now, if you were to put this dilemma before this representative group, what might these individuals suggest as the "best" decision?

nonconsequentialist approach focuses on principles that appear to rights, duties, and promises

categorical imperative the obligation to consistently apply a rule, standard, or principle by which we make decisions

The Nonconsequentialist Approach   Another kind of moral theory emphasizes a **nonconsequentialist approach** to morality. Instead of looking at the consequences of a decision, this approach focuses on principles that appeal to rights, duties, and promises. Immanuel Kant, an eighteenth-century philosopher, was one of the most famous nonconsequentialists. Kant developed a principle called the **categorical imperative**, that "focuses on principles that appeal to rights, duties, and promises" (cited in Jaksa and Pritchard 1994, p. 70). In other words, if we develop a rule, a standard, or a principle by which we make decisions, we are obligated to apply that principle to anyone or any similar circumstance. We cannot use standards for ourselves that we are unwilling to use for others, and vice versa. Using Kant's nonconsequentialist approach to our dilemma of the take-home exam, what would be the "right" decision? Would it be possible to create a standard by which anyone in similar circumstances would have the right to use another's work? What would it mean for our country's educational system if it was acceptable to submit plagiarized work because you didn't have the time to do your own? Can you think of any circumstances where this "standard" would be acceptable?

degree of ethical quality an alternative to simplistically labeling words or deeds as ethical or unethical; each situation should be assessed individually

Jensen (1997) suggests that we need "to think in terms of the ethical quality, not in terms of simplistically labeling words or deeds as either ethical or unethical, automatically eliciting a yes or no response" (p. 7). In any communication situation, we must ask, "How ethical is it?" We can then assess the **degree of ethical quality**. Jensen believes that by refining our judgments and continually probing the possible variables and potential outcomes in a given situation, we can become more effective and ethical communicators. Continuing with our situation of the exam, how could you increase the ethical quality of your decision? Would simply talking to the person who took the course the prior semester about his answers, then writing your own based upon this conversation increase the ethical quality? Would it increase the ethical quality enough to make it "right"? This example shows that what we believe are simple decisions are often more complex than we first realize.

Goals of Studying Communication Ethics

Ethicists James Jaksa and Michael Pritchard provide four overriding goals for studying the ethics of communication. First, a study of ethics *stimulates our moral imagination*. Each of us needs to be prepared for meeting the moral challenges that will inevitably confront us in our families, our jobs, and our lives. Second, studying ethics helps us understand and *recognize ethical issues* in a given situation. Unless we recognize an issue in terms of its consequences for ourselves and others, we are bound to underestimate the impact of a decision. Third, the more time we spend examining fundamental ethical concepts and principles, the more we *develop the analytical skills* necessary to make more effective and ethical decisions. When we analyze a situation thoroughly, we begin to see how our decisions impact others, and we take greater responsibility for our choices. Finally, developing effective and competent communication skills such as good listening, thinking reflectively about our and others' communication, and maintaining interpersonal sensitivity allow us to more effectively *tolerate disagreement* and differences of choice in others. This tolerance prevents us from labeling our choices as "moral" and opposite choices as "immoral."

ETHICAL COMMUNICATION AS COMPETENT COMMUNICATION

*I*n the final analysis, ethical communicators are more competent communicators. We hope that you are taking a class in human communication, in part, to become a more effective and competent communicator since *the success of every relationship in your lifetime will depend upon your communication competence*. Whether it is your partner, coworker, best friend, boss, children, parents, or mechanic, you will need to communicate ethically and competently. Communication competence occurs when individuals communicate in ways that are responsible, effective, appropriate, and result in shared meaning between communicators. (Figure 2.1 summarizes important information about competent communication). Can you see that competence includes an ethical component? "Appropriateness" and "responsibility" ask us to make choices about our communication behavior for ourselves and others. Today, we extend communication competence expectations to relationships that are negotiated exclusively in a computer-mediated environment, where there is no face-to-face interaction. We believe that the basic definition of *competence* does not change simply because the channel of communication is computer-mediated (see the box Computer Links: Ethics on "the Net").

FIGURE 2.1	Guidelines for Competent Communication

- Knowledge of rules, norms, expectations, similarities, and differences among communicators and communication situations
- Sensitivity to and respect for others as humans, not as objects to be manipulated in a communication interaction
- Awareness and understanding of the ethical standards needed to judge the moral correctness and appropriateness of our communication

The effective and competent communicator knows that communication isn't just something we "do" but something we are constantly learning to "do better." Competent communication requires a set of skills that maximize the appropriateness and effectiveness of our communication interactions.

Ethics on "the Net"

The following is a summary of ethical guidelines for "computer etiquette" or "Netiquette," originally in a book written by Virginia Shea (retrieved from www.albion.com/netiquette/). She suggests that there are rules and standards for "appropriate" communication on the Internet:

- **Rule 1: Remember the human.** When you're holding a conversation online—whether it's an e-mail exchange or a response to a discussion group posting—it's easy to misinterpret your correspondent's meaning. And it's frighteningly easy to forget that your correspondent is a person with feelings more or less like your own. A useful test for anything you're about to post or mail [is to ask] yourself, "Would I say this to the person's face?" If the answer is no, rewrite and reread. Repeat the process till you feel sure that you'd feel as comfortable saying these words to the live person as you do sending them through cyberspace.

- **Rule 2: Adhere to the same standards of behavior online that you follow in real life.** Don't believe anyone who says, "The only ethics out there are what you can get away with." But if you encounter an ethical dilemma in cyberspace, consult the code you follow in real life. Chances are good you'll find the answer.

- **Rule 3: Know where you are in cyberspace.** What's perfectly acceptable in one area may be dreadfully rude in another. For example, in most TV discussion groups, passing on idle gossip is perfectly permissible. But throwing around unsubstantiated rumors in a journalists' mailing list will make you very unpopular there. When you enter a domain of cyberspace that's new to you, take a look around. Spend a while listening to the chat or reading the archives. Get a sense of how the people who are already there act. Then go ahead and participate.

- **Rule 4: Respect other people's time and bandwidth.** It's a cliché that people today seem to have less time than ever before, even though (or perhaps because) we sleep less and have more labor-saving devices than our grandparents did. When you send e-mail or post to a discussion group, you're taking up other people's time (or hoping to). It's your responsibility to ensure that the time they spend reading your posting isn't wasted.

- **Rule 5: Make yourself look good online.** You will be judged by the quality of your writing. For most people who choose to communicate online, this is an advantage; if they didn't enjoy using the written word, they wouldn't be there. So spelling and grammar do count.

- **Rule 6: Share expert knowledge.** The strength of cyberspace is in its numbers. The reason asking questions online works is that a lot of knowledgeable people are reading the questions. And if even a few of them offer intelligent answers, the sum total of world knowledge increases. The Internet itself was founded and grew because scientists wanted to share information. Gradually, the rest of us got in on the act. So do your part. . . .You do have something to offer. Don't be afraid to share what you know.

- **Rule 7: Help keep flame wars under control.** "Flaming" is what people do when they express a strongly held opinion without holding back any emotion. It's the kind of message that makes people respond, "Oh come on, tell us how you really feel." Tact is not its objective. Does Netiquette forbid flaming? Not at all. Flaming is a long-standing network tradition (and Netiquette never messes with tradition). Flames can be lots of fun, both to write and to read. And the recipients of flames sometimes deserve the heat. But Netiquette does forbid the perpetuation of flame wars—series of angry letters, most of them from two or three people directed toward each other, that can dominate the tone and destroy the camaraderie of a discussion group. It's unfair to the other members of the group. And while flame wars can initially be amusing, they get boring very quickly to people who aren't involved in them. They're an unfair monopolization of bandwidth.

- **Rule 8: Respect other people's privacy.** Of course, you'd never dream of going through your friend, roommate, or colleagues' desk drawers. So naturally you wouldn't read their e-mail either. Unfortunately, a lot of people would. Unless you want to lose your friend, your roommate, or your job, don't do it.

- **Rule 9: Don't abuse your power.** Some people in cyberspace have more power than others. There are wizards in MUDs (multi-user dungeons), experts in every office, and system administrators in every system. Knowing more than others, or having more power than they do, does not give you the right to take advantage of them. For example, sysadmins should never read private e-mail.

- **Rule 10: Be forgiving of other people's mistakes.** Everyone was a network newbie once. . . . So when someone makes a mistake—whether it's a spelling error or a spelling flame, a stupid question or an unnecessarily long answer—be kind about it. If it's a minor error, you may not need to say anything. Even if you feel strongly about it, think twice before reacting. Having good manners yourself doesn't give you license to correct everyone else.

Source: "Ethics on 'the Net'" from *Netiquette* by Virginia Shea. Reprinted by permission of Albion.

ETHICS, RESPONSIBILITY, AND COLLEGE STUDENT LIFE

s a college student, you are now immersed in a community in which a broad array of moral issues confront you daily. For example, what is your school's policy on each of the following issues?

Academic dishonesty or plagiarism

Tolerance and hate speech

Privacy and security

Drinking and drug use

On a more personal level, what do you believe characterizes true friendship during college? Have you modified your value system in terms of appropriateness of sexual intimacy in college relationships? What role do prior sources of your ethical guidelines play now that you are in college? Finally, how tolerant are you of the ideas, feelings, and behaviors of others?

Tolerance at a basic level implies that we respect one another. Respect doesn't mean we must agree with everything someone else says or does but simply that we believe every human being has value. And because they have value, they are entitled to equal treatment, rights, and justice. Because we respect others, we also tolerate differences in viewpoint and choices, again, not because we agree with the choice or point of view, but because we believe humans are moral agents who are responsible for their own decisions. Respect doesn't mean that we permit people to violate the rights of others; tolerance doesn't mean we tolerate intolerance. The *Credo for Ethical Communication* developed by the National Communication Association (NCA) illustrates this clearly: "We condemn communication that

tolerance respect for one another and the belief that every human being has value

dialogue communication *with* each other, not *to* each other; the foundation of effective, competent, and ethical communication

**N A T I O N A L
COMMUNICATION
A S S O C I A T I O N**

NCA is a scholarly society that promotes the "study, criticism, research, teaching, and application of the artistic, humanistic, and scientific principles of communication" (www.natcom.org).

degrades individuals and humanity through distortion, intimidation, coercion, and violence and through the expression of intolerance and hatred."

The NCA credo is the ethical code endorsed by the largest communication association in the United States (see the box, Communication Links: The National Communication Association Credo for Ethical Communication). Ultimately, the credo provides a set of principles that allow each of us to support the notion of **dialogue** as a foundation of effective, competent, and ethical communication. In dialogue, we communicate with each other, not to each other. Strike and Moss (1997, p. 194) provide four reasons to support dialogue as fundamental to effective communication:

1. Dialogue makes moral judgments more reasonable by bringing evidence and argument to bear on our opinions.
2. Dialogue is a way of affirming the equal right of people to participate in decisions that affect them.
3. Dialogue recognizes that sometimes what counts as the right thing to do is the product of an open and uncoerced agreement, a contract.
4. Dialogue accepts people's right to their own understanding of the meaning of respect and helps us to understand one another.

Strike and Moss summarize their support of dialogue by saying, "Why dialogue? Your character depends upon it" (p. 195). As a college student, a professional, a family member, and a citizen, your character represents your moral decision making. For example, someone who tells a lie once is not usually perceived as "a liar," but someone who habitually tells lies is perceived as having a weak or untrustworthy character. Ethicist Karen Lebacqz suggests, "[E]ach choice about what to do is also a choice about whom to be—or, more accurately, whom to become" (1985, p. 83). Our character, then, is the accumulation of our choices about what it means to be a moral and ethical person.

◎ SUMMARY

In this chapter, we have stressed that an ethical component is inherent in every communication situation where individuals have choices about whether and how to communicate and whenever that behavior could significantly impact other persons.

- Ethics is the moral responsibility to choose the values in a communication situation that are "right" for ourselves and for others. Each individual develops a set of values and beliefs that act as ethical guidelines for making these communication choices.
- The sources of these guidelines vary from families to schools to churches and to the larger culture of which we are a part.
- For most of us, basic values of honesty and truthfulness, fidelity, confidentiality, fairness, and significant choice guide our communication.
- Moral theories reflecting either a consequentialist or nonconsequentialist orientation can also assist us in developing an ethical orientation.
- Understanding the role of communication ethics in our communication can assist us by stimulating our

moral imagination; helping us recognize the ethical issues in any communication situation; providing the analytical skills necessary to make effective, ethical decisions; and, ultimately, helping us tolerate disagreement.

- Ethical, effective, and competent communication isn't something we just "do" but something we are constantly trying to "do better."
- Ethical issues such as lying, cheating, privacy, sexual intimacy, and tolerance are a part of the community of college life and confront you on a daily basis. Studying ethical communication can assist you in maneuvering through the maze of moral issues within this community.
- Ultimately, the ethical and competent communicator will develop an approach to communication founded on dialogue. The dialogic approach to communication will also help develop in you a fundamental, ethical character.

Questions for Discussion

1. What do you think are the most significant areas of ethical concern to college students?
2. Do you believe that most people want to know the truth, or do they want to be left in ignorance if the truth would be harmful?
3. Is it morally objectionable to lie to the elderly? To children? Under what circumstances?
4. According to survey data compiled for the past twenty years, Americans have turned cheating into a national "pastime." Americans cheat on tests, tax returns, diets, spouses, car sales, loans, and so on. Do you think that since "everyone cheats," you need to cheat just to stay "in the game"?
5. Do you believe the values necessary to develop and maintain intimate relationships are different from those that develop and maintain social relationships?
6. Do you think Sissela Bok's principle of veracity is possible? How?
7. Contrast the consequentialist and nonconsequentialist approaches to ethical decision making. Which do you believe is the most effective guideline?
8. What are the limits to tolerance of other points of view? When you are confronted by others who practice intolerance, what would or should you do?

EXERCISES

1. List and prioritize the sources of your ethical guidelines. Make a list of relevant quotes from these various sources (i.e., religious documents, teachers, parents, cultural icons).
2. Write an essay about the one person who has had the most significant impact on you as a "moral citizen."
3. Write an essay that describes a situation in which two (or more) of your basic values were in conflict. For example, truthfulness vs. confidentiality.
4. If your employer asked you to lie or mislead the public regarding some product or service, what would you do? Under what circumstances would you "blow the whistle" on a situation in your workplace?
5. Argue for or against the use of gender-neutral or politically correct language as appropriate, competent communication.
6. The NCA credo states, "We promote communication climates of caring and mutual understanding that respect the unique needs and characteristics of individual communicators." What are the limits to "caring" and "mutual understanding" in communication?

KEY TERMS

Honesty
Truthfulness
Fidelity
Confidentiality
Fairness

Significant choice
Consequentialist approach
Principle of veracity
Nonconsequentialist approach
Categorical imperative

Degree of ethical quality
Tolerance
Dialogue

REFERENCES

Barada, Paul W. *Honesty is still the best policy*. Retrieved June 8, 2007, from http://hr.monster.com/articles/honesty/.

Bok, S. 1978. *Lying: Moral choice in public and private life*. New York: Vintage Books.

Jaksa, J. A., and Pritchard, M. S. 1994. *Communication ethics: Methods of Analysis*. 2nd ed. Belmont, CA: Wadsworth.

Jang, S. A., Smith, S. W., and Levine, T. R. 2002. To stay or to leave? The role of attachment styles in communication patterns and potential termination of romantic relationships following discovery of deception. *Communication Monographs* 69:236–252.

Jensen, J. V. 1997. *Ethical issues in the communication process*. Mahwah, NJ: Lawrence Erlbaum.

Johannesen, R. L. 2002. *Ethics in human communication*. 5th ed. Prospect Heights, IL: Waveland.

Kluckhohn, F. K., and Strodtbeck, F. L. 1961. *Variations in Value Orientations*. Evanston, IL: Row, Peterson.

Lebacqz, K. 1985. *Professional ethics: Power and paradox*. Nashville: Abingdon Press.

National Communication Association. 1999. *NCA Credo for ethical communication*. Retrieved May 8, 2007, from http://www.natcom.org/policies/External/EthicalComm.htm.

Niemoller, Martin. 1976. *First they came for the Jews*. Retrieved May 8, 2007, from http://www.telisphere.com/~cearley/sean/camps/first.html.

Nilsen, T. R. 1966. *Ethics of speech communication*. New York: Bobbs-Merril.

Perry, W. G. Jr. 1970. *Forms of intellectual and ethical development in the college years: A scheme*. New York: Holt, Rinehart, and Winston.

Strike, K. A., and Moss, P. A. 1997. *Ethics and college student life*. Boston: Allyn and Bacon.

CHAPTER 3

Perception
Self, Others, and Communication

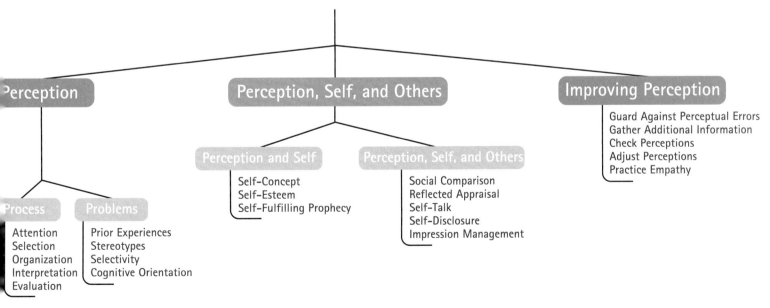

Perception

Process
- Attention
- Selection
- Organization
- Interpretation
- Evaluation

Problems
- Prior Experiences
- Stereotypes
- Selectivity
- Cognitive Orientation

Perception, Self, and Others

Perception and Self
- Self-Concept
- Self-Esteem
- Self-Fulfilling Prophecy

Perception, Self, and Others
- Social Comparison
- Reflected Appraisal
- Self-Talk
- Self-Disclosure
- Impression Management

Improving Perception
- Guard Against Perceptual Errors
- Gather Additional Information
- Check Perceptions
- Adjust Perceptions
- Practice Empathy

Knowledge Checklist

✔ To understand the process of perception
✔ To recognize potential problems with perception
✔ To acknowledge the reciprocal relationship between perception and communication
✔ To be aware of the relationship between perception, self-concept, identity, and communication
✔ To comprehend the role of perception in communicating with others
✔ To appreciate the role of perception in college and career success

THE PROCESS OF PERCEPTION

CLARENCE: "Wow, that tastes so good!"

BRAD: "Are you kidding? I don't know how you stomach that stuff!"

LATISHA: "Why would anybody ever wear a dress like that?"

ROBIN: "Because it's a cool dress."

JOEY: "Let's get in line again. I just love riding this roller coaster."

ANN: "Not me! I hate those huge drops and upside-down turns!

You have probably heard or been engaged in conversations like this before. In each of these examples, both people tasted the same food, saw the same dress, and rode the same amusement park ride, and yet they had completely different responses. You may experience the same tastes, sights, or movements but perceive them very differently than someone else. For example, you and your roommate may disagree about the "best" time of the day. Maybe you're a morning person while your roommate is a night owl. So, you want to study at 11:00 A.M. in the mornings before class, and he wants to study at 11:00 P.M. at night. While 11:00 is the same number on your clocks, it means completely different things to both of you: You perceive time differently. In this chapter, we discuss the process of perception and its problems, consider the reciprocal relationship between communication and perception, examine self-perception and the perception of others, and suggest ways to apply the chapter's insights to college and career contexts.

perception the process of becoming aware of people, events, or objects and attaching meaning to that awareness

Perception is the process of becoming aware of people, events, or objects and then attaching meaning to your awareness. The process involves attention, selection, organization, interpretation, and evaluation. Let's consider each of these steps.

Attention and Selection

attention the first stage of perception; awareness of certain stimuli

Attention, the first stage in the perception process, refers to something that catches your eye or another one of your physical senses. For example, you may pass someone on your way to class who is wearing an appealing fragrance that stimulates your olfactory sense. This is especially true if you associate a pleasant memory with a particular scent. Attention means that you are aware of certain stimuli. You are bombarded by a host of stimuli every day that involve your senses of sight, smell, hearing, taste, and touch. A colorful bouquet of carnations, a freshly baked pizza, a blaring car alarm, a warm chocolate chip cookie, or the rough stubble on a beloved grandfather's face—these stimuli assail you during your every waking moment.

selection the second stage of perception; focusing on specific stimuli

While you may be aware of all these stimuli, you do not consciously attend to them all; you select some over others. **Selection**, the second stage of perception, refers to those stimuli that you focus on. You probably choose those that impress you in some way—for example, you notice the smell of fresh bread coming from a cafeteria because you are hungry. In this case, you select a stimuli related to your needs. You may also pay attention to sensory information because of your interests. For example, while you are heading across campus, you see a good friend walking with a group of students. Despite the crowd around her, you focus on your friend to see if she is wearing the new baseball cap you bought her. You also tend to select stimuli that are intense or novel. For instance, if you hear a bloodcurdling scream in the middle of the night, you'll wake up with an adrenaline rush. The intensity and uniqueness of the experience grab your attention.

Organization

Because we are surrounded by so many stimuli, we seek to **organize** them in order to help make sense of our world and reduce uncertainty (Berger 1979). Our brain uses some shortcuts to help us organize these stimuli. First, we rely on prior experience and arrange stimuli in simple categories that serve as representative examples for all other similar experiences. To illustrate, you likely have an idea of what makes a "good" course in your college career. Or you have a clear idea of what constitutes a "good teacher." As noted in the box Campus Links: Student Perceptions of Teachers, Lim (1996) verifies that students grade their college professors based on these kinds of organized patterns.

organize creating relationships among stimuli

 Campus Links

Student Perceptions of Teachers

Cooper and Simonds (2002) summarize Lim's (1996) study of student evaluations of college professors. How would you rate your professors using these guidelines?

The "A" Professor: An Outstanding Professor

Preparation: Well-organized syllabi; lectures that are thorough and efficient based on a complete set of class notes

Enthusiasm: Enthusiastic about teaching; makes students feel welcome in seeking personal or academic help; genuine interest in the subject he or she teaches

Clarity: Answers questions clearly, accurately, and specifically. Makes homework assignments clear and to the point

Research: Possesses up-to-date information; able to introduce the latest research in class; keeps an eye on the latest technology and prepares students for the future

Assignments: Gives relevant assignments regularly to reinforce class material; ensures students have the tools and knowledge to complete assignments; grades assignments promptly and offers adequate comments

Humor: Uses humor to make class more fun to attend; employs a level of dynamics to keep the class interesting even if the material is dry

Fairness: Treats students fairly; grades students according to performance and effort; unbiased and impartial in grading

The "C" Professor: An Average or Typical Professor

Preparation: Does not prepare lectures well; does not have syllabi students can follow; misplaces or forgets to bring class notes; does not know where he or she is in the flow of the course content; does not have a clear plan for class sessions

Enthusiasm: Does not show strong commitment toward the class; halfhearted about teaching; not focused on the task at hand

Clarity: Students feel lost during lectures; vague about requirements for assignments

Research: Not up-to-date in his or her field of study; does not have full command of the subject matter but tries to conceal it

Assignments: Gives minimal assignments; does not provide prompt feedback but waits weeks to return graded work; piles up assignments all at once without proper warning; gives unreasonable assignments that are not in line with student knowledge and skill level; provides poor guidance on assignments

Humor: Presents materials in a monotone voice and manner; makes even an interesting subject boring; appears aloof and intimidating

Fairness: Not necessarily fair in treating students; favors students he or she knew prior to class and gives some sense of inequality in the classroom

Source: From *Communication for the Classroom Teacher*, 7e, by J. Cooper and C. J. Simonds. Published by Allyn and Bacon, Boston, MA. Copyright 2002 by Pearson Education. Reprinted by permission of the publisher.

We organize our perceptions according to prior experience, particularly to the principle or similarity and difference, and we rely on patterns. For example, in a parking lot full of cars, you typically perceive just a mass of cars rather than different makes and models. However, if you are looking for your own car, you will scan the mass of cars looking only for the red one or the one with a tennis ball on the antenna.

scripts mental organization patterns that help arrange information and inform behavior

You also rely on **scripts** or mental organizational patterns to help arrange information and inform behavior. For instance, different cultures have unique greeting and leave-taking behaviors that convey certain meaning. When Korean students come to the United States to study and greet their professors for the first time, they often bow and then shake hands. In the Korean culture, and in other Asian cultures, bowing is the appropriate way to greet someone of higher status. U.S. professors, unaware of this cultural script, may return the bow, working off their own script, which reads, "Mirror the greeting you receive." In this case, the cultural scripts collide, because if the professor bows, the students will be required to bow once more, only more deeply than the first time. As you can see, we respond to observed behaviors by drawing on our own experiences and the mental scripts we have created from our cultural backgrounds. Often, these differing perceptions cause confusion or uncertainty.

Interpretation and Evaluation

interpret assign meaning to information

evaluate decide on the worth or value of information

As we attend, select, and organize information, we also interpret and evaluate it—that is, we assign meaning (**interpret**) and decide on the information's worth or value (**evaluate**). Consider the following information:

1, 500, 000

€1,500,000

£1,500,000

$1,500,000

Which piece of information holds the most meaning and value for you? If you live in the European Union, the second number has greater meaning and value. If you live in the United Kingdom, the third symbol is more meaningful. And if you live in the United States, the fourth number holds more value. Of course, the process of interpretation and evaluation is more complex than this simple illustration.

As we will discuss in Chapter 5, language encompasses layers of meaning, which are interpreted and evaluated. To make the point simply, consider the word *snaps*. What does this word make you think of—a sound, a type of candy, or a photograph? Depending upon where you live and how you were raised, this word *snaps* will have different meanings for you. This example illustrates an important point that we will consider next. Perception has limitations and problems.

PROBLEMS WITH PERCEPTION

*O*ur perception is limited. While people with physical, cognitive, or learning disabilities are often thought of as limited, in reality, we are all limited. For example, some people have a stronger sense of taste, hearing, or smell, while others have greater visual acuity. In fact, as we age, our senses become more limited. Furthermore, if we compare ourselves to other species, we discover that our hearing, for example, pales in comparison to that of an owl, a whale, or a dog. As humans, we face sensory boundaries; however, most problems with perception are not linked to these limits but to prior experience, stereotypes, selectivity, and cognitive orientation.

Prior Experience

As we noted in our discussion of scripts, our prior experiences frame our perceptions. To illustrate, you may avoid going to the dentist because you once had a very painful tooth extraction and, as a result, are frightened and anxious about visiting the dentist. In another example, if your experiences with older people have been friendly, encouraging, and enjoyable, you may be more likely to get to know your elderly neighbors. In

Avoid stereotyping your coworkers by listening to what they are suggesting and keeping an open mind.

short, our prior experiences with specific events, people, or places frame our perceptions but may also lead to misperceptions, stereotypes, prejudice, and discrimination.

Stereotypes

Stereotypes draw conclusions about individuals based on a generalization about a group of people. For example, stereotypes may be based on ethnic, racial, gender, sexual, religious, or even physical attributes. Sheldon (1942) asserted that there were three different body types and that people with these body types possessed certain personality characteristics. For example, overweight people are often labeled "jolly"—look at the strong cultural figure of Santa Claus. Obviously, these stereotypes are inaccurate and even offensive.

    However, not all stereotypes are negative. For example, the idea that "all Hispanics are family oriented and warmhearted" is a positive stereotype. Regardless of whether stereotypes are positive or negative, they are problematic. While they may help us organize information neatly, they also create false categories that lead to **prejudice**, a definitive negative attitude toward a given group, which in turn can lead to **discrimination**, or unfair treatment of a given group of people. As a result, a host of "isms" may ensue, including ageism, sexism, racism, ableism, and ethnocentrism. All of these "isms" rest on the assumption that one group is superior to another, which supports harmful stereotypes that lead to prejudice and discrimination. For example, if you were raised in India under the caste system, you would hold specific beliefs about people in each of the five castes, such as knowing that people marry into and die in the caste into which they were born and that a member of the merchant class (Vaishya) would never consort with an "untouchable" (Harijan). In short, if you believe that a certain group of people is better than another, you harbor prejudicial attitudes.

stereotypes conclusions drawn from generalizations

prejudice a definitive negative attitude toward a group

discrimination unfair treatment of a given group of people based on prejudice

Selectivity

As we noted in our discussion of the process of perception, you select certain stimuli more than others. This leads to an additional problem: You tend to see what you choose to see. In other words, your experiences, cultures, beliefs, values, and other factors cause you to focus on the information that you find the most comfortable, credible, or compelling. Therefore, if you expect a certain person or group of people to behave in a particular manner, you will see exactly what you expect. This creates a potentially vicious cycle: Your perceptions create your expectations, and your expectations confirm your perceptions. Selectivity, then, makes it very difficult to gain new information or insight; this hinders open-mindedness and perception checks, both of which we will discuss later in this chapter.

Cognitive Orientation

cognitive orientation how a person processes information—visual, auditory, or kinesthetic; also termed *learning style*

brain dominance refers to the side of the brain a person is more likely to use, left (logic and writing based) or right (visual and feeling based)

Cognitive orientation refers to how you process information and is directly tied to perception. We usually think of cognitive orientation as *learning style* or **brain dominance**. *Brain dominance* refers to the side of the brain you tend to use. The following list of qualities may help you determine your learning style or perceptual preference: If you prefer information that is logical, orderly, well planned, evidence based, and written, you are likely left-brained. In this class, you will probably find outlining, organizing, and supporting your ideas relatively easy. If you prefer information that is visual, feeling based, and shared conversationally, you are likely right-brained. In this class, you will probably find ideas about interpersonal communication particularly interesting and share your feelings easily in class discussions.

Brain dominance is also reflected in our learning styles. There are various learning styles, which we cover in depth in other chapters. However, to simplify, think of yourself as a visual, auditory, or kinesthetic learner. If you prefer to learn by sight and then re-create mental pictures in your mind, you are likely a visual learner. If you prefer to learn by listening and then focusing on words to help you remember information, you are likely an auditory learner. If you prefer to learn by doing and then mentally reenacting what you've done in order to remember it, you are likely a kinesthetic learner. Table 3.1 summarizes information about these learning styles. To learn more about your cognitive orientation, including your brain dominance and learning styles, consult the numerous resources listed in the box Computer Links: Using the WWW to Discover Yourself.

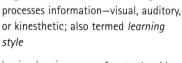

Computer Links

Using the WWW to Discover Yourself

Self-discovery is fun and helpful. There are many things to learn about yourself. Finding out if you're left- or right-brained, your learning styles, and how to use this information to help you succeed in college is particularly useful information for you right now. We encourage you to use your computer to discover some important information about how you perceive your world.

Brain Dominance Links
Information about brain dominance:
1. http://www.web-us.com/brain/LRBrain.html
Brain dominance test links:
1. http://brain.web-us.com/brain/braindominance.htm
2. www.ipn.at/ipn.asp?BHX
3. www.sil.org/lingualinks/LANGUAGELEARNING/OtherResources/YorLrnngStylAndLnggLrnng/TheBrainDominanceInventory.htm

Learning Style Links
These links provide numerous other links to learning styles information and/or inventories.
www.engr.ncsu.edu/learningstyles/ilsweb.html
www.ldpride.net/learning_style.html
www.chaminade.org/inspire/learnstl.htm
www.engr.ncsu.edu/learningstyles/ilsweb.html

Table 3.1   Learning Styles

This chart helps you determine your learning style. Read the word in the left column and then answer the questions in the successive three columns to see how you respond to each situation. Your answers may fall into all three columns, but one column will likely contain the most answers. The dominant column indicates your primary learning style.

When you . . .	Visual	Auditory	Kinesthetic & Tactile
Spell	Do you try to see the word?	Do you sound out the word or use a phonetic approach?	Do you write the word down to find if it feels right?
Talk	Do you dislike listening for too long? Do you favor words such as *see*, *picture*, and *imagine*?	Do you enjoy listening but are impatient to talk? Do you use words such as *hear*, *tune*, and *think*?	Do you gesture and use expressive movements? Do you use words such as *feel*, *touch*, and *hold*?
Concentrate	Do you become distracted by untidiness or movement?	Do you become distracted by sounds or noises?	Do you become distracted by activity around you?
Meet someone again	Do you forget names but remember faces or remember where you met?	Do you forget faces but remember names or remember what you talked about?	Do you remember best what you did together?
Contact people on business	Do you prefer direct, face-to-face, personal meetings?	Do you prefer the telephone?	Do you talk with them while walking or participating in an activity?
Read	Do you like descriptive scenes or pause to imagine the actions?	Do you enjoy dialogue and conversation or hear the characters talk?	Do you prefer action stories or are not a keen reader?
Do something new at work	Do you like to see demonstrations, diagrams, slides, or posters?	Do you prefer verbal instructions or talking about it with someone else?	Do you prefer to jump right in and try it?
Put something together	Do you look at the directions and the picture?	Do you prefer having someone read the directions aloud to you?	Do you ignore the directions and figure it out as you go along?
Need help with a computer application	Do you seek out pictures or diagrams?	Do you call the help desk, ask a neighbor, or growl at the computer?	Do you keep trying to do it or try it on another computer?

Source: From *Accelerated Learning* by Colin Rose, copyright © 1987 by Colin Rose. Used by permission of Dell Publishing, a division of Random House, Inc.

What have these ideas about cognitive orientation got to do with perception? Since you "see" information in a particular fashion, you are likely to positively perceive information that is organized according to your preferences and negatively perceive information that is, in your view, disorganized. For example, if you are a left-brain, auditory learner, you probably have a negative impression of a professor whose lectures are not well organized and whose assignments ask you to create a visual product such as a collage or a diagram. On the other hand, if you are a right-brained, visual learner, you are likely to find this same professor an excellent teacher.

These orientations can create tensions between people. However, you can develop your skills to compensate for your orientations and avoid the problems that may result. One way to do this is by taking courses or engaging in activities that don't necessarily match your cognitive orientations. Even though they would be challenging, these classes or activities will help you become a well-rounded learner. To summarize, differing cognitive orientations determine your preferred ways of attending, selecting, organizing, interpreting, and evaluating the multiple stimuli in the world around you, and they frame your perceptions about your world. These perceptions, in turn, guide your responses and create learning and relational challenges.

PERCEPTION AND COMMUNICATION: A RECIPROCAL RELATIONSHIP

*N*ow that you have a basic understanding of the process of and problems with perception, you can think more about the impact of perception on communication and vice versa. Campbell and Hepler (1970) assert that every communication encounter includes six people:

how I see myself

how you see yourself

how I see you

how you see me

how I think you see me

how you think I see you

As we communicate, our prior, immediate, and ongoing perceptions of ourselves and of one another inform our communication. To illustrate, if, when we first meet, I perceive you as friendly and open, then I might strike up a conversation or make small talk in an attempt to be sociable. However, if you perceive my attempts at conversation as intrusive, you are likely to think of me as pushy or forward, and in response you might lower your eyes or refrain from responding. After our initial meeting, I will adapt my perceptions of you, while you may continue to hold your perception of me. As a result, we will both consider each other unapproachable. The consequence of this communication will continue because it will inform our subsequent encounters and impact our self-perceptions—I will internalize your impression of me, and vice versa. This, in turn, will create a round of self-talk, or what some scholars call **intrapersonal communication**. This self-talk may confirm the self-perceptions that we brought with us to our initial encounter (e.g., "Everyone thinks I'm a jerk!") or create questions (e.g., "Do people respond to me like this because there's something wrong with me?"). Perception and communication, then, are reciprocal: One influences the other.

While perception's influence on communication is a dynamic process, in order to understand it more completely, let's consider how we perceive ourselves and others. We'll conclude this chapter by exploring ways to improve our perception and will examine the role of perception in college and career.

Perception, Self, Identity, and Communication

How you perceive yourself influences how you communicate with yourself and with others. We first consider how we view ourselves by focusing on the important elements of self-perception as well as how we distinguish ourselves from others. Then we examine how self-perception influences communication. In order to understand self-perception, we must think about three important related concepts: self-concept, self-esteem, and self-fulfilling prophecy.

Self-concept refers to the relatively stable mental image you hold of yourself; this self-image includes how you view your personality as well as your strengths and weaknesses. Your self-concept is like a compass that always points to your perceived "true personality." For example, believing that you are a shy person is part of your perceived self-concept. **Self-esteem**, on the other hand, refers to how you

---

intrapersonal communication internalizing messages and communicating with yourself about yourself; also termed *self-talk*

self-concept the relatively stable mental image a person holds of him- or herself

self-esteem the value or worth a person places on him- or herself

self-fulfilling prophecies events that are more likely to transpire because someone expects them to

feel about yourself or the value or worth you place on yourself. Some refer to self-esteem as *self-respect*. To expand on the previous example, if you believe you are *too* shy, then you are evaluating a part of your perceived self-concept, which affects your self-esteem accordingly.

Self-concept and self-esteem influence each other, because who you believe you are influences how worthy you feel, and how worthy you feel influences who you believe you are. These powerful psychological influences can lead to **self-fulfilling prophecies**, events that are more likely to transpire because you expect them to. For example, if you expect to do poorly on your first speech in this class, you increase the likelihood that you will, indeed, not do as well as you could had you not expected a substandard performance. If you possess low self-esteem, you are likely to fall prey to the power of negative self-fulfilling prophecies. Your expectation becomes your reality.

While these are important and powerful concepts, it is important to clarify that you cannot suddenly become proficient in a given area simply by thinking more positively about yourself. Rather, first you must be aware of your strengths and weaknesses as fully as possible. Know what you do well and what requires more work on your part. Then set realistic goals, accomplish those goals, and congratulate yourself for reaching them. This will provide a strong sense of self and self-worth based on sound expectations, thereby creating a motivating self-fulfilling prophecy. The box Career Links: Using the Self-Fulfilling Prophecy reviews another way to think about self-fulfilling prophecy as you move into the world of work and provides insights for your college career.

Your self-concept, the mental image you hold of yourself, is the sum of your perceived abilities, attitudes, and beliefs.

Career Links

Using the Self–Fulfilling Prophecy

Read the following article by Max Garfinkle of Capability Snapshots, Inc., a Canadian organizational consulting firm (see www.capsnap.com/max/maxarticle1.asp?ID=7). After you read the article, reflect on the questions at the end of this box.

Expectations Shape Reality

In 1932 the American public lost faith in the ability of the banks to guarantee their deposits. People ran to the banks trying to get their money out before the banks became insolvent. This mass behavior did indeed force banks, even those with sufficient funds, to close their doors on frantic depositors.

The sociologist Robert K. Merton coined the term "the self-fulfilling prophecy" to explain this turn of events. Once the public perceived the situation as a threat, their subsequent behavior turned those fears into a reality. He defined a self-fulfilling prophecy as "a false definition of a situation evoking a new behavior which makes the originally false perception come true."

However, self-fulfilling prophecies can be based on true as well as false definitions of a situation. They can be used for positive as well as for negative outcomes. Another sociologist, W. I. Thomas, stated this funda-

mental truth about human nature: "If men define situations as real, they are real in their consequences." In essence, expectations shape reality.

The nature of the expectation of success by an individual, a group, or an organization as a whole leads to the kind of striving that is likely to result in outcomes supporting the initial prophecy. This principle can be demonstrated by viewing the sales achievements of four types of salespersons:

- The AVERAGE ACHIEVER sets limited goals and puts forth moderate effort to achieve these goals. The prophecy is fulfilled with the achievement of these limited goals.

- The OUTSTANDING ACHIEVER sets stretch goals and puts forth strenuous effort to achieve these goals. Again, the prophecy is fulfilled with the achievement of the stretch goals.

- The ANXIOUS ACHIEVER sets limited goals and puts forth strenuous effort. The salesperson is afraid to aspire higher for fear of failure. The self-fulfilling prophecy is based on the expectation that hard work is needed to assure even limited success.

- The SELF-DEFEATING ACHIEVER sets stretch goals to gain approval, but puts forth only moderate effort, never coming near to the goals set. This sales rep starts with an expectation of personal inadequacy that gets reinforced by continuously disappointing performance. Even the moderate effort is more a show of work, more a display of rote behavior than of looking after the essentials.

Types of Managers

This concept of a "self-fulfilling prophecy" can be applied to the leadership behavior of any manager by keeping in mind one distinction. The sales rep sets *personal* goals and is *personally* responsible for his/her own effort. The manager sets the direction toward *unit* goals [department, division] and endeavors to mobilize *unit-wide* effort on behalf of these goals. Leadership effectiveness is determined by the extent that the unit achieves its unit goals. There are four types of managers analogous to the four types of sales reps:

- The AVERAGE manager sets limited goals for the unit and mobilizes moderate unit-wide efforts to achieve these limited goals.
- The OUTSTANDING manager sets stretch goals for the unit and mobilizes strenuous unit-wide efforts to achieve these strenuous goals.
- The ANXIOUS manager sets limited goals for the unit and mobilizes strenuous unit-wide efforts to achieve these limited goals. What a waste of potential!
- The SELF-DEFEATING manager sets stretch goals for the unit but mobilizes only moderate unit-wide effort. The unit learns not to take the stretch goals too seriously.

In both situations we can portray a 2 × 2 table based on the interaction between "Level of Aspiration" and "Degree of Effort," leading to four prototypical cases. The following table illustrates these cases.

Four Types of Achieves			
		Level of Aspiration	
		Limited Goals	Stretch Goals
Degree of Effort	Moderate	AVERAGE	SELF-DEFEATING
	Strenuous	ANXIOUS	OUTSTANDING

Coaching Managers

The leader who understands the dynamics of the self-fulfilling prophecy can use it to coach managers to become outstanding achievers. The process is a gradual, step-by-step change.

- The self-defeating manager can be helped to become an average manager. The leader has to put this manager on a "guaranteed success" program, lowering the goals to make them fit the actual moderate effort. The expectations of failure, disappointment, and a sense of personal inadequacy have to be broken. Once success comes to be expected, the moderate efforts become more functional, replacing the earlier superficial style.
- The average manager has to pass through the stage of being an anxious manager en route toward eventually becoming an outstanding achiever. The leader has to help the manager get his/her unit to put forth more strenuous effort while still retaining limited goals. The unit comes to expect success as a result of the hard work.
- The anxious manager, whose unit is accustomed to strenuous effort, can now be converted into an outstanding manager. The leader has to help the manager gradually raise the bar and let go of the security blanket of readily achievable targets. Not

only the manager but also the whole unit becomes higher performing, constantly trying to surpass its best achievements.

- Outstanding managers and units should have their successes recognized and be properly compensated.

For the sales rep the difference between moderate and strenuous effort lies in the effort to cultivate the personal competencies required for sales success. For the manager of a unit, the difference between modest and strenuous effort lies in the effort to build unit capabilities required for unit success.

The CEO directs toward organization goals and endeavors to mobilize organization-wide effort on behalf of these goals. For the CEO, the difference between modest and strenuous effort lies in the effort to build organization capabilities essential for strategic success.

Expectations lead to efforts to shape reality in the direction of the expectations.

Questions

1. What is Garfinkle's main point?
2. How is this point relevant to your future career, even if you do not intend to enter business?
3. How can Garfinkle's insights assist you as you complete your college education? To help in answering this question, review the table in the article.

Self and Others

Your self-perception does not exist in a vacuum: Your self-perception develops as you interact with others, and your self-concept and self-esteem develop as you communicate. When other people praise your abilities or point out the areas where you need to develop your skills, you take this information to heart and, especially after repeated similar responses, adjust your self-concept. Therefore, our definition of *self-concept* is relatively stable; however, it changes as you learn more about yourself from others. Likewise, your self-esteem increases when others affirm your value and worth as a person. Of course, conversely, if people denigrate you, make fun of you, or disconfirm your worth, your self-esteem suffers.

Social Comparison

Social comparison, or how we see ourselves in comparison to others, also impacts our self-esteem (Festinger 1954). Typically, you compare yourself to people who are like you, but if you engage in *upward social comparison*—meaning you compare yourself to people you perceive to be superior—then your self-esteem will plummet. For example, if you compare your speaking abilities with those of Martin Luther King Jr., you are likely to come away severely disappointed. On the other hand, if you engage in *downward social comparison*—meaning you compare yourself to someone whom you find less impressive—then your self-esteem grows. For example, if you compare your speaking abilities with those of an average ninth grader, you are likely to come away with an inflated sense of self-esteem. To illustrate further, several studies (see Abell & Richards 1996; Faith, Leon, & Allison 1997) note that people, especially adolescents, evaluate their body images by comparing themselves with others (Rosenblum & Lewis 1999). Additionally, media, including magazines (Jones, Vigfusdottir, & Lee 2002) and television (Botta 1999) influence how male and female children and adolescents view their bodies. Research indicates that eating disorders and other body-image difficulties are also linked to the results of social comparison (Cash & Deagle 1997) and influence self-esteem (Abell & Richards 1996). In short, social comparison is a powerful method for determining our self-concept and self-worth and can dramatically influence our behavior.

social comparison how a person sees him- or herself in comparison with others

Reflected Appraisal

Reflected appraisal refers to accepting how others define or describe you and impacts self-perception. So, for example, you may compare how much you weigh with how much others your age weigh and conclude that you are either "too thin" or "too overweight"; this is social comparison. If you then comment to your best friend, "You know, I think I'm too skinny," and your friend says, "Yeah, I think you are too," then you may reflect this appraisal; you internalize what others say. Of course, this is not automatic, because you may also respond with greater **self-efficacy,** which means that you have a strong sense of self and respond accordingly. If you have greater self-efficacy, you will be less likely to reflect others' appraisals and, as a result, can cope with setbacks, accomplish your goals, enhance your sense of well-being, and possess a greater sense of self-control over situations (Bandura 1994). Therefore, while social comparison and reflected appraisal exert powerful influences, you can balance their potency by having a sense of greater self-efficacy. To summarize, your perceptions are dynamic and formed by your experiences and by your interactions with others and how you respond to these influences.

reflected appraisal accepting how others define or describe you

self-efficacy sense of self

Self and Communication

Self-Talk As you interact with others and examine yourself, you internalize messages and communicate with yourself about yourself. As previously mentioned, some people refer to this as *self-talk,* or *intrapersonal communication.* Some argue that intrapersonal communication is not authentic communication, but we can all agree that self-talk certainly occurs; indeed, emerging research reveals that intrapersonal communication is a viable field of inquiry in the discipline of communication (see Aitken & Shedletsky 1995). Perhaps more importantly, however, research indicates that self-talk has a powerful impact on the state of your self-concept and mental health, even after suffering traumatic life events (see Kubany et al. 2004). For example, after the death of a loved one, you will be extremely sad. Instead of berating yourself for being weak or emotional, you could tell yourself, "Feeling this sadness is normal and is to be expected. I just need to work through these feelings as part of my grief." Intrapersonal communication, therefore, helps frame and form our self-perception. Of course, this self-talk is not a solo conversation; others dramatically influence our self-talk as well.

Self-Disclosure Our self-perception influences how we communicate with others. Specifically, we share our self-perceptions through **self-disclosure,** which is the process of purposefully sharing personal information with others. If you feel good about yourself, you are more likely to disclose information. However, if you doubt yourself or feel unworthy, you are more likely to be protective, uncertain, or guarded.

The **Johari window,** named for its creators Jo Luft and Harry Ingham, provides a way for you to analyze your level of self-disclosure (Luft 1970). Figure 3.1 depicts their model, which contains four quadrants, or panes. The "open" pane refers to all the information that both you and someone else knows about you, information you have self-disclosed; the "secret" pane contains information you have not disclosed with anyone; the "blind" pane contains information that others may know about you that you do not know about yourself; and the "unknown" pane refers to information that neither you nor anyone else knows. As you self-disclose and receive feedback from others, the various panes enlarge so that others learn more about you and you learn more about yourself. However, how you view yourself will impact what, how much, and with whom you disclose information. In other words, your sense of self will, in part, determine the size of the panes in your personal Johari window.

The **social penetration model** (Altman & Taylor 1973) provides yet another way to think about self-disclosure. This model, also termed the *onion model,* depicts self-disclosure as a process that gradually reveals both breadth and depth of information. We are like onions in that we have layers, which we reveal as we get to know one another. In this process, we disclose more information about ourselves and include a broader range of topics and more detailed information about these

self-disclosure process of purposefully sharing with others information that they would not otherwise know

Johari window a tool for analyzing a person's level of self-disclosure

social penetration model depicts self-disclosure as a process that gradually reveals both breadth and depth of information

---

FIGURE 3.1   The Johari Window

	Known to Self	Not known to Self
Known to Others	1 OPEN	2 BLIND
Not known to Others	HIDDEN 3	UNKNOWN 4

Source: "The Johari Window" from *Group Processes: An Introduction to Group Dynamics* by J. Luft. Reprinted by permission of the McGraw-Hill Companies.

topics. However, the depth and breadth of these revelations relates directly to our self-concept.

Impression Management   We adjust our self-disclosure as a result of our self-concept, and we monitor our interactions with others. **Impression management** (Goffman 1959) refers to strategies we use to positively influence others toward us. Some refer to this as *self-enhancement* or "putting your best foot forward." This is not dishonest; it is a conscious attempt to make a positive impact on others. For example, if you interview for a job, you should be well-groomed, speak articulately, and be ready to sell yourself to a prospective employer. However, your self-concept will influence how you manage your impressions. If you judge yourself unworthy, you may appear and act in a manner that more likely ensures you will not get the job. Therefore, it is important to manage your impressions toward others and your self-image so that you can present your best self without feeling fake or phony.

impression management strategies people use to positively influence others towards them; also termed *self-enhancement*

Perception of Others and Communication

We communicate based on our self-perceptions, and we interact with others based on our perceptions of them. Specifically, as you observe others, you rely on your perceptual biases and attributions in order to make conclusions about them. Let's consider these ideas in greater detail.

Observation   When you walk into a new class at the beginning of a new academic term, you probably look for people you already know and try to find out some things about the professor. In other words, you begin to observe the people around you and start drawing conclusions about them; you engage in the process of perception. For example, if a male professor came to the first class of the semester wearing a white shirt, a black tie, a black jacket and pants, and highly polished black shoes, what would be your first impression? No doubt you would draw some conclusions about his personality just from his attire, because how teachers dress impacts students' perceptions (Morris et al. 1996).

According to **implicit personality theory**, we rely on deductions based on a combination of physical characteristics, personality traits, and behavior to draw conclusions about others (Bruner & Taguiri 1954). Specifically, we tend to believe that certain traits, behaviors, or personality characteristics go together, and we draw several conclusions about an individual based on observing a single factor; this is termed the **halo effect.** The halo effect occurs when you take one outstanding trait and create an overly favorable perception of the whole personality. Therefore, you may conclude that the professor wearing a blue cardigan and open necked shirt is relaxed, open, and friendly based only on his attire. Whatever your perceptions, you draw conclusions based on limited observation.

implicit personality theory the idea that people rely on deductions based on a combination of physical characteristics, personality traits, and behaviors to draw conclusions about others

halo effect drawing conclusions about an individual after observing a single factor based on the belief that certain traits, behaviors, and personality characteristics belong together

Perceptual Influences   Why do we organize and interpret our perceptions of others in patterns such as seen in the previous example? Knowing more about scripts, closure, and attributions can help you understand this process more clearly. Scripts, as we noted earlier, are mental organizational patterns we use to help us move more easily through the world. For example, you have expectations about what to do when you get into an elevator: You step to the back, face forward, and stand apart from others. These scripts inform our perception of others. If someone enters an elevator and faces you, you are likely to question the appropriateness of their behavior because he or she violated a nonverbal communication norm.

We also rely on **closure** or filling in the blanks. For example, what if you saw the following on a license plate?

closure filling in the blanks

HNRS STDNT

first impressions conclusions based
on an initial meeting

Even though there are no vowels on the license plate, you would probably conclude that the plate reads "HONORS STUDENT." In other words, you provide the missing information. So, when we first meet others, we draw conclusions, or **first impressions**, and then fill in the blanks. To illustrate, when you go for an interview and meet your prospective boss, you may say to yourself, "She seems very nice; I think I'd like working with her." Based on your first impression, you fill in the blanks about the kind of boss you think she will be.

attributions meanings assigned to
actions

Additionally, we rely on **attributions**, or assigning meanings to actions. Attribution theory is based on Heider's (1944) work on social perception that suggests we assign meanings to others' behavior based on either external or internal explanations. So, for example, if you like the woman who is nominated as the representative for nontraditional students on your campus, you are likely to attribute her success to her skills or personality. If, on the other hand, she loses the election, you are likely to attribute her lack of success to external factors, such as poor advertising. However, if you dislike the nominee and she wins the election, you are likely to say it was because the other candidates were weak; whereas, if she loses the election, you are likely to blame her. Interestingly, this tendency results in a series of perceptual biases, which are summarized in Table 3.2. The point is that our perceptions are highly influenced by limited observations, scripts, closure, and attribution. In addition to these limitations, culture also impacts our perceptions, as explained in the box Cultural Links: The Influence of Culture on Perception.

Perception and Communication with Others

Given the reciprocal link between perception and communication, it is not surprising that we communicate with others based on our perceptions and that we adjust our perceptions of others based on communication encounters. For example, you perceive Susan, who is in your math class, as someone who truly understands college algebra. Consequently, you are more likely to ask her questions about course content. However, if you approach Susan and discover that she is dismissive and unfriendly, you will probably change your perceptions and actively avoid any future communication with her. In other words, your original perception motivates you to

Table 3.2   Attribution Biases

Bias	Explanation	Example
Fundamental Attribution Error	Overestimating internal factors to the exclusion of external factors	"I know Jared is late to dinner because he didn't plan time well, not because he's stuck in traffic."
Self-Serving Bias	Overestimating external factors to explain personal failure and overestimating internal factors to explain reasons for personal praise	"I did well on the test because I studied really hard" versus "I did poorly on the test because the professor wrote an unfair test."
Attractiveness Bias	Thinking better of people who we find physically attractive as compared to people we find unattractive	"Sharon is really beautiful AND she's also nice; it's just not her fault that she can't seem to pass math."
Similarity Bias	Thinking others we like are similar to us; attributing our own motivations to someone else	"Jeff and I are a lot alike; I bet he really likes J. R. Tolkien books as much as I do."

Cultural Links

The Influence of Culture on Perception

Culture is like a lens through which we view the world. It includes our background, values, beliefs, and attitudes gleaned from our upbringing and shared with us by others with whom we live. These influences, like the tools a lenscrafter uses to make eyeglasses, influence the way our cultural lens is ground. Consequently, our perceptions are formed by our cultures.

Samovar and Porter (2001) explain this difference in generalized terms that may not necessarily equally apply to all cultural groups or individuals within cultures. In the United States, for example, most people hold to individualism and believe in independence. This individuality in turn gives rise to a strong sense of self-concept and self-esteem. However, in many Asian countries, people emphasize collectivism; the group and especially the family are more important than individuals. Therefore, many Asians value self-effacement, cooperation, and responsiveness to others' needs.

Think how these different cultural perspectives might, for example, influence who you choose to marry. In the United States, while you may be concerned to some degree with what family members think, for the most part, marriage is a decision between two individual people. In other words, you perceive marriage as an individualized decision. However, in many cultures around the world, marriage is a family decision. In fact, in many cultures, marriages are arranged by parents and family members. In these cultures, marriage is perceived as a collective decision that includes family members' insights, opinions, and involvement.

To summarize, culture powerfully influences our perceptions, which, in turn, directly impacts our communication, choices, and behavior.

communicate, but your subsequent communication alters your perceptions and affects future communication. This simple illustration demonstrates the reciprocal power of perception and communication.

IMPROVING PERCEPTION

*G*iven the multiple factors that frame our perceptions, our observations can be very flawed. You have probably had the unfortunate experience of discovering that your first impressions about someone were totally wrong. To use a previous example, upon meeting your prospective new boss for the first time, you may conclude that she would be pleasant to work with, only to later discover that she is more focused on her own career and sacrifices the well-being of others to ensure that she succeeds.

How can you improve your initial and subsequent perceptions and, thereby, enhance your communication abilities? Consider these suggestions.

Guard against Perceptual Error

It is easy for us to absolve ourselves of responsibility. For example, if you insist, "I know what I saw" and contend that your conclusions are valid, you give little room for error. However, since you know that perceptions can be erroneous, recognize that you might have a different perspective than someone else. Also, acknowledge that perceptions matter, because we treat them as reality. In fact, some argue that perception *is* reality. To guard against perceptual errors, it is important to consider others' perceptions and to be open to ideas other than your own.

Gather Additional Information

As we have explained in this section, knowing more can often adjust your perceptions. So, rather than take first impressions at face value or draw conclusions based on limited information, seek multiple sources of information that can help you adjust your perspectives. Of course, talking with others is one of the best ways to do this. While you may be uncertain about or uncomfortable talking with others who are different from you, doing so can help you glean important information and help you avoid stereotypes, which lead to discrimination and prejudice. The box Communication Links: Communicating with People with Disabilities (PWD) offers insights on communicating with people who are disabled, which may present perception and communication challenges.

Communication Links

Communicating with People with Disabilities (PWD)

What is your first reaction when you see someone who uses a wheelchair, a white cane, a hearing aid, or a communication board? Do you feel pity? Do you feel grateful that you're not in their situation? Do you feel uncertain? Research confirms that many nondisabled people feel all of these emotions and more when communicating with a person with a disability (PWD). However, these reactions are rooted in perceptions of PWD as people whose entire identity is not as a *person with a disability* but as a *disabled person*. At first reading, "disabled person" does not seem much different from "person with a disability," but notice the order of the words. When we refer to someone as a PWD, we are emphasizing their personhood, but when we refer to someone as "disabled," the phrasing emphasizes the disability. In other words, the varying language reflects our perception of what we believe is most important to PWD. In order to shape our perceptions appropriately and thus inform our communication with PWD, here are some suggestions:

1. Remember that PWD are people first; their disability is part of their lives but not their whole lives. Treat PWD with the same regard and respect you treat others. PWD are *people* first.
2. Speak with PWD directly. Do not address questions or comments to someone who is with the PWD; speak directly with the person, make eye contact, and stand at an appropriate distance.
3. Use the appropriate language to help frame your perceptions:

DO NOT SAY	SAY
disabled person	person with a disability
wheelchair-bound	uses a wheelchair
handicapped	disabled
crippled	disabled

4. Don't avoid speaking with PWD because you're uncomfortable or uncertain; they probably understand how you feel from previous experience. Avoidance is disconfirming to anyone.
5. Do not make inquiries about someone's disability or explain that "you understand" their situation if you are not a PWD. Do practice the principles of appropriate self-disclosure.

6. If your conversational partner uses a wheelchair, do not touch or lean on the wheelchair or stand farther away. Do use appropriate nonverbal distances.

7. Don't assume PWD cannot do what they need to for themselves; don't force your help on them. Do offer assistance if you feel it is appropriate and let the PWD tell you if and how they would like your assistance.

Use Perception Checking

One of the best ways to avoid perceptual error is to use **perception checking**. Perception checking is based on a simple but powerful communication principle: Ask questions first and make statements later. Here's how it works:

1. Describe the behavior you observe that you wish to clarify ("It seems like you're really down today.")
2. Offer at least two possible explanations for the observed behavior ("Maybe you're just extra tired today, or perhaps something is wrong.")
3. Ask a clarifying question ("Is there something you'd like to talk about?")

Notice how this approach acknowledges your perceptions but also recognizes that there may be multiple explanations for them, without assuming that your perceptions are necessarily accurate. Moreover, this approach encourages communication as a way to clarify your perceptions, while also potentially advancing your relationship development with someone else.

perception checking a process that acknowledges initial perceptions, but also recognizes that there may be multiple explanations for them

Adjust Your Perceptions

As you glean additional information and clarify your perceptions, you can adjust your perceptions. Moreover, by practicing some simple principles, you can learn to adjust your perceptions and avoid the potential pitfalls we have identified. In the book, *People in Quandaries*, Johnson (1946) offers two such principles: dating and indexing. **Dating** refers to assigning specific time periods to perceptions in order to emphasize that perceptions can shift over time. Consider this example of dating:

dating assigning specific time periods to perceptions in order to emphasize that perceptions can shift over time

> Undated statement: Professor Lambert is concerned about student success.
> Dated statement: Professor Lambert was concerned with student success when I took interpersonal communication with her *last year*.

Notice that this statement adjusts perception based on personal experience in a specific time frame.

The other principle, **indexing**, qualifies generalizations when they are applied to specific circumstances. For example:

indexing qualifying generalizations when they are applied to specific circumstances

> Generalized statement: You'll have a hard time in Professor Lambert's interpersonal communication class. I sure did!
> Indexed statement: While I had a hard time in Professor Lambert's interpersonal communication class, *you may do better than I did*.

Notice the difference in the two statements: the first generalizes the speaker's experience to everyone else's, while the second recognizes that not everyone may share the same experience. Qualifying your thinking and speaking in this manner allows you to avoid some of the problems associated with perception by recognizing that perceptions change over time and circumstances.

Practice Empathy

empathy a purposeful attempt to understand another person's perspective

Empathy, or attempting to see experiences from someone else's perspective, helps you avoid drawing firm conclusions without considering how others may see a given situation. Even though you may disagree with someone else's perceptions, by practicing empathy, you demonstrate respect for another person, enlarge your perspective, glean additional information, and check your perceptual biases. As a result, you are more likely to communicate ethically as well.

PERCEPTION IN COLLEGE AND CAREER

*A*s you pursue your college career and then move into the world of work, the power of perception will play a significant role. While we have mentioned these connections throughout this chapter, we want to highlight some important areas.

Perception, Self-Concept, and Academic Success

While we understand that you have multiple goals for your college experience, we believe that your college education is primarily about learning. While this learning takes many forms, your academic performance remains vitally important. Research confirms that a reciprocal relationship exists between how you perceive yourself and your academic success (Bassett & Smythe 1979). In their research, Gage and Berliner (1992) assert that a positive sense of self alone is not enough to ensure academic success; self-esteem is not a panacea. However, a positive attitude is crucial. Seligman (1996) suggests that optimism is an important variable that ultimately impacts self-concept and academic achievement. Moreover, Bandura (1997) notes that self-efficacy is an important measure of academic success. Specifically, research suggests that when you increase your sense of self-expectancy, based on your prior academic experience, you can impact your success in specific subject areas like math, science, or reading.

So, what does all this mean for you? Believing in yourself is important, equal measures of positive attitude, personal expectation, and hard work are vital to academic success. Since you can't rely on positive thinking alone to graduate, you must be realistic about your strengths and weaknesses and respond accordingly. You can do this by monitoring and adjusting your self-perceptions based on external and internal feedback and using what you learn to strengthen your performance in college.

Perception and the Workplace

When you believe your input matters, it is easier to be open with your coworkers.

When you hear the word *work*, do you look for a way to postpone, avoid, or shuffle the task to someone else, or do you consider work a challenge, an opportunity, or a way to make a difference? Some students think that once they get through college and go to work, life will be much better, because they won't have to deal with the demands of mountainous homework, tight deadlines, or demanding professors. In actuality, many of the same aspects of college work transfer to the working world: You will often have to work overtime to complete tasks, you will still have deadlines to meet, and you must continue to work hard to please your boss. One distinct difference, however, is that you will be paid to work at your job rather than paying to learn! Nevertheless, how you perceive work will impact your level of enjoyment, personal progress, and even your health (Schaubroeck, Jones, & Xie 2001). Recognizing the power and place of perception and knowing how to assess and adjust your perceptions will help you make the most of your working life.

Being receptive to a friend's viewpoint helps you view the situation emphatically.

SUMMARY

In this chapter, we focused on the important role of perception and communication. Specifically we have noted that

- perception is a process that includes attention, selection, organization, evaluation, and interpretation;
- perception is problematic due to prior experience, stereotypes, selectivity, and cognitive orientation;
- a reciprocal relationship exists between perception and communication;
- there are important concepts related to self-perception, including self-concept, self-esteem, self-fulfilling prophecies, social comparison, reflected appraisal, and self-efficacy, as well as their impact on communication with self and others, particularly intrapersonal communication, impression management, and self-disclosure;
- as we observe others, we rely on our perceptual biases and attributions in order to make conclusions about them;
- perceptual flaws can be strategically offset by using tactics such as guarding against perceptual errors, gathering more information, using perception checking, adjusting our perceptions, and practicing empathy;
- college and career are both significantly impacted by the power of perception.

Questions for Discussion

1. Identify a stereotype that you relied upon, and explain how this stereotype proved to be helpful or harmful.
2. Provide your own example of the intersection of self-concept, self-esteem, and self-fulfilling prophecy. If appropriate, draw on your own experience to illustrate the connection.
3. Using the principles of appropriate self-disclosure, analyze a time when someone inappropriately self-disclosed information to you. What principles did they violate? How? What advice would you offer them now given what you have learned in this chapter?
4. Evaluate our discussion of the role of self-perception and academic success. Do you agree or disagree with our analysis? Why?

EXERCISES

1. Interview someone who is in a career similar to the one you would like to engage in after you graduate. What are his or her perceptions of work? How does this influence his or her sense of self and success?
2. Identify a time in your life when you misperceived someone else. How were you wrong? Why were you wrong?

How might you use the principles in this chapter to help you avoid this same misperception in the future?
3. Read the following and then explain what this poem teaches us about perception.

American poet John Godfrey Saxe (1816–1887) based the following poem on a fable that was told in India many years ago.

It was six men of Indostan
  To learning much inclined,
Who went to see the Elephant
  (Though all of them were blind),
That each by observation
  Might satisfy his mind

The First approached the Elephant,
  And happening to fall
Against his broad and sturdy side,
  At once began to bawl:
"God bless me! but the Elephant
  Is very like a wall!"

The Second, feeling of the tusk,
  Cried, "Ho! what have we here
So very round and smooth and sharp?
  To me 'tis mighty clear
This wonder of an Elephant
  Is very like a spear!"

The Third approached the animal,
  And happening to take
The squirming trunk within his hands,
  Thus boldly up and spake:
"I see," quoth he, "the Elephant
  Is very like a snake!"

The Fourth reached out an eager hand,
  And felt about the knee.

"What most this wondrous beast is like
  Is mighty plain," quoth he;
"'Tis clear enough the Elephant
  Is very like a tree!"

The Fifth, who chanced to touch the ear,
  Said: "E'en the blindest man
Can tell what this resembles most;
  Deny the fact who can
This marvel of an Elephant
  Is very like a fan!"

The Sixth no sooner had begun
  About the beast to grope,
Than, seizing on the swinging tail
  That fell within his scope,
"I see," quoth he, "the Elephant
  Is very like a rope!"

And so these men of Indostan
  Disputed loud and long,
Each in his own opinion
  Exceeding stiff and strong,
Though each was partly in the right,
  And all were in the wrong!

Poem retrieved July 13, 2006, from
www.wordinfo.info/words/index/info/view_unit/1/?letter=B&spage=3.

◎ KEY TERMS

Perception	Brain dominance	Impression management
Attention	Intrapersonal communication	Implicit personality theory
Selection	Self-concept	Halo effect
Organize	Self-esteem	Closure
Scripts	Self-fulfilling prophecy	First impressions
Interpret	Social comparison	Attributions
Evaluate	Reflected appraisal	Perception checking
Stereotypes	Self-efficacy	Dating
Prejudice	Self-disclosure	Indexing
Discrimination	Johari window	Empathy
Cognitive orientation	Social penetration model	

◎ REFERENCES

Abell, S. C., and Richards, M. H. 1996. The relationship between body shape satisfaction and self-esteem: An investigation of gender and class difference. *Journal of Youth and Adolescence* 25:691–703.

Aitken, J., and Shedletsky, L., eds. 1995. *Intrapersonal communication processes.* Plymouth, MI: The Speech Communication Association and Midnight Oil Multimedia.

Altman, I., and Taylor, D. 1973. *Social penetration: The development of interpersonal relationships.* New York: Holt, Rinehart and Winston.

Bandura, A. 1994. Self-efficacy. In *Encyclopedia of human behavior,* ed. V. S. Ramachaudran, Vol. 4, 71–81. New York: Academic Press.

Bandura, A. 1997. *Self-efficacy: The exercise of control*. New York: Freeman.

Bassett R., and Smythe, M. J. 1979. *Communication and instruction*. New York: Harper & Row.

Berger, C. R. 1979. Beyond initial interaction: Uncertainty, understanding and the development of interpersonal relationships. In *Language and social psychology*, eds. H. Giles and R. St. Clair. Oxford: Basil Blackwell.

Botta, R. A. 1999. Television images and adolescent girls' body image disturbance. *Journal of Communication* 49:22–41.

Bruner, J. S., and Taguiri, R. 1954. *The perception of people*. In *Handbook of social psychology*, ed. G. Lindzey, Vol. 2. Reading, MA: Addison-Wesley.

Campbell, J., and Hepler, H. 1970. *Dimensions in communication: Readings*. Belmont, CA: Wadsworth.

Cash, T. F., and Deagle, E. A. 1997. The nature and extent of body-image disturbances in anorexia nervosa and bulimia nervosa: A meta-analysis. *International Journal of Eating Disorders* 22:107–125.

Faith, M. S., Leon, M. A., and Allison, D. B. 1997. The effects of self-generated comparison targets, BMI, and social comparison tendencies on body image appraisal. *Eating Disorders* 5:128–140.

Festinger, L. 1954. A theory of social comparison processes. *Human Relations* 7:117–140.

Gage, N., and Berliner, D. 1992. *Educational psychology*. 5th ed. Boston: Houghton Mifflin.

Garfinkle, M. 2004. Using the self-fulfilling prophecy: Expectations shape reality. Retrieved October 10, 2004, from www.capsnap.com/max/maxarticle1.asp?ID=7.

Goffman, E. 1959. *The presentation of self in everyday life*. New York: Doubleday.

Grammatis, Y. 1998. *Learning styles*. Chatsworth, CA: Chaminade College Preparatory. Retrieved July 29, 2006, from www.chaminade.org/inspire/learnstl.htm.

Heider, F. 1944. Social perception and phenomenal causality. *Psychological Review* 51:358–374.

Johnson, W. 1946. *People in quandaries: The semantics of personal adjustment*. San Francisco, CA: International Society for General Semantics.

Jones, D. C., Vigfusdottir, T. H, and Lee, Y. 2004. Body image and the appearance culture among adolescent girls and boys: An examination of friend conversations, peer criticism, appearance magazines and internalization of appearance ideals. *Journal of Adolescent Research*, 19:323–329.

Kubany, E. D., Hill, E. E., Owens, J. A., Iannce-Spencer, C., McCaig, M. A., Tremayne, K. J., and Williams, P. L. 2004. Cognitive trauma therapy for battered women with PTSD (CTT-BW). *Journal of Consulting and Clinical Psychology* 72(1):3–18.

Lim, B. 1996. Student expectations of professors. *The Teaching Professor* 10(4):3–4. In *Communication for the classroom teacher*. Cooper, P., and Simonds, C., 58: 2003. Boston: Allyn and Bacon.

Luft, J. 1970. *Group processes: An introduction to group dynamics*. Palo Alto, CA: Mayfield.

Morris, T. L., Gorham, J., Cohen, S. H., and Huffman, D. 1996. Fashion in the classroom: Effects of attire on student perceptions of instructors in college classes. *Communication Education* 45:135–148.

Rosenblum, G. D., and Lewis, M. 1999. The relations among body image, physical attractiveness, and body mass in adolescence. *Child Development* 70(1): 50–64.

Samovar, L. A., and Porter, R. E. 2001. *Communication between cultures*. Belmont, CA: Wadsworth.

Schaubroeck, J., Jones, J. R., and Xie, J. L. 2001. Individual differences in utilizing control to cope with job demands: Effects on susceptibility to infectious disease. *Journal of Applied Psychology* 86(2):265–278.

Sheldon, W. H. 1942. *The varieties of temperament: A psychology of constitutional differences.* New York: Harper & Brothers.

Seligman, M. 1996. *The optimistic child: How learned optimism protects children from depression.* New York: Houghton Mifflin.

CHAPTER 4

Effective Listening

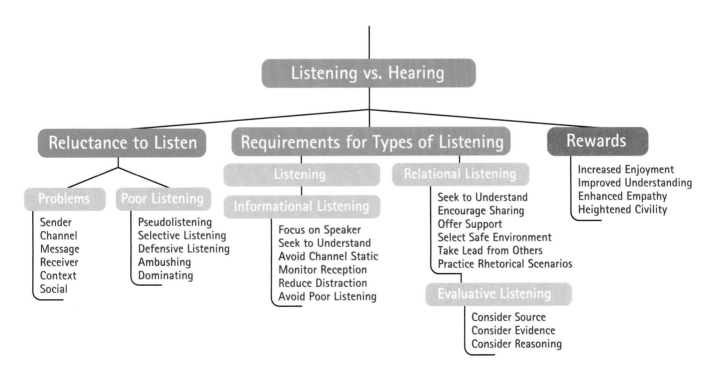

Listening vs. Hearing

Reluctance to Listen

Problems
Sender
Channel
Message
Receiver
Context
Social

Poor Listening
Pseudolistening
Selective Listening
Defensive Listening
Ambushing
Dominating

Requirements for Types of Listening

Listening

Informational Listening
Focus on Speaker
Seek to Understand
Avoid Channel Static
Monitor Reception
Reduce Distraction
Avoid Poor Listening

Relational Listening
Seek to Understand
Encourage Sharing
Offer Support
Select Safe Environment
Take Lead from Others
Practice Rhetorical Scenarios

Evaluative Listening
Consider Source
Consider Evidence
Consider Reasoning

Rewards
Increased Enjoyment
Improved Understanding
Enhanced Empathy
Heightened Civility

65

Knowledge Checklist

✓ To understand the difference between listening and hearing
✓ To recognize the multiple problems in listening
✓ To identify types of poor listening
✓ To understand how to listen well, given the four kinds of listening
✓ To recognize the many rewards of effective listening
✓ To appreciate the role of listening in college and career experiences

THE RELUCTANCE TO LISTEN

few years ago, one of your authors invited the dean to attend an orientation for new graduate teaching assistants and to welcome them to the campus. In his brief remarks, the dean mentioned that he had just returned from a symposium where academics and business professionals discussed the changes that need to be made in higher education to better prepare college students for the workplace. The dean related that listening was the primary communication skill college graduates needed but seemed to lack the most.

Certainly, listening is the communication skill we use the most and learn the least about. In this chapter, we offer information that highlights the importance of listening in the communication process. As we explained in Chapter 1, human communication is a transactional process in which we create and share meaning. As with other aspects of communication, listening is reciprocal; it is important to listen and be listened to. Therefore, we need our parents, partners, professors, and peers to listen to us, and they need us to pay attention to them. In this chapter, however, we will focus specifically on receiving messages, even though both sending and receiving messages happen simultaneously. In the box Cultural Links: Silence as Responding, you will note that communication occurs even in the absence of sound.

Cultural Links

Silence as Responding

Silence is an important part of listening. We must be truly quiet in order to artfully listen to others. In this sense, silence is not just the absence of spoken words; it is also "tuning in" or attending to the other person. Consider this paragraph found in the *Hindu*, India's national newspaper, which aptly explains the role of silence in listening:

The words "listen" and "silent" are both made up of the same letters, but they're very different. If we're simply silent, we'll end up listening like a stunned stonefish. We need to listen with our hearts, our eyes and our minds, as well as our ears. Listening, as opposed to being silent, does three things for us. It helps us build better relationships, which makes us happier. It helps us find out what's really going on and what people are really thinking, which makes us more effective, persuasive and influential. And if you're still not convinced, listen to this: listening carefully to others obliges them to listen carefully to us. (www.hinduonnet.com/thehindu/mp/2002/08/01/stories/2002080100920400.htm)

While silence is a vital part of the listening process, cultures differ regarding the role of silence in responding, the final step in listening. To illustrate, you tell your best friend, "I'm really having trouble with my math class. I just can't seem to understand it. I'm worried I may fail the class, which will create all kinds of problems." Assume your friend just remains silent. How will you interpret her silence? If you are a member of the U.S. dominant culture, you are likely to interpret this silence as unsupportive. You may even think that your friend has not listened to what you've been saying. However, in Native American cultures, this silence may reflect careful listening or an empathic response, since words are not as trusted as silence in their culture (Martin & Nakayama 2001). Consider this quote from Ohiyesa (Charles Alexander Eastman), a Wahpeton Santee Sioux, which summarizes the Native American view of silence:

> *The Wise Man believes profoundly in silence—the sign of a perfect equilibrium. Silence is the absolute poise or balance of body, mind and spirit. The man who preserves his selfhood ever calm and unshaken by the storms of existence—not a leaf, as it were, astir on the tree, not a ripple upon the surface of the shinning pool—his, in the mind of the unlettered sage, is the ideal attitude and conduct of life. Silence is the cornerstone of character. (www.greatdreams.com/wisdom.htm)*

Listening is hard work. While you may *hear* with little difficulty, unless you are deaf or hearing impaired, listening requires concentration and effort. While **hearing** is a physical process that allows us to perceive sounds in our environment, **listening** is a mental process that requires us to focus upon specific sounds in a certain time and place in order to create meaning—we must be **mindful** (Wood 1997). When we are mindful, we are paying attention. Notice that this phrase assumes that we are *paying* attention. In other words, it costs us to listen.

As an experiment in hearing and listening, stop reading and focus upon the variety of sounds in your physical environment. You may hear birds outside the window, music playing in the next room, or the mechanical noise created by an air conditioner or heater. These sounds have likely been present the entire time you have been in this environment. However, when you listen to these sounds, you concentrate on them, or you become mindful of them. Because concentration requires time and energy, and because we have a limited amount of both, we are more likely to give our time and attention to what we find interesting, unique, or appealing.

hearing the physical process that allows people to perceive sounds

listening the mental process that requires a person to focus upon specific sounds in a certain time and place in order to create meaning

mindful paying attention

Internal or external distractions during a big game can cause you to miss key information.

For example, think about how you pay attention to a lecture in one of your general education classes as opposed to the comments of a person you find attractive. You probably listen more carefully to your attractive acquaintance than to your professor's lecture because you find this person much more interesting, unique, or appealing. While this does not necessarily mean the lecture is boring, it does mean that when compared to an enjoyable conversation, you are more reluctant to listen to the lecture. By understanding this reluctance to listen and the problems associated with this reluctance, we can develop strategies to improve our listening skills.

Problems in Listening

Listening is difficult for many reasons. In this section, we identify some of the specific listening problems or challenges we face. In general, listening is difficult because it is a complex process. Consider the listening model in Figure 4.1.

As you can see, listening consists of seven overlapping stages, including hearing, selecting, attending, understanding, evaluating, remembering, and responding. The overlapping circles that form the model, along with the model's circular shape, reinforce that the seven stages and the entire act of listening are, indeed, a process; each stage is integrally related to the others. At any point in this process, we may encounter various types of noise that interfere with, or even block, our ability to listen effectively. Consider each of these stages briefly:

- Hearing is physically receiving sound waves.
- Selecting is choosing to focus on certain sounds.
- Attending is paying close attention to the sounds that we choose.
- Understanding is assigning meaning to the sounds we choose and pay attention to.
- Evaluating is analyzing and making decisions or judgments about the sounds we choose, attend to, and understand.
- Remembering is retaining the sounds we have chosen, attended to, understood, and evaluated for later recall.
- Responding is offering feedback to the sounds that we have chosen, attended to, understood, evaluated, and remembered.

FIGURE 4.1   Listening Model

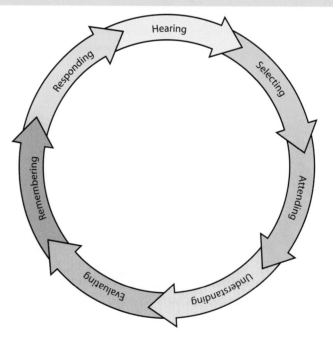

Given these necessary skills, you can see that listening is complex and creates many potential problems for effective listening. This is especially crucial in the workplace, as described in the box Career Links: The Costs of Poor Listening on the Job.

The Costs of Poor Listening on the Job

While we can espouse the value of listening and the importance of listening on the job, perhaps the following illustrations make the point more graphically. Consider this information drawn from Fisher (1996).

A Hypothetical Calculation

- Most workers spend about 50 percent of their working hours listening.
- Studies indicate that workers, on average, listen with a 25 percent efficiency rate.
- There are approximately 100 million workers in the United States.
- If each of the 100 million workers in the United States makes a mistake in listening each year that results in a cost of ten dollars, the cost would be 1 billion dollars per year.

A Tragic Incident

On March 27, 1977, a 747 with 248 passengers and DC 10 with 380 vacationers prepared to take off from a fog-shrouded airport in the Canary Islands. The control tower directed the pilot of the 747 to taxi up the runway, make a 180-degree turn, and stand by for takeoff clearance. Meanwhile, the DC 10 was directed by the same control tower to taxi up the same foggy runway and turn off at the third ramp. The DC 10 crew, however, considered the first turnoff to be inactive because it was blocked by another aircraft. So the DC 10 crew headed for the fourth exit rather than the third. The pilot of the 747 misunderstood his instructions because he started to take off before receiving clearance from the tower. As the pilot of the 747 was attempting to take off, he saw the DC 10. The 747 was approaching the DC 10 at 186 mph; there was no way to avoid a collision. According to the nine-minute tape recording of the exchanges between the control tower and the aircraft,

- both planes and the control tower were tuned to the same radio frequency and should have heard the various communications among the tower and the two pilots;
- the 747 was not, at any point, given clearance to take off.

The costs of this tragic failure to listen were

- 581 lives;
- over 500 million dollars in lawsuits;
- the destruction of two planes worth a total of 63 million dollars.

Source: "The Costs of Poor Listening on the Job" from *Effective Listening* by S. Fisher. © 1996. Used by permission of the publisher, HRD Press, Inc. Amherst, MA. www.hrdpress.com

Another way we can identify listening problems is to recall the communication model we examined in Chapter 1. That model contained several important elements, including sender, message, channel, receiver, feedback, noise, and context. To better understand problems with listening, we can reconsider these elements and identify how particular aspects of each of these elements contribute to listening problems.

Sender-Based Problems   Sometimes we face listening problems because of the sender's credibility or clarity. The credibility, or **ethos**, of a communicator rests primarily upon the listener's perception of his or her goodwill, trustworthiness, competence, and appropriateness. If we believe a sender has our best interest at heart, we consider him or her to have goodwill. We are more likely to trust the advice of our best friend rather than someone we do not know very well, because we believe that our best friend is truly interested in our welfare. Moreover, if we believe someone is honest, we consider him or her trustworthy. To illustrate, you are probably more likely to loan money to someone you believe will pay you back than to someone who has not returned the money you loaned them two weeks ago, although he promised to do so repeatedly. In other words, these two borrowers' different levels of honesty make a difference in their respective trustworthiness and how reliable you perceive their promises to be.

While listening is impacted by our perceptions of a communicator's goodwill and trustworthiness, we are also impacted by competence and appropriateness.

ethos a speaker's credibility, based upon the perception of his or her goodwill, trustworthiness, competence, and appropriateness

While competent people know what they are talking about, speakers who are sensitive to the audience and the occasion demonstrate appropriateness. For example, special speakers for graduation are usually chosen because of their reputations, intelligence, or success. However, some speakers seem to forget that students attend graduations to receive their diplomas, not to listen to speakers, and end up speaking too long! In this instance, the speaker may be competent but is insensitive to the occasion and the audience. However, when a communicator embodies competence, appropriateness, goodwill, and trustworthiness, we are more likely to pay attention to the message because we consider the speaker credible. Likewise, if a sender uses clear language that we understand and seeks feedback from us to ensure that we *do* understand, we are also more likely to listen.

The standards of goodwill, trustworthiness, competence, and appropriateness apply to others, and they also apply to *us* when we send messages. If we are credible, clear communicators, we help others listen to us.

Channel-Based Problems   As we discussed in the Chapter 1, there are several types of channels we use to share messages with one another, including verbal and nonverbal communication shared via mass media. When we think of the relationship between listening and channels, focusing on the *nature* and the *number* of channels helps us understand this relationship and the listening problems that may occur.

From our own experience with communication, we know that the *number* of channels we use can enhance or complicate listening. Particularly, when we use multiple channels, we enhance the likelihood that others will listen. For example, think about how difficult it is to create shared meaning when you play a game like *Pictionary* or charades. You may find this difficult because players rely only on the nonverbal channel to send or interpret messages. It is difficult not to speak as we attempt to cue others in this game, because if we add the verbal channel, or spoken words, to the nonverbal channel, the gestures we use, we know that our partners are more apt to guess correctly.

Additionally, think about the conclusions you make about professors or peers based on their speech or appearance. For instance, we may find a teacher who speaks very slowly or with a strong nasal quality quite annoying. On the other hand, peers who dress stylishly or who are physically attractive are more likely to catch our attention; studies indicate that even from childhood, we are more likely to listen to them because we find them appealing (Ramsey & Langlois 2002). But we will find it easier to listen if we forego drawing conclusions based solely on nonverbal channels, such as vocal quality and attire, and gather additional information, including *how* a person speaks and *what* the person says. In short, by paying attention to multiple communication channels, we can enhance our listening.

Additionally, think about the *nature* of the channels that influence our listening. If all you know about a particular class comes from only reading the syllabus, you may draw incorrect inferences about the course. However, by asking questions of the teacher or talking with other students who have taken the class, you can gain additional information that will help you draw better conclusions. Therefore, by using both the written and oral verbal channels, you can adjust your perceptions and avoid listening problems created by drawing conclusions from insufficient information. The lessons in this section, then, are simple but important:

* Use more than one channel in order to enhance your listening and to ensure that you send clear messages that help others listen to you.
* Use more than one type of channel in order to enhance your listening and to ensure that you send clear messages that help others listen to you.

To further illustrate these two important principles, think about how media influences your listening. Much of television advertising and even the news relies upon **sound bites**, which *American Heritage Dictionary* defines as "a brief statement, as by a politician, taken from an audiotape or videotape and broadcast especially during a news report." This approach may initially help you gain information;

sound bite a brief statement taken from an audiotape or videotape and broadcast especially during a news report

however, reducing complex ideas, events, or feelings to brief messages tends to compromise rather than help us listen. Therefore, to listen more carefully, it would be helpful to listen to the sound bites and to gather additional information through reading, talking with others, or listening to other media sources that offer in-depth information about a given issue. In doing this, we are adding listening channels that improve our listening. Likewise, while we may use sound bites to catch others' attention, by using additional channels we can ensure that others receive our messages clearly and completely. The box Computer Links: Listening and Computer-Mediated Communication (CMC) explains some of the challenges, as well as the benefits, of using new technologies to send and receive messages.

Computer Links

Listening and Computer-Mediated Communication (CMC)

As we indicated in Chapter 1, the channel of communication you choose to use dramatically impacts human communication. We also indicated that CMC (computer-mediated communication) has dramatically transformed the landscape of human communication. But how does CMC impact listening? Does listening even play a role in CMC? As we continue to increasingly rely upon CMC and other forms of technology such as cell phones and iPods, we are faced with new insights and challenges in listening.

Some contend that we are so bombarded by information that our listening skills are rapidly declining. *Multitasking* has become the buzz word for many people who talk on their cell phones while driving a car or who respond to e-mails and talk on the phone simultaneously. No doubt our listening skills are compromised by our failure to give full attention to one another, but are computers and other technology the true culprits in this decline? Others offer different perspectives, as follows.

CMC may be seen as a call to greater listening, rather than the demise of effective listening. For example, there are many forms of aural information on the Web, including the various audio and video formats, streaming, Web telephone, and computer-based video conferencing. All of these channels of communication require effective listening skills, as much as face-to-face conversation, even though some of them are asynchronous, or not happening simultaneously.

Additionally, assistive technological devices help the deaf and people with hearing impairments listen more effectively. Therefore, technology for these people represents the opportunity to listen.

But what is the role of listening, if any, in text-based CMC? Do we "listen" to e-mails, instant messages, or blogs? Interestingly, Daisley (http://wac.colostate.edu/rhetnet/rdc/daisley16.html) notes that "lurkers" may actually be thought of as listeners to Internet communication and that CMC may actually call upon us to develop turn-taking and listening skills that are directly transferable to face-to-face conversation. In his book *The Future Does Not Compute: Transcending the Machines in Our Midst*, Talbott (1995) offers these observations.

The Ability to Listen

I mean an active sort of listening—the kind that enables and encourages, eliciting from the speaker an even better statement than he knew he was capable of producing. The kind that enters sympathetically into the gaps, the hesitations, the things left unsaid, so that the listener can state the speaker's position as effectively as his own. To listen productively is to nurture a receptive and energetic void within which a new word can take shape. Such listening is half of every good conversation, perhaps the most creative half.

Needless to say, listening expresses a deep selflessness. And, if my own experience is any guide, the discipline required is far from natural. In fact, it usually seems impossible. But this does not prevent our working toward it, as toward any ideal.

What about computer-mediated communication? Clearly, listening is still more difficult here. The speaker is no longer physically present. He no longer demands so insistently that I attend to his words, nor is my listening immediately evident to him. If I wish, I can more easily conceal my disinterest.

However, the situation is not hopeless. Even in face-to-face communication I must "overcome" the physically detached word if I would find my way to the mind of the speaker. So it's not as if the computer confronts me with an altogether new challenge. It's just that I must make a more conscious effort of attention, actively seeking out the speaker behind the words on my screen. When I do this well, my response can still convey a quality of listening. Listening is in any case more than a mere visible blankness. It is a receptive participation that colors all aspects of the conversation.

What is your opinion of the impact of CMC on listening? Do you think technology has negatively impacted listening ? If so, how? Has it offered an alternative way to develop listening skills?

Source: "The Ability to Listen" from *The Future Does Not Compute* by S. Talbott. © 1995, O'Reilly Media, Inc. All rights reserved. Used with permission.

Message-Based Problems

message overload receiving too many messages at the same time, making it difficult to listen

Messages also impact your listening. Receiving too many messages at the same time, for example, creates **message overload** and makes it more difficult to listen. Perhaps you experience message overload in the classroom. Given that college students spend up to 53% of their time in listening (Barker, Edward, Gaines, Gladney, & Holley 1980), you probably often feel like a fully saturated sponge, even though your brain is very capable of processing more information. Consequently, listening to more information becomes practically impossible because you wrestle with processing a great deal of information in a relatively short period of time.

message complexity containing complicated ideas, numerous details, or new skills

Message complexity also creates a listening challenge. For example, think about the most difficult course you are taking this semester. It probably contains complex ideas, numerous details, or new skills. In short, the course contains many complex messages that require you to listen carefully and consistently. We all find this difficult to do. One of your authors remembers taking Greek as a first-year student in college. Here is his experience:

> *Trying to master a new alphabet and learn vocabulary and grammar was difficult enough. But when the teacher used English grammar as a way to help students understand the equivalent parts of speech in Greek, I was utterly lost! In other words, language got in the way of learning language!*

This anecdote indicates another problem with listening to some messages. At times, words themselves present a listening barrier. Complex vocabulary, technical jargon, or loaded words make it more difficult to listen. Messages that employ simple, direct language and avoid using **trigger words**—words that stimulate a negative emotional reaction in listeners—can help others listen to us and can help us as we listen to others.

trigger words words that stimulate a negative emotional reaction in listeners

Receiver-Based Problems

As listeners, we face numerous problems receiving messages. Have you had a conversation with a friend in which you realized, after the conversation ended, that you had little recall of what your friend said? What happened? Perhaps your mind raced ahead, given that you can think much faster than your friend can speak. During this time gap, your mind easily wandered and you ceased to listen. Maybe you were preoccupied with other matters, such as an upcoming event or concern about how well you did on the test you took earlier in the day. You may have been cold, hot, hungry, or had a headache. In these cases, external and internal physical noise distracted you from listening. You may have also found your friend difficult to hear or understand and decided that what she was saying was not important anyway. Or you may have assumed that you already knew what she was going to say and thought, "I've heard this all before!" In either case, you made a prejudgment and ceased to listen.

You may also have experienced **receiver apprehension** or "the fear of misinterpreting, inadequately processing and/or not being able to adjust psychologically to messages sent by others" (Wheeless 1975, p. 263). However, whatever the explanation, all of the listening problems discussed in this section are receiver-based difficulties—that is, the primary source of your listening problem was *you*, not the sender's ethos, too few channels, or complex messages with troublesome language. You did not listen because you did not effectively manage physical or mental noise. This is not a matter of blame but of responsibility. In other words, sometimes we do not listen because we are physically or mentally distracted or we choose not to listen.

receiver apprehension the fear of misinterpreting, inadequately processing, and/or not being able to adjust psychologically to messages sent by others

Context-Based Problems

Remember that *context* refers to the various environments that surround a given communication event, including the physical, linguistic, cultural, and social environments. Each of these environments potentially creates listening challenges. Obviously, if we are unable to hear a message because of physical noise, we cannot listen. Simply changing the physical environment by moving to another space, turning down the CD player, or turning off the television can dramatically impact listening.

If we do not share the same language with someone, it may be impossible to truly listen. As a result, the linguistic environment creates a listening barrier. We may be able to hear what is said but be unable to understand. As our communities increasingly become multicultural, linguistic barriers are more likely to appear. And even when people of other ethnic backgrounds speak English, their accents may make it challenging for us to listen. For example, some students find it difficult to understand international students or teachers who speak accented English. Moreover, **co-cultures**, or cultures that exist within a more dominant culture (Martin & Nakayama 2001), may use words in unique ways or speak with dialects that sound foreign to our ears. If we focus on these differences, we are likely to be distracted from listening.

co-cultures cultures that exist within a more dominant culture

Cultural environments also impact listening. A colleague explains that he chose to stay in the United States to teach because he enjoys student–teacher interaction. He was not inclined to return to the lecture-based teaching typically found in his native country. In his culture, listening includes limited feedback from students. Note how the role of listening shifts in this example. Students in Japan and in many other nations are expected to absorb information from the professor by listening to lectures. While lecture is very common in college classrooms in the United States, discussion, small group projects, and other interactive instructional methods are used more often. In this case, listening becomes a matter of attending to and absorbing information, and of dealing with numerous voices, offering more personal feedback, and evaluating ideas, opinions, and learning information.

The cultural context that influences classroom communication in Japan and the United States creates different types of listening problems. In Japanese higher education, passive listening is the norm; it requires students to attend carefully to the presentation of information. However, in U.S. college classrooms, students are expected to actively engage in listening by providing immediate feedback through exchanging and examining ideas (Martin & Nakayama 2001).

Social-Based Problems

Deborah Tannen (1990) notes how gender influences or impacts listening. In her book *You Just Don't Understand: Women and Men in Conversation*, Tannen suggests that men, in general, interrupt their conversational partners more often than women and prefer to focus more on information; women, in general, emphasize relational issues and focus more on people. As listeners, then, women are prone to provide support for their conversational partners by giving encouraging feedback (smiles, nods, or vocal support) while men are less likely to provide supportive feedback and even interrupt their conversational partners more often. Why do these listening differences exist? Are men, by nature, rude? Are women, by nature, more nurturing? To make such assumptions fails to understand the influence of the social context and overgeneralizes. Most likely, men and women speak and listen differently because of the ways in which they are socialized. In short, the social context dramatically impacts how people listen.

Poor Listening

Given the reluctance with which we listen, no wonder many of us listen poorly. However, understanding poor listening behaviors is the first step in improved listening. In this section, we identify several problems that lead to poor listening.

Pseudolistening   As professors, we often see students in our classes who appear to be listening but are not. They may keep eye contact with us, nod, or even smile, while they are actually mentally far removed from the classroom conversation. As another example, perhaps your boss or coworker tries to leave the impression he is listening, when in fact he could not repeat what you have said. This is termed **pseudolistening,** or pretending to listen.

Selective Listening   **Selective listening** occurs when we focus on parts of a message that appeal to us because we like or dislike the topic. For example, many speakers know that audiences are more likely to listen to stories, anecdotes, or examples, so they include several of these in their speeches. The novelist Andrew Greeley gave one of the most effective commencement speeches at Northern Michigan University. Rather than deliver a typical speech for such an occasion, which often puts an audience to sleep, Greeley told a story that kept the audience's attention and left an important insight for the graduates to consider.

This happens in public speaking and in conversation. Think of how often you fail to listen to a friend, romantic partner, or family member until he or she mentions something that you find particularly interesting. Or, conversely, you may tune out something that you find distasteful or difficult to handle. In such instances, you are listening selectively.

Defensive Listening   "I can't believe you would say something like that to me!" Have you ever received this kind of a response and wondered what you said to provoke it? Perhaps you know people who often respond this way. These people are possibly engaged in **defensive listening,** which is the practice of attributing criticism, hostility, or attacks to the comments of others even when these comments were not meant to be offensive. Low self-esteem, feelings of inadequacy, or an assumption that another person distrusts us may prompt defensive listening.

Ambushing   **Ambushing** is essentially the opposite of defensive listening and occurs when we listen carefully to others in order to attack what they say. While listening includes evaluating what others say, evaluation is not equivalent to attack. When we authentically listen, we attempt to truly understand the person's intended message, not actively look for ways that we can attack the other's position. While we may disagree with someone's position, our purpose in constructive listening is not to find ammunition for our conversational war, but to give a "fair hearing" to others and respond accordingly.

Dominating   **Dominating,** also termed *monopolizing* or *stage hogging,* happens when others consistently refocus attention on themselves, even if they must

Improve your listening habits by encouraging dialogue rather than avoiding it.

pseudolistening pretending to listen

selective listening occurs when listeners focus on parts of a message that appeals to them because they like or dislike the topic at hand

defensive listening the practice of attributing criticism, hostility, or attacks to the comments of others even when they are not intended

ambushing occurs when a person listens carefully in order to attack what the speaker says

dominating occurs when others consistently refocus attention on themselves, even if they must interrupt others to do so; also termed *monopolizing or stage hogging*

interrupt others to do so. Dominators may use interruptions like, "Well, if you think that's something, let me tell you what happened to *me*." Unlike supportive listeners who interrupt to clarify or encourage another to continue to speak, dominators interrupt to recapture the conversation. One of your authors worked with a colleague who dominated conversations so often that at one point he confronted the colleague kindly and said, "I don't know if you realize it or not, but you simply don't listen to me. Every time I try to speak with you, you interrupt or talk over me." Interestingly, this colleague received the information very well, but even during the conversation, when his dominating behavior was explicitly mentioned, he continued to control the conversation. This person did not even listen closely enough to accept constructive criticism about his listening behaviors!

THE REQUIREMENTS FOR LISTENING

*N*ow that you have some understanding of the problems that accompany listening and some of the poor listening habits that result, let's think about the requirements for effective listening. Particularly, we will focus on specific, practical strategies that you can employ in order to improve your listening skills. However, in order to understand these strategies, we need to understand the basic types of listening, including **pleasurable listening, informational listening, relational listening,** and **evaluative listening.**

pleasurable listening listening for appreciation

informational listening listening to discern

relational listening listening to understand, support, and empathize with others

Pleasurable Listening

When we listen to music, television, or a joke, we are engaged in pleasurable listening, or listening for appreciation. This type of listening calls for less focused concentration but nevertheless still requires us to tune in to the source. In short, you can't fully enjoy much of your world without truly listening.

Informational Listening

When people are seeking to understand others' messages, they are reengaged in informational listening, or listening to discern. Given the nature of human communication and the problems that accompany listening, this is much more complicated than it may at first appear. As a college student, it is especially important that you develop a keen ability to listen for information since you spend much of your time in this endeavor. When you attend class, talk with your RA about housing regulations, obtain financial aid information, or visit the student health center, you are listening to information. We will have more specific suggestions later in this chapter, but here are some initial suggestions to improve your informational listening.

Focus on the Speaker Position yourself so that you can easily make eye contact with the speaker. When your mind begins to wander, catch yourself and refocus your attention on the speaker. Make it your aim to understand what the speaker has to say rather than on how she says it or her appearance.

Seek to Understand the Message Look for main ideas rather than details. In some cases, such as a lecture, take notes and seek to organize the information in a way that helps you understand and remember it. Use memory devices such as acronyms and acrostics. Ask questions as you listen. Don't judge the value of the message by your impression of the speaker. The box Campus Links: Use a Recall/Cue System of Note-Taking offers some helpful suggestions for improving note-taking.

Careful listening is the first prerequisite for success on the job.

◎ Campus Links

Use a Recall/Cue System of Note-Taking

Using a recall/cue system with your notes is one way to make your outline notes work harder for you—it makes them easier to review and helps you retain information. John Gardner and his colleagues A. Jerome Jewler and Betsy Barefoot (2007) describe the recall/cue system of note-taking in the seventh edition of their book *Your College Experience: Strategies for Success*. The steps are as follows:

1. *Set up your notebook paper.* Draw a line down from the top of your page to the bottom about two inches in from the left-hand margin. This will divide your paper into two parts. The recall/cue space (on the left side of the paper) and the note-taking area.

2. *Take outline lecture notes.* Jot down your notes as you normally would, using the right-hand two-thirds of your sheet. Be sure to use good outline format by employing indentation and spacing to help you see relationships between and among main points and details.

3. *Set aside a brief, daily study session to review notes and develop recall cues.*

4. *Write the main ideas in the recall column.* Gardner et al. (2006) suggest that you review the notes you took in lecture for five or ten minutes first. Then, they suggest you go back through your notes and identify or highlight key terms or phrases and then write them in the recall column next to the material they represent.

5. *Use the recall column to review your ideas.* Cover up the notes on the right-hand side of your page with a blank piece of paper and use the prompts from the recall column to review your material. Reciting *out loud* or writing out the ideas on the sheet you are using to cover the right-hand side of the notes are excellent ways to really actively learn the material rather than passively review it.

6. *Review the previous day's notes just before the next class session.* Arrive at class early for lecture and take a few moments to review your two-column notes. Again, begin by covering up the right-hand side and only using the recall cues on the left-hand side to trigger or prompt your review. This will help you not only to review the material you've previously covered but also to prepare for what will be covered next in class.

If you have back-to-back classes and can't review immediately before class, try doing your periodic review during breakfast, in the hallway before class, riding the bus to school, or while doing a load of laundry. Using little bits of time to review prior to and after class will increase your understanding and will help you retain the information in your notes.

Avoid Allowing the Channel to Decide How You Listen   You may find a lecture with visual aids, demonstrations, or dynamic delivery more interesting. However, do not allow your preferences to decide whether you listen. Choose to listen regardless of the channels being used, even though you may find it challenging.

Monitor Your Reception   Decide to listen and reinforce this decision by catching yourself as your mind begins to wander. Avoid trying to read speakers' minds or concluding that you already know or dislike what they are going to say. Since you can listen much faster than someone can speak, use this lag time to pose questions or summarize main points in your notes. Getting enough rest and attending to those hunger pangs will also help you monitor your listening.

Reduce Contextual Distractions   Dress appropriately for the physical environment. Seat yourself away from as many physical distractions as possible. Mentally block out background noise. Don't become so focused upon the words the speaker uses or the ways in which the speaker forms words that you miss the message.

Avoid Poor Listening Behaviors   Don't pretend to listen or listen only to those parts of the message you like or that you find interesting. Give speakers the benefit of the doubt rather than assuming they are opposed to you or that you need to find fault with the message.

Relational Listening

In relational listening, we listen in order to understand, support, and empathize with others. As noted in Chapter 3, **empathy** refers to an attempt to understand other people's perspectives and to place yourself in their situation. When we listen relationally, we focus upon the feelings, needs, and desires of others as they attempt to make decisions, solve problems, or get to know each other better. Later, when we focus more on listening and learning, we will provide additional insights about empathic listening. However, here are some first steps to consider when listening in order to enhance relationships.

empathy a purposeful attempt to understand another person's perspective

Seek to Understand   When you listen to what others say, you may respond in any number of ways. Sometimes you may make quick *judgments* that are either positive ("Hey, that's a good plan!") or negative ("That's a really stupid way to feel!"). Or you may offer *advice* ("Well, if I were you, I would . . ."). At other times, you may provide an *analysis* of the situation ("As I think about it, it seems to me that the real problem here is . . .") or pose *questions* that help the other person think about the issue at hand ("Why do you think this happened at this particular point in time?").

While any of these responses may be helpful in certain situations, initially it is best to attend to what the other person has to say. To let others know you are listening, you can offer various forms of feedback. **Paraphrase** or restate the speaker's ideas or feelings in your own words. This can help you check your understanding while also assuring the speaker you are listening.

paraphrase restate a someone's ideas or feelings in your own words

Encourage Others to Share More   Responses like "Tell me more," "Uh-huh," and "I see," prompt speakers to reveal what they are thinking or feeling and add important clarifications that will help you understand them better. Even a brief silence offers the speaker a chance to share more information.

Offer Support   As someone once noted, "People don't care how much we know until they know how much we care." In other words, the people who are important in our lives need to know that we are committed to them regardless of their problems or decisions. Providing verbal and nonverbal feedback—such as posing questions, paraphrasing, encouraging response, maintaining eye contact, smiling, nodding, and touching (when appropriate)—communicate interpersonal support.

Select a Safe Environment   Some information is much too personal to share in a public setting. Recently, two of your authors were in a restaurant where a man and woman were arguing about their relationship. They were talking so loudly about personal issues that we became uncomfortable both for them and for ourselves. We encourage you to deal with personal issues in private so that you can listen and respond appropriately.

Conversing with others going through the same things you are helps you to feel welcome and supported.

Take Your Lead from the Other Person   Often conversational partners will ask for your evaluation or opinion if they want it. Therefore, it's best to wait until you are invited to share your viewpoint. Even then, however, it is important to weigh your words carefully.

Practice Rhetorical Sensitivity   **Rhetorical sensitivity**, a concept developed by Hart, Carlson, and Eadie (1980), refers to "concern for self, concern for others, and a situational attitude" as cited in Littlejohn (1996, p. 107). In other words, as we listen empathetically, we are focused on ourselves, the other person, and the situation; in this way, we can provide appropriate, supportive verbal and nonverbal feedback to the speaker. To learn more about this concept, see the box Communication Links: Rhetorical Sensitivity.

rhetorical sensitivity concern for self, concern for others, and a situational attitude

Communication Links

Rhetorical Sensitivity

The idea of rhetorical sensitivity rests on the belief that all people hold attitudes toward communication—that is, they like to talk with others, they dislike talking with others, or they think everyone who tries to start a conversation is after something, and so on. Rhetorical sensitivity embraces a particular approach composed of the following assumptions:

- When talking, people should *balance* their needs and the needs of others.
- People should sharply distinguish between all thoughts and thoughts-for-communication.
- People should assume that there are many different ways to say the same thing.
- There is no "real self," as each of us is composed of multiple selves and we speak with multiple voices.
- Flexibility, strategy-making, and adaptation to others are the keys to successful communication.

The Rhetorical Sensitivity Scale (RHETSEN) developed by Hart, Carlson, and Eodie (1980) taps into our attitudes about communication and works from these assumptions. Although it takes a little time to score the scale, it is a useful way to get to know yourself and your attitudes toward communication. The scale gives each respondent three scores that represent three different attitudes toward communication. First, some people are rhetorically sensitive (RS)—that is, they largely agree with the assumptions bulleted above. Others hold the attitude that some researchers refer to as the "noble self" (NS; Hart, Carlson, and Eadie [1980]). These are people who believe in speaking their minds at all costs, who believe in the "real self," who won't try to make others feel good just to be kind, and who believe if you think it, you should say it. Still other people are referred as "rhetorical reflectors" (RR; Hart et al.). These people try to adapt to others, relying on their communicative partners to give them important cues about how to respond. RRs analyze communication as it happens and believe that being likable is important to being persuasive with others. Over one-half of the people who take the RHETSEN actually express a mix of these three types of attitudes and are not, therefore, clearly RS, NS, or RR. Some interesting overall trends have emerged, however:

- Trained counselors tend to have higher RS scores than noncounselors.
- Nurses tend to have higher RR scores than people in other professions.
- Over 3,000 college students' scores reveal the following:
  - Students who score high RS are male, have higher SAT scores, have low church attendance, are politically independent, have a low sense of ethnic identification, and are from the professional socioeconomic class.
  - Students who score high NS are typically single rather than married, are more often Democratic than Republican, tend to major in liberal arts, come from urban areas, are less financially well-off, and possess a high sense of ethnic identification.
  - Students who score high RR are typically female, tend to be older, are often married, have lower SAT scores, exhibit high church attendance, come from the laboring socioeconomic class, are often conservative Protestant, and possess a low sense of ethnic identity.

Perhaps without even completing the scale, you see your attitudes reflected in these descriptions. Nevertheless, we encourage you to complete the RHETSEN for an even better sense of your attitudes toward communication.

Evaluative Listening

Evaluative listening, or critical listening, refers to analyzing a message in order to judge its validity, reliability, or usefulness. Evaluative listening critiques information, viewpoints, opinions, and evidence. Rather than accepting a message at face value, evaluative listeners carefully think about a message and weigh its merit. As a college student, you are bombarded with many media messages that attempt to persuade you to purchase certain products or services because they are "cool." For example, think about how media influences the clothes we choose to wear or what kinds of music we listen to. While you certainly make personal choices dependent upon your unique preferences, your choices are framed in part by your peers' choices. These choices are directly influenced by various advertisements and marketing initiatives sponsored by businesses that seek to persuade you to purchase their products or services. When you listen critically, however, you can be aware of these messages and can evaluate them for yourself, given your own preferences or the state of your pocketbook.

> **evaluative listening** analyzing a message in order to judge its validity, reliability, or usefulness; also termed *critical listening*

While the products or services we buy may not be critically important decisions (unless we are creating an unmanageable debt), other issues are much more important and potentially affect our safety and the well-being of our society. For instance, certain hate groups or gangs have become more prevalent on college campuses and seek to recruit students as new members. Are you acquainted with the messages of such groups? Do you accept their claims? If so, why? If not, why not? As an evaluative listener, you must be aware of these messages and analyze them carefully. Here are some suggestions for doing this (You will find others in the "Persuasive Speaking" chapter 9).

Listen Before You Evaluate

Before we can judge a message's quality, we must first understand a message. Just because a message comes from the media, a particular group, or a certain person does not mean that the message is necessarily suspect or reliable. By seeking to first understand the message, we are then better able to assess its merit.

Consider the Source

Even though the source may not cause us to doubt or accept a message's validity, we must consider the credibility of the message's originator. Is the source biased? Does the source have a known agenda that impacts the message? Is the source competent? Is the source trustworthy? Does the source have a reputation for goodwill toward the audience? Does the source use appropriate messages for the occasion? Asking such questions will help you think about the validity, reliability, or usefulness of the message.

Consider the Evidence

Is the evidence accurate or recent? Is there a sufficient amount of evidence? Is the evidence drawn from an unbiased source? Is the evidence open to multiple interpretations? Is the evidence an appeal to emotions or does the evidence include reason and logic? These kinds of questions can help you evaluate the claims that others make.

Consider the Reasoning

While we further discuss faulty reasoning in the "Persuasive Speaking" chapter, it is important that an evaluative listener think about how a source develops an argument. Does the speaker focus on attacking another person or addressing the issue? Does the speaker draw hasty conclusions without sufficient evidence? Does the speaker appeal to popular opinion or use the argument, "Everybody is doing it"? Does the speaker appeal to an authority as being "right"? Does the speaker draw a cause–effect relationship that is not necessarily valid? Does the speaker present a case as being an either/or situation without considering other possible alternatives? Asking these kinds of questions can help you begin to understand whether the speaker's reasoning is sound.

THE REWARDS OF LISTENING

*N*ow that we have considered the reluctance to listen, the problems that led to this reluctance, the results of poor listening, and the requirements necessary to improve listening, let's think about the rewards of listening. Why should we listen? While there are many possible answers, we will address four primary benefits of listening. Learning to listen well can increase our enjoyment, improve our understanding, enhance our empathy, and heighten civility.

Increased Enjoyment

As we noted when we discussed pleasurable listening, enjoyment and listening are linked. However, the more carefully we attend to a variety of types of stimuli such as the tones, pitches, or words, the more enjoyment we are likely to obtain. For example, as you learn more about music as a part of your general education, you will likely have a new appreciation for a greater range of music, because you can listen to it with an attuned ear. This does not, of course, mean that you will suddenly prefer Beethoven over your favorite popular music artist, but you can gain more enjoyment from a variety of music by listening more carefully to what makes each genre unique. Learning, then, to stretch your listening preferences can truly increase your enjoyment.

Improved Understanding

Consider this scenario: A student questioned a grade he received in a communication class because it was affected by his unexplained, excessive absenteeism. Although the attendance policy was clearly explained in the syllabus for the course, orally reinforced by his instructor, and even separately detailed in a document especially written for the student to clarify the policy, he still did not abide by the policy, and offer any explanations for his absenteeism, or even speak with his instructor about the situation as the syllabus directed him to do. Moreover, when the policy was explained to the student in greater detail and he was given a fresh start in the course, he continued to miss class. As a result, his grade was considerably reduced. In short, if the student had listened, he would have understood the policy and been able to keep a higher grade. Listening, then, is vital to improving our understanding of many types of information. Whether we are learning information in the classroom, on the job, or in conversation with others, improved listening will help us better understand ourselves and others and the situations we encounter every day. With improved understanding, we can make decisions, answer questions, and solve or even prevent problems. This can mean improved grades, job promotions, or higher salaries. It can also mean better work situations or personal relationships with others. Such rewards are certainly worth the effort of listening with greater care to the information we encounter.

Enhanced Empathy

As you have likely noted, nothing brings more pleasure—or pain—than personal relationships. Empathy is one of the most important skills we can develop in order to gain the most from relationships. Earlier we noted that empathy refers to the ability to feel as another person feels or to see as another person sees. This complex behavior includes our choices, intelligence, and emotion—that is, we must seek to understand and appreciate another person's perceptions. Listening is a vital first step in this process. When we listen carefully to what others say and cue into the words and the manner in which they are spoken, we start to develop empathy. As we do so, we increase the pleasure in our relationships because we can build relationships founded on shared understandings.

Furthermore, when we are hurt by relationships, we also learn from our own experience how others feel in similar situations. We can, as a result of our experiences with pain, enter into others' disappointments and provide genuinely meaningful support by listening and empathizing.

Additionally, by developing empathy, we are more likely to gain the acceptance and appreciation of others. Although we do not empathize to increase our own influence or to have others affirm us, nevertheless, when we learn to carefully and compassionately listen to others, we are likely to enhance our skills in empathy and gain the acceptance and affirmation of others. In other words, empathy has reciprocal benefits.

Heightened Civility

How easy it is to become angry, rude, and self-centered! All of us understand this tendency. We also know that as the world becomes more diverse and people of different cultures, backgrounds, and lifestyles interact more frequently, the potential for personal and large-scale conflict escalates. Road rage and ethnic or cultural wars are examples of this kind of conflict. Sadly, **civility**, an attitude of respect for other people as unique individuals, is often uncommon both in the world at large and in our own communities. For example, recently in the Midwest, a college student killed several international students in a series of drive-by shootings before committing suicide. Investigators revealed that this young man had connections with a right-wing group that stressed white supremacy as a central tenant of its belief system. These ideas had so influenced this young man's thinking that he exploded in a violent manner.

civility an attitude of respect for other people as unique individuals

In response to this disturbing trend of violence, Arnett and Arneson (1999) propose **dialogic civility** as a communicative antidote to the despair, cynicism, and cycle of hatred that too often mars contemporary life. *Dialogic civility* refers to a set of communication behaviors that include understanding the importance of public dialogue, needing to respect one another, extending grace to one another, and committing to keeping the conversation going (Worley & Worley 2000). As Arnett and Arneson phrase it, we need to "reach out to one another using behaviors that are civil and that keep the conversation going in the midst of difference" (p. 76).

dialogic civility a set of communication behaviors that include understanding the importance of public dialogue, the need for respect for one another, the extension of a sense of grace to one another, and the commitment to keep the conversation going

But this is easier said than done. How can we begin such a seemingly complex process? The first step is to begin to genuinely listen to one another. Genuine listening communicates respect and provides us with important opportunities to gain understanding and develop empathy. Civil communication, then, along with the resulting social and personal benefits, begins with practicing the principles of effective listening. After all, isn't it fair to listen to what someone else has to say before we decide how to respond? To do less strikes us as unethical and uncivil for all concerned. Using effective listening principles is essential in many settings, especially when working with groups, as seen in the box Community Links: Community Listening Sessions.

Community Links

Community Listening Sessions

As one of your authors surfed the Web while working on this chapter, he came upon an interesting and useful idea—community listening sessions. This idea has powerful possibilities for forging and facilitating links among community members. Here are a variety of ways listening sessions are presently being used:

- The State of Oklahoma uses community listening sessions to address the concerns and perspectives of the citizen who live in the state's various counties. See www.dasnr.okstate.edu/oces/ocls/.

- Various U.S. representatives have used listening sessions to address a number of concerns. See www.house.gov/search97cgi/s97_cgi/index.jsp?QueryText=listening+sessions&ResultCount=25&Page=0.
- Calvin College hosts listening sessions that address a variety of issues relevant to both the college and the community. See www.calvin.edu/admin/community/listening.htm.

These just represent many listening session initiatives. Consider how this approach might be useful on your campus or in your community. This could, for example, provide a useful focus for a service learning project, or it may be a useful way to address some immediate problem on your campus or in your dorm.

We prefer to spend the majority of our time with people who are like us and whom we already know; therefore, we can easily attend to our own lives and never even realize the perspectives of others, because we do not give time to listening to one another. If you are interested in learning how to organize and conduct a listening session, visit Community Toolbox at http://ctb.ku.edu/tools/en/1021.htm. However, as a first step, we suggest you have a mini listening session with your roommate, partner, friend, family member, or another person with whom you would like to build or repair a relationship. What would happen in that relationship if you truly listened to the other person's perspective? We believe that by practicing the effective listening skills outlined in this chapter, you can start building a community one relationship at a time.

THE ROLE OF LISTENING AND THE COLLEGE EXPERIENCE

To this point we have thought about the reluctance to listen, the requirements for listening, and the rewards of listening. But how is this information relevant to your experience as a college student? Although we have already offered several ways that listening is important to your life, let's think about how listening specifically applies to your experience in learning and in relationships with your peers.

The Role of Listening in Learning

As we noted earlier, you invest a tremendous amount of your time listening in college. Particularly, you are called upon to listen both inside and outside the classroom as you negotiate your college experience. Here are some suggestions to help you sharpen your abilities to learn through listening.

1. *Listen to teacher instructions.* College professors usually have syllabi or course outlines that explain major assignments and their due dates. They also often explain the assignments and reinforce the due dates orally. Be sure to cue in to this information. It is your responsibility to understand what you are to do and when you are to have assignments completed. Explaining that you didn't know an assignment was due or that you missed class the day a test or quiz was given will not generally persuade professors to give you an opportunity to make up the work. By listening carefully, you can avoid such difficulties.

2. *Reduce forgetting.* Studies indicate that we generally lose 50 percent of what we learn or hear within the first hour after encountering the new material and that we normally lose 70 percent of what we heard seventy-two hours after hearing it (McWhorter 2006). Therefore, to combat forgetting, you must capture and retain as much information as possible during lectures and other learning situations.

3. *Keep all class handouts.* If your instructor gives you copies of notes or provides you written instructions for assignments, keep a copy of this

information. It will help you listen to any oral explanations and remind you of important ideas as you prepare to complete assignments.

4. *Get and stay organized.* Staying organized in college takes time; however, the end result is worthwhile. Being able to get right to work or to find the right handout will save priceless study time and unnecessary frustration. Be sure to purchase a good three-ring binder, two inches wide or larger; section dividers; and a three-hole punch. Use the tabs to delineate the different courses you are taking or units you are studying in a certain subject. Keep all your subjects and materials (lecture notes, handouts, returned work, textbook notes) in this binder. This way you'll always have all your materials with you, which you can review when you have extra time.

   Additionally, many students find that noting important dates on a calendar or assignment notebook helps them keep track of their workload. You can also use a calendar or the programs on your computer to remind you of other appointments, meetings, or social events. Practicing these organizational skills will help you prepare to enter the world of work where organizational skills are even more important.

5. *Practice the principles for effective informational listening.* Earlier in this chapter we offered some guidelines that will help you listen for information. Using these will truly help you in the classroom. Consider writing short reminders about these principles on a 3 × 5 card and putting them in your notebook for easy review. Effective listening, like most habits, requires persistent practice. Do you consider yourself a good listener? Could you use some additional listening practice? Check out the box Communication Links: Are You Listening? to sharpen your skills even more.

Communication Links

Are You Listening?

You may think you are an effective listener, but are you? Here are some tools to help you evaluate and improve your listening.

1. Go to the following link and take the brief listening self-evaluation. www.taft.cc.ca.us/lrc/quizzes/listtest.htm
2. Here's a tool to help you discern how well you listen empathically. Go to www.gov.mb.ca/agriculture/homeec/cba20s04.html and take the survey.
3. Visit these websites for strategies and suggestions to improve listening in class:
   www.geocities.com/Athens/Forum/7908/listenin.htm
   http://kish.cc.il.us/lsc/ssh/listening.shtml

Listening on Campus

Not only must you listen in class, but you must also listen to various people in a variety of places on campus. When you need assistance with a particular question or problem, you will often receive information about where to go or with whom to speak. By paying careful attention, you can save time, energy, and frustration for yourself and others. For example, financial aid is often confusing given the number of forms and the amount of information you need to gather. While some of the complexity that accompanies financial aid is inevitable, with careful and cordial listening, you can avoid unnecessary complications and frustrations. Specifically, consider the following suggestions:

- *Ask the person's name with whom you are speaking.* Being able to address someone by name personalizes your encounter and allows you to get to know someone in that office.

- *Ask clarifying questions.* If you don't understand the information, ask questions until you do understand. Try to rephrase what you've heard to make sure that you have heard correctly. You might try saying, "If I heard you correctly, you want me to do three things . . ." or "So, what I need to do is . . . Is that correct?"

- *Practice civility.* When you are confused or frustrated, it is easy to become angry or rude. Take a deep breath and remember that if you want the information you need, it is best to avoid anger or outbursts, especially if the person with whom you are speaking is in the best position to help you.

- *Jot down notes.* As we noted earlier, psychological studies indicate that we all have problems with forgetfulness. Jotting down names, numbers, addresses, or directions will give you a better chance of recalling important information, and you will tend to listen better as you initially receive the information.

THE ROLE OF LISTENING IN COLLEGE AND CAREER RELATIONSHIPS

*I*n order to enjoy a successful college or workplace experience, you must develop relationships with your peers. Researchers who interviewed college students (Terenzini et al. 1996) learned that receiving interpersonal validation from friends and other students is particularly important to staying in and succeeding in college. **Interpersonal validation** refers to when someone offers to help us, expresses interest in us, or supports us. As we have already seen, listening is one way to offer such support. By listening to our peers, both at school and at work, we offer them support and develop relationships that will provide us the opportunity to be listened to when we need support. Perhaps your college has special programs, clubs, or activities that encourage you to interact with other students. If so, make use of these special opportunities and learn to develop an empathetic ear. By listening to others, you will help them and help yourself. Moreover, you will begin to develop skills that are important in your relationships with your family, life partners, and employers.

interpersonal validation the times when someone else offers to help us, expresses interest in us, or supports us

@ SUMMARY

In this chapter, we have emphasized that listening is vital in human communication. In doing so, we have stressed these main ideas:

- The rewards for listening—enjoyment, understanding, empathy, and civility—are significant enough to encourage us to become effective listeners.

- Improved listening abilities will pay dividends now in your college experience and in your personal relationships and later in your professional lives.

Questions for Discussion

1. Consider this scenario: John and Gloria are sharing a deep-pan pizza in the Student Center. As they decide who should have the last slice, John says, "Professor Raja is so frustrating. I had to miss two labs for my aunt's funeral, and she won't let me make up the time. Now, my grade is really suffering."

   "Have you talked to her about it?" Gloria inquires.

   "I tried! I showed her the obituary and tried to get her to understand how important my aunt was to me, but she just wouldn't listen. And to top it off, I'm not sure she even understands what I'm saying since she doesn't speak English all that well to begin with. Then, because she speaks English with that funny accent, when she does try to explain why she won't excuse my absences, I have the same problem understanding her as I do when she lectures in class. I don't know what to do. If I don't get at least a B in that class, it could affect my financial aid, and then my parents will freak for sure!"

   What listening problems do you identify in this scenario? What suggestions do you have for Jack, Gloria, and Dr. Raja in order to improve their listening?

2. Consider the remainder of this scenario: After his lunch conversation with Gloria, John went to his communication course where his teacher explained the idea of using multiple channels to help ensure shared meaning between communicators. John realized that he had only tried talking to Professor Raja and had never attempted to use another channel. Immediately after class, he went to the computer lab and sent an e-mail message to Professor Raja, trying to be as respectful as possible and to explain his concerns. What is your opinion of John's new course of action? Given

the principles in this chapter, what additional advice would you offer him? What other communication strategies may help him resolve this situation in a manner that is mutually acceptable to both him and his professor?

3. Why is listening transactional?

4. Where do you find the greatest listening challenges on your campus? Why? What strategies are offered in this chapter that might help you improve your listening in this context?

5. Recall a recent incident when you and your friend, roommate, or parent strongly disagreed with each

other. What listening challenges did you face in this situation? How would listening relationally help you deal with this situation more effectively when it occurs again?

6. What do you think about the current state of civility in our society? Does this impact your personal experience? Do the ideas that we offer here sound helpful? What role does communication play in helping to enhance civility in our interactions with others? What additional suggestions would you offer?

EXERCISES

1. Listen to the song "American Pie." Write down the lyrics as you listen. Did you encounter difficulties writing these lyrics? Analyze any specific problems with listening you encountered.

2. Using this chapter's model for listening, analyze a recent lecture in one of your classes. How does each stage apply to the listening process in this situation? What specific listening challenges do you face in listening to lectures? How might you improve your listening in this situation?

3. In pairs, tell a story about a recent time when you believe that someone with whom you were speaking was not listening. How do you know he or she was not listening? How did this make you feel? What lessons for your own listening can you draw from this experience?

4. To understand pleasurable listening and its relationship to family communication, tell one of your favorite family stories to a small group of your classmates. Make sure the story is appropriate to repeat to others. After telling the story, discuss as a group some of the following questions:

   a. When does your family engage in storytelling?
   b. Who surfaces as the "orator" in your family?
   c. In addition to pleasurable listening, what listening skills are enhanced by storytelling? Explain.
   d. What are some of the stories you have heard that have stayed with you all your life? Who was the storyteller? How did these stories make you feel about the storyteller? What have you learned about the person? What did they teach you through their stories?
   e. Do you see yourself as a storyteller for your family? Why or why not? (Bowles & Gee 2000).

5. In order to practice listening nonjudgmentally, Collins (2000) suggests that we get interested in something so that we can attend to ideas or feelings of others as they talk. She refers to this as "playing the inner game of listening." To do this, try the following exercise: Engage in a conversation in pairs. One of you should

be the "talker" and the other the "listener." The talker should talk for three to five minutes about anything she wishes. The listener should close his eyes and listen for the talker's interest level while focusing on a way to become truly interested in what the talker is saying. After three to five minutes, the listener should reflect on the following questions: On a scale of zero to ten, how interested is the talker? How do you know? What other observations can you make about the person talking? Do not share your observations yet but make some notes about your insights. Now reverse roles and repeat the exercise. Once again, the listener should jot down notes about his observations. Next, together discuss your observations: What did you hear? How did you get interested in what the talker was saying? How did you change your personal listening experience to make it more fulfilling? What kind of inner games did you find yourself engaging in to improve your interest level and your listening?

6. Interview five to ten peers who are not in your class about their listening behaviors. Write down their responses to the following questions. When you have completed all the interviews, summarize the responses for each question by noting what is similar or unique among them.

   1. What is the main reason you listen to classroom lectures?
   2. During which class period of the day do you listen best?
   3. What physical classroom characteristics influence your listening the most?
   4. Where do you sit in the classroom if you really want to listen to what is being said?
   5. What single characteristic of the instructor most influences your listening?
   6. What single characteristic of your own most influences your listening?
   7. What single behavior on your part helps you listen?
   8. What single characteristic about the lecture or message most influences your listening?

◎ KEY TERMS

Hearing

Listening

Mindful

Ethos

Sound bites

Message overload

Message complexity

Trigger words

Receiver apprehension

Co-cultures

Pseudolistening

Selective listening

Defensive listening

Ambushing

Dominating

Pleasurable listening

Informational listening

Relational listening

Empathy

Paraphrase

Rhetorical sensitivity

Evaluative listening

Civility

Dialogic civility

Interpersonal validation

◎ REFERENCES

Arnett, R. C., and Arneson, P. 1999. *Dialogic civility in a cynical age*. Albany, NY: State University of New York Press.

Barker, L., Edwards, R., Gaines, C., Gladney, K., and Holley, F. 1980. An investigation of the proportional time spent in various communication activities by college students. *Journal of Applied Communication Research* 8:101–110.

Bowles, K. and Gee, F. H. 2000. *The benefits of storytelling to listening*. Retrieved May 18, 2004, from www.listen.org/pages/exercises.html.

Collins, J. 2000. *Listening nonjudgmentally*. Retrieved May 18, 2004, from www.listen.org/pages/exercises.html.

Fisher, S. 1996. *Effective listening*. Amherst, MA: Human Resource Development Press.

Gardner, J., Jewler, A. J., and Barefoot, B. 2007. *Your college experience: Strategies for success*. 7th ed. Belmont, CA: Thomson Wadsworth.

Hart, R. P., Carlson, R. E., and Eadie, W. F. 1980. Attitudes toward communication and the assessment of rhetorical sensitivity. *Communication Monographs*. 47:1, 1–22.

Littlejohn, S. 1996. *Theories of human communication*. 5th ed. New York: Wadsworth.

Martin, J. N., and Nakayama, T. K. 2001. *Experiencing intercultural communication: An introduction*. Mountain View, CA: Mayfield.

McWhorter, K. 2006. *College reading and study skills*. 5th ed. Upper Saddle River, NJ: Pearson Education.

Ramsey, J. L., and Langlois, J. H. 2002. Effects of the "beauty is good" stereotype on children's information processing. *Journal of Experimental Child Psychology* 81:320–340.

Talbott, S. 1995. *The future does not compute: Transcending the machines in our midst*. Retrieved May 18, 2004, from www.praxagora.com/~stevet/fdnc/ch19.html.

Tannen, D. 1990. *You just don't understand: Women and men in conversation*. New York: William Morrow.

Terenzini, P. T., Rendon, L. I., Millar, S. B., Upcraft, M. L., Gregg, P. L., Jalomo, R., Jr., and Allison, K. W. 1996. Making the transition to college. In *Teaching on solid ground: Using scholarship to improve practice*, eds. R. J. Menges, and M. Weimer, 42–73. San Francisco: Jossey-Bass.

Wheeless, L. R. 1975. An investigation of receiver apprehension and social context dimensions of communication apprehension. *The Speech Teacher* 24:261–268.

Wood, J. 1997. Diversity in dialogue: Communication between friends. In *Ethics of communication in an age of diversity*, eds., J. Makau, and R. Arnett, 5–26. Urbana: University of Illinois Press.

Worley, D. W., and Worley, D. A. 2000. *On religious wars: Wieman's concept of creative interchange and Arnett and Arneson's dialogic civility*. Paper presented at the Sixth Annual Communication Ethics Conference. Gull Lake, MI.

Verbal Communication/Language

```
Understanding Language
```

Properties	Powers	Language Sensitivity	Guidelines
Symbolic Arbitrary Structured Abstract	Shape Culture Create Meaning Confuse Meaning Classify People Clarify Meaning	Denotative / Connotative Gender Sensitivity Cultural Sensitivity	Adapt to Audience Attend to Context Employ Rhetorical Sensitivity

Knowledge Checklist

✓ To understand the arbitrary nature of language

✓ To describe the properties of language in human communication

✓ To understand the power of language in human communication

✓ To distinguish between denotative and connotative meaning

✓ To become more sensitive to the challenges of language within cultural and gendered contexts

✓ To develop strategies for overcoming the challenges of language use

✓ To develop skills in competent and ethical use of language

UNDERSTANDING LANGUAGE

We live in a world of words. Actually, it is more accurate to say that we live in many "worlds of words." This is because language is embedded in a particular culture. To put it another way, there are some words that can be translated into a different language, and others for which there is no direct translation.

In this chapter, we explore the nature of language and its impact on our lives. Although we sometimes take for granted that people who "speak our language" will understand the words we use, we must also understand that each of us creates personal meaning for our language; therefore, our meaning can never exactly match the meaning of another person. It is also important to emphasize that it is impossible to study either verbal or nonverbal communication in isolation. When we communicate, we experience all of the verbal and nonverbal elements together. When you engage in conversation, your tone of voice communicates to the listener important information about how to interpret your words: as a joke, as a serious remark, or as sarcasm.

Communication scholar John Stewart (1995) suggests we think of verbal and nonverbal communication as existing on a continuum. At the "primary verbal" end of the continuum are written words; at the opposite end are "primary nonverbal" elements such as gestures, facial expression, touch, and appearance. At the continuum's midpoint are what Stewart refers to as "mixed" elements, including vocal pacing, pause, loudness, and silence. Stewart emphasizes the relationship between the two when he suggests, "the verbal and nonverbal elements of communication are completely interdependent, which means that the verbal affects the nonverbal and the nonverbal affects the verbal, but that neither *determines* the meaning of the other" (p. 52). We discuss the nature of verbal communication in this chapter and the nature of nonverbal communication in the next chapter.

We use words to describe ourselves, and the ways we describe ourselves both reflect, and are a reflection of, our self-concept. In turn, our self-concept influences how we dress, behave, and interact. In this sense, language is an activity that influences who you are and how you behave. Words affect what we perceive; they reduce uncertainty; they allow us to express abstract, complex ideas; and they both promote human contact and create barriers between persons. Language allows us to express feelings and emotions, as well as assert individual and social identity. Our personal meaning can be explained by the fact that language has certain properties we need to understand.

PROPERTIES OF LANGUAGE

Symbolic

symbolic representative of a particular thing, idea, concept, or event

First, we need to understand that language is **symbolic**. In other words, a particular set of letters represents a particular thing, idea, concept, or event. Thus, language is a system of symbols that allows us to relate sounds or writing to meaning in ways that facilitate our understanding of each other and ourselves. But there is no relationship between the symbols and the "thing." Symbols stand for things, but they are not "the thing." A map, for example, is a symbolic representation of the "territory" you are traveling; it is not the actual route or destination.

Second, these language symbols are **arbitrary**. Meaning is created in individual persons or through cultural associations. Meaning does not exist in a word. Did you ever stop to think about who decides which symbols stand for which things? For example, why do the letters *D-O-G* stand for the four-legged, drooling pet we love? At some point in history, someone used these letters to describe this animal. Over time, and by mutual consent, more people used this set of symbols to refer to the animal. And we now know this is the "correct" set of symbols for our pet because the dictionary uses these letters to represent the word for this animal. This combination of letters for this animal is also what we learned in school. In preschool or kindergarten, we might have had flash cards with a picture of the animal on one side and the letters *D-O-G* on the other. We had books that explained that the picture should be referred to by the word *dog*. However, in French-speaking countries, the symbols for this animal are *CHIEN*; in Spanish, *PERRO* or *PERRA*, depending upon whether the dog is male or female; and in Chinese, *QUAN*.

> arbitrary meaning is created in individual persons or through cultural associations

When we forget that the word is not the thing, we engage in the act of *reification*. We reify something when we regard something that is intangible or abstract as tangible or concrete. We may also think of it as characterized by consistent parts of a static entity. Take the example of "woman." What is a woman? If you attempt to describe this "thing" as having certain parts or certain characteristics, you have engaged in reification. A woman is not a thing to be described. A woman is a person with distinctive and often unique feelings, thoughts, and behaviors. Reification of words causes potentially damaging misunderstanding. When we reify a word, we often engage in what is called *bypassing*. This refers to using different words with the same meaning or the same words with different meanings—instead of making sure we understand what a speaker intends by a word or what a listener interprets in a word, we "pass each other by." Stewart and Logan (1993) describe what may be the most catastrophic example of bypassing, which occurred at the end of WWII:

> *Before the United States dropped atomic bombs on Hiroshima and Nagasaki, the Japanese government knew that they had lost the war. Government leaders were meeting almost constantly, and they had agreed to surrender; the only question was exactly when and how. Surrender negotiations were also under way with Russia, which meant the Japanese government had received detailed ultimatums from both Russia and the Allied Forces. So as not to upset the negotiations with Russia, the Japanese cabinet decided that their first response to the Allied ultimatum would be noncommittal. The key word in its reply was* mokusatsu, *a term which can be translated as "no comment." Unfortunately, the Japanese word is made up of two characters, one meaning "silence" or "ignore." Allied translators understood the Japanese to have "ignored" the ultimatum and were furious. The punishment came quickly, tens of thousands of people died, and the world was propelled into an age of weapons we still haven't completely figured out how to manage. (p. 115)*

Triangle of Meaning

It is impossible to speak of language and the meaning we develop without understanding that language is **structured**. The way we put words together into sentences (syntax), sentences into paragraphs, and paragraphs into essays is governed by a set of rules that is culture bound. Individuals who are bilingual or trilingual understand how different the structure of languages can be. A change in a sentence's structure affects how the meaning will be interpreted.

> structured governed by a set of rules

FIGURE 5.1   Triangle of Meaning

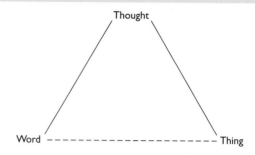

Communication theorists Ogden and Richards (1993) developed a "triangle of meaning" to help us understand how language works (see Figure 5.1). The triangle explains the relationship between the *thought*, the *word*, and the *thing*. The symbol/word is designated to refer to some thought or feeling. The symbol stands for or references the actual object or what the symbol stands for. Thoughts and feelings are shaped by past experience. The solid line between the word and the thought implies a direct connection between the letters we see (word) and our interpretation (thought) of the word. The solid line between the thought and the thing implies a direct relationship as well. However, the dotted line between the word and the thing tells us that there is no direct connection.

abstract complex and open to varied interpretations and understanding

Language is also **abstract**. Some words are clear, simple, and commonly understood across a particular cultural group. On the other hand, some words or concepts are much more complex and are open to varied interpretations and understandings. Despite these inherent problems, the ability to categorize and abstract is ultimately part of what separates us from "lower" animals. Hayakawa (1990) developed an "abstraction ladder" to help us understand this concept. The least-abstract words are positioned at the ladder's lowest rungs, the most abstract at the top. As you move up the abstraction ladder, you encounter more meanings for any word. When our language becomes abstract, we are better able to describe the world. The more our language allows us to describe the world, the more we are able to understand it. When we understand the world, we are able to manipulate our environment and, hopefully, make the world a better place.

Denotation and Connotation

denotative meaning the objective, agreed-upon definition of a word

Understanding a word's two types of definitions, denotative and connotative, can help you avoid using arbitrary language. A word's **denotative meaning** is the objective, agreed-upon definition that we find in a dictionary. Thus, the *American Heritage Dictionary* defines *dog* as "a domesticated canid related to foxes and wolves and raised in many breeds" or "Any of various other animals, such as the prairie dog" or "a contemptible person." So how do we decide which is the correct or fitting definition?

connotative meaning the meaning of a word as influenced by an individual's personal history or cultural experience

We have to understand that each of us has some personal history or cultural experience that will influence the meaning we create for the word. This is our **connotative meaning**. Our connotative meaning is subjective and individual and built upon our experiences with that word. For example, have you ever owned a dog? Was it your best friend, a beast that shared space in your house, or a being to fear? Was it large, small, friendly, mean, loving, standoffish, young, old, thin, fat? When you think of a dog, does a specific mental picture come to mind? The connotative meaning we give to words, symbols, and "things" originated within this personal relationship. For each word, we create a set of personal "signifiers" that become a set of characteristics for the word. For many of us, "dog" is something we "signify" as loving, loyal, funny, or protective. It may be our best buddy, a comforting

What does the word "dating" mean to you? What does it mean if you are "going out" with someone?

friend, or even a member of the family. For others, a dog is something we signify as ferocious, mean, dangerous, hurtful, or wild. Depending upon your experience with dogs, your signifiers for *dog* could be very different from either of these lists. Thus, some words have many connotative definitions, especially concepts such as freedom, love, and justice; other words may have fewer connotations—for example, *chair, book,* or *apartment.*

Perhaps you are wondering why it matters what we use to signify a particular word. Because language allows us to **associate** or signify language in very personal ways, we must understand how some words have enormous power in our relationships, cultures, and lives. Words become meaningful to us through a very complex process of association over time. When we are children, the associations we make between words and things are simple; later in life, we expand our range of associations with a word to create more complex combinations of meanings. For example, to a child, water may be associated with a bath or a drink from a faucet. The child may be conscious of the water's temperature and may have experiences with it, such as playing in a pool or running under a sprinkler. Later in life, we can associate water with experiences both in our lives and beyond the immediate world in which we live—for example, it may be associated with massive flooding, beachside vacations, or community picnics or with the place where we fell in love, were rejuvenated at a retreat, or spread a loved one's ashes. In sum, competent communicators need to be aware of the associations of the words they use.

associate signify language

POWER OF LANGUAGE

Many of you have heard the childhood saying, "Sticks and stones may break my bones, but names will never hurt me." Do you believe this is true? Do words sometimes hurt? Of course they do. Language allows us to do more than just convey facts or find information. Trenholm and Jensen (1992) suggest that there are eight basic functions of language: (1) Language allows us to "conquer silence," thus allowing us to reduce fear. Through language, we reduce our uncertainty about ourselves, others, and relationships; (2) language allows us to express and control emotion. By talking about emotions, we can regulate them; (3) language can either reveal or hide our thoughts and motives. We can "tell it like it is," or we can "tell it like we want another to know"; (4) language permits us to either connect with or avoid others. Language bridges differences or divides; (5) language enables us to be unique individuals, to create our own "style." We can grow closer to others by "sharing" a language or vocabulary; (6) language allows us to share information. Sharing with others allows us to feel we belong; (7) language allows us to control and be controlled by the world. Once we name or describe something, we know what to expect from it; and (8) language can be used to monitor or analyze our communication. As human beings, we have the power of "metacommunication"—we can "talk about our talk."

Language Shapes Culture

Language has the power to *shape culture* and has the potential to create who we are and how we define ourselves and are defined by others. We need to understand the **authoritative nature of language**. Language is authoritative because it tells us the rules of communication with particular others in certain communication contexts. It tells us who people are, their position in society, and how we should interact with them. Sometimes these rules are appropriate and understood by individuals across the entire culture; at other times, they create barriers between individuals and groups.

Edward Sapir and Benjamin Lee Whorf (1956) developed the **Sapir-Whorf hypothesis**; they theorize that language is the most significant factor in determining what we see in the world and how we think and evaluate what we see. At a very basic level, this means that if we do not have a word to describe something, we do not see it as important. Once we have developed words to describe a phenomenon, we can discuss, analyze, label, and evaluate it. Language is bound by culture, a system of symbols governed by the rules and patterns of the culture.

Think about the word *work*. What does this signify to you? In your experience, is work something you must do to survive? Is it something you take for granted or depend upon to make ends meet? Is your work your life? Or is your life your work? What is the difference between these two questions? Do you believe in the "Protestant work ethic," defined by Wikipedia (www.wikipedia .org) as "a biblically based teaching on the necessity of hard work, perfection, and the goodness of labor." Is work what we do so we'll have the money to really enjoy life? Is work the ticket to respect and self-esteem? How you signify this word will influence almost every other aspect of your life. It will determine what you study in college and what career you aspire to. It will influence the friendships you create and the romantic partners you have. It will influence how you analyze and evaluate public policies such as welfare and affirmative action. It will, perhaps, even impact your civic engagement and determine which political party you support.

Language Creates Meaning

Language, as an element of culture, helps us *create meaning*. And we, in turn, use that meaning to modify, adapt, and change our culture. We use it to create, maintain, and evaluate relationships. Any *Seinfeld* fan will remember the phrase, "Yada yada yada," which was the essence of an entire episode and which became one of the show's "signature" phrases. The *Encarta Dictionary* defines "yada yada yada" as "boring, trite, superficial, unending talk" and "used in speaking as a filler for unstated material or to indicate boredom or distaste for things others are saying or have just said" (cited in Dobkin and Pace 2003). Why *yada yada yada*? When the writers of *Seinfeld* were developing the script, they thought the phrase sounded right for the characters. Although the Seinfeld writers were not the first to use this phrase, their incorporation of this funny utterance on an episode of a TV sitcom has come to have its own place in our language. We now have a term to describe a behavior that we did not have before. We have named it, we can understand it, and we can create meaning from it. It has become part of our shared popular culture experience.

authoritative nature of language
the rules of communication with particular others in certain communication contexts as dictated by language

Sapir-Whorf hypothesis
language is the most significant factor in determining what we see in the world and how we think about and evaluate what we see

As a supervisor, the words you use can enhance or inhibit open communication.

Language Confuses Meaning

Language also has the *power to confuse* us, especially if it is **equivocal**. Equivocation includes language that is **ambiguous**. Sometimes there are so many different meanings for a word that we do not know which one to choose. Using language ambiguously can be seen as a form of language power, because occasionally we might be intentionally ambiguous in order to strategically deceive another. Sometimes we are ambiguous with language because we are careless or because we don't want to hurt someone's feelings. What does it mean when your instructor says you are a "good" speaker? Our students often tell us they want to be communication professionals because they are "good" with people. What does that mean? Our dog is "good with people." Does this mean he would make a great communication professional? When people say, "Hi, how are you?" are they asking for a summary of your health and well-being, or do they mean "hello"? When a politician says, "Vote for me because I care about this country," what does he or she mean by "care" or "country"?

equivocal (or ambiguous) having multiple meanings

What do the words *almost never, frequently, seldom, now and then*, or *occasionally* mean? How many are *a few, several, not many*, or *a lot*? Each of these words or phrases is open to interpretation based upon the context, the individuals in conversation, and the relationship between those individuals. Language, thus, is often very subjective. The following are headlines taken from newspapers and news reports in the last twenty years:

"Man Found Dead in Graveyard"

"Local Man Has Largest Horns in Texas"

"20-Year Friendship Ends at Altar"

"Massive Organ Draws a Crowd"

Sometimes a word is ambiguous because its meaning or interpretation has changed over time. For example, what does *gay* mean? *Encarta* provides the following definitions: 1. homosexual; 2. merry (dated); 3. bright in color (dated); 4. carefree (dated); and 5: debauched (dated). The most common meaning of the word *gay* today is "homosexual," but the other four meanings are correct, although associated with a different time in history and thus "dated." Competent and effective communicators know that there is a difference between "what words mean" and "what people mean by words." And competent communicators also know that you should never assume that you understand what people actually mean in their ambiguous language. When words do not have a clear meaning, it is a good idea to ask for clarification.

Other forms of ambiguous communication often strategically used to confuse or soften meaning are doublespeak and euphemisms, respectively. **Doublespeak** is often associated with governmental, military, and corporate institutions and is employed to obscure the speaker's true meaning or intention—as in using "downsizing" for "firing of many employees" or deliberately ambiguous phrases such as "wet work" for "assassination." A **euphemism** is a strategic choice, often used to "soften" or "be sensitive" to another person. For example, we might say that someone has "passed away" instead of "died," or we say that someone has gotten "pink-slipped" rather than "laid off." Euphemisms are considered to be more "socially acceptable" alternatives to direct speech. If your friend asks, "How do you like my new hairstyle?" and you don't like it but want to spare her feelings, you might reply, "It's really unique!" rather than saying something more direct like, "It really makes your ears stand out."

doublespeak language deliberately constructed to disguise or distort its actual meaning

euphemism language used to soften or be sensitive to another person

Language Classifies People

Language also has the power to *classify people*, such as by labeling them. We must not underestimate the power of **labels**. Sometimes labels tell us about a group someone belongs to. For example, which of the following labels most correctly identifies your political philosophy: liberal, democratic, socialist, republican, libertarian, conservative, communist, fascist, internationalist, utilitarian, environmentalist, or

labels words used to classify

nationalist? What does it mean to say that someone is a liberal or a conservative? It depends upon your position, doesn't it? Does the word *liberal* refer to someone who is tolerant and open-minded or does it mean someone radical and pushy? Does the word *conservative* refer to someone who is closed-minded or fiscally responsible? Labels are most powerful when you are the one who controls the definition associated with them. If you are the one stuck with the label, especially an incorrect one, you may become angry and resentful at someone who attempts to define you as something you are not. The box Communication Links: Gender Labels provides opportunities for futher exploration of the powers of labels.

Communication Links

Gender Labels

Have you ever noticed how many terms or labels are used to describe men and women? Think of the categories at our disposal. In the following categories, how many terms for each can you think of?

Food (e.g., cupcake, sweetcakes, sucker, etc.)
Animals (e.g., ham, pig, cow, chicken, pussycat, etc.)
Plants (e.g., clinging vine, rose, etc.)
Playthings or toys (e.g., dollface, Barbie, etc.)

Does one list look longer than another? Are more of the terms associated with men or women positive? Negative? Are some dominant and others passive? What are the implications of any "imbalance" in your lists? What is the objective of using these labels to describe men and women?

stereotypes oversimplified categories that people associate individuals with in order to reduce uncertainty about them

Stereotypes are a more extreme form of classifying people. Some stereotypes are simply oversimplified categories in which we associate individuals in order to reduce uncertainty about them. When we meet someone for the first time, we often rely on stereotypes to determine how we should approach or interact with them. We attempt to find a "rule" that will help us act appropriately with that person. What are the "rules" for approaching your professor for the first time? Should you approach male and female professors differently? Does it make a difference if you are much younger than your professor or if you are a nontraditional student who is about the same age? If your roommate is from Southeast Asia, how should you establish the physical territories you each will inhabit in the dorm room? If you are on a predominantly commuter campus and want to create a carpool to school, which individuals would you be most comfortable approaching about sharing rides? In each of these examples, we use a "group" as a baseline to provide information about how we should communicate with one another.

Some stereotypes, however, are not mild. According to the Conflict Research Consortium at the University of Colorado, "the term 'prejudice' refers to stereotypes which lead parties to view their opponents as threatening adversaries who are inherently inferior or are actively pursuing immoral objectives. Such prejudices lead the parties to view others as enemies who must be actively opposed. This results in a persistent level of destructive tension which can easily escalate into a highly destructive, all-out confrontation" (www.colorado.edu/conflict/peace/treatment/prejred.htm).

Some prejudice arises from ignorance regarding a particular group and is often the result of fear or hatred. Racism stems from the beliefs that people from particular groups have qualities and abilities that are superior or inferior to others. Once we have created stereotypes that result in prejudicial feelings or beliefs, we create labels that define and demean that group.

Sexism is a form of prejudice regarding issues of gender, expectations of what is appropriate female and male behavior, and assertions on gender superiority. **Heterosexism** is a form of prejudice regarding issues of sexual orientation and the issue of whether attraction to the same sex is by choice. Both sexism and heterosexism create tensions in relationships when individuals "impose" on others certain characteristics or moral values. Sexism and heterosexism are particularly harmful forms of prejudice that prevent people from truly knowing one another as individual, valuable human beings. In the box Career Links: Creating Nonsexist Environments, we explore ways to eliminate sexist language at work and in our daily lives.

sexism a form of prejudice regarding issues of gender, expectations of what is appropriate female and male behavior, and assertions on gender superiority

heterosexism a form of prejudice regarding issues of sexual orientation and the issue of whether a person's attraction to the same or opposite sex is one of choice or not

 *Career Links*

Creating Nonsexist Environments

A greater equality exists in terms of job access today, but there is not always agreement about what that means for the communication behavior of women and men in the workplace. Is there such a thing as "women's work" or "men's work"? Should men try to adopt a more "feminine" style of leadership? Should women be more masculine or feminine in the workplace? What are the rules?

Should men "walk on eggshells" in the workplace in order to avoid inadvertent sexual harassment? What is a sexist remark? Here are some suggestions for both women and men in nonsexist treatment of all persons in a workplace:

- Avoid typecasting in careers and activities and in hiring policies. (Are all of your secretaries female but the administrative assistants male?)
- Represent members of both sexes as whole human beings: characteristics praised in males should be praised in females, and vice versa.
- Pay closer attention to your words; take responsibility for your words and for the meanings you and others may ascribe to them. Clarify, ask questions.

- Accord women and men the same respect and avoid either trivializing women or describing them by physical attributes when men are described by mental attributes:
  - Avoid sexual innuendos
  - Avoid female gender word forms
  - Avoid references to the general "ineptness" of men in the home
  - Treat women as part of the rule, not the exception, as in "woman doctor"
  - Avoid describing women as needing male permission to act
  - Use inclusive language (i.e., "humankind")
- When confronted by what you perceive to be sexist language, both women and men should confront the situation by
  - focusing on the event, not the person
  - offering positive criticism
  - owning your thoughts and feelings
  - stating your concern for the other
  - being specific and using examples
  - avoiding mind reading

The enormous power of our labels and stereotypes lies in the ways they influence our attitudes and, ultimately, our actions. If our attitudes about an individual's sexual orientation, ethnicity, or religion are based on stereotypes, we may refrain from establishing relationships with them. How many times in your life have you tried *not* to get to know someone because of your stereotypes? If we are honest with ourselves, we will admit that the answer may be many times. Thus, our *attitudes* influence our *behaviors*, which in turn are *communicated* to the individuals we stereotype—through our words and actions and by what we *do not* say and what we *do not* do.

Language Clarifies Meaning

Much of this discussion has been focused on the negative power of language. Yet it is important to remember that competent communicators use language to *clarify meaning*, create relationships, and break down the barriers that separate us. When we expand our language, we enhance our relationships and our lives. The more words we have to describe and analyze a situation, an object, or a concept, the more opportunities we have to know the world and ourselves, to understand the past and present, and to predict the future. Language is the fundamental building block to all relationships. Education is fundamentally about developing more sophisticated language that we can use to generate new ways of thinking, products to market, and services to provide. More precise language may also help us to make the world better by reducing the misunderstandings between people who speak "different languages."

GENDERED LANGUAGE

Some theorists believe that the first "language barrier" each of us must negotiate is the "different world of words" inhabited by men and women. Sociolinguist Deborah Tannen (1990) suggests that the ways boys and girls grow up in the world and the language used to socialize them is a primary factor in our tendency to misunderstand one another. It is important to recognize the distinctions between the words *sex* and *gender*. *Sex* is a biological factor based upon the chromosomes in our DNA. *Gender* is a social construct that creates a set of expectations for appropriate behavior. Language, according to Tannen, is "gendered." Women and men, she suggests, approach the world differently. Men often approach the world as individuals in a hierarchical social order in which they are either one-up or one-down. They commonly use negotiation to try maintaining the upper hand, taking charge of situations, or solving problems and offering solutions. Conversely, women often view the world as a network of connections. Their conversations are negotiations for closeness, confirmation, and support. They protect themselves from others' attempts to push them away, struggle to preserve intimacy, and work to avoid isolation.

The language used by men tends to conform to a "hierarchy of power," and the language used by women tends to conform to a "hierarchy of friendship." These are different but equally valid language styles. It's important to remember that trying to treat women's and men's language "the same" hurts both. Imposing a male hierarchy on women is devaluing; imposing a female hierarchy on men sparks resentment and anger. Both of these approaches to conversation and relationships are a means to the same end. Both status (male) and connection (female) can be used to get things done by talking. Most meaning in conversation does not reside in the words spoken but is filled in by the person listening. Yet it is important to understand that women and men often have very different reasons for carrying on a conversation. Men tend to converse to impart information (report talk); women converse to indicate relationship (rapport talk). Women are also more likely to exchange personal and relational talk than men. For example, in your experience, is a man or a woman more likely to talk about a troubling experience? Who is more likely to share a secret? Who is more likely to give advice? Who is more likely to challenge an expert in a public forum? If you answered "woman" to the first two questions and "man" to the second two, you can understand the differences between rapport talk and report talk. Understanding how women and men engage in conversations and use language is the first step. Realizing how our language creates inequality in perceptions is also important.

Other distinguishing characteristics of male and female language include vocabulary, adjective use, and use of questions and hedges. Stewart, Cooper, and Friedley (1986) report that women, in general, have a larger number of words to describe things that interest them. For example, women use a broader array of words to describe colors and tend to use a broader array of adjectives to describe things. Women are much more likely to use words like *adorable, charming,* and *lovely* (p. 53). Women also tend to "qualify" their language with the use of tag questions ("don't you think?" or "isn't it?") and hedges ("I wonder if" or "kind of"). These qualifiers, according to Stewart, Cooper, and Friedley, are used more by women because they have been socialized to believe that assertive language is "unladylike" or "unfeminine" (p. 54).

In the English language, the male pronoun has historically been used to include both male and female referents, such as in *mankind, he, his,* and so on. The problem with the masculine pronoun as all-inclusive is that it isn't. When we hear, "The professor should treat all of his students fairly," we do not "see" both men and women professors; we "see" a male professor. The female professor becomes invisible. Man-linked terms are interpreted as male, not as "all." Sexist language conveys that women are less valued than men.

Gender bias in language occurs in the titles we use to address men and women. Are all men to be addressed as "Mr."? How do you address a woman? Does the fact that she is married matter in the form of address used? Should it matter? In our culture, it is still common to see a woman change her name when she gets married. The reason for the name change is associated with a time in history in which a woman was considered the legal property of a man, either her father or her husband. The use of "Mrs." to refer to a woman also dates back to a time when women were defined by their relationships to men. The use of "Ms." has been an attempt to move away from defining a woman by her relationship. For some, however, the term "Ms." is associated with "feminism," which has both positive and negative connotations, depending upon your point of view.

Another way women become invisible in language is the use of masculine forms for certain titles, such as *mailman, fireman, policeman, workman, chairman,* and so on. When the female is invisible in our language, the implication is that male is "normal" and female is "other." Another common form of biased language is the use of nonparallel terms such as "man and wife" or "male students and coeds." Gender bias also shows up in language when we have different terms for males and females in the same professions, such as "actor and actress" or "tailor and seamstress" or "waiter and waitress." These are examples of how female suffixes create a secondary category for the female profession. Men, it is implied, are the "real" thing; women are inauthentic copies.

Utilizing these different terms creates artificial barriers where none exist. Competent communicators use gender-neutral language to create a more inclusive culture, using such terms as *mail carrier, firefighter, police officer, worker,* and *chairperson*. When we modify our language, we modify our cultural expectations and build bridges that bring us closer together in our relationships and in our understanding of one another. In the box Cultural Links:

Cultural Links

Transmission of Culture to Children

One of the ways that culture is communicated across generational lines is through nursery rhymes, fables, and myths and legends. We learn nursery rhymes in preschool and kindergarten. The books that are read to us as children play an important part in who we become and how we compare ourselves to others in our culture. Compare the two versions of this popular nursery rhyme. Which version do you like best? Why or why not?

There Was an Old Woman

There was an old woman who lived in a shoe.
She had so many children she didn't know what to do.
She gave them some broth without any bread.
She whipped them all soundly and put them to bed.

The Old Couple Who Lived in a Shoe

There was an old couple who lived in a shoe,
They had so many children they didn't know what to do.
So they gave them some broth and some good whole wheat bread,
And kissed them all sweetly and sent them to bed.
There's only one issue I don't understand.
If they didn't want so many why didn't they plan?

Source: Copyright Girls Incorporated of Greater Santa Barbara. Reprinted with permission of Advocacy Press, P.O. Box 236, Santa Barbara, CA 93102. Not to be duplicated in any other form.

Transmission of Culture to Children, you'll find a humorous rendition of a popular nursery rhyme that serves as a reminder of how culture impacts our views of the world.

Competent communicators also understand that nonsexist language reflects nonsexist attitudes. Nonsexist language is unambiguous and strengthens our ability to share meaning. It demonstrates sensitivity to others and empowers them. Since we know that language shapes our thinking, when we change our language, we can change our thinking. Nonsexist language reinforces the belief that men and women have equal status in our society.

LANGUAGE AND CULTURE

linguistic determinism the power of language to influence interpretations of the world in a specific culture

Each culture in the world has developed a language that assists its members in creating meaning. **Linguistic determinism** is a term used to describe the power of language to influence interpretations of the world in a specific culture. For example, the Inuit tribes in northern Canada have more than fifty words for *snow*. In the world of the Inuit, the ability to make fine distinctions between the type of snowfall and snow pack is a life-and-death issue. Here are just a few examples:

Innuit snow lexemes

1. apun—*snow*
2. apingaut—*first snowfall*

3. aput—*spread-out snow*

4. kanik—*frost*

5. anigruak—*frost on a living surface*

6. ayak—*snow on clothes*

7. kannik—*snowflake*

8. nutagak—*powder snow*

9. aniu—*packed snow*

10. aniuvak—*snowbank*

(Retrieved July 12, 2006, from www.ucalgary.ca/~kmuldrew/cryo_course/ snow_words.html)

Language is the element of culture that allows people to develop values and beliefs and to name them. Language allows us to share our customs, which binds individuals together into a collective identity.

Culture shapes perceptions by telling us how to perceive and name what we see. At its most powerful, culture provides us the road map for what we should pay attention to and what we should ignore. Once our values, beliefs, and customs are developed and named, culture affects our role identity, telling us how to categorize individuals inside our culture. Culture affects how we identify our goals and how we achieve them. Finally, culture explains how we should evaluate the aspects of communication competence. When we communicate with individuals who have been acculturated by a different set of values, beliefs, and customs, we must make a greater effort to understand and clarify meaning. Intercultural conversations require new rules for negotiating meaning.

In the past, most humans were born, lived, and died in limited geographic areas. Indeed, some parts of the United States are still relatively homogeneous because people live and die in the same place. Today, people have the ability to travel, explore, study abroad, or relocate virtually anywhere in the world, and if you do not want to travel physically, technology allows you to do so "virtually." Even within a country like the United States, there are subcultures that exist in isolation. The more isolated we are from others, the more we tend to think of our group as the "best" or "most moral."

Ethnocentrism is the view that one's own culture or group is the center of the universe; it is seen as the most valuable, the most advanced, and the most moral. Ethnocentrists view their culture as having the "best" of everything and label individuals from other groups with such terms as *alien, intruder, foreigner, outsider, newcomer,* or *immigrant.* Many of us may be guilty of ethnocentrism when we have imposed these labels on unknown or unfamiliar persons.

> **ethnocentrism** the view that one's own culture or group is the center of the universe

One of the most interesting and important dimensions of culture is the degree to which the culture identifies an individualist or collectivist orientation. Reynolds and Valentine (2004) suggest that **individualist cultures** like the United States and Great Britain emphasize the importance of individual success. Values such as freedom, independence, and autonomy are at the heart of these cultures. For example, North Americans believe in their "inalienable rights" as guaranteed by the Constitution, which are "life, liberty, and the pursuit of happiness." Within an individualist culture, independence and autonomy are highly valued. Members of individualist cultures take pride in being self-reliant, assertive, and direct. Individualist cultures support the goal of equality, regardless of race, class, religion, gender, and so on. Think about the power these words have for you. Language in individualist cultures is direct. U.S. citizens are known for "speaking their minds" when in conversation with others, and U.S. history books are filled with the stories of adventurous individuals who have fought against incredible odds to prevail and succeed.

> **individualist cultures** cultures that emphasize the importance of individual success

In contrast, according to Reynolds and Valentine, **collectivist cultures** emphasize the group, not the individual. Harmony within the group is highly valued. In conversation, politeness is often a goal. Language is indirect and implicit, and communicators depend more often on what is not spoken. Words are less important to the overall meaning within an interaction than the nonverbal elements. Silence has

> **collectivist cultures** cultures that emphasize the group, not the individual

more value in collectivist cultures. The Japanese proverb, "You have two ears and one mouth" implies that listening is twice as important as speaking. Important values in collectivist cultures include stability, tradition, and authority. For example, in Japan, exchanging business cards is one of the first and most important interactions in a business transaction. This is because one's title determines the nature of the interaction with that person. The businessperson with the lower rank must perform the lower bow. In contrast to English, the Sino-Tibetan family of languages, spoken by most Asian cultures, "is multi-valued, complex, and subtle, allowing for many shades of gray. There is no firm belief in objective reality; language seeks to capture impression, an overall emotional quality, and subjective, experiential thinking. Communication is fluid, indirect, inexplicit, nonlinear, and self-effacing" (p. 61).

Each culture tends to emphasize its positive elements. Yet there is also the tendency to believe "my" culture is the best. When cultural ethnocentrism becomes extreme, language can deteriorate into **hate speech**. Hate speech is commonly used by individuals or groups to express their belief that their point of view and their place in society is superior and to express their need to develop a "pure" society (one that includes only members of their cultural group). Hate speech attacks or denigrates the status of entire groups—whites, blacks, gays, Jews, homosexuals, and so on. The Internet has made dissemination of denigrating speech much easier and more widespread. Should such speech be stifled? Read more about it in the box Computer Links: Hate Speech and Indecent Speech.

hate speech speech aimed at attacking or denigrating the status of entire groups—whites, blacks, gays, Jews, homosexuals, and so forth

◎ Computer Links

Hate Speech and Indecent Speech

The Internet as a medium for communication has gained much attention recently by Congress, organizations supporting freedom of speech, and others. Two types of speech on the Internet have become the focus of much attention: hate speech and indecent speech.

There has been enormous debate over whether hate speech should be allowed the same freedoms as other types of political speech. Restrictions on hate speech have been attempted in workplaces, universities, cities, and states.

Depending on who is counting, there are between 250 to 1,500 "hate" sites on the Internet. Find a site that has been listed as a "hate site" by the American Civil Liberties Union (ACLU) or the Wiesenthal Center. Do you believe that the content of the sites should be restricted? By whom?

In 1996, Congress passed the Communications Decency Act (CDA), a federal law that outlawed "indecent" communications online. However, the Supreme Court struck down the law.

Ruling unanimously in *Reno v. ACLU*, the Court declared the Internet to be a free-speech zone, deserving of at least as much First Amendment protection as that afforded to books, newspapers, and magazines. The government, the Court said, can no more restrict a person's access to words or images on the Internet than it could be allowed to snatch a book out of a reader's hands in the library or cover over a statue of a nude in a museum.

The importance of the Internet as the "the most participatory form of mass speech yet developed" requires that the courts perpetually uphold the freedom of speech. The Court said that "content-based prohibitions of speech have the constant potential to be a repressive force in the lives and thoughts of a free people."

Do you believe there should be restrictions on indecency and pornography on the Internet? Who are the groups in need of protection from this type of speech?

Regardless of the targeted group, the goal is to humiliate and harm with words. Hate speech hurts those who send hateful messages as well as those who receive them. It hurts communities in which it occurs, creating community divisions and harming the culture in which it occurs; it may also cause some groups to become more isolated, fearful, or dangerous. For example, the Southern Poverty Law Center reports an increase in neo-Nazi extremists in the U.S. military and suggests these individuals pose an "elevated threat" to the military's ability to succeed in the war in Iraq (www.splcenter.org/intel/news/item.jsp?site_area=1&aid=197).

GUIDELINES FOR COMPETENT AND ETHICAL USE OF LANGUAGE

*I*f we are to begin to distinguish between "what words mean" and "what people mean by words," then we must understand the numerous influences on how we create meaning and some of the pitfalls to competent and effective communication. One of the first characteristics of competent and ethical use of language is understanding and adapting to one's audience.

Adapting to One's Audience

What does it mean to "adapt to one's audience" when using language? At a very basic level, it means understanding the cultural influences that play a role in how someone interprets meaning. In order to understand how a different culture influences the interpretations of its members, you need to understand the influences of your own culture on your interpretation. You must recognize the cultural or ethnocentric stereotypes you have regarding the value of a particular worldview. For example, consider some of your personal biases. Do you think that elderly people are burdensome, that the working poor deserve low pay, or that only the best and brightest students should get college scholarships? One of the results of failing to recognize the cultural and other biases we have is called **mindlessness**. Someone who is communicating in a "mindless" way uses fairly habitual or scripted ways of communicating regardless of the others in the communication experience. Mindless communication uses stereotyped categories to make inferences about others instead of attempting to clarify in a specific communication situation what others mean or understand.

In contrast, competent communicators operate from a perspective of **mindfulness**. Mindful communicators are willing to create new categories of meaning and understanding in communicating in new situations. They choose words carefully, and when communicating cross-culturally, select simple, concrete words with commonly recognized meanings. Mindful communicators also try to avoid jargon and "buzzwords" that create confusion and misunderstanding.

Mindful communicators are open to new information, are aware of more than one perspective, and are able to make finer distinctions about individual differences of interpretation. They take greater care to accommodate the other in the conversation, to "meet them halfway." Active listening is a sign of competent and mindful communication and is characteristic of rhetorically sensitive communicators.

In developing the ability to be mindful of your communication, you must make an effort to examine your thoughts and actions critically, looking for new solutions, new explanations, and new perspectives on language and its impact on your communication success. Finally, mindful communicators make an effort to be aware of the impact of the communication context on meaning and interpretation.

mindlessness the use of fairly habitual or scripted ways of communicating regardless of the others in the communication experience

mindfulness willingness to create new categories of meaning and understanding in communicating in new situations

Attending to Context

As we discussed in Chapter 1, the communication context is a critical element in the communication model. Context is critical to how we understand and create meaning.

jargon a language strategy used by a specific group to create a sense of community among group members

To become a competent communicator, we must understand the cultural "rules" that impose themselves on a particular communication context. When is it appropriate, for example, to use jargon? **Jargon** is a vocabulary that is shared by members of a group to create a sense of community among its members. It becomes a sort of "shorthand" for individuals, allowing for more efficient communication. For example, consider the jargon of these individuals:

Politicians—wonk, GOP, spin

Police officers—10-4, perpetrator, JD

Attorneys—briefs, subpoena, motion

Newspapers—pica, layout, production, paste-up, storyboards

Jargon can be the source of much misunderstanding by individuals who are not members of the group. To identify whether using jargon is appropriate or inappropriate, ask yourself whether the intention is to include or to exclude.

Employing Rhetorical Sensitivity

rhetorical sensitivity the ability to adapt to the widest range of communication experiences with skill, considering the most appropriate response based upon a comprehensive understanding of the entire communication experience

Rhetorical sensitivity describes communicators who can adapt to the widest range of communication experiences with skill, considering the most appropriate response based upon a comprehensive understanding of the entire communication experience. Imagine you are hired at your "ideal job." You have been in this position for two months. As a part of your orientation to the job, you have been reviewing a variety of print materials produced by your company. In chatting with your boss one day, she asks for your opinion of the materials in general. You do not think they are very interesting, visually appealing, or representative of the organization overall. What do you tell her? In constructing a rhetorically sensitive response, what are the critical questions you must ask yourself about this communication situation?

In addition to knowing how to adapt your language to the specific context, rhetorical sensitivity also includes taking risks in exploring and communicating in a broad range of communication contexts. Rhetorically sensitive communicators are curious about others and attempt to explore their beliefs, values, and worldviews. Curiosity about others does not imply that we are abandoning our beliefs and values; it merely allows us to broaden our vocabulary and to expand our ways of analyzing, explaining, and interpreting the world.

confirming language language that acknowledges and directly supports the contributions of another person

Rhetorically sensitive communicators characterize their conversation with **confirming language**. Confirming language acknowledges the other person. Individuals who use confirming language clearly and directly support the contributions of another person (i.e., "That was a great idea, Michelle" or "Angelo, we haven't heard your position on this issue; would you like to share it with us?"). Communicators who use confirmation ask questions and respond directly. In contrast, **disconfirming language** evaluates or judges the contributions of others (i.e., "That's a stupid idea" or "Doesn't somebody have a *good* idea for a change?").

disconfirming language language that evaluates or judges the contributions of others

A final characteristic of rhetorically sensitive communicators is that they take responsibility for their own feelings, thoughts, beliefs, and actions. Instead of blaming others for a thought or feeling (i.e., "You make me mad."), rhetorically sensitive and competent communicators take ownership of the ways they create meaning (i.e., "I feel angry when you ignore me."). Ownership of individual thoughts, feelings, and actions translates blame (a "you" message) into responsibility (an "I" message). Stewart and Logan (1993 suggest that true understanding of the close connection between what you say and who you are is critical to respectful language. Thus, they suggest to "watch your tongue . . . be careful about your speech; revere talk for what it is—a direct reflection and a clear indication of who you are and what's important to you. Talk is how you make yourself present to others" (p. 70).

How rhetorically sensitive are you? How well can you detect bias? Try out your skills in the box Community Links: Who's in the News?

Community Links

Who's in the News?

Obtain copies of your local newspaper for the last week. Analyze the articles to find who in your community is identified with an activity done for the greater good. Can you identify any consistent racial, ethnic, religious, or gender bias in these stories?

Now look at the articles for those responsible for the "failures" in the community. Who are the "have nots" in your community? Who is responsible for the crime? Is racial, ethnic, religious, or gender bias obvious in these stories?

LEARNING AND USING "COLLEGE LANGUAGE"

As a student on a college campus, you are experiencing a unique communication "culture" every day. The language of college will provide you with some of the most potentially satisfying and perhaps frustrating experiences of your life thus far. In some ways, learning this new language is as alien as any other foreign language.

Understanding Typical College Language

What is "typical" college or academic language? College language incorporates a wide range of topics and a jargon that can create a sense of community but can also cause misunderstanding. Let's explore the titles people have on your campus. In your classroom, you might have an instructor, an adjunct, a teaching assistant, an assistant professor, an associate professor, a full professor, or even a dean. What is the difference between these titles? One of the primary differences is the type of degree the person holds. Instructors, typically, do not have what is called a "terminal degree" or the highest degree that can be obtained in a particular field—doctor of philosophy, doctor of education, doctor of arts, jurist doctorate, or doctor of psychology; these are the individuals who should be addressed by "Doctor." Another factor that distinguishes the title is the number of years that person has been teaching at the institution and whether he or she has received tenure (meaning the person has a permanent appointment or "job security"). Most assistant professors do not have tenure; normally, associate and full professors do. In either case, rhetorically sensitive communicators are encouraged to address all their teachers as "Professor" unless advised otherwise. This title of respect is always correct.

If you do not know exactly what you want to study, there are offices on your campus where people can help you. You may have a Career Center where you can explore a range of options with regard to your field. When you identify the degree you want to obtain, you must declare your major, and in many cases, your minor, or secondary area of study. Your program of study might be housed in a school or a college. Your degree may be in the arts, humanities, social sciences, natural sciences, education, technology, business, health, sports, medicine, or law. Once you have a major, you will be assigned an advisor who will assist you in choosing classes and identifying career goals.

Outside of the classroom, you may have already dealt with people in Admissions (who helped you with your entrance into your school) and Student Affairs. Student Affairs professionals may be those you encounter in Housing and Residence Life, Student Activities, Diversity Services, and the like.

Whether you are learning on campus or online, there is a plethora of new language to get used to.

If you are on a residential campus (where some students live in dorms or student housing on campus), you will likely have met the coordinators or supervisors called *resident advisors* (RAs) or *resident directors* (RDs). If you attend a primarily commuter campus (where most students drive to and from classes), you will probably find Commuter Student offices where staff members can assist you with issues like transportation and child care. The Financial Aid office is where you fill out paperwork to request grants (assistance you do not pay back), loans (financial assistance you must pay back), or work-study (payment you receive for work you do on campus). Other offices provide information about scholarships (gifts of tuition, books, or other assistance to candidates who qualify under certain conditions).

The key to successfully negotiating the college campus "world of words" is to think of the experience as similar to the cross-cultural communication experience. Learn where the important offices, services, and professionals are, and be sure to ask faculty and staff to explain this new world's jargon to you. Much of this jargon is conveyed in your college's student handbook. Be sure to check out an online or hard copy of your school's handbook. Check to see whether your school has policies governing communication. If it does, you may want to try the activities described in the box Campus Links: Combating Hate Speech on Campus.

◎ Campus Links

Combating Hate Speech on Campus

Find your college's student handbook and locate any information regarding hate speech on campus. Is there a definition of hate speech in the handbook? Are there policies that sanction hate speech?

Locate the student handbooks from a range of colleges in your state or region. How do they compare to your campus handbook with regard to definitions of and rules or policies regarding hate speech? Are there similarities or differences in the definitions, standards, or degree of punishment (or lack thereof) for violations?

SUMMARY

Effective communication involves negotiating a "world of words." In this chapter, we have identified concepts important to your understanding of effective and rhetorically sensitive verbal communication:

- Each of us creates personal meaning for our language, and therefore, our meaning can never exactly match the meaning of another person.
- When we communicate, we experience all of the verbal and nonverbal elements together.
- Language is symbolic. A particular set of letters together comes to represent a particular thing, idea, concept, or event. Symbols are arbitrary. Meaning is created in individual persons or through cultural associations.
- Language is structured. The way we put words together into sentences, and sentences into paragraphs, and paragraphs into essays is governed by a set of rules that is culture bound.
- Language is abstract. Some words are clear and simple, and the meaning for the word is shared across a particular cultural group.
- The *denotative definition* is the one we find in our language dictionary.
- The *connotative definition* is the personal, experiential meaning we have for a word.
- Language allows us to be associative.
- The Sapir-Whorf hypothesis theorizes that language is the most significant factor in determining what we see in the world and how we think and evaluate what we see.
- Language is equivocal and often ambiguous. Doublespeak is language deliberately constructed to disguise or distort its actual meaning.
- A euphemism is also a strategic choice, but more often used to "soften" or be sensitive to another speaker.
- Language is gendered. Women and men growing up in different worlds of words have different purposes for verbal communication and often very different styles.
- *Linguistic determinism* is a term used to describe the power of language to influence interpretations of the world in a specific culture, whether the culture is individualistic or collectivistic.
- Ethnocentrism is the view that "my" culture or group is the center of the universe and is the most valuable, the most advanced, and the most moral. When cultural ethnocentrism becomes extreme, language can deteriorate into hate speech.
- Competent communicators operate from a perspective of mindfulness.
- *Rhetorical sensitivity* is the term used to describe someone who can skillfully adapt to the widest range of communication experiences.

Questions for Discussion

1. In your experience, how are men's friendships (with men) and women's friendships (with women) similar and different? To what degree do you believe the stereotypes (i.e., of female "nurturance/passivity" and male "logic/aggressiveness") have affected patterns of communication in your friendships?
2. Why is it important to understand the ways in which our language influences our words and actions? Can you think of times when you were communicating with a person from another culture and one or the other of you confused meanings?
3. What are some of the best reasons for using ambiguous language? For example, consider corporations' slogans or logos. For example, what does Ford's company slogan, "Quality is Job 1," mean?
4. What is reification? Can you think of an example from your experience?
5. How are language and perception interrelated?
6. Have you heard anyone on your campus use hate speech? What was your response?

EXERCISES

1. Develop a Top 10 list of U.S. cultural rules for conversation between women and men who are interested in a potential romantic relationship.
2. Do you belong to a group or organization on or off campus? Identify the jargon used by members of the group. Describe an experience where use of jargon by a group member caused misunderstanding by someone who was an "outsider."
3. Translate the following statements from "you" language to "I" language:
   - You hurt my feelings.
   - You make me sick.
   - You are embarrassing me.
   - You make me happy.
4. Make a list of ten terms that describe you. Identify the origin of the descriptor. In other words, is this a label that has been imposed by another (parent, friend, media) or one you have created independently?
5. Identify the jargon on your campus that creates the most confusion among students. Who might help you to "learn" the jargon?

◎ KEY TERMS

Symbolic
Arbitrary
Structured
Abstract
Denotative meaning
Connotative meaning
Associate
Authoritative nature of language
Sapir-Whorf hypothesis
Equivocal

Ambiguous
Doublespeak
Euphemism
Labels
Stereotypes
Sexism
Heterosexism
Linguistic determinism
Ethnocentrism
Individualist cultures

Collectivist cultures
Hate speech
Mindlessness
Mindfulness
Jargon
Rhetorical sensitivity
Confirming language
Disconfirming language

◎ REFERENCES

Dobkin, B. A., and Pace, R. C. 2003. *Communication in a changing world: An introduction to theory and practice.* New York: McGraw-Hill.

Father Gander [Douglas W. Larche]. 1985. *Father Gander's Nursery Rhymes: The Equal Rhymes Amendment.* Santa Barbara, CA: Advocacy Press.

Hayakawa, S. I. 1990. *Language in thought and action.* 5th ed. New York: Harcourt Brace.

Ogden, C. K., and Richards, I. A. 1993. *The meaning of meaning.* New York: Morrow.

Reynolds, S., and Valentine, D. 2004. *Guide to cross-cultural communication.* Upper Saddle River, NJ: Pearson/Prentice Hall.

Stewart, J. 1995. Verbal communicating. In *Bridges not walls,* ed. J. Stewart, 50–53. New York: McGraw-Hill.

Stewart, J., and Logan, C. 1993. *Together: Communicating interpersonally.* New York: McGraw-Hill.

Stewart, L. P., Cooper, P. J., and Friedley, S. A. 1986. *Communication between the sexes: Sex differences and sex-role stereotypes.* Scottsdale, AZ: Gorsuch Scarisbrick.

Tannen, D. 1990. *You just don't understand: Women and men in conversation.* New York: Ballantine Books.

The Real Mother Goose, 2004. Available at www.gutenberg.org/files/10607/10607-h/10607-h.htm.

Trenholm, S., and Jensen, A. 1992. *Interpersonal communication.* 2nd ed. Belmont, CA: Wadsworth.

Whorf, B. 1956. *Language, thought, and reality,* ed. J. Carroll, Cambridge, MA: MIT Press.

CHAPTER 6

Nonverbal Communication

Understanding Nonverbal Communication

Fundamentals
Not Formally Structured
Culture Bound
Continuous
Adds Meaning

Functions
Modifies Verbal Communication
Exposes Feeling
Regulates Interaction

7 Types
1. Kinesics
2. Physical
3. Haptics
4. Paralanguage
5. Proxemics
6. Artifacts
7. Chronemics

Nonverbal Sensitivity
Gender
Culture

Guidelines
Self-Presentation
Mindfulness
Respect
Accuracy
Immediacy

UNDERSTANDING NONVERBAL BEHAVIOR

*H*istorically, there have been many attempts to define nonverbal communication. These efforts are complicated by the fact that we try to define nonverbal communication using words (verbal communication). Attempting to separate verbal and nonverbal communication into discrete areas further complicates definitional attempts. In reality, our verbal and nonverbal communication is intricately woven together, and when we create meaning about our own or another's communication behavior, we cannot separate the two. Many times our verbal and nonverbal communication "match"—what communication scholars call **congruent messages**. At other times, however, messages don't match, and our communication has **incongruent messages**. Consider the following exchange:

> Pat: *"I don't understand why you always get so angry when we talk about the future."*
> Kelly: *"I am NOT angry!" (With raised voice, fists clenched, face taut . . .)*

In interpreting Kelly's response, which do you believe—the verbal message or the nonverbal message?

Thus we might "define" nonverbal communication as vocal or non-oral messages not expressed linguistically. We might also suggest that nonverbal communication is the process by which nonverbal behaviors are used in the exchange and interpretation of messages. Dance (1967) provides this clarification on the verbal/nonverbal distinction:

> *A verbal symbol can be either vocal or nonvocal. A vocal sound need not always be symbolic. A scream, for instance, may be vocal and nonverbal on the reflex discharge level. On the other hand, a scream, when interpreted by a passerby in terms of circumstances, may be vocal and also may have meaning for the passerby beyond the meaning of the screamer. . . . The essential attribute of verbal is not the existence of sound in acoustic space, but the representation of abstractions of many specific instances by one sign that then becomes a sign or a symbol. (p. 290)*

congruent messages messages in which verbal communication and nonverbal communication match

incongruent messages messages in which verbal communication and nonverbal communication do not match

Table 6.1 Verbal	Nonverbal
Verbal/Vocal	*Nonverbal/Vocal*
Word Symbols	Paralanguage (tone, pitch, rate)
Verbal/Nonvocal	*Nonverbal/Nonvocal*
Sign language/tribal or ceremonial language	Space, body language, eyes, face, touch, time, etc.

In order to clarify the distinctions here, we must examine several fundamental characteristics of nonverbal communication that distinguish it from verbal communication.

FUNDAMENTALS OF NONVERBAL COMMUNICATION

One of the most significant differences between verbal and nonverbal communication concerns structure. Verbal communication is highly structured. We learn verbal communication by understanding and applying the formal rules of grammar to generate "correct" speaking and writing. Nonverbal communication, in contrast, has no formal structure. Thus, a variety of different meanings can be assigned to any nonverbal message.

As we discussed in Chapter 5, verbal communication is culture bound. In the United States, we speak English; the French speak French; the Russians speak Russian; and so on. While some nonverbal symbols or gestures have meaning that is culture bound, a large number of nonverbal symbols and messages have universal meaning. For example, some of what we call the more "innate" communication (facial expressions denoting happiness, fear, disgust, or surprise) is interpreted similarly across many cultures. We call this type of nonverbal communication "innate" because infants at birth use these expressions prior to any "learning" and because

What nonverbal messages are conveyed in this business meeting?

Cultural Links

Nonverbal Communication between Asian and Western Cultures

Scollon and Scollon (1995) point out the importance of kinesics and proxemics:

Kinesics is the movement of our bodies. One example . . . is that Chinese tend to smile more easily than [W]esterners when they feel difficulty or embarrassment. A smile because of embarrassment by a Chinese might be interpreted as being friendly by a [W]esterner and cause problems in Intercultural Communication (ICC). Another example is that Chinese tend to avoid direct eye-contact in face-to-face interaction out of respect while they might be perceived as not paying attention or even disrespectful by [W]esterners.

Proxemics refers to the use of space. One point that is of particular interest is the concept of "'bubble' of space" by Hall (1959), which is the space a person moves and in which he or she feels comfortable. Scollon and Scollon (1995) point out Asians in general have a smaller sphere of personal space than [W]esterners. With different expectations of personal space, a Chinese speaking to an American might find that he or she is trying to keep a distance while on the other hand the American might feel that the Chinese is intruding into his or her personal space. This inevitably affects the evaluation of each other and interpretations of interactions.

In their article, the Scollons point to Chan's (1992) summary of the contrasts in communicating styles between Asian and [W]estern cultures which are as follows:

Asian	Western
Indirect	Direct
Implicit, nonverbal	Explicit, verbal
Formal	Informal
Goal-oriented	Spontaneous
Emotionally controlled	Emotionally expressive
Self-effacing, modest	Self-promoting, egocentric

Source: "Non-verbal communication between Asian and Western cultures" from www3.telus.net/linguisticsissues/problemschinese.html. Reprinted by permission of Manfred Wu Man-fat.

infants from every culture use similar expressions at birth. In the box Cultural Links: Nonverbal Communication between Asian and Western Cultures, we provide additional information on learned nonverbal differences between these two cultures' use of kinesics, body movements, and proxemics (the use of space).

A third distinction refers to the fact that nonverbal communication is a continuous communication phenomenon. We don't "stop" communicating nonverbally, even when we stop talking. Thus, we say, "We cannot not communicate." Verbal communication, however, occurs in discrete, often disconnected units. Related to this characteristic is the fact that verbal communication is always "intentional." We speak because we choose to. Nonverbal communication, however, can be both intentional and unintentional. Much of our nonverbal communication is spontaneous and occurs outside of our awareness.

A final distinction between verbal and nonverbal communication concerns the "what" that is communicated through verbal and nonverbal means. Verbal communication, for example, expresses primarily factual information. The nonverbal dimension adds feeling or relational information that creates meaning in our communication interactions.

THE FUNCTIONS OF NONVERBAL COMMUNICATION

*A*nother way to clarify the relationship between verbal and nonverbal communication is to consider the three primary functions of nonverbal messages: to modify verbal communication, to express feeling, and to regulate interaction.

Modifies Verbal Communication

First, nonverbal communication serves to *modify* verbal communication in four basic ways: (1) to *complement* or *clarify*, (2) to *contradict* (incongruence), (3) to *repeat* or *reinforce*, and (4) to *substitute* for verbal messages. For example, when you give someone directions to a destination, your nonverbal hand gestures and body movements complement your oral instructions. When you shout, "I am NOT angry!" your nonverbal message contradicts your verbal message. When you are immersed in a conversation and want to make your point clear, your hand gestures again reinforce the verbal message. And, finally, sometimes our nonverbal message replaces a verbal message, such as nodding your head instead of saying, "Yes." These nonverbal messages are very important, especially when trying to determine if a person is telling the truth. The box Communication Links: How Can You Tell if Someone Is Lying? provides some examples of nonverbal behaviors that may indicate a person is not being truthful.

◎ Communication Links

How Can You Tell if Someone Is Lying?

How good are you at lying? How good are you at detecting when someone else is lying? How do we learn how to lie? These are questions that concern a wide range of researchers, law enforcement personnel, teachers, and others who have had to deal with liars. Research on lying and college students suggests that students lie to teachers about 25 percent of the time.

Interestingly, more lying occurs over the phone and via e-mail, suggesting we are less successful at lying in person. Probably the best reason for this is that lying is communicated physiologically. When threatened, humans react with a "fight or flight" mentality. So when placed under emotional stress, the body has trouble remaining still; movement helps (subconsciously) us deal with the threat.

Because of the fight-or-flight reaction, some people, when asked difficult questions, subconsciously assume a "fleeing" position. When asked a difficult question or when lying to a teacher, boss, or police officer, people may visibly shift their position, moving their whole body in the process. It is therefore easier to get away with a lie if we are not communicating face-to-face.

Some indicators of lying include rapid eye movement, crossed arms, eyes focused to the right, staring, rubbing eyes, crossing legs, fidgeting hands, touching face, playing with hair (females), and gripping an object.

But before you decide that someone is lying, remember that communication comes in a package and that one of these identifying cues is not enough to convict someone of lying. Your ability to detect lying will increase with the depth of the relationship. The more you know someone, the more likely you will know when they aren't acting "normally."

Expresses Feelings

A second function of nonverbal communication is to *express our feelings* about several relational dimensions. Three relational dimensions may be communicated through our nonverbal message: (1) the degree of like or dislike we have for another, (2) our perceptions of the status or power within the relationship, and (3) our degree of awareness or responsiveness (sometimes called "attending to") to the other. Our eyes and facial expressions are the primary channels of nonverbal communication regarding attending to (or not) another.

A variety of nonverbal messages communicate how much we like someone; for example, we sit closer to them, look them in the eye, smile, or nod our heads in response. Or when communicating with a superior at work, we express our status in a variety of nonverbal means such as not keeping a supervisor waiting or allowing the boss more "speaking time" in a conversation. As many of you may be aware, emoticons, or expressions of emotion in Internet communication, are able to convey nonverbal messages as well. Review the box Computer Links: Nonverbal Communication on the Internet to see if you can identify the meaning behind each of the emoticons in the left-hand margin.

Computer Links

Nonverbal Communication on the Internet

Is nonverbal communication possible on the Internet? According to the website www.muller-godschalk.com/emoticon.html, nonverbal cues are alive and well in the form of emoticons ("smileys"). Here is a sample of basic emoticons:

:-)	Standard smiley (you are joking; satisfied)
:)	Standard smiley for lazy people
,-)	Winking smiley. You don't mean it, even if you are joking
;-)	Winking smiley. See above
:->	Follows a really sarcastic remark
(-:	Left-handed smiley
:-(	Sad smiley. You aren't joking; you are not satisfied

| :< | Very sad smiley |
| :C | Very sad smiley |

Here is a sample of action emoticons:

:X	Kissing smiley
:-*	Kissing smiley
:-<>	Kissing smiley
;-<>	I-want-to-kiss-you smiley
:-@	French kiss
:-)~~(-:	French kiss
:-)~~~~	French kiss
:-@	Screaming; swearing
:-()	Yelling
XD	Laughing hilariously
:^):<	Is naked
>8D	Evil or crazed laughter

Have you used smileys in your Internet communication? In what ways do they increase shared meaning?

Regulates Interaction

The third function of nonverbal communication is perhaps the most fundamental. We use nonverbal communication to *regulate interaction*. As infants and toddlers, most of us learn the "rules of interaction"; however, for some individuals, this is a lifelong struggle. These rules of interaction, unfortunately, are not written down somewhere but are learned intuitively through experience. Communicators learn to regulate interactions in two crucial ways: by using turn-taking cues and start/stop cues. To illustrate, when we run into friends on our way to class, we know that the appropriate way to begin an interaction is to attempt to make eye contact. Sometimes we recognize them before they see us, and we will perhaps touch them lightly on the shoulder in order to get their attention. Later in the interaction, we use our eyes and voices to signal that we are finished with our turn in a conversation, or we signal that we want to add to the conversation through facial expression, eye movements, hand gestures, and body movement.

Each of these functions of nonverbal communication highlights the importance of understanding communication as a "package." It is also highlights that while there are no formal rules regarding the appropriateness of nonverbal communication, there are implicit or intuitively understood informal norms that guide our interactions. These norms affect all types of nonverbal behavior, from eye contact to styles of dress to arrangement of our living spaces. Most of us know immediately when someone has violated a nonverbal communication norm such as standing too close to someone in a checkout line or staring directly at stranger. Let's explore some of these types of nonverbal communication and their roles in our interactions. Before doing so, we urge you to check out the box Campus Links: Nonverbal Communication in "Casual" and "Involved" Dating to examine some of your own relationships in light of your nonverbal communication practices.

◎ Campus Links

Nonverbal Communication in "Casual" and "Involved" Dating

In a study conducted by McGinty, Knox, and Zusman (2003), 233 never-married undergraduates at a large southeastern university completed a forty-five item questionnaire designed to assess nonverbal and verbal communication differences in "involved" and "casual" dating relationships. Two-thirds (67.3%) of the respondents were female; 32.7% were male. In regard to relationship status, most (56.6%) were casual daters with 43.4% dating someone exclusively, engaged, or married (referred to as involved). Whites comprised 78% of the sample, blacks 20%, and 2% reported mixed race/heritage.

Findings revealed that "involved" daters, females, and whites are significantly more likely to be concerned about nonverbal communication than "casual" daters, males, and blacks. Analysis of the data revealed several significant findings:

1. Involved daters value nonverbal communication more than casual daters.
2. Involved daters work on nonverbal behavior more than casual daters and were more likely than casual daters to "work hard" to insure that their nonverbal behavior reinforced their verbal behavior.
3. Partners of involved daters also worked on nonverbal communication more.
4. Involved daters are "less confused than casual daters" when their partner says one thing and does another.
5. Involved daters are happier than casual daters. Respondents were told that the lower the number they assigned, the higher their satisfaction. The mean value for the "involved" and "casual" daters was 3.08 and 5.08, respectively.
6. Females value nonverbal behavior more than males. When females were compared with males, the females were significantly more likely than males to report that nonverbal behavior "should" be regarded as important.
7. Females engage in more nonverbal behavior. When females are compared to males, females were more likely to look their partners straight in the eye and to nod their heads when their partners spoke.
8. Whites value nonverbal behavior more. Whites were significantly more likely than blacks to believe that nonverbal behavior is and should be important to a relationship. The hypothesis regarding this finding is that blacks face enormous pressure to adapt to the mainstream white culture even with little to no attention given to nonverbal communication. Hence, blacks may feel more predisposed to believe in the verbal, the literal. Meanwhile, whites may feel no such pressure and feel more "free" to focus on nonverbal aspects of communication.

Source: "Nonverbal and verbal communication in 'involved' and 'casual' relationships among college students." *College Student Journal*, March 2003, by Kristen McGinty, David Knox, and Marty E. Zusman. Reprinted with permission of Project Innovation, Inc.

TYPES OF NONVERBAL COMMUNICATION

Knapp (1978) created a list of nonverbal communication types to assist us in understanding the role of nonverbal messages in the communication process but reminds us that we should not study nonverbal communication in "discrete" units; rather we should understand the important role that nonverbal communication plays in the "total communication system, the tremendous quantity of information cues it gives in any particular situation, and . . . its use in fundamental areas of our daily life" (p. 38). We add the concept of time as nonverbal communication to Knapp's list of kinesics (body movement), physical characteristics, haptics (touch), paralanguage, proxemics (use of space).

Body Movement (Kinesics)

The body movement category of nonverbal communication includes a broad range of messages communicated through the human body, including the eyes, face, gestures, and posture. The term **kinesics** refers to this area of nonverbal behavior. Kinesics or body behaviors assist communicators in several ways, including the use of emblems, illustrators, affect displays, and adaptors.

kinesics body behaviors including the eyes, face, gestures, and posture

How many gender differences can you detect in these two women's communication?

emblems communication behaviors that substitute for words

illustrators communication behaviors that accompany words to add vividness or power to them

affect displays the facial movements or expressions that convey emotional meaning as well as the posture or gesture cues that convey our emotions at any given moment

adaptors a wide range of movements intended to hide or "manage" emotions that we do not want to communicate directly

Emblems, for example, are communication behaviors that substitute for words and have a specific verbal translation. Some examples are nodding your head to communicate yes, using the A-OK gesture, giving the slash across your throat to communicate "cut," raising your hand to signal you wish to speak, or holding your hand to your ear to say, "Speak up. I can't hear you."

The second type of kinesic behavior includes a variety of **illustrators** that accompany our words to add vividness or power to what we're saying. Illustrators include our use of gestures when speaking. Many people use their hands continuously while they speak, and others use few gestures. These gestures do not have a specific meaning in and of themselves; they simply add meaning to the total message.

Affect displays are the facial movements or expressions, as well as posture or gesture cues, that convey our emotions. Consider the ways we communicate anger, happiness, sadness, fear, and disgust. Anger shows in our eyes (the glare), our face (the intense frown), our clenched fists, and our rigid body posture. Happiness shows in our raised eyebrows, our wide smiles, our open arms, and our loud laughter.

A final category, called **adaptors**, includes a wide range of movements that are intended to hide or "manage" emotions that we do not want to communicate directly. Adaptors come in two forms: self-adaptors and object-adaptors. Self-adaptors are the ways we manipulate our bodies, such as chewing nails, twisting hair, cracking knuckles, or biting the inside of our cheeks. When we experience anxiety, stress, uncertainty, or other negative feelings, we use adaptors to help us reduce these feelings. Object adaptors serve a similar purpose, except we manipulate an object such as a pencil or pen, our glasses, or a cigarette. What each of these kinesic movements or adaptors have in common is that they operate primarily at the subconscious level (on the sender's part). The adaptors can either help or hinder our communication effectiveness, depending upon the communication context or relationship. Since we usually communicate these messages unconsciously, and since receivers are more often aware of these messages, we may be sending messages we do not really want to send. For example, have you ever watched someone who you believed was lying nervously manipulate pencils, pens, or other objects?

Physical Characteristics

In this category of nonverbal behavior are such characteristics as physical attractiveness; body shape, size, color, and smell; and our clothing and personal adornment.

Perhaps more than any other factor in nonverbal communication, we are bombarded daily with information about what constitutes "attractiveness" in our culture. In fact, every culture has standards about what is considered attractive or unattractive. Consider how much time you spend each day "preparing" yourself to be seen by others. How often do you see someone who looks like you represented in the mass media?

For many years, scholars have been researching the role of attractiveness in human communication. Studies have shown fairly conclusively that attractiveness does matter in many communication interactions such as job interviews, dating, and marriage, and impacts persuasion, attitude change, and perceived credibility. This does not mean that you have to look like a cover model to get a job. It just means our perceptions of others are influenced by their physical characteristics.

Body shape and height, for example, influence our perceptions of someone's personality. Research suggests that individuals with "soft, round, fatter" body shapes are more often seen as easygoing, happy, and good-natured. Individuals with a "tall, thin, fragile" build are seen as more tense and nervous, more conscientious, and more meticulous than others. And finally, those with a "strong, muscular, athletic" build are more often seen as adventurous, mature, and self-reliant. In other words, we seem to have a "physique-temperament stereotype" (Knapp 1978, p. 165).

We also seem to be overly conscious of body color. The tremendous growth in tanning salons attests to the fact that many individuals are unhappy with their skin color. We are also aware of the racial and ethnic stereotypes associated with people of color. Related to skin color and perception is the influence of body smell. We refer to the influence of smell in human communication as **olfactics**. In the world today, Americans are the least tolerant of "normal" body odors. In fact, Americans spend more money annually on products created to mask their body odors than any other culture in the world today.

olfactics the influence of smell in human communication

Touch (Haptics)

Touch, or *haptics*, is perhaps one of the most powerful methods of communicating nonverbally; it is the most basic form of communication and the one we learn first. Positive touch is at the very heart of our most intimate and accepting relationships, and when touch turns violent and negative, it has the greatest power to hurt, both physically and mentally. Touch is perhaps the most "regulated" of our nonverbal behaviors, although this regulation occurs more through cultural and family norms than through official "rules" of touch behavior. Touch is also one of the most contextualized nonverbal behaviors. In other words, touch is directly related to the situation in which it occurs. For example, we endure "functional-professional" touch when we go to our hairdresser, chiropractor, or physician. We engage in "social-polite" touch when we shake hands with a stranger or an acquaintance. We hug or kiss a dear friend whom we have not seen in a long time during "friendship-warmth" touch. Finally, we engage in "love-intimacy" touch within our most personal and meaningful relationships. Yet touch communicates much more. For example, we communicate status and power differences with our touch (high-status individuals touch lower-status individuals more than the reverse). The ways we interpret the meaning of touch are impacted by when (in what context), where (on our bodies), how long, and in what manner we are touched.

Paralanguage

Paralanguage, or **vocalics,** is the use of the voice to communicate. The qualities of the voice (loudness, pitch, rhythm, intensity, and inflection) are an extremely important part of how we create meaning in communication. Vocalizations such as crying, whispering, moaning, screaming, laughing, and whining are also important in paralanguage. Fillers or "disfluencies" are also included in this category. What we know is that *what* is said is often less important than *how* it is said.

vocalics the use of the voice to communicate

pitch how high or low a voice is

Pitch refers to how high or low a voice is. We associate higher voices with females and lower voices with males. When we meet someone who does not "match" this expectation, we alter our perceptions about that person. Volume or loudness also affects how we perceive another. We view someone who is too loud as boisterous and pushy; someone whose voice is too soft as meek or ineffectual. *Rate* is the speed at which one speaks, and this affects our perception of the speaker's attitude or intelligence. For example, someone from the Midwest might meet a New Yorker and conclude that this person is pushy and loud ("I couldn't get a word in!"). The New Yorker, on the other hand, thinks the Midwesterner is slow and dull since that person doesn't seem capable of contributing to the conversation! Our perceptions of "appropriateness" related to the speed of speech are also very much dependent upon the situation. Rates of speech differ dramatically, as evidenced in the pacing of classroom instruction, funeral eulogies, and auction bidding.

disfluencies the fillers that some individuals add within their conversations (e.g., *um, uh, you know*)

Disfluencies are the "fillers" that some individuals add within their conversations, such as *um, uh, you know, hmm, ahh*, and others. Too many of these in our conversation may signal to others that we are nervous, anxious, or unprepared. Many senders fail to "hear" their disfluencies but receivers hear every one of them; in fact, sometimes we are so distracted by these disfluencies that we no longer hear the message itself. Ultimately, it is important to understand what your vocal qualities communicate about you, because your voice has a powerful influence on others' perceptions of you.

Proxemics

proxemics the study of the use of space to communicate

Proxemics, or the study of spatial environments in which people communicate, includes a number of dimensions. At one level, *proxemics* refers to communication messages within environmental settings such as lighting, noise, color, textures, temperature, and so on. At another level, proxemics includes aspects of our "territoriality" or "ownership" of certain physical spaces. Finally, proxemics includes what anthropologist Edward T. Hall (1959, 1966) referred to as "personal space." What areas of your world can you truly call your own—your dorm room, apartment, office, or garage? When you walk into a classroom, do you sit in the same seat each day of class? When you go to the library, do you spread your books, papers, book bag, or other personal items out on the table so that no one will "invade" your space? Have you ever found yourself crowded in a room or elevator and felt uncomfortable because people were too close? Each of these questions reflects the importance of understanding how proxemics is part of our nonverbal communication behavior.

The environments of many public and private spaces communicate a great deal of information about those who live and work in them. Have you ever noticed, for example, that restaurants or bars are the most comfortable places in an airport? Why? If you are more comfortable in those areas of the airport, you are more likely to spend money. Look around your campus. Can you locate the president's office? How many administrative assistants must you speak to before you can see him or her? What do the offices of your faculty look like? Some are probably large, include windows, or are nicely decorated. Others perhaps are in a basement and are dark and maybe even damp. Which ones are the most "inviting" to you as a student? Think of your classrooms. What color are the walls? How old is the furniture? Is there a particular smell? There is a relationship between the classroom environment and your level of motivation to learn. Recognizing that some environments are not conducive to learning may assist students, faculty, and staff in helping to create more effective surroundings to enhance learning.

territoriality the characteristic of marking one's environment

Territoriality is a term coined by ethologists, scientists who study animal behavior. Many animals stake out a particular territory, mark it, and declare ownership. Humans also "mark" their territories. The closer to home (our familiarity with a particular place), the more territorial we are. Territory is something we don't often think about until someone "invades" it. When we feel invaded, we respond. Sometimes we react by defending our territory; sometimes we try to insulate ourselves from further invasion and withdraw. Have you ever seen someone in your library spread his or her materials out on a table, then go to retrieve a book and return to find someone else "sharing" his or her space? How does the person returning react?

Hall's Zones of Personal Space   The final element of proxemics refers to our personal or "informal" space. Hall (1966) identifies four types, or zones, of personal space: intimate, personal, social, and public. **Intimate space**, which Hall suggests is from zero to about eighteen inches, is the zone into which we allow only those with whom we are most intimate, such as a parent, lover, child, or close friend. Do you feel odd in crowded elevators where you have no room to move? What do you do? Our discomfort in this type of situation reflects the fact that when strangers are in our intimate zone, we respond negatively. **Personal space**, Hall's second zone, ranges from eighteen inches to about four feet. In this space, we are comfortable with friends and family or good friends. **Social space** ranges from about four to twelve feet, and we reserve this zone for impersonal business, classroom interactions, and general interactions. Finally, **public space** ranges from twelve feet to the limits of our visibility or hearing. Public performances or presentations fall into this spatial zone. It is important to understand that Hall developed his zones based on his observations of adult, middle-class Americans and that the actual limits of each zone vary by geographic region, culture, gender, age, and other factors.

Artifacts

The way we dress and the adornments we choose affect the perceptions of those with whom we interact, and research suggests that our dress affects our self-image. Therefore, our clothing and **artifacts** are both a reflection of our self-image and a means of communicating messages about the wearer. Our clothes may encourage or discourage certain patterns and types of communication. What is your perception of someone who wears an "inappropriate" outfit? Have you ever been in a situation where you were either overdressed or underdressed? How did you feel? Aiken (1963) conducted research to determine whether there was any relationship between clothing selection and personality traits. The results of his study suggest that clothing is related to personality. For example, Aiken found that males and females who scored high in clothing consciousness were more guarded, inhibited, and compliant when confronted by authority figures. Both males and females who scored low in clothing practicality were considered independent, serious, mature, and aloof.

In addition to the relationship between clothing, self-concept, and personality, research also suggests that we intentionally communicate through personal artifacts such as badges, tattoos, jewelry, and cosmetics. While exactly *how* we communicate through these artifacts is not known, we do know that our appearance impacts the ways we communicate and how we interpret the messages communicated by others. We know that our appearance impacts our ability to influence others and that we have developed a set of stereotypes related to physical appearance.

Chronemics

Chronemics refers to the study of how people use time as a nonverbal communication channel. There are two ways we can discuss how we think about and interpret communication behavior chronemically. First is our psychological time orientation. There are three main categories of time orientation: past, present, and future. Do you spend more time contemplating past experiences, activities in your present life, or events that may transpire in the future? Are you always on time or chronically late? Do you wear a watch or refuse to own one? Are you "preoccupied" by time, or do you give it little consideration? Do you complete tasks ahead of time or wait

intimate space the zone of comfort only for those with whom a person is most intimate, such as a parent, lover, child, or close friend; about 0 to 18 inches

personal space the second zone of comfort, for family and good friends; about 18 inches to 4 feet

social space the third zone of comfort, for impersonal business, classroom interactions, and general interactions; about 4 to 12 feet

public space the fourth and widest zone of comfort, for public performances and presentations; 12 feet to the limits of our visibility or hearing

artifacts a person's dress and adornments, which are a reflection of self-image and a means of communicating messages about the wearer

chronemics the study of how people use time as a nonverbal communication channel

until the last minute? What does your orientation toward time and your use of time say about you? What messages are you sending to others about how you value their time?

We also communicate status and power differences through time. Higher-status individuals keep lower-status individuals waiting. For example, does your campus have a "rule" about how long you should wait in a classroom for an instructor to arrive? Often it depends upon the instructor's rank. On some campuses, students are advised to wait five minutes for a nontenured faculty member and ten minutes for a tenured faculty member!

A second aspect of time communication refers to the differences between our "formal" and "informal" time. Our **formal time** is most likely scheduled. During formal time, we schedule for certain exchanges of services and goods. For example, we call for appointments with doctors, lawyers, psychologists, counselors, hairstylists, and so on. In contrast, our **informal time** is often spontaneous. During our informal time, we are more likely to drop in on a friend, call a friend at the spur of the moment just to chat, or decide to go for a walk with a colleague.

While this is but a brief look at a number of nonverbal communication behaviors, by now you should understand that nonverbal messages are equal to, if not more powerful than, verbal messages. Nonverbal communication comes in many forms. The most competent communicators exhibit sensitivity and interpret the complexities of nonverbal messages. There are, however, two additional concepts to understanding and interpreting nonverbal cues: gender and culture.

formal time scheduled time; used for appointments with paid professionals such as doctors, lawyers, and psychologists

informal time unscheduled time, often spontaneous; used for activities like dropping in on a friend or calling someone just to chat

GENDERED NONVERBAL COMMUNICATION

Women and men often communicate in dissimilar ways and interpret communication behavior differently. Nonverbal communication is no exception. One of the first distinctions in women's nonverbal communication behavior is they are usually more sensitive to the nuances of nonverbal communication than men. Stewart, Cooper, and Friedley (2002) suggest that one of the reasons for this may be that mothers display and encourage a wider range of emotions with girls than with boys. Because girls are exposed to a wider range of emotional communication as infants, they are more likely to "read" that emotional communication as adults. Hall (1976) asserts that greater nonverbal sensitivity is required of those persons who are oppressed in society. Thus, women and minorities are more likely to be better at interpreting nonverbal behavior in order to survive the inequities still operating in our society. There is not absolute agreement on whether either of these theories is correct, yet they do acknowledge that women and men communicate nonverbal messages differently. How these differences manifest themselves on the job are shown in the box Career Links: Gender and Nonverbal Communication in the Workplace.

Career Links

Gender and Nonverbal Communication in the Workplace

Consider the following table, which shows differences between women and men regarding nonverbal communication. What are the implications for these "gendered" differences in nonverbal communication in the

workplace? According to Deborah Tannen (1995) in her book *Talking 9 to 5*, those who speak in ways that claim attention tend to be heard more often, and their suggestions are more likely to influence decision making. In the following table, which set of styles is more likely to be heard? Who is perceived as more credible and assertive?

Females	Males
Stand closer to each other in conversation	Maintain greater distance from each other
Use more eye contact than men	Use less eye contact
Use more facial expression and are generally more expressive	Reveal less emotion through facial expressions
More likely to return a smile when smiled at—generally smile more than men	Smile less often than women
Take up less space—hold legs more closely together and keep arms close to their bodies	Tend to have legs apart and hold arms farther from their bodies
Use fewer gestures overall than men—use more gestures with men than with other women	Use more gestures in general social situations—use about the same amount of gestures with women or men
Women are approached by both sexes more closely than men	Men have more negative reactions to crowding
More likely to lower eyes, avert eyes, look away, and watch another speaker while listening	More likely to look or stare aggressively at others, to look elsewhere while speaking
More likely to wear more constraining, formfitting clothing	More likely to wear loose, comfortable clothing

Gendered Space and Territory

Let's examine some instances in which men and women convey nonverbal messages. For example, in terms of personal space and territory, men tend to control more area and invade another's personal space more freely. When a man and woman sit next to each other in a movie theater or airplane, men usually use the armrest. In another example, research suggests that women are also kept waiting more often than men. In your experience, do women still wait to be asked out on dates? Who is responsible for asking someone on a date in today's world? Is this an equally shared expectation or might it vary depending upon one's age, gender, culture, and so on?

Gendered Fashion

Regarding fashion, are expectations the same for men and women? Today, women wear jeans, pants, and suits, yet it's not socially acceptable for men to wear skirts and dresses. Why is this? Men and women also have different ranges of colors that are acceptable. For example, how do people react when they see a little boy wearing pink? How acceptable is it for a man to wear a flowered shirt, a lavender tie, or colorful socks? Men and women also wear different clothing styles. Men wear looser, more comfortable clothes in a wider area of contexts. Women, on the other hand, tend to wear more constraining clothes in more form-fitting styles. Consider how these customs, colors, and contexts impact male and female communication. How many examples can you cite that illustrate gender's influence on communication?

Gendered Touch

Gender also influences other nonverbal behaviors such as touching, eye contact, and movement. In tactile communication (haptics), women are still more likely to be touched than to touch, except with children. Thus, you can see that status is an issue in this nonverbal area too. When a man touches a woman, she is more likely to interpret the touch as casual while men are more likely to interpret a woman's touch

Maintaining direct eye contact and turning toward the person you are speaking with conveys your openness to other viewpoints.

high-contact cultures cultures that engage in communication that encourages interaction, physical proximity, large gestures, and warm greetings (e.g., Arab, Latin American, and Mediterranean)

low-contact cultures cultures that maintain more distance, use smaller gestures, and more formal greetings (e.g., American, German, Scandinavian)

monochronic cultures cultures that generally prefer a linear approach to activities (e.g., American, English, Swiss)

polychronic cultures cultures that generally prefer to do multiple things at once and view time as a flexible concept (e.g., Bolivian, African, Samoan)

as having some sexual intent. It is also more socially acceptable for a woman to touch a woman than for a man to touch a man, except, of course, at funerals or sporting events, for example.

Gendered Eye Contact

Considering eye contact, who looks at whom more often? Surprisingly, women use more eye contact than men. Regarding movement, what is the role of nodding the head in conversations between women and men? Women tend to nod to signal, "I hear you," whereas men tend to nod to signal, "I agree with you." Think about the potential misunderstanding that could occur in this situation. Women also tend to smile more than men and use a smile in the same way they use a head nod—to communicate listening.

These examples show that gender differences and expectations exist in nonverbal communication. In general, women read more nonverbal cues into communication situations than men. Expectations for appropriate nonverbal communication are gendered. Recognizing the differences, however, may lead to a broader range of behaviors and interpretations of nonverbal cues, which may decrease the potential for misunderstanding and miscommunication.

NONVERBAL COMMUNICATION AND CULTURE

While different cultures may share some of the same nonverbal communication cues, the interpretation of those nonverbal cues is culture bound. As a result, understanding the ways culture influences nonverbal communication and interpretation is important to developing effective communication skills. Becoming more sensitive to differences in nonverbal cues across cultures is one of the most important competencies you can develop.

In the same way that cultures exist on a continuum in regards to verbal behavior as we discussed in the previous chapter, they also exist on a nonverbal continuum from high contact to low contact. **High-contact cultures** are those that engage in communication that encourages interaction, physical proximity, large gestures, and warm greetings such as hugs and kisses. **Low-contact cultures** maintain more distance and use smaller gestures or more formal greetings. Hugs and kisses are reserved for intimate relationships and nonpublic spaces. The personal space for individuals in high-contact cultures (Arabic, Latin American, Mediterranean) is less than for low-contact cultures (American, German, Scandinavian).

Cultures also exist on a time continuum, ranging from monochronic to polychronic. Individuals from **monochronic cultures** (American, English, Swiss) prefer to do one thing at a time, concentrating on a linear approach to a task. People from these cultures value being on time and tend to develop a larger number of short-term relationships. People from **polychronic cultures** (Bolivian, African, Samoan) prefer to do many things at once. Time is a much more flexible concept, and being on time is based upon the relationship or commitment between people. Interruptions are expected. These people also tend to build life-long relationships more than transitory ones.

The appropriateness of direct eye contact also varies a great deal from culture to culture. Very direct eye contact is highly valued in the Middle East, Latin America, and most of North America. A more moderate level of eye contact is expected in Northern Europe and Britain. Minimal eye contact is considered appropriate in Southeast Asia, India, and in Native American cultures (Chaney and Martin 2004).

Olfactics also plays an important role in nonverbal communication. Most Americans react negatively to body odor, bad breath, or soiled clothing and go to extraordinary lengths to be "clean." Many other cultures, however, consider Americans' obsession with masking body odor to be unnatural. One interesting finding in the research on cross-cultural communication suggests that people from cultures that include little meat (Chinese and other Asian) feel that people who

Competent and Ethical Nonverbal Communication

consume meat on a regular basis (Europeans and Americans) emit a very offensive odor (Samovar and Porter 2001).

Cultures also differ in the ways individuals greet each other. For example, in Hindu cultures, individuals greet each other with hands together and head bowed to indicate respect. In Thailand and Laos, a similar gesture is used to show respect for higher-status individuals. Of course, in the United States we greet with a handshake (if in business or formal settings), as do people in the Netherlands, France, and some Asian countries. In many Mediterranean and eastern European cultures, individuals greet each other (even strangers) with kisses on both cheeks, hugs, and shoulder pats (Reynolds and Valentine 2004).

These are but a few examples of the distinctive cultural expectations for a variety of nonverbal behaviors. There are countless ways in which nonverbal communication differs across cultures, and understanding these cross-cultural differences enhances your communication skills in personal, business, and social relationships.

COMPETENT AND ETHICAL NONVERBAL COMMUNICATION

*T*here are ethical issues surrounding the communication of nonverbal messages. Competent and ethical communicators attend to the consequences of their nonverbal communication. Next, we discuss three ways an ethical communicator can ensure that nonverbal messages result in mutual understanding and shared meaning in the communication interaction.

Self-Presentation

Stewart and Logan (1993) suggest that you can enhance the quality and ethicality of your interpersonal communication by attending to the ways in which you present personal aspects of yourself. These authors identify three "distinct attitudes" that can improve your **self-presentation**. First, you must adopt an "availability attitude" toward your interactions. Being available to another means that you present your concerns and questions and attend to the concerns and topics of another. There are critically important nonverbal availability skills that may enhance your interpersonal relationships: Direct eye contact, for example, is an important indicator of availability in Western cultures. Facial expressions that show interest in the other also enhance the quality of interaction. Body orientation that meets the other openly and directly also communicates attention and availability. Being on time for appointments communicates a subtle but critical message that the other's time and needs are important.

self-presentation the ways in which a person presents some of the more personal aspects of him- or herself

The second attitude is flexibility. When we are flexible, we create meanings for the verbal and nonverbal messages that are tentative, open to new information, and dependent upon perception-checking before understanding is assured. When confronted by unclear or uncertain nonverbal messages, remaining open to the possibility of new interpretations, to different cultural foundations, or to gendered interpretations will improve relationships.

The final "attitude" is commitment to the conversation. Commitment does not mean you must agree with every message the other person communicates. Instead, commitment means being involved in the interaction and communicating that you value the other, whether or not you agree with him or her.

Mindfulness and Respect

When we are consciously aware of our nonverbal messages and pay attention to how others interpret them, we are being "mindful" of our communication. The opposite of mindfulness is thoughtlessness, not paying attention to what we communicate verbally and nonverbally. Thoughtlessness is often reflected in our habitual communication behaviors. Stereotyping others' communication is one form of

Engaging in perception-checking will enable you to become a more effective communicator academically and professionally.

thoughtlessness. When we are willing to create fresh categories instead of relying on stereotypes, when we are open to new information, and when we are available to others' perspectives, we are engaging in mindful and respectful communication.

Accuracy and Immediacy

For each of us, interacting with someone new is likely to produce a certain level of anxiety. We may worry about what this newcomer may think about us or about our ability to communicate effectively. Engaging in nonverbal behaviors that communicate **immediacy** will help to lower your anxiety and enhance the ethicality of your communication. Some examples of nonverbal immediacy behaviors include using direct eye contact, showing a smile, facing the other directly, and using vocal variety. The results of using these nonverbal immediacy behaviors are increased accuracy and understanding of the messages you send as well as increased accuracy of your interpretations of other's messages.

immediacy behaviors such as direct eye contact, smiling, facing the other person directly, and using vocal variety

NONVERBAL COMMUNICATION IN COLLEGE AND LIFE

*A*s a new or returning student, the success of your communication in college and beyond frequently depends upon your ability to negotiate the complex communication relationships that surround you. Chaney and Martin (2004) suggest that

effective negotiators are observant, patient, adaptable, and good listeners. They appreciate the humor in a situation but are careful to use humor only when appropriate. Good negotiators are mentally sharp. They think before they speak, and they are careful to speak in an agreeable, civil manner. . . . Good negotiators praise what is praiseworthy and refrain from criticizing anything about the [other] negotiators. (p. 197)

What are the important relationships you must negotiate during your college experience? You will encounter teachers; roommates; family members; financial aid personnel; records and registration personnel; and individuals in student life, the health center, the counseling center, and many more. Each of us comes to these negotiations with a "cultural mind-set" that influences what and how we perceive another. How you attend to the nonverbal messages within each of these negotiations dramatically impacts your success in college and in the world beyond your college experience.

As Chaney and Martin suggest above, being an observant, patient, and careful listener is important. What are other important nonverbal cues you must be aware of about yourself and observe in others in college? In the following true story about your author's encounter with students in a group project, what cues were being sent?

> *Scenario: A group of students in a communication class is assigned to work on a project; its task is to develop a communication plan to increase student-voter turnout for the upcoming election. Prior to beginning the project, the team develops a contract that delineates responsibilities for each member of the team. The contract spells out what each member must do for the project and what principles guide interactions between group members. During the first weeks of the project, one group member is habitually late turning in work and routinely turns in work that other team members perceive as substandard (i.e., not edited carefully, lacking major portions of a section, etc.). This group member also misses several meetings without contacting fellow group members and shows up bleary-eyed and half-asleep. When confronted by other group members about violating the contract, this group member responds with angry facial expressions, stony silence, and crossed arms.*

If you were the teacher, what would you think about this communication exchange? What responsibilities do group members have to negotiate in this situation? What role should the teacher play to monitor the negotiation? What role does nonverbal communication play in the success or failure of the negotiation?

While this situation actually occurred in the college context, it could just as easily have occurred in the workplace. Does the changed context of the situation alter the responsibilities of the participants? If so, how? Clearly this situation escalated into a significant conflict for all participants, including the wayward group member. In Chapter 8, we cover conflict management and ways to manage conflict successfully. The self-presentation skills of this errant student played a critical role in the escalation of this conflict. Mindfulness and immediacy are lacking in this communication situation as well.

In order to ensure greater success and accuracy in the creation and interpretation of nonverbal communication, we must pay careful attention to the detailed nonverbal messages within the environment of the communication. These messages include such things as setting, space, and décor, as well as eye contact, facial expressions, body posture, personal artifacts, touch, and vocal variety. Developing the habit of perception-checking will enhance your ability to negotiate the complex relationships in college and in the world beyond. In the box Community Links: The Role of Ceremony and Ritual in Building Community, you will see how these activities and events carry meaning.

◎ Community Links

The Role of Ceremony and Ritual in Building Community

In his book *Body, Identity and Interaction: Interpreting Nonverbal Communication*, Allan Canfield, PhD (text available at http://canfield.etext.net/) explains the role of ceremonies and rituals in building communities, which, in turn, influence the behaviors of those who live within them. After reading this excerpt, discuss both the positive and negative communication consequences of "ritualized" communication.

> *People create a milieu and live within it; both the built and the natural environment are part of the context that influences human behavior. Artifacts, such as buildings, clothes and communicative technologies are created by humans; these artifacts influence their behaviors in turn. The built environment includes houses and public structures. Cultural thoughtways influence how buildings are structured. For example, Frank Lloyd Wright,*

a prominent American architect, designed homes that fit into the environment; the Navajo designed the hogan, a round-shaped building that grew out of their values, beliefs and practices.

Ritualistic and ceremonial behaviors are usually collective events. Customs and holidays are celebrated by social gatherings, special foods, games and other activities. They reflect cultural values and folkways and they exist separately from the individual who takes part in them.

Rituals are often associated with religious activities, although much everyday behavior can be ritualized. Rituals are social events, usually jointly performed, that are nonverbal in nature. Going to church, attending synagogue, going to the football game and so on can become ritualized, yet deeply imbued with meaning. They are recognizable, patterned activities that exist in all cultures in different forms.

Ceremonies, similar to rituals, are usually public events that are jointly produced. The wedding ceremony, the funeral, rites of passage, births, and so on are ceremonialized according to social custom. For the individuals involved, they take on meaning according to the experiences, life construals, and frames of references of the individuals involved.

Ceremonies and rituals occur in all societies, conveying deeply held meanings with which the individual must come to terms. Ceremonial events may be quite structured although they may be altered from one generation to another; they may convey joy, bonding or togetherness, or enact or depict myths, depending on their function in society. Ceremonies involve life and death and all that falls in-between. They can act as rites of passage.

Source: "The role of ceremony and ritual in building community," by Allan L. Canfield, PhD, from *Body, identity and interaction: Interpreting nonverbal communication.* Reprinted by permission of Allan L. Canfield PhD.

◎ SUMMARY

In this chapter, we have identified concepts important to your understanding of effective and ethical nonverbal communication, including these important points:

- We define *nonverbal communication* as oral and non-oral messages not expressed linguistically.
- Verbal and nonverbal messages can be congruent or incongruent.
- Nonverbal communication serves to modify verbal communication, to express our feelings about a number of relational dimensions, and to regulate interaction.
- Kinesic messages are those communicated through the human body, including the eyes, face, gestures, and posture.
- Touch, or haptics, is perhaps one of the most powerful methods of communicating nonverbally.
- Paralanguage, or vocalics, is the use of the voice to communicate.
- Proxemics, or the study of the use of space to communicate, includes how environmental settings such as lighting, noise, color, textures, temperature, and so on affect our communication, as well as how

aspects of our "territoriality" or "ownership" of certain physical spaces and personal space are shown.
- *Chronemics* refers to the study of how people use time as a nonverbal communication channel.
- *Olfactics* refers to communication based on smell.
- Women are usually more sensitive to the nuances of nonverbal communication than men.
- High-contact cultures are those that engage in communication that encourages interaction, physical proximity, large gestures, and warm greetings with hugs and kisses.
- Low-contact cultures maintain more distance and use smaller gestures and more formal greetings.
- Self-presentation includes three important "attitudes"—availability, flexibility, and commitment.
- When we are consciously aware of our nonverbal messages and pay attention to how others interpret them, we are being "mindful" of our communication.
- Engaging in nonverbal behaviors that communicate immediacy will help to lower your anxiety and enhance the ethicality of your communication.

Questions for Discussion

1. Do you remember when and how you "learned" nonverbal behavior and what certain nonverbal cues meant? Explain some of the lessons you learned in childhood.
2. We argue that women are more sensitive to nonverbal cues than men. Do you agree? Why or why not?
3. Have you ever been accused of sending a sexual signal when you did not? How is this possible?
4. Think about the places in your home that are yours (others are not allowed or must seek permission to enter). What are they? If you have a life partner, what are his or her spaces? How are they similar or different to yours?
5. Think about the people who keep you waiting in your life. What can you say about them in terms of education, status, importance, and so on. Who do you keep waiting? Why?
6. What is the most appropriate clothing to wear for a job interview? What are the reasons for wearing particular attire in that communication setting? What are you trying to communicate to the prospective employer through your mode of dress?
7. What is the difference between a "gaze" and a "stare"? Who stares more, women or men? Why do women tend to smile more than men?

EXERCISES

1. A young man is fairly successful at getting first dates but second and third dates are extremely rare. The general consensus is that he is cold, unemotional, and, especially, unromantic. What advice for nonverbal communication would you give him to make him a more successful dating partner? What nonverbal dating faults would you point out? Organize your advice around the following areas of nonverbal communication: body communication, facial and eye communication, spatial communication, and tactile communication.
2. In a group, identify how the following attitudes are communicated nonverbally. Be as specific as possible: machismo, sexism, love, hatred, loneliness, happiness, dogmatism, authority, high status, sensuousness.
3. In a group, identify as precisely as possible what individuals from Canada, China, England, Saudi Arabia, Japan, Brazil, and Germany would say is the time frame for the following list of terms:

- Immediately
- Soon
- Right away
- As soon as possible
- Later today
- In the near future

4. Draw a diagram of your ideal office. Where is it located in the building in which you work? What is the décor like? Who will be allowed to enter without your permission?
5. Identify three rules of body communication and gesture operating in U.S. culture that are uniquely masculine. [Note: Rules may be conceived of as prescriptive (indicating what should be done) or as proscriptive (indicating what should not be done)]. Identify three rules of body communication and gesture in U.S. culture that are uniquely feminine.

KEY TERMS

Congruent messages
Incongruent messages
Kinesics
Emblems
Illustrators
Affect displays
Adaptors
Olfactics
Vocalics

Pitch
Disfluencies
Proxemics
Territoriality
Intimate space
Personal space
Social space
Public space
Artifacts

Chronemics
Formal time
Informal time
High-contact cultures
Low-contact cultures
Monochronic cultures
Polychronic cultures
Self-presentation
Immediacy

REFERENCES

Aiken, L. 1963. The relationship of dress to selected measures of personality in undergraduate women. *Journal of Social Psychology* 59:119–128.

Canfield, A., n.d. *Body, identity and interaction: Interpreting nonverbal communication.* http://canfield.etext.net/

Chan, S. 1992. "Families with Asian roots." In E. W. Lynch and M. J. Hanson (Eds.) *Developing cross-cultural competence: A guide for working young children and their families* (pp.181–257). Baltimore: Brookes.

Chaney, L. H., and Martin, J. S. 2004. *Intercultural business communication.* 3rd ed. New Jersey: Pearson Prentice Hall.

Dance, F. E. X., ed. 1967. *Human communication theory.* New York: Holt, Rinehart and Winston.

Hall, E. T. 1959. *The silent language.* Garden City, NY: Doubleday.

Hall, E. T. 1966. *The hidden dimension.* Garden City, NY: Doubleday.

Hall, E. T. 1976. *Beyond culture.* Garden City, NY: Anchor Press.

Knapp, M. L. 1978. *Nonverbal communication in human interaction.* 2nd ed. New York: Holt, Rinehart and Winston.

Knox, D., McGinty, K., and Zusman, M. E. March 2003. Nonverbal and verbal communication in "involved" and "casual" relationships among college students. *College Student Journal.* 68–71.

Reynolds, S., and Valentine, D. 2004. *Guide to cross-cultural communication.* New Jersey: Pearson Prentice Hall.

Samovar, L. A., and Porter, R. E. 2001. *Communication between cultures.* 4th ed. Belmont, CA: Wadsworth.

Scollon, R., and Scollon, S. W. 1995. *Intercultural communication: A discourse analysis.* Oxford, England: Blackwell.

Stewart, P. J., Cooper, L. P., and Friedley, A. D. 2002. *Communication and gender.* Boston: Allyn and Bacon.

Stewart, J., and Logan, C. 1993. *Together: Communicating interpersonally.* 4th ed. New York: McGraw-Hill.

Tannen, D. 1995. *Talking 9 to 5.* New York: Harper.

CHAPTER 7

Understanding Interpersonal Communication

Impersonal vs. Interpersonal

Intimacy

Relationship Development Stages

Concepts
- Attraction

  Need fulfillment
  - Maslow's Hierarchy
  - Schutz's Theory of Interpersonal Needs

Stages
- Initiating
- Experimenting
- Intensifying
- Integrating
- Bonding

Dialectics
- Type of Relationship
- Degree of Dependence
- Type of Messages
- Communication Climate
- Degree of Assertion
- Degree of Flexibility

Relationship Dissolution Stages
- Differentiating
- Circumscribing
- Stagnating
- Avoiding
- Terminating

Phases of Model
- Intrapsychic
- Dyadic
- Social
- Grave-Dressing

Relationships, Intimacy, and Conflict

Types
- Student/Professor
- Men/Women
- Different Cultures

127

Knowledge Checklist

✓ To understand the role of intimacy in relationship development and dissolution

✓ To understand the role of attraction in relationship development

✓ To understand the role of need-fulfillment in relationship development and dissolution

✓ To recognize the stages of relationship development and dissolution

✓ To understand the role of intimacy in relational conflict

✓ To recognize the gender and cross-cultural differences in communication and conflict style

✓ To understand the ethical implications of relational development and dissolution

IMPERSONAL VS. INTERPERSONAL RELATIONSHIPS

Our lives are shaped and formed by the varied and often complex relationships we have with others. From the very first relationships we develop within our families, we branch out to create relationships with friends, schoolmates, coworkers, lovers, and others. Some develop into long-term, intimate relationships while others are short-lived. What factors influence the longevity of some relationships and not others? This chapter discusses several issues that impact our competence as communicators in our interpersonal relationships. At one level, **interpersonal (dyadic) communication** can be defined as a relationship context involving two persons, or a *dyad*. *Inter* is a prefix that means "between." We can distinguish the interpersonal context from, say, groups or public-speaking contexts. But not all dyads are equally interpersonal. A more useful way to understand interpersonal relationships is to distinguish them from impersonal ones.

> **interpersonal (dyadic) communication** a relationship context involving two persons *(a dyad)*

Think of interpersonal and impersonal communication as two ends of a relationship continuum. Both require interaction with at least one other person. But at the impersonal end of the continuum, the information we exchange with the other is superficial, lacks depth, and does not provide us or the other any authentic information. The degree that we develop relationships beyond impersonal interaction depends upon many factors described earlier in this text, such as self-disclosure, self-concept, and listening.

> **developmental approach** includes three levels of rules—cultural, sociological, and psychological—that tell us how to communicate with others

Miller and Steinberg (1975) outline the **developmental approach** to interpersonal communication. They identify three levels of "rules" that tell us how to communicate with others. *Cultural rules* are general rules we apply to all members of a culture. When most Americans meet a stranger for the first time, they are usually polite, shake hands, exchange names, and choose topics that are very general, like the weather. Cultural rules include a society's beliefs, values, and language. For example, while some Americans feel a person who doesn't make eye contact is untrustworthy, in some cultures, not making eye contact is a sign of respect for someone's age, position, or experience. A student from South Africa found it difficult to make eye contact with others, because in his background, eye contact invited confrontation, not interest or engagement. Another student, who had worked in Russia for several months, found that if he made eye contact, especially with women, his intentions were misread as a sexual overture.

We use *sociological rules* with individuals who belong to certain groups. For example, you communicate one way with other college students and another way with faculty members. We associate the set of rules with the group, and each group's rules are different.

We use *psychological rules* when we begin to learn something about a person as an individual. These rules are developed by the individuals and are unique to that relationship. We joke around with friends or "insult" them. We sit closer or maybe even develop our own language that others outside the relationship cannot understand. As Miller and Steinberg suggest, the more we develop a relationship beyond exchanging basic factual information and begin to tell others about our feelings, values, dreams, and goals, the more we move toward a truly interpersonal relationship. The more we move away from a general, culturally proscribed set of rules for interaction to more personal ones, the more we are willing to invest ourselves in the relationship; likewise, the more confident we are in disclosing personal, intimate information, the more interpersonal the relationship. The more we listen to others, the more we can respond to them with appropriate, timely, relationship-based information, thereby expanding and developing the relationship interpersonally.

THE KEY CONCEPT OF INTIMACY

*S*o what motivates you to continue a relationship beyond the impersonal level? Fundamentally, we are motivated to continue those relationships that help us develop a more comfortable, confident sense of self. The more comfortable we are in establishing **intimacy** with another, the more likely the relationship will grow beyond impersonal communication. In this sense, we do not primarily mean physical intimacy, but also the process of coming to know the other and yourself as the relationship develops. We refer to *intimacy* as the willingness to risk sharing information in order to create a unique and personal relationship.

intimacy the process of coming to know the other and yourself as a relationship develops

Intimacy and Attraction

Several factors influence and motivate us toward intimacy in developing interpersonal relationships. One is **attraction**. At a very basic level, each of us is *attracted* to some individuals and not others. Every individual, for example, develops a basic criteria for what makes others physically attractive. Our society places a great emphasis on physical beauty as a measure of attractiveness. Each individual, in turn, identifies certain physical characteristics with what he or she finds attractive. But other issues impact how we identify another as "attractive." We are attracted to those who share our values, hobbies, or personality characteristics and to those in close physical proximity to us. The sheer "opportunity factor" of proximity means we will have greater opportunities to get to know others if we often run into them in classes, in apartments or residence halls, or in groups we belong to. We are also attracted to those who share our past or present experiences. We are motivated to develop relationships more interpersonally when we have something in common. And finally, we are attracted to those who assist us in achieving goals. Is there a group or organization you want to be involved with because you admire its work? Do you want to position yourself to advance in your career? Or do you simply want to be associated with certain people? For example, if you want to be a member of the Greek society on your campus, on what basis do you choose the sorority or fraternity you will rush? On the other hand, if you have no interest in being a member of a Greek organization, why do you hold such an opinion? Or to take another example, if you are a mature learner, have you sought out organizations on your campus where you can meet other students like yourself? What is the basis of your decision to seek or not seek such engagement? In the final analysis, we are much more likely to be attracted to individuals who help us achieve these goals. So, the more knowledge we have of others and the more attraction we feel toward them, the more likely we are to develop those relationships interpersonally.

attraction one of the factors that motivates individuals toward intimacy in an interpersonal relationship

Different concepts of intimacy exist among ethnic, cultural, age, and other groups.

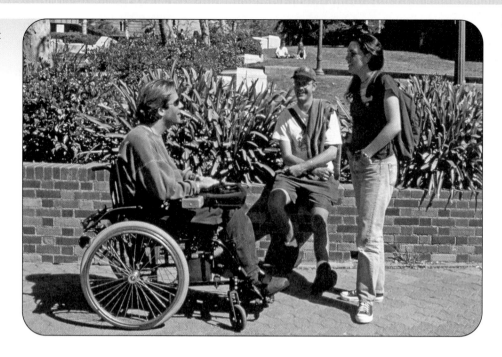

While each of these elements of attraction move *us* toward developing interpersonal relationships, our expectations for how *others* will act also influences our motivation to maintain or continue those relationships. Our expectations of a friend may differ vastly from those we expect of a life partner. Thus, the more we invest of ourselves in an interpersonal relationship, the more expectations we have for the other in that relationship. However, this, too, may shift depending on one's culture. For example, many people throughout the world use the word *friend* to describe what many U.S. residents would call a *close friend* (Martin & Nakayama 2001). Additionally, research verifies that different concepts of friendship exist among specific ethnic or cultural groups (Elbedour, Shulman, & Peri 1997; You & Malley-Morrison 2000), age groups (Adams, Blieszner, & DeVries 2000), and between people with and without physical disabilities (Meyer et al. 1998; Novak 1993). Moreover, such differences impact how well people perceive one another's communication ability (Collier 1996) and even the topics they will engage in during friendly conversation (Goodwin & Lee 1994).

Intimacy and Need Fulfillment

Clearly we are more attracted to some individuals than others, and an important consideration in deciding how, where, and with whom we develop relationships involves what those relationships do for us. The function of an interpersonal relationship in our lives is to fulfill our various needs. Abraham Maslow and William Schutz are two theorists who discuss our needs and how we fulfill them.

Maslow's Hierarchy of Needs Abraham Maslow (1970) developed a hierarchy that classifies our needs into seven categories—physiological, security and safety, love and belonging, self-esteem, knowing and understanding, aesthetics, and self-actualization. Maslow believed that each of the levels provides us with certain motivations that characterize our behavior. These motivations constrain our behavior until we have fulfilled those needs. The categories are hierarchical in the sense that we must be at least partially fulfilled at each level in order to move toward a higher level (see Figure 7.1). In other words, we must fulfill our physiological needs before we are motivated to fulfill our safety needs.

    Physiological needs are biological needs necessary to sustain life and include air, food, water, sleep, and sex. Once we satisfy these basic needs, we can address our needs

physiological needs biological needs necessary to sustain life, including air, water, food, sleep, and sex

FIGURE 7.1   Maslow's Hierarchy of Needs

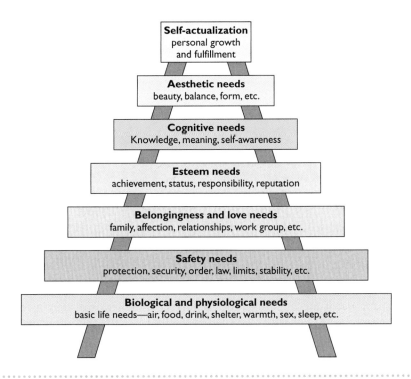

for safety and security. However, as indicated in the box Campus Links: Physiological Needs and Self-Care, how we meet these needs impacts our well-being. In turn, our well-being impacts our ability to develop and maintain healthy relationships.

Safety and security needs include feeling free from violence and having a sense of stability in our lives. Safety needs are physical; security needs are psychological. For many of us, physiological and safety concerns are not issues because we live in fairly

safety and security needs feeling free from violence and feeling a sense of stability in life

Campus Links

Physiological Needs and Self-Care

College life creates new demands on your mind and body. How you meet these needs dramatically impacts your well-being, which, in turn, impacts your ability to learn and to attend to or develop meaningful, healthy relationships. Gardner and Jewler (2003) suggest the following strategies for helping to ensure your ongoing well-being:

- Get enough rest. Try to get at least eight hours of sleep each night and rest when you need to.
- Get enough exercise. Engage in a physical activity you enjoy four to six days a week, and exercise for at least twenty to thirty minutes. If you are a traditional college age student, between 18–23, reach a pulse rate of about 120; if you

are a little older, reach a pulse rate of about 105–108.

- Get sufficient, appropriate nutrition. Eat a balanced diet, avoid caffeine, and eat only when you are hungry, not for emotional satisfaction or comfort.
- Make wise sexual decisions. Issues such as birth control, sexually transmitted diseases, and AIDS are only some of the issues you should consider.
- Think carefully about your use of alcohol, tobacco, and other drugs, since these have considerable physical and emotional health consequences.

safe neighborhoods and have food and shelter. However, many people in the world are not so lucky. Abject poverty and lack of affordable housing means that individuals and families spend a considerable amount of time simply trying to find enough to eat or a place to sleep. Just a few hundred miles off U.S. shores you will encounter indescribable poverty in countries like Haiti, Guatemala, and Honduras.

And we are not exempt from this problem within our own country. Consider the number of people today in the United States who live in homeless shelters. According to the Urban Institute (2000), 2.3 million people, or 1 percent of the population, face homelessness at least one time during any given year. In addition, the rate of people living in poverty is 6.3 percent. We may take for granted our livable houses or apartments, while thousands of families in this country go without decent, affordable housing or even lack indoor plumbing.

So for most of us, our behavior is not motivated by physiological or safety and security needs. Maslow believed that once we meet these first two levels of needs, we then seek to fulfill **love and belonging needs**. *Love and belonging* refers to our needs for affection, support, approval, and love from friends and family. This level of motivation is perhaps the most significant in our search for meaningful interpersonal relationships. Many of us have felt strong support and love from our families all our lives, while others have had these needs withheld or provided only conditionally. Once some of our needs for love and belonging have been satisfied, we move toward the need for self-esteem and respect.

Self-esteem needs are our needs for confidence or self-worth; they motivate us toward our careers and toward accumulating the things in life that show we are successful, such as homes, cars, and other worldly goods. Have you identified a career goal? What type of job do you think you are suited for and that would give you satisfaction? Think about what you have accumulated in your life to date and what you still yearn for, and consider all the advertisements you see on a daily basis that portray "successful" people in our culture. Consider the importance of what people *think* of you. Are you liked and respected? By whom? Whose respect matters to you? Your parents? Your teachers? Your friends? Your boss? Much of your behavior is motivated by these important, and perhaps as-yet-unsatisfied, self-esteem needs. Consider the shoes you are wearing today. People prefer certain styles over others. For example, students often wear brand-name athletic shoes. Why? What motivates college students to choose certain kinds of shoes over others? While it may seem that shoes and self-esteem are hardly related, on closer examination, perhaps they *are* related, because how others perceive us, including whether we wear the right shoes, influences how we think of ourselves.

Once we have partially satisfied the need for self-esteem and respect, Maslow believes we move toward the need for knowing and understanding and the need for aesthetics and beauty. **Knowledge and understanding needs** make us curious about the world and about others. We seek out others, develop relationships, and expand our knowledge just because it is possible to do so and because we feel more confident about ourselves with that knowledge. Some of the greatest learning occurs by interacting with our peers. For example, your authors go to conferences, attend professional development meetings, and chat at lunch with colleagues because we have learned how much we can gain from our colleagues and peers. Moreover, we have found that we learn from our students every semester! Curiosity and conversation are the ways to connect with others and to enhance our learning. Look at the person sitting next to you in class; imagine all the knowledge they have that you do not. There's only one way to tap into their knowledge and experience—communicate with them! Ask questions. Engage a conversation. You may be pleasantly surprised at what you'll learn, and besides, you may make a friend.

According to Maslow, **aesthetic needs** encompass the need to see beauty for its own sake. Have you ever been on a vacation and just stopped to enjoy a view? Do you remember the feeling you had just standing there and surveying what was before you? In order to truly appreciate what we see before us, we need to understand and value what is inside us. To illustrate, while you may consider some of

love and belonging needs the need for affection, support, approval, and love from friends and family

self-esteem needs the need for confidence or self-worth; they motivate individuals toward success

knowledge and understanding needs needs that make individuals curious about the world and about others

aesthetic needs the highest level of needs; the need to see beauty for its own sake

your general education courses to be less important than those directly related to your major, these courses provide you the opportunity to meet aesthetic needs as described by Maslow, since you will have the opportunity to examine various forms of art, including poems, paintings, theatrical productions, or musical scores.

The level of self-actualization is the highest level of motivation, according to Maslow. Maslow described **self-actualization needs** as encompassing our drive to be the best we can be and to live our lives in the best ways we know how. At this level, we are comfortable and satisfied with who we are, where we are, and what we have achieved. This level is actually quite difficult to achieve, and many of us spend our entire lives searching for true fulfillment.

self-actualization needs encompass an individual's drive to be the best that he or she can be

Schutz's Theory of Interpersonal Needs

William Schutz (1958) developed his theory from similar considerations as Maslow, but he focused more specifically on what motivated each of us toward how and why we create relationships with particular people. Schutz identified three interpersonal needs that motivate us— *affection, inclusion,* and *control.*

Like Maslow, Schutz identified our need for affection as basic to our development of relationships. We need to feel liked, loved, and respected. We join groups for this purpose, and we seek out friends and life partners because of these needs. While some people develop those affectionate relationships on their own, others may contract with a dating service or ask friends to "set them up." Essentially, we seek out emotional commitments because we cannot feel truly satisfied without them, even though they may often be unsatisfying in the long run. And while we make mistakes in some of our relationships, we still try to find "the one" for us.

Schutz also identified our need for inclusion as a primary motivator of our behavior. We need to feel that we are making a difference, that we have some significance in the world or in someone else's life. Think of the types of groups you would most like to join or be involved with. Do you seek out this group because of what might be changed or improved in your community (i.e., Habitat for Humanity, the Boys and Girls Clubs of America, etc.)? You may also have an opportunity to join a variety of campus groups, including service, academic, student government, religious, or Greek groups. You should find groups that are in harmony with your personal goals or interests, since these groups can add a great deal to your academic experience and can meet your need for inclusion. We had one student who recently said, "When I first came to campus, I made a lot of friends, and then most of them joined a sorority during their first year at school. I didn't really want to join a sorority, but after a year, I did, because I lost contact with so many of the friends I made my first year." You will be faced with these decisions, and you will need to think clearly about what *you* want to do. If you are returning to school later in life, you, too, will face similar decisions. While you may not be faced with joining a sorority, you will likely have to juggle time between study or social groups, your family, friends, or your social group outside college. Clearly, some of us are more motivated to be "joiners" than others. Schutz suggests that we each have a different level of needing to belong, which makes us more or less social.

Finally, Schutz identifies our need for control as a primary motivator. At a basic level, this means we must be able to predict what will happen to us in our jobs, our relationships, and in our lives. But taken to a higher level, our need for control encompasses our need to be leaders and to be responsible for jobs and tasks. Some of us are more motivated toward leadership than others, which may result in new challenges or opportunities in our college experience.

Each of these needs—affection, inclusion, control—motivates our communication and development of relationships with others. These needs also motivate us to gain knowledge of the world and our role in it. Knowing these needs exist and understanding how much of each need we must fulfill can help us understand why we seek out certain relationships and not others. In the next section, we explore the factors that impact the depth of relationship development, including intimacy.

A variety of needs motivate our communication and development of relationships with others.

INTIMACY AND THE STAGES OF RELATIONSHIP DEVELOPMENT

*K*napp and Vangelisti (1992) have developed a ten-step model to describe the stages of relationship development and dissolution. These stages can assist us in seeing how increasing and decreasing levels of intimacy impact the way relationships succeed or fail. The model's first five stages describe how relationships "come together" and will be discussed below, while the last five describe the stages of "coming apart" and will be discussed later in the chapter under "Relationship Dissolution." The full diagram can be seen in Figure 7.2.

Initiating

initiating the stage of a relationship in which the parties attempt to create an impression

The **initiating stage** of relationship development is where the parties involved attempt to create an impression. Each of us pays careful attention to the other, in an attempt to pick up any cues that would provide information about who the other is and how the other

FIGURE 7.2 **Knapp's Relational Development and Dissolution Model**

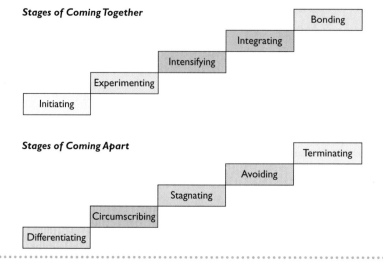

will respond to us. For some, this is one of the most difficult stages of the relationship. Like the apprehension many of us feel when giving a public presentation, we may also feel significant apprehension in any social setting where we meet another for the first time. This **social anxiety** can be quite difficult for people to overcome. Anxiety, in general, is caused by uncertainty. Uncertainty is "what we don't know about a situation" and "what we don't know about how the other will react" in the encounter. Our inability to predict what the other might do in a social situation threatens our self-concept and self-esteem because we fear being seen as foolish, incompetent, or stupid. Social anxiety often stems from how we compare ourselves to others and the fact that these

social anxiety a feeling of apprehension in any social setting in which an individual meets another for the first time

Computer Links

Dating and Relationship Development Online

Communication technologies have dramatically influenced our lives and relationships. For example, here are some interesting facts about online dating, drawn from two research organizations and summarized at http://answers .google.com/answers/threadview?id=157428. (You can find the actual reports upon which the summary is based at www.mkt-data-ent.com/datingtoc.html, although the report in its entirety costs $1,695.)

- Why is online dating booming? Online dating services (ODS) make over $900 million a year, indicating there is a market for these services.
- Who uses online dating services? Out of 1,000 respondents (500 male/500 female),
  28 percent were ages 18–34;
  42 percent were ages 35–54;
  28 percent were ages 55 and older;
  40 percent had an annual income of $50K or greater;
  29 percent had an annual income of $25K–$49K;
  20 percent had an annual income of less than $25K;
  35 percent were from the South;
  23 percent were from the Midwest;
  21 percent were from the West;
  19 percent were from the Northeast;
  62 percent had children;
  71 percent had some college or a degree;
  81 percent were white.
- Why do people use online dating services?
  Fifty-two percent felt that they had a better or equal chance of meeting someone online than in a singles bar.
  Only 40 percent felt that a relationship started online had a better or equal chance of success.
  Seventy percent would not recommend using online dating services to their friends.
  A key reason given for the increase in ODS is September 11. People feel safer at home, yet they need interaction. These services allow for some anonymity, yet create a sense of interaction with others. Another reason is control over the pace of the relationship, being able to truly learn about someone (though some would argue that fact), and other control factors.

What is your opinion of online dating? Do you think an online romance can work? Why or why not? How do online relationships differ from face-to-face relationship development?

social comparisons how an individual compares him- or herself to others

social comparisons often find us lacking in a certain area. Social anxiety also stems from what we see or think we see about ourselves reflected in the eyes of others, and the more importance we invest in others' perceptions of us, the more anxiety we are likely to feel. As you can see in the box Computer Links: Dating and Relationship Development Online, technology has dramatically affected the ways we initiate relationships.

Experimenting

experimenting the stage of a relationship in which individuals begin to look for commonalities

phatic communication small talk

If some initial positive responses help to reduce our anxiety, we will be more likely to continue to stage two, the **experimenting stage**. Each individual in the dyad cautiously begins to look for commonalities, primarily through small talk, or what some communication scholars term **phatic communication** (introduced by Malinowski 1923). The primary goal at this stage is to reduce some of the uncertainty that comes from not knowing the other. This is a critical stage in relationship development because our "first impressions" often determine very quickly whether or not there is reason to develop the relationship.

Intensifying

intensifying the stage of a relationship in which individuals begin to disclose in a more personal manner

If we decide to continue, we move to the **intensifying stage**, where we finally risk disclosing in a more personal manner. The relationship is often more relaxed, and we feel free to joke and tease. We begin to speak in terms of "we" instead of "I." We develop a level of comfort with the other because we can now predict how that person will respond to our self-disclosure. This is often the most exciting and satisfying period because both parties are having fun investing time and energy in the relationship.

Integrating

integrating the stage of a relationship in which two individuals become a couple

In the fourth stage, the **integrating stage**, the two individuals become a "couple." Outsiders to the relationship begin to identify the two as "a couple" or as "friends." The two have become so familiar with each other that they begin to speak their own language. They are often so synchronous that nonverbal signals communicate more between them than verbal signals.

Bonding

bonding the stage of a relationship that signifies to the outside world a commitment to maintain intimacy

At this point, the parties in the dyad may want to publicly ritualize their movement into the **bonding stage**. Lovers unite through a marriage ceremony. Friends may create a different type of ritual to show their ultimate commitment to each other. For example, the notion of "blood brothers" emerged from the practice of two friends intermingling their blood as a physical sign of interpersonal commitment. Likewise, those who join sororities or fraternities speak of one another as "brother" and "sister" as a way to linguistically formalize a bonded relationship. Some religious groups also use family labels, such as "brother," "sister," or "father," to express their interpersonal bonds. In any case, the bonding stage signifies to the outside world a commitment to maintaining intimacy. At this point, the parties have worked out several critical issues in terms of the expected communication patterns of the relationship. The box Communication Links: The Spiritual Child relates the process of relational development to the nurturing required to raise a healthy child. How does this metaphor help you to understand the role of competent communication in relational development?

INTERPERSONAL COMMUNICATION DIALECTICS

dialectics tension or opposition between interacting forces or elements

 f it is to survive, each relationship must work out many dialectics. **Dialectics** means tension or opposition between interacting forces or elements. Use Figure 7.3 to assess one of your important relationships.

The Spiritual Child

John Stewart, author of *Bridges, Not Walls,* uses the metaphor of the "spiritual child" to describe the process of creating and maintaining a relationship. When we meet someone for the first time, the relationship is like the birth of a child. The parents of the child are the ones who control whether the child will grow and develop into a healthy adult. All children must be fed, clothed, loved, and nurtured if they are to reach adulthood in good health. In this way, each partner in the relationship is responsible for providing what the child needs to survive. Both parties must take the time and energy required by the child. If the child is stimulated, the result is a happy, growing, healthy relationship. If the child is ignored, lacks care, is confronted by aggression and disconfirmation, or is always being criticized, the relationship will stagnate and suffer and may ultimately fade away and die. In other words, communication about and to this child determines its growth, health, and longevity. Consider a relationship that is important to you. How would you describe the health of this "spiritual child"? Begin by thinking about how you communicate with the other "parent" of this child. What communication patterns can you identify?

Every relationship must contend with several issues, or dialectics, in the negotiation of communication between the parties. The first issue is whether the relationship will be complementary or symmetrical in nature. **Complementary relationships** are those that are based on difference; each person brings characteristics that balance or complement those of the other. For example, you may be very logical and systematic in how you study for tests or complete assignments. You create a schedule or a checklist and mark off each task as you complete it. You begin several days before the assignment is due. Your best friend, roommate, or relational partner, however, may like to spend considerable time thinking about how to best understand the material. She may work on many assignments or tasks at the same time. At the last minute, she pulls it all together and finishes the assignment. The relationship is

complementary relationships
relationships based on difference; each person brings characteristics that balance the characteristics of a relational partner

FIGURE 7.3 Relational Dialectics in Interpersonal Communication

Name of Other _____

Type of Relationship _____

| Complementary | Symmetrical |

Examples:

| Dependent | Interdependent | Independent |

Examples:

Messages

| Rejection | Disconfirming | Confirming |

Examples:

| Defensive | Supportive |

Examples:

| Agresssive | Nonassertive | Assertive |

Examples:

| Rigidity | Flexibility |

Examples:

symmetrical relationships relationships based on similarity; both individuals share traits, interests, and approaches to communication

independent relationships relationships in which the partners live separate and disconnected lives

dependent relationships relationships in which the partners rely so much on one another that their identities are enmeshed with one another

interdependent relationships relationships in which the partners rely on one another, but are not so dependent that they cannot make independent decisions when warranted

disconfirming messages messages that deny the value of a relational partner by refusing to acknowledge his or her presence and communication

confirming messages messages that value the partner's presence and contributions

rejection messages messages that acknowledge the partner's presence and communication, but do not fully accept or agree with the partner

defensive climate a climate in which partners feel threatened and seek to protect themselves from attack

supportive climate a climate in which partners feel comfortable and secure

complementary because each of you balances out the strengths and weaknesses of the other as you interact, live, or work together.

Symmetrical relationships are based on similarity; both individuals share traits, interests, and approaches to communication that are essentially alike. Perhaps you and your best friend share the same idea of what constitutes a "real" vacation: throw some clothes together, jump in the car, and drive until you get to someplace interesting. Or perhaps you both like to sit down and thoroughly plan where you'll go and what you'll see.

A second issue is the nature of independence, dependence, or interdependence the parties will have. In **independent relationships**, partners live separate and disconnected lives. In other words, they have different hobbies or interests; they may take separate vacations. Should the relationship terminate, the partners would not be dramatically impacted by the loss. In **dependent relationships**, partners rely so much on each other that their identities are enmeshed. One of the partners may not be able to make any decision without consulting the other. Should the relationship terminate, the partners would lose essential support and face an identity crisis. Parties in **interdependent relationships** rely on each other and possess mutual influence and importance, but they are not so dependent on the other that they cannot make independent decisions when warranted. Should an interdependent relationship terminate, the partners feel the loss keenly but have sufficient personal identity to rebuild.

A third key issue or dialectic involves the routine types of relational messages that constitute the ongoing relationships between the parties. The individuals may communicate through disconfirming, confirming, or rejection messages. **Disconfirming messages** deny a relational partner's value by refusing to acknowledge the partner's presence and the importance of the partner's communication. Messages can be disconfirming in many ways. One person might simply ignore the other or change the subject in the middle of a conversation.

Confirming messages, by contrast, value the partner's presence and contributions. We send confirming messages when we look directly at another, nod in response to a message, ask for additional information, or share a similar experience. **Rejection messages** acknowledge but do not fully accept the partner's presence and communication, such as when one person calls another's contribution "stupid" or "nonsense."

Messages possess two important characteristics: *effectiveness* and *appropriateness* (Spitzberg & Cupach 1984). Effective messages accomplish the communication's intended goal, while appropriate messages demonstrate responsiveness to the message's relational and contextual aspects. While some messages lack one or the other of these characteristics, rhetorically sensitive messages communicate both effectively and appropriately.

Related to effectiveness versus responsiveness is a fourth dialectic concerning the type of atmosphere that is maintained between the parties and that is important to the dyad. The atmosphere may be defensive or supportive. A **defensive climate** is an atmosphere in which partners feel threatened and seek to protect themselves from attack. Defensiveness usually develops if our relational partner behaves in an evaluative, controlling, manipulative, uninvolved, superior, or dogmatic manner. One of the most common examples of defensiveness in a relational atmosphere occurs when one or both partners show extreme jealousy. Extremely jealous partners may question their partner's fidelity every time they interact with another person, or they may attempt to control or block their interactions with anyone outside the relationship.

A **supportive climate** is an atmosphere in which partners feel comfortable and secure. Understanding, honesty, empathy, equality, and flexibility characterize a supportive climate. Equality and flexibility are the most critical of these qualities. Equality in the relationship means that each partner's experience, knowledge, and relational expectations will be considered when important decisions must be made. Flexibility means that both partners show a willingness to change or modify interests, plans, and expectations when circumstances change.

A fifth dialectic concerns the need for partners to negotiate the degree of **nonassertiveness, assertiveness,** or **aggressiveness** that each individual will communicate in the relationship. *Nonassertive* partners feel powerless and keep their feelings and thoughts to themselves; they are often unable to express honest feelings comfortably. *Assertive* partners know and communicate their feelings and thoughts straightforwardly and honestly with others; they do not let others speak for them or tell them how they should feel, even though they remain concerned about others' perspectives. *Aggressive* partners assert themselves to an extreme without concern for others' concerns or needs; they stand up for themselves even at another's expense. They have the tendency to force others to believe as they do and engage in verbal attack marked by strong disconfirming messages.

Two final dialectics concern the degree of rigidity or flexibility that characterizes the relationship, and the interaction, domination, or passivity each partner will exhibit. **Rigid partners** lack the ability to adapt and cope with changes that occur in a relationship; they possess neither the motivation nor the inclination to learn new ways of interacting. **Flexible partners,** by contrast, adapt and alter their behaviors in order to accommodate the changes that occur in relationships since all relationships change. **Interactive conversation** remains an important aspect of relational initiation and development. Turn-taking that allows each partner an opportunity to engage the conversation promotes interaction. However, when people **dominate** the conversation and do not permit their partners to speak or when one of the partners is **passive,** and therefore reticent or unwilling to enter the interaction, effective communication becomes virtually impossible.

Within each of these dialectics, what style is most comfortable to you? It is important to remember that the individuals in the dyad, not outsiders to the relationship, decide what will constitute the basic communication between each other. Does your style change within these dialectics in different types of relationships? Are you more passive with your romantic partner than you are with your best friend? The key to successful and competent interpersonal communication is how the individuals in the dyad negotiate the various dialectics we have discussed. The ways in which the parties negotiate and agree with each other's behavior within each dialectic will assist in maintaining and expanding the relationship over a number of years—or may contribute to the relationship's eventual dissolution.

nonassertiveness feeling of powerlessness and inability to express feelings honestly and comfortably

assertiveness ability to communicate feelings honestly and in a straightforward manner

aggressiveness asserting oneself to an extreme without concern for others

rigidity inability to adapt and cope with changes that occur in a relationship

flexibility ability to adapt and alter one's behaviors in order to accommodate changes in a relationship

interaction turn-taking that allows each partner to engage a conversation

domination one partner does not allow the other to speak

passivity one partner is reticent or unwilling to enter the interaction

INTIMACY AND STAGES OF RELATIONSHIP DISSOLUTION

*W*hile the stages of relational development are seen as exciting, stimulating, and satisfying, the stages of relational dissolution are more often characterized by anger, insecurity, and pain. The communication skills used by the partners during the dissolution phases significantly impact the effectiveness of the process and the ability to successfully engage in future intimate relationships. To achieve competent and effective communication, partners must be honest, empathic, and adaptable to the constraints of the situation. Each partner must be willing to talk openly without accusation. As hard as this might sound, the more each partner represses his or her feelings or engages in hurtful, aggressive accusations, the more painful and long-lasting the consequences of the breakup.

The development, maintenance, and dissolution of relationships impact your everyday life, especially in terms of your friendships or romantic relationships. Many of you can testify to the excitement and subsequent pain of becoming good friends with someone in your class, dorm, neighborhood, or workplace, only to have the relationship end in disappointment.

The stages of relational dissolution are often characterized by anger, insecurity, and pain.

Stages of Relationship Dissolution

Knapp and Vangelisti (1992) describe five stages of relationship dissolution. While the stages of relationship development show how intimacy contributes to the growth and expansion of the relationship, the stages of relationship dissolution show how withholding and diminishing intimacy may contribute to the ultimate termination of the relationship.

Differentiating   If one or more parties begin to *withhold* or *retreat* from intimacy in a relationship, the relationship may enter the **differentiating stage**. It is often at this point that some of your partner's behavioral traits go from tolerable to annoying, or where activities that used to be enjoyable are now something you simply endure. Instead of using "we" or "us," you may start saying "you" or "I." One of the major causes of relationship differentiation is lack of negotiation and agreement on the dialectics we previously discussed. Sometimes in our rush to develop relationships, we ignore some of our partner's behaviors because we don't want to appear too critical. If, however, you or your partner is unwilling to negotiate critical dialectic issues, the relationship will inevitably move to the differentiating stage.

differentiating a relationship stage that occurs when one or more of the parties withholds or retreats from intimacy

Circumscribing   If differentiation continues and the parties are still unwilling to renegotiate the critical dialectics, then the relationship may move to the **circumscribing stage**. The most significant characteristic of this stage is that the parties' communication with each other is significantly lessened. Instead of communicating about critical issues, they are ignored or identified as "off limits." Ultimately, this lack of communication means significantly fewer expressions of commitment between the parties.

circumscribing a relationship stage in which the parties' communication with each other is significantly lessened

Stagnating   If this lack of communication continues, the parties quickly move to the **stagnating stage**. For the most part, communication disappears, or communication becomes awkward or overly formal. It also means the individuals engage in virtually no activities together. They may continue to inhabit the same living space, but each acts as if communication with the other is a "waste of time." Perhaps at some time in your life you have either received or given the "cold shoulder treatment" or the "silent treatment" as an indication of relational dissatisfaction; this is an early form of stagnating that can eventually spiral downward to the avoiding stage if not addressed.

stagnating a relationship stage in which communication disappears

Avoiding   When the relationship gets to the **avoiding stage**, each individual goes his or her own way or makes independent decisions, without consulting or communicating with the other. What has been subtle avoidance now becomes more direct. One of the parties will move out, or if that is impossible, psychological avoidance becomes more direct. In the case of friends, one of the individuals may stop answering the phone or be too busy to get together.

avoiding a relationship stage in which parties go their separate ways

Terminating   Ultimately, this spiral continues to the **terminating stage** if no significant intervention is attempted. Sometimes the termination is a relief; sometimes, however, it is the most painful experience imaginable. Ultimately, the communication in this stage focuses on all the partners' faults and problems and on what may happen in the future to either or both parties.

terminating occurs when no significant intervention is attempted at the avoiding stage

Knapp and Vangelisti's model describes the potential process that relationships may evolve through, but the process is not inevitable. Moreover, each dyad, and each individual in that dyad, has the opportunity to change the course of the relationship if he or she chooses. Each dyad is unique in the speed with which the stages are negotiated and the degree of success within that negotiation. It is also true that individuals in a dyad are often not in the same stage as their partner during the course of the relationship. The degree of relationship success or failure and the speed of the process are determined by the ability of the individuals in the dyad to negotiate the dialectics previously described.

Relational Dissolution Model

relational dissolution model identifies the intrapsychic, dyadic, social, and grave-dressing phases of relationship dissolution

Duck's (1982) **relational dissolution model** provides another perspective with which to view the stages of relationship dissolution. Duck describes four types of behavior that individuals engage in when a relationship is ending.

Intrapsychic Phase   Individuals must first come to terms with their sense of "grievance and distress" at the possibility of relational dissolution and at a partner's faults and weaknesses. Duck calls this the **intrapsychic phase** (*intra* meaning "within"). In this stage, the costs and benefits of staying and leaving are explored. Partners will review the relationship over and over in their minds and will engage in a sort of cost-benefit analysis, comparing the "costs" of the other partner's faults and weaknesses with the "benefits" of staying in the relationship. This is a sort of "what's in it for me" approach to analyzing the relationship.

intrapsychic phase the stage in which an individual explores the costs and benefits of leaving a relationship

Dyadic Phase   While the intrapsychic phase is an introspective, individualistic phase, the next step, the **dyadic phase**, involves the other partner. Partners confront each other, talk about the relationship's strengths and problems, and try to find ways to fix what is wrong. Sometimes this phase involves the parties sitting down together to calmly explore what is bothering them. At other times, the confrontation may be loaded with emotion, accusation, and insult.

dyadic phase the stage in which partners confront one another, talk about the relationship's strengths and problems, and try to identify solutions to the problems

Social Phase   The third phase, the **social phase**, involves talking with friends and family about the possibility or actuality of the dissolution. This social phase is a sort of test to see how others will react to the potential breakup. The partners will also explore what others feel should be the nature of the relationship with the "former" partner after they break up.

social phase the stage in which partners discuss the possibility or actuality of dissolving the relationship with friends and family

Grave-Dressing Phase   Finally, Duck describes the last stage in the dissolution process as **grave-dressing**. In grave-dressing, partners must come to terms with their perceptions of the relationship, the problems that occurred, who was at fault, and how they should "remember" the relationship. This involves a sort of perception-checking of self and others in order to make sense of how and why the breakup occurred. Duck believes we must compare our feelings to others who are important to us to help confirm our decisions or our rationalizations about the relationship.

grave-dressing phase the stage in which each partner must come to terms with his or her perceptions of the relationship, its problems, and how they should remember the relationship

RELATIONAL DEVELOPMENT BETWEEN PROFESSORS AND STUDENTS

While friendships and romantic relationships are important in your college experience, your relationships with your professors are equally important. Cooper and Simonds (2003) adapt and apply Knapp's relational development model to teacher–student relationships. Teachers and students *initiate* relationships on the first day of class, when first impressions play an important role. So if you are a student who misses the first class, you may want to think again, since you leave a first impression by your absence, especially if you have not contacted your professor ahead of time to explain your nonattendance.

Teachers and students also engage in *experimenting* as they develop relationships. This phase is earmarked by testing: Students test teachers to discern their expectations, while teachers test students to assess who they are, what they want from a class, and what might be the best teaching methods for reaching the students. After initiating and testing have been charted, teachers and students may *intensify* their relationships. No doubt you have had a teacher who has left a long-lasting impression on you. You probably developed a different level of intimacy with this teacher that permitted you both to get to know each other in a more personal and yet appropriate fashion. In short, you got to know this teacher as a person as well as an instructor, just as the teacher got to know you. This experience illustrates intensification well.

According to Cooper and Simonds (2003), while your friendship with a teacher may exist beyond your classroom interaction, eventually all teacher–student relationships deteriorate and dissolve. In other words, unlike other interpersonal relationships, teacher–student relationships have definitive endings because all courses or programs end. If the friendship continues beyond the course or program, the relationship has moved to a different level, but the teacher–student bond is no longer motivating the relationship. Others would argue that during the lifetime of this relationship, there is always recognition of this relational dialectic as fundamentally important to both parties.

INTIMACY AND CONFLICT

Conflict, unfortunately, is inevitable in any relationship. Issues arise that lead to conflict, and partners vary in their responses to it. Some partners avoid conflict and refuse to deal with issues; they are more likely to surrender. Other partners go on the attack and seek to shift the blame or defeat the other partner; they want to win at all costs. Still other partners confront the issue in order to solve the problem rather than sidestep the issues or adopt an "I win, you lose" strategy. In order to make sure your relationships run as smoothly as possible, you must first understand the inevitability of conflict. If you try to avoid conflict, your relationships will suffer. Successful conflict management can ensure the relationship survives and grows more satisfying over time. The existence of conflict does not mean the partners in a relationship are having trouble; conflict exists because we are linked to each other, involved with each other, connected with each other.

conflict the perception of incompatible goals

By definition, **conflict** is the perception of incompatible goals and the belief that in order for one partner to reach his or her goal, the goals of the other partner cannot be met (see Hocker & Wilmot 1997). Sometimes conflict is out in the open, but sometimes it is hidden. When we confront someone directly about a perceived conflict, the conflict is said to be *overt*. When conflict is hidden or *covert*, we sometimes act in passive-aggressive ways that send mixed messages. For example, you may be angry at a roommate for not pulling his share of the responsibility for keeping the apartment clean or upset with your spouse or children who know you have to study yet don't take the initiative to start supper or throw in a load of laundry. You may say nothing in these situations but act coolly toward the person or people with whom you are upset. However, when you respond to conflict in these passive-aggressive ways, the conflict remains unresolved, and the relationship suffers.

The way an individual responds to conflict reflects past experiences, which are often a product of family history. Think about the ways your family resolves conflict. Do family members ignore the problem and hope it goes away? Is there competition to see who can "win"? Does your family encourage constructive engagement and discussion of conflict? How you manage conflict will be reflected in your words and actions. While conflict is inevitable, it is also manageable. When you approach conflict as a problem to be solved, and not a challenge for you to win at all costs, you can develop and expand your relationships with others and increase your confidence and self-esteem. A key to becoming more effective at managing conflict is your ability to be adaptable. This is easier said than done. While you may be able to control your feelings and actions during conflict, you cannot control someone else's. In the face of anger, tears, shouting, or accusation, however, we often find it difficult to remain calm. Conflict can spiral out of control if neither party in the relationship is willing to listen and adapt to the needs of the conflict situation. Perhaps even a time-out to cool down and collect your thoughts can help keep a heated conflict from becoming even more destructive. The old practice of counting to ten before you speak is still valuable.

One of the basic values essential in important relationships is honesty. We expect honesty in the relationship no matter what the situation. When we deceive people we care about, we lose trust in them and in the relationship. Trust is a critical building block in any interpersonal relationship. When we are trying to manage conflict, it takes courage to remain honest and to trust another. You must describe your feelings honestly and ask the other person to do the same. You must also avoid lashing out with hurtful, aggressive comments, despite how you might feel at the moment. Focus on the positive side of the relationship and its potential for better understanding of yourself and the other. When we are calm and in control of our emotions, we know this is possible. Yet, it is easy to fall back on deception when emotions run high or

when we don't want to admit we've made a mistake. The box Campus Links: Five Ways to Say "I" provides some examples of ways that you can prevent conflict from escalating into a "win at all costs" war of words. You may find these skills valuable as you negotiate problems with your roommate or juggle the multiple demands of being a student, spouse, and parent, since these and other issues can create conflict. Obviously, there are numerous reasons why conflict can emerge in relationships. Therefore, conflict is inevitable but manageable and even potentially beneficial.

◎ Campus Links

Five Ways to Say "I"

Conflict is inevitable in any relationship, but how you respond verbally is within your control. Using "I" messages rather than "you" messages will help the other person hear what you have to say without feeling attacked or demeaned. Here are five ways that David Ellis, author of *Becoming a Master Student*, suggests that college students respond to conflict by using "I" messages:

- *Observation*: describes what you can see, hear, touch, and experience, and focuses on facts. Instead of saying, "You are eating like a pig," you can say, "We spent twenty dollars again this shopping trip on junk food like chips and cookies."

- *Feelings*: describes your own feelings. Rather than saying, "You make me feel stupid," say "I feel foolish when you remember more than I do from our chemistry lecture."

- *Wants*: describes what you want or need instead of hoping that others will guess what you want them to do or what you need from them. Avoid using the word *need*, if possible. Change your comment from, "You are so lazy around here," to "I would like you to help me with the dishes and the laundry before we go to the movies."

- *Thoughts*: describes your thinking. Beware of "I" messages that are really judgments, such as "I think you are insensitive," or "I know that you hate my cooking." Try messages like, "I feel secure when you tell me you love me more often," or "I like it when you tell me whether or not you enjoyed the meal I cooked."

- *Intention*: describes what you plan to do. Rather than depend on the other, state your intentions. Instead of saying, "We have a lot of chores this weekend," say, "I intend to wash the car and vacuum the carpet before studying this weekend. What would you like to do?"

To summarize, thus far we have described several issues that reflect the complex nature of interpersonal relationships. Successful negotiation of each of the dialectics will create an atmosphere where conflict can be managed successfully and relationship development and growth can be assured. But before we leave this discussion of how to successfully negotiate these issues, there is one more issue we must explore.

GENDER AND CULTURE IN RELATIONSHIPS

Communication between Women and Men

Does it sometimes seem that women and men inhabit different worlds of feelings, thoughts, and behaviors? Many researchers have suggested that is, in fact, the case. Sociolinguist Deborah Tannen (1990) suggests that boys and girls grow up in "different worlds of words" and that this difference significantly impacts communication style in adults. Boys, for example, learn to play with other boys in groups where the goal is to see who can be at the top of the status hierarchy—boys play games where they can show their status by being "better than" the other boys. Girls, by contrast, are more likely to play in smaller groups or pairs where the goal is to see how they can be more "like each other." While boys work through *status* issues in their play, the girls are more focused on *connection*. Adult males, then, who have grown up in a world focused on status, may attempt to manage conflict by showing their knowledge and experience as "experts" who have all the information needed to "solve" a problem. For men, intimacy develops from what partners "do" with each other. That may mean responding to their female partners by trying to "fix" a problem.

Adult females, having grown up in a world of connection, may attempt to manage conflict by showing how their feelings and experiences are similar to another. Women tend to focus more on feelings in managing conflict while men tend to focus more on facts. Women rarely want to be told how to "fix" a problem; instead they want to share with their partner and to hear his feelings in order to develop closeness and intimacy. So who's right and who's wrong here? Neither. But in order to understand each other and to manage conflict successfully, both women and men need to understand these differences in style.

Recognition of these differences in how men and women manage conflict can help us understand and adapt to differences in style. Engaging in direct, open discussion can reduce the frustration and misunderstanding that prevents successful conflict management. For women, this means recognizing that "solutions" to a problem are worth discussing. For men, this means discussing feelings in addition to solving problems.

Communicating across Cultures

Like the cultural differences in communication between women and men, there are communication style differences among individuals from diverse cultures both within and outside the United States. Assumptions, beliefs, and perceptions about communication and conflict must be recognized. For example, the United States is characterized as a **low-context culture**, where self-expression is valued and messages are primarily communicated verbally. In contrast, Asian cultures such as in China, Japan, Korea, and Malaysia are characterized as **high-context cultures**, where more value is placed on indirectness and social harmony and where nonverbal aspects of communication play a much more significant role (Gudykunst & Lee 2002; Hall 1976).

The consequences of the cultural lenses through which we see the world impact the ways we manage conflict as well. Where directness is valued, an individual may be more likely to stake out a position in the conflict and defend it. Where indirectness is valued, an individual may be more likely to downplay the conflict in an attempt to "save face" (Ting-Toomey & Oetzel 2002). There is never only "one right way" to send a message, yet we often evaluate another's message based on "our" way of communicating. The more we know about the communication style

low-context culture culture in which individual self-expression is valued, and messages are primarily communicated verbally (e.g., the United States)

high-context culture culture in which more value is placed on indirectness and social harmony, and nonverbal aspects of communication play a significant role (e.g., China, Japan, Korea, Malaysia)

of someone from another culture, the more opportunities we have for successfully interpreting a message's meaning and for responding appropriately to the other. It is important to understand that differences exist and to remain adaptable to the conflict participants and situation.

Additionally, cultures share different values, perceptions, and attitudes (Martin & Nakayama 2001). These orientations inform interpersonal communication. For example, different cultures emphasize the role of the family differently. The movie *My Big Fat Greek Wedding* humorously portrays the culturally based family perspectives that can complicate romantic relationships. In this movie, the bride is enmeshed in her large, culture-bound family in which all activities (work and play) involve all members of the immediate and extended family. In contrast, the groom comes from a small family in which ethnicity, religion, and extended family play a minimal role in the relationships among mother, father, and son. The ways in which these families "come to know each other" involved comedic misperceptions, misunderstandings, and social blunders. Due to our enculturation, we are likely to see romantic relationships differently (Dion & Dion 1996; Quiles 2003). As the box Cultural Links: Intercultural Romantic Relationships points out, there are similarities and differences in how romantic relationships are viewed in different cultures.

Cultural Links

Intercultural Romantic Relationships

According to Martin and Nakayama (2001), there are similarities and differences in how romantic relationships are viewed in different cultures. The similarities across cultures include the importance of openness, involvement, shared nonverbal meanings, and assessing the relationship. The differences, according to the authors, are related to distinctions between individualist and collectivist cultures. In the United States, for example, students focus on physical attraction, passion, love, and autonomy as important elements in romantic relationships. These characteristics reflect our individualist U.S. culture. In contrast, many other cultural groups focus on the importance of family acceptance of a potential partner, reflecting a more collectivist orientation. In collectivist cultures, the romantic partner's lives are likely to be much more integrated into the larger family group.

Martin and Nakayama suggest that too much individualistic orientation among Americans can be problematic when trying to balance the needs of two individuals in the relationship. An extreme individualistic perspective makes it hard for either partner to justify sacrifice or accommodation to the other. Dion and Dion (1991) suggest that the fundamental conflict of partners trying to reconcile the need for personal freedom with marital obligations is more difficult in relationships where one or both partners has an extreme individualistic orientation. These authors also suggest that individuals with an extreme individualist orientation may experience less love, care, trust, and physical attraction with their partners in their romantic relationships. In collectivist cultures, these types of relational problems are much less common.

In cross-cultural dating and romantic relationships, the degree of independence versus interdependence may be more problematic because of the difference in individualistic versus collectivist cultural orientation. Do you believe that cross-cultural romantic relationships can work? What recommendations would you give to an American who is beginning to date someone from Japan? What recommendations would you give to someone from Indonesia who is beginning to date an American?

COMPETENCE AND ETHICS IN INTERPERSONAL COMMUNICATION

*B*ecause interpersonal relationships have the greatest meaning for our personal lives and for our professional success, it is essential that we understand the ethical implications and consequences of our communication in these relationships. Because these are the most personal relationships we develop, and because we take the greatest risks in sharing ourselves with others, there also exists the greatest danger in being hurt or in hurting others. When strangers lie to us, we feel anger, but when our close friends or family members lie to us, the hurt is much deeper and lasts longer. We feel betrayed.

Ethical interpersonal communication is competent communication. When we look at another and see a unique human being who deserves consideration and care, we take the first step toward ethical interpersonal communication. When we are willing to engage in dialogue with another and to take responsibility for our com-

Community Links

Interpersonal Relationships and Community

This chart (taken from www.communitycollaboration.net/id53.htm) identifies the differences in a strong versus weak sense of community. Note how many of the differences are directly related to the nature of the interpersonal relationships that exist among community members. We cannot have strong communities without strong interpersonal relationships that are based on shared common ground and the ability to dialogue with one another. Many structured initiatives already exist, including study circles, the Public Conversations Project, the Public Dialogue Consortium, and National Issues Forum. These encourage people to gather for conversation about important community issues. However, these endeavors rest upon the assumption that we will not just talk *to* one another, but *with* one another, consequently developing relationships that will form a solid foundation for our communities.

Indicator	Strong Sense of Community	Weak Sense of Community
Sense of membership	The active participants proudly display symbols of membership in the community.	The active participants do not view themselves as a community.
Mutual importance	The active participants recognize, cherish, and support the contributions of each other.	Participants are active only because one or a few powerful persons are involved.
Shared world views	The active participants hold common beliefs and promote shared values important to them.	The active participants hold fundamentally different beliefs and values and cannot reconcile their differences.
Bonding/networking	The active participants enjoy one another and look forward to time spent together.	The active participants have no affinity for each other, and relationships are formal or superficial.
Mutual responsibility for the community	The survival and health of the community is a primary concern of all its active participants.	One or only a few persons struggle to keep the group together.

Source: From *Effective Community Mobilization, Lessons from Experience.* Published by the Department of Health and Human Services Substance Abuse and Mental Health Services Administration.

When we are willing to engage in dialogue with another, we increase the potential for a meaningful relationship.

munication, we increase the potential for meaningful and satisfying relationships. The foundation of ethical interpersonal communication is honest, authentic dialogue. **Authentic dialogue** (Buber 1970) is characterized by *empathy* and *confirmation*. It involves a willingness to become fully involved with the other, a belief in the equality of each participant, and a climate of supportive communication. Authentic dialogue adds a level of intimacy that helps develop our relationships in mutually satisfying ways. Finally, authentic dialogue tolerates difference and disagreement as part of the process of expanding knowledge of self and others. As the box Community Links: Interpersonal Relationships and Community suggests, strong communities depend upon interpersonal relationships that are based on shared common ground and the ability to dialogue.

authentic dialogue dialogue characterized by a willingness to become fully involved with the other, a belief in the equality of each participant, and a climate of supportive communication

Ethical and competent communication starts with you. You must explore your attraction to the other and your motivations and goals within the relationship. You must understand what motivates you within the relationship and what motivates the other. Ethical and competent communicators balance self-motives with others' motives. You must communicate effectively and appropriately with the other and remain flexible and adaptable as the relationship develops.

INTERPERSONAL COMMUNICATION IN COLLEGE AND LIFE

Whether you are a traditional student entering college right after high school or a nontraditional mature learner, successfully negotiating the college environment means understanding and applying the dialectics discussed in this chapter in a number of "new" interpersonal relationships. No matter what type of educational institution you are in (i.e., community college, private four-year college, public university), one of the relationships that you must negotiate is that between you and your instructor. It is hard to think of these relationships as "intimate"! Yet if you are willing to share a little of yourself with your instructors, your college success, and particularly your learning, will increase (Chen 2000). This doesn't mean you should follow your instructors around every day or ask them deeply personal questions, but you should look for opportunities to develop mentoring and mutually respectful, empathic relationships with them. Gardner and Jewler (2003) advise students to find a mentor or someone who expresses a special interest and offers meaningful support. But how do you do this? How do you develop an appropriate relationship with a professor so that you can gain the most from your academic experience? The box Communication Links: Important Characteristics of a Possible Mentor-Professor identifies some teacher characteristics that will help you find a teacher with whom you can develop a mentoring or interpersonally warm relationship.

There will be times when you need clarification and additional information on an assignment, a test, or a project. While some of your classes will take place in large lecture halls, many will be in smaller classrooms, and the climate of the class will be interactive and involve dialogue and experiential activities. The interpersonal communication dialectics we have discussed will need to be negotiated in these classes and in conversation with your instructor outside of class. Your success in college depends upon your willingness to use *confirming* responses to others both in and out of class.

Communication Links

Important Characteristics of a Possible Mentor-Professor

While there are numerous teacher characteristics related to both classroom and interpersonal communication, some characteristics are more critical than others when seeking to establish a mentoring relationship with one of your professors. Here are a series of questions that will help you search for someone to assist you.

1. **Does the professor truly listen?** All of us can hear but do not necessarily listen. Good mentors know how to actively listen, which means they are involved in the communication process and refuse to be distracted; they focus on you and can empathize with you. A true mentor is someone who listens, frequently asks questions, encourages you to say more, paraphrases your comments, and clarifies your comments by posing questions. Listeners will be nonverbally supportive; they will typically make eye contact, smile, nod their heads, and lean forward.

2. **Is the professor immediate?** *Immediacy* refers to both nonverbal and verbal behaviors that indicate that one is approachable, friendly, warm, and available for communication (see Andersen 1979). Therefore, immediate professors are people who strike you as likable and approachable. They may, for example, regularly invite students to visit during office hours or stop by as needed. Take them up on the offer!

3. **Does the professor appropriately self-disclose?** *Self-disclosure* means telling people something about yourself that they would not otherwise know. Professors who disclose appropriate information about themselves are more likely to be open to being known and getting to know others.

4. **Is the professor credible?** According to Cooper and Simonds (2003), credibility consists of competence and character. In other words, a credible professor demonstrates expert knowledge in a given field, and, at the same time, is someone you perceive as trustworthy, ethical, and concerned for others' well-being. If you want a mentor, you need someone who has the knowledge you need and who has your best interests at heart.

5. **Does the professor use power appropriately?** Teachers possess considerable power, or the ability to influence students (Barraclough & Stewart 1992). Research demonstrates that teachers can use different types of power, which, in turn, impacts student learning (see McCroskey & Richmond 1983; Richmond, McCroskey, Kearney, & Plax 1987). In order to have an effective mentoring relationship with a professor, you need someone who will advise you, not dominate you.

Your success also depends upon the degree of assertiveness you can develop. *Assertiveness* means being able to ask for what you want and not giving in to others who try to make you do something you don't want to. It means saying no when you mean no and standing up for yourself without denying other people their rights. So if you're at a party and someone shoves a beer at you and you don't want it, say so. If you've come home from a long day of work and classes and the house is a mess, tell your family that you need their help. If someone pressures you into sexual activity and you're not ready, tell him or her how you feel. Assertiveness also means that once you explain how you feel, you are not required to repeatedly justify your feelings. Once explained, your feelings should be respected. Assertive people act responsibly and accept responsibility for what they will and will not do. It means you're not afraid to speak up, ask questions, or seek information, and you make your own decisions.

If you are a college student living away from home, you will need to negotiate new relationships with roommates. For many people, this is one of the most difficult relationships they experience in college, while others find friends for life. How you negotiate these relationships in the first weeks of your first semester will be critical to your success in many of your other relationships during college. Remember, you can control your communication and your response to others. You have some of the responsibility in the relationship's outcome. Developing effective and appropriate communication strategies in your college relationships is the best practice you could possibly have for relationships later in life.

Employers today want employees who can engage in effective and appropriate communication with coworkers, supervisors, customers, and many others. What do you want in your professional relationships? You will spend a good deal of your professional life interacting with others in the workplace. Many of you will spend more hours at work than at home. The most critical interpersonal skills needed to negotiate the numerous relationships in the workplace are the same ones that are important for ensuring college success. Does intimacy play a role in relationships at work? Yes. When you are willing to appropriately and effectively share yourself with coworkers and supervisors, ask for information and assistance, and stand up for your beliefs and values and allow others to do the same, you will develop the communication skills needed to ensure success in your career and in your long-term relationships. And as box Career Links: Feedback: Essential to Interpersonal Communication in the Workplace tells us, feedback is the key to effective relationships at work.

Career Links

Feedback: Essential to Interpersonal Communication in the Workplace

Feedback refers to the verbal and nonverbal messages we offer to one another as we converse. As you listen or as others listen to you, comments, eye rolls, shrugs, or questions all serve as feedback. While feedback is essential to the process of communication in general and to interpersonal communication in particular, it is especially significant in the workplace, since it is common to receive feedback from our employer or supervisor. Here are some simple but important principles for giving and receiving feedback, drawn from a PowerPoint presentation found at www.tki.org.nz/r/assessment/.

To be useful, feedback should

- be specific, rather than general—focus on concrete, observed behaviors;
- be descriptive, not judgmental—describe what the person has done, rather than evaluate what the person has or has not done;
- focus on the consequences—tell the person how it made you feel. This cannot be argued with and allows the receiver to appreciate the consequences of his or her actions;
- be helpful—identify a behavior the person can do something about; point to areas of possible change;
- be limited—limit the amount of feedback so that it is manageable; offer two or three observations at the most;
- use sandwich psychology—start with a positive observation, offer a constructive observation, and close with a positive observation.

According to *Management for the Rest of Us* (www.mftrou.com/giving-receiving-feedback-job.html), there are seven principles for receiving feedback.

1. **Do Welcome Constructive Feedback.** Your powers of self-perception only go so far. People around you notice things, both good and bad, which you don't and you might learn from their input. There is a "virtuous circle" of feedback whereby the more you actively seek it out, the less you can hide bad behavior, and generally your feedback is better. eBay seller feedback is an excellent example of a transparent feedback process, encouraging positive behaviors.

2. **Don't Justify Your Position.** Telling the person why [their] feedback is wrong will not work.

Ever. Arguing, justifying your position, or denial are all powerful negative emotions, making the conversation more challenging than it need be. The only way for the conversation to go is downhill, with tempers flaring and insults flying.

3. **Do Accept Feedback at Face Value.** Although the feedback might feel like a personal insult, challenging your whole identity, keep some perspective. The feedback relates to specific instances, in one part of your life, AND now you know about it, you have the opportunity to do something about it.

4. **Don't Ruminate on Feedback.** Only cows need ruminate before they digest. Chewing over feedback again and again will not make it clearer or easier to understand, particularly if the feedback is less than glowing. Avoid the temptation to reenact the conversation to a friend as this only makes you feel ten times worse. Do talk about it with someone else, but make sure you're emotionally detached first.

5. **Do Evaluate Feedback Before Responding.** Feedback often tells you more about the person saying it than it does about you. For example, a person who says you never praise his or her work might have difficulty evaluating his or her work by him- or herself. Teaching this person to give him- or herself "marks out of ten" for his or her own work may be a better approach than simply praising him or her ad nauseam. In the long run, you'll be giving him or her a more powerful boost to his or her self-esteem.

6. **Don't Throw Your Toys from the Pushchair.** Sulking, stonewalling, or withdrawing from the person giving the feedback is childish. If need be, give yourself some space from the person, allowing you to calm down and deal with the feedback, and person, as a rational adult.

7. **Do Make Your Choice How to Use the Feedback.** Feedback can be a gift allowing you to grow and develop as a person, in a job, or in a relationship. But some feedback is downright useless and best ignored. Yes, ignored. It is ultimately your choice how to act, or not, upon feedback received.

SUMMARY

Interpersonal communication can be defined as another communication context involving two persons in face-to-face interaction or, more appropriately, as a developmental process involving increasing intimacy in developing a unique, personal set of rules for interaction with another. In this chapter, we have identified concepts important to your understanding of effective interpersonal communication:

- Increasing the intimacy within a relationship involves moving from cultural-level rules to sociological-level rules to psychological-level rules for appropriate behavior in the relationship.
- *Intimacy* refers to our risk-taking within the relationship as we self-disclose more feelings, beliefs, values, dreams, and expectations for the other, the relationship, and ourselves.
- We are attracted to certain others based on physical characteristics, similar attitudes and values, similar activities, and physical proximity.
- Abraham Maslow developed a hierarchy of needs that suggests we are motivated by various needs to create and maintain relationships; these needs include physiological, safety, love and belonging, self-esteem and respect, and self-actualization.
- William Schutz identified three basic needs that motivate individuals: inclusion, affection, and a degree of control and predictability in our lives.
- Relationships develop through five stages as intimacy is increased: initiating, experimenting, intensifying, integrating, and bonding.
- Relationship dissolution also involves five stages: differentiating, circumscribing, stagnating, avoiding, and terminating.
- The ability of the parties to negotiate a variety of dialectics will significantly impact each partner's willingness to grow together, including complementary versus symmetrical relationships, the degree of independence of each party, what constitutes appropriate and effective messages within the relationship, and the degree of flexibility required to keep the relationship functioning.
- Conflict is inevitable in relationships, but it can be managed successfully.
- Gender and cultural factors impact how we develop relationships and what we expect from ourselves and from the other in the relationship.
- Ethical issues play a critical role in interpersonal relationships because of the increased risks attached to both parties when intimacy increases between the partners.
- To create and maintain effective interpersonal relationships, the partners must be more sensitive to and flexible in responding to the unique needs and expectations of the self and the other.
- Ethical and effective interpersonal relationships are characterized by open, continuous dialogue in the give-and-take between the partners.

Questions for Discussion

1. What do you think are the most important "intimacy behaviors" between close friends? Roommates? Lovers?
2. Do you think it is possible to end a relationship without engaging in angry accusations? Can "old lovers" become "new friends"?
3. Consider the "little white lie" and its role in relationship development and dissolution. Are we more apt to tell them during the first stages of relationship development or when the relationship is more fully developed? Are little white lies ever appropriate? Why or why not?

EXERCISES

1. Practice with "I" messages. Imagine that you are talking with someone who has really irritated you. First, write out your messages as a "you" statement. Then convert them to "I" messages, keeping in mind Ellis's "five ways to say 'I'" ideas. Be sure to state what you observe, how you feel, and what you want in your message.

2. Using Miller and Steinberg's three levels of "rules" for interpersonal communication, think of a primary relationship that you are currently involved in (i.e., son or daughter, employee, parent, student, etc.) and give examples of cultural, sociological, and psychological rules that govern your communication and behavior.

KEY TERMS

Interpersonal (dyadic) communication

Developmental approach

Intimacy

Attraction

Physiological needs

Safety and security needs

Love and belonging needs

Self-esteem needs

Knowledge and understanding
  needs
Aesthetic needs
Self-actualization needs
Initiating stage
Social anxiety
Social comparison
Experimenting stage
Phatic communication
Intensifying stage
Integrating stage
Bonding stage
Dialectics
Complementary relationships
Symmetrical relationships

Independent relationships
Dependent relationships
Interdependent relationships
Disconfirming messages
Confirming messages
Rejection messages
Defensive climates
Supportive climates
Nonassertiveness
Assertiveness
Aggressiveness
Rigidity
Flexibility
Interaction
Domination

Passivity
Differentiating stage
Circumscribing stage
Stagnating stage
Avoiding stage
Terminating stage
Relational dissolution model
Intrapsychic phase
Dyadic phase
Social phase
Grave-dressing phase
Conflict
Low-context culture
High-context culture
Authentic dialogue

◎ REFERENCES

Adams, R. G., Blieszner, R., and DeVries, B. 2000. Definitions of friendship in the third age: Age, gender, and study location effects. *Journal of Aging Studies* 14(1):117–134.

Andersen, J. 1979. The relationship between teacher immediacy and teaching effectiveness. In *Communication yearbook 3*, ed., D. Nimmo. 543–561. New Brunswick, NJ: Transaction Books.

Barraclough, R. A., and Stewart, R. A. 1992. Power and control: Social science perspectives. In *Power in the classroom: Communication, control, and concern*, eds., V. P. Richmond and J. C. McCroskey, 1–18. Hillsdale, NJ: Erlbaum.

Buber, M. 1970. *I and thou*. Trans. W. Kaufmann. NY: Scribner.

Chen, Z. J. 2000. The impact of teacher-student relationships on college students' learning: Exploring organizational cultures in the classroom. *Communication Quarterly* 48(2):76–84.

Collier, M. J. 1996. Communication competence problematics in ethnic friendships. *Communication Monographs* 63(4):314–337.

Cooper, P. J., and Simonds, C. J. 2003. *Communication for the classroom teacher*. 7th ed. Boston: Allyn & Bacon.

Dion, K. K., and Dion, K. L. 1991. Psychological individualism and romantic love. *Journal of Social Behavior and Personality* 6:17–33.

Dion, K. K., and Dion, K. L. 1996. Cultural perspectives on romantic love. *Personal Relationships* 3:5–19.

Duck, S. W. 1982. A topography of relationship disengagement and dissolution. In *Personal relationships 4: Dissolving personal relationships*, ed., S. W. Duck, 1–30. London: Academic Press.

Elbedour, S., Shulman, S., and Peri, K. 1997. Adolescent intimacy: A cross-cultural study. *Journal of Cross-Cultural Psychology* 28:5.

Ellis, D. 2000. *Becoming a master student*. 9th ed. Boston: Houghton Mifflin.

Gardner, J. N., and Jewler, A. J. 2003. *Your college experience: Strategies for success*. 5th ed. Belmont, CA: Wadsworth.

Goodwin, R., and Lee, I. 1994. Taboo topics among Chinese and English friends: A cross-cultural comparison. *Journal of Cross-Cultural Psychology* 25(3):325.

Gudykunst, W. B., and Lee, C. M. 2002. Cross-cultural communication theories. In *Handbook of international and intercultural communication,* 2nd ed., eds. W. B. Gudykunst and B. Moody, 25–50. Thousand Oaks, CA: Sage.

Hall, E. T. 1976. *Beyond culture.* Garden City, NY: Doubleday/Anchor.

Hocker, J. L., and Wilmot, W. W. 1997. *Interpersonal conflict.* 5th ed. New York: McGraw-Hill.

Knapp, M., and Vangelisti, A. L. 1992. *Interpersonal communication and human relationships.* 2nd ed. Boston: Allyn & Bacon.

Malinowski, B. 1923. The problem of meaning in primitive languages. In *The meaning of meaning: A study of the influence of language upon thought and the science of symbolism,* eds., C. K. Ogden and I. A. Richards, 451 510. London: Routledge & Kegan Paul.

Martin, J. N., and Nakayama, T. K. 2001. *Experiencing intercultural communication: An introduction.* Mountain View, CA: Mayfield.

Maslow, A. H. 1970. *Motivation and personality.* 2nd ed. New York: Harper & Row.

McCroskey, J. C., and Richmond, V. P. 1983. Power in the classroom I: Teacher and student perceptions. *Communication Education* 32:175–184.

Meyer, L. H., Park, H., Grento-Scheyer, M., Schwartz, L. S., and Harry, B., eds. 1998. *Making friends: The Influences of culture and development.* Baltimore, MD: Paul H. Brookes.

Miller, G. R., and Steinberg, M. 1975. *Between people: A new analysis of interpersonal communication.* Chicago: Science Research Associates.

Novak A. A., ed. 1993. *Friendships and community connections between people with and without developmental disabilities.* Baltimore, MD: Paul H. Brookes.

Quiles, J. A. 2003. Romantic behaviors of university students: A cross-cultural and gender analysis in Puerto Rico and the United States. *College Student Journal* 37(3):354–367. Retrieved February 3, 2004, from www.findarticles .com/cf_dls/m0FCR/3_37/108836901/p1/article.jhtml.

Richmond, V. P., McCroskey, J. C., Kearney, P., and Plax, T. G. 1987. Power in the classroom VII: Linking behavior alteration techniques to cognitive learning. *Communication Education* 36:1–12.

Schutz, W. 1958. *Firo: A three-dimensional theory of interpersonal behavior.* New York: Holt, Rinehart & Winston.

Spitzberg, B., and Cupach, W. 1984. *Interpersonal communication competence.* Newbury Park, CA: Sage.

Stewart, J. 1977. *Bridges not walls.* 3d. ed. New York: McGraw-Hill.

Tannen, D. 1990. *You just don't understand: Women and men in conversation.* New York: Balantine.

Ting-Toomey, S., and Oetzel, J. G. 2002. Cross-cultural face concerns and conflict styles. In *Handbook of international and intercultural communication,* 2nd ed., eds., W. B. Gudykunst and B. Moody, 143–164. Thousand Oaks, CA: Sage.

Urban Institute. February 2000. Millions still facing homelessness in a booming economy. Retrieved January 28, 2004, from www.urban.org/url.cfm? ID=900050.

You, H. S., and Malley-Morrison, K. 2000. Young adult attachment styles and intimate relationships with close friends: A cross-cultural study of Korean and Caucasian Americans. *Journal of Cross-Cultural Psychology* 31(4):528–534.

CHAPTER 8

Applying Interpersonal Communication
Principles and Practice

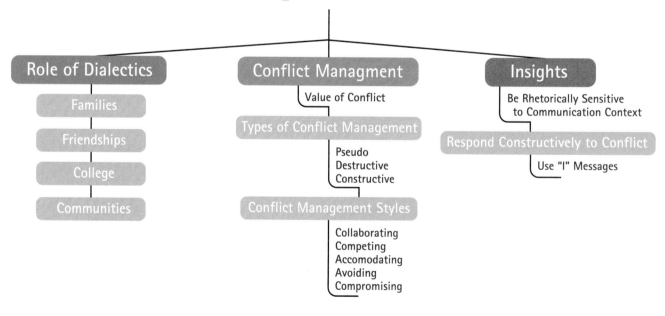

Role of Dialectics
- Families
- Friendships
- College
- Communities

Conflict Managment
- Value of Conflict

Types of Conflict Management
- Pseudo
- Destructive
- Constructive

Conflict Management Styles
- Collaborating
- Competing
- Accomodating
- Avoiding
- Compromising

Insights
- Be Rhetorically Sensitive to Communication Context
- Respond Constructively to Conflict
  - Use "I" Messages

Knowledge Checklist

✓ To understand the role of interpersonal communication (IPC) dialectics in various relational contexts

✓ To utilize understanding of intercultural differences and expectations to appropriate interpersonal relationship development

✓ To understand and appreciate rhetorically sensitive interpersonal communication skills

✓ To understand the various approaches to conflict management

✓ To develop effective conflict-management skills in various interpersonal contexts

THE "REALITY" OF RELATIONSHIPS

Because interpersonal relationships are so important to us—whether within our families, friendships, intimate partnerships, or workplaces—many of us spend our lives searching for information that will help us create the "perfect" relationship. Go into any bookstore and you will find entire sections dedicated to books that will help us attract the perfect partner, develop lifelong friendships, or deal with a nasty boss. Television sitcoms show us "life" in an enormous variety of "normal" or "dysfunctional" relationships, depending on your point of view. One of the most recent phenomena to hit television is the so-called reality show, where seemingly random strangers are stuck together in one situation or another and must "survive" the season. Have you ever noticed, though, that the purpose of the show is never to have the strangers develop positive, healthy interpersonal relationships? These shows find every way possible to create competition, jealousy, conflict, and dissatisfaction among the participants. And if the "survival" of strangers together isn't bad enough, you can now potentially find and marry the man or woman of your dreams, all on television. Is the ultimate goal of these shows to find true love and long-lasting happiness in a committed partnership? Most of us don't believe so—especially when the title of the show is something like *How to Marry a Millionaire*.

Yet despite reality shows dominating in the media, healthy and long-lasting interpersonal relationships in a variety of contexts are possible. In order to develop and maintain these healthy relationships, however, we must understand how to balance the interpersonal dialectics discussed in the last chapter in each of the following contexts.

INTERPERSONAL DIALECTICS AND FAMILIES

There are two types of families: those we are born into and those we create. The families we are born into become the fundamental building blocks of who we are today. The patterns of interaction within our families are the models for the families we create. Think about the type of relationship your parents or primary caregivers modeled for you. Where did these individuals fall on the complementary/symmetrical dimension? How dependent/independent/interdependent was their relationship? What was the nature of the confirming or disconfirming communication within your family unit? Would you characterize the climate in your family as mostly supportive or mostly defensive? What degree of assertiveness did your parents or caregivers communicate to you, to each other, to others outside the immediate family? Were the rules in your family somewhat rigid or more flexible and changeable over time? Overall, was there a sense of a dominant hierarchy within your family or a feeling of more equal participation among all members?

Families model and form interpersonal communication practice.

It is important to remember that no single family dynamic is necessarily better than another. The key to successful and healthy family relationships is the agreement and cooperation among its members about these important dialectics. Healthy family communication is characterized by emotional and physical support between the members—this is a "functional" family. In a "dysfunctional" family, communication is closed, and members are not allowed to express their feelings, needs, hopes, fears, and dreams to each other.

The model your "first" family communicated to you impacts your "second," or created, family. How you approach your romantic relationships and future long-term partnerships will, to some extent, be adapted from this first model. Make a list of your basic expectations for your romantic relationships. Does your list consist primarily of what you want your romantic partner to do and be for you? Does your list include what you want your partner to allow you to do and be for him or her? As we discussed in the last chapter, it is important to remember that men and women may not always have the same expectations for the relationship, particularly in terms of "the talk" that is used to negotiate healthy and long-term support of each other. Men are more likely to suppress feelings and to not talk about relationships, and this is not always healthy.

Anyone who suppresses feelings may ultimately jeopardize their physical health and, ultimately, a relationship. Yet disclosing feelings also has risks. Self-disclosure must be appropriate to the relationship and the immediate situation. However, honestly expressing your feelings can potentially add multiple benefits to the relationship. You confirm both yourself and the other through your honesty; you set an example for the climate in the relationship with supportive and honest self-disclosure; you can become more aware of your own strengths and weaknesses in communication and of your own feelings through self-disclosure; and you can be proactive in managing conflict within the relationship.

INTERPERSONAL DIALECTICS AND FRIENDSHIPS

We meet any number of other people on any given day. How is it that some of these people become our friends? What differentiates an "acquaintance" and a "friend"? We run into acquaintances and have a chat. We seek out friends because we like to be with them. We communicate, for the most part, only superficially with acquaintances; we self-disclose more deeply to our friends. The degree of trust that operates in a true friendship impacts how we accept each other, support each other, and even criticize each other. A strong trusting friendship allows us to criticize each other when needed, because we know the friendship can survive honest critical assessment. As the friendship moves from acquaintanceship into true friendship, we must work out important relational dialectics. Must we think alike on all things, or can we complement each other with our unique habits, quirks, and personalities? Do we have to see each other every day? Week? Year? In what ways do we need our true friends to communicate confirmation? How do we show our support to one another? Will this friendship be characterized by one person being more dominant and the other more passive? How do we negotiate each of these characteristics of the relationship?

The most effective and healthy friendships are characterized by understanding about these dialectics. Notice that we did not say "talking about" these dialectics. Some friendships seem to just naturally move into a level of comfort with the way the dialectics emerge, without the need to speak about them directly. In others, however, the friends may freely talk about expectations and comfort about some aspect of a dialectic. In both of these types of friendships, one of the most important skills for both parties in developing the health of the relationship is assertiveness. Remember that assertiveness is the ability to express your rights or views without judging the rights or views of another. When you are assertive, you do not become overly sensitive to the other's point of view, and you don't take disagreements personally. You do not make *your* assertions personal or judgmental about the other. When both parties in a friendship are assertive, they can remain friends even through times of disagreement about a topic, issue, or situation.

INTERPERSONAL DIALECTICS AND COLLEGE

*W*hether you are entering college right after high school or returning after several years, there is a good chance that you will develop friendships and even romantic relationships during this time. These interpersonal relationships in the college context are unique in that you are exposed to a much more rich and varied group of individuals. Because many campuses are composed of persons from a wide variety of cultural, ethnic, and geographically varied origins, it may be more challenging to develop friendships and/or romantic relationships.

Expectations for appropriateness in interpersonal relationships are strongly influenced by culture. As we have discussed earlier in this text, culture is a pattern of perceptions, values, and behaviors shared by a group of people. In other words, culture is the unique way in which we engage in the everyday behaviors—such as eating, socializing, and creating and maintaining relationships—as American, Chinese, or French; male or female; white or Hispanic; and so on. Yet cultures are not homogeneous; they are dynamic and heterogeneous. This means that every individual in a cultural group is also unique. Race, gender, class, and sexual orientation provide additional layers of culture that impact the ways each of us negotiate the world we live in.

Cultural characteristics impact the interpersonal dialectics we have discussed. Martin and Nakayama (2001) argue that the values of a cultural group represent a worldview, a particular way of looking at the world. They distinguish between individualistic and collectivist cultural worldviews. **Individualistic cultures** place more importance on the individual within certain types of relationships. These cultures value direct, open forms of communication. **Collectivist cultures** value less direct communication and tend to avoid conflict. These cultures emphasize the importance of the group (i.e., family, work, or social) and value the group's success rather than any individual in that group. Later in this text, we discuss several cultural influences on group communication.

Dutch social psychologist Geert Hofstede (1980) has identified a number of distinctions between cultural groups. One of them refers to the long- or short-term orientation to life. Some individualist cultures are more likely to value a "short-term orientation" to life. These cultures emphasize the importance of quick results and of finding an immediate solution. Some Americans, for example, are more likely to want to establish relationships quickly by "telling all" about themselves in the first few interactions.

individualistic cultures cultures that place more importance on the individual within certain types of relationships; value direct, open communication

collectivist cultures cultures that emphasize the importance of the group; value less direct communication and tend to avoid conflict situations

Cultural Links

Intercultural Relationships on Campus

Ask yourself the following questions concerning your potential to establish a face-to-face friendship with someone from another race or culture:

1. Would you invite a student from another country who is in one of your classes to join you for lunch? How would you go about extending the invitation? Would you just jump right in and ask or would you need to talk to them informally over a number of weeks?

2. If you were paired as a research partner for a class project with a person of another race or ethnicity, how would you approach the assigned task? Would you try to get to know a little bit about the person first, or just start working on the project? How would you know whether this person would be a good partner for the project?

3. You have identified a group on campus that you want to join. There are a dozen people from several different racial and ethnic groups in the room. You show up for the first meeting, and the group's leader asks everyone to introduce themselves and to include information such as name, class in school, major, hometown, and so on. What information would you add to your introduction? Would you be likely to return to the group for a second meeting? Why or why not?

In contrast, collectivist cultures are more likely to value a long-term orientation to life. They emphasize slowly developing relationships over time, tenaciously working toward long-term goals, and practicing the virtue of thrift. What do you think it means to be "thrifty" in developing and maintaining interpersonal relationships? Use the questions in the box Cultural Links: Intercultural Relationships on Campus to assess your ability to create healthy intercultural relationships. In addition, the box Computer Links: Expanding Your Knowledge of Cultures provides websites useful for broadening your knowledge of other cultures and establishing cross-cultural friendships.

Computer Links

Expanding Your Knowledge of Cultures

While many of you will meet individuals from across the world in your classes or jobs, there are many other ways to expand your knowledge of other cultures and establish cross-cultural friendships. Several online sites let you correspond with individuals around the world. Here are two examples:

1. Europa Pages (www.europa-pages.com/penpal_form.html): "A great way to make friends around the world and to practice your language skills is to get an international pen friend. [This] website [offers] this FREE service to everyone: students wishing to meet other language learners, teachers wanting to exchange ideas, or anyone keen to make new contacts in other countries."

2. Pen Pal Party (www.penpalparty.com/): Also offers opportunities to meet and establish friendships with others around the world.

If you were interested in establishing an online friendship that crosses cultural boundaries, how would you introduce yourself online?

Another unique communication context operating in college concerns the relationships among faculty, staff, and students. As we will discuss later in this text, the college or campus is a unique organization with a hierarchy of power relationships. At a very basic level, instructors have the power to assign you a grade for the value of your work in their classes. Do you think it is appropriate to develop a friendship with an instructor? What should be the boundaries for appropriate interpersonal relationships? Some faculty like to have students call them by their first names and are willing to tell students about their background and experience, and even disclose some information about their life history; other faculty are not. Which style are you most comfortable with? Is it appropriate for you to socialize with a faculty member outside the classroom? See the box Communication Links: So, What Do You Call Your Professor? for insight into this issue.

◎ Communication Links

So, What Do You Call Your Professor?

When one of your authors was an undergraduate, professors referred to students as "Mr.," "Miss," or "Mrs." This was before the introduction of "Ms." In response, students used formal address ("Mr.," "Mrs.," or "Dr.") when speaking to or about their professors. However, these cultural guidelines are no longer as clear as they once were. College students and professors often refer to one another by first names. Many instructors, including your authors, actually encourage students to use their first names. However, you may not have such clear signals from your instructors. Moreover, depending on the type of institution you attend, teachers may range from graduate students to distinguished professors. Here are some suggestions to assist you in deciding how to address your teachers:

1. Always take your lead from the teacher. If you are invited to use your teacher's first name, do so if you feel comfortable. If not, you can explain your reluctance at an appropriate moment. For example, when one of your authors, David, said to a student with whom he had a long-term relationship, "When are you going to call me David instead of Dr. Worley?" she replied, "You've worked so hard for that title, and I want you to know that I respect you and what you've done to become a doctor." This was a kind and appropriate way for the student to explain her reluctance to use David's first name.

2. If you are unsure of how your teacher prefers to be addressed, be more formal and use instructors' titles, if you know them. If they hold a doctoral degree (PhD, PsyD, EdD), it's always best to use the title "Dr." If you're unsure whether they hold a doctoral degree, check your school's directory, or visit the instructor's or department's website and find out. Failing all else, use the title "Professor," because this can be used in a more general sense. While it may not matter all, some of your instructors who hold a doctoral degree may be insulted if you refer to them as "Mr." or "Ms.," so unless you know for sure that these titles are acceptable, avoid them.

3. If you're still unsure, ask. For example, you may say something like, "I have not had an opportunity to find out how you prefer to be addressed, and I don't want to be insensitive, so how do you prefer students to address you?" This is a wise communication choice when addressing your professors, and it's good practice for the working world and a very useful general principle of communication. When in doubt, simply and politely ask.

Your relationship with your advisor can be one of the most important during your college career.

Your campus may assign you to an advisor within your major's department, and this person assists you in identifying classes that meet your major's requirements. What other expectations do you have for your advisor? Is it important for this person to know something about you personally in order to more effectively provide counsel on your career or life goals? Is it important for you to know something about your advisor's experience and credibility in order to accurately assess his or her advice? Like most communication situations on your campus, the faculty–student communication context will be varied and heterogeneous. In other words, some faculty may be more willing than others to know and understand you and to disclose information about themselves. The box Campus Links: Choosing an Academic Advisor offers some additional insights about advising and advisors. (You may also access information on advising at the National Academic Advising Association (NACADA) Clearinghouse of Advising Resources website at www.nacada.ksu.edu/Clearinghouse/AdvisingIssues/Core-Values.htm).

Campus Links

Choosing an Academic Advisor

While you may be initially assigned an academic advisor, you will probably have an opportunity to select one during your college experience. How do you select a sound, helpful advisor? Consider this information in choosing and working with your academic advisor.

First, advisors hold core values, as explained by the National Academic Advising Association. One of these values is particularly important for you to consider:

Advisors are responsible to the individuals they advise. Academic advisors work to strengthen the importance, dignity, potential, and unique nature of each individual within the academic setting. Advisors' work is guided by their beliefs that students

- have diverse backgrounds that can include different ethnic, racial, domestic, and international communities; sexual orientations; ages; gender and gender identities; physical, emotional, and psychological abilities; political, religious, and educational beliefs;
- hold their own beliefs and opinions;
- are responsible for their own behaviors and the outcomes of those behaviors;
- can be successful based upon their individual goals and efforts;
- have a desire to learn;
- have learning needs that vary based upon individual skills, goals, responsibilities, and experiences;
- use a variety of techniques and technologies to navigate their world.

In support of these beliefs, the cooperative efforts of all who advise include, but are not limited to, providing accurate and timely information, communicating in useful and efficient ways, maintaining regular office hours, and offering varied contact modes.

Advising, as part of the educational process, involves helping students develop a realistic self-perception and successfully transition to the postsecondary institution. Advisors encourage, respect, and assist students in establishing their goals and objectives. Advisors seek to gain the trust of their students and strive to honor students' expectations of academic advising and its importance in their lives.

George D. Kuh, author of *Student Success in College*, states,

> *Academic advisors can play an integral role in promoting student success by assisting students in ways that encourage them to engage in the right kinds of activities, inside and outside the classroom. Advisors are especially important because they are among the first people new students encounter and should see regularly during their first year. (Kuh 2006)*

He adds that there are four important common themes regarding advising that arise from his Documenting Effective Educational Practices (DEEP) study of twenty schools, which you may wish to consider in choosing and working with your advisor:

1. **Advisors know their students well.** Subscribing to a talent development perspective on education, advisors believe their primary task is to help change students for the better by making certain they take full advantage of the institution's resources for learning. To do this, many advisors go to unusual lengths to learn as much as they can about their students—where they are from, their aspirations and talents, and when and where they need help.

2. **Advisors strive for meaningful interactions with students.** Another way advisors contribute to the quality of student learning and campus life is by helping to develop, support, and participate in mentoring programs. Mentee–mentor relationships help create close connections with one or more key persons, relationships that are especially important for students in underrepresented groups on campus. Also, because connecting *early* with advisees is essential, advisors at DEEP schools are involved in planning and delivering first-year orientation programs and experiences.

3. **Advisors help students identify pathways to academic and social success.** In addition to assisting students with choosing the right courses, advisors encourage students to take advantage of the learning and personal opportunities their school makes available. They make a point of asking students to apply what they are learning in their classes to real-life issues, thereby enhancing student learning in ways that many academic courses alone may not be able to accomplish. Among the high-quality cocurricular experiences that have powerful positive effects on students and their success are service learning, study abroad, civic engagement, internships, and experiential learning activi-

ties. Another key to navigating college effectively is for students to learn the campus culture—the traditions, rituals, and practices that communicate how and why things are done at their school.

4. **Advising and student success is considered a tag team activity.** At high-performing schools, the educational and personal development goals of advising are shared across multiple partners, not just the person "assigned" this task. Faculty, student affairs staff, and mentors along with professional academic advisors make up the multiple early alert and safety net systems for students in place at DEEP schools—particularly for students who institutional research studies indicate may be at risk of dropping out. Such team approaches go a long way toward keeping students from falling through the cracks and getting students the information they need when they need it.

Source: Excerpt from "Thinking DEEPly about academic advising and student engagement," by George D. Kuh from *Academic Advising Today*, June 2006, 29, 1, 3. Reprinted by permission of the National Academic Advising Association (NACADA) and the author.

INTERPERSONAL DIALECTICS AND COMMUNITIES

*M*any colleges today are attempting to incorporate a variety of service learning or problem-based learning initiatives into the life of the campus and surrounding community. Many of these initiatives have been sponsored by the American Association of Colleges and Universities (AAC&U). The AAC&U believes that every student deserves to receive a "liberal education," which they define as

> one that prepares us to live responsible, productive, and creative lives in a dramatically changing world. It is an education that fosters a well-grounded intellectual resilience, a disposition toward lifelong learning, and an acceptance of responsibility for the ethical consequences of our ideas and actions. Liberal education requires that we understand the foundations of knowledge and inquiry about nature, culture and society; that we master core skills of perception, analysis, and expression; that we cultivate a respect for truth; that we recognize the importance of historical and cultural context; and that we explore connections among formal learning, citizenship, and service to our communities. (Adopted by the Board of Directors of the Association of American Colleges & Universities, October 1998)

Liberal education is a student-learning and problem-centered approach to preparing students for life beyond the campus, preparing them for the issues of society and the workplace: "Quality liberal education prepares students for active participation in the private and public sectors, in a diverse democracy, and in an even more diverse community. It has the strongest impact when studies reach beyond the classroom to the larger community, asking students to apply their developing analytical skills and ethical judgment to concrete problems in the world around them, and to connect theory with the insights gained in practice" (*Greater*

As a student, your work may move beyond the classroom to engage in the life of your surrounding community.

Expectations 2002, p. 26). The liberal education approach eliminates the artificial distinctions between studies deemed "liberal" (i.e., unrelated to job training) and "practical" (assumed to be related to a job). "A liberal education is practical because it develops just those capacities needed by every thinking adult: analytical skills, effective communication, practical intelligence, ethical judgment, and social responsibility" (p. 26). To clarify, the concept of a liberal education should not be confused with a liberal arts college. Any two-year community college, four-year private college, four-year public university, research-intensive university offering advanced degrees, or any other can offer students a liberal education.

Practically speaking, this means that student work moves beyond the classroom (either utilizing problem-based cases in classrooms or through service-learning projects in the community) to engage in the life of the community in which the campus resides. Whether your campus has this type of initiative or not, you will in your lifetime become a member of some collective community. You may be a parent negotiating with teachers and administrators in your child's school. You may purchase a house and find yourself confronted by a reassessment of property values. You may be a member of a church that has undertaken a project to assist a less-privileged group within the community. Your ability to be sensitive to the interpersonal dialectics operating within this communication context will be regularly tested. The box Community Links: Teaching Tolerance provides a resource for community projects that can enhance trust and relationships among diverse groups with different interests.

◎ Community Links

Teaching Tolerance

The Southern Poverty Law Center was founded in 1971 as a small civil rights law firm. Today, the Center is internationally known for its tolerance education programs, its legal victories against white supremacists, and its tracking of hate groups. To combat the causes of hate, in 1991 the Center established Teaching Tolerance, an educational program to help K–12 teachers foster respect and understanding in the classroom. Teaching Tolerance is now one of the nation's leading providers of antibias resources, both in print and online. Its award-winning magazine is distributed free twice a year to more than 500,000 educators, and its free innovative multimedia kits are provided to thousands of schools and community groups.

Tolerance.org is an online destination for those wanting to dismantle bigotry and promote diversity in their communities. Launched in 2001, Tolerance.org offers a wide variety of resources to support antibias activism. Its outreach component provides on-site help to concerned individuals and organizations who are working for unity in their communities.

Information, community activist activities, and updates on programs around the world dedicated to creating greater understanding and sensitivity to our expanding diversity can be found at www.splcenter.org/center/about.jsp. This is a great resource for developing service-learning activities in your classrooms, service organizations, or churches.

CONFLICT MANAGEMENT IN INTERPERSONAL RELATIONSHIPS

The Value of Conflict

We cannot, nor should we, try to avoid all conflict. Avoiding conflict will not make problems go away. Let us return to the definition of *conflict* we developed in Chapter 7. First, conflict is an *expressed struggle*. This means that both parties in a conflict must recognize the conflict and communicate to the other about the conflict. Next, the conflict occurs between *interconnected* individuals. It can hardly be a conflict if the communication occurs between complete strangers who will never see each other again after their brief interaction. The parties' interconnectedness implies that these individuals mean something to each other. The relationship could be between parent and child, life partners, best friends, boss and subordinate, coworkers, teacher and student, or any configuration where the relationship matters to the parties. Finally, conflict exists because the parties see incompatibility between one person's success and another's: If I reach my goal in this situation, you cannot reach yours. You see my success as interfering with your success. We perceive that any win by one of us will be at the expense of the other. At the heart of the conflict is the critical role of *perception*, as we discussed in Chapter 3. We may be able to find a solution that meets both parties' needs, but our perceptions prevent us from seeing that as a possibility.

From the outset, we must understand that conflict has the potential to enhance the health and growth of our interpersonal relationships. If managed effectively, our relationships grow and prosper, becoming healthy, long-term, and satisfying. The absence of conflict is not healthy for any relationship.

Pseudo-, Destructive, Constructive Conflict

Conflict is inevitable but not inevitably destructive. Some conflicts are actually only perceptual misunderstandings. **Pseudo-conflict** occurs when the parties are actually in agreement, but perceptions and misunderstanding prevents them from seeing the areas of agreement and compatibility. One or more parties mistakenly believe that goal attainment is impossible for all. Pseudo-conflict is easy to resolve if the parties are rhetorically sensitive to the misunderstanding. If the parties are not willing to listen to each other, however, the escalation intensifies.

Destructive conflict occurs when we allow the communication to escalate and spiral out of control. Wilmot and Hocker (2001) characterize destructive conflict as that which escalates; encourages each party to retaliate against the others; causes one or more individuals to dominate and compete with others; and increases the potential for defensiveness, inflexibility, and cross-complaints. The aim becomes to hurt another. Destructive conflict is both unethical and incompetent communication.

pseudo-conflict situation in which the parties are actually in agreement, but perceptions and misunderstanding prevent them from seeing the areas of agreement and compatibility

destructive conflict conflict in which communication escalates, and hurting one another becomes the goal

Obviously, there are numerous reasons why conflict can emerge in relationships. Smith and Walter (1995) identify several roadblocks that can impede the academic success of adult learners, many of which can also induce conflict:

- Family resentment because of frequent absence from home
- Resentment from coworkers because of absences and trying to improve one's self or one's skill
- Resistance from a spouse who doesn't support a career change, the costs of money or time invested in attending college, or the potential for developing new friends or life directions

Acknowledging that conflict exists is one of the first steps in preventing the escalation of destructive conflict. This expression of the conflict is important. The box Career Links: 5 Steps to Reduce Conflict at Work provides some examples of ways that you can prevent conflict from escalating into a "win at all costs" war of words. You may find these skills valuable as you negotiate problems with your roommate or juggle the multiple demands of being a student, spouse, and parent, since these and other issues can create conflict in relationships.

Career Links

5 Steps to Reduce Conflict at Work
by Margot Robinson

Conflict is in everyone's life. But it's very hard to work in an environment where conflict exists. First of all, you're not very excited to get out of bed in the morning and go to work. Second, unresolved conflict can cause health problems due to stress.

So what can you do about it? Rethink how you handle conflict. It might be difficult to implement at first, but if you and your coworkers practice the following five steps, you'll enjoy work more by minimizing destructive conflict.

Step One: Honor the diversity of others' opinions. Most people have a different opinion than yours. What tends to happen is we seek out only those who have the same opinion as we do. Then we create "groupthink." That means that the same thing happens again and again. If we can look at situations with a different eye, we not only grow and stretch but our service/product improves.

Step Two: Avoid put-downs, blaming others, and labeling. There's no such thing as a perfect person. We all make mistakes. But what happens when we do make mistakes is we learn from them and move on. If we are put down for our mistakes and made to look stupid in the eyes of others, we get very angry. That creates a good breeding ground for conflict.

Have you ever thought that when we put someone else down, we are trying to make ourselves look better? Most people with low self-esteem do this frequently. In the long run we are the ones who won't look good. So put-downs, blaming, and labeling only make things worse.

Step Three: Listen until the other person is finished. Listening is a skill that we all need to develop. Stephen Covey, author of *Seven Habits of Highly Effective People,* says we listen not to understand but to answer. In a conflict situation, we only want to be heard. We don't care how the other person thinks. It is the "me" who we think is the most important. Conflicts can be resolved faster if both parties listen to the other person.

Step Four: When communicating in a conflict situation, use "I" statements like "I think . . . I feel . . . I need." When we use "you" statements, we put the other party on the defense. Each person in a conflict situation needs to own their feelings and opinions and let other people speak for themselves. When we get upset, we have a tendency to say something like, "You make me so mad!" or "You don't know what you are doing." If a conflict situation gets out of hand, usually someone is on the defense. Become aware of the messages that are being given.

When listening, try to hear all the messages from your heart. Listening from the heart creates compassion and will soften any conflict. Saying something like, "Bless your heart" verbally or nonverbally will make a conflict situation lessen.

Step Five: Give yourself permission to state your needs. No one is a mind reader. I hear over and over from unhappy employees, "Well he should have known what I wanted!" Well, he probably can't read your mind! Only you can tell him what's on your mind.

If your normal style is a talker, during conflict you'll naturally talk faster and put a lot more emotion in the words being spoken. Why not invite that other person to speak? Listen to what their thoughts and needs are. If your normal style is to be more quiet, take a risk and let the other party know what your ideas are. This will build trust that will help each of you come to a resolution faster.

Conflict is here to stay. It will never go away. Carl Jung once wrote, "All the greatest and most important problems of life are fundamentally unsolvable. They can never be solved, but only outgrown." If you can get a handle on how to reduce conflict situations, you'll look forward to going to work, have less stress, and produce more.

Source: "5 Steps to reduce conflict at work," by Margot Robinson. *From Innovative Leader,* 7, 2, February 1998. Reprinted by permission of Margot Robinson.

Constructive conflict begins with recognition of the conflict and starts the process of managing it by one individual's willingness to own his or her feelings. Turning the tide of destructive conflict means you must recognize when you are being selfish and stupid, and to say so to the other. Constructive conflict begins with recognizing the basic importance of the relationship and valuing the relationship more than the conflict. While we still may disagree with another during the conflict, the goal is one of problem solving, not hurting the other. Each participant in the conflict must be flexible and strive to find the best solution for the relationship.

constructive conflict conflict in which the goal is problem solving, not hurting one another

Conflict-Management Styles

Thomas-Kilmann (1974), drawing on the work of Blake and Mouton (1964), have identified five possible styles of managing conflict. They base these five styles on the possible combinations of two important elements: concern for self and concern for people. Figure 8.1 shows the possible combinations.

FIGURE 8.1 Thomas-Kilmann Conflict Mode Instrument

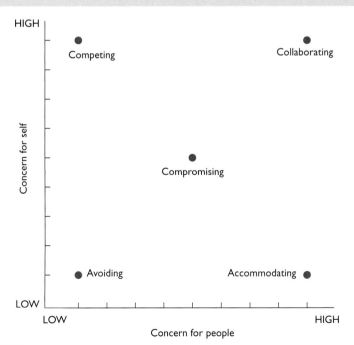

Source: Adapted from K. Thomas, "Conflict and Conflict Management," Handbook of Industrial and Organizational Psychology, Ed. by Marvin Dunnette, 1976.

collaborating style characterized by high concern for self and high concern for people

A **collaborating style** is characterized by high concern for self and high concern for people. *Collaboration* means to work together. Both parties share concern for solving a problem in a cooperative manner and consider the ultimate goal to be win-win. Although both parties may initially identify different solutions to the problem, both work together to ultimately develop a different solution that meets the needs of all individuals involved. The collaborating style takes work, time, and energy. Collaboration is characterized by assertiveness, perceptions of equality among the participants, belief that all parties and their opinions have value, and the motivation to see the conflict through to a satisfying end. This conflict-management style is usually the most effective. However, it may not be appropriate in times of emergency, when an immediate decision must be made.

competing style characterized by high concern for self and low concern for people

A **competing style** is characterized by high concern for self and low concern for people. Generally, individuals who utilize a competing style engage in a win-lose approach to the conflict. They must win, and others must lose. These individuals dominate others involved in the conflict and insist that their own opinions and solutions are more valuable than those of others. The dominating individual's communication is aggressive and depends on threats, sarcasm, overt hostility, and disconfirming statements to others. Engaging in a competing style increases the likelihood of destructive conflict.

However, under emergency situations, when an immediate decision must be made, this style might be useful. When individuals in the relationship recognize that emergencies are a part of life and have agreed that under certain circumstances one party may make a decision without communication with the other, this style may be effective. It is critical, though, to understand that this must be agreed upon in advance. Here is an example. Perhaps you and your life partner have agreed that neither of you will make a major purchase, say of over $100, without discussing it with the other. But one day when you're traveling on a trip away from home, your car breaks down, and you've got to get repairs in order to meet your client and return home. The repairs, as you'd expect, are considerably more than $100. In this type of circumstance, discussing the options with your partner isn't a consideration.

accommodating style characterized by low concern for self and high concern for people

An **accommodating style** is characterized by high concern for people and low concern for self. When we accommodate another, we yield to their wishes, needs, desires, or solutions. Accommodation is associated with a nonassertive communication approach. Accommodating is effective if you really do not care about the outcome of a particular circumstance or situation as much as your partner might. For example, if you want to see a movie this weekend and there's something that your partner really wants to see but you're not interested in it, you agree to go because you don't really care all that much. The downside of too much accommodation is the tendency to become a pushover for everyone else's ideas but never stand up for your own. The accommodating style is more likely to be utilized by individuals from collectivist cultures rather than individualistic cultures. Remember, collectivist cultures attach more value to the group than to individuals, so they are more likely to yield to the group's will.

avoiding style characterized by low concern for self and low concern for people

An **avoiding style** is characterized by low concern for self and low concern for people. The most common behavior associated with avoidance is withdrawal, either physically or mentally. We avoid a conflict by withdrawing physically or emotionally. We ignore phone calls or e-mails or simply refuse to respond to a request. Or we change the subject when an uncomfortable situation arises. Avoidance is all too common in many relationships, because the parties fear that any type of confrontation will damage the relationship. Avoidance is very common in the initial stages of a relationship where one party doesn't want to be the first one to cause an argument. Unfortunately, avoidance only intensifies the possibility of a more intense conflict.

gunnysack adding to the "weight" of avoided conflict

Avoidance causes us to **gunnysack** our problems and concerns. Think about an invisible gunnysack that you carry around on your back. When it is empty, it doesn't

Individuals who use a competing style of conflict management are more interested in winning than in solving a problem collaboratively.

weigh anything, but every time we avoid a confrontation, swallow a criticism, or ignore a problem in our relationship, we add it to our sack. Every time we do this, the sack gets heavier. Eventually the gunnysack fills up, and the result is not pretty. Say your partner always leaves the tube of toothpaste on the edge of the sink and never puts the cap back on, always takes off work clothes and tosses them on the bedroom floor, or always leaves the car on empty so you have to fill it up. In the early stages of your relationship, you may consider these to be "quirks" in his personality, nothing major. One day, though, you're amazed to find that you've been really angry for the six months you've been picking up those work clothes, and you're sick of doing it. You're tired of wiping up toothpaste from the sink, and you don't have time to fill the car up with gas today because you're in a hurry and late for a meeting. You explode. What is your partner's likely reaction to your anger?

The **compromising style** is the final conflict-management style and is characterized by moderate concern for self and moderate concern for people. When we compromise, we give up something to gain something. Compromise may be the most often used conflict-management style. However, it can be very dangerous. The most critical difference between collaborating and compromising styles is the parties' degree of satisfaction with the outcome. In collaboration, we modify our decision, but we are satisfied by both the process and the outcome of the decision. In a compromise, we give something up, but we are not particularly happy about it. We do it to expedite the situation, perhaps to avoid a drawn-out conversation or meeting. One of the most common reasons for compromise is that we are too lazy to put the energy and time into the process of collaboration. Compromise as a long-term strategy to conflict management may have the same results as accommodation. Yet compromise can be effective under some circumstances. If the parties see compromise as a short-term approach to a problem, or when the situation is not critical to either party, compromise can work. But it needs to be used only rarely, and only until a more comprehensive solution can be found.

compromising style characterized by moderate concern for self and moderate concern for people

RHETORICALLY SENSITIVE INTERPERSONAL COMMUNICATION IN COLLEGE AND LIFE

*B*eing able to adapt your communication to the unique requirements of a particular communication context is one of the most critical skills of the competent communicator. **Rhetorical sensitivity** is the ability to adapt a message to the people, place, and timing of the communication. We are not

rhetorical sensitivity the ability to adapt a message to the people, place, and timing of the communication

implying that you so dramatically change your message that you compromise your ethical standards. Rhetorically sensitive communicators understand the unique elements of each communication situation and audience and adapt their messages accordingly. Morreale, Spitzberg, and Barge (2001) put it this way: "Communication is the process of making community. This means that the choices we make about how to communicate influence what we create and the kinds of personal lives, relationships, and communities we build" (pp. 22–23). Yet even when we act in the most communicatively competent manner possible, we cannot control someone else's communication behavior. As we discussed in the previous chapter, conflict is inevitable. Yet we also have the tools to manage it effectively.

Today's college classroom learning environment may be characterized by more active student involvement through small group activities and problem solving. Small groups often present unique difficulties, including interpersonal conflict as a result of personality clashes or differences of opinion. Inter-role conflicts often occur because members share some of the same responsibilities without a clear understanding of how to divide the tasks involved or because they simultaneously compete for the same functions.

How may group members respond to conflict? In some cases, groups ignore, prevent, squelch, or, as a last resort, use a leader's status or power to suspend conflict; in most cases, collaboration, which strives for a negotiated settlement between the conflicting parties, proves most beneficial to all concerned. Members focus on solving the problem rather than defending or attacking one another.

Another potential interpersonal conflict involves the nonparticipating member of a group. Groups often have members who, through disinterest, shyness, fear, selfishness, or defensiveness do not actively or verbally participate in discussion, decision making, and problem solving. Typically, this person shows up to group meetings but says nothing and waits for others to discuss and decide issues to which they readily consent.

The flip side to this potential conflict is the overachieving member. Some group members, whether unconsciously or purposefully, seek to dominate groups with their ideas, opinions, or talk. Motivations for this behavior can range from a desire to be helpful to a desire to be the center of attention or create conflict. In any case, these people tend to bring the free exchange of ideas to a standstill and hinder the group's creativity and task functions. Some strategies for addressing both nonparticipating and overparticipating members include the following:

* Assign the problem member a specific task or responsibility, especially one well suited to his or her skills or interests (e.g., "Marcie, would you please

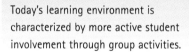
Today's learning environment is characterized by more active student involvement through group activities.

prepare a report that provides and explains the demographic of our student body so we can structure our membership drive more carefully?")

- Attend to nonverbal cues so that you sense when a member is about to speak and can respond accordingly to encourage participation or silence (e.g., "Noriko, I noticed that you frowned a bit at what Susan just said. Did you have something to add?")

- Arrange the group's seating to provide encouragement or control of members by sitting them near the leader (e.g., "Jenda, would you please sit next to me for this meeting? I may need to consult with you during the meeting, and it would be helpful to have you physically near.")

- Invite more silent members to share their insights, thereby encouraging them to speak while helping to monitor those who may speak too much (e.g., "Jan, what do you think about using tickets to control the number of people who attend our open house?")

- Redirect the talk in the group to encourage more silent members to share (e.g., "That's very interesting, Laughton. Thank you. Nate, what's your opinion on providing additional funds for undergraduate research projects?")

- Talk privately with the problem member (e.g., "Sally, I usually don't hear you speak up in our group on a regular basis. Is there something wrong? I would really like to hear from you." Or, "Patrick, have you noticed that it seems like some of our members are reluctant to speak up during the meeting? I was wondering if you would be willing to help me get the others members to add their thoughts by asking the quieter members questions or inviting them to speak?")

- Directly request change or voluntary self-removal of the problem member (e.g., "Mike, may I ask you to help me out? While what you share in our group is always worthwhile, would you be offended if I asked you to let others talk as well?" Or, "Joe, you really seem to have a problem relating to our group. I wonder if you would feel more comfortable working on another project or with another group. How do you feel about that?")

Conflict is inevitable in any relationship, but how you respond verbally is within your control. Using "I" messages rather than "you" messages will help the other person hear what you have to say without feeling attacked or demeaned, as we discussed in Chapter 7.

The success of group communication depends upon effective IPC.

◎ SUMMARY

In this chapter, we have discussed the importance of applying your understanding of the dialectics of interpersonal communication in a variety of communication contexts. We have identified concepts important to your understanding of effective interpersonal communication:

- Individualistic cultures place more importance on the individual within certain types of relationships. Individualist cultures value direct, open forms of communication.
- Collectivist cultures value less direct communication and tend to avoid conflict situations. Collectivist cultures emphasize the importance of the group (i.e., family, work, or social group) and value the group's success rather than any individual in that group.
- Pseudo-conflict is when the parties actually are in agreement but perceptions and misunderstanding prevent them from seeing the areas of agreement and compatibility.
- Destructive conflict is that which escalates; encourages each party to retaliate against the other; causes one or more individuals to dominate and compete with others; and increases the potential for defensiveness, inflexibility, and cross-complaints.
- Constructive conflict begins with recognition and starts the process of managing the conflict by one individual's willingness to own his or her feelings.
- A collaborating style of conflict management is characterized by high concern for self and high concern for the other. *Collaboration* means to work together.
- A competing style of conflict management is characterized by high concern for self and low concern for the other. Generally, individuals who utilize a competing style engage in a win-lose approach to the conflict.

- An accommodating style of conflict management is characterized by high concern for the other and low concern for self. When we accommodate to another, we yield to their wishes, needs, desires, or solutions.
- An avoiding style of conflict management is characterized by low concern for self and low concern for the other. The most common behavior associated with avoidance is withdrawal, either physically or mentally.
- Avoidance causes us to gunnysack our problems and concerns. Eventually our gunnysack overflows with increased destructive conflict.
- A compromising style of conflict management is characterized by moderate concern for self and moderate concern for the other. When we compromise, we give something up to gain something.
- Rhetorical sensitivity is this ability to adapt a message to the people, place, and timing of the communication.

Questions for Discussion

1. What is the most critical issue that can cause misunderstanding within cross-cultural friendships?
2. If you are a member of the dominant cultural group in your campus, organization, or community, do you believe it is ever possible to truly understand what it feels like to live in a minority or ethnic culture?
3. Look around your campus and examine the "integration" of your institution. Are individuals of different racial, ethnic, or religious groups interacting with each other outside of classes? Why or why not?

◎ EXERCISES

1. Summarize a recent conflict you had with a friend or romantic partner. Utilizing the grid summarized in Figure 8.1, identify the strategy you utilized within this conflict. What other strategy might you have utilized to manage the conflict more successfully?
2. You have been seeing an individual who is of a different race, ethnicity, or religion. You believe that this relationship has the potential to become a deeper, long-term partnership. You have not told your parents because you believe they would be very upset. What steps might you take to continue nurturing this new relationship without causing harm to your relationship with your parents?
3. Contact your local United Way and identify a not-for-profit or social service agency in your community in need of volunteers. What communication skills are most critical to assisting you in your volunteer work for this agency?

◎ KEY TERMS

Individualistic cultures	Constructive conflict	Avoiding style
Collectivist cultures	Collaborating style	Gunnysack
Pseudo-conflict	Competing style	Compromising style
Destructive conflict	Accommodating style	Rhetorical sensitivity

REFERENCES

Association of American Colleges and Universities. 2002. *Greater expectations: A new vision for learning as a nation goes to college.* Washington, DC: Association of American Colleges and Universities.

Blake, R., and Mouton, J. 1964. *The managerial grid.* Houston: Gulf Publishing.

Hofstede, G. 1980. Culture's consequences: International differences in work-related values. Newbury Park, CA: Sage.

Kuh, G. 2006. Thinking DEEPly about academic advising and student engagement. *Academic Advising Today* 29:1, 3. Retrieved June 15, 2006, from www.nacada.ksu.edu/AAT/NW29_2.pdf.

Martin, J. N., and Nakayama, T. K. 2001. *Experiencing intercultural communication: An introduction.* Mountain View, CA: Mayfield.

Morreale, S. P., Spitzberg, B. H., and Barge, J. K. 2001. *Human communication: Motivation, knowledge, & skills.* Belmont, CA: Wadsworth.

NACADA. 2004. NACADA statement of core values of academic advising. Retrieved June 15, 2006, from the NACADA Clearinghouse of Academic Advising Resources website, www.nacada.ksu.edu/Clearinghouse/AdvisingIssues/Core-Values.htm.

Robinson, M. 1998. 5 steps to reduce conflict at work. *Innovative Leader* 7(2), 325. Retrieved September 1, 2004, from www.winstonbrill.com/bril001/html/article_index/articles/301-350/article325_body.html.

Smith, L. N., and Walter, T. L. 1995. *The adult learner's guide to college success.* Belmont, CA: Wadsworth.

Wilmot, W. W., and Hocker, J. L. 2001. *Interpersonal conflict.* New York: Random House.

CHAPTER 9

Public Speaking
Process, Purposes, Topics, and Audiences

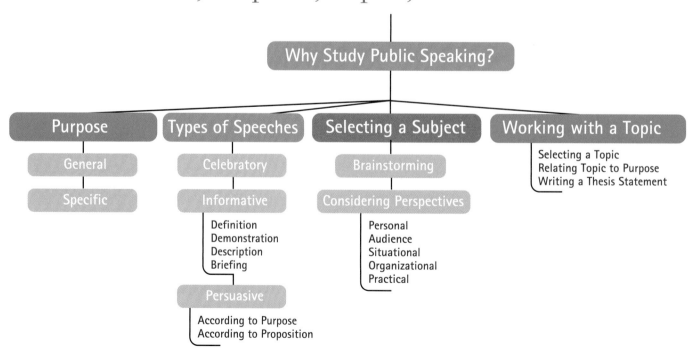

Why Study Public Speaking?

Purpose	Types of Speeches	Selecting a Subject	Working with a Topic

Purpose
- General
- Specific

Types of Speeches
- Celebratory
- Informative
  - Definition
  - Demonstration
  - Description
  - Briefing
- Persuasive
  - According to Purpose
  - According to Proposition

Selecting a Subject
- Brainstorming
- Considering Perspectives
  - Personal
  - Audience
  - Situational
  - Organizational
  - Practical

Working with a Topic
- Selecting a Topic
- Relating Topic to Purpose
- Writing a Thesis Statement

Knowledge Checklist

✓ To appreciate the value of public speaking skills

✓ To understand and learn to deal with communication apprehension

✓ To understand the process of developing a speech

✓ To learn the three general purposes in public speaking

✓ To identify and draft specific purpose statements that relate to the three general purposes in public speaking

✓ To know how to select a speech subject and topic

✓ To understand how to relate speech subjects, topics, and purposes

✓ To learn how to write an effective thesis for a speech

✓ To identify the various types of informative, persuasive, and celebratory speeches

✓ To appreciate the significance of public speaking in the college experience

WHY STUDY PUBLIC SPEAKING?

*I*n this chapter, we discuss reasons *why* you should study and develop your public speaking skills and *how* to craft and deliver an effective speech. We'll introduce a model for public speaking and address the initial aspects of developing a speech, namely, identifying a clear purpose for your speech, selecting a subject for your speech, and articulating a narrowed topic suitable for your speech and your audience.

First let's think about reasons for studying public speaking. Preparing to give a speech helps you develop important academic skills. Although we'll discuss each of these ideas in greater detail, for now just consider the skills required to prepare an effective speech:

- Develop a simple, clear sentence that summarizes your main idea
- Identify main ideas relevant to your thesis
- Support your ideas adequately with current, reliable, and relevant research
- Organize your ideas in a way that makes them accessible and reasonable
- Articulate your ideas clearly so that others can understand your message

While this list is incomplete, it emphasizes many of the skills you need as a college student, including engaging classroom discussion, thinking critically about what you read, supporting your ideas, and writing and speaking articulately with greater precision and clarity. Kanar (1998) includes the ability to make oral presentations as one of the "five essentials for classroom performance" (p. 45). However, only 36.3 percent of 276,449 first-year students consider themselves above average in public speaking skills (Young 2003). Therefore, developing your public presentation skills is an important area of communication for you to focus on.

Studying public speaking helps you in your studies and prepares you to enter the work world. (See the box Career Links: Public Speaking as Marketing Strategy for additional insights.) Recent surveys confirm that effective oral communication is one of the most important job skills you can obtain (Darling & Dannels 2003; Peterson 1997). However, many students do not receive adequate communication education (Burk 2001) or resist integrating communication skills into their education (Dannels, Anson, Bullard, & Peretti 2003). Given that you will spend a great deal of your working hours listening, conversing, making presentations, working in small groups, and relating to other workers, developing your public speaking skills will provide you a keen advantage as you enter the job market. You may be thinking, "How can public speaking help me do all the things? Giving a speech doesn't

Public Speaking as Marketing Strategy

Many business professionals use public speaking as a way to contact prospective clients or customers and to build their businesses. For example, brokers often offer free investment seminars or underwrite a dinner to which they invite potential customers. At the meeting or after the meal, the broker explains some basic information about investing and then notes how he or she can assist in this important process. Doctors, dentists, attorneys, insurance agents, and other professionals are using the same approach to identify and recruit new clients. They often offer to speak at service clubs or other community meetings in order to provide explanation. In other words, public speaking can be used to market a business. As a result of these endeavors, unforeseen opportunities to provide keynote speeches, conduct training sessions, or offer seminars may result.

require me to do all these things." However, public speaking does not just include the actual presentation; it also requires preparation. You must gather information about your audience, often through listening and interviewing, and must collect other forms of evidence and support. Additionally, you are most likely speaking in front of a small group and seeking to relate to your audience. Public speaking skills help you develop a wider range of abilities than you might first believe, which, in turn, are important to other contexts of communication.

Additionally, developing your public speaking skills enables you to fulfill your responsibilities and privileges as a member of various groups, as highlighted in the box Community Links: Public Speaking and Community. As a voter, you may need to speak to issues in your local community. As a parent or future parent, you may need to respond to school policies or interact with other parents, teachers, or coaches who work with or care for your child. As a member of a mosque, synagogue, church, or civic group, you may be called upon to participate in a religious service or a public meeting. All of these commonplace events require public speaking skills and, more importantly, include your contribution to the public dialogue.

Community Links

Public Speaking and Community

It is easy to think of public speaking as "linear communication." Perhaps you think of public speaking as a single person standing in front of others who sit passively or who, depending on the topic, audience, and culture, respond visually, vocally, or verbally. For example, in many African American churches, the speakers and the audience share a call-response strategy that includes comments of support and encouragement from the audience toward the speaker. However, regardless of whether we speak to an animated audience or not, public speaking creates and sustains community at at least three levels.

The Immediate Community

As we speak with an audience, we develop an immediate community—that is, we seek to find and make connections with our audience. We seek to address topics of concern that we all share. Moreover, what we say and how we say it has the potential to significantly impact our audience and how they respond to us. Even though we may disagree, we still share the same space; we are a community. This is especially true in classrooms where community can be realized, even if only for a few weeks. Working toward community proves especially helpful in a communication class and helps you prepare, practice, and present speeches. A sense of classroom community will help you build solidarity with your classmates, enhance your credibility, and encourage greater audience response, while also reducing apprehension, which, in turn, can often help you obtain a higher grade.

The Local Social Community

Public speaking, even in your classrooms, has importance for the larger social community. As you prepare to speak, think about questions, problems, issues, or possibilities that exist in your campus or geographic community. How can you address one of these matters in a way that will add to the body of information and the communal conversation? Too often students choose trivial or relatively unimportant speech topics. We encourage you to speak to issues that truly matter to you and to your peers. Use the opportunity you have in this class to find and share knowledge that will help shape opinion, solve problems, or engage possibilities. In doing so, you will strengthen the immediate community and help forge links with the local community. In our experience, this is the path to become a student leader now and a leader in your future profession later.

The Larger Social Community

Public speaking also engages the larger conversation. To use an image from Kenneth Burke (1973), engaging social dialogue is like coming to a party late and entering a passionate conversation, where people are so engaged they have no time to tell you the topic of the conversation. As you listen, you catch the elements of the argument well enough to contribute your own views, and then, given the pressure of time, you must leave, although the conversation continues. As you share your ideas in your class, in your community, and perhaps even in broader contexts, you contribute to the ongoing dialogue. Learning to engage this dialogue with skill, through your work in this class, provides you with important first steps in entering and maintaining the conversation. Never forget that words matter! Think about it. Our social fabric is based upon the words we find in revered documents such as the Constitution of the United States and the Declaration of Independence. Words are the means by which we resolve conflicts, pass and adjudicate laws, and explain and understand social policy. While others' words may seem more important than our insights or contributions, to remain silent squelches the conversation. Never underestimate the value of what you have to share. We urge you to think, speak, and act, and to join the conversation. What you learn here will let you do this with excellence. Your engagement in civic and community life truly matters. Learning to speak with skill is one way to be engaged.

As a member of various communities, you have a social and personal responsibility to engage the issues of your time. While it is easy for us to become complacent or even cynical about our role as citizens, failure to engage the important questions that face our communities only ensures that our opinion goes unheard and that the voices of others, with whom we may well disagree, prevails. Eventually, these issues will directly impact our day-to-day lives (and those of future generations) since the people who engage in civic dialogue decide laws, work policies, community standards, and a range of other issues. For example, the decisions made by lawmakers in your state directly impact the amount of tuition you pay, while state and federal law also impacts the availability of financial aid to pay your tuition. Have you been frustrated by the process of obtaining financial aid? Rather than complain, what have you done about your frustration? How could you engage this issue that impacts your life and the lives of future college students? You could choose a topic like this for your informative or persuasive speech in this class so you can learn more about the issues and develop skill in addressing them. Use this communication class to engage the public dialogue. Recent information indicates

(Young 2004) that many first-year students are more politically aware, so you are likely to have an audience interested in the political and civic issues of the day in your communication class.

Moreover, public speaking skills enable you to engage not only in civic but also in social life. At a recent wedding, the best man was expected to toast the newly-weds, even though he had not been informed of this until just after the ceremony. Sweating, literally and figuratively, he approached the minister and poured out a stream of concern and complaint: "What am I going to do? What am I supposed to say? I've never done this before! I just can't do it. Will you please do it for me?" Although the minister tried to help him see that giving the toast was not that difficult, he utterly refused. In the end, the minister gave the toast because the best man believed he could not. While a basic communication course would not necessarily address all of this young man's concern, he would have gleaned some experience before an audience and probably would have been more prepared to toast his best friends on their wedding day.

COMMUNICATION APPREHENSION

*A*n officer in the military gets ready to deliver his speech to a basic oral communication class. He begins by speaking in a clear, strong voice and appears to be doing well, until suddenly he stops speaking and runs from the room with tears streaming down his face. He explains to his teacher, "I don't know what happened; I couldn't think what to say next, and I felt everyone looking at me. I froze and couldn't keep going. Please don't make me do that again!" Many people experience "fear or anxiety associated with either real or anticipated communication with another person or persons" (McCroskey & Richmond 1979), or what we term **communication apprehension (CA)**. Researchers have studied CA and developed many insights about its origins and effects, including the fact that high CA interferes with a speaker's ability to deliver a speech. The possible combination of confused thought, sweaty palms, shaky knees, dry mouth, breathlessness, and nausea combine to create a frightening physical and psychological reaction. If you have such reactions, we suggest speaking with your instructor, who will have strategies to assist you. However, as Dr. Michael T. Motley (1997) notes, reframing your attitude toward delivering your speech will help you begin to deal with CA. He suggests thinking of giving your speech not as a performance but as a communication event. Performances, as Motley notes, are often memorized and charged with expectations of perfection, while communication events are an ordinary part of everyday interaction and therefore do not have the same purpose or expectations as performances. The box Communication Links: Dealing with Communication Apprehension summarizes some suggested ways for dealing with CA. These strategies will give you an idea of ways to begin addressing your anxiety. You can also measure your level of anxiety about public speaking by completing the PRPSA available online at www.jamescmccroskey.com/measures/prpsa.htm. Simply print the survey, complete it according to the directions, and follow the scoring directions at the bottom of the page.

communication apprehension (CA) the fear or anxiety associated with either real or anticipated communication with another person(s)

⊚ Communication Links

Dealing with Communication Apprehension

Communication apprehension refers to anxiety or fear about oral communication, which people experience in a variety of communication situations, including public speaking. Some people refer to this fear as "stage fright." While most everyone feels some anxiety before speaking, there are some steps you can take to help reduce the anxiety that may hinder you from speaking as well as you would like. Using a combination of these approaches usually works best.

1. *Explanation.* In explanation, you basically seek to understand why you are afraid of public speaking. By identifying the fear, you can then face it realistically, which helps you see that the fear is not well founded. Sometimes people say, "If I have to give a speech, I'll just die." But you realize that this won't really happen; it's an irrational fear. This understanding helps reduce fear.

2. *Rationalization.* Through rationalization, give yourself messages that replace negative thoughts with positive ones. So substitute "I'm scared to death about this" with a statement like, "I'm ready to speak; I've planned and practiced, and I can do this." When a negative thought comes to mind, immediately replace it with a positive message. Persistence in this practice reduces apprehension.

3. *Relaxation.* Before you speak, find a quiet, comfortable place where you can sit down. Beginning with your toes, tighten, hold, and release muscles and work your way up to each area of the body, clenching and releasing your muscles. Concentrate only on your body as you tighten and release muscles; pay attention to the sensation of tension in your body. As you release the muscle tension, take deep breaths and let the tension go. This helps relieve the physical symptoms that accompany anxiety.

4. *Visualization.* How do you see yourself in your mind before you speak? Are you succeeding by speaking fluently and engaging your audience? Through visualization, you create a "mental movie" in which you picture yourself delivering a successful speech from beginning to end. In this way, you can then actually *do* what you've pictured in your mind and help reduce your fear.

5. *Education.* Often you have important things to say but lack the communication skills necessary to say them as well as you'd like. Through education such as communication classes, you can learn and develop these skills that increase your confidence. As your confidence increases, your fears decrease. By reading your text thoughtfully, attending class regularly, participating in exercises, practicing the delivery of speech, and continuing to work on your communication skills, you can reduce your communication apprehension by building your speaking skills.

Public speaking skills help you engage in civic and social life.

Of course, you may not have high CA but still experience some measure of it. If so, please remember that this is a natural response and that you can actually use this energy to help you deliver your speech more effectively. The emotions and physical responses you experience when you are excited are very similar to those you have when you are somewhat nervous. Therefore, reframe your response from anxiety to anticipation and look forward to the opportunity to share with others what you have learned or believe. After all, how many times do you have an opportunity to present your ideas to an audience? We encourage you to seize this chance.

THE PROCESS OF PUBLIC SPEAKING

Now that we have discussed some of the advantages gained from developing your public speaking skills and addressed one of the major concerns with public speaking, let's consider a process you can use to prepare to speak. While you could prepare in many different ways given your culture, audience, and personal preferences, consider the model in Figure 9.1. This model summarizes the important steps you must take to speak effectively and emphasizes that *preparing* to speak is a *process* that requires time and energy. By referring to public speaking as a process, we are implying that you must work at developing both individual speeches and your speaking ability over time. Even people who may seem to speak with ease and assurance must employ this or a similar process. As you gain practice, you will be able to implement these steps more easily, but you will continue to use the steps in this process if you are to speak effectively. Make a strong commitment now to engage this process and the work required to speak effectively. Preparation will pay off in increased confidence and in positive responses from your listeners.

Before we discuss specific aspects of this model, let's consider some key characteristics of the model as a whole in greater detail. First, the model depicts the entire public speaking process, from developing a focus for your speech to presenting it. Because we may get so involved in one aspect of the process that we forget the larger picture, this model helps us remember that public speaking is a multifaceted process and that every aspect of preparation is important to the whole process.

Second, this model incorporates both single and double arrows. The single arrow indicates those aspects of preparation that logically move you forward toward the

FIGURE 9.1   A Model for Speech Preparation

ASSIGNMENT/PURPOSE

SUBJECT

BRAINSTORMING

TOPIC

THESIS

RESEARCH

OUTLINES/VISUAL AIDS

PRACTICE

PRESENTATION

next step. The double arrows indicate that, at times, as you move forward in your preparation, you will return to a former step in order to refine what you previously completed. For example, consider the first double arrow located between the words *subject* and *brainstorming*. While you may have a subject in mind as you begin preparing, you may find a more suitable subject when you actually brainstorm. Therefore, brainstorming may help you refine your subject. These double arrows also emphasize that preparation is a process requiring time, careful thought, and strategic planning.

Third, considering each part of the model briefly permits us to examine the overall process important to public speaking:

- Assignment: You may receive an assignment to speak as a result of an invitation from a particular group, responsibilities on the job, participation in a ceremony or ritual, or as a requirement for a particular class. Given that you are enrolled in a communication course, your instructor will have clear assignments for you to complete. If, however, you are invited to speak by an organization or if you make a presentation at work, it may be helpful to ask some basic questions of the contact person or your supervisor about the occasion, audience, or purpose of the talk.

- Purpose: The purpose of the speech refers to *why* you are giving the speech. What are you seeking to accomplish in a particular speech? You should be able to state your purpose clearly. In the model, *purpose* and *assignment* are placed on the same line because if you are given an assignment, the purpose for your speech will either be explicit or implicit. For example, if your boss asks to you to update management on the progress your work team has made in completing a marketing plan, the assignment delineates that management wants information. However, you may not always receive a clear assignment. In this case, you must consider other factors such as the occasion, the audience, your expertise, and the amount of time you have to speak in order to identify a suitable purpose.

- Subject: A subject consists of a broad area of knowledge that could yield several potential topics. A subject is much too broad for a single presentation and must be narrowed to a topic, which, in turn, must also be refined to a single main idea for your speech.

- Brainstorming: Brainstorming allows you to let ideas flow without evaluating them so that you can generate many possible ideas.

- Topic: While a subject consists of a broad area of knowledge, a topic represents a particular and narrowed focus on that subject.

- Thesis: A thesis statement summarizes the essence of your speech in a single, declarative sentence. The thesis is the speech's central idea, the theme to be developed, or the proposition to be proven that flows from the purpose of the speech.

- Research: If your ideas are to be clear and useful to your audience, you must develop and support them thoroughly. Research will provide you with the needed information and evidence to frame and bolster your ideas and will also help you refine your thesis, as indicated by the double arrow. In Chapter 10, we offer additional practical advice on conducting and using research.

- Outlines and visual aids: Outlines help organize your ideas in order to assist in your speech's preparation and presentation, while visual aids help provide illustration and impact. In Chapters 10 and 11, we discuss organization and delivery in more detail.

- Practice: There is no substitute for repeated, focused practice in preparing your speech. In our discussion of delivery, we suggest specific techniques that will make the most of the time you devote to practice.

- Presentation: You have planned, prepared, and practiced, and now it is time to make your presentation.

As you can see from this brief explanation of the public speaking process, making effective presentations requires an investment of time and energy. Given the demands on your time, you will be tempted to short-circuit this process. You may even believe that you can delete some of the steps we have outlined here or disregard the entire process. Many beginning speakers think they can generate an effective presentation with minimal or even no preparation, but if you avoid or neglect this process, you will fail to gain the skills you need for academic, career, and personal success that we outlined earlier in this chapter. Moreover, you will insult your audience. How do you feel when you are listening to a speaker who rambles or who speaks in a monotone? You will place your audience in the same position if you do not adequately prepare. Therefore, we urge you to commit yourself to gleaning as much as possible from your study of public speaking. Many students will testify that they benefited greatly from making such a commitment.

PUBLIC SPEAKING PURPOSES

Why are you giving a speech? What is your purpose? Answering these questions is central to success in both your preparation and presentation. To assist you in answering these questions, consider that speeches have both general and specific purposes.

General Purposes

general purposes (1) to entertain, inspire, or celebrate; (2) to inform; and (3) to persuade

epideictic speeches speeches that celebrate occasions; also known as **celebratory, ceremonial,** or **special occasion speeches**

informative speeches speeches that instruct or assist the audience in gaining understanding

persuasive speeches speeches that stimulate an audience to reaffirm or alter beliefs or encourage the adoption of new behaviors or the continuation of past behaviors

General purposes are meant to (1) entertain, inspire, or celebrate; (2) inform; and (3) persuade. For example, graduation speeches, after-dinner speeches, and eulogies all celebrate occasions and are therefore referred to as **epideictic speeches** and **celebratory, ceremonial,** or **special occasion speeches.** While some of these speeches celebrate an event, others honor people for their work or lives. **Informative speeches** instruct or assist the audience in gaining understanding. A well-prepared and effectively delivered lecture or a briefing illustrates informative speeches. **Persuasive speeches** stimulate an audience to reaffirm or alter beliefs or encourage them to adopt new behaviors or continue to behave as they have in the past. While we categorize speeches according to these general purposes, it is important to note that this is, to some degree, an artificial distinction, particularly with regard to informative and persuasive speeches.

By selecting a particular topic and using specific information, even when we are not *directly* persuading, we present a particular perspective that may *indirectly* persuade. For example, a student who delivers an informative speech on creation science advocates a particular view about the origin of the world just by using the term *creation science* and by drawing on information from those who espouse this perspective. While the speaker may not seek to persuade us that his or her ideas are valid or that we should also believe in creation science, the topic and the evidence is, by its very nature, indirectly persuasive.

Further, persuasive speeches must use information effectively. A persuasive speech that lacks explanation and evidence, or information, will lack credibility and fail to persuade. Therefore, informative and persuasive speeches share important characteristics.

So, you may be asking, if there isn't much difference between informative and persuasive speeches, why even bother making the distinction in the first place? That's a valid question. The short answer is this: While informative and persuasive speeches share similar territory, *each speech bears a different burden.* An informative speech teaches; it does not seek to convince or actuate. Any persuasion in an informative speech is clearly indirect and not purposeful. On the other hand, persuasive speeches use information purposefully to reinforce or change listener's beliefs or behaviors. This is an important distinction because it helps you to envision your goal in giving either an informative or persuasive speech.

Table 9.1   Comparison of Informative and Persuasive Speeches

	Informative Speech	*Persuasive Speech*
Intent of Speech	To explain, define, demonstrate	To alter belief or action; reinforce
Topic	A process, concept, or activity	A proposition or claim
Desired Audience Response	To understand	To believe or do
Speaker's Role	Teacher	Advocate
Appeals	Mostly credibility and logic	Credibility, logic, and emotion

Table 9.1 summarizes the differences between informative and persuasive speeches and notes several differences, including the intent, topic, desired audience's response, role of the speaker, and the types of appeals used in each type of speech.

Specific Purposes

In addition to general purposes, your speech also needs a **specific purpose**. Obviously, if you are going to celebrate an occasion, you need to know what kind of occasion you are commemorating. If you are delivering an informative speech, it is logical to ask, "What do I want my audience to learn from this speech?" If you are delivering a persuasive speech, you may well ask, "What do I want my audience to believe, or how do I want them to behave?" Answering these questions requires you to have a clear sense of your topic and have a full understanding of how your topic meshes with your purpose. We will address this link further in a subsequent section. At this point, let's focus on your speech's specific purpose.

specific purpose the purpose of a speech in relation to its specific topic

To assist you in identifying and writing specific purpose statements, we suggest that you use a template to draft your first specific purpose statement. The formula below represents one way to draft your specific purpose statement:

> *Specific purpose statement = "I want my audience to . . ." + informative or persuasive descriptor + topic*

Consider each aspect of this template. The clause "I want my audience to . . . " allows you to focus on what you want your audience to gain from your presentation and reminds you that public speaking is a "speaker–audience partnership" (Andrews, Andrews, & Williams 1999, p, 93). In other words, as you consider your specific purpose statement, you must also consider how this statement relates to your intended audience.

Table 9.2 provides a list of celebratory, informative, and persuasive descriptors that you can use to draft your specific purpose statement. A brief summary of your topic provides the last part of the specific purpose statement. Review the following example of a specific purpose statement in order to see how the parts of the statement relate.

["I want my audience to"]	+	*[descriptor]*	+	*[summary of topic]*
↓		↓		↓
"I want my audience to		*understand*		*three reasons why educators believe that working while attending college negatively impacts students."*

Table 9.2   Descriptors for Specific Purpose Statements

Celebratory Speeches	Informative Speeches	Persuasive Speeches
Celebrate	Understand	Believe
Recognize	Learn	Agree
Remember	Know	Begin to
Enjoy	Comprehend	Cease to
Laugh at	Appreciate	Choose to
Reflect upon	Absorb	Purchase
Dedicate	Explain	Select

If this was your specific purpose statement, it would reveal that your speech's general purpose is to inform and that your specific purpose is to help the audience *understand* the speech's topic.

If you used the same topic but wrote a specific purpose statement for the general purpose of persuading, consider how the statement would change: "I want my audience to agree that there are three solid reasons for not working while attending college." The opening phrase, descriptor, and topic statement in this specific purpose statement identify this as a persuasive presentation. Also, notice how the focus or burden of the speech shifts. Now you want the audience to agree with your position on the issue of working while attending college. Although you may use some of the same information during an informative or a persuasive speech on this topic, *how* you use the information shifts. In the informative speech, you target understanding, but in the persuasive speech, you seek to lead the audience to agree with you.

How could you reframe this topic in order to make it a celebratory speech? Consider this specific purpose statement: "I want my audience to celebrate their success at balancing college and employment." This statement would be suitable for a banquet or an awards ceremony where working college students are recognized for successfully balancing multiple demands. In this speech, you do not explain why working and attending college simultaneously is demanding, nor do you seek to persuade your audience that both working and attending college is a problem to avoid. Rather, you celebrate their success at doing both even in the face of the difficulties of their choice. While you may use some of the same information that you would for an informative or persuasive speech on this topic, you will employ it much differently in this speech—to enhance the celebration.

HOW TO SELECT A SUBJECT

Once you have a sense of your purpose and the type of speech you will deliver, you are still faced with numerous decisions in preparing your speech. Logically, the next question you need to answer is, "What will I talk about?" This requires you to consider the speech's subject and then the topic. Earlier, we noted that the **subject** is a broad area of knowledge. To begin, you must identify several such subject areas that can, in time, yield narrowed topics. Brainstorming can help you generate these subject areas.

subject a broad area of knowledge

Brainstorming

brainstorming allowing the thought process to flow freely

Brainstorming refers to letting your thought process flow freely. Write down any possible subjects or topics that come to mind. If you have trouble getting started, use categories to jump-start the process. For example, think about people, places, events, movies, computers, books, TV, controversies, beliefs, opinions, or the latest news stories; these are all subject areas. At this point, don't eliminate any possible ideas; just write until you have no more ideas or until you have filled two or three pages with ideas. Then, begin to work through these ideas using the information in the next section. When you find a subject that has strong possibilities, circle it and move on. However, don't throw away the ideas you have worked to create; keep them in case you need to go back and consider other possibilities.

Perspectives to Consider in Choosing Your Subject

You have numerous possible subjects for your speech. Which should you choose? Consider the following perspectives as you work through the possible subjects one by one (Worley 2000). Remember to circle those that appropriately consider each of these perspectives. Table 9.3 summarizes these perspectives and suggests questions to help you analyze your chosen subjects.

The Audience Perspective Begin your subject selection by considering your audience. What issues matter to them? What questions do they have that you may be

Table 9.3   Questions to Ask in Choosing a Subject

Perspectives to Consider	Questions to Ask
Audience perspective	What does my audience consider important? What does my audience want to know? How does my audience feel about particular issues, problems, or interests? What issue is currently being debated or investigated as reported in the media?
Personal perspective	What subjects interest me? What problem concerns me? What issue would I like to learn more about? What can I learn from my personal inventory?
Situational perspective	What is the nature of the event? Where will I be speaking? At what time will I be speaking? What expectations does the audience have for this event? How many people will attend the event?
Organizational perspective	How will this subject reflect on my organization? How would the leaders in my organization want me to represent them? What subject should I avoid in order not to misrepresent my organization? What subjects may need clarification in order to offset any misperceptions of my organization?
Practical perspective	How much time do I have to speak? How soon am I to speak? How much research have I gathered? How much time will I need for additional research? What subjects do I already know a lot about? Will the subject I know a lot about interest my audience? How interested am I in the subjects I know a lot about? How motivated am I about them?

Table 9.4   Analyzing Your Audience

The following graphic depicts the issues you need to consider in analyzing your audience in order to help you select an appropriate subject and narrowed topic.

AUDIENCE CHARACTERISTICS

Demographics
Age
Gender
Ethnicity
Level of education
Physical ability level
Group memberships

Psychological Profiles
Attitudes
Beliefs
Values

Learning Styles
Feelers
Watchers
Thinkers
Doers

AUDIENCE TYPES

Friendly
Neutral
Apathetic
Unsupportive
Opposed

---

audience perspective considers the listeners' multiple characteristics and the resulting type of audience they comprise

able to answer? Additionally, the **audience perspective** considers your listeners' multiple characteristics and the resulting type of audience they comprise. Audience *characteristics* include the group's demographics and psychological profiles. Audience *type* refers to the listeners' basic disposition. (Table 9.4 summarizes the information about audiences.) However, because analyzing your audience is essential to choosing your topic and to preparing and presenting your speech, let's consider it in more detail by briefly reviewing each of the audience characteristics; we then conclude this section by considering audience types.

Demographics refer to an audience's observable or readily available characteristics—age, sex, gender, ethnicity, education level, physical ability levels, and group affiliation. Some of these characteristics are readily defined while others may be less clear. *Age* refers to how old people are, which, at least in a general sense, often influences how they look at the world due to their experiences. For example, elders who were born near the turn of the twentieth century have a very different view of the world than children born at the turn of the twenty-first century.

Sex refers to whether one is biologically male or female, while *gender* refers to the learned behaviors we develop as a result of our socialization. Wood (1994) refers to *gender* as the socialized tendencies of women and men to perceive, believe, and behave differently. Although gender roles are more flexible in contemporary society, there are still relatively stable expectations for male and female behavior (Kirtley & Weaver 1999; Sellnow & Golish 2000).

Ethnicity refers to individuals' cultural background. While some people refer to race as a distinguishing characteristic, race is a problematic idea because it cannot be easily defined, especially in view of the diverse world in which we now live

(Martin & Nakayama 2005). But ethnicity, which includes a mix of characteristics such as skin color, facial features, native language, rites and rituals, and core values, helps us think more accurately about the people with whom we may speak. Culture also impacts how individuals communicate, as the box Cultural Links: Rhetorical Traditions explains.

Rhetorical Traditions

Culture influences every aspect of life, including all types of communication. Public speaking, too, differs among cultures. We admit that the principles of public speaking we offer in this text are based on Western presuppositions that rely on linear thinking. For example, look again at the model of public speaking in this chapter (Figure 9.1); it is a straight line that moves methodically from one step to the next. However, other cultures have different assumptions about public address. Although stereotyping individuals in a group is problematic, nevertheless, these patterns help us understand how speakers of various languages construct thought differently and therefore approach public speaking differently both in preparation and presentation. R. B. Kaplan (1984) explains some of the differences in cultural thought patterns and resulting speech.

> *The following illustration graphically represents typical paragraph structures by speakers of several languages: extensive parallel constructions in the Semitic group, an "indirect" approach to the topic in the Oriental group, and frequent digressions in Romance and Slavic groups. Although it is now often criticized for being too simplistic and for assuming the English rhetorical model to be "straight" or "normal," Kaplan's theory is still extremely valuable because it points out the nature of those rhetorical differences which, although obvious to English native speakers, are often "felt" rather than understood.*

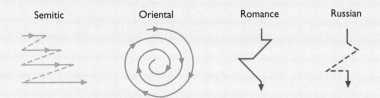

For more information about non-Western rhetorical traditions, check out the "NetLabs" at http://college.hmco.com/communication/daly/presentations/2e/students/netlabs/nl01-1.html.

Source: Rhetorical Tradition figure by Robert Kaplan from "Cultural thought patterns in intercultural education," from *Language Learning*, copyright 1966, p. 15. Permission granted by the author and Language Learning.

Education level usually refers to the amount of formal education your audience may have received. However, education may also be thought of in terms of life experience and should not be discounted.

Physical ability level refers to whether people have disabilities. With the passage of the American Disabilities Act and the subsequent research that has emerged regarding the experiences of people with disabilities (see Braithwaite & Thompson 2000), we have become aware of the importance of attending to this audience characteristic in shaping our presentations.

Effective speakers always consider the audience they will address in preparing and presenting a speech.

Group affiliation, according to Osborn and Osborn (2000), includes membership in religious, political, social, and occupational groups. In short, knowing the kinds of groups to which your audience belongs can cue you to the types of beliefs, attitudes, and values they hold.

These demographic characteristics can help you understand your audience and, thereby, assist you in choosing a topic. For example, if you are speaking with mature, single mothers who have returned to college later in life, you have some important information about your audience that can help direct your choice of topics. On the other hand, if you are speaking with a group of teenage males who are avid listeners of rap music, you have a very different audience. Let's assume that one of your top five topics is to relay some of what you learned during a recent ten-day trip to England. You would certainly structure your speech differently for mature, single mothers than you would for the group of teenagers. For the first group, you may concentrate on government support for child care in the UK, while for the second group you might focus on the major influence of the "British Invasion" on American music.

Stereotyping is a significant problem with this approach to audience analysis. As we've discussed before, a stereotype is a biased opinion of a group, often based on overgeneralizations. For example, thinking that all women are emotional while all men are logical are stereotypes of both groups. Concluding that all Asian students study more than U.S. students is also a stereotype, as is believing that all college students drink heavily. Therefore, it is important to avoid making assumptions about your audience based on demographic characteristics. To return to our example, you may well find some single mothers who are interested in rap music and teenage males who are interested in child-care issues. It is important, therefore, to avoid biases in your speech preparation.

Psychological profiles include your audience's attitudes, beliefs, values, needs, and learning styles. Let's give each of these more attention.

Attitudes, beliefs, and *values* refer to the ethical characteristics of your audience. **Values** are deeply held convictions about the undeniable worthiness of a certain ideal. For example, after the September 11, 2001, tragedy, President Bush appealed to the value of justice in response to the terrorist acts because many U.S. citizens hold to the ideal of justice. **Beliefs** are strongly held ideas about the nature of truth. For example, some people express a belief in God, while others, of equally strong

values deeply held convictions about the undeniable worthiness of a certain ideal

beliefs strongly held ideas about the nature of truth

persuasion, do not believe in God. Beliefs, then, are even more specific than values. To keep to our example, some people believe in God as conceptualized by Christianity, while others believe in God as explained in Judaism, Islam, Buddhism, Hinduism, or other religions. An **attitude** refers to a favorable or negative inclination toward a person, place, event, or object. For example, some people have a favorable response to NFL football and are avid fans while others find football unimportant or boring.

As you might expect, values, beliefs, and attitudes relate to one another. For example, many undergraduates are concerned about grades. In some courses, midsemester and final exams scores largely determine final grades. If you hold to the *value* of fairness, you probably *believe* that midterm and final tests should represent the content of the course as reflected in classroom lectures and assigned readings. Therefore, if you take a midterm and notice that several of the questions are not drawn from classroom lectures or the assigned readings, you may well consider this unfair and thereafter harbor a definitively unfavorable *attitude* toward the course and the instructor. In the future, if the course or the instructor is mentioned, you will probably experience a distinctively negative emotional response and communicate this to others by saying, "Don't take the course with her; she doesn't give fair tests."

As a speaker, if you deny, question, or slight your audience's values, beliefs, and attitudes, you will complicate the speaking situation. Therefore, it is important to be aware of your audience's ethical predisposition so you can build common ground with them by identifying shared values, beliefs, and attitudes. Even if, in the end, you wish to question or disagree with some of your audience's ethical positions, building common ground with them is an important step in persuasion. In other words, you need to identify common areas in order to enhance your credibility so that later you can speak with your audience about those ideas that you do not share in common. For example, your audience may not share your view that convicted prisoners should be allowed conjugal visits with their spouses. However, your audience is likely to believe in the ideal of justice. Even though your audience may disagree with your argument, you share the common value of justice, which you can use to help increase the reasonableness of your argument.

Audience *needs* refer to the basic motivations of audiences. Earlier we discussed Maslow's hierarchy of needs. Recall that, according to Maslow, people have needs that range from basic physical needs to self-actualization. It is important to note that all of these needs, however, center in the self to some degree. As Osborn and Osborn (2000) explain, "People will listen, learn, and remember a message only if it relates to their needs, wants or wishes" (p. 90).

People learn differently; they prefer to process information in different ways. There are a variety of approaches to understanding how people learn (Reiff 1992). As Sellnow (2002) explains, learning styles can be thought of as "a four-stage cycle of feeling, watching, thinking and doing" (p. 17). As you prepare to speak, remember this important information. Even if you do not have demographic information or insight about your audience's values, beliefs, and attitudes, you can appeal to various learning styles in your audience by using anecdotes, examples, or stories that have an emotional quality. Use visuals in order to catch the attention of those who prefer to watch. Rely on strong evidence such as facts, statistics, or expert testimony to appeal to those who prefer to think with you as you speak. And provide an activity for your audience to appeal to those who prefer hands-on learning. This might be something as simple as completing a short survey or engaging in bodily movement. If you find a way to drive home the main point of your speech in these four different ways, you will leave an impression on your audience. The box Communication Links: Using Multiple Intelligence Theory in Public Speaking offers another way to think about learning styles and how they may influence your speech preparation.

attitude a favorable or negative inclination toward a person, place, event, or object

Communication Links

Using Multiple Intelligence Theory in Public Speaking

Howard Gardner (1993), a Harvard psychologist, asserts that people have nine different basic mental preferences for solving problems and producing a relevant response to the problem. Gardner views these mental processes as abilities, talents, or mental skills and terms them *intelligences*. The following chart summarizes information about the nine types of intelligences and offers suggestions about how to appeal to them when giving public speeches. To appeal to all nine intelligences in one speech is certainly a challenge; however, if you prepare well and think carefully, you will find you can relate to many of the nine intelligences at different points in your speech. If not, target as many different intelligences as you can in order to include as many members of your audience as possible at some point during your presentation.

Intelligence	Description	Use in Public Speaking
Bodily	Ability to control one's body movements and to handle objects skillfully	Appeal to listeners' "gut reactions;" use description to touch listeners' five senses; ask audience to physically move or respond (e.g., "Will you please raise your hand?" "Try this simple exercise.")
Verbal	Well-developed verbal skills and sensitivity to the sounds, meanings, and rhythms of words	Use language carefully; craft stories or examples for listener appeal; include eloquent quotes, poetry, or prose
Logical	Ability to think conceptually and abstractly; capacity to discern logical or numerical patterns	Organize ideas carefully; avoid logic errors; use statistics as evidence
Musical	Ability to produce and appreciate rhythm, pitch, and timber	Include an "aural" rather than visual aid by playing music; incorporate song lyrics; work on vocal variety and vary rate of speech for effect by using carefully planned pauses
Visual	Capacity to think in images and pictures, to visualize accurately and abstractly	Use visual aids; paint mental pictures; screen a movie clip
Interpersonal	Capacity to detect and respond appropriately to the moods, motivations, and desires of others	Use interviews to gather supporting material and refer to them; relate personal information, anecdotes; show relationship between your topic and people's lives; emphasize the human aspect of your topic (e.g., "This problem affects over one-half of college students.")

Intrapersonal	Capacity to be self-aware and in tune with inner feelings, values, beliefs, and thinking processes	Reveal appropriate information about yourself; link your topic to others' potential personal goals; emphasize the importance of how your audience feels or the value of their beliefs, views, and opinions
Naturalistic	Ability to recognize and categorize plants, animals, and other objects in nature	Use topical organization; link topic to environmental welfare; stress the worth and value of the outdoors; use figurative language with natural connections (e.g., "strong as an oak tree" or "fresh as a spring rain")
Existential	Sensitivity and capacity to tackle deep questions about human existence, such as the meaning of life, why do we die, and how did we get here	Choose topics with "deeper" significance; avoid shallow treatment of ideas; use weighty evidence; show how your topic "matters"

Source: Gardner, H. (1993). Frames of the mind: The theory of multiple intelligence. New York: Basic Books. Schaller, K. A., & Callison, M. B. (1998). Applying multiple intelligences theory to the basic public speaking course. Basic Communication Course Annual, 10, 90–104. Disney Learning Partnerships and Thirteen Ed Online (n.d.) Tapping into multiple intelligences. Retrieved February 11, 2004 from http://www.thirteen.org/edonline/concept2class/month1/

Types of Audiences Typically, your audience will be one of four types, depending upon their characteristics and psychological profiles. Figure 9.2 depicts the four types of audiences and places them on a continuum.

Friendly audiences are those who hold positive regard for you or your topic. If, for example, you deliver a persuasive speech, a friendly audience already agrees with your position; you already share values, attitudes, and beliefs. You will likely simply reinforce those ideas that the audience already agrees with in order to encourage the listeners to continue holding their position. For example, members of sororities or fraternities already agree in the value of the Greek system. If a speaker supports this position, then he or she will speak with a friendly audience.

In contrast, audiences toward the other end of the continuum disagree with your position or doubt your credibility; they are opposed to your position. In this case, you must find common ground in order to help them appreciate an alternative perspective, even though they probably won't change their minds. To keep to our example, if your speech emphasizes the value of the Greek system for beginning college students, and your audience consists of former members of sororities and fraternities who consider the Greek system discriminatory rather than inclusive, and abusive rather than supportive, then the audience is strongly opposed to a position you are advocating.

Of course, audiences may be located at any point along the continuum and, therefore, be inclined toward friendliness or opposition without being deeply committed to a definite posture. *Neutral* audiences are at the continuum's center; they remain unde-

FIGURE 9.2   Types of Audiences

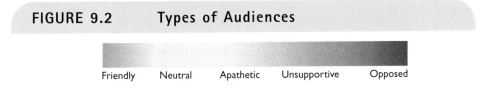

Friendly   Neutral   Apathetic   Unsupportive   Opposed

cided about you or your topic, although they may be interested in the topic. When addressing neutral audiences, consider offering a wide range of appeals in order to nudge the audience toward greater friendliness. Remember that you can always appeal to needs and learning styles as a strategy for enhancing audience responsiveness.

Unlike neutral audiences, *apathetic* audiences are disinterested in your topic and/or you as the speaker. They simply don't care. Consequently, they appear to be more opposed than they truly are. When speaking to apathetic audiences, increase their interest by relating the topic more directly to them and by delivering the speech skillfully. In other words, to overcome the "So what?" mentality of the apathetic audience, help the audience see and feel that what you have to say directly impacts their lives. Again, remembering your audience's basic needs can help you strengthen their interest.

Unsupportive audiences are not strongly opposed to a position because they possess a less definitive degree of disagreement. Unlike neutral audiences, unsupportive audiences hold a defined position on your topic, and unlike apathetic audiences, unsupportive audiences care about the topic. However, because they are less opposed to you or your position, they may be swayed by carefully crafted arguments and appeals.

By attending to the demographics, psychological profiles, and the subsequent types of your audience, you can refine your choice of subjects. After you identify those subjects that appeal to you, carefully think about your audience. What will they find interesting, novel, alluring, familiar, comfortable, or provocative?

The Personal Perspective The **personal perspective** considers your knowledge, attitudes, interests, experiences, and beliefs to help generate speech topics. By choosing a subject that you are personally invested in, you can maintain your enthusiasm in both preparing and presenting your speech. However, it is essential that you select a subject that interests both your audience and you. Begin with your listeners and link your interests with theirs. A personal inventory form, which helps you identify areas of personal interest, can help you think through possible topics.

> personal perspective takes into account an individual's knowledge, attitudes, interests, experiences, and beliefs to help generate speech topics

Other Perspectives While the audience perspective and personal perspectives are central, there are other perspectives you should consider in choosing your topic. First, the **situational perspective** focuses upon the context for your speech. You must consider the time, occasion, place, and size of your audience. It's helpful to know when, where, and why you are speaking, because these will help you plan your speech carefully and select an appropriate subject and tone for delivering the speech.

> situational perspective focuses upon the context of a speech in selecting a topic

Choose a subject for your speech in which you are personally interested.

Second, the **organizational perspective** recognizes that speakers may directly or indirectly represent the firm or organization for which they work; therefore, speakers may need to be sensitive to the subject they choose since there are public relations overtones related to the choice.

Third, the **practical perspective** considers the ready availability of adequate and recent research material as well as time limits for preparation and presentation of your speech. While all of us must manage our time in order to accomplish multiple tasks, this is especially true for college students since they have many demands on their time. Therefore, you must be practical about your choice of subject, given the time you have to prepare for your speech—either you manage your time or your time will manage you.

Now that you have identified potential subject areas using the five perspectives we have discussed, go back through your brainstorming list and write down all the circled subject areas on a piece of paper. As you read them again, rank them using the perspectives we just discussed. Which topic seems best considering each of these perspectives? With these rankings before you, select the speech subject you find most suitable and commit to using it. You may be tempted to go back to this list and start over again, but you are likely to lose valuable preparation time.

> **organizational perspective** recognizes that speakers may represent an organization and, as a result, may need to be sensitive in choosing a subject
>
> **practical perspective** considers the availability of adequate, recent research materials and time limits for the preparation and presentation of a speech

HOW TO SELECT A TOPIC

*N*ow that you have a subject, you must narrow it to a **topic**, or the specific focus of your speech. You will not have enough time to share all the information about a given subject. Moreover, your audience does not have the patience or endurance to listen to all that information. As someone noted, "The mind can only contain what the seat can endure." So, how do you begin to narrow a subject into a topic? As our model in Figure 9.1 indicates, brainstorming can once again be very helpful. Using clean sheets of paper, again start to generate specific ideas related to your subject. Ask basic information questions like Who? When? Where? Why? How? This will help you think about ideas related to your topic. As you did before, let your thoughts flow uninterrupted; don't exclude any possibilities. Keep this worksheet to use later in the process of developing your speech.

> **topic** the specific focus of a speech

Once you have a list of possible topics for your speech, return to the perspectives we discussed and apply them again. Which topics seem to mesh well with these perspectives? As you did with the subjects, rank the topics you have generated and commit to one. If you have carefully thought through the process, you should have confidence that the topic you have chosen will interest you and your audience and you should have sufficient enthusiasm to begin crafting your speech. As a final litmus test, ask yourself, "Do *I* truly care about this topic? Am *I* genuinely interested in this topic?" Without a personal commitment to the topic, you will lack the enthusiasm to effectively prepare and present your speech.

You also need to consider if your selected topic is narrow enough. A key tip here is to consider the amount of time you have to speak. Understand the time limits for the speeches you will give in this class. While these limits may seem long at first, the time will pass very quickly. Furthermore, as a general guideline, plan to share more information about a focused idea rather than less information about a greater number of ideas. Consider this example:

Insufficiently narrowed topic: College roommates

Sufficiently narrowed topic: How to get along with college roommates

The topic "college roommates" is much too broad, because there are many possible topics related to this subject. Generate as many topics or ideas as you can about college roommates. How many emerged as you brainstormed? Now, think about strategies for getting along with college roommates. How many ideas can you generate? As you will likely see, the narrowed topic provides fewer and more specific ideas and, therefore, suggests that it is limited sufficiently. As the box Computer Links: Computer Help in Finding a Topic points out, there are many resources to assist you in your brainstorming and topic selection process.

Computer Links

Computer Help in Finding a Topic

Are you having problems finding a topic for your speech? Check out the following websites for assistance in finding a subject or topic. Even though these sites may help you get started, remember that you must analyze your audience and adapt the topic well to them.

www.hawaii.edu/mauispeech/html/infotopichelp.html

www.bedfordstmartins.com/publicspeaking/topic.htm

http://faculty.cinstate.cc.oh.us/gesellsc/publicspeaking/topics.html

HOW TO RELATE A TOPIC TO PURPOSES

You now have a subject and a narrowed topic. But what is your speech's goal? Remember that the goal of your speech is related to the assignment you receive and/or the three general purposes we discussed earlier in this section. At this point, you must be clear as to whether you are to celebrate, inform, or persuade. This defines your general purpose.

You also need a specific purpose, which you can frame by using the formula we offered earlier: *Opening clause + descriptor + topic.* Also review Table 9.2, which provides appropriate descriptors for each general purpose. As an example, let's use the topic we identified earlier: how to get along with college roommates. Consider each of these specific purposes:

Celebratory speech: *I want my audience to laugh at ways we use to get along with college roommates.*

Informative speech: *I want my audience to understand how to get along with a college roommate.*

Persuasive speech: *I want my audience to begin to use known ways to get along with college roommates.* (This is a speech to actuate.)

OR

Persuasive speech: *I want my audience to agree with me that the known ways to get along with college roommates are useful strategies.* (This is a speech to convince.)

The general and specific purposes for a speech help to craft the topic even more clearly, although the essential topic remains the same. This reminds us that while the process of crafting a speech follows the logic identified in our model, the steps influence one another; it is an iterative process. Remember that the general and specific purpose of your speech is fundamentally important since it is the rudder; it sets the direction of your speech and helps to ensure that you stay on course. You must know what you want to achieve before you can effectively reach your goal and link this purpose to your topic.

HOW TO WRITE A THESIS STATEMENT

At this point in the process, you know your assignment and, therefore, your general purpose. You have also identified a subject and a topic and sufficiently narrowed the topic, and you have crafted a specific purpose statement that integrates and refines the links between your general purpose and your topic. While this statement provides you with important direction, you still need to develop its content by creating a thesis statement. A **thesis statement** summarizes the essence of your speech in a single, declarative sentence. The **thesis** is the speech's central idea, the theme to be developed, or the proposition to be proven. A solid thesis statement should contain the single, main idea of the speech, stated in clear language. Using again the topic we identified previously, consider these two thesis statements:

> Ineffective thesis statement: *How to get along with college roommates.*

> Effective thesis statement: *There are three important strategies that will help us get along with college roommates.*

The first statement is not a sentence and lacks focus and clarity. The second statement, on the other hand, is a complete, clear sentence that offers specific information.

You may be asking, "How did I know there were *three* important strategies?" At this point, you may not be sure that there are three, but you do know that because the speech must be short, you must limit your main ideas to no more than three. This is just a beginning thesis statement; it isn't the final draft you'll write on your preparation outline. Also realize that you can refine the thesis statement as you gather research and develop the body of your speech. You may well write several drafts of your thesis statement as you develop your topic. The double arrow in our model between thesis and research is a reminder that the thesis at this point is a work in progress. However, it is still important to write a first draft so you remember that your speech needs a clear, single idea from which all the other ideas flow.

thesis statement a single, declarative sentence that summarizes the essence of a speech

thesis the central idea of a speech

CELEBRATORY, INFORMATIVE, AND PERSUASIVE SPEECHES

 ow that we have considered some of the fundamental steps necessary to develop your speech, let's give more detailed consideration to celebratory, informative, and persuasive speeches.

Celebratory Speeches

Celebratory speeches are typically given to recognize a person, place, or event. For example, **speeches of tribute** include eulogies, roasts, toasts, welcomes, and award presentations that celebrate a person or a group of people. Other celebratory speeches that focus on people include introductions, welcomes, and nominations, while dedications, ribbon-cuttings, or opening ceremonies tend to focus on a particular structure, location, or memorial. Commencement addresses and acceptance speeches celebrate a particular event. **Speeches to entertain and inspire** are general in nature and may occur in a variety of settings. For example, an organization may host an annual convention and invite a keynote speaker whose sole purpose is to inspire or entertain the organization's members. Table 9.5 summarizes some of the basic types of celebratory speeches. We encourage you to study this information, because you are very likely to deliver a celebratory speech at some point in your life, such as a toast at a wedding.

speeches of tribute speeches that celebrate a person, a group of people, or an event

speeches to entertain and inspire celebratory speeches that are general in nature and may occur in a variety of settings

We have offered only basic information about celebratory speeches; it takes considerable time and energy to gain skill in crafting and delivering these speeches. We urge you to take additional public speaking courses to help develop your skills more thoroughly. There are also several excellent resources you can consult. We encourage you to review the references on public speaking found at the end of this chapter or to search the Internet to identify other resources.

Informative Speeches

Informative speeches include speeches of explanation, definition, description, and briefings.

Speech of Explanation

A **speech of explanation** explains an idea, concept, or process. For example, a speech of explanation may help listeners understand the difference between a republic and a democracy, thereby clarifying both ideas. It might also

speech of explanation a speech that explains an idea, concept, or process

Table 9.5 Types of Celebratory Speeches

Type of Speech	Focus of Speech	Purpose of Speech	Example
Tributes	Person/People	To honor a person or group for service or accomplishment	Address by dean at Honor's Day for students on Dean's List
Eulogies		To honor a person recently deceased	Reflections on life of grandparent
Roasts		To humorously honor a person and his/her contribution/work	Comments at retirement of your immediate supervisor
Toasts		To celebrate a person's life, work, or future (e.g., a wedding)	Toast to best friend at his/her wedding
Award		To honor excellence in performance	Presentation of MVP athletic award
Introductions	Person	To introduce a speaker and help establish his/her credibility	Introduction of guest speaker for sorority induction ceremony
Welcome	Person/Group	To officially acknowledge the presence or participation of people	Official welcome by university president to visiting scholars from another country
Nominations	Person	To present a person for office or an award	To officially nominate a classmate for president of student government
Dedications (ribbon-cuttings, opening ceremonies)	Place	To name a building or structure in honor of a person/group	Dedicating a new laboratory in honor of a donation to fund the new facility
Commencement Speeches	Event	To recognize and inspire graduates	Valedictorian address
Acceptance Speeches	Event	To acknowledge and express appreciation for an award or honor	Accepting an MVP award
Speeches to Entertain	Various	To engage listeners with appropriate humor and share a specific message	After-dinner speech for a campus organization or club focusing on the continuing value of the group's work
Speeches to Inspire	Various	To move listeners to appreciation, resolution, and/or motivation	Address at honor society induction ceremony encouraging continued academic excellence

help listeners understand concepts such as spontaneous generation or the process of solving a quadratic equation. For the most part, speeches of explanation concentrate on abstract notions and are, therefore, very challenging to develop and deliver. Very often a lecture, a form of speaking with which you are well acquainted, is essentially a speech of explanation. Although some college students consider a lecture a boring presentation, it can be an engaging and interesting informative speech if it is prepared and presented effectively, as the box Campus Links: Approaching Lectures as Informative Speeches explains. It is important to remember that when you give speeches of explanation, you need to provide clear definitions of key terms in language that listeners can comprehend, along with numerous, relevant examples that illustrate your ideas.

⊚ Campus Links

Approaching Lectures as Informative Speeches

Like many other students, perhaps you would rather watch a fly on the wall than attend a lecture class. However, lecturing is a very real part of college learning, even though active learning, service learning, and Web-based learning are also becoming equally important. Perhaps thinking of a lecture as an informative speech may adjust your approach to lectures and help you learn more at the next class. How can this approach help? Consider these suggestions.

First, by thinking of a lecture as an informative speech, you can focus on the lecture's thesis. In other words, what is the topic of the lecture? Rather than assume your professor is rambling on without any goal, try to summarize in one sentence the major point of the lecture. Your professor may provide this information, but if he or she does not, you can probably identify the thesis by thinking about the readings assigned in preparation for the class and the information the instructor shares during the class. In most instances, your professor will give a clear indication of the lesson's topic at the beginning of the lecture. Therefore, it is to your advantage to listen when the class begins and to attend to the information immediately. Arrive a few minutes early and prepare to listen and learn. If you think of attending class as though you were going to hear an important speech, you will adjust your attitude, which will positively impact your learning.

Second, listen for the lecture's main points. An effective lecture, just like an appropriately organized informative speech, identifies and develops main points related to the topic and thesis. Your professor may provide these ideas by offering key terms or highlighting the most important ideas through visual aids. In general, words, objects, diagrams, or other information your professor offers are typically important points you should glean from the day's session. So, attend to what is written on the board, overhead, or included in PowerPoint slides. (Hint: If possible, ask your professor to e-mail you his or her PowerPoint slides or visuals in order to ensure that you have a complete set of notes.)

Third, listen for examples, stories, anecdotes, or other illustrative material. Many times a story or an example will capture the essence of a main idea and help clarify the thesis of the lesson. According to research, effective teachers are often storytellers (Collins & Cooper 1997), so you may find it particularly interesting to listen to your professor's stories. In our case, we often draw on our own life experiences or research to help illustrate ideas as we teach. These stories may seem like "filler" material, but attending to them can help you enjoy the lecture more and "get the point" of the lecture more readily.

Fourth, pay attention to the lecture's conclusion. Your professor will often repeat the topic and the main ideas of the lesson before closing class. This provides you with an important summary and gives you a thumbnail sketch of the ideas for the day. Additionally, many professors will leave time for posing questions at the end of a lecture. By attending to the lecture as an informative speech, you will be able to identify any concepts that remain unclear to you; consequently, you can pose a relevant question for clarification. Your teacher will appreciate your meaningful question and will likely positively remember you for posing it!

As soon as possible after the lecture, review your notes. Using a notation system that employs color-coding, marginal notes, or computer transcription, highlight the main ideas and important details that your professor stressed with visual aids, examples, or explanations. In this way, you will have a valuable set of notes readied for study before the next exam or project.

Additionally, by approaching a lecture as an informative speech, you can provide important feedback to your professor. At some point, you will likely have an opportunity to provide feedback to your professor about his or her teaching. Using informative speaking principles, you can provide valuable, specific feedback that will help your professor continue to improve his or her teaching. This allows you to use your public speaking instruction not only for your own development, but also to assist your teachers.

speech of definition an informative speech that helps an audience understand what something means

Speech of Definition

A **speech of definition** focuses on helping your audience understand what something means. To achieve this goal, you may address the connotative or denotative meanings of words, or you may analyze the history or use of key terms essential to the definition you are considering. To make your definitions clear, you may employ contrast or comparisons or identify terms that are similar to or very different from the key notion you choose to focus upon. For example, although we are all acquainted with the term *justice*, upon close examination, we realize that this is not an easy concept to define. A speech focused on defining *justice* would, therefore, require careful thought, specific research, and an ability to make the topic interesting for the audience. As an example, consider an informative speech on date rape that offers a legal definition of the term in order to help college students understand this serious and illegal behavior—without attempting to influence their opinion.

speech of demonstration an informative speech that shows how something is done using visual aids and movement

Speech of Demonstration

A **speech of demonstration** is a third type of informative speech. Most communication teachers can point to a time when a student presented a speech entitled, "How to Make Scrambled Eggs" or a presentation on another mundane topic. However, speeches of demonstration can be interesting and informative. For example, do you know how to Rollerblade? Obviously, not everyone does, at least not with skill! Demonstrating the steps for learning how to Rollerblade properly may well provide listeners with new or interesting information. However, in a demonstration speech, you do more than just *explain* how something is done; you also *show* how it is done through the use of visual aids and movement. One student we had was a scuba diver. For his informative assignment, he chose a demonstration speech. He brought his scuba-diving equipment, and by the time he finished his speech, he was attired in all of the necessary gear. Of course, his speech ended with silence when he put the mouthpiece in place, peered at us through his diving mask, and opened his arms wide as if to say, "Here's what it looks like, folks!" As you can imagine, his conclusion drew a hearty laugh from his peers.

speech of description an informative speech that relies on mental pictures created by pictorial language

Speech of Description

Speeches of description rely on mental pictures created by strategic use of pictorial language. Rather than relying heavily on visual aids to help an audience envision a scenic vista or an imposing structure, the speaker uses language to help the audience "see" the color, size, shape, texture, and characteristics of the place of interest or object. For example, consider a speech that describes the incredible poverty in Guatemala. The speech might describe how people literally fight huge, black vultures for the garbage expelled from the back of garbage trucks into the city dump and live in houses constructed of cardboard and sheets of tin. The purpose of such a speech is to paint a picture for the audience by recounting the sights, sounds, and smells of a disturbing experience.

briefing a short presentation in an organizational setting

Briefings

Osborn and Osborn (2000) define a **briefing** as "a short presentation in an organizational setting" (p. 343). Briefings usually provide an update, report on a specific project, or provide information necessary for others to complete a task. For example, nurses brief one another at shift changes so that patient care can continue. Marketing directors brief other members of a manufacturing company on the latest attempts to sell a particular product. Managers explain policy changes to employees. Resident assistants in college dorms provide information to other student-life personnel regarding activities or incidents on their respective floors in weekly meetings. In short, briefings occur in a variety of organizational settings in order to ensure that the people in the organization understand important information.

Persuasive Speeches

Types of Persuasive Speeches According to Purpose

As we noted earlier, unlike informative speeches, persuasive speeches fulfill one of three purposes: (1) to reinforce, (2) to change beliefs/to convince, and (3) to change behavior/to actuate.

Health-care workers are often involved in briefings, which are a specific type of informative speech.

While all persuade, these three types of persuasive speeches differ in their specific purposes. Let's consider each of these three specific purposes in more detail.

Have you heard the phrase, "Preaching to the choir?" When people preach to the choir, they reinforce beliefs or behaviors to which the audience already ascribes. Since this is often the purpose of sermons, this phrase utilizes the image of preachers delivering a message to the choir, who agrees with their words. This is a **speech to reinforce or stimulate**. However, using the same example, if a sermon challenges the audience to alter widely accepted beliefs, the specific purpose changes from reinforcement to motivation to accept new beliefs or alter present beliefs, even though the overall intent or general purpose remains persuasive. This is a **speech to convince**.

In another example, if a candidate for student government asks students to cast their ballots for him, the general purpose is persuasive but the specific purpose is to motivate voters to behave in a particular manner. This is a **speech to actuate**. On the other hand, if the president of your university asks the student body to believe that a proposed tuition increase is a necessary response to economic needs, even though the general purpose is persuasive, the specific purpose changes. In this instance, the president *speaks to convince* or to alter the audience's beliefs.

Although these three specific purposes for persuasive speeches differ, in each case the speaker acts as an advocate for a particular proposition or supports a specific claim. In doing so, the speaker draws on his or her credibility (ethos), employs logic and evidence (logos), and often seeks to touch the audience's emotions (pathos).

Types of Persuasive Speeches According to Proposition Persuasive speeches are by nature propositional; they propose and advocate a particular belief or behavior. However, the nature of the proposition for a speech may differ. Persuasive speeches may be categorized according to these various propositions: fact, value, and policy.

Propositions of fact are debatable issues that a single piece of objective evidence cannot resolve. In other words, persuasive speeches that focus on propositions of fact focus on whether a given interpretation of evidence is or is not true. Propositions of fact seek to answer the question, "Is this true or false?" For example, consider these propositions of fact:

Global warming continues/does not continue to increase as a result of changes in the ozone layer.

WorldCom executives did/did not purposefully ensure their economic fortunes at the expense of stockholders.

speech to reinforce or stimulate a speech that reinforces the beliefs or behaviors to which the audience already ascribes

speech to convince a persuasive speech that challenges the audience to alter widely accepted beliefs

speech to actuate a persuasive speech that motivates the audience toward a particular behavior

proposition of fact a debatable issue that a single piece of objective evidence cannot resolve

proposition of value focuses on the worth or value of a particular person, idea, event, or object

proposition of policy advocates a particular response or specific course of action

Legislators frequently use the various types of propositions in persuasive speeches.

Propositions of value focus on the worth or value of a particular person, idea, event, or object. Propositions of value seek to answer the question, "Is this good or bad, right or wrong, ethical or unethical?" For example, consider these propositions of value:

The Internet is/is not a morally compromised environment due to the widespread presence of pornography.

Alternative health-care practitioners do/do not take advantage of sick people.

Many propositions of value rest on propositions of fact—that is, you cannot argue the value of a certain proposition without also providing evidence regarding certain assumptions. For example, you cannot argue that the Internet is a morally compromised environment in view of the widespread presence of pornography without first establishing that pornography is, indeed, widespread on the Internet.

Propositions of policy advocate a particular response or specific course of action. They are concerned with what course of action should be taken in response to a particular question. For example, consider these propositions of policy in response to propositions of fact and value we have already introduced:

The U.S. Congress should pass legislation to ensure that executives of corporations do not propagate the kind of fraud exemplified by the executives of WorldCom.

All parents should be required to use a child protective software program on home computers in order to ensure that children are not exposed to pornography.

Propositions of policy espouse and argue for a specific response to a given problem. You can often identify propositions of policy by the presence of the word *should*, although some propositions of value may also employ this key word.

Understanding the various types of speeches and their purposes will help you craft your own speeches and understand and analyze other speakers and speeches.

CONNECTING COLLEGE AND PUBLIC SPEAKING

efore we leave this chapter, it is important to emphasize that giving a speech in your communication class is an authentic and relevant speaking event.

The College Classroom as a "Real" Audience

Often students complain that giving a speech to their peers isn't "real" because the class doesn't comprise a "real" audience. This is a misunderstanding. Every aspect of a genuine speaking situation exists in your classroom. All the aspects of the communication model are present, including a speaker, listeners, a message, channels, feedback, and contexts. Furthermore, if you think of your peers as an authentic audience and plan your speech with them in mind, you can craft a speech that will engage them. For example, what do you know about your classmates? Every generation has its own unique characteristics (Table 9.6 summarizes some of these). Understanding these may help you address the various members of your classroom audience and craft your message accordingly. If you are speaking with traditional-college-age students, you are addressing the "millennial generation," people born in or after 1982 who began entering the college classroom after 2000. Howe and Strauss (2000) summarize the millennials in these words:

As a group the millennials are unlike any other youth generation in living memory. They are more numerous, more affluent, better educated, and more ethnically diverse. More important, they are beginning to manifest a wide array of positive social habits that older Americans no longer associate with youth, including a new focus on teamwork, achievement, modesty and good conduct. (p. 4)

Being aware of this information; gathering information through surveys, class discussions, and conversations will help you get to know your classmates. Also,

■ Table 9.6   Understanding Basic Generational Differences

1. "Baby Boomers" (born 1943 to 1960, ages 44 to 61)

Core Values	Assets	Liabilities
Optimism	Service-oriented	Not naturally "budget-minded"
Team orientation	Driven	Uncomfortable with conflict
Personal gratification	Willing to go "extra mile"	Reluctant to go against peers
Health and wellness	Good at relationships	May put process ahead of result
Personal growth	Want to please	Overly sensitive to feedback

2. Generation Xers (born 1960 to 1980, ages 24 to 44)

Core Values	Assets	Liabilities
Diversity	Adaptable	Impatient
Thinking globally	Technoliterate	Poor people skills
Balance	Independent	Inexperienced
Technoliteracy	Unintimidated by authority	Cynical
Fun	Creative	
Informality		
Self-reliance		
Pragmatism		

3. Generation Next, or "Y" also called "Millennials" (born since 1980, ages 24 and younger)

Core Values	Assets	Liabilities
Optimism	Collective action	Need for supervision/structure
Civic duty	Optimism	Inexperience handling difficult
Confidence	Tenacity	people
Achievement	Heroic spirit	
Sociability	Multitasking capabilities	
Morality	Technologically savvy	
Street smarts		
Diversity		

Source: "Understanding basic generational differences," from *Generations at work: Managing the clash of veterans, boomers, Xers, and Nexters in your workplace,* by Ron Zemke, Claire Raines, and Bob Filipczak. AMACOM Books, 2001.

listen intently to your classmates' speeches; this will help you plan your speech and make genuine connections with your peers. Don't sell your peers short; they are a genuine audience.

Relevance of Celebratory, Informative, and Persuasive Speaking to the College Experience

While the immediate relevance of public speaking to your course work is evident since you are enrolled in this communication class, the various types of public speaking that we discussed earlier in this chapter extend to other aspects of your college experience. You will have numerous opportunities to use these various types of speeches in ceremonial, social, and academic settings while in college. For example, most colleges have commencement exercises that include a student speaker. While this honor is often limited to one or two students, you may, nevertheless, be the valedictorian of your graduating class or participate in your graduation ceremony as an officer of a student organization that "passes the torch" to the next graduating class.

In other situations in college, you may be called upon to present or receive an award or nominate a colleague to an office in an organization. Or you may be the person nominated by others to fill a position in student government or in your sorority or fraternity. As a result, you will need to articulate your vision with other students whose votes or support you will need in order to serve your college community. In most cases, if you hold any leadership position, you will be expected to speak publicly in some manner.

Additionally, you will probably be required to deliver informative speeches in other classes, especially in institutions that emphasize speaking across the curriculum. For example, in our institutions, students give reports individually or in groups in a variety of academic areas ranging from the sciences to the humanities. In other instances, you may be called upon to teach a class for a day or to develop your presentation skills in other assignments, especially if you are pursuing a career in areas such as education, business, or law that require excellent oral communication skills. In short, involvement in campus life means that you will be a public speaker. Learning public speaking skills, then, can improve your social and academic success and enhance your college experience.

As we have noted, when you graduate, you will need public speaking skills. While you may not be required to make public presentations, the variety of skills you glean from developing your public speaking skills are transferable immediately and directly to the working world. Those who work full or part-time have already likely learned that the ability to speak clearly and appropriately in work settings matters to your personal satisfaction with your job, as well as the likelihood of recognition or promotion.

 ## SUMMARY

In this introductory chapter to public speaking, we have identified some essential elements of effective public speaking. Specifically, we have

- explained why public speaking is important for the college experience and your future career;
- considered the problem of communication apprehension;
- identified public speaking as a process and illustrated the process in a model;
- discovered how to craft an appropriate specific purpose statement;
- considered the various types of celebratory, informative, and persuasive speeches;
- explained how to select a subject and a topic using brainstorming and considering four important perspectives;
- discussed how to craft a clear, succinct thesis for your speech;

- examined the three general purposes for public speaking: to entertain, to inform, and to persuade;
- examined the relevance of the public speaking classroom audience;
- reviewed the relevance of the three types of public speaking for college and career.

Questions for Discussion

1. Kanar (1998) asserts that making presentations is one of the five essential academic skills for students. Do you agree? Why?
2. Revisit the model for public speaking we introduced in this chapter. How might this model change if people from other cultures were constructing it? Why?
3. Evaluate Osborn and Osborn's (2000) statement: "People will listen, learn, and remember a message only if it relates to their needs, wants or wishes" (p. 90).

EXERCISES

1. Create a list of all the ways public speaking is used as a means to inform and persuade you from day to day. What conclusions do you draw from this list about the role of public speaking in everyday life?
2. Find the written text of a speech that you find interesting. You can find speech texts on the Web or in your library. For example, check a publication such as *Vital Speeches* or check these websites: www.uiowa.edu/~commstud/resources/speech.html, links to various

speakers; http://gos.sbc.edu/, speeches by women; www.americanrhetoric.com, collection of numerous American speeches; http://library.ups.edu/research/spchtxt.htm, collection of speeches.

When you find a speech you like, print it out and then identify its general purpose, specific purpose, subject, topic, and thesis. Highlight these and bring them to class for further discussion.

KEY TERMS

Communication apprehension
General purpose
Epideictic speeches
Celebratory, ceremonial, or special occasion speeches
Informative speeches
Persuasive speeches
Specific purpose
Subject
Brainstorming
Audience perspective
Values

Beliefs
Attitude
Personal perspective
Situational perspective
Organizational perspective
Practical perspective
Topic
Thesis statement
Thesis
Speeches of tribute
Speeches to entertain and inspire

Speeches of explanation
Speeches of definition
Speeches of demonstration
Speeches of description
Briefing
Speeches to reinforce or stimulate
Speeches to convince
Speeches to actuate
Propositions of fact
Propositions of value
Propositions of policy

REFERENCES

Andrews, P. H., Andrews, J. R., and Williams, G. 1999. *Public speaking: Connecting you and your audience.* Boston, MA: Houghton Mifflin.

Braithwaite, D. O., and Thompson, T. L. 2000. *Handbook of communication and people with disabilities.* Mahwah, NJ: Lawrence Erlbaum.

Burk, J. 2001. Communication apprehension among Master's of Business Administration students: Investigating a gap in communication education. *Communication Education* 50:51–58.

Burke, K. 1973. *The philosophy of literary form: Studies in symbolic action.* 3d ed. Berkeley, CA: University of California Press.

Collins, R., and Cooper, P. 1997. *The power of story: Teaching through story-telling.* Boston: Allyn & Bacon.

Dannels, D. P., Anson, C. M., Bullard, L., and Peretti, S. 2003. Challenges in learning communication skills in chemical engineering. *Communication Education* 52:50–56.

Darling, A. L., and Dannels, D. P. 2003. Practicing engineers talk about the importance of talk: A report on the role of oral communication in the workplace. *Communication Education* 52:1–16.

Disney Learning Partnerships and Thirteen Ed Online. n.d. *Tapping into multiple intelligences.* Retrieved February 11, 2004, from www.thirteen.org/edonline/concept2class/month1/.

Gardner, H. 1993. *Frames of the mind: The theory of multiple intelligence.* New York: Basic Books.

Howe, N., and Strauss, W. 2000. *Millennials rising: The next generation.* New York: Vintage Books.

Kanar, C. C. 1998. *The confident student.* 3d ed. Boston, MA: Houghton Mifflin.

Kaplan, R. 1984. Cultural thought patterns in intercultural education. In *Composing in a second language,* ed., S. McKay. Rowely, MA: Newbury House Publishing 43–62.

Kirtley, M. D., and Weaver, J. B. 1999. Exploring the impact of gender role self-perception on communication style. *Women's Studies in Communication* 23:190.

Martin, J., and Nakayama, T. 2005. *Experiencing intercultural communication: An introduction.* 2nd ed. New York: McGraw-Hill.

McCroskey, J. C., and Richmond, V. P. 1979. The impact of communication apprehension on individuals in organizations. *Communication Quarterly* 27:55–61.

Motley, M. T. 1997. *Overcoming your fear of public speaking: A proven method.* Boston, MA: Houghton Mifflin.

Osborn, M., and Osborn, S. 2000. *Public speaking.* 5th ed. Boston, MA: Houghton Mifflin.

Petersen, M. S. 1997. Personnel interviewers' perceptions of the importance and adequacy of applicants' communication skills. *Communication Education* 46:287–291.

Reiff, J. C. 1992. *What research says to the teacher: Learning styles.* Washington, DC: National Educational Association.

Schaller, K. A., and Callison, M. B. 1998. Applying multiple intelligences theory to the basic public speaking course. *Basic Communication Course Annual* 10:90–104.

Sellnow, D. D. 2002. *Public speaking: A process approach.* Fort Worth, TX: Harcourt.

Sellnow, D., and Golish, T. 2000. The relationship between self-disclosure speech and public speaking anxiety: Considering gender equity. *Basic Communication Course Annual* 12:28–59.

Wood, J. 1994. *Gendered lives: Communication, gender, and culture.* Belmont, CA: Wadsworth.

Worley, D. W. 2000. An acrostic for public speaking. *Basic Communication Course Annual* 12:193–209.

Young, J. R. June 30, 2004. Students' political awareness hits highest level in a decade. *Chronicle of Higher Education* A30.

CHAPTER *10*

Organization, Development, and Support

Organization, Development, and Support

Organization

Principles

Clarity
Simplicity
Parallelism
Balance
Practicality
Orderliness

Parts

Introduction
Body
Transitions
Conclusion

Patterns

For Informative Speeches
For Persuasive Speeches

Development/Support

Finding Materials

Evaluating Materials

Types of Supporting Materials

Facts
Statistics
Testimony
Examples
Narratives

Effective Use of Materials

Relatedness
Relevance
Respect

Citing Sources

In Writing
Orally
Plagerism

Outlining

Types of Outlines

Planning
Preparation
Presentation

Alternatives to Outlining

Concept Map
"Tree" Outlines

Knowledge Checklist

✓ To understand the principles of effective organization
✓ To understand the parts of a speech: introduction, body, transitions, and conclusion
✓ To identify and use various types of organizational patterns
✓ To identify and use effective patterns for informative and persuasive speeches
✓ To know how to find various types of supporting material
✓ To know how to select credible source materials
✓ To learn how to cite sources
✓ To learn how to use supporting materials to effectively support ideas
✓ To appreciate the importance and purpose of clear organization
✓ To learn and use the principles of effective outlining
✓ To learn how to organize ideas using outlines, concept maps, and flowcharts
✓ To understand the importance of organizational skills for college learning and life

ORGANIZING YOUR SPEECH

Put the following ideas into a logical order: (1) starting college, (2) choosing a college, and (3) applying to college. How did you arrange these ideas? Most of you probably put them in this order: (1) choosing a college, (2) applying to college, and (3) starting college. You likely put them in this order because we have been taught that events occur in chronological order. In this chapter, we consider how to organize, develop, and outline the important information in a presentation. (See the box Communication Links: Clarifying Terms for additional information regarding our use of terms in this section.) Refer back to Figure 9.1 where we considered the early parts of this model—namely, purpose, subject, topic, and thesis. We are now ready to discuss the continuation of this process, which includes research and outlining. In Chapter 11 we will discuss the final aspects of this model, which include visual aids, practice, and presentation. (Did you notice that we just organized our ideas so that you understand where we are in the process of developing public speaking skills? We are using the same ideas we wish to teach you.) Before we move on, please notice the double arrow between *thesis* and *research* in Figure 9.1. This arrow emphasizes the relationship between developing your presentation's thesis and your research. As you gather information, you may wish to adjust your thesis, which will, in turn, inform the main ideas for your speech and how you support these ideas.

Understanding and using the principles and patterns of organization will help your listeners and you. Remember that unlike reading a paragraph in a book or a magazine, your listeners have one opportunity to understand your message. If your presentation is clearly organized, they will be able to follow your speech. Additionally, clear organization can help offset communication apprehension by ensuring that your speech has a clear sense of direction, thereby increasing your confidence. Moreover, understanding these will assist you in listening, reading, and writing more effectively (Andrews, Andrews, & Williams 1999).

Principles for Effective Organization

Organizing ideas rests on some basic principles which can help you understand how to craft your presentation ideas and assist you to listen, read, and write more effectively.

Communication Links

Clarifying Terms

Perhaps you have noticed that we use the words *presentations* and *public speaking* interchangeably. However, some consider these different approaches to *public address*, or in some cases, *rhetoric*, which are broader terms used to describe the study and practice of speaking to groups of people either in person or via technology.

Osborn and Osborn (2006) identify public speaking as a form of public address that possesses distinctive features. First, the speaker's and listeners' roles are clearly defined, because the spotlight is on the speaker, who is the primary sender of messages. Second, public speakers craft their messages carefully through preparation and practice. Third, the context of communication can change due to unforeseen physical or psychological factors. Fourth, public speaking has the power to transform the speaker, the listener, and the public by providing additional knowledge.

Engleberg and Daly (2005) prefer to think of public address as "presentation speaking." In their view, public speaking is a "special type of presentation speaking that occurs when speakers address public audiences in community, government, and/or organizational settings" (p. 5). Such events are typically open to the public and press and seek to influence the opinion or behavior of others who are not necessarily present when the speech is delivered. On the other hand, these scholars note that "presentation speaking is a broader term and refers to *any* time speakers use verbal and nonverbal messages to generate meanings and establish relationships with audience members who are usually present at the delivery of the presentation" (pp. 5, 6).

While these distinctions may seem unimportant, there are some significant assumptions about each of them that should help inform how you think about and plan for speaking in a variety of settings. In other words, if you speak in a more formalized setting, such as a public hearing, you may need to think in terms of public speaking, while in less formal settings, such as a business briefing to a small group, you may find the presentational speaking approach more effective. The point is this: by learning multiple approaches to speaking in front of others, you can adapt your style to the occasion and the audience in order to deliver the most effective and appropriate message possible.

Clarity   Ideas should be clear. Your ideas are clear when they are directly related to the purpose of your presentation and are complete. Each main thought in your speech should clearly flow from the thesis statement and relate to your speech's purpose statement. Second, each main idea should be a complete sentence, not a phrase or fragment. Consider this example:

Purpose: To persuade my audience

Thesis: The death penalty should be abolished.

Main Ideas:

1. Cost
2. Closure
3. Deterrent

While you may be able to guess what a speaker using this sparse outline wishes to say, the ideas are not clear because the thesis and the main ideas are both incomplete. Furthermore, we are not sure how the ideas relate to the thesis. Now, consider this example, using the same topic:

Purpose: I want my audience to agree that the death penalty should be abolished.

Thesis: The death penalty should be abolished because it is not cost-efficient, it does not bring closure to victims' families, and it is not a deterrent.
Main Ideas:

I. The death penalty does not cost more than housing a prisoner for life.
II. The death penalty does not bring closure to the victims' families.
III. The death penalty is not an effective deterrent to crime.

Notice how the ideas clearly relate to the purpose and the thesis, while they are also complete, clear thoughts.

Organizing your speech is similar to putting together the pieces of a puzzle.

Simplicity   Read this excerpt from *Alice in Wonderland* by Lewis Carroll:

> "I quite agree with you," said the Duchess; "and the moral of that is— 'Be what you would seem to be'—or, if you'd like it put more simply— 'Never imagine yourself not to be otherwise than what it might appear to others that what you were or might have been was not otherwise than what you had been would have appeared to them to be otherwise.'"

In your own words, explain what the Duchess means by these words. Having difficulty? Why? As you can see, ideas should be simply stated. Complete sentences help clarity, but they also help simplicity. If you use very complex sentences, your audience will find it difficult to listen well. Attempting to sound intelligent by using as many words as possible complicates your message and typically does not impress your audience. Furthermore, if you truly know your topic well, you will be able to explain it clearly. On the other hand, if you're having difficulty explaining your ideas, you may not have a grasp of the ideas yourself.

Parallelism   Look back to our example of clear main ideas. Note that each main idea begins with the same words: "The death penalty." This phrasing illustrates the principle of parallelism, which helps listeners identify the main ideas you wish to emphasize. Moreover, parallelism assists clarity and simplicity.

Balance   As we will discuss shortly, your presentation should consist of an introduction, body, and conclusion. You should devote most of your speaking time to developing the ideas in the body of your speech. However, while each point may deserve the same amount of development and thereby receive *equal emphasis*, you may find that either your first or last main point requires more development. Perhaps your audience is unaware of the persistence of a problem, like global warming. In this case, your *first* main point must establish the reality and persistence of this problem; this is called *descending order*. On the other hand, your audience may agree that global warming is a very real threat but need you to identify practical solutions to the problem that they can employ. In this case, your *last* main point may need more emphasis; this is called *ascending order* (Osborn & Osborn 2006).

Practicality   Importantly, your organization should help your audience to understand and remember your message and, perhaps, decide how to respond. Additionally, your organization should help you plan, prepare, and present your speech. As you organize your presentation, think about how it can help your audience to listen and help you to speak.

Orderly   Your presentation should follow a clear, logical, consistent pattern from beginning to end so that your audience can easily comprehend your ideas. Perhaps you have listened to a professor or a visiting speaker lecture and struggled to understand what they were saying. Did they skip from one idea to another? Were you unsure of how one thought related to another? If so, you've experienced a disorderly presentation and know how frustrating it can be, especially if you truly need to know the information. Later we will discuss organizational patterns that work well for both informative and persuasive speeches, but at this point it is important to realize that organizing your entire speech and your main points is critical to successful speaking. Therefore, let's consider how to organize your entire speech before we discuss appropriate and effective organizational patterns.

Understanding the Parts of a Presentation

For your speech to be effective, you need a strong introduction, body, and conclusion connected by clear transitions; these constitute the main portions of any well-crafted speech. Even though we advise you to develop the body first, let's consider each part in order.

The Introduction   A speech's introduction is vital, because it is the first impression you leave as a speaker. You need the introduction to capture your audience's attention, state your topic clearly, give your audience a reason to listen, establish your credibility, and offer a preview of your main points. Consider this example:

> *You're lying on a beach, listening to your favorite CD. You roll over on your stomach so that you can get a little more sun on your back. The rays warm your shoulders and you drift off to sleep. You wake up a half hour later and attempt to roll over to your back. Ouch! Your back is red and burned. Oops—you forgot your sunscreen! How often has this happened to you? I know it's happened to me more times than I care to count. Not only does forgetting your sunscreen result in a nasty sunburn, but it can also increase your chances of getting skin cancer. After a skin cancer scare last summer, I realized the importance of sunscreen, which helped me to learn about the long-term effects of sunburns, especially skin cancer, and the importance of sunscreen in protecting against these potentially serious effects.*

Notice how the student begins by gaining attention. This is your first goal in the introduction of your presentation—attract your audience's attention. Table 10.1 provides some time-tested strategies to help you capture audience attention.

Table 10.1   Attention-Getting Devices

Strategy	Description/Example
Quote	"We have nothing to fear but fear itself."
Story	"When I was a boy on the farm …" An extended narrative that is either true or hypothetical
Humor	An amusing but appropriate anecdote, saying, or one-liner
Startling statement	An arresting statement that relies upon some unusual fact, statistic, or alarming choice of words
Greeting	A warm greeting that identifies you with the audience, establishes common ground, and expresses your appreciation
Rhetorical questions	"Have you ever seen money fly out a window? That's what's happening every winter in your house if you don't have thermal-pane windows from Acme."
Creating curiosity	Through description, narrative, or question, the speaker does not clearly identify a referent and creates curiosity in the listeners. "The only thing he does is sit behind a highly polished mahogany desk day by day and talk on the phone. Yet he controls transactions worth millions of dollars each day that reap him enormous profits."
Illustration	A case or incident that helps the speaker point the audience toward his or her topic

After you gain attention, you should clearly state your topic by indicating the specific subject you want to address and how you intend to address it. However, the most effective way to state your topic is not by saying, "My specific purpose is . . ." or "Today I want to talk with you about . . ." Find a creative way to state your idea while also engaging your audience. Again, notice how the example above illustrates this principle. The speaker indirectly leads us to consider the importance of sunscreen by relating a personal example and linking it to something that has likely happened to us.

Additionally, your introduction should give your audience a reason to listen. Given our electronic age, most people are surrounded by hundreds of messages every hour. How can you get people to listen to *you*? Give them a good reason to. By appealing to the needs of your listeners, you can help your audience focus on what you have to say. For example, in the above introduction, the speaker addressed the audience's concern about cancer. Many people realize that wearing sunscreen is important, so they may have become immune to the message. But, if you can provide them with reasons to listen more carefully, most will likely give a fresh ear to the information.

Many audience members silently ask, "Why should we listen to *you?*" The answer is to establish your credibility. In the above example, the speaker referred to her personal experience with a skin cancer scare. You, too, likely possess experience or areas of expertise that can help you establish your credibility. If not, you can reference your research of the subject or your concern for the topic area and the audience. By helping your audience trust you, they will be more likely to trust what you have to say.

Finally, your introduction should provide a clear preview of your main points before you proceed with your speech. Give the essence of your speech in simple statements in order to identify the path along which you intend to lead your listeners. In our example, the speaker cues us that she will focus on the long-term effects of sunburns, skin cancer, and the importance of sunscreen to protect us from these effects. There are other ways to offer your preview as well. Many prefer what is termed an **enumerated preview**, which means arranging your main points in order (e.g., first, second, third). Here's an example of an enumerated preview for the same speech topic of skin cancer:

> *The first thing to consider is the relationship between sunburns and skin cancer. Second, I'll discuss the serious risks associated with skin cancer. Third, I'll give you some practical tips on how to use the right type and amount of sunscreen in order to help you avoid this risk.*

While not all speeches have such clear previews, this basic approach to speaking works well. Remember that your perspective as a speaker and your audience's perspective differ considerably. If you have adequately prepared, you know the information in your speech very well, but your listeners do not; they need clear verbal markers so they can follow your ideas and stay interested. The time-tested strategies we have shared with you for crafting an introduction will truly help you speak and will help your audience listen. Therefore, when you capture audience attention, state the topic, give the audience a reason to listen, establish credibility, and provide a preview, the introduction to your speech tends to be very effective. As someone once said, "You only get one chance to make a first impression." As a speaker, that one chance comes with your introduction; craft it carefully.

The Body The body of your speech consists of the main points, transitions, and supporting material you have gathered through your research that explains, illustrates, and bolsters your ideas. We will discuss supporting material more thoroughly later in this chapter, but for now let's consider principles that will help you craft strong main points and effective transitions.

The main points in your speech are the primary ideas you want your audience to remember. But how do you identify, craft, and organize main points for the greatest

enumerated preview arranging the main points of a speech in order (e.g., first, second, third)

effect? Because your main points are so important, be sure to identify strong main ideas around which to build your speech. Do this by considering your specific purpose statement that we discussed in Chapter 9; the most important ideas you want to emphasize may already be stated or implied here. For example, consider the specific purpose statement, "I want my audience to vote in the next election." With this persuasive focus, you may decide to present your speech by discussing the reasons to vote, the effects of not voting, and ways for students to vote. As you can see, you have three main points suggested by this approach.

In addition, as you do initial research, common themes may repeatedly occur in your reading. These repetitive ideas are probably the most important concepts to address in your speech and may, therefore, cue you as to the main ideas you should cover. If these approaches do not yield potential main ideas, brainstorming can help generate possibilities. As we noted before, in brainstorming you produce ideas without evaluating them. In order to identify main points, write down everything you know or would like to know about your topic and then look for themes among your ideas. These themes can yield main points.

After you identify your speech's main ideas, you are ready to write them. Main ideas should be simple, independent sentences. Rather than allowing the main ideas to become too complicated, break them into subpoints or, in some cases, divide them into additional main points. Let's return to our earlier example topic of the death penalty. Consider this summary of the topic as one speaker approached it: "The death penalty should be abolished because, contrary to popular belief, it does not cost more money to house prisoners than to execute them, it does not bring closure to the victims' families, and it is not an effective deterrent to crime." This complex sentence could be broken down into three main ideas:

The Death Penalty Should Be Abolished
 I. The death penalty does not cost more than housing a prisoner for life.
 II. The death penalty does not bring closure to the victims' families.
 III. The death penalty is not an effective deterrent to crime.

If the purpose of this speech extends beyond considering the abolition of the death penalty to motivating us to protest the death penalty, the organization could change and result in two main points, with supporting subpoints:

 I. There are three concrete reasons to abolish the death penalty.
   A. The death penalty does not cost more than housing a prisoner for life.
   B. The death penalty does not bring closure to the victims' families.
   C. The death penalty is not an effective deterrent to crime.

 II. There are three effective ways we can all protest the death penalty.
   A. We can join a group that is antideath penalty, such as Amnesty International.
   B. We can join an on-site protest when a state or federal execution takes place.
   C. We can write our state and federal officials.

Notice how the language of the main points is clear, simple, and parallel, which reinforces the principles we discussed in the beginning of this chapter. If you use these principles, you will help your audience listen. However, you also need to limit the number of main points. For most speeches, including those in this class, you usually need no more than two or three main points. Too many main points creates information overload for your audience that, in turn, creates confusion.

Place your main points in some kind of logical order. For the most part, the organizational design you use for your speech will help guide the organization of your main points. In the next section, we discuss various organizational patterns that will help you decide how to arrange your main points so they adhere to the principles of balance and order, the other two principles we discussed at the outset of this chapter.

The main points of your speech are too important to leave to chance. Be sure to identify, craft, and organize them well in order to ensure the strength of your speech's body.

Table 10.2   Purposes of Speech Transitions

1. Transitions to summarize the main points that precede them. For example, "To this point, I have offered you a brief analysis of the problem."

2. Transitions reinforce your organizational approach, whether topical, spatial, temporal, and so on, by linking ideas together. For example, here is a transition that reemphasizes a topical approach: "Not only do persons with AIDS face economic difficulties, but they also must deal with social ostracism."

3. Transitions preview what is ahead in the upcoming main point. Consider the example above. Note that the transition summarizes one main point (the economic difficulties of persons with AIDS) while it introduces the next (the social ostracism of persons with AIDS).

4. Transitions often employ cue words like those in this list:

moreover	consequently	in the first place
furthermore	therefore	secondly
by contrast	as a result	now consider
in comparison	in view of	however
additionally	similarly	now turn to

Transitions   Just as a preview helps map the territory for your listeners as you begin your speech, transitions within the speech provide important markers that ensure your listeners follow you as you proceed. In essence, a transition builds a listening bridge between ideas. Transitions do not provide additional information or evidence but, rather, help lead listeners from one idea to the next. Transitions are especially important (1) between the end of the introduction and the beginning of the body, (2) between main points, (3) between subpoints within the body, and (4) at the end of the body and the beginning of the conclusion.

Moreover, there are two important elements in any transition: (1) *what* is said and (2) *how* it is said. In other words, the content and delivery of transitions are crucial to their success. The content of a transition consists of the actual words you use. Table 10.2 summarizes suggestions for how to word your transitions well.

Transitions are like bridges that help lead your listeners from one idea to another.

Whatever your approach in developing your transitions, avoid using "bare-bones" transitions like these: "Now that I have talked about *X*, let me talk about *Y*." While these are better than no transitions, they tend to be uninteresting. To make your transitions the most effective, incorporate the principles in Table 10.2 and pay as much attention to your transitions as to your main ideas. In other words, solid transitions, like clear main ideas, are a part of planning and practicing your speech. For additional help with the content of your transitions, consider Table 10.3.

While *what* you say in a transition is important, *how* you say it is equally important. To indicate transitions, you can increase your direct eye contact, slow down your speech rate, vary your pitch, and pause either before or after stating the transition. (Chapter 11 provides you with much more information on effective delivery). Like every other part of your speech, practicing your delivery of transitions will help make them more effective.

The Conclusion   While your introduction is your first impression on your listeners, your conclusion is the last. To make the best of your last impression, your conclusion should accomplish two goals. First, you should summarize your speech's content. Second, you should bring the speech to a close so the audience knows you are finished speaking.

To summarize, you should briefly review your speech's main points in one or two sentences. The conclusion should not contain any new information or a lengthy

---

Table 10.3   Types of Transitions

1. **Signposts** alert your listeners to important ideas by verbally pointing to them much like street signs or billboards direct the attention of drivers. Signposts may include a number, question, or a short phrase. Here are some examples:

The first question is	Don't forget
Mark this idea!	This is important!
Hold on to that thought.	But what is the best solution?
The final issue . . .	Secondly, . . .

2. **Internal Previews** offer a brief introduction of the next main point you are about to introduce. Consider this internal preview offered by a student whose speech focused on explaining the power of language to impact our attitudes toward people with disabilities.

   Example: "Not only does our use of language, such as 'wheelchair bound,' reflect our attitudes about people with disabilities, our choice of language also helps form our attitudes toward people with disabilities. Let's consider how this occurs."

3. **Internal Summaries** review the main ideas you have already presented in your speech and serve as transitions to new ideas. In particular, internal summaries are valuable between main points in a speech.

   Example: "As we have seen, persons with AIDS face many problems. Among them are, first, personal economic difficulties; second, social ostracism; and third, dealing with their own impending death. While these problems seem overwhelming, there are important steps we can take as a nation and as individuals to alleviate these problems. Let's consider some of these solutions."

   You may be confused by the difference between internal previews and internal summaries. The difference is this: Internal previews review the idea that has immediately preceded the idea you want to introduce, while internal summaries review *all* the main ideas you have discussed prior to introducing a new idea. In practice, you may find internal previews useful when you're moving from a first to a second main point and internal summaries more valuable as you move from a second main point to a third main point. The important thing is to help your audience follow your thoughts with ease.

Table 10.4	Strategies for Effective Conclusions
Strategy	**Description/Example**
Quote	Uses a statement by another person that emphasizes the theme of your speech. If you are speaking on the value of silence: As one wise man advised, "Foolish people speak all that is in their minds; wise people keep a part back."
Reference to the introduction	Relates back to the words or tone found in the introduction
Call for action	An appeal for the audience to respond in some specific way presented in the body of the speech
Rhetorical question	Ask the audience a "thought question." Example: "If you were a person with AIDS, what response would you desire?"
Combination	Blends any of the above devices together for effect

restatement of information you shared in the body. Make the summary concise and clear. Here's an example once again using the topic of sunburns and skin cancer:

Sunburns are, then, not just temporarily painful, they can have serious, long-term effects on your appearance and health. However, you can avoid these risks by using the appropriate type and amount of sunscreen every time you will be exposed to the sun for more than a few minutes.

Along with a summary, you must also cue your audience that you have completed your speech. This "wrap-up" gives the audience psychological closure and provides an interesting and memorable point of reference for them. See Table 10.4 for concluding devices that can help you craft a clear and compelling closure.

Patterns of Organization

Organizing your speech is vital. Organizational patterns are important strategies for arranging your material in a recognizable manner. Additionally, these patterns of thought will help you craft the flow and language of your entire speech. One of the early decisions you should make in your speech preparation is how to organize your information. While there are several organizational patterns, some are well suited to either informative or persuasive speeches, while others are more suited to informative or persuasive speeches.

Suggested Organizational Patterns for Informative Speeches
Some organizational patterns or designs yield themselves well to informative speeches, and all are based on a clear logic. We discuss several of these in the following paragraphs.

chronological design speech design that arranges ideas according to time

A **chronological design** arranges ideas according to time. Speeches that employ this design usually move either forward or backward in time—that is, they discuss events moving from earlier to later or from later to earlier in time. For example, if you were discussing the development of country music, you might begin by talking about contemporary country music and then explain how it is similar to and different from the country music of the original days of the *Grand Ole Opry*.

spatial design speech design that relies on a geographical or spatial relationship

Spatial designs rely on geographical or spatial relationships. Spatial designs include patterns such as top to bottom, east to west, front to back, or side to side. For example, if you were explaining the components in a computer, you may begin from the inside and work to the outside or vice versa. This is a spatial design. Or you may introduce students to your campus by moving from east to west; this design reflects a geographic yet spatial approach. As another example, you may discuss the places of battle that occurred at Gettysburg during the Civil War.

Topical or categorical designs are very common in informative speeches. In a topical design, you deal with topics or categories that relate to a main theme. For example, if you discuss the main challenges in applying for financial aid, you may choose to use a topical or categorical organizational pattern. In this case, you may choose from several challenges that would include collecting information, filling out the forms, submitting the applications at the appropriate time, communicating with your college's financial aid office, waiting for the response, and appropriately using the aid when it arrives. You probably won't have time to cover all of these related topics, so you must be sure they flow from your narrowed topic and thesis statement.

topical or categorical design speech design that deals with topics or categories that relate to a main theme

Problem–solution designs describe or define a problem and then offer ways that the problem may be solved. It is difficult to use this organizational pattern for an informative speech if you seek to promote one particular solution over another. In doing so, you take on a persuasive burden and change the speech's intent. However, you can easily change this design for an informative speech as long as you can remember to teach your listeners about the problem without taking a position on the advisability or applicability of any particular solution. As an example, you may examine the problem of rising tuition costs at your college, and then identify possible solutions to the problem without arguing for any one solution to be adopted.

problem–solution design speech design that describes or defines a problem and then offers potential solutions

Cause–effect designs identify how a certain set of conditions brings about a particular result. Or, conversely, you may use this pattern to focus on the effects and then consider the cause. The difference in the two approaches has to do with whether you discuss the cause or the effects first. The danger with this design is that you may oversimplify a serious problem and indicate only one cause, while many causes may actually create a known effect. It is also possible to infer cause, and effect when no such link actually exists. When you cannot firmly establish a clear link, you should use another design to avoid endangering your credibility. As with the problem–solution design, you must also avoid arguing a case rather than presenting insight. For example, you may identify some of the effects of being a first-year college student (the cause). The effects may include homesickness, lack of friends, uncertainty, financial difficulties, and stress. Or you may wish to focus on other more positive effects, such as forming new friendships, intellectual growth, and future career possibilities.

cause–effect design speech design that identifies how a certain set of conditions brings about a particular result

Suggested Organizational Patterns for Persuasive Speeches

While any of the designs we discussed when we considered informative speech organizational designs might be used for persuasive speeches, some additional patterns are especially applicable to persuasive speaking. These include the motivated sequence design, the refutative design, and the state-the-case-and-prove-it design.

The **motivated sequence design** was developed by a salesman who wanted people to purchase his products and is therefore especially useful for speeches that motivate people to act. There are five sequential steps in this design. Table 10.5

motivated sequence design speech design that motivates people to act

Table 10.5	Monroe's Motivated Sequence	
Step	**Function**	**Audience Response**
Attention	Getting attention	"I want to listen."
Need	Showing the need: describing the problem	"Something needs to be done (decided or felt)."
Satisfaction	Satisfying the need: presenting the solution	"This is what to do (believe, or feel) to satisfy the need."
Visualization	Picturing the results	"I can see myself enjoying the satisfaction of doing (believing or feeling) this."
Action	Requesting action or approval	"I will do (believe or feel) this."

refutative design speech design that presents the arguments that oppose the speaker's proposition or claim and show how they are fallacious, inadequate, inconsistent, or deficient

summarizes each of the steps, along with the step's function and the desired audience response.

The **refutative design** is another organizational design that is particularly useful for persuasive speeches. In this approach, you present the arguments that oppose your proposition or claim and show how they are fallacious, inadequate, inconsistent, or deficient. In order to use this design, you must know your opponents' arguments well and be able to use evidence and reasoning to effectively counter them. By doing this, you are then able to establish credibility and adequacy of your position since it withstands the opposing position's ineffective arguments. So, for example, if you wanted to argue that gun control is necessary for increased protection of human life in the United States, you could establish your case by examining and defusing the arguments of those who oppose gun control.

state-the-case-and-prove-it design speech design in which the speaker sets forth a proposition or claim and then proves it systematically by offering evidence and reason to support the arguments

State-the-case-and-prove-it design provides a third organizational approach to persuasive speaking. In this pattern, you set forth your proposition or claim and then systematically prove it by offering evidence and reason to support your arguments. For example, if you contend that protecting our natural environment is the first social issue we should address, you can use this design to straightforwardly state your claim and then go about providing arguments to support the claim backed by evidence and reasoning.

While you may find the chronological, spatial, or topical designs useful for persuasive speeches, you will probably discover that one of the three previously mentioned designs or the problem–solution or cause–effect designs are most suitable. Whatever design you choose, make sure you understand it and know how to make the most of it to ensure that your speech achieves your intended purpose.

SUPPORTING YOUR PRESENTATION

*Y*ou now have a narrowed topic, a clear thesis, and some sense of how you will organize your presentation. However, you must gather information, which provides the substance of your speech. As you read about your specific topic, you may find information that helps you write your thesis, identify your main points, and discover supporting material. In other words, the process of developing your speech does not necessarily move in a straight line; it may double back upon itself. Effective speakers realize that they continue to refine their topic choice, specific purpose, and thesis by way of research. Be alert to how you can improve your speech as you proceed; don't get locked into a single way to approach your topic. But how do you find appropriate supporting material? To answer this question, we discuss where to search, how to search, and what to search for as you conduct your research. Then we will explore how to effectively use what you found. (The box Cultural Links: Culture and Evidence outlines important factors to consider when choosing evidence for various audiences).

Finding Supporting Materials

There are numerous ways to find information to support your topic. These often include electronically available information, as the box Campus Links: Doing Research explains. For example, you may enter key terms into an Internet search engine such as Yahoo! or Google to find some initial information. However, for the most part, the best sources are still contained in your college library. Use the computerized card catalog, electronic encyclopedias such as *Encarta,* and electronic databases you find there. For example, databases such as ProQuest, Academic Premier, ERIC, or EBSCO will often provide you with numerous and credible "hits." You can also find statistical information in such sources as *Facts on File* or leads to various periodicals and newspapers in resources such as the *Reader's Guide to Periodical Literature* or LexisNexis. Additionally, you can find supporting materials in print resources such as books, pamphlets, or brochures.

Cultural Links

Culture and Evidence

What constitutes credible evidence? The answer depends on your cultural background. According to Kearney and Plax (1999), the credibility of evidence among co-cultural groups within the United States is directly related to one's cultural background. The following chart summarizes some of these differences.

Cultural Group	Preferred Form of Evidence
Euroamericans ("white")	Objective evidence: statistics, experts
African Americans	Emotional appeals: humor, stories, personal testimony
Latino/Latina	Parables, stories, vivid descriptions
Asian Americans	Traditions, oral histories, indirect appeals
Native Americans	Stories, myths, legends
Middle-Eastern Americans	Tribal history, poetry, religious references, personal experience

While it is always inappropriate to stereotype individuals, knowing what appeals to various ethnic groups can help speakers choose supporting material that will ring true for the audience. This can also assist audience members in adapting their expectations of speakers with various ethnicities.

People are often also equally valuable resources. Librarians can be very valuable resources to help you find material; talk with them. You may also interview a person who has strategic knowledge about your topic, or you may even draw on your own observations or experiences to help flesh out ideas. Carefully organize your materials so you can refer to them later. Even a manila folder can help keep your information together and save you time later. While it may seem much simpler to just "Google it,"

Campus Links

Doing Research

Throughout your college career, you will need to conduct research in order to complete course requirements. For example, research papers, English essays, and oral presentations all require effective research skills. In addition to those ideas we provide in this chapter, here are some pointers to help you begin researching effectively and efficiently:

1. **Tour your library.** During the first two weeks of your first semester in college, tour your campus library. Many libraries offer either a self-guided or group tour to get you acquainted with its layout and resources.

2. **Focus on what you need to know.** You will probably have a glut of information for any topic

that you are interested in pursuing. Save time by refining what you need to know. Gardner and Jewler (2003) offer a series of questions that will help you refine your information search:

- What do you already know about the topic?
- Who would be likely to write about your topic? What scholars, researchers, professionals, or groups might be interested? In what publications would you likely find articles about your topic?
- What do you want to know about the topic? Work on refining your topic or central question for your assignment.
- What important vocabulary do you need to know given your topic?

- What do you want to do with the information you gather? Do you want to inform, persuade, debate, interview?
- What level of information do you need? Do you need a broad overview or very specific, detailed information? Do you need historical or contemporary information?

3. **Learn how to conduct searches using the computers in your library.** While your reference librarian can help you with these searches, you can often find what you need by using various types of searches. For example, your library probably allows you to search by subject, author, title, or keyword. Trying these various approaches may help yield results. Learning to use a search string can also be helpful. In general, you can use connectors such as *AND* to search for multiple terms or *OR* to search for either term. So, for example, you might search for *college AND freshmen,* or *college freshmen* or *college first-year students,* since these terms are still used interchangeably. You can also use quotation marks to help search for a specific term such as "nontraditional students." Additionally, if you are using a search engine like AltaVista, you can add terms by using a plus sign (+) or omit terms by using a minus sign (-). For example, you might have terms like "+ Greeks + college," or if you wanted to retrieve information about Greek society and ensure that you did not retrieve information about fraternities and sororities, you could use "'Greeks' – college".

4. **Learn to take clear and concise notes.** As you conduct research, be sure to take appropriate notes. Whether you use a laptop, pen and note cards, or e-mail yourself information, be sure you have a system and use it consistently. At the very least, your notes should provide complete citation information; there's nothing more frustrating than having to search a second time because you forgot to get information necessary for citing your source. Also, you should summarize important information and record word for word any quotes you wish to use. While this may seem time-consuming, in the end you save time by gathering, recording, and reflecting upon the information you find. Most of us find more information than we can use, but it's better to have too much than not enough. To help avoid overload, however, keep asking yourself, "How will this information fit with my topic?"

it is important to remember that your supporting materials need to be reliable, credible, and varied. So, let's talk about how to find credible sources before we discuss various types of supporting material. (See the box Community Links: Community Resources and Supporting Materials for suggestions for finding helpful resources.)

Evaluating Materials

Not all supporting materials are created equal. In fact, some are outright ludicrous. If you use offensive, questionable, or suspect supporting materials, you will compromise your credibility and lose your audience's respect and attention. In general, sources should be credible, recent, and objective. Because Internet sources can be especially troublesome, consider these questions as suggested by David Boraks (1997) to help you evaluate them:

- What is the site's purpose?
- Is its information unbiased?
- Who sponsors the site?
- What are the organization's values or goals?
- Can you contact the sponsors should questions arise?
- Is the information in the site well documented?
- Does it provide citations to sources used in obtaining the information?
- Are individual articles signed or attributed?
- When was it published? Is the date of the last revision posted somewhere on the page?
- What are the author's credentials?
- Is the author frequently cited in other sources?
- How does the value of the Web-based information you've found compare with other available sources, such as print?

Community Links

Community Resources and Supporting Materials

As you look for supporting materials, don't neglect the numerous community resources available to you. For example, newsletters, brochures, reports, or other printed materials may provide excellent information about an organization, business, or event. Nonprofit organizations, governmental agencies, or Chambers of Commerce can provide numerous immediate resources and can help you find other materials. For instance, assume you decide to focus on domestic abuse as a subject area for a speech in your class. Local community agencies and nonprofit organizations that assist abused women can help you find information that will aid you in narrowing the subject to a focused topic, while also helping you link your subject with your own locale and your audience. To illustrate, as a result of gathering information on domestic abuse, you could consider topics such as (1) agencies in your community addressing the problem; (2) the cycle of domestic abuse; (3) events such as "Take Back the Night" that, in part, address the issue of women's safety; or (4) the effects of domestic abuse on women and families. By brainstorming, you can likely create several other possible topics or ideas. In short, gathering readily available information in your community may help you find a subject and topic that will provide your audience with valuable information and insights.

Also, talking with people can provide you with important information. For example, speaking with someone who works at a women's shelter can provide insight that humanizes and personalizes a difficult but significant topic. Attorneys, law enforcement officials, and professors in various fields such as sociology, women's studies, or criminology can also provide you with important information, along with suggestions for further research. Use your community resources well to help craft your topic and find relevant, readily available supporting material.

Types of Supporting Material

To help you find both a sufficient number and variety of materials to support your ideas, consider the various types and effective uses of supporting materials.

Facts   **Facts** are objective, verifiable information, which you can typically find in sources such as encyclopedias or almanacs. For example, as you enter college for the

fact a piece of objective, verifiable information

Using a computer will help you find needed supporting material for your speech.

first time, you face multiple new challenges. What you *think or feel* about these challenges is not a fact per se; however, that you face specific, identified challenges is a fact verified both by research and by such organizations as the National Center for the First Year. Even though some facts are common knowledge, to enhance your credibility, be sure to find and cite reliable sources when you use facts to support your ideas. While we discuss how to cite sources later in this chapter, it is important to make this observation now.

statistics numeric facts that include such information as percentages, averages, or amounts of money

Statistics   While facts are objective pieces of information, **statistics** are basically numeric facts that include such information as percentages, averages, or amounts of money. Therefore, your grade point average (GPA) is an arithmetic average that reflects how well you are performing in your classes; it is a fact. While you may not *think* your GPA accurately reflects your abilities or your performance, your opinion of your GPA is not a fact, however much you would like it to be. To take another example, the percentage of U.S. citizens who make more than $75,000 per year is also a statistic. Statistics, when used sparingly, provide strong support for certain ideas; however, it is best to place the statistic in context so your audience can appreciate the power of your information. For example, the U.S. Department of Health estimates that in 2003, there were 4 million deaths worldwide due to tobacco use (see www.globalhealth.gov/tobacco.shtml). However, to stress the power of this number, put it in context:

> *According to the U.S. Department of Health, worldwide deaths due to the use of tobacco resulted in approximately 4 million deaths in 2003. Given data from the U.S. Census Bureau this is akin to almost every person in the State of Kentucky dying in a year's time. (See http://factfinder.census.gov/home/saff/main.html?_lang=en.)*

Notice that this statement cites sources and offers a comparison so the audience can comprehend the magnitude of the problem.

testimony the words or ideas of another person used to support a speaker's points

direct quotations word-for-word repetition of what someone has said

expert testimony the insights of someone who has specialized knowledge or experience and is therefore a recognized authority on a given subject

lay testimony the views of people who are not, necessarily, experts

Testimony   **Testimony** refers to using the words or ideas of another person to support your points. While you may paraphrase these ideas, you may choose to use **direct quotations**—repeating verbatim what someone has said. Direct quotations are most useful if the quotation is brief or especially powerful.

Of course, not all testimony is necessarily equal. **Expert testimony** refers to the insights of someone who has specialized knowledge or experience and is therefore a recognized authority on a given subject. For example, Dr. John Gardner is a recognized expert in first-year college student issues because of his research and experience in this field. Likewise, many of your professors are experts in their respective fields because of their education and research.

However, at times you may not need or want expert testimony; you may want to use **lay testimony**, or the views of people who are not necessarily experts. Lay testimony typically focuses on peoples' feelings or opinions. Therefore, if you want to know what it feels like to be a first-year college student, you do not necessarily need an expert; you can speak with students on your campus who can share their opinions and experiences. Lay testimony is useful for helping your audience understand the human dimension of your topic, while expert testimony provides you with more objective support. It's often wise to include both in your presentation in order to appeal to your audience both intellectually and emotionally.

examples illustrations that help an audience visualize your point

personal examples examples drawn from the speaker's own experience

Examples   **Examples** are illustrations that help make your ideas clearer and engage your audience's interest; they help your audience visualize your point. Examples can be personal, actual, or hypothetical. **Personal examples** are drawn from your own experience. Assume your speech topic is learning how to simultaneously manage working and attending college. You may relate an example such as this:

> *I remember leaving the restaurant where I worked as a server one night after midnight, dreading the history reading assignment and the beginning*

speech outline I still had to complete before my class schedule, which began at 8:00 A.M. the following morning. While I tried to do both after I got back to my apartment, I couldn't stay awake. So I went to both my history and communication classes unprepared and it cost me points in both classes. After I did this a few more times, I came to grips with the reality that I would have to find ways to manage my time differently if I was going to succeed in college.

Actual examples are drawn from real-life events. For example, you may relay an illustration from current events, history, or the experiences of another person. In this case, using the same speech topic as above, rather than recount your own experience, you would interview a family member or friend who attempted to balance the demands of both work and college and then relay their experience and clearly cite your source. In contrast, you may also use **hypothetical examples**, which are examples you create from information you have collected. Typically, hypothetical examples are created by blending events and experiences that are likely to have occurred. Again using our above example, you would relate the same information but rather than tell it in the first person, you would invite the audience to picture or imagine the scene. The phrasing therefore would change: "Imagine leaving the restaurant where you work as a server …"

actual examples examples drawn from real-life events

hypothetical examples examples created from information the speaker has collected

Narratives   **Narratives** are much like examples in that they illustrate a point or idea. However, narratives tell stories rather than relate incidents and usually have a clear introduction, body, and conclusion. Like examples, they can be stories drawn from your own life or the lives of others, since, in most cases, these make the best stories. Folk tales, oral traditions, or children's books also offer excellent resources. In addition, you can find numerous storytelling resources online. Just remember that if you choose to tell a story, take the time to tell it well and make sure it clearly communicates the theme of your speech and engages your audience.

narratives stories that illustrate a point or idea; usually have a clear introduction, body, and conclusion

Now that you have some idea of the kinds of supporting materials you can use to help flesh out your ideas, let's consider how to use them effectively. Specifically, you will need to use your supporting material well and cite your evidence clearly.

Using Supporting Material Effectively

You must use supporting material well in order to make the thesis and main points of your speech both clear and compelling. Therefore, select supporting material carefully and use it effectively to ensure that you share your message with your audience. Consider these guidelines for using your supporting material effectively.

Relatedness   Assume you find a truly engaging story that you want to use in your presentation. Even though the story may be excellent, if you force it to fit a point, it detracts from your presentation. Therefore, be sure the information you choose is directly and clearly related to your topic, your thesis, and your point. This means you should choose your supporting material with care and then craft your ideas equally carefully.

Relevance   Choose material that relates to your audience. Obviously, different kinds of materials appeal to groups of children, teens, and adults. Therefore, the same topic may result in a very different presentation as you adapt to your audience's interests and nature. While your thesis and main points may remain similar, the supporting material will change significantly.

Respect   Choose supporting materials that respect your audience's prior knowledge and their values. You can often introduce new ideas by comparing or contrasting them with established or well-known ideas. For example, assume you are speaking to your class about study strategies that will help them succeed in college.

The students in your class have already developed some strategies from their prior years of schooling; however, some of these strategies may not be sufficient for the challenges of college-level work. Therefore, you can compare and contrast the strategies you wish them to consider with their default study strategies. In this way, you respect what they already know and show them how to draw on and adapt their prior knowledge.

In addition to respecting your audience's prior knowledge, you must also be aware of their values. To avoid offending your audience, do not use supporting material that includes profanity, sexism, racism, or other offensive material. Also, use humor carefully since it can easily backfire and alienate your audience. Therefore, use appropriate, credible sources to support your main ideas. For example, consider a student who cites *Playboy* magazine as a credible source on sex education. You can easily see the difficulties such a choice might create for the audience, the speaker, and your teacher. (See the box Career Links: Critical Skills in an Information Age for additional information on the importance of choosing suitable sources.)

◎ *Career Links*

Critical Skills in an Information Age

Most of you want a well-paying, fulfilling job when you leave college. Do you know the skills you need to find, obtain, and keep that job? You'll find a comprehensive list created by experts Randall and Katharine Hansen at www.quintcareers.com/job_skills_values.html. Here are the categories of skills employers most want, copied directly from this website:

Communications Skills (listening, verbal, written). By far, the one skill mentioned most often by employers is the ability to listen, write, and speak effectively. Successful communication is critical in business.

Analytical/Research Skills. Deals with your ability to assess a situation, seek multiple perspectives, gather more information if necessary, and identify key issues that need to be addressed.

Computer/Technical Literacy. Almost all jobs now require some basic understanding of computer hardware and software, especially word processing, spreadsheets, and e-mail.

Flexibility/Adaptability/Managing Multiple Priorities. Deals with your ability to manage multiple assignments and tasks, set priorities, and adapt to changing conditions and work assignments.

Interpersonal Abilities. The ability to relate to your coworkers, inspire others to participate, and mitigate conflict with coworkers is essential given the amount of time spent at work each day.

Leadership/Management Skills. While there is some debate about whether leadership is something people are born with, these skills deal with your ability to take charge and manage your coworkers.

Multicultural Sensitivity/Awareness. There is possibly no bigger issue in the workplace than diversity, and job-seekers must demonstrate a sensitivity and awareness to other people and cultures.

Planning/Organizing. Deals with your ability to design, plan, organize, and implement projects and tasks within an allotted time frame. Also involves goal setting.

Problem Solving/Reasoning/Creativity. Involves the ability to find solutions to problems using your creativity, reasoning, and past experiences along with the available information and resources.

Teamwork. Because so many jobs involve working in one or more work groups, you must have the ability to work with others in a professional manner while attempting to achieve a common goal.

As you review these skills, note how many of them are directly related to the goals of this and other courses you are taking. However, especially consider the second skill in the list: analytical/research skills. As Gardner and Jewler (2003) note, the ability to "find, evaluate, and analyze information is critical" (p. 166) to careers in an information age filled with rapid change. Developing your research skills, along with the ability to evaluate information is, therefore, relevant to this course and to your college experience and future job-market potential.

_____

Source: "Critical skills in an information age" from www.quintcareers.com/job_skills_values.html. Reprinted by permission of Randall S. Hansen, Ph.D.

Citing Sources

As we noted earlier, clearly citing your sources is important in both researching and presenting your topic. It is therefore important to learn how to cite sources in writing and orally.

Citing Your Sources in Writing
As you gather research and prepare your outline, you should use one of several accepted forms of citation or style. These most commonly include styles of the Modern Language Association (MLA) and the American Psychological Association (APA), although your teacher may ask you to use another form, such as *The Chicago Manual of Style*. While you can purchase style manuals, you can also retrieve a great deal of information from online resources. For example, your college library probably has a site with this information, or you may find a site such as http://panther.indstate.edu/tutorials/apa/ very helpful. Use the style your teacher suggests and use it consistently. While you may find it frustrating to learn and use the details of citing sources, it is an important skill you need in your college career and in your future work.

Citing Sources Orally
You will also need to cite sources as you speak in order to enhance your credibility; your audience wants to know that you have done your homework. While you do not want to include every detail of a written citation, you do need to give sufficient information to clearly identify your source. Consider these examples:

"According to Dr. Arnold Speckler ..."

"*Time* magazine, July 22, 1996, reports ..."

"In the book *A Road Less Traveled*, Dr. M. Scott Peck writes ..."

"In a personal interview I conducted with my best friend ..."

"A recent article in *Contemporary Education* asserts that ..."

Notice that each citation offers enough information to identify the source, without giving complete citation information. In all likelihood, your teacher will ask you to clearly cite sources as you speak and will grade you accordingly.

Plagiarism
Failing to cite sources you use either in writing or when speaking is tantamount to stealing someone else's ideas without giving them appropriate credit—it is **plagiarism**. In many colleges, plagiarism, intentional or not, can result in severe penalties. Students have failed courses or even been academically dismissed from colleges for plagiarism. More importantly, it is unethical and illegal to use someone else's ideas, even if you change a few words, without giving them credit. Consult the academic dishonesty policies and talk with a librarian at your college in order to clarify any questions. Your teacher may also have a clear statement in her or his syllabus about the consequences of plagiarism.

Carefully citing your sources during your speech will enhance your credibility.

plagiarism using someone else's ideas without giving them appropriate credit

OUTLINING

Speech outlines are like our skeletal system: They provide structure, connections, and support. Don't neglect this important aspect of speech preparation. Outlines will ensure that you develop a strong speech that your audience can follow and provide you with the necessary structure to prepare and deliver your speech effectively.

Planning, Preparation, and Presentation Outlines

As you develop your speech, you will probably write a rough outline as you jot down ideas and gather supporting material. Think of this as your **planning outline**. It may not look like a conventional outline and may just be a collection of notes and related ideas or a concept map, like the ones you find at the start of each chapter in this book. We'll have more to say about concept maps later, but for now it is

planning outline a rough collection of ideas and supporting material

important to realize that you must blend all the aspects of the process in developing your speech into a coherent whole; outlines will help you do this.

In addition to the planning outline, you must develop a preparation and a presentation outline before you actually speak. A **preparation outline** is the formal, typewritten outline that clearly identifies an introduction, body, and conclusion along with the required portions in each section. This outline is the blueprint for your speech; it provides the structure and the detail for what you will say when you deliver your speech *without writing out the speech word for word*. While you will certainly work on phrasing your main points and key ideas, you should not construct a manuscript of the speech; rather, create a detailed plan of your presentation to ensure that you speak extemporaneously or conversationally.

Wise speakers and experienced speakers know that a preparation outline is essential to an effective speech. Don't shortchange yourself or your audience by taking a shortcut. Furthermore, you will, in most instances, need to hand in a copy of your preparation outline to your teacher. In many communication classes, your outline is your ticket to the front of the room because it evidences your preparation to address your class.

On a technical note, the preparation outline should be typed and contain full sentences arranged in a proper outline format. You should also include references after the conclusion of the outline, along with citations in the outline's text. Figure 10.1 illustrates an outline format sheet that may serve as a template for writing your speech outlines. Note that the outline uses Roman numerals for main ideas, capital letters for subpoints related to main ideas, Arabic numbers for supporting material related to subpoints, and lowercase letters for the final level in the outline. These format rules are standard outlining procedure and can be useful in preparing for your speech and in developing an outline for research papers in other classes. While your instructor may ask you to adapt or change the outline to some degree in order to follow the requirements of your course, the outline format sheet provides a recognized and classroom-tested pattern you can follow, and it can serve as a checklist for your outline. For additional help, consult Figure 10.2, which shows a student outline that employs the outline format sheet.

While a preparation outline is important to planning your speech, a **presentation outline (skeletal or keyword outline)** is vital to your speech delivery because most people get too nervous when speaking to rely solely on memory. This outline helps you stay on track when delivering your speech. Unlike the preparation

preparation outline the formal, typewritten outline that clearly identifies an introduction, body, and conclusion as well as the required portions in each section

presentation outline the outline that contains cue words or phrases that help you recall what you have planned and practiced when you actually deliver the speech; also called the **skeletal** or **keyword outline**

FIGURE 10.1   Outline Format Sheet

Specific Purpose: Stated in terms of audience response
Organizational Pattern:
Intended Audience:

Introduction
I. **Attention-Getting Device:** Full sentences giving actual attention-getter to be given in speech.
II. **Orientation Phase:** (all in complete sentences)
    A. **Point:** Statement of topic
    B. **Adaptation:** Reason for audience to listen
    C. **Credibility:** Explains why we should listen to you speak on this subject
    D. **Enumerated Preview:** Prestates your main points
Transition to first main point

Body
I. First main point as stated in preview in a complete sentence
    A. Supporting information for first main point in a complete sentence
        1. First detail of support for A in a complete sentence
        2. Second detail of support for A in a complete sentence (transition)
    B. Supporting information for first main point (Flanders 1990, p. 63)
        1. First detail of support for B in a complete sentence

    2. Second detail of support for B in a complete sentence (transition)
  C. Supporting information for first main point in a complete sentence
Transition statement connecting first and second main points

II. Second main point as stated in preview in a complete sentence
  A. Supporting information for second main point in a complete sentence
    1. First detail of support for A in a complete sentence (Croug, personal interview, 1992)
      a. Further detail of 1
      b. Further detail of 1
    2. Second detail of support for A in a complete sentence (transition)
  D. Supporting information for second main point
    1. First detail for B in a complete sentence
    2. Second detail for B in a complete sentence
Transition statement connecting second and third main points

III. Third main point as stated in preview in a complete sentence
  A. Supporting information for third main point in a complete sentence (transition)
  B. Supporting information for third main point in a complete sentence (transition)
  C. Supporting information for third main point in a complete sentence
    1. First detail of support for C in a complete sentence
      a. Further detail of 1
      b. Further detail of 1
      c. Further detail of 1
    2. Second detail of support for C in a complete sentence
Transition to conclusion

Conclusion

I. Review of main points
II. Closure

FIGURE 10.2   Sample Preparation Outline

Specific Purpose: After my speech, my audience will know how to get along with their roommates.
Organizational Pattern: Topical
Intended Audience: Communication 101 Class

Introduction

I. Attention-Getting Device: They can be your best friends or your worst enemies. They can respect your space or they can go digging through your closet. They can make your bed when you're running late or they can pile their dirty dishes on your clean laundry. Do you know this person? It's someone, who at one time or another, we have all had to deal with—a roommate.

II. Orientation Phase:
  A. *Point:* Today, I want to give you some tips on getting along with your roommate.
  B. *Adaptation:* Most of us will have to room with someone at some point. Learning how to live with someone is not only important for college life, but for further relationships, too.
  C. *Credibility:* A roommate can be someone you come to love and trust, or he or she can become your worst enemy. In my case, my last roommate became my worst enemy. To keep this from happening again, I have found research that identifies ways to make living with someone easier.
  D. *Enumerated Preview:* This research identifies three main ways to keep the peace while living with a roommate—don't lie, don't assume anything, and remember that each roommate should have an equal voice and equal power in the relationship.

Transition: The first way to make living with someone better is to remember not to lie.

Body

I. Lying can cause several problems while living with a roommate.

  A. According to the September 1994 issue of *Seventeen Magazine*, there are three common lies that roommates tell each other (Barry 1994, p. 123).

    1. The first lie roommates tell is, "I'm not uptight about neatness."

      a. If you're a slob, admit it and keep your mess to your space.

      b. If you're a neat freak, try to understand the other person isn't like you.

    2. The second common lie is, "I don't care if guys/girls sleep over."

      a. You should set rules about what nights members of the opposite sex may spend the night.

      b. You should also set rules about how much prior notice the other person gets to find another place to sleep.

    3. "We're best friends" is the third lie roommates tend to tell.

      a. Don't feel like you have to invite your roommate to go along wherever you go.

      b. It takes a while to become friends, so take your time in developing a friendship.

  B. Usually lying to your roommate creates problems for both of you.

    1. Your roommate will feel betrayed if you lie to him or her, and he or she may not trust you again.

    2. Lying creates an emotional backlash, so in the end, you will feel worse.

Transition: Lying is not the only way to miscommunicate with your roommate. Assuming anything about the person you're sharing your living space with can cause just as many problems.

II. Remembering not to assume anything about your roommate will make living together much easier ("Crowd Control," E3).

  A. You should always ask before you use anything of your roommate's.

    1. For example, one of the major problems my old roommate and I had was assuming we could always use each other's things.

      a. I thought I could borrow her Monopoly game one weekend while she was gone.

      b. She assumed she could use my computer anytime she wanted.

    2. Another example occurred when we first moved in.

      a. My roommate assumed that since my stereo took up the whole top of the bookcase, she could take the whole top of the dresser.

      b. I assumed that since she chose the bed she wanted, I had first dibs on which closet I wanted.

  B. If you're ever unsure about anything, wait until your roommate gets home and ask him or her in person!

  C. And if something happens that disturbs you, as the *Princeton Review* online recommends, speak up. If you let issues go unaddressed, they typically only get worse or continue to upset you.

Transition: Lying and assumptions create problems, but you can create a positive atmosphere in your living space by remembering that each roommate is equal.

III. The June 26, 1994, issue of the *LA Times* states that the best way to get along with your roommate is to create a place where equality rules ("Crowd Control," E4).

  A. Each roommate should always have a say in all matters.

  B. Each roommate has the right to voice his or her opinions.

  C. It is important, however, to actually talk about the issues that need to be addressed, including who will clean what parts of the room or house, how utility bills will be paid, or what guidelines you will agree to regarding having others in your room or apartment (www.college-student-life.com/dorm_life.htm).

Transition: These tips should make living with a roommate easier and more enjoyable.

Conclusion

I. **Summary:** Never lying, never assuming anything, and remembering that everyone is equal are three of the essentials for living with anyone.

II. **Concluding Device:** By remembering these suggestions, living with your college roommate, or even someone further down the line, should be an enjoyable and rewarding experience.

FIGURE 10.3   Sample Presentation Outline Card

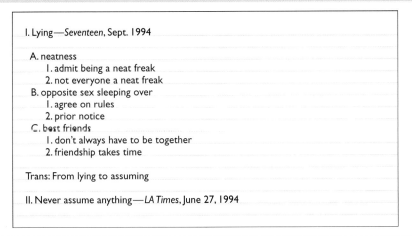

I. Lying—*Seventeen*, Sept. 1994

   A. neatness
      1. admit being a neat freak
      2. not everyone a neat freak
   B. opposite sex sleeping over
      1. agree on rules
      2. prior notice
   C. best friends
      1. don't always have to be together
      2. friendship takes time

Trans: From lying to assuming

II. Never assume anything—*LA Times*, June 27, 1994

outline, the presentation outline does not contain detail, but cue words or phrases that help you recall what you have planned and practiced. Here are some important features of the presentation outline: (1) the outline consists of keywords or phrases, *not* sentences to be read; (2) the outline should be written in letters large enough to be easily read at a glance; (3) the outline should be written on sequentially numbered note cards, not paper. See Figure 10.3 for an illustration of a presentation outline card. The card illustrates how one speaker might create a presentation outline for the first main point of the speech outlined in Figure 10.2.

Alternatives to Outlining

Although you will usually need a formal preparation outline in your communication class, you may find it helpful to use alternatives to outlining as a way to organize your ideas and research. Concept mapping, or what Ron Curtus calls "graphical outlines," are another way to organize information. The main idea of concept maps is relatively simple. Put your topic in the center of the page and jot down ideas as you think, read, and gather information. Then begin linking ideas together by drawing circles or arrows to show the relationship of the ideas. See Figure 10.4 for an example of a concept map.

FIGURE 10.4   An Example of a Concept Map: Forms of Water

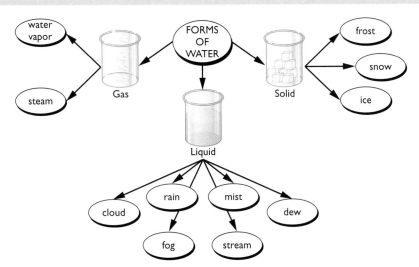

Retrieved July 30, 2006, from www.studygs.net/mapping/mapping1.htm.
Source: Reprinted by permission of Kendra Grant.

FIGURE 10.5   Tree Outline

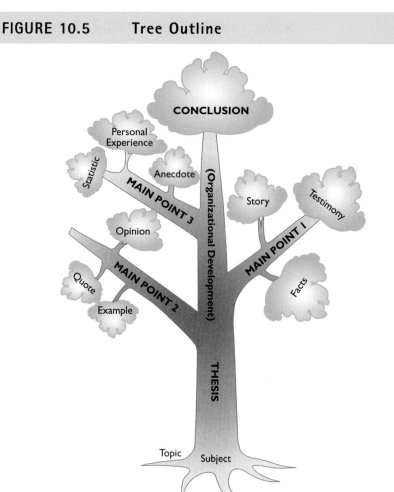

Engleberg and Daly (2005) also suggest using tree outlines (see Figure 10.5). These outlines use the structure of a tree to graphically depict how ideas relate to one another. The tree's trunk is your thesis, the limbs are the main points, and the branches and leaves represent the supporting material. As you develop the tree outline and you find no connection between a leaf and a branch, or a branch and a limb, you can "see" that you have an organizational problem that needs attention. As the box Computer Links: Software for Speakers explains, you can also use computer programs to help with organizing ideas.

Computer Links

Software for Speakers

If you struggle with organizing ideas or developing outlines, there are numerous resources to assist you. For example, Inspiration Software (www.inspiration.com) offers programs to help visualize ideas and create concept maps. Another program is MindMapper (www.mindmapper.com). You can also purchase numerous outlining programs, some of which are reviewed at http://john.redmood.com/organizers.html. While MS Word or WordPerfect provides an outline format, it does not actually assist you in linking ideas, as some software does.

You may also find outlining help online in a variety of places, including colleges, universities, and textbook online sites. Regardless of whether you use computer software sites or just paper and pen to help with your work, you must learn to connect ideas in an organized manner so that your audience can easily follow your logic and evaluate your presentation. There's no shortcut to thinking!

THE IMPORTANCE OF ORGANIZATIONAL SKILLS FOR COLLEGE LEARNING AND LIFE

*A*s a college student, you are bombarded with demands. Learning to organize your learning and your life will help you succeed both now and later. Many of the principles we have discussed in this chapter are relevant to your overall college and future career experience. Consider these suggestions from Smith and Walter (1995) and note how they are directly related to organizing your presentations.

1. **Plan on paper.** Write down your plan for college, just like you draft a concept map or outline for your presentation. A written plan becomes visual and therefore more tangible.

2. **Create a method of organization.** Many students toss materials in their backpacks and then later search through the bag for what they need. This is an ineffective method of organization. As we mentioned when discussing supporting materials, you must create and systematically use a method of organization that works for you and that helps you keep track of important materials. If nothing else, buy different-colored pocket folders and place your course materials in them. Then keep all these materials for future reference in the same file cabinet, closet, or drawer.

3. **Plan to plan.** Just like you take time to plan your speech, you must also take time to plan your college career. Your advisor can be very helpful in this process, but ultimately you are responsible for meeting graduation requirements. This is *your* college education; don't just float through it— engage it.

4. **Plan to change.** As we noted earlier, planning your presentation is a process, and as you gain fresh insights from research, you may well adapt your thesis or your main points. Likewise, remain flexible in your college planning. What seems right today may not fit you well as you continue to grow and develop. Many college students change majors because they find unforeseen opportunities. Your plan, therefore, needs to be adaptable.

5. **Develop a step-by-step action plan.** Your speech outline is your master plan, but it resulted from attending to a detailed process as depicted in our model of speech preparation. Likewise, your college career is a step-by-step process that requires not only a semester-by-semester plan, but also a monthly, weekly, and daily plan in order to achieve measurable goals. We suggest you use a planner to help ensure that you stay on track.

While these suggestions are immediately relevant to your college experience, they are equally important as you transfer into the work world. Organizational skills will be important now and for the rest of your life, and learning to prepare and present speeches can help you learn some of these important principles.

Learning to organize your time will help you succeed in college.

SUMMARY

This chapter has reviewed important information about organization, supporting materials, and outlining. To review, we have discussed

- principles of effective organization, including clarity, simplicity, parallelism, balance, practicality, and orderliness;
- the introduction, body, transitions, and conclusion of a presentation and the important functions of each of these important parts of a speech;
- various patterns of organization for both informative and persuasive speeches;
- finding, evaluating, using, and citing various types of supporting materials to build your speech's body;
- how to avoid plagiarism;
- planning, preparation, and presentation outlines and how to develop each;
- alternative methods of organizing ideas, other than outlines, including concept mapping and tree outlining;

- the importance of organizational skills for college life and work.

Questions for Discussion

1. We emphasized the importance of evaluating all supporting materials, but especially online sources. Why is it necessary to carefully evaluate Internet sources?
2. What steps can you take to learn to use your library more effectively and efficiently?
3. What types of evidence appeal to you? Why? What role does your cultural background play in your preference?
4. Consider the job skills identified in the box Career Links: Critical Skills in an Information Age. How does this course help you gain some of these skills? What do your conclusions suggest about the role of communication in college and career?

EXERCISES

1. Consider this complete introduction written by a student in a basic speech course and see if you can identify the five essential components of an effective introduction:

   Have you ever not had enough money to pay the telephone bill or electricity bill? Have you ever bought a new car and wondered if you could make the payments? Have you bought something on a credit card and wished later that you hadn't? These are not uncommon occurrences, and you shouldn't feel inferior for letting things like this happen. There is one simple reason for not being prepared for these types of expenses. That is the lack or insufficiency of a personal budget. With the accounting background that I have, along with the reading that I have done, I am prepared to tell you how you can prepare a good budget. This might seem to be a tremendous undertaking at first, but it is really quite simple. In order to prepare a personal budget, we need to first look at some of the reasons for having a budget; then explain how you go about developing a budget; and finally, look at some warning signs for potential poor budgeting.

   Use the following codes to identify each part of this introduction. Write one of the codes above each sentence.
   1. AG = attention-getter
   2. ST = stating the topic
   3. LR = listening reason
   4. EC = establishing credibility
   5. EP = enumerated preview

2. Integrate some of the principles you have learned about preparing a speech, including developing clear, main points. You've chosen the subject of social opportunities for college students in your town for an informative speech. With this subject in mind, answer the following questions:
   1. What will be the specific purpose of this speech?
   2. What topic will I develop from this subject?
   3. What is my thesis for this speech?
   4. What are the main ideas I want to share in my speech?
   5. How will I organize these main ideas? What design will be most useful?
   6. How can I craft these main ideas so that they are clearly stated in parallel fashion?

   Now, write your main points and provide the appropriate outline symbols.

3. Using the death penalty topic we referred to in this chapter and the outline format below, write an introduction and conclusion. Also, write transitions between the introduction and main points and the main points and the conclusion.

   The Abolition of the Death Penalty

   Introduction
   1. Attention-getter:
   2. Statement of topic:
   3. Credibility:
   4. Listening reason:
   5. Enumerated preview:

Transition
  I. The death penalty does not cost more than housing a prisoner for life.
Transition
  II. The death penalty does not bring closure to the victims' families.
Transition
  III. The death penalty is not an effective deterrent to crime.
Transition

Conclusion
  1. Review of topic
  2. Closure
4. Review the topic in Exercise 2. Write main points for an informative speech using the same topic. This time, change the organizational design from the one you originally used and rewrite the main points using this new organizational pattern.

◎ KEY TERMS

Enumerated preview
Chronological design
Spatial design
Topical or categorical design
Problem–solution design
Cause–effect design
Motivated sequence design
Refutative design
State-the-case-and-prove-it design

Facts
Statistics
Testimony
Direct quotations
Expert testimony
Lay testimony
Examples
Personal examples
Actual examples

Hypothetical examples
Narratives
Plagiarism
Planning outline
Preparation outline
Presentation outline (skeletal or keyword outline)

◎ REFERENCES

Andrews, P. H., Andrews, J. R., and Williams, G. 1999. *Public speaking: Connecting you and your audience.* Boston: Houghton Mifflin.

Barry, R. 1994. Welcome to roommate hell. *Seventeen* 9: 123–4, 129.

Boraks, D. 1997, March 27. Checklist: Internet sources. *Amarillo Globe News*, p. 18A. In *Creating competent communicators: Activities for speaking, listening, and media literacy in Grades 7–12*, eds. P. Cooper, and S. Morreale, 2003. Scottsdale, AZ: Holcomb Hathaway.

Croug, Nicole. 06 May, 1992. Personal Interview.

Crowd Control. 1994, June 27. *Los Angeles Times*, E3–4.

Curtus, R. *Enhancing writing creativity using graphical outline.* Retrieved September 6, 2004, from www.school-for-champions.com/writing/graphicaloutlines.htm.

Engleberg, I. A., and Daly, J. A. 2005. *Presentations in everyday life: Strategies for effective speaking.* 2nd ed. Boston: Houghton Mifflin.

Flanders, J. 1990. *The art of conversation.* New York: Jakers.

Gardner, J. N., and Jewler, J. A. 2003. *Your college experience: Strategies for success.* Belmont, CA: Wadsworth.

Kearney, P., and Plax, T. 1999. *Public speaking in a diverse society.* Mountain View, CA: Mayfield.

Living in the Dorm—Surviving College Dorm Life. Retrieved on June 11, 2004, from www.college-student-life.com/dorm_life.htm.

Osborn, M., and Osborn, S. 2006. *Public speaking.* 7th ed. Boston: Houghton Mifflin.

Personal experience, 1994, Fall.

Smith, L. N., and Walter, T. L. 1995. *The adult learner's guide to college success.* Rev. ed. Belmont, CA: Wadsworth.

The Roommate Issue: Eight Tips for Success. *The Princeton Review* [online]. Retrieved on June 11, 2004, from www.princetonreview.com/college/research/articles/life/roommatetips.asp.

Delivery and Visual Aids

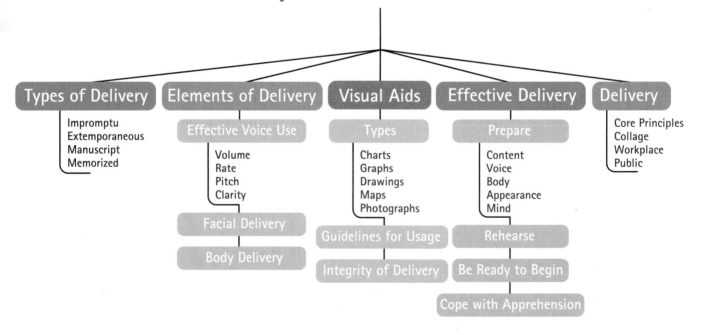

Types of Delivery	Elements of Delivery	Visual Aids	Effective Delivery	Delivery
Impromptu Extemporaneous Manuscript Memorized	**Effective Voice Use** Volume Rate Pitch Clarity	**Types** Charts Graphs Drawings Maps Photographs	**Prepare** Content Voice Body Appearance Mind	Core Principles Collage Workplace Public
	Facial Delivery	**Guidelines for Usage**	**Rehearse**	
	Body Delivery	**Integrity of Delivery**	**Be Ready to Begin**	
			Cope with Apprehension	

Knowledge Checklist

✓ To appreciate the importance of delivery in presentations

✓ To learn the main types of delivery and when to use them

✓ To learn how to prepare for effective delivery

✓ To understand how to use your voice for effective delivery

✓ To understand how to use your face to enhance delivery

✓ To understand how to use your body to enhance delivery

✓ To understand how to use visual aids to complement and enhance delivery

✓ To learn the types of visual aids

✓ To reflect upon the appropriate use of PowerPoint

✓ To understand and respond to the impact of communication apprehension on delivery

✓ To appreciate different delivery styles in different communicative contexts

TYPES OF DELIVERY

A student returned from a debate angry because many students attending the event considered one side's arguments more credible than another. The student fumed, "The opposition's arguments were not as strong as the proponent's; he was just a better speaker, so a lot of the students thought he made a stronger case." This incident highlights an important point: delivery in presentations matters. Delivery should never be a replacement for substance; however, *how* you deliver your message obviously impacts whether your audience grasps your message. In this chapter, we consider the important aspects of delivery and how visual aids impact your delivery and the effectiveness of your message. To this point, if you have been following our process, you have put a lot of work into your presentation. You have found a subject, narrowed the subject to a topic, developed a clear thesis with related main points, organized your ideas, conducted research, and prepared your outlines. However, you are now ready to put all of this behind-the-scenes work onstage; you are ready to present your speech. Just as you invested time in planning and researching your speech, you must now invest time in preparing to deliver it effectively. To do so, think about the type of delivery you will employ and the various elements essential to effective delivery, as well as how you will practice this delivery. You will also need to learn how to deal with communication apprehension, which can impact your delivery.

You can deliver your speech in one of four ways: impromptu, extemporaneous, manuscript, or memorized. All of these have their uses, although in most communication classes you will likely be asked to develop your extemporaneous speaking skills. However, because you will use your speaking skills throughout your college experience and later in your career, knowing the different delivery options allows you to plan for effective presentations now and in the future.

Impromptu speeches are presentations that you must give in the moment, without prior planning or practice. Although you do not have time to prepare, you can quickly draw on some of the basic principles you have already learned in this textbook and from your communication course: have a clear purpose, identify main ideas, and use your experience to provide supporting information. You may think that you will never have to give an impromptu speech. However, you may be in a meeting where you are faced with a serious issue that dramatically impacts your life, livelihood, or the well-being of your neighborhood or family. Will you sit quietly by and allow decisions to be made without your voice? If you intend to address the matter, you will be called upon to speak. Moreover, a job interview is, in reality, much like an extended impromptu speech, as explained in the box Career Links: Job Interviews as Impromptu Speaking. While you may get a job without an interview, it's highly unlikely.

impromptu speeches presentations that are given at a moment's notice, without prior planning or practice

Career Links

Job Interviews as Impromptu Speaking

Career Services at Virginia Polytechnic and State University identifies several typical interview questions (see www.career.vt.edu/JOBSEARC/interview/questions.htm). Consider some of the questions on their list:

1. What are your long-range goals and objectives?
2. Why did you choose the career for which you are preparing?
3. Describe a situation in which you had to work with a difficult person (another student, coworker, customer, supervisor, etc.). How did you handle the situation? Is there anything you would have done differently in hindsight?
4. In what ways have your college experiences prepared you for a career?
5. Describe a situation in which you worked as part of a team. What role did you take on? What went well and what didn't?
6. Do you think your grades are a good indication of your academic achievement?

Notice that each of these questions asks for a response. In fact, practically all job interview questions ask you to create a response in the moment, without having time to prepare or practice. In other words, you are called upon to speak impromptu. Therefore, learning this skill is important preparation for job interviews. Daly and Engleberg (2001) review two valuable skills for impromptu speaking:

1. Use simple, ready-made organizational patterns to craft your response. These include

   - past, present, and future. In this response, you explain your answer in terms of the flow of time. For example, if you were answering question 3 above, you could discuss the event of the past and how you responded, how the experience presently influences you, and what you would likely do in the future in a similar situation.

   - yes/no: here's why. In this response, you basically state your position or belief and then outline the reasons for it. This is much like the state-the-case-and-prove-it pattern we discussed in Chapter 10. For example, in question 6, you could answer the question and then briefly list your reasons why you believe your grades are or are not a reflection of your academic achievement. You may also want to speak to how academic achievement is related to your promise as an employee. Obviously, how you answer this question may depend on your GPA!

2. Buy time. Pause and reflect as necessary and/or rephrase the question. This will give you time to think on your feet, while also demonstrating that you are a thoughtful person who does not respond quickly but wishes to ponder at least a moment. In most instances, this will also enhance your credibility.

---

extemporaneous speeches planned presentations that are delivered using a keyword outline that helps the speaker deliver his or her prepared comments

manuscript speeches speeches in which the speaker reads the presentation word for word

memorized speeches presentations that speakers write word for word and then memorize

Extemporaneous speeches are planned presentations that are delivered using a keyword outline that helps you deliver your prepared comments. This mode of delivery allows you to engage your audience by employing a conversational style earmarked by effective delivery techniques. It also allows you to remain flexible and adapt to your audience, especially if they become restless.

In delivering **manuscript speeches**, you read your presentation word for word. This allows you to prepare every detail carefully, craft your use of language artfully, and time your speech exactly. If you need to be extremely careful because of language or time constraints, a manuscript speech is an appropriate choice. Beginning speakers may prefer to read presentations because they are nervous, but in most cases this compromises many of the elements of effective delivery that we will discuss later in this chapter. Therefore, your instructor will probably not allow you to read your speech to the class.

Memorized speeches are presentations that speakers write word for word and then memorize. While memorized speeches allow for greater freedom in delivery, we do not recommend them to beginning speakers for several reasons. First, it takes considerable time to memorize even a four-minute presentation; your time is already strained as a college student. Second, if you forget a part of the speech, you are likely to be faced with disaster. Third, you are liable to recite rather than speak with your audience, which negatively impacts effective delivery. While you may find it useful to memorize certain portions of your speech, such as your introduction or the way you want to phrase your main points, memorizing the entire speech is, in most instances, not appropriate as you begin to develop your presentation skills.

ELEMENTS OF EFFECTIVE DELIVERY

Now that you have a basic understanding of the delivery types you might employ, let's consider the various elements of effective delivery before we look at some guidelines for preparation and practice. In this section, we will consider how to use your voice, face, body, and visual aids to enhance your delivery.

Using Your Voice Effectively

Have you ever sat in a lecture and drifted off to sleep? While there may be many reasons for this response, you may have been nudged into a nap by the speaker's monotone delivery. *How* the speaker vocally delivers his or her message impacts how well the message is received. In like fashion, even though you may have strong content, you must engage your audience by delivering the content using appropriate breathing, volume, rate, pitch, and clarity.

Breathing   You must breathe well in order to deliver your speech well. Without proper breathing, you cannot use your voice effectively. Moreover, if you control your breath, you can reduce apprehension. The box Communication Links: Proper Breathing in Public Speaking provides important information about breathing correctly.

Communication Links

Proper Breathing in Public Speaking
by Katherine Axtell

In public speaking situations, delivery is as important, if not more so, than content. Many speakers practice certain aspects of delivery, including eye contact, vocal tone, and use of the hands. However, few pay attention to the most fundamental part of speaking: breathing. Neglect of this aspect of delivery often results in fast, breathless speech, the creation of strange noises during the inhaling process, and plain old discomfort on the part of the speaker. By paying attention to three components of breathing, specifically posture, initial air intake, and mouth position during repeat inhalation, speakers can easily make a positive difference in this critical aspect of delivery.

In order to speak, it is necessary to breathe. To see this for yourself, try this simple experiment. Try to inhale and speak at the same time. Can't do it? That's because the outward movement of air created by exhalation helps the vocal cords do their work. Here's another little experiment: exhale as far as you can. Let the air out of your nose and mouth, and push it out of your lungs. Now try to speak. You can produce some tone, but not very much, and not of a good quality. And it definitely doesn't feel good to speak this way. So, you can see now how important it is for a speaker to have a proper air supply, traveling in the proper direction.

It's not hard to develop correct breathing techniques. The first step in the process is to learn to use the maximum lung capacity. To allow the lungs to expand fully, a proper, upright posture is essential. Stand firmly, body directly centered over the feet. Straighten the spine by imagining that your vertebrae are balanced along a string which runs from the floor to the ceiling. Alternatively, imagine that a string, connected to the top of your head, is pulling you upward, forcing you to straighten. The next step in increasing lung capacity is to "open the chest." Straighten your shoulders by pulling back on the shoulder blades. Imagine that you're trying to make the tips of the shoulder blades touch in the middle of your back. Next, lift the rib cage. Male or female, thinking of the phrase "boobs up" helps accomplish this step. Finally, turn your attention to the muscles of the neck and throat. Your head should be in a comfortable position, neither held stiffly nor tilted up or down. A tilted head will restrict the movement of air as you breathe, and a stiff neck will just not feel good. This complete posture may feel unnatural at first, especially to those of you inclined to be couch potatoes, but with practice you will discover that it's just about the most comfortable way possible to hold the body.

Now that you've achieved the correct posture for maximum inhalation, it's time to fill those lungs. The first breath a speaker takes is by far the most important one, because it's the one that establishes the maximum lung capacity that the speaker will be able to achieve during the speech. In other words, if your first breath is a shallow one, the air won't last long. You'll have to breathe sooner and more often, and you won't be able to increase the lung capacity because you'll be more concerned about maintaining the pace of your speech than about taking extra time in there somewhere to take a deep breath. But if you start out with a good, deep breath, that air will last longer. You won't need to stop talking so often to breathe, and the tendency when you DO take a new breath will be to maintain the lung capacity you established with the first breath. So, make that first breath a good one. Keeping the body in the position I have already described, inhale slowly through the mouth. As you inhale, relax the muscles in your lower body. Let the stomach and the muscles of the lower back expand. Feel your lungs filling. Take in a good amount of air, but when you feel yourself straining against continued expansion, stop.

It's important that breathing be as inaudible as possible. No one wants to be so distracted by the breathing noises made by a speaker that they forget, or are unable, to listen to the speech. For most people, the inhalation noise is high-pitched and fast, somewhat like a hiss. I know a girl who, when she's nervous, actually *squeaks* when she inhales. It's awfully distracting. These hissing and squeaking problems are caused by the position of the tongue, jaw, and lips at the moment of inhalation. When the lungs are open to maximum capacity, they are drawing in a tremendous amount of air. The position of the mouth must be such that the air has room to pass through. The tongue and lips, especially, act as barriers to the air trying to enter the lungs. When the air rushing into the lungs comes in contact with the tongue, for example, a noise is made because not all the air can get past.

The solution to this problem, then, is to get the mouth parts—tongue, lips, and teeth—out of the way. The lower teeth are the ones that cause the problem, and they are attached to the lower jaw, so the way to get them out of the way is to move the lower jaw. It's helpful to think of letting the jaw drop slightly, rather than straining to open it. It might feel silly at first to let the mouth open, but as long as you are letting the movement happen naturally, you will still look OK. It's when you *focus* on opening the jaw that you look silly, because conscious effort here inevitably creates too much movement. Just relax the lower jaw and it will take care of itself. The other mouth parts, the tongue and lips, can be moved simultaneously. Even better, they can be moved in a way that will increase lung capacity in addition to reducing breathing noise! Here's another fun experiment. Position your mouth to say "E." Don't actually make any sound yet, just put your face in that position. Notice where your lips and tongue are. Now, go ahead and make the sound. Be sure to notice any changes that happen in the position of your tongue and lips. Now, return to the original mouth position, form an "E," and inhale. Aha! A hissing sound, right? It's not especially noticeable now, probably, but I can guarantee that when you're nervous and inhaling improperly and often, that little hissing noise will grow. And that noise will be increased by a microphone system (if you're using one). Now, go back to the beginning of this section and repeat these little experiments, replacing the sound "E" with the sound "OH." You will find that, by forcing the body to make this second sound, the problems with lips and teeth and tongue will all be resolved. This is because the syllable "OH" automatically relaxes the jaw, moving the teeth out of the path of the incoming air. It rounds the lips, covering the hard surface of the teeth that is a major factor in hiss production. And finally, the "OH" sound puts the tongue lower in the mouth so that it's not obstructing the intake of air. So, by thinking of the syllable "OH" while breathing, you will not only reduce the annoying noises that are caused by the frequent mouth position "E," but you will also be able to breathe more deeply more quickly because the obstructions of mouth parts have been removed.

Well. You thought you knew how to breathe, didn't you? You weren't necessarily wrong. Since you're alive to read this, you obviously have mastered breathing skills to some degree. But the breathing techniques required in public speaking do differ from those required to simply keep the body going. When you're in a stressful speaking situation, the most important thing you can do for yourself is to breathe correctly. Start with good posture, take in enough air at the beginning of your speech, and when you replenish that supply later, be sure to inhale while thinking of the relaxed syllable "OH." If you follow this advice, you will automatically set a better pace for your speech, and increase your physical comfort during the time you're in front of the audience. Your lungs and your audience will both thank you for learning to breathe correctly in a public speaking situation. ◎

Source: "Proper breathing in public speaking," by Katherine Axtell from www.whitman.edu/rhetoric/84zbreathing.htm. Reprinted by permission of Katherine Axtell.

Volume Remember how the media reported presidential contender Howard Dean, who exuberantly shouted a portion of his speech as he rallied his supporters? Although his message reached millions of people, the volume with which he delivered it turned many people off; they found his delivery comical or disturbing. This incident reminds us that appropriate **volume**, or how loudly or softly one speaks, is an important aspect of delivering a speech. If you speak too softly, the audience cannot hear you. Therefore, you must *project* your voice. Think of your voice as a ball that you must bounce off the room's back wall. While you may think you're speaking too loudly, you will often find that you need to add vocal energy to your delivery so the people in the back row can hear you. Of course, if you are in an auditorium with a microphone, you need not be as concerned with vocal projection, but in many instances you will need to project in order to be easily heard. At the same time, you must also avoid shouting, since this tends to alienate your audience. Most listeners don't want to be shouted at; they want you to speak directly and clearly with them. Of course, you can also adjust your volume at various points in your presentation for emphasis or effect. For example, if you wish to stress an idea, enhancing your volume can make this idea stand out for your listeners. In general, you should speak loudly enough to be easily heard and to add impact to certain portions of your speech.

volume how loudly or softly one speaks

Rate Just before their turn to speak in a communication class, students often comment, "Okay, I'll go next so I can get it over with." They begin their speech with

rate how rapidly one speaks

this attitude and race through their speech, only to realize that a speech that was to last five minutes lasted only three. In response, they may say, "But when I practiced at home, my speech lasted five minutes. What happened?" Typically, students speak considerably faster when they deliver speeches to their classes than when they practice at home. To avoid this, you must consciously focus on how rapidly you are speaking, or your **rate**. If you speak too quickly, you will lose your audience through disinterest. If you speak too slowly, you will lose your audience through boredom. So what should you do? First, breathe through your diaphragm. Breathing deeply will help pace your speech rate. Second, remind yourself to slow down. You are speaking too rapidly if you stumble over words or begin to feel out of breath. If this happens, take a deep breath and slow down. We also recommend that you practice and time yourself so that you have a feel for how quickly you should speak. Let this guide your decisions as you speak. Also remember that like volume, you can use rate for effect. For example, sports announcers respond to exciting moments in a game by increasing their rate of speech. In other words, the announcer uses rate to emphasize the events. You, too, should use rate, in conjunction with volume, to emphasize important points of your speech. For example, to stress an important point, enhance your volume and slow down your rate; this will give your point vocal emphasis.

vocal inflection frequently changing the pitch of one's voice

monotone rarely changing the pitch of one's voice

Pitch Listen carefully to your favorite radio DJ. Notice how the DJ frequently changes the pitch of his or her voice; this is called **vocal inflection** and is the opposite of a **monotone** voice, where one rarely changes pitch. For example, in the film *Ferris Bueller's Day Off*, Ben Stein is teaching a high school history class to a group of unresponsive students. His monotone voice, along with the variety of student responses, makes the scene very funny. However, it's not as funny if you're a member of an audience listening to a monotone speaker. To avoid a monotone voice, we suggest that first you recognize the range of pitch you can employ. As a test, stand up, take a deep breath, and slide your voice along a musical scale. Begin at the highest tone you can produce and slide your voice down to the lowest tone you can produce. While you obviously will not want to speak with a high, falsetto voice or attempt to speak in an abnormally low voice, this exercise can help you identify a comfortable vocal range, which still includes numerous pitches you can employ to make your speech more effective. Second, think about how you can use inflection to emphasize keywords or ideas. For example, repeat the following sentences and change your voice to emphasize the words in bold.

> **I** just got out.
>
> I **just** got out.
>
> I just **got** out.
>
> I just got **out**.

How does the meaning of the sentence change given the change in your voice? Can you add a different "tone" to each of the messages and alter the meaning yet again? For example, how might you say "I **just** got out" with frustration or as an apology? Note how the inflection changes as you purposefully change the meaning of this simple sentence. Inflection adds emphasis, interest, and expressiveness that will help you communicate your message and engage your listeners.

Clarity Not only do you need to speak with sufficient and varied volume, rate, and pitch, but you also need to speak clearly. We have already discussed how to use language more carefully for clarity. However, clarity is also a matter of delivery and refers, specifically, to articulation, pronunciation, and fluency. Let's consider each of these terms in greater detail.

articulation saying the sounds within words clearly

pronunciation saying words correctly

First, **articulation** refers to saying the sounds in words clearly. For example, poor articulation occurs when "going to" becomes "gonna" and "get out of here" becomes "gitouttahere." Second, **pronunciation** refers to saying words correctly. Mispronunciation occurs frequently because of adding, subtracting, reversing, or substituting sounds, as well as accenting the wrong syllable. Yourdictionary.com

Table 11.1	Examples of Commonly Mispronounced Words	
Incorrect	**Correct**	**Type of Problem**
athelete	athlete	adding a sound
cannidate	candidate	dropping a sound
birfday	birthday	substituting sounds
aks	ask	reversing sounds
mis*chiev*ous	*mis*chievous	misplaced accent

(www.yourdictionary.com/library/mispron.html) provides a list of the one hundred most commonly mispronounced words. Consider the examples in Table 11.1 to help you address this common problem with clarity.

Fluency refers to a smooth flow of speech without frequent verbal stumbles or fillers. Beginning speakers often add words such as *you know, like, okay*, or *uhs* and *ums*. While some *disfluencies* are a part of natural, conversational speech, when they are used excessively and repeatedly, they become highly distractive to listeners. We recommend that you have a solid grasp of your ideas, work carefully on the language of your speech, and omit fillers as you practice in order to maintain fluency. In our experience, you are most likely to insert unnecessary fillers at the beginnings and ends of sentences. To avoid this repetitive pattern, work carefully on the language of your main ideas and your transitions between these ideas. Also remember not to obsess over an occasional "uh" or "um." Additionally, you may be concerned about accents or dialects. The box Cultural Links: Dialects and Accents offers some insight and advice about this issue of clarity.

fluency a smooth flow of speech without frequent stumbles or fillers

(◎) Cultural Links

Dialects and Accents

We develop rules for language from our upbringing and cultural background, which include such things as how words are spoken and joined together. The differences that exist among native English speakers are commonly referred to as *dialects*. So, for example, someone from the eastern United States may pronounce the word *idea* as "idear." On the other hand, someone from the southern United States may use "y'all" rather than *you*, while in the Midwest someone may say "youins" for *you*. As another example, you will hear people from various parts of the country use the words *carry, take,* and *bring* to mean the same thing. In the South, one is "carried" to the store, while in other parts of the United States, one is "taken" or "brought" to the store. In reviewing a film focusing on dialectical differences, Schroeder (2004) notes that the question of dialects and what is acceptable is much more than just a matter of speech sounds; it is also a matter of power, education, and resources. In other words, dialectical differences are as complex socially as they are linguistically.

In contrast, people who speak English as a second language (ESL) often have *accents*. So, for example, the "r" sound is often difficult for ESL speakers from Asian countries. Therefore, the word *rice* sometimes sounds like "lice" to native English speakers. Likewise, the "w" sound is often replaced by a "v" sound by native speakers of German or Eastern European languages. Consequently, *work* is pronounced "vork."

Given these co-cultural and cross-cultural differences, what impact do dialects and accents have on public speaking? How should one respond to them? We suggest the following guidelines:

1. As much as possible, use standard American English when addressing U.S. audiences. While we recognize that there is an ongoing debate about this advice, research suggests that in most cases, standard American English enhances one's credibility (Glen, Glen, & Forman 1998).

2. Adapt to your audience. In some instances, using a distinct dialect with a given audience actually enhances your credibility. Therefore, if you are addressing a group with whom you share a dialect, you may enhance your credibility by drawing on your common language background. However, if you try to become someone you are not, you will probably undermine your credibility. So, be yourself and then adapt to a given audience in ways that do not compromise your identity and that avoid potentially offensive words, phrases, or humor.

3. If you speak English as a second language, concentrate on being understood rather than getting rid of your accent. In most cases, you can't and shouldn't try to get rid of your accent but rather work toward speaking intelligibly. Consider, for example, the success of Arnold Schwarzenegger as both a movie star and a politician, even though he speaks with accented English.

Using Your Face Effectively

eye contact looking at everyone in the audience

facial expressions the ways in which an individual animates his or her face

Facial delivery refers, for the most part, to **eye contact** and **facial expressions**. While eye contact, like language, differs among cultural groups, in most speaking situations, frequent, sustained, and comprehensive eye contact will help you link with your audience. This means that you should regularly share eye contact with everyone in your audience without relying on your keyword outline or note cards. Beginning speakers tend to look at their notes as a way to avoid eye contact, thus reducing their apprehension, even though they know the content of their speech well. This strategy typically backfires because you will be more apt to continue looking at your notes rather than your audience. You may also be tempted to focus on your instructor or one friendly face in the audience, but this excludes a large portion of your audience as well. Remember, as Andrews, Andrews, and Williams (1999) point out, eye contact helps you enhance your credibility with the audience, while, at the same time, you can watch how your listeners respond to your presentation and adapt accordingly. Your eyes are an important gateway to audience feedback.

Additionally, think about your facial expressions. When all eyes are on you, you may become less expressive than you are in everyday conversation. Therefore, focus on your message and allow your speech's content to help direct your facial expressions. If your speech reflects a note of humor, sorrow, or surprise and you respond accordingly, you will come across as more natural and believable; however, if you focus on practicing your nonverbal expressions, you are likely to come across as unnatural. In most instances, a smile will relax you and your audience, and your audience is likely to reciprocate, especially considering that smiling is a universal human behavior (Ekman & Friesen 1987). Of course, a smile is not always appropriate if it violates the tone or content of your speech, but it is often an effective default facial expression, especially as compared to a consistently solemn or terrified facial expression.

Using Your Body Effectively

gestures movements of the hands, arms, or sometimes the shoulders, legs, or feet

posture overall stance

movement encompasses whether the speaker stands still or moves his or her entire body

Physical or bodily delivery typically includes gestures, posture, and movement. **Gestures** refer to movements of the hands, arms, shoulders, legs, or feet. **Posture** refers to your overall stance, whereas **movement** usually encompasses whether you stand still or move your entire body. With these basic definitions in hand, let's consider some principles that can enhance your physical delivery.

Just as your speech's content should direct your facial expressions, it should also give rise to natural gestures. Forced or overly planned gestures look robotic and are distracting, if not downright laughable. We have seen beginning speakers make a point and then suddenly remember they were intending to employ a specific gesture and do so a split second after making the point. However, with practice, you can plan for some gestures that harmonize well with your speech's content. For example, if you use an ordinal approach to organization (e.g., first, second, third), you can hold up the appropriate number of fingers to help emphasize your transition between points. If you wish to emphasize a particular point, simply pointing your right index finger into the palm of your left hand helps to nonverbally underscore your point. Above all, remember to be yourself and to blend your gestures with your message.

As for your posture, stand up straight but not rigidly, flex your knees, and firmly place both feet on the floor. Some speakers visualize chewing gum on the bottom of their shoes, so the image of something tugging on their feet reminds them to move their feet purposefully. Avoid slumping or leaning on or clinging to the podium. Standing straight and keeping your knees unlocked will assist your breathing and keep you from becoming dizzy while you also strike a confident, relaxed pose.

If you wish to move as you speak, keep your movement natural and linked to your speech's content. For example, as you move from one main point to another, you may wish to step left or right in order to help physically reinforce your verbal transition. You can also use movement to enhance a description or to help your audience focus on a visual aid. For example, you may move from the podium to a poster, chart, or overhead transparency to point to a specific diagram or piece of information. If you do this, continue facing your audience and stand to the side of your visual aid as you draw attention to it.

Above all, avoid distracting movement. Playing with your hair or a pen, jingling the keys in your pocket, tapping your finger on the podium, rocking back and forth or from side to side, picking at or adjusting your clothing, or pacing all distract from your message. Focus on integrating your movement with the content of your speech and maintaining a professional, poised appearance without distracting mannerisms.

Appropriate facial expression enhances the delivery of a speech.

USING VISUAL AIDS TO ENHANCE DELIVERY

*V*isual aids are intended to assist the delivery of information, not replace it. Too often we have seen a visual aid *become* the speech rather than aid in the delivery. Consider the types of visual aids you may choose from, and learn some fundamental guidelines for using them and ways to effectively integrate them into your delivery.

Types of Visual Aids

Visual aids come in many forms, including charts, graphs, tables, drawings, pictures, maps, photographs, and other less common forms. **Charts and graphs** often focus on helping an audience understand *how much* and compare parts to the whole. You may, for example, use a pie chart to demonstrate proportions (see Figure 11.1) or a bar or line graph to show your audience how trends have changed over time (see Figures 11.2 and 11.3). The Math League offers some valuable insight on the purpose and format of graphs at www.mathleague.com/help/data/data.htm. Charts also sometimes contain only text. For example, a poster, flip chart, chalkboard, or software slide that previews or summarizes key ideas or concepts are **text charts**, while **tables** help *summarize information*. In sum, text charts help listeners see a main point, while tables summarize a larger amount of information using words and sometimes graphics.

Drawings are often used to depict how things work. For example, if you are explaining the parts and functions of a personal computer, a drawing or diagram of a

charts and graphs visual aids that help an audience understand *how much* and offer comparisons of part to a whole

text charts a poster, flip chart, chalkboard, or slide that previews or summarizes key ideas

tables visual aids that summarize information

drawings visual aids that depict how things work

FIGURE 11.1   Pie Chart

This pie chart shows the ingredients used to make a sausage and mushroom pizza. The fraction of each ingredient by weight is shown. We see that half of the pizza's weight comes from the crust. The mushrooms make up the smallest amount of the pizza by weight, since the slice corresponding to the mushrooms is smallest. Note that the sum of the decimal sizes of each slice is equal to 1 (the "whole pizza").

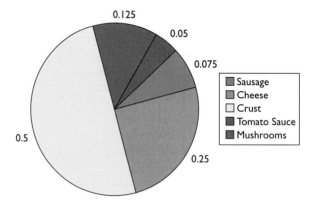

Source: From www.mathleague.com/help/data/data.htm. Reprinted by permission of Mathematics Leagues, Inc.

maps visual aids that help an audience understand where things occur

computer can help clarify your explanations. **Maps** focus on helping your audience understand *where* events occur or *where* landmarks are. In addition, maps may graphically explain where a given group of people live or the geographic relationship of one place to another. While we often think only of road maps that help us find

FIGURE 11.2   Number of Police Officers in Crimeville, 1993 to 2001

The number of police officers decreased from 1993 to 1996 but started increasing again in 1996. The graph makes it easy to compare or contrast the number of police officers for any combination of years. For example, in 2001 there were nine more police officers than in 1998.

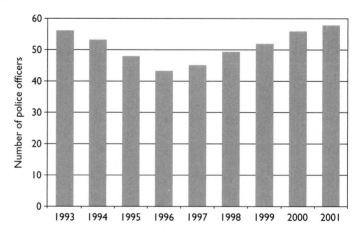

Source: From www.statcan.ca/english/edu/power/ch9/bargraph/bar.htm. Statistics Canada information is used with the permission of Statistics Canada. Users are forbidden to copy this material and/or redisseminate the data, in an original or modified form, for commercial purposes, without the expressed permission of Statistics Canada. Information on the availability of the wide range of data from Statistics Canada can be obtained from Statistic Canada's regional offices, its World Wide Web site at http://www.statcan.ca, and its toll-free access number 1-800-263-1136.

FIGURE 11.3   A Line Graph

A line graph is used to show continuing data—how one thing is affected by another. It's clear to see how things are going by the rises and falls a line graph shows. This kind of graph is needed to show the effect of an independent variable on a dependent variable. This graph shows a person's pulse rate changing over time.

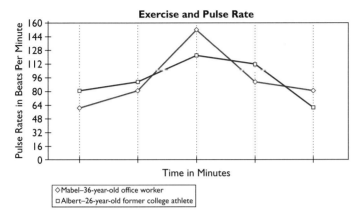

Exercise and Pulse Rate

Pulse Rates in Beats Per Minute: 160, 144, 128, 112, 96, 80, 64, 48, 32, 16, 0

Time in Minutes

◇ Mabel–36-year-old office worker
□ Albert–26-year-old former college athlete

Source: www.twingroves.district96.k12.il.us/ScienceInternet/ChartsGraphs.html.

directions, there are several types of maps, including physical, political, climate, economic, topographic, and so on. However, in general, maps typically show placement. **Photographs** tend to show *what* by preserving a snapshot of reality that may include, for example, a person's face, a landscape, or the action in a dramatic event. Remember, however, that a four-by-six photo you had processed at the local drugstore is not usually an effective visual aid because your audience cannot see it as you hold it, and passing it around during your speech distracts individual members of your audience.

Other visual aids include an audio or video clip, handouts, objects, or even a demonstration, although you will need to exercise care in how you use these particular visual aids, since they can create more problems than benefits if not used wisely. Whatever visual aids you decide to use, be sure that they truly aid your speech and follow some basic guidelines.

photographs visual aids that show what the speaker is discussing

PowerPoint® can be an effective visual aid in public speaking when used appropriately.

Guidelines for Using Visual Aids

Here's a checklist you can use to help ensure that your visual aids are well chosen, well prepared, and well used.

1. Does your visual aid relate well to and assist in explaining your topic? Visual aids should contribute to and support a main point in your speech by making the point memorable or more powerful.

2. Have you prepared the visual aid so that it is readable and appeals to the eye? Choose an easily readable typeface such as Arial or Times Roman and use contrasting, dark colors so that any text is easily seen. While pastel colors may seem attractive, they "wash out" when you put them on paper or an electronic slide. Keep your visual clear, simple, and direct; avoid cluttering it with graphics or too many words. In most cases, less is better. Also, be sure it is large enough so that everyone in the audience can see. As the size of the audience increases, so must the size of the visual.

3. Does your visual aid need to be placed on an easel or attached with tape or a tack? If you have to hold a visual aid and refer to it, you may encounter a number of practical problems. Moreover, holding a visual inhibits your physical delivery, so tack it, tape it, or put it on an easel.

4. Will your visual aid draw too much attention? Visual aids should not be the focus of the speech or create unforeseen difficulties that distract the audience.

This is why you should avoid using live animals, shocking pictures, or inappropriate displays or videotapes. If your aid may cause mishaps, create audience distraction, or be offensive, choose another type of aid.

5. Can you keep your visual aid covered, use it, and then lay it aside? Effective visual aids will not be used for your entire speech but employed at a particular point in the speech. Therefore, keep them out of sight until you are ready to use them, and make sure you can easily retrieve them and just as easily put them aside.

6. Can you avoid using handouts? Speakers who distribute handouts provide the audience with potential distractions. If you feel that handouts are useful and particularly necessary, plan to distribute them after your speech. If information from the handout is important to your speech, represent the information on a chart, overheard transparency, or blackboard.

7. Have you planned for any needed assistance in advance? Especially large or cumbersome visual aids may require someone else's help; be sure this is pre-arranged. Moreover, if you intend to conduct a demonstration that requires someone else's assistance, be sure to arrange this in advance.

8. Have you made sure that any equipment you need is readily available? At times, speakers may want to use audiovisual equipment. Be sure that these are available, economically feasible, and in good working order if you need them. In certain instances, securing equipment is prohibitively expensive; plan accordingly.

9. Have you practiced with your visual aid? As with every other aspect of speech preparation, it is important to practice delivering your speech while using your visual aid. If this is not done, unforeseen problems may result.

10. What does the audience expect? In some instances, your audience may expect a particular type of visual aid, such as a computerized slide show. Get a sense of the types of visual aids prior speakers have employed when addressing a given audience.

Integrating Visual Aids with Delivery

Once your visual aid is ready, think about how to use it to enhance your delivery. Here are a couple of tips. First, *focus the audience on you, not your visual aid*, as you begin your speech. We have seen several student speakers use a visual aid to gain attention and lose the opportunity to build common ground or connect with their audience. For example, this is why we advise you to avoid using video clips. Sometimes audience members want to continue watching the movie rather than listening to you. Therefore, use the first minute of your speech to gain your audience's attention through effective use of language and delivery. Additionally, this strategy will help you gain confidence, establish eye contact, and get your speech well started, which will, in turn, help focus and energize the remainder of your speech.

Second, *use your visual to clarify an important idea in your speech*. While in many professional settings it is common to dim the lights and talk through a series of electronic slides, we find this approach problematic because it separates the speaker from the audience, turns a speech into a slide show with a "voice-over," and essentially omits many of the aspects of physical delivery we talked about earlier. Avoid this approach, unless it is absolutely the expected norm. Even then, make adjustments by having the lights as bright as possible and creating significant pauses in the slide show that move the focus from the visuals to you. (See the box Computer Links: The Problem with PowerPoint® as a Visual Aid for additional information about the ongoing PowerPoint® controversy). In general, use your visual aid to strengthen a major point in your speech and at the same time enhance audience interest.

Third, *use the visual aids you truly need*. At times, a single visual aid is sufficient for your speech, but at other times, you may need more than two or even more; use what you need to communicate your message effectively. Also remember that using appropriate visual aids helps engage your audience's attention and assists their memory. Ultimately, keep in mind that visual aids are, indeed, aids, not the substance of your speech; *you* are the speaker, and your aids are your assistants.

Computer Links

The Problem with PowerPoint® as a Visual Aid

Read the following article from the *New York Times*.

PowerPoint Makes You Dumb
by Clive Thompson

In August, the Columbia Accident Investigation Board at NASA released Volume 1 of its report on why the space shuttle crashed. As expected, the ship's foam insulation was the main cause of the disaster. But the board also fingered another unusual culprit: PowerPoint, Microsoft's well-known "slideware" program.

NASA, the board argued, had become too reliant on presenting complex information via PowerPoint, instead of by means of traditional ink-and-paper technical reports. When NASA engineers assessed possible wing damage during the mission, they presented the findings in a confusing PowerPoint slide—so crammed with nested bullet points and irregular short forms that it was nearly impossible to untangle. "It is easy to understand how a senior manager might read this PowerPoint slide and not realize that it addresses a life-threatening situation," the board sternly noted.

PowerPoint is the world's most popular tool for presenting information. There are 400 million copies in circulation, and almost no corporate decision takes place without it. But what if PowerPoint is actually making us stupider?

This year, Edward Tufte—the famous theorist of information presentation—made precisely that argument in a blistering screed called the Cognitive Style of PowerPoint. In his slim 28-page pamphlet, Tufte claimed that Microsoft's ubiquitous software forces people to mutilate data beyond comprehension. For example, the low resolution of a PowerPoint slide means that it usually contains only about 40 words, or barely eight seconds of reading. PowerPoint also encourages users to rely on bulleted lists, a "faux analytical" technique, Tufte wrote, that dodges the speaker's responsibility to tie his information together. And perhaps worst of all is how PowerPoint renders charts. Charts in newspapers like the *Wall Street Journal* contain up to 120 elements on average, allowing readers to compare large groupings of data. But, as Tufte found, PowerPoint users typically produce charts with only 12 elements. Ultimately, Tufte concluded, PowerPoint is infused with "an attitude of commercialism that turns everything into a sales pitch."

Microsoft officials, of course, beg to differ. Simon Marks, the product manager for PowerPoint, counters that Tufte is a fan of "information density," shoving tons of data at an audience. You could do that with PowerPoint, he says, but it's a matter of choice. "If people were told they were going to have to sit through an incredibly dense presentation," he adds, "they wouldn't want it." And PowerPoint still has fans in the highest corridors of power: Colin Powell used a slideware presentation in February when he made his case to the United Nations that Iraq possessed weapons of mass destruction.

Of course, given that the weapons still haven't been found, maybe Tufte is onto something. Perhaps PowerPoint is uniquely suited to our modern age of obfuscation—where manipulating facts is as important as presenting them clearly. If you have nothing to say, maybe you need just the right tool to help you not say it.

What is your reaction to Thompson's observations? Given this article, would you use PowerPoint as a visual aid for your speech? Why or why not? If so, how would you use it? What guidelines would you follow? For more information on using PowerPoint effectively, you can visit numerous websites by using any search engine.

Source: "PowerPoint Makes You Dumb" by Clive Thompson first appeared in *The New York Times* Magazine, December 14, 2003. Reprinted by permission of Feature Well.

PREPARING FOR EFFECTIVE DELIVERY

*N*ow that you understand the various modes of delivery and the critical elements of effective delivery, you must prepare and practice to deliver your speech effectively. This section contains some guidelines for preparation in advance and just before addressing your audience, as well as some other practical suggestions.

Guidelines for Effective Preparation

While there are several specific steps you can take to prepare for effective delivery, here are some basic guidelines to consider. First, *prepare your content*. While we addressed this point in detail in Chapters 9 and 10, we again urge you to develop a clear preparation and presentation outline on a topic that you find interesting and worthwhile. Knowing what you're going to say because you have mastered the content will improve your self-confidence as a speaker. Believing that you have something important to share with your listeners is equally important to your confidence. Also, be sure to prepare any visual aids you intend to use. We will say more about visual aids later in this chapter.

Second, *prepare your voice and practice speaking clearly*. As you practice your speech, think about how you can use the pitch and volume of your voice, the rate at which you speak, and the emphasis you place on certain words to enliven your presentation. Strive to say your words clearly and correctly. If possible, practice your speech in the room where you will deliver it and have a friend sit in the back row. Your friend can help you be sure you're speaking at an appropriate volume, rate, and with sufficient vocal variety.

Third, *prepare your body*. As you practice your speech, think about how you can use your face, hands, posture, and bodily movement to enhance the impact of your words. While any movement needs to be natural and not forced, some planning can help you focus on your nonverbal behavior. Consider placing reminders on your keyword outline to prompt desirable gestures, facial expressions, or movement. Additionally, be sure to get a good night's rest and eat a light but nutritious breakfast, lunch, or dinner on the day you are to speak to maintain your blood sugar level and thereby provide you with needed energy.

Fourth, *prepare your appearance*. Think about and plan how you want to be dressed and groomed for your presentation. Your appearance impacts your credibility. Wearing caps or letting long hair fall in your face can make it difficult for the audience to see your eyes and face. Your instructor may have other helpful guidelines.

Fifth, *prepare your mind*. It's natural to be nervous before you speak. But you can use your nervousness as energy to draw upon rather than as "mental noise" that interferes with your presentation. Be positive. See yourself doing well. Tell yourself that your nervousness will help you think and speak better. For additional help, re-read the section on communication apprehension in Chapter 9.

Sixth, *prepare by practicing*. There is no substitute for regular, appropriate practice in order to ensure the delivery of your speech. We discuss practice further in the next section.

Seventh, *prepare before you begin*. Before you take the podium for your presentation, be sure nothing is in your mouth (such as gum) or hand (such as a pencil or pen); bring only what you need for the speech. After you reach the front of the room, take a moment to collect your thoughts before you begin speaking. Don't start talking before you reach the front of the room and don't continue speaking as you walk back to your seat toward the conclusion of your speech. Deliver your entire speech from the front of the room.

How to Practice for Effectiveness

There is simply no substitute for practice if you want to deliver your speech effectively. Consider these ideas for practice.

- Work on the parts of your speech privately and aloud. You may find it useful to practice portions of your speech in shorter time periods as you begin. For example, deliver your first main point aloud to yourself. As you do, you may find a better way to phrase your main point or to adapt your supporting material to make it more effective. You can make these changes to your outline. Then practice the major sections of your speech, specifically, the introduction, body, and conclusion.

- After you practice each major section aloud, put the entire speech together and practice it aloud. At this point, time yourself and make any changes necessary to meet the stipulated time limits or to improve the speech's flow. Make sure these are your final edits to the content of the speech.

- Continue to practice the entire speech aloud. At this point, you should have made necessary changes in the content, so focus now on delivering your content effectively. While some people recommend practicing in front of a mirror, we find this method often interferes with focusing on your message, since the mirror too often prompts you to focus on yourself. However, continue to practice aloud, and be sure to use any visual aids you have prepared for the speech.

- You may wish to record a practice session when you are basically satisfied with the speech. Listen to yourself and identify specific aspects of your delivery you want to change. We recommend this step only if you have heard your recorded voice. Otherwise, you may become too distracted.

- As a final step, ask your roommate, a friend, or a family member to listen to your speech and provide feedback. You may also have a speech lab where you can practice and receive even more focused, helpful feedback. If you have such an opportunity, use it; research indicates that speech labs make a measurable difference in student performances and the resulting grades (Hunt & Simonds 2002).

See the box Community Links: Labs for Ongoing Practice for even more suggestions for "lab" opportunities during your college career.

To be well prepared, practice your speech with your friends.

Community Links

Labs for Ongoing Practice

Realistically, we know that this single course in communication will not help you fully develop your skills as a competent communicator or as a public speaker. If you have ever attempted to learn a new musical instrument or a foreign language, then you know that learning new skills takes frequent, sustained practice. Likewise, you will need multiple opportunities to practice your public speaking skills if you are to develop them sufficiently. In other words, you need some labs outside of class where you can practice. Fortunately, you have numerous such opportunities. Consider these suggestions:

- Speak up in your classes. When you have opportunities to share your ideas, pose questions, or work on a group project, engage the conversation rather than sit back and wait for others. Sharing your thoughts in class will help you think, speak, and listen.

- Get involved in a literacy initiative. With little effort, you can find opportunities to read aloud to children or to help teach people to read. While you may not think of this kind of work as a way to develop your delivery skills, think again. For example, most children's books are full of emotion. Reading the books aloud can help you enhance various aspects of your delivery, including your vocal and physical expressiveness. We remember, for instance, an old *M*A*S*H* episode in which Dr. Potter read a manual on how to dismantle a rifle to a little Korean child in such an expressive way that even though the child did not understand English, he enjoyed the delivery of the "story." Imagine what you can do with children who understand English.

- Seek out student organizations. Your campus probably has numerous student organizations, many of which offer opportunities to become involved in campus life and to share your ideas with others. For example, student government organizations are often involved in making, changing, or applying policies. This process requires various forms of public speaking and offers you an opportunity to develop your skills. Group leaders on your campus would probably welcome your participation. By choosing to become involved, you enhance not only your links with your campus, but also your opportunities for developing your communication skills.

- Look for other community links. Consider the number of religious, political, nonprofit, and service organizations in your community. Many of these organizations actively seek participants who will speak to and for them. For example, you may find a chance to share spiritual insights or information at your local church or synagogue, or to speak to a local service club about an initiative in which you are involved, or to represent a nonprofit organization to a group of community members. With little effort, you can find numerous opportunities to use and develop your public speaking skills outside the classroom.

Preparing a speech takes a considerable investment of time, but it is an investment that will pay valuable dividends in developing your skills and improving your grades. Furthermore, in many ways, the time-management skills necessary to prepare to speak effectively parallel your overall college experience, as indicated in the box Campus Links: Time Management.

Campus Links

Time Management

To successfully complete the process of speech preparation, you must allow yourself sufficient time to brainstorm in order to identify your subject and topic, conduct sufficient research to construct the content of your outline and speech, and still save time for practicing aloud. In other words, you have to manage your time in order to be an effective speaker. The same skills required for completing your speaking assignments are also required for college and professional success. Learning how to manage your time now will yield important dividends in your college and career, as well as in your communication class.

So, consider this piece of advice: *You can never FIND time; you must MAKE time.* But how do you *make* time? Consider these practical suggestions for time management for completing your speech assignments and for college and career success.

1. **Find out how you are spending your time.** Analyze where your time is going by completing a time analysis sheet. Here's a link to help you, as a college student, get started in analyzing your time: http://istudy.psu/FirstYear Modules/Time/Time/TimeManagementLesson .htm. Remember that there are only 168 hours in a week. You may be surprised to find that you have more time on your hands than you thought, or, like some very busy folks, that you've exceeded the 168 hours and are overcommitted. This analysis will allow you to identify how much time to commit to preparing your speech. As a general guideline, you need two hours of preparation time for every hour you spend in class. So, if you're taking a three-semester credit hour communication class, you need to spend at least six hours a week studying. Effective speech preparation is likely to take even more!

2. **Plan your time.** Once you know what activities you are currently spending your time on, you can make choices about how to spend your time in the future. Invest in a monthly and a daily planner. Begin by reading through the syllabi or course outlines for each of your classes and then record all your test, quiz, or paper due dates in your monthly planner. Use different colors for each class so you can quickly note what you must do for each class. The major advantage of a monthly planner is that you can see what's coming up and can plan accordingly. After you've filled in your monthly

planner, use your daily planner to write down all reading assignments, lecture topics, and other information. Keep your daily planner filled out at least two weeks in advance so you can keep on top of your homework load. Include your speech preparation time in your planner using the guidelines below.

3. **Combat procrastination.** According to McWhorter (2001), procrastination is one of the main enemies of successful time management. Here are some specific steps to help combat this enemy:

   Set aside weekly plan time. Keep your monthly and daily planners up-to-date by setting aside an hour or half-hour time block to plan each week. Use this time to update your calendars, plan what needs to be done, and set weekly and daily goals. Jot down what you wish to accomplish on a daily "sticky" note. That way you can easily add to it and will get the satisfaction of crossing off things you have accomplished. Setting realistic daily "to do" tasks provides a checklist as well as positive feedback, since you will feel so much better when you can check off one of your assignments or projects.

   Establish "soft" deadlines. "Soft" deadlines are due dates that you establish for yourself that allow you to complete your work ahead of time, ensuring you meet your instructor's "hard" deadline. For example, if you need to write a research paper that's due in four weeks, you could set a soft deadline to complete your research by the end of week 1, to create an outline or a rough draft by the end of week 2, and to have reworked your rough draft and completed your bibliography by the end of week 3. By setting soft deadlines, you've allowed extra time in your schedule for the real-life occurrences such as getting called into work, running out of ink cartridges for your printer, or getting clarification on your paper from your teacher.

   Use these same strategies in planning your speech preparation, using specific days rather than weeks, because typically you will not have as much time to prepare your speech as to complete a research paper. So, for example, if you have a week of preparation time for your speech, identify specific goals for each day. Here's a suggested timetable, assuming you have a week's preparation time:

Day 1: Commit to a subject and topic and start your research. Consult your instructor or speech lab about your topic (two hours).

Day 2: Conduct your research and write a preliminary thesis statement (two hours).

Day 3: Complete your research and refine the preliminary thesis statement and write your first-draft preparation outline. Start to work on your visual aids (two hours).

Day 4: Consult with your instructor or speech lab about your outline and refine your preparation outline and visual aids. Make your keyword outline and put it on note cards. Practice aloud and make changes to your note cards as you go, noting any areas that need special attention either in your use of language or your delivery goals (two hours).

Day 5: Finalize your visual aids. Practice aloud by yourself, even if it's in the shower (one hour); at a speech lab; or with your instructor and/or in front of roommates, family, or other class members using your note cards and visual aids (one hour). Make any changes to your note cards and or visual aids.

Day 6: Practice aloud and make your final draft of keyword outline cards (two hours).

Day 7: Practice aloud one more time for reinforcement as close as possible to your speech delivery time and then deliver your speech.

Of course, you may need to adjust this schedule depending on intervening factors; that's why we offer these as soft deadlines. For example, you may need more time for research. However, if you use this schedule and adjust it as necessary, you will avoid waiting until the last minute to prepare your speech. Don't forget, an excellent speech rests on excellent preparation!

Give yourself just a few minutes to start. Often, just starting is the most difficult thing for you to do. This can be true from starting a weight-loss program to cleaning your closet, but it is especially true when it comes to studying and preparing for your speech. If you give yourself just a few minutes to start, you may make progress on your task and find that working just a few more minutes isn't as difficult as you thought. The most important step to take when preparing your speech is to get started now!

4. **Fight disorganization.**

Use a three-ring-binder system. Rather than using separate notebooks and folders for each class, invest in a two-inch-wide D-ring binder and a three-hole punch. Buy some section dividers and loose-leaf paper as well. Create a separate section that is chronologically organized (according to the date the assignment was completed) for each of your classes in which to keep all your lecture notes, handouts, text notes, and returned work. In addition to keeping you organized, carrying your binder allows you to use brief moments to study (like between classes or when a class is canceled) and prevents you from having to run back to your residence hall or to your car to get what you need. Former students have indicated that this is the most important organizational strategy they have learned.

In order to assist your speech preparation, here are some additional specific organizational suggestions to consider. Keep all your work for the speech together, including your brainstorming sheets, copies of your research, your preliminary outline, and your note cards. An inexpensive folder can be a valuable organizational tool. You can save time just by having everything together in the same place. Additionally, save any research you gather under your "favorites" on your computer, save it to a disk, and e-mail articles to yourself for future use. You may also find it very useful to print hard copies of your research if you use a computer lab or the library and cannot easily access the information elsewhere. If you are using information gathered from print copies of magazines, journals, or books, photocopy the information. As you find research, carefully note the citation information so you do not have to retrieve it later, since you will need this for your outline. If you are using printed information, you can always copy the page from the book, journal, or magazine that has the essential citation information. Or you can simply write down the bibliographic information on note cards and put them in your organizational folder. These simple strategies can truly save time in the long run.

EFFECTIVE DELIVERY FOR DIFFERING CONTEXTS

*A*s we noted in Chapter 1, all human communication is contextualized; it occurs in unique settings. Therefore, you must adapt your delivery to a variety of settings as you continue to employ your public speaking skills. While there is a wealth of information about numerous contexts, we offer a summary and some fundamental principles for contexts you are most likely to encounter in this section. First, we offer some reliable, time-tested principles that cut across all contexts, and then we provide some insights for the college, workplace, and public contexts.

Common Core Principles

Context is one of the essential components of any communication situation. Therefore, you should be keenly aware of public speaking contexts. We will say more about this in the next section, but at this point, consider these core principles of delivery that are applicable across contexts:

- Be clear. Your first goal in delivery is to be understandable. Speak with appropriate volume, pitch, rate, and gestures for the size of the audience and the room you are speaking in.
- Be concise. In a highly technological age, your audience is conditioned to sound bites and relatively brief oral explanations. Therefore, be conscious of the time you are allotted to speak and how you use it. Make your points as cleanly and directly as possible.
- Be correct. While some contexts are more relaxed and allow for greater flexibility in delivery, in most instances you need to use correct grammar, pronunciation, and articulation.
- Be courteous. In every speaking situation, your audience expects you to be appropriate, sensitive, and nonoffensive. Treat your audience with courtesy by avoiding any slurs that might offend.
- Be controlled. Avoid overt movement, gestures, and facial expressions that distract your audience. Smooth, flowing movements and gestures are, in most cases, appropriate and engaging. Remember that speaking is not acting or performing; it should be conversational in appearance and tone.
- Be captivating. Work at gaining and maintaining your audience's attention. Think about how you can use language and nonverbal delivery to help seize and hold attention. Sometimes this may be as simple as moving a step closer to your audience; it need not be dramatic to be effective.

College and Public Speaking

The college classroom, as we noted in Chapter 1, is a viable, real-life communication context. Rather than treat your classroom audience as a training ground for a "real audience" that you will face later in life, approach public speaking in your classes by carefully considering your audience. Given what we know about college student experiences, plan to deliver your speech energetically by employing considerable vocal variety, gestures, and strong visual aids. Moreover, Dr. Charles Schroeder (1993) suggests that present-day college students prefer concrete, well-organized information presented in a personalized manner. Consequently, think about how to make the ideas in your speech specific, clear, and practical. This will require real-life examples backed by helpful visual aids that make your ideas accessible. Additionally, carefully organize your speech so your ideas flow together, thereby allowing your audience to easily follow them. In most cases, your peers need you to lead them from one idea to another. Finally, speak with your audience in a friendly vocal tone, smile, and build common ground with them; they want a personal touch, not an overly polished orator.

Public speaking is an important skill in the workplace.

The Workplace and Speaking

Whole courses are committed to helping you develop your skills in business and professional communication, and we highly recommend that you consider such a course in the future. While it is beyond the scope of this book to offer you a complete review of speaking in the workplace, we encourage you to read Appendix A in Andrews, Andrews, and Williams's (1999) book, which provides detailed information about workplace communication. However, here are some important delivery principles to consider that are applicable across a variety of presentations in the workplace:

- Understand the organization's culture. To craft your delivery appropriately, you must have a working knowledge of how a given business or organization is structured, how decisions are made, and how the organization's members relate to one another. There is simply no substitute for doing your homework about an organization, department, or team that you will speak with.

- Deliver your presentation extemporaneously. Prepare, practice, but be spontaneous and adapt so that you reach every audience member.

- Consider the physical context. You may be in an office, boardroom, or larger conference area; adapt your nonverbal delivery accordingly. In most instances, it is best to stand as you present, although you may sometimes be seated at a conference table.

- Use visual aids. Most organizations expect computer-generated visual support for presentations, although, in some cases, other forms are equally acceptable. Be sure that your aids are clean, clear, correct, and appealing to the eye; they should look truly professional. We recommend you take a workshop on how to use PowerPoint effectively.

- Respect time limits. People in organizations are faced with multiple tasks and hard deadlines; therefore, time is often strained. Remember this and reflect it in your presentation.

- Be ready to answer questions. You must have a command of the information and be ready to respond to questions in an impromptu fashion. Refer to your prepared information as much as possible in order to repeat and reinforce it, but be sure to maintain a cooperative, professional attitude as you respond to potentially difficult questions; don't get rattled or, worse, angry or defensive. Monitor your nonverbal responses and adjust them in order to manage your impressions appropriately.

Public forums are often an important place to voice your opinions.

The Public and Speaking

Although many of you may not see yourself speaking publicly, life has a way of providing you with surprises. For example, your college may consider instituting a new fee in order to offset some of the expenses of labs or technology purchases and plans to open public hearings so that interested people can express their opinions. Will you speak or remain silent? While it may be easy to cynically complain, we suggest you think about a constructive response and speak up!

Much of what we have already said applies to speaking in a public forum, but we would like to emphasize some principles for delivery that are especially applicable in public forums. First, in public forums there are often differences of opinion. Therefore, it is important to present your position clearly and carefully; say what you mean as directly as you can, using clear, specific language. Pay particular attention to your articulation, pronunciation, and the vocal nonverbal elements we discussed in this chapter, because these will likely impact your credibility with the audience. Even though you may hold strong opinions about a given issue, it is important to remain controlled and rational when making your point. Ranting, raving, or accusing will allow listeners to label you a "crackpot" and disregard what you have to say.

Second, while you may have prepared comments, deliver them extemporaneously—speak with your audience, don't read to them. This will allow you to make eye contact and employ appropriate gestures to help reinforce your point.

Third, make your point clearly and concisely by using the principles of organization we discussed in Chapter 10. Carefully use the limited time you have.

◎ SUMMARY

This chapter has focused on delivery and visual aids as essential elements in public speaking. In review, we have considered the following:

- Types of delivery, including impromptu, extemporaneous, manuscript, and memorized
- Elements of effective vocal delivery, specifically volume, pitch, rate, pronunciation, articulation, and fluency
- Elements of effective physical delivery, particularly eye contact, facial expressions, gesture, posture, and movement
- Various types of visual aids, including charts, graphs, maps, and photographs
- Guidelines for effectively using visual aids in order to assist your presentation, not overshadow it

- Strategies for effective preparation and practice well before and just before you deliver your speech
- Principles and specific suggestions for speaking in college, workplace, and public contexts

Questions for Discussion

1. In this chapter, we have repeatedly emphasized the value of extemporaneous speaking. To what degree do you agree with your position? When might extemporaneous speaking not be the best mode of delivery for you?

2. What principles of practice have you identified in playing sports, learning a video game, or playing a musical instrument that you believe are equally applicable to effective speech preparation?

3. What is your opinion of PowerPoint given your own experience as an audience member? For example, how do you react when your professor uses PowerPoint during a lecture?

4. What is your greatest challenge in effectively delivering a speech? What steps can you take to help you address this challenge and improve your skill?

◎ EXERCISES

1. Present an impromptu speech. Then engage in a mock interview with one of your peers in class, using some of the typical interview questions provided in the box Career Links: Job Interviews as Impromptu Speaking. In what ways does your experience in completing this exercise parallel delivering an impromptu speech? How is the experience different? How does giving an impromptu speech help you with interview questions and vice versa?

2. As a relaxation technique to prepare for your speech delivery, sit comfortably in a chair. Beginning with your toes, contract the major muscle groups in your body, moving up toward your shoulders. Hold your contraction and count to ten, then slowly release the muscles. As you contract, breathe in deeply, and as you release your muscles, breathe out fully. How does this exercise affect your tension level? What differences can you tell in your body and emotional state from this exercise?

◎ KEY TERMS

Impromptu speeches	Articulation	Charts and graphs
Extemporaneous speeches	Pronunciation	Text charts
Manuscript speeches	Fluency	Tables
Memorized speeches	Eye contact	Drawings
Volume	Facial expressions	Maps
Rate	Gestures	Photographs
Vocal inflection	Posture	
Monotone	Movement	

◎ REFERENCES

Andrews, P. H., Andrews, J. R., and Williams, G. 1999. *Public speaking: Connecting you and your audience.* Boston: Houghton Mifflin.

Axtell, K. nd. *Breathing in public speaking.* Retrieved March 6, 2005, from www .whitman.edu/rhetoric/84zbreathing.htm.

Daly, J. A., and Engleberg, I. A. 2001. *Presentations in everyday life: Strategies for effective speaking.* Boston: Houghton Mifflin.

Ekman, P., and Friesen, W. V. 1987. Universals and cultural differences in judgments of facial expressions of emotion. *Journal of Personality and Social Psychology* 53:712–717.

Glen, E. C., Glen, P. J., and Forman, S. 1998. *Your voice and articulation.* 4th ed. Boston: Allyn & Bacon.

Hunt, S. K., and Simonds, C. J. 2002. Extending learning opportunities in the basic communication course: Exploring the pedagogical benefits of speech laboratories. *Basic Communication Course Annual* 14:60–86.

McWhorter, K. 2001. *College reading and study skills.* 8th ed. New York: Longman.

Schroeder, C. S. 1993. New students—new learning styles. *Change* 25(5):21–26.

Schroeder, W. 2004. Do you speak American? *Humanities* 25(2):10–14.

CHAPTER 12

Groups in Discussion

Characteristics
- Size
- Purpose
- Mutual Influence
- Interdependence
- Norms
- Collective Identity
- Cohesion
- Commitment

Goals

Types of Goals
- Individual
- Group

Types of Groups
- Learning
- Therapy
- Problem Solving
- Social

Roles
- Task
- Social
- Individual

Stages
- Forming
- Norming
- Storming
- Performing

Culture, Values, Gender
- Group Culture
- Value System
- Equifinality

Leadership Approaches
- Trait
- Styles
- Functional
- Situational

Climate, Conflict, Decision Making

Types
- Supportive
- Defensive

Decision-Making Strategies
- Reflective Thinking
- Brainstorming
- Group Thinking

Types of Conflict
- Pseudo
- Content
- Ego

Conflict Resolution
- Assertiveness
- Aggressiveness
- Nonassertiveness

Knowledge Checklist

✔ Identify the characteristics of effective group communication

✔ Recognize and understand that groups are interdependent

✔ Understand the stages of group development

✔ Understand how goals and roles affect the group process

✔ Recognize the unique communication constraints and opportunities of working in a group

✔ Understand the importance of effective leadership in groups

✔ Use group concepts to make effective group decisions

CHARACTERISTICS OF GROUPS

As a student, you will spend much of your time working in groups. Some groups are exciting and motivating; others are just plain frustrating. What makes some groups a success and others an exercise in frustration? And why all of this group work anyway? Many of your classes will require you to work in groups because today's workers participate in more group projects and attend more meetings than ever before in history. More and more organizations utilize teams to make decisions that were once handled by individuals. Because organizations are utilizing groups to develop products and services and to make important organizational decisions, understanding the critical characteristics of effective group communication in decision making is essential.

You've actually spent a great deal of time in groups throughout your life. Your family is a primary group in your life, and the decision-making strategies your family uses have set the stage for how you experience other groups. Were all members of your family involved in discussion, or did your parents make the decisions and then convey them back to you? Were all opinions valued and encouraged, or were some members more credible and thus given more "speaking time" than others?

As a member of a class, you belong to a group; if you belong to a church, you are also a member of that group; in your residence hall or apartment, you belong to another group. Each of these groups exists for different purposes and each provides you with varying levels of satisfaction. Think of the most successful groups you belong to. What makes them successful? How do the groups define who you are?

A **small group** usually includes three or more persons who interact together for a certain purpose, influence one another over a period of time, operate interdependently, share certain standards and norms, develop a collective identity, and derive certain satisfaction from the cohesion and commitment in the group. Let's take this definition one concept at a time.

small group three or more persons who interact together for a purpose, influence one another over a period of time, operate interdependently, share standards and norms, develop a collective identity, and derive satisfaction from the cohesion and commitment in the group

Group Size

Group size dramatically impacts the nature of the interaction among individuals. There is some disagreement among scholars as to what *small* means in small groups. Groups, by definition, must have at least three members; two individuals are a *dyad*. Moreover, when there are more than two members, there is always the possibility of an alliance between two members against the other.

So when does a small group stop being small? Some researchers suggest that small groups are most effective when each of the participants can observe and interact with every other member. The *optimal* small group is probably between three and seven members; however, the optimal number will vary depending upon the task but will likely not exceed twenty.

Interaction for a Purpose

Group members *interact* with one another for a certain *purpose*. Individuals who happen to be in the same place at the same time do not necessarily constitute a group. The interaction within the group occurs verbally and nonverbally, and more and more today, it occurs through some type of technology (e-mail, teleconferencing, etc.). Again, the group exists for some purpose. For example, did you join a fraternity or sorority because of its philanthropy? Did you join your college or university chapter of Habitat for Humanity to solve the problem of substandard housing?

Mutual Influence

As a member of the group, you will *influence* and be influenced by every other group member. The knowledge and experience each member brings to the group provides opportunities to teach one another. The *attitude* you bring about yourself, your priorities, and your willingness to invest time and energy in the group process can also influence the attitudes of other members. This influence is essential to understanding the next element of our definition—interdependence.

Interdependence

The concept of **interdependence** is at the heart of the group process and involves mutual influence. The behavior of each group member influences every other member. When you are in a group, are you the one who remains silent and listens to others? Do you take charge of the group and attempt to directly influence the decision? Do you intentionally or unintentionally speak only to certain group members and ignore others? In each of these cases, who you communicate with and how you choose to become involved influences the way the group operates. Interdependence also means that no one person is responsible for the group product or outcome. Your level of motivation for your group's project, the manner and timing of your communication with other group members, your attitude toward your group and its members, and the investment you make (or choose not to make) in the process are impacted by every other member of the group and vice versa. While these insights are relevant to your college experience and the group work you likely encounter in a variety of situations, it will become even more important as you move into the working world. The box Career Links: Dependence, Independence, Interdependence discusses the role of mutual influence in effective group process.

interdependence mutual influence

Career Links

Dependence, Independence, Interdependence

Groups function well when members are interdependent, which we have defined as *mutual influence*. Here are some additional insights that may help you communicate in groups. Some of this information is drawn from Stephen Covey's book *The Seven Habits of Highly Effective People*.

Dependence

Dependence means that you depend on others to get what you want; you are reliant. As a result, if you don't get what you want, you complain and blame. It's always someone else's fault. You do not see yourself as being in control of your own life; rather, your life is controlled by other people or outside forces. This difference is sometimes referred to as "the locus of control," or where you place control—in yourself or in others. If you locate control in yourself, then you have an "internal locus of control"; if you believe others control your life, you have an "external locus of control." If you are dependent, you stress the external locus of control and your keyword of reference is *you*. As a result, like most dependent people, you will make statements such as, "It's my boss's fault that I didn't get the job done in time; he didn't give me enough time" or "My coworker makes me so mad when he isn't considerate of my feelings!" or "I didn't really want to go to the departmental picnic, but everyone else seemed to be going so what was I supposed to do?" We can symbolize dependent people by the letter *A*. The letter *A* has two stems that lean on each other and one stem that connects them. If we remove any of the three stems, the letter collapses; it cannot stand alone. If you are a dependent person, you are like the letter *A*; you cannot stand alone without the support of others.

Independence

Independence means that you rely on yourself to get what you want; you are self-reliant. As Covey (1989) puts it, "You act rather than being acted upon." Or to use another of Covey's favorite words, you are "proactive." As a result, you hold yourself accountable for your behavior and the subsequent results. You recognize that you, not others, control your life. As an independent person, you possess an internal locus of control and your keyword of reference is *I*. As a result, you make statements such as, "I didn't get the job done in time because I didn't anticipate the time demands adequately" or "I feel angry at my coworker when he is inconsiderate of how I feel" or "I decided not to go to the departmental picnic, even though I knew several others were intending to go." We can symbolize independent people by the letter *I* because this letter stands alone without requiring support.

Interdependence

Interdependence means that you rely on yourself, but you recognize the value of working harmoniously with others to get what everyone wants. As a result, you don't abandon your own ideas, but you look for ways to understand and to develop mutually beneficial results for all concerned. You recognize that when people work together effectively, they can reach a new level of problem solving that joins ideas in a creative and unforeseen result. To again use Covey's (1989) language, you "think win-win"; you "seek first to understand and then to be understood," and you "synergize." While you still possess an internal locus of control, your keyword of reference is *we*. Consequently, you make statements such as, "My boss and I can work together to ensure that I finish projects in a timely fashion" or "When I feel angry at my coworker for being inconsiderate, we can work on it together so that our relationship grows" or "I can shift my view of the departmental picnic and see it as a time to work on networking and building trusting relationships, rather than satisfying an implied directive." We can symbolize interdependent people by the letter *H*. Notice that the letter *H* essentially has two *I*s and a connecting stem. The two major stems *can* stand alone, but because they are connected and can provide mutual support, they work together to create a new symbol.

The following chart summarizes this information:

	Locus of Control	Keyword	Symbol	Communication Result
Dependence	External	You	A	Complaining and blaming
Independence	Internal	I	I	Personal responsibility
Interdependence	Internal	We	H	Cooperative problem solving

Group Norms

norms standards that guide a group

explicit norms norms that are verbally discussed and agreed upon

implicit norms norms that occur through repetition of behavior that is not questioned

As members come to know one another throughout the group process, the group begins to develop a set of standards, or norms, that guide the group. **Norms** can be either **explicit** (verbally discussed and agreed upon) or **implicit** (occur through repetition of behavior that is not questioned). However they are developed, norms operate like a set of rules for what is appropriate or inappropriate behavior for members throughout the group process. Norms also encompass the shared values and beliefs of the group. Ultimately, they become the procedures by which the group operates. More often than not, the norms evolve implicitly—that is, they are not directly stated but are "accepted" by members through their silence. If Maribeth routinely arrives for group meetings fifteen minutes late, and none of the group members object, a norm has been created that implicitly accepts Maribeth's tardiness. If Rodney is silent throughout the majority of the group meetings, and other members simply "talk around him," Rodney may rightly presume that his silence is acceptable to the group.

In other cases, group members explicitly state norms. Some of your instructors probably state in their syllabi that a certain number of absences from class during the semester may lower your grade. Your university has a set of expectations, or the do's and don'ts, that were given to you in the Student Code of Conduct. These rules probably reflect expectations regarding such issues as academic dishonesty, alcohol use in the residence halls, sexual harassment, and a variety of other student behaviors and responsibilities. The key to group effectiveness with regard to norms is the degree to which they are *explicitly stated and agreed upon* by members. If members know what is expected of them, they are more likely to act in accordance with the rules and to function more effectively as participants. Norms help us predict behavior and reduce our uncertainty regarding the group process. To the degree that the group depends upon implicit or unstated norms only, individuals may not be operating on a common understanding, and thus, the potential for misunderstanding and frustration increases.

It is helpful to think of norms in three categories. **Social norms** guide the relationships among group members. To what degree do we self-disclose personal information during meetings? Can we express our feelings toward one another? Is disagreement acceptable to the group? How? The second type of norm is a **task norm**, which focuses on how decision making and problem solving occur. Will the group collaborate on a solution until all agree? Will one person's position on a subject or task simply be imposed on other group members? The last category is **procedural norms**, which govern how members coordinate tasks. Will someone take notes at meetings? Who should group members call if they will miss a meeting? Who will call to remind members of a meeting? Groups frequently state procedural norms more explicitly; in contrast, social norms are more often understood implicitly. However, norms, from all three categories, that are explicitly discussed can enable the group to be more creative and, ultimately, more satisfied with the outcome.

It is difficult, however, to point out to other group members when the process is not working effectively or when frustration is building. We usually show our frustration and uncertainty nonverbally, while at the same time saying everything is all right. This inconsistency between nonverbal and verbal messages only increases frustration and uncertainty and often works to push members away from the group instead of drawing them into the process.

social norms norms that guide the relationships among group members

task norms norms that focus on how decision making and problem solving occur

procedural norms norms that govern how members coordinate tasks

Collective Identity

Throughout the group process, as members interact, influence one another, and develop rules for member behavior, the group begins to establish a **collective identity**. This is established as a result of how the group balances two critical dimensions of the process—the social and task dimensions. See the box Communication Links: Group Contracts for ways to establish a group identity early in the group process.

collective identity established as a result of how the group balances social and task dimensions

Communication Links

Group Contracts

It is challenging to identify and clarify group norms. However, when group members share in creating and enforcing expectations, groups can offset from the beginning some of the problems they typically encounter. In other words, by being proactive, groups can work toward mutually satisfying outcomes. A group contract is often a useful, proactive step toward creating meaningful results and member satisfaction. Therefore, when you are assigned to work on a group or team project in the classroom or workplace, consider suggesting that, together, the group first create a written, detailed contract, which all agree to sign.

Your contract should identify group member responsibilities and roles, group goals, and consequences for any member who does not meet the expectations discussed in the contract. Your group should begin the process of developing the contract by discussing what each member would like to see the group accomplish during the task. From each member's goals and expectations, develop a group list that all the members agree upon. Every member and every effective group as a whole should pay attention to both the task dimension of the group (the job you have) and the social dimension (the relationships between members). Once you have identified and agreed upon "group expectations," begin identifying the important roles needed by the group such as, group leader, recorder, coordinator, researcher, and so on. In addition to identifying and labeling each group role, identify the specific responsibilities of the individual in the role. Finally, decide which group member will fill each role.

Now the group must articulate the process of motivating group members who, for whatever reason, do not conduct themselves in accordance with the contract. What will you do when members are late, don't show up, or don't do work on time? How will you encourage all members to contribute to discussions and activities? This section of the contract does not have to be a list of "punishments"; it can be a set of strategies that motivate group members to participate and pull their weight. However, it should also discuss the responsibilities of all group members in communicating with reluctant or uncooperative group members. The communication component of this section of the contract should be clear and comprehensive. For example, you may decide that your group cannot "fire" an uncooperative group member without extensive communication first. Once the group has discussed the contract and has come to a consensus regarding all its elements, type the contract and have every member sign it. Make copies for all group members.

Groups have social purposes and task purposes. The **social dimension** involves the personal relationships among members, the socialization process within the group, and ways in which we allow others opportunities to participate in the group process, or not. The **task dimension** involves the ways groups make decisions and solve problems. How much each member becomes involved with other members, recognizes the social and task dimensions, and works toward a common purpose ultimately impacts the overall effectiveness and success of the group. The group's social and task dimensions must be recognized as having equal influence on the group.

social dimension the personal relationships among group members

task dimension the ways groups make decisions and solve problems

Group Cohesion

When members of your group are willing to work together to accomplish goals, the group becomes more cohesive. **Cohesion** refers to the attraction that group members feel for one another and the degree to which they are willing to work together. When your group simply divides up the tasks and allows individuals to work alone, you are ignoring the importance of cohesion. Of course, some tasks are best accomplished alone, but at some point the group must come together to accomplish its goals. Cohesive social relationships among group members are just as important as accomplishing the task.

cohesion the attraction that group members feel for one another and the degree to which they are willing to work together

Commitment to the Group

A final concept of critical importance to effective groups is **commitment**. This commitment must focus on the accomplishment of the task and on the development of relationships among group members. Have you ever participated in a group where members focused on everything else but the group? Perhaps their other classes, their significant others, or their jobs take precedence. We communicate commitment, or lack of commitment, both directly and indirectly. However, remember that the greater the level of commitment among members, the greater the potential for success and

commitment group members' willingness to accomplish a task and develop relationships with each other

Groups have both social and task purposes.

effectiveness of the group. When we are committed to the group, we would rather remain in the group and work toward the goal rather than leave the group.

GOALS IN GROUPS

*M*any types of groups exist in society, and each exists based upon the group's goals. Group goals provide the focus for the task that must be accomplished. As we mentioned earlier, both individual goals and group goals operate throughout the group process.

Individual and Group Goals

Individual goals are the motivations of individual members, whereas **group goals** involve the whole group seeking to accomplish a task. As individuals, we join groups for various reasons. They help us satisfy important psychological and social needs, such as those for affection and attention. Groups allow us to accomplish purposes that we would be unable to accomplish alone. They provide us with greater self-knowledge and awareness as well as world knowledge by the diversity of information group members bring to the discussion. Groups also provide us with a sense of security and belonging. They provide a safe and welcoming environment and contribute to our social identity, providing us with another view of how others see us; this in turn influences our self-concept, self-esteem, and self-respect.

In essence, the group goals become the group's collective purpose. For example, many academic honor societies not only honor achievements but also assist the community through volunteer efforts. Advocacy groups like Greenpeace attempt to change or influence national policy regarding the environment. Other religious and social groups seek to influence the value systems by which we operate as citizens within a community. Ultimately, the most effective groups are those in which the individuals learn to meet their individual goals while also staying focused on the group goals. Effective groups also learn to incorporate the individual goals of members within the group process.

Learning, Therapy, Problem Solving, and Social Groups

Groups come in all types, including **learning groups**, which focus on increasing members' knowledge and skills; **therapy or growth groups**, which assist members in

individual goals the motivations of individual group members

group goals the outcome the whole group seeks to accomplish

learning groups groups that focus on increasing the knowledge and skills of their members

therapy (or growth) groups groups that assist members in learning about themselves and solving personal problems

problem-solving teams groups that focus on a project external to the group

social groups groups that focus primarily on the belonging needs of the participants

learning about themselves and solving personal problems; **problem-solving teams,** which may focus on a project external to the group, like research and development teams who design new products or services for organizations; and **social groups,** which focus primarily on the belonging needs of the participants. However, many groups cross over these categories and do not easily fit into just one. For example, the box Computer Links: Online Support Groups discusses one unique type of group.

Groups vs. Individuals

By now you should recognize the important role of groups in your personal and professional lives. Groups allow us to use a greater variety of resources in working through complex issues and problems. But when should a group make decisions?

Computer Links

Online Support Groups

Research suggests that online support groups can help connect people who face physical and/or emotional problems (Barnes 2001). King (1995) suggests that these groups provide a focus for a mutually recognized need for emotional support and feedback. Online support groups are particularly helpful for those individuals with physical limitations, or who are separated from others geographically. A sense of community may be established for these individuals through the use of Internet technology.

According to http://answers.google.com/answers/threadview?id=2531, there are approximately 1,300 support groups in Google's directory support groups. There are many support group directories, but all of them list online support groups together with groups that don't have any online presence. The most comprehensive ones are:

American Self-Help Group Clearing House (lists over 800 support groups): www.selfhelpgroups.org and www.mentalhelp.net/selfhelp/

Patient UK Self-Help and Support Groups: www.patient.org.uk/selfhelp/groups.htm#non-uk

U.S. Government's Healthfinder: Support Groups: www.health.gov/nhic/NHICScripts/Hitlist.cfm?Keyword=Support%20Groups

Case Management Resource Guide (over 2,000 health organizations, including support groups): www.cmrg.com/ and www.cmrg.com/cmrg_cfmfiles/healtho.cfm

King and Moreggi (1998) write,

"It is the social aspect of computer assisted communication, the interpersonal exchange with others, that is so stimulating, rewarding and reinforcing that some people are finding it hard to know when to stop (see http://netaddiction.com). Internet communications offer people an opportunity to experience a form of social contact, with no real social presence. The significant difference between Internet relationships and ones maintained by other existing technologies (telephones, mail, fax's) is the new culture values of Internet virtual communities. They have social norms that allow for, and even encourage, contact with relative strangers. The level of concern for fellow participants in Internet forums is remarkable. These online groups are distinct from f2f (face-to-face) meetings in their ability to engender a sense of community among people who hardly know each other or are in fact total strangers. There is a higher degree of feeling connected than would be expected from interpersonal relating devoid of body language and other nonverbal clues."

Are some decisions best made by individuals? Think back to the decision you made on where to go to college. What information did you need to make that decision, and who else was involved? Teachers? Coaches? Parents? Friends?

When a decision is complex, a group is more likely to make a better decision than an individual. Each person in the group may contribute important information and experience that any sole individual simply does not have. In the group process, we pool our resources, taking advantage of others' knowledge and experience. This pooling of resources also allows the group to identify errors and incomplete information. Working through a complex decision with others also increases our motivation to participate and, ultimately, leads to a more rewarding and satisfying experience. We develop the satisfaction of accomplishing the task and of the companionship that develops among members. When others listen to what we have to say and confirm our knowledge and experience, our self-esteem and self-confidence increase.

But while groups can be rewarding, they can also be frustrating. Probably one of the most significant potential disadvantages of working in groups is that the process simply takes more time. When groups work effectively, every individual should have the opportunity to participate and contribute to the process. Allowing everyone this opportunity is time consuming. However, the potential for effective and creative decision making is more likely when collective time and energy are invested.

Another common disadvantage of working in groups is the potential for any individual to sit back and let others do the work. A lazy group member can increase the frustration and anger of others. **Social loafing** occurs when an individual allows others to carry the workload. When the workload of another is increased, he or she may label the loafer a "troublemaker" and ostracize him or her from the process. Social loafing can cause stress, frustration, and ostracism and can ultimately lead to poor task attainment and dysfunctional relationships among members.

> **social loafing** occurs when an individual sits back and allows other group members to pick up the workload

As we mentioned earlier, sometimes individual and group goals are different. Group members who feel their personal goals are more important than the group's might dominate and attempt to control the group process. When personal goals become more important than group goals, the selfish member usually has a **hidden agenda** (he or she does not explicitly state that his or her goals take precedence over those of the group); this also causes increased frustration and stress. Deciding to use a group to make a decision should be based upon the task itself—whether simple or complex—and on whether the group has enough time to reach a good decision. All group members should be encouraged to participate in order to alleviate the potential for social loafers or hidden agendas.

> **hidden agenda** the unstated personal goals of a selfish group member

ROLES IN GROUPS

*R*oles refer to the patterns of behavior each individual may utilize in the group process. Like norms, some roles are "official" or assigned by the group. In many groups, there are offices like president, vice president, secretary, treasurer, and so forth. Other roles are understood more informally and, like norms, develop throughout the interaction process among members. Three types of roles impact group dynamics—task roles, maintenance or social roles, and individual roles. **Task roles** assist group members in goal accomplishment, **social roles** help members shape the relationships within the group, and **individual roles** offer group members opportunities to interfere with effective group process. Role behavior describes what individuals do, not the positions they hold. Roles are rarely assigned and are often not even acknowledged. Roles, like norms, belong to the group, not to individuals, though different individuals often share or trade roles at different times in the process.

> **task roles** roles that assist group members in goal accomplishment
>
> **social roles** roles that help members shape the relationships within the group
>
> **individual roles** roles that offer group members opportunities to interfere with effective group process

People who assume task roles *propose* new ideas, *clarify* concepts, or *provide information* to other members in the form of facts, examples, statistics, and so on. In addition, these individuals assist group discussion by offering opinions and examples based on experience. Ultimately, utilizing task roles helps to energize the group

Social loafing occurs when one individual allows others to carry the workload.

process, motivates others to participate, and helps to organize the process of task accomplishment. For example, if LaTia makes an effort to ask other group members what they think of a specific issue or problem as a possible group presentation topic, she is exhibiting an effective task role.

People who assume social or maintenance roles focus on the *relationships* among group members. These individuals offer praise or acceptance, mediate disagreements, or encourage less talkative members to participate—all behaviors that impact the group's social dimension. If Jarod makes an effort to thank group members for contributing to a lively and stimulating conversation during a meeting, he is exhibiting an effective social role. Conversely, individuals may assume roles that disrupt the group process by attempting to focus the group's attention on their own agenda rather than on the group process. Examples of individual role behavior include taking credit for someone else's contribution, attacking another member's remark, or acting in a stubborn or uncooperative manner. Behavior that shows cynicism or lack of enthusiasm for the group, or behavior that attempts to gain sympathy from other members also represents individual roles.

Role behavior patterns may either assist the group process or work to inhibit effective group decisions. Every group member must be conscious of the importance of task and maintenance role behavior in the group. And the group should confront individual role behavior immediately in order to prevent that behavior from causing communication problems for the group.

LEADERSHIP IN GROUPS

The emergence of leadership within the group constitutes the most critical role challenge. **Leadership** refers to the ability to influence others. In the small group, leaders guide followers in reaching goals. Researchers have studied the phenomenon of leadership for several decades and have identified many approaches to it. In early research, social scientists viewed leadership as a set of traits that an individual exhibited. In the **trait approach**, leaders were either born with or cultivated a set of behaviors that "guaranteed" they would assume leadership positions. The needed traits included confidence, social skills, intelligence, and charisma. However, in today's society, even if you possess these traits, there is no guarantee that you will become a leader, nor is there a guarantee that these traits will help you become a leader in all situations.

leadership the ability to influence others

trait approach presumes that leaders are either born with or cultivate a set of behaviors that guarantee they will assume leadership positions

In the **styles approach** to leadership, three different styles were commonly identified with leaders: (1) autocratic, (2) democratic, or (3) laissez-faire. Autocratic leaders give orders and try to control others. Democratic leaders engage in collective decision making by working toward consensus among group members. Laissez-faire leaders rely on a "hands-off" approach to leadership and let the group process flow without assistance or input.

styles approach identifies three different leadership styles—*autocratic, democratic,* or *laissez-faire*

In the **functional approach** to leadership, two categories of functions are necessary for effective leadership: task functions and process or relational functions. The basic assumption underlying this theory is that groups vary in the type of task they want to accomplish, the time they have to accomplish it, the skills group members have to accomplish the task, and the nature of relationships among group members. Each of these factors determines the type of leadership behavior needed in the group. When the group is under pressure to solve a problem, the leader coordinates the group's activity and makes sure members have all available information. When the task involves understanding differences, perhaps related to gender or culture, the leader needs to focus on interpersonal communication issues such as honesty, respect, and support.

functional approach identifies two categories of functions that are necessary for effective leadership— *task functions* and *process* (or *relational) functions*

Over time, scholars have come to understand leadership not as a set of *characteristics* associated with an individual, but as a *process* that can be utilized by any group member or by members collectively. Researchers such as Hersey and Blanchard (1993) suggest that a more effective way of thinking about leadership is to look to **situational factors,** or group context. Leaders adopt a style or approach that meets the requirements of the situation or task as well as those of the individual group members. Critical to this analysis is the group members' "readiness" or maturity. Readiness involves an individual's motivation, willingness to take responsibility, knowledge levels, and skills and experiences related to the task that needs to be accomplished. This theory suggests that groups change over time, and leadership should adapt appropriately to these changes. A group beginning a new task, with which it is unfamiliar, needs leadership that can clarify and simplify the task. Later in the process, once the task is clarified, leadership should focus more on the social or relational dimension of the group. Effective leadership in the group should vary depending upon the nature of the task, the individuals who make up the group, and the person engaging in leadership behavior. In addition, leadership skills can be learned, and any group member can adopt leadership behavior. Leadership is thus a set of skills, including the ability to understand the nature of the group and its task and the ability to adopt and modify leadership behavior depending upon the group's unique requirements.

situational factors group context that influences a leader's style or approach

Power and leadership are linked in the group. As mentioned in an earlier chapter, every relationship has a power dimension. In the small group, power is not something a member "has" but something that is given in the context of interaction. Power is distributed throughout the group; it rarely belongs to just one person. Group members hold power in differing degrees. Finally, power that is shared by group members has the potential to increase among all participants. Effective leaders, then, must adapt their communication behavior to the power relationships among group members as well as to task or situational factors.

STAGES OF GROUP DEVELOPMENT

*R*oles often change depending upon the phase of the group process. According to many researchers (Tuckman 1965; Tuckman & Jensen 1977; Wheelan & Hochberger 1996; Wheelan & Kaeser 1997), groups go through four phases—forming, norming, storming, and performing. Communication in each of the phases is distinct and serves a specific purpose (Moosbrucker 1988; Wellins, Byham, & Wilson 1991). Researchers may call these phases by different names, but essentially every group experiences, to some degree, each of these stages. The stages do not necessarily occur in order; in fact, some groups may get "stuck" in a particular stage. Other groups may revert to an "earlier" stage during the decision-making process. So while no two groups are identical in terms of the group process, each group will experience some aspects of each of the four stages, which we will now consider in greater detail.

Forming Stage

forming stage the stage in which group members get to know one another and determine how the group process will occur

In the **forming stage**, group members try to get to know one another and to understand how the group process will occur. Like the beginning of all relationships, this is a stage of "feeling our way," of understanding and being able to predict one another's behavior. Group members begin by exchanging basic factual information such as age, hometown, major, and so on.

Norming Stage

norming stage the stage in which group rules and roles are developed

In the **norming stage**, the rules and roles (often implicitly understood) are developed. Some procedures are adopted, while others are eliminated. At this stage, group members may try out different patterns of interaction to see which might fit the group. Tomoko may be silent in the meetings, and yet no group member discusses the silence directly with her; as a result, a group norm has been developed that essentially states, "Tomoko can be silent."

Storming Stage

storming stage the stage in which group conflict emerges as members react to norms and rules negatively

In the **storming stage**, conflict emerges as members negatively react to norms and roles. If norms are implicitly accepted, as with Tomoko's silence, and individual members fail to speak out about this as an issue, the effectiveness of the process is compromised. Also, if members feel a role they are uncomfortable with has been thrust upon them, they will rebel, either directly through verbal confrontation or indirectly by withdrawing from interaction with certain members. Storming is a critical stage in the group process. If the group ignores or fails to resolve conflict within this stage, decision making and satisfaction are negatively affected. Groups that are willing to risk confrontation and work to resolve conflict during this stage are more creative and effective in the long run.

Performing Stage

performing stage the stage in which group members risk confrontation and resolve conflict or ignore conflict

In the **performing stage**, groups have decided to either risk confrontation and resolve the conflict or ignore the conflict and act as if nothing is wrong. At this stage, how individuals "perform" toward each other or how the group performs toward outsiders becomes the focus of the group process. The deadline is fast approaching, the presentation is due in two days, and the group has got to get on with it. The critical challenge to the group is whether to "act" through the storming (by ignoring problems) or to address the conflict and work to resolve it.

Through each of these stages of group development, attention to both the group's task needs and social needs is critical. Group members should not rush the task just to "get it done." They should also nurture the relationships among group members in order to increase motivation and satisfaction with the process and with the outcome. Attending to the group process is even more critical for groups that have long-term associations. In addition to these four phases of the group process, groups are also influenced by variables such as gender differences in communication and cultural influences within and outside the group.

CULTURE, VALUES, AND GENDER IN GROUPS

group culture the values and beliefs shared by group members

The group process of developing norms, roles, and collective identity culminates in the development of a **group culture**. This encompasses the values and beliefs shared by members, the language or symbols used in interaction, the rituals that group members enact in the group process, and the behaviors that evolve from these elements. This culture, or personality, is created and maintained by the group and influenced by the larger culture in which it belongs. The larger culture significantly influences group structure and dynamics and provides a second way of examining the concept. Culture is not static but changeable, depending upon the situation and needs of group members.

At the heart of group culture is the **value system** that guides the development of norms, roles, and structure. Each of us interacts in our relationships based upon our individual moral principles and values. Values guide us to determine what behavior is right or wrong, and thus ethical or unethical. Values flow from the larger culture to which we belong and from the nature of the significant relationships in our lives. We come to the group and engage in interaction based on our value system, and yet we must also understand the value systems of others in order for the group to develop its own unique process. When individuals share their values and work collaboratively and explicitly to develop a larger set of values for the group, they maximize the potential for group effectiveness.

value system guides the development of norms, roles, and structure within a group

How can the group develop a set of values and principles that guide appropriate and ethical behavior? The principle of **equality** is at the heart of ethical groups. *Equality* refers to such things as the right to speak and be heard, and to the way group norms should be applied to every group member. Philosopher Immanuel Kant suggests the rules should be created and applied to everyone with equal weight. He also admonishes us against using others to achieve our own selfish desires. Rather, every human being should be valued for his or her unique knowledge, experience, and potential.

equality applying group norms to every member

Most of us also believe in the principle of honesty in communicating with others. What does it mean to you to be honest or dishonest with someone? If we are honest, we do not intentionally deceive another. When we are dishonest, we intentionally deceive directly (by direct misstatement) or indirectly (by omitting information that leads to misinterpretation). Where and how might honesty and sensitivity to others come into conflict? What other ethical principles do you think should guide interaction among group members? Review the principles of ethical communication in Chapter 3. How do these ethical principles apply in group communication?

Gender is another significant factor that influences group interaction and the development of a group culture. According to psycholinguist Deborah Tannen (1990), men and women communicate differently. As we stated in earlier chapters, the issue is not who are "better" communicators; the issue is trying to understand the nature of the differences in communication and working through these differences to reach a common understanding. Gender research suggests that in mixed-sex groups, men tend to determine topics of conversation and to talk more. Men also tend to focus more on the group's task dimension. In contrast, women tend to be more affirming or positive in response to others' comments and tend to focus more on the nature of the relationships among members. While there are differences in how women and men communicate, research has found little difference between the ability of women and men to solve problems or make decisions.

Women, in general, tend to use a more cooperative style when interacting with group members and are more likely to share resources. For instance, when Kara gives an example from her experience, Sela shares a similar story. In this way, Sela confirms Kara's example, in effect saying, "We're the same." This type of sharing similar stories, however, is often perceived by men as being weak. In contrast, men tend toward a more competitive style, often seen by women as aggressive. When Dominic tells the group of his experience, Kyle tries to "top" the story with one of his own. Kyle is saying, in effect, "My experience is even more relevant to our discussion." The point is that neither gender's approach is right or wrong in this instance. Group members must recognize that differences in style are a product of ways of thinking and behaving that have developed since early childhood. The goal for group members, then, is to understand how differences in style affect interpretation of meanings between women and men. The most effective groups are those that recognize what particular style is most appropriate to the interaction. If commitment and cohesiveness are to characterize an effective group, then a range of style options for communicating maximizes the potential for the group to succeed.

Gender is a significant factor in group interaction.

GROUP CLIMATE, CONFLICT, AND PROBLEM SOLVING

*P*erhaps the most important goal of every group is to develop a process by which problems may be solved, decisions may be made that prove worthwhile to the task, and satisfaction with the group process may be derived. Every group must establish a strategy that optimizes good solutions and decisions. The process developed by the group to make decisions is a reflection of the goals, norms, roles, and the group's structure and culture. Is there one perfect problem-solving strategy? No. Yet, having any strategy is better than having no strategy at all. In the next section, we explore a range of approaches that may assist groups in working toward good decisions.

Supportive and Defensive Climates

climate the degree of cohesiveness among group members, their willingness to communicate with each other, and the tone of that communication

Before exploring how groups make decisions, we must discuss the issue of **climate**. Climate is the "feel" of the group and involves the degree of cohesiveness among members, their willingness to communicate with one another, and the tone of that communication. Gibb (1961) described two ends of a continuum in terms of climate. At one end are *supportive* climates where members feel positively toward each other and toward the group task. At the other end are *defensive* climates, characterized by individuals who monopolize the process and discount one another.

To develop a supportive climate, effective groups must have individual members who can describe one another's point of view, focus their discussion on the best solution for a problem, react honestly and spontaneously to other members' contributions, show empathy toward fellow members, minimize status differences, and remain flexible to the changing needs and information obtained by others.

In contrast, defensive groups are characterized by *evaluation,* where group members judge one another in words or tone of voice. For example, a defensive group member may show superiority and a belief in the rightness of her own opinions and not those of others. Defensiveness occurs also when group members lack sensitivity for the feelings of others or use deceit to manipulate group members. As a result, the degree to which the group develops a supportive or defensive climate significantly impacts the amount of conflict the group will encounter and will determine how that conflict is managed.

Whether the group develops a more supportive or more defensive climate will impact many other elements in the group process. For example, the group that develops a more defensive climate will likely also develop norms more implicitly than explicitly, and the potential for misunderstanding and frustration will increase. Groups that are characterized by defensiveness will find accomplishing the task much more difficult. The social dimension of defensive groups is poorly developed, and individuals will likely lack interest or motivation in the final outcome. Defensive climates encourage social loafing and free riding, as discussed earlier. Therefore, the level of satisfaction with the process is much lower in defensive groups.

In the group that has developed a supportive climate, however, the social dimension is considered as important as the task. Group members feel a strong sense of cohesion and gain energy and motivation in belonging. Creativity is the most important advantage in groups with a supportive climate. Members in supportive groups are willing to engage in more creative brainstorming and are willing to take more creative risks that can lead to a more innovative and effective outcome. Supportive climates also encourage group members to engage in the process in more appropriate and ethical ways. When we communicate a sense of equality and spontaneity, and when we encourage others to do the same, we enhance the ethics of our communication and relationships. In addition, supportive group climates encourage more effective management of conflict.

Types of Conflict

The ways the group manages or mismanages conflict inevitably flow from its implicit or explicit norms. Yet conflict resolution is critical to group effectiveness and creativity. The group's ability to develop a process that will allow it to effectively proceed through the phases of the group is dependent on its ability to manage conflict. Conflict is inevitable. It is not a matter of *if* the group will experience conflict, but rather *how* it will develop strategies to deal with the conflict effectively. Think back to how conflict was handled in your family. Were you taught to ignore the conflict and hope it would resolve itself? Did your family "argue it out" until consensus was reached or until participants were exhausted and gave up? Did one individual dominate the conflict process? In our culture, it is common to not manage conflict at all. Women in particular are taught that it is unacceptable to engage in conflict. Men are often taught that they must stand up for themselves and fight it out, or they're not men.

There are different types of conflict and various ways to resolve it. Miller and Steinberg (1975) have identified three types of conflict: pseudo-conflict, simple or content conflict, and ego conflict.

Pseudo-Conflict   **Pseudo-conflict** is due to misperceptions; participants perceive they have a conflict, but in reality participants are in agreement. Pseudo-conflict often involves the mistaken notion that participants are in a win-lose situation. If I win, you lose, and if you win, I lose. To illustrate, Janine and Stephan are constantly misunderstanding each other in group discussions because they come from different religious backgrounds. These perceived differences cause them to listen poorly and misinterpret information. If they were to set aside their differences, they might realize they are in agreement on the group's proposed solution to the task. Pseudo-conflict is often called "fake" because it really doesn't exist. It is often resolved by clarifying issues and recognizing where agreement exists. One possible source of pseudo-conflict may be a difference in communication style across cultures. We have mentioned several times in this text that cross-cultural communication can provide opportunities for increased knowledge, as well as problems between communicators who are unwilling to understand cultural differences. Misunderstanding as a result of cross-cultural communication is pseudo-conflict because the participants in the conversation perceive disagreements and problems that are not truly intended by the other. See the box Cultural Links: Cultural Differences among Group Members for sources of possible misunderstanding in mixed-culture groups.

pseudo-conflict situation in which the parties are actually in agreement, but perceptions and misunderstanding prevent them from seeing the areas of agreement and compatibility

Cultural Links

Cultural Differences among Group Members

Increasingly, each of us must deal with multiple ethnic groups with different cultural expectations and with co-cultural groups with very different cultural beliefs, values, language, and behaviors. In your classes, you are likely to be in a group with students from many different countries and with different racial and ethnic groups from your own communities. Your workplace will likely be one of the most diverse places in your life. It is important to recognize that people from different cultures and co-cultures are different in a variety of ways. Some dimensions along which cultures vary are:

Dependence upon verbal vs. nonverbal communication?
Some cultural groups value things made explicit, and there is considerable dependence on what is actually said or written. Other cultures assume a great deal of commonality of knowledge and views, so less is spelled out explicitly and much more is implicit or communicated in indirect ways. Is the speaker or the listener more responsible for the success of the communication interaction? Cultures that explicitly value verbal communication can find other cultures to be

secretive, devious, and unforthcoming with information. Cultures that value the nonverbal elements of communication more significantly often find the direct approach to be offensively blunt.

Solution: Monitor your dependence upon words or implicit assumptions in a group. Use perception-checking to clarify your perceptions.

Importance of "timing"?

Some cultures and co-cultural groups like to do just one thing at a time. They value a certain orderliness and sense of there being an appropriate time and place for everything. They do not value interruptions. Others like to do multiple things at the same time. Some individuals can have an open door, a ringing phone, and a meeting all going on at the same time. Others may not understand why the person he or she is meeting is so interruptible by phone calls and people stopping by.

Solution: Monitor your expectations regarding the meaning of time. Clarify your expectations and perceptions. In groups, time is a valuable resource; make sure each group member is aware of others' class schedules, work hours, or other commitments.

Power distance?

This is the extent to which people accept differences in power and allow this to shape many aspects of life. Is the boss always right because he is the boss, or only when he gets it right? Do you believe power should be equally shared? Or do some individuals "earn" more power through a title or experience?

Solution: When working in groups in the United States, expect that power will be perceived as something all members are entitled to equally. Outside the United States, these expectations may not be operating. Know the cultural expectations.

Individualism vs. collectivism?

Some of us value individual uniqueness and self-determination more than many other important factors. A person is all the more admirable if they are a "self-made person" or "make up his or her own mind" or show initiative or work well independently. In contrast, some cultures expect people to identify with and work well in groups. The groups then protect each individual in exchange for loyalty and compliance. Paradoxically, individualist cultures tend to believe that there are universal values that should be shared by all, while collectivist cultures tend to accept that different groups have different values.

Solution: Remember the importance of interdependence in the group process. In this unique and important communication context, the individual must find a balance between individual and group goals. This is not the place for selfish individualism. However, every group will benefit from all group members' constructive critical evaluation of group decision making.

content (or procedural) conflict occurs when people disagree over facts, definitions, implications, solutions, or procedure

Content Conflict **Content** (or **procedural**) **conflict** occurs when people disagree over facts, definitions, implications, solutions, or procedure. For example, your group's project is to investigate homelessness in your city by researching its causes and effects. As your group begins, your first question might be, "What is the definition of homelessness?" Can someone be homeless for a night? A week? Does it mean no permanent address? The group might also ask, "What subgroups make up the homeless population?" If individuals in your group disagree over the definition of homelessness or the types of people who are most likely to be homeless, the group is experiencing content conflict. Group members can resolve this type of conflict with solid research that utilizes credible sources in defining basic facts and implications. When individuals attempt to verify facts, test inferences, and develop concrete criteria for solutions, this conflict is managed effectively.

A related but more complicated type of conflict may occur in the group when individuals hold different values on some issue. This is more difficult to resolve because our values are personal and deeply held. For example, in your group's discussion of homelessness, members might disagree on the role of government in this issue. Some may value government intervention in the lives of those who are less fortunate. Other members might believe that individuals must take responsibility for their own lives. Often resolutions are effective when participants "agree to disagree" about which values are *most* important and focus instead on solutions that meet the needs of as many parties as possible. Participants also must listen to one another and allow others to express their values without needing to agree.

Ego Conflict   Finally, groups also may encounter **ego** (or **power**) **conflict**. This type of conflict has the greatest potential for destroying the group process. In this case, participants are so intent on "winning" that they tie winning and losing to their self-concept and self-worth. The conflict becomes one of who has the most power and influence over other members. For individuals who want to win more than they want the group to win, it is unacceptable to "lose" the conflict. The issue, problem, or task becomes lost in the fight for position. Alexa wants the group to choose the portrayal of women in advertising as its topic because she has done extensive research in this area for another class. She dominates group discussions and finds problems with any other topic under discussion. It is only when participants recognize the relationship between ego and conflict strategy that resolution is possible. If this conflict is to be managed, group members must focus on the process of resolution, not on the positions of participants. Identifying the common ground among group members is essential.

ego (or power) conflict a conflict in which the issue, problem, or task becomes lost in the fight for position

Styles of Conflict Resolution

Emotions play a large role in whether conflict will be managed successfully or not. Emotions are hard to control and easy to inflame. Most of us have not been taught effective conflict management strategies, and thus we feel helpless when conflict arises. But conflict can be managed successfully in the group process. Group members may choose to manage conflict through assertiveness, aggressiveness, or nonassertiveness.

Assertiveness   The **assertive style** is often referred to as a "caring selfishness." Assertiveness's intent is to communicate honestly and explain clearly your ideas and beliefs without harming another. When you are assertive, you refuse to become a victim, yet you allow the other group members the same degree of opportunity to assert their ideas and beliefs. Assertive people recognize that rights and responsibilities apply equally to all participants. The primary focus of assertiveness is on negotiating for a solution that meets the needs of all participants.

assertive style communicating honestly and clearly explaining one's ideas and beliefs without harming another

Aggressiveness   The **aggressive style** of conflict management forces positions on others without allowing for their input. Aggressive group members are insensitive, selfish, stubborn, and pushy. The aggressive individual ignores other people's beliefs and values, refusing to recognize their validity. Often these individuals believe that to allow others their point of view automatically means they must agree with them. Usually the individual simply refuses to listen. But simply because we listen to others' points of view does not imply we must agree with them. We listen because other human beings have value. If equality is to be a principle that guides the group, every opinion, position, or point of view must be heard.

aggressive style forcing one's position on others without allowing for their input

Nonassertiveness   Group members who exhibit a **nonassertive style** suppress their own feelings. Individuals are afraid other group members may no longer like them if they express their feelings. Sometimes group members are simply too shy to speak up for their beliefs. Other times, group members are nonassertive because they are

nonassertive style suppressing one's own feelings because of shyness, laziness, or fear that other group members will dislike you

lazy. Both aggressive and nonassertive styles prevent effective conflict resolution and prolong the conflict. Both of these styles stem from too much focus on self and not enough on the others involved in the conflict. However, each of us must develop a degree of assertiveness if our communication is to be effective, satisfying, and ethical. Assertiveness is an honest yet caring communication style. It is a communication strategy with many rewards, both for individuals and for the group process. If a group develops a norm of using an assertive style of conflict management, its task is accomplished more effectively with the maximum resources shared among group members. Also, the relationships among group members are more satisfying when individuals communicate with honesty and care.

Refer back to our discussion of conflict management in Chapter 8. Group members also may try to manage conflict by avoiding, competing, accommodating, or compromising. The most appropriate strategy for the greatest number of decisions, however, is collaboration. In this next section, we discuss the critical role of collaboration in the group decision-making process.

MAKING QUALITY DECISIONS IN GROUPS

Our democratic society loves the vote. Despite the fact that many Americans do not vote in elections, we still use the vote as one of the easiest ways to make a group decision. When all else fails, take a vote. After all, majority rules, right? A related strategy in choosing a solution to a problem is to flip a coin. What movie do we see tonight? Flip a coin. What restaurant shall we go to? Flip a coin. When we are trying to be more objective about a situation, we'll call in an expert. Then the decision is out of our hands. If the solution doesn't work, we can say it was the expert's fault, not ours.

In small groups, we often defer to the leader for his or her position on the issue. Again, if the solution doesn't work, we can blame it on the leader. Organizations often create a subcommittee that is charged with making decisions. Other groups simply refuse to make a decision or stall until the decision is unnecessary. In each of these cases, the strategy of choice has many problems. Ultimately, someone is dissatisfied with the outcome, either because his or her voice wasn't heard or because it was ignored. In each of these examples, the solution is dependent upon one individual, and the group has failed to fulfill a critical obligation of effective group process—collaboration.

Collaboration involves assertiveness and cooperation. A collaborative group makes an effort to hear all sides of an issue, all information relevant to a decision, and all members' points of view. Collaborative groups believe that the best decisions are those that look creatively at solutions and information, and members attempt to develop solutions that meet the parameters of the problem and the needs of the participants. Collaboration involves input from all members to work toward a solution. The following model of effective decision making is an approach that has excellent potential for maximizing group collaboration.

collaboration incorporating assertiveness and cooperation in decision making

The Reflective-Thinking Approach

A standard process in small groups occurs when the assignment has been given or the task identified; group members jump straight to the solution stage without thoroughly analyzing the situation. Often these solutions are attempts to maximize efficiency (speed) not effectiveness (suitability). The more group members are willing to work creatively and suspend judgments about a specific solution, the more the process will flow smoothly and generate the best solution in the end. The *reflective-thinking framework* was developed by John Dewey (1910) at the turn of the century in recognition of this tendency to jump to solutions. While not a perfect strategy, it is one of the most effective and commonly used means of small-group decision making. The components of the framework include the following:

1. **Characterize the problem.** In this step, the group looks objectively at the nature of the problem. The wording of the problem or task significantly

impacts the possible solutions, so carefully and objectively wording the problem is critical. "When and how is this campus going to care about its students and solve the parking problem?" is different than "What are the perceived strengths and weaknesses of parking on campus, and how might current policies be modified to improve the situation?"

2. **Understand the facts of the situation.** A more thorough analysis of the situation occurs in this step. The history of the situation is reviewed. Who is impacted? How? What are the causes of the situation? This step calls for effective research and critical thought.

3. **Develop criteria for an effective solution.** Until the group develops a set of criteria for the solution, it will not recognize a good solution when it sees one and will have no way to distinguish the best solution from a range of options. Here the group selects the requirements for solutions and ranks criteria. Once again, solid research and understanding the problem's complexity can benefit from generating criteria for possible solutions.

4. **Generate possible solutions.** It is not until the situation has been thoroughly analyzed that solutions can be discussed. As solutions are generated, strengths and weaknesses are discussed. The degree to which each meets solutions criteria is also assessed.

5. **Choose the best solution.** Once a comprehensive list of possible solutions is generated, group members further analyze options and rank them from strongest to weakest in terms of the solution criteria generated in step 3. Further, in this step, the group combines elements of various solutions.

6. **Implement and evaluate the solution.** In this step, the implementation process must be examined. While some solutions may appear to be better than others, the reality is that some solutions are impossible to implement due to cost, time, or other factors. The group must understand the steps required for implementing its chosen solution. If the chosen solution has implementation problems, return to step 5. Finally, the group must be able to evaluate the degree of implementation success. What parts of the solution did or did not work? The group must return to the "criteria" step (step 3) and ask important questions about whether or not the solution successfully met the criteria.

So, as we stated before, when group members are willing to work creatively and suspend judgments about a specific solution, the process will flow more smoothly and provide the best opportunity for the most effective solution. This process involves research and a clear understanding of the problem or task. Moreover, all the group's resources must be utilized to maximum advantage for the process to be successful. This means group members must be willing to provide input, to become part of the process, and to be committed to a collaborative group effort.

Brainstorming: Creativity Is the Key

One of the most common roadblocks to the group decision-making process is when group members fail to suggest, or refuse to think imaginatively about, possible solutions. Contemporary theorists on problem solving refer to this creativity as "thinking outside the box." Many of today's organizations now seek to recruit divergent thinkers or those who come up with new and original ideas. Divergent thinkers take risks, and brainstorming involves risks. The premise of brainstorming is that all ideas are relevant, at least initially. The group must create a supportive culture that encourages every member to provide his or her ideas. The first rules of brainstorming are that no idea is unacceptable and no ideas are judged. Members are encouraged to work off of one another's ideas to build, not dismantle. When judgment is suspended, members are less inhibited in making suggestions. Motivation is increased; members become more enthusiastic and, thus, take more creative risks. It is critical that group members truly suspend judgment.

In brainstorming, all ideas are relevant, at least initially.

Groupthink and Decision Making

Some groups, however, may get caught up in simply expediting the task or in focusing on agreement instead of on quality decision making. Psychology professor Irving R. Janis (1972) believes that ineffective decision making is often the result of a phenomenon he calls **groupthink**. Dr. Janis defines groupthink as "a mode of thinking that occurs when people are deeply involved in a cohesive group, when desire for unanimity overrides a realistic appraisal of alternatives." Thinking alike and groupthink are two different matters. Engaging in a discussion that clarifies people's positions and experiences is helpful to group decision making. Groupthink leads to bad decisions within the group.

groupthink a mode of thinking that occurs when people are deeply involved in a cohesive group and desire for unanimity overrides a realistic appraisal of alternatives

On January 28, 1986, the space shuttle *Challenger* lifted off from the Kennedy Space Center in Florida but exploded seventy-three seconds later, killing all seven astronauts and a civilian on board. The civilian, Christa McAuliffe, was to become the first "teacher in space." On Saturday, February 1, 2003, the space shuttle *Columbia* broke up as it returned to Earth after a sixteen-day mission. The investigating bodies for both of these shuttle disasters concurred that in addition to mechanical causes for both accidents (a faulty O-ring seal for *Challenger* and foam striking a wing on *Columbia*), faulty decision making played a role. Both of these tragedies are classic cases of groupthink that resulted in catastrophe—the lives of fourteen astronauts and the image of the space program were just two of the many negative consequences of these bad decisions.

Janis offers eight symptoms the group must be alert for when trying to avoid groupthink:

1. **Illusion of invulnerability:** We often feel that our knowledge and experience will shelter us from bad decisions. NASA had launched twenty-four successful shuttle flights with faulty O-ring seals prior to the *Challenger* mission. *Columbia* was the oldest shuttle in the fleet and had landed "successfully" on each prior mission. The decision makers simply did not believe that the launches would fail.

2. **Belief in the group's inherent morality:** Group members believe they are right because they are on the "right" side or because they feel their values and beliefs are supported by some higher authority. NASA officials became so caught up in the importance of space flight and of the need to expand knowledge that they failed to recognize the safety concerns of engineers.

3. **Collective rationalization:** If we believe we are invulnerable to failure or that our decision stems from the only appropriate value system, we engage in lengthy rationalization in order to support our decision. Decision makers at the Marshall Space Flight Center on the night before *Challenger*'s launch went to great lengths to justify the pro-launch decision. After the *Columbia* tragedy, NASA repeatedly suggested that foam couldn't possibly damage the shuttle wing tiles.

4. **Stereotyped views of "out-group" members:** If "outsiders" raise objections or suggest reevaluation of the decision, groups often ridicule or downplay the outsider's motivation, knowledge, or credibility. There were two engineers at Morton Thiokol (the manufacturer of the faulty O-ring seal) who argued against the launch of *Challenger* due to cold temperatures expected at the time of the launch. Tragically, upper-level decision makers at NASA succeeded in discounting the engineers' objections because the engineers could not prove absolutely that the launch would fail. After *Columbia*, memos surfaced suggesting NASA engineers also were concerned about wing tiles (Tompkins 2005).

5. **Direct pressure on dissenters:** If group "insiders" raise objections, other members may apply pressure through direct or indirect threat. In this way, dissenters are "shouted down" and may decide objections are unsafe. During the decision-making process the night before the *Challenger* launch, engineers reported that they saw a "look" in the eyes of their superiors at Morton Thiokol. Said engineer Roger Boisjoly, "You know that look; it's the look you get just before you get fired."

6. **Self-censorship of dissenters:** When we look at other members of the group and think they are in agreement, we simply decide not to speak, whether we have objections or not. As other engineers at Morton Thiokol observed the reaction to Boisjoly, the engineer who argued against the launch, they decided their objections would carry no weight and refused to speak up. Even Boisjoly reported that once management had overruled his objections, there was no point in pushing the subject any further, and he remained silent.

7. **Shared illusion of unanimity:** When members engage in self-censorship and fail to raise objections, their silence implies consent. We have no choice but to interpret silence as consent to our point of view without any other evidence of disagreement. Once the teleconference between Morton Thiokol and Marshall Space Flight Center was over and the decision to launch *Challenger* had been approved, no information was passed to the next decision-making level regarding the objections of Thiokol engineers. The highest-level decision makers at NASA thus believed that the decision to launch *Challenger* had been unanimous.

8. **Emergence of mindguards:** When we believe that our position or opinion has little or no value to others, we refrain from any dissent. Over time, this feeling is modified to the point where we do not even entertain critical thoughts. Mindguards prevent us from considering another point of view; we simply "block" information from our mind or avoid sources of information that might contradict our point of view. NASA officials who were part of the *Challenger* decision refused to explore additional sources of information that might have been relevant to the issue of temperature on the launchpad at the time of the scheduled launch. Similarly, when engineers expressed concern over possible tile damage on *Columbia* missions, NASA disregarded the potential dangers of the foam.

Groupthink is a very dangerous phenomenon that group members must be aware of when making decisions. There are several ways the group can prevent groupthink. First, all members must understand and be alert to the symptoms of groupthink. Second, engaging in critical assessment of all decisions is crucial. At least one group member must be willing to play devil's advocate during the decision-making process in order to guard against faulty decisions. Using outside experts, considering alternative scenarios thoroughly, and setting aside the decision until members can consider it further are also strategies that can serve to prevent groupthink.

MAKING GROUPS WORK IN COLLEGE, COMMUNITY, AND CAREER

As you begin your college career, consider investigating the numerous groups on campus that can add to your college experience. Check your college website for a list of student organizations. There are a variety of student groups on campus that address a range of interests, activities, and concerns. Given that involvement with college life is fundamentally important to a student's learning, satisfaction, and development (Astin 1984), student organizations provide an immediate way for you to become linked to your campus. Investing some time in discovering and linking with student groups can help offset problems, while immeasurably enhancing your college experience.

Campus Links

How to Engage Classroom Discussion

Drawing on the work of Deemer (1986), Tiberius (1990), and Gardner and Jewler (2003), here are some suggestions to enhance your participation in classroom discussion.

Guidelines for Interacting with Your Teacher

1. Listen for and learn the ground rules of classroom discussion as either clearly established or implied by the teacher. For example, are you expected to raise your hand before speaking?
2. Avoid asking the same question repeatedly in class. If you don't understand a concept or explanation and you've attempted to clarify with a question or two, make an appointment with your instructor during his or her office hours for further clarification.
3. Prepare for class by reading assigned materials, making appropriate notes (especially drafting questions), and looking for connections with your own experience to offer examples. Your instructor will appreciate thoughtful questions or insights that indicate you have adequately prepared for class.

Guidelines for Directing Your Participation

1. Avoid characterizing your questions as "stupid" before you ever ask them, because very often someone else has the same question.
2. Work at following the conversation so you can put ideas together and make links between them. Offer your insights.
3. Provide examples drawn from your own experience or from information you gleaned in another class or through the media.
4. Ask open-ended question that further discussion, rather than squelch it with decisive statements.

5. Stick to the subject and speak briefly.
6. Avoid long stories or anecdotes.
7. Don't shift topics until there's a lull in the conversation and doing so seems appropriate. You can even ask, "Does anyone else have something to say on this subject, since I want to move to another topic?"
8. Don't wait to speak until every idea is complete. Speaking will often help you form your ideas in the moment.
9. Don't be afraid to disagree. If you don't share another's view, say so, and explain why.
10. Offer reasons, not just reactions, although it's okay to express how you feel and how you think.

Guidelines for Responding to Your Classmates

1. Criticize ideas, not people. You may disagree with someone's ideas without being unkind or uncivil to them as a person.
2. Encourage everyone to participate. Leave room for others to speak and kindly invite others who are quiet to add their comments.
3. Listen to everyone's ideas even if you don't particularly like them or their ideas.
4. Try to paraphrase, pose a question, or encourage your classmate to say more if you don't understand what he or she has said.
5. Invite others to disagree with you and assure them that you are receptive to it.
6. Don't interrupt others while they are speaking.
7. Focus on gaining information or insight, not on winning an argument or being right.
8. Work at linking your comments to the previous speaker's insights; develop a fabric of ideas that are knitted together rather than disjointed.

Additionally, given that many campuses are stressing service learning and experiential learning, you are likely to be engaged in group class projects that focus on serving the needs of organizations in your community. In many courses, your instructors will expect you to engage in classroom discussion. As one international student explained, "My father told me before coming to America to the university, 'They don't care how much you know; they just want you to talk about what you do know.'" While this may be an overstatement, it is true that higher education in the United States relies heavily on oral interaction. The box Campus Links: How to Engage Classroom Discussion offers some ways to effectively engage classroom discussion. Though you may find it difficult, we encourage you to engage in classroom discourse—offer your opinions, ask questions, draw links between classroom content and your lived experience.

When you graduate and enter the work world, group and team projects will probably be part of your job. Many corporations and businesses have moved to a "flatter" organizational structure, rather than a hierarchical one. This means that employees are often in work teams or productivity groups and have a greater share of decision making. This suggests that you should not focus on merely surviving the group experience, but on making that process work for you, the group, and the organization.

Groups are also fundamentally important to community endeavors. Never underestimate the power of a group to influence a decision, accomplish a task, or address a community need. For example, the Boys and Girls Clubs of America—which serves 3.6 million young people in all fifty states, Puerto Rico, the Virgin Islands, and military bases at home and abroad—began in 1860 as the result of several women in Hartford, Connecticut, who decided to provide a positive alternative for boys who roamed the streets. Similar stories abound. Therefore, as you pursue your college education and, later, your work, remember the enduring value of community engagement as a way to contribute and receive from others. As many testify, you are likely to find that you receive considerably more than you give. One of the primary reasons we engage in work in our communities is explained in the box Community Links: Contribution and Reward.

Community Links

Contribution and Reward

Reflection

Consider this quote from the famous psychologist, Alfred Adler:

> And since true happiness is inseparable from the feeling of giving, it is clear that a social person is much closer to happiness than the isolated person striving for superiority. Individual Psychology has very clearly pointed out that everyone who is deeply unhappy, the neurotic and the desolate person stem from among those who were deprived in their younger years of being able to develop the feeling of community, the courage, the optimism, and the self-confidence that comes directly from the sense of belonging. This sense of belonging that cannot be denied anyone, against which there are no arguments, can only be won by being involved, by cooperating, and experiencing, and by being useful to others. Out of this emerges a lasting, genuine feeling of worthiness. (From a new translation of *Individual Psychology* [*Einführung in die neuere Psychologie*] 1926, in the AAINW/ATP Archives. Retrieved April 22, 2004, from http://ourworld.compuserve.com/homepages/hstein/qu-comm.htm.)

What is your reaction to this quote? Do you agree or disagree with Adler? Why? Are you presently involved in community groups? If so, what are your experiences? If not, what do you anticipate if you choose to become involved with community groups?

Action

For additional information and a student perspective, go to www.ccsse.org/ to view some online videos of community college students who have invested time in community service. Search out the office on your campus that coordinates civic and community engagement and/or service learning. If your campus does not have such an office, get in touch with the local United Way headquarters and find out where community volunteers are needed. Agree to donate a small amount of time to a community group as a first step to assess your interest and how you might respond further.

All of us know what it feels like to work in a group that lacks cohesion and commitment. Maybe someone's individual goals became more important than the group's goals. Maybe you felt voiceless in the group process and decided to withdraw from interaction completely. The point is that, despite your past familiarity with negative group experience, you can develop more effective group communication skills.

The group communication process is inevitably complex. While you are in college, you will join some groups because of your interest in their activities and because you desire to create and maintain friendships. However, some groups will be formed for class projects and activities, and the group membership may be beyond your control. You cannot control the personalities of other group members, but you can control your communication responses to their personalities and behaviors. You can also control the ways in which you communicate, both verbally and nonverbally, about your expectations of others and of the group process, and how you communicate your value judgments of others and of the group process. And finally, you can control how you manage the inevitable conflict that will arise during the group process.

 ## SUMMARY

Think about the groups you encounter in college not as something you must endure, but as a way to practice the critical skills you must utilize in your life after college. In Chapter 1, we reported on research that suggests that communication remains among the top skills required by employers. If you utilize the skills and concepts described in this chapter and improve your communication in the groups you are involved with now in college, you will enhance your opportunities for employment after college, and you will position yourself to move up the career ladder faster than those who do not. But don't take our word for it—ask the successful professionals in your chosen career!

In this chapter, we have identified some essential elements of effective small-group communication:

- Important characteristics of groups include size, interaction for a purpose, mutual influence, interdependence, norms, collective identity, cohesion, and commitment.
- Every group must balance both individual and group goals.
- Types of groups include learning, therapy, problem-solving, and social groups.

- Groups are more effective than individuals in solving complex decisions.
- Roles in groups encompass the task and social dimensions of the group.
- Dysfunctional behaviors such as hidden agendas, social loafing, and individual roles prevent effective group process.
- Leadership research has resulted in the traits approach, the styles approach, the functional approach, and the situational approach to leadership.
- Stages of group development include forming, storming, norming, and performing.
- Each group develops a unique culture and values.
- Gender plays an important role in a group's culture and decision making.
- A group's climate may develop on a continuum ranging from defensive to supportive.
- Types of conflict include pseudo-conflict, content conflict, and ego conflict.
- Styles of conflict resolution include assertiveness, aggressiveness, and nonassertiveness.

- Making quality decisions in groups requires collaboration and the avoidance of groupthink.
- The reflective thinking process components include define, analyze, criteria, solutions, evaluation, and implementation.
- Brainstorming: creativity is the key.
- Groupthink prevents effective decision making.
- Making groups work in college will maximize your career success and help you contribute to your community.

Questions for Discussion

1. What are the advantages and disadvantages of working in groups and teams?
2. How can individuals more effectively manage stress throughout the group process?
3. Describe individuals who in your experience make good leaders. What makes them stand out?

⟳ EXERCISES

1. Using the reflective thinking model, outline the process for a group research project that would reduce drinking on your campus. Or, develop a list of the most irritating habits of a small group's members. Brainstorm possible individual and group responses to these habits.

2. As a group, discuss group or organizational experiences where cultural or gender differences surfaced. Brainstorm strategies for understanding and adapting to these differences. Which "differences" are the most difficult to understand and adapt to? Discuss how stereotypes inhibited the communication between participants.

⟳ KEY TERMS

Small group	Commitment	Social roles
Interdependence	Individual goals	Individual roles
Norms (explicit or implicit)	Group goals	Leadership
Social norms	Learning groups	Trait approach
Task norms	Therapy (or growth) groups	Styles approach
Procedural norms	Problem-solving teams	Functional approach
Collective identity	Social groups	Situational factors
Social dimension	Social loafing	Forming stage
Task dimension	Hidden agenda	Norming stage
Cohesion	Task roles	Storming stage

Performing stage
Group culture
Value system
Equality
Climate

Pseudo-conflict
Content (or procedural) conflict
Ego (or power) conflict
Assertive style
Aggressive style

Nonassertive style
Collaboration
Groupthink

◎ REFERENCES

Astin, A. W. 1984. Student involvement: A developmental theory for higher education. *Journal of College Student Personnel* 25:297–308.

Barnes, S. B. 2001. *Online connections: Internet interpersonal relationships.* Cresskill, NJ: Hampton Press.

Covey, S. R. 1989. *The seven habits of highly effective people: Restoring the character ethic.* New York: Simon and Schuster.

Deemer, D. 1986. Structuring controversy in the classroom. In *Strategies for active teaching and learning in university classrooms,* ed., S. F. Schomberg. Minneapolis, MN: Office of Educational Development Programs, University of Minnesota.

Dewey, J. 1910. *How we think.* Boston: D.C. Heath.

Gardner, J. N., and Jewler, A. J. 2003. *Your college experience: Strategies for success.* Belmont, CA: Wadsworth.

Gibb, J. R. 1961. Defensive communication. *Journal of Communication* 11:141–148.

Hersey, P., & Blanchard, K. H. 1993. Management of organization. Englewood Cliffs, NJ: Prentice Hall.

Janis, I. R. 1972. *Victims of groupthink.* Boston: Houghton Mifflin.

King, S. 1995, May 1. *Commentary—interpersonal cyberspace relationships.* Electronic message to Interpersonal Computing and Technology Discussion List, archived at ipctl@guvm.georgetown.edu.

King, S. A., and Moreggi, D. 1998. Internet therapy and self-help groups—the pros and cons. In *Psychology and the Internet: Intrapersonal, interpersonal, and transpersonal implications*, ed. J. Gackenbach, 77–109. San Diego, CA: Academic Press.

Miller, G. R., and Steinberg, M. 1975. *Between people: New analysis of interpersonal communication.* Chicago: Science Research Associates.

Moosbrucker, J. 1988. Developing a productivity team: Making groups at work work. In *Team building: Blueprints for productivity and satisfaction,* eds. W. B. Reddy and K. Jamison, 88–97. San Diego: National Institute for Applied Behavioral Science and University Associate.

Tannen, D. 1990. *You just don't understand: Women and men in conversation.* New York: Morrow.

Tiberius, R. G. 1990. *Small group teaching: A trouble-shooting guide.* Toronto: Ontario Institute for Studies in Education Press.

Tompkins, P. K. 2005. *Apollo, Challenger, Columbia: The decline of the space program.* Los Angeles: Roxbury.

Tuckman, B. W., and Jensen, M. A. C. 1977. Stages of small-group development revisited. *Group & Organization Studies* 2:419–427.

Tuckman, B. 1965. Developmental sequence in small groups. *Psychological Bulletin* 63:384–389.

Wellins, R. S., Byham, W. C., and Wilson, J. M. 1991. *Empowered teams: Creating self-directed work groups that improve quality, productivity, and participation.* San Francisco: Jossey-Bass.

Wheelan, S. A., and Hochberger, J. M. 1996. Validation studies of the group development questionnaire. *Small Group Research* 27:143–170.

Wheelan, S. A., and Kaeser, R. M. 1997. The influence of task type and designated leaders on developmental patterns in groups. *Small Group Research* 24:60–83.

CHAPTER *13*

Communication in Organizations

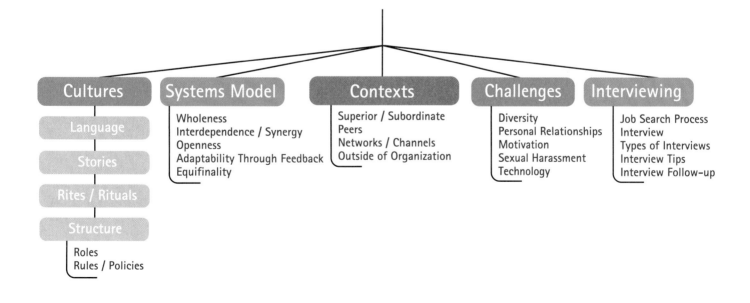

Cultures	Systems Model	Contexts	Challenges	Interviewing
Language	Wholeness	Superior / Subordinate	Diversity	Job Search Process
Stories	Interdependence / Synergy	Peers	Personal Relationships	Interview
Rites / Rituals	Openness	Networks / Channels	Motivation	Types of Interviews
Structure	Adaptability Through Feedback	Outside of Organization	Sexual Harassment	Interview Tips
Roles	Equifinality		Technology	Interview Follow-up
Rules / Policies				

Knowledge Checklist

✓ To describe the characteristics of organizational cultures

✓ To describe the elements of an organizational system

✓ To understand the various communication contexts in organizations

✓ To recognize the critical communication challenges in contemporary organizations

✓ To apply your knowledge of effective interpersonal, group, and public speaking skills to communication in organizations

✓ To identify the various types of interviewing used in organizations

✓ To develop effective interviewing strategies

THE IMPORTANCE OF COMMUNICATION IN ORGANIZATIONS

One of the primary reasons you are in college is to get that perfect job, to become a professional in a chosen career. As a professional, you will spend a significant portion of your time associated with one or more organizations. In the workplace today, organizations are constantly changing: structures are changing, organizational decision making is changing, and requirements for employee productivity are also changing. Indeed, one of the key variables in employee success is communication effectiveness. Much of what you have learned thus far in this text will allow you to be an effective organizational communicator. In this section, we explore several additional concepts that will assist you in fine-tuning your communication skills to meet the complex organizational demands. Like groups, organizations play a very important role in our lives.

Today's organizations require more teamwork than in past decades. The business world is expanding, and new markets are opening around the world; this globalization requires employees to understand and adapt to a multicultural world. Communication in this multicultural world means knowing, understanding, and adapting to different communication rules across cultures. Management theorist Peter Drucker (1992) believes that contemporary organizations are now looking for "the new knowledge worker," who possesses four key characteristics: (1) a college education, (2) the ability to apply analytical and theoretical thinking, (3) a commitment to lifelong learning, and (4) good communication skills. Drucker suggests that the single most important characteristic of this "new knowledge worker" is his or her *ability to communicate with others who do not share the same worldview.*

Information technology is also dramatically changing the nature of the workplace. Computers and telecommunications allow us to communicate instantly across geographic boundaries. Thus, the complexity of organizational life and the rapidly changing role of technology mean more demands upon individual organizational members than ever before. Those who are successful in this changing world of work are those who develop what organizational theorist Pamela Shockley-Zalabak (1999) calls "communication competency": knowledge, skills, values, and sensitivity. Employees must possess knowledge about the organization's communication environment. They must be sensitive to others and understand their feelings and meanings. Values reflect concern for the well-being of others in the communication situation and an understanding of responsibility within those situations.

Organizations today depend upon creative and flexible people, workers who can solve problems working with others who may not share their points of view. To prepare for these complex organizations, communication competency is critical. Your present educational experiences provide an excellent opportunity to learn communication competency in organizations, since the school you attend is a distinct organization that you must negotiate successfully. Many of the skills you are now developing will prepare you for the workforce. The first step in developing communication competency in organizations is understanding the cultural and systemic components of organizations.

ORGANIZATIONAL CULTURES

*I*t is critical to understand that organizations operate as distinct cultures. An **organization's culture** represents the actions, practices, language, and artifacts of a group. A culture is revealed *symbolically*. We understand a culture in numerous ways—by the way people explain the culture, by the tools used to create and maintain that culture, and by the values and beliefs that guide actions and practices. An organization's culture results from the accumulation of learning and behavior among a group of people and of how those individuals communicate their understanding of each other as members of the culture. Organizational culture persists through the organization's personnel changes. As a result, communication creates and sustains culture, while simultaneously influencing how individuals communicate and interact. Many symbolic practices make up culture, including language, stories, rites and rituals, and structure.

organizational culture the actions, practices, language, and artifacts of a group

Language

Each organization develops its own vocabulary with which it refers to its members' activity. One of the first ways organizational members learn expressed values is through the organization's mission statement. Have you read your university's mission statement? What does it tell you about the organization's value system? The vocabulary or language expresses the organization's past, present, and future values. The box Cultural Links: Organizational Cultures and Mission Statements describes the role of mission statements in organizations.

◎ *Cultural Links*

Organizational Cultures and Mission Statements

Organizations are unique cultural systems that share a set of beliefs, values, and norms, which are communicated among the people within the organization. These powerful, unifying forces are typically reflected in the heroes, villains, rites, rituals, communication flow, symbols, and stories of the organization. However, most organizations outline their values, beliefs, and objectives in carefully crafted mission statements in an attempt to capture and reflect the essence of its culture. A mission statement, according to Radtke (1998) should be an inspiring, goal-oriented, clear, jargon-free, succinct paragraph that resonates with the people inside and outside the organization. A mission statement should answer at least three questions:

1. What are the opportunities or needs that we exist to address? (the purpose of the organization)

2. What are we doing to address these needs? (the business of the organization)

3. What principles or beliefs guide our work? (the values of the organization)

As a part of a university or college, you are part of an organization with a mission. Do you know that mission? Find your school's mission statement. In some cases, it may be challenging to find these statements; they may not even exist. If you discover these mission statements, analyze them carefully. How well does the mission statement answer the three questions above? How well is it drafted? How well does your experience in this organization reflect the mission statement? If there is a discrepancy, why does it exist? How well is the mission statement communicated to members of your college or university community? How well is the mission statement communicated to external constituents?

Analyzing university, college, or departmental mission statement(s) will help you practice for analyzing mission statements in organizations, businesses, or companies to which you apply for employment. By identifying and analyzing mission statements, you have one immediate way to discern whether or not there is "fit" between you and a potential employer. Moreover, mission statements will give you some clear clues as to the culture of the organization you are interested in; they can also help you communicate more effectively in your cover letter and interview to get the position and in your performance reviews once you secure it.

As an example, consider this mission statement: "We are a global family with a proud heritage passionately committed to providing personal mobility for people around the world. We anticipate consumer need and deliver outstanding products and services that improve people's lives." What kind of business is reflected in this mission statement? What values are suggested? Does this sound like an environment in which you would like to work? Why? If you find this mission statement appealing, then you might want to consider working for Ford Motor Company, since this is its mission statement (found at www.ford.com/en/company/about/overview.htm).

---

language the vocabulary that is used to refer to the activity of group members; the level of formality between members of different statuses

Language also reveals a great deal about such things as power relationships among members. How people are addressed provides information about their status. The level of formality or informality of language tells individuals how to act with peers, supervisors, or customers. Are supervisors in the organization referred to by their first names or addressed as Ms. Johnson, Mr. Obama, or Dr. Singh? Whether language is formal or informal may also provide insights about how organization members should dress or whether people are encouraged to discuss personal or social interests while at work. What special language or vocabulary have you come to understand as part of your university experience?

Stories

stories and myths tales of past successes and failures and of past and present heroes that help socialize new members of an organization

One way organizational members talk about their culture is through **stories and myths**. Organizational history is explained through corporate stories. These tell of past successes and failures, helping organizational members understand the type of risks that are acceptable. They provide members with an opportunity to recognize past and present "heroes" as well. Stories provide a critical socialization function for new members of the organization. They provide information about how work is done, about the appropriateness of many kinds of communication, and about the values and beliefs among organizational members. While new employees are normally provided with rule books or "standard operating procedures," stories allow new members to compare what is "written" with what is unwritten but "understood" by its members. A final function of stories is that they provide opportunities for members to feel connected to one another and to the organization as a whole.

Rites and Rituals

rites and rituals practices that symbolize the tools organizational members use to create and maintain culture

The organization's **rites and rituals** often symbolize the "tools" members use to create and maintain culture. Examples include the annual holiday party, the company picnic, or performance reviews. The most famous "rituals" of university life might include surviving registration, learning the maze of financial aid, and, of course, participating in graduation with all its pomp and circumstance. There are also other annual or seasonal rituals on college campuses such as homecoming parades, fund-raisers for nonprofit agencies, or tailgate parties.

Structure

An organization's structure is revealed in two ways—through the roles that individuals play and the rules and policies that govern the organization. Thus, in order to communicate effectively within the organization, employees must understand the roles, rules, and policies that make up the organization's underlying support and framework.

Roles

Just as power relationships are revealed by how employees address one another, organizational structure can also be identified by individuals' titles or by the **roles** they play in the group. In the university system, faculty have many titles that refer to such things as their level of education, their longevity, and their level of professional standing among their peers. A lecturer or adjunct, an instructor, an assistant professor, an associate professor, or a full professor may teach one of your classes. These titles reflect the person's teaching responsibilities, his or her rank within the organizational hierarchy, and to some degree, his or her status among other faculty. There are, of course, other titles in the hierarchy, such as associate dean, dean, vice president, provost, president, chancellor, and trustee. These titles reflect an individual's job description and levels of responsibility within the university. Organizational charts that depict the relationships among the various offices and roles in your university will help you understand who's who and will give you a better sense of how communication flows within the organization.

roles titles and/or job responsibilities

Rules and Policies

Another example of structure is in the **rules and policies** by which organizational members make decisions. Every organization has a set of operating policies that are mandated by various authoritative figures or bodies such as the board of trustees, the president, or department heads. When you entered your college, you probably received a student handbook or code of conduct containing your school's rules and policies. Rules are more or less formal, depending upon the organization and the type of product or service they provide. Like our earlier discussion of group rules and norms, organizational rules also may develop either implicitly or explicitly. As with groups, the more explicitly the rules are developed in the organization and the more rules members agree upon, the more effective the organizational communication may be. Policies are formal statements about what is and is not expected of organizational members. The most common types of policies in any organization refer to such things as pay, benefits, hiring and firing, promotion, leave, and so on.

rules and policies standards by which organizational members make decisions

One of the most important rituals of college culture is the graduation ceremony.

Once individuals in organizations learn how to "read" the culture, they can interpret "what it means to work here" much more effectively. Think about the last job you had. Did you learn what was expected of you by reading the corporate manual or by observing the company's day-to-day standard operating procedures? Did you get more information from watching others and hearing stories about "heroes and villains"? When individuals can interpret cultural symbols correctly, they begin to establish the knowledge and skills needed to succeed in that organization.

Understanding that an organization develops its own unique cultural characteristics can assist all members in developing a greater comprehension of the organization's "work life." Grasping the language, stories, rites, rituals, and structure can allow members to reduce uncertainty about their jobs and help them shape and adapt relationships within the organization. As a result, individuals come to know their place within the organizational system through knowledge of its culture. The box Communication Links: Uncertainty Reduction Theory describes the ways in which new employees attempt to understand the cultural characteristics of an organization new to them.

Communication Links

Uncertainty Reduction Theory

Berger and Calabrese (1975) developed uncertainty reduction theory (URT) to explain the discomfort that arises when people meet one another and the subsequent desire to reduce the discomfort through communication strategies. These researchers assert that people use three types of strategies: passive, active, and interactive. Let's consider how each of these strategies play out in an organization where daily rumors indicate that the company is planning to downsize.

First, the employees are likely to use passive strategies. Usually this means they will try to silently analyze what's going on; they will be more alert to the climate and who talks to whom. They may also try to pick up bits of conversation and piece together an explanation of the situation. They will likely begin investing significance in everyday behaviors and reflecting upon them (e.g., "You know, the boss wouldn't make eye contact with me today in the hall; I wonder if that means I'm on the 'hit list' for the upcoming downsizing?"). This first phase may be considered the silent phase, when others' communication is carefully monitored and when nonverbal communication carries more weight.

Second, the employees will likely use active communication strategies if they want more information. In this phase, they will analyze the situation together, talk among themselves, and try to gain more information through the grapevine. They may gossip, backbite, or blame others for the impending downsizing in order to vent frustrations, especially if there's an absence of direct information from credible sources. If information is not forthcoming, some employees may even try to connect with people from other departments or sectors of the organization in order to "get a feel" for what's going on and what to expect. This second phase may be considered a venting phase, when information is withheld; or it may be the investigative phase, when people begin talking with one another to gain more information indirectly. In either or both cases, verbal communication becomes more important.

Third, the employees will likely engage in interactive strategies to gain more concrete information. In this phase, employees will go directly to a credible and qualified source to find out whether the rumors are true. For example, the employees may approach their immediate supervisor, a union representative, or someone in a position of higher authority in order to find out the facts. Like the second phase, this phase relies on verbal communication; however, rather than relying on speculation and assumption or indirect communication, the employees use direct communication. This strategy, like the active strategies, relies more heavily on verbal communication.

While these strategies may not necessarily be used in order, they provide a template for understanding how people respond in organizations when uncertain situations develop. As you move into the work world, remember these principles, because they will help you understand, as well as select, communication strategies in uncertain times.

ORGANIZATIONAL SYSTEMS: THE SYSTEMS MODEL

environment the larger system surrounding an organization that provides resources and utilizes products and services.

Understanding organizations as systems means recognizing that every organization exists within a larger environment. A *system* is a set of parts (individuals) that are interconnected (relationships) within its environment. The larger **environment** provides resources to the organization (input) and utilizes the products or services the organization creates (output). What the organization does with these products and services is called *throughput*. To illustrate, a university system depends upon the larger environment for a variety of human, information, or fiscal resources such as students, faculty, and other employees; knowledge and information; and money from the state, benefactors, grants, and tuition fees. The university also depends upon such physical resources as electricity, computers, books, equipment, and furniture. The university system generates output through its graduates, who are potential employees, and through additional knowledge and information from research, community service endeavors, and tax dollars paid by university workers. The university processes all the resources from the environment in classrooms, meetings, research projects, and other types of activities, and this becomes the essence of "throughput" at a university. Every system is unique, just like every college or university is unique. And every individual within the organization is connected with one another in the system.

In order to understand the way a system operates, we will discuss several characteristics, including wholeness, interdependence, openness, adaptability, and equifinality. Systems theorists Daniel Katz and Robert Kahn (1966) suggest that a systems approach focuses on problems of relationships, structure, and interdependence rather than on concrete objects in the organization. Let's look at the relationships between the parts (individuals) of a system and the way individuals understand and process feedback to understand the system.

Wholeness

The first characteristic of a system is **wholeness**, or the unique configuration of the system's parts. Most organizations have different departments, offices, or individuals, but the way these elements coordinate activities constitutes the system. Restructuring the system will not threaten the wholeness of the organization. Some universities, for example, are organized by the college structure. The university has several colleges. Each college consists of several departments. In our universities, for example, the Communication Department is a part of the College of Arts and Sciences. The chair or head of our department is responsible to the college's dean. Some larger universities, on the other hand, have an entire College of Communication that consists of several different departments such as broadcasting, film studies, journalism, communication studies, and others. Though uniquely configured, each of our institutions remains a whole organization; it is not a loose coalition of independent, autonomous units.

wholeness the unique configuration of the parts in a system

Interdependence and Synergy

It is necessary to understand how the parts of the system function together in an **interdependent** fashion to create the whole. In a family, team, or business, the relationships among people make the group a system. As we discussed in the chapter on group communication, every part in the system can impact every other part of the system. Thus, systems theorists suggest, "the whole is greater than the sum of its parts." Collective energy, or **synergy**, increases when the parts work together. This synergy can be negative or positive. Negative synergy results from ineffective communication and misunderstanding. Positive synergy results from recognizing the interdependence between system components and competent communication within the system.

interdependent components of a system rely upon one another in order to function properly

synergy collective energy

Openness

Every organization interacts differently with the environment. Environments are dynamic and changing. Today's organizations must monitor the environment and adapt to changing resources in that environment. The concept of **openness** refers to

openness the way a system uses feedback to adapt to changes in the larger environment

how the system uses feedback to adapt to changes in the larger environment. For example, changes can be economic (changes in the stock market, in number of customers, or in cost of supplies), political (changes in legislation that affect the organization), or human (changes in technology require more worker training). Openness also means that organizations that exist in a larger system are constantly impacted by events in that larger system.

On September 11, 2001, the tragedies in New York and Washington reverberated around the world and in our schools. Many of us knew someone connected to another person working in the World Trade Center or in the Pentagon, so the events caused shock waves on our campuses. Many faculty at our universities canceled classes, called loved ones just to hear their voices, or talked with coworkers about their feelings. The outpouring of assistance—from raising money to donating blood—reverberated across the country and solidified our commitment to fellow Americans in need. The events of September 11 also demonstrated the incredible diversity in our American system and showed the variety of our feedback in response to tragedy. Some individuals traveled thousands of miles to assist with the rescue efforts in New York City. And while some Americans responded by reaching out to Arab Americans, others responded with hatred and violence against these individuals. We are diverse in how we give, in how we love, and in how we hate. Most of these responses are related to our individual levels of openness. In the same way, organizations respond differently to the environment depending on their respective levels of openness. For the most part, organizations that are not flexible and adaptable begin to solidify.

Adaptability through Feedback

Changes in the larger environment, then, require organizations to adapt quickly and responsibly. In order to adapt to changes, the organization must become more proactive in seeking out information and must adopt a flexible approach to larger environmental change. **Adaptability** is critical to contemporary organizations, which must constantly adopt new policies, procedures, products, and services to respond to the rapidly changing global environment. After September 11, airports around the country were closed for days, and some airlines laid off thousands of employees. Other organizations set up funding mechanisms and matched employee contributions to the "September 11th Fund," which assisted victims and their families. General Electric Corporation, for example, donated $10 million to the fund. In other words, these organizations adapted to the crisis at hand with philanthropic feedback.

adaptability the ability to change in response to a rapidly changing global environment

September 11, 2001 brought about a variety of organizational feedback.

Organizations must also recognize that strategies that work in one situation will not necessarily work in another. Strategies are contingent upon many environmental factors. For example, today's organizations must monitor the environment and create unique ways of adapting. A range of new jobs that focus on monitoring the environment—marketing, sales, public relations, and others—have opened up in organizations. Individuals in these jobs must have effective communication skills in order to recognize changes and to communicate those changes to others in their organization.

Equifinality

The final characteristic of any system is **equifinality**. This refers to recognition that the end product (whatever output the organization produces) can be produced in several ways. Every system has the capacity to identify and develop several ways to reach its goals. For example, think of the number of options you have when choosing an Internet provider. No matter which provider you choose, you accomplish virtually the same thing—the ability to send e-mail, surf the Net, join a chat room, and so on. Each provider, though, has *some* unique features. Another example of equifinality can be seen in the number of colleges and universities that offer communication degrees. Although there are many different ways colleges or universities might offer this degree, each may require slightly different courses or experiences within their programs. Students achieve the same goal but travel somewhat different paths to achieve it, depending on the program's focus.

equifinality recognition that the end production can be produced in a number of ways

Communication in the System

Through organizational communication, we gather, interpret, and utilize information from the environment outside the system. Communication allows the organization to coordinate the interdependent parts within the system. Openness to feedback allows an organization to adapt and adjust itself to environmental change. Communication and creativity within and throughout the system open a range of options in developing, modifying, marketing, and selling the organization's products and services. Think back to the types of advertising or marketing strategies that convinced you to attend your college or university. Did admissions counselors come to your school? Was the institution's website creative and interesting? Did you watch videos or receive a DVD? Did you receive brochures or letters? Did you go to campus and take a tour guided by a student representative? Did you speak with a faculty member? You can probably identify some key communication strategies that helped guide your decision.

COMMUNICATION CONTEXTS IN ORGANIZATIONS

Competent organizational communication must consider its many contexts within the organization. We communicate interpersonally with peers, supervisors, and subordinates. We also communicate with customers, clients, suppliers, and others outside the organization. Additionally, gender and cultural differences add a level of complexity to each of these contexts. Interpersonal relationships at all levels are crucial to individual and organizational success, and they are a prerequisite for effective job performance.

Superior–Subordinate Communication

Riley and Eisenberg (1991) suggest that the key to successful communication with superiors is advocacy. Employees must understand the needs of superiors and adapt communication accordingly. One of the critical principles of effective advocacy is connecting arguments to supervisors' needs and expectations. Eisenberg and

Goodall (1997) suggest the following principles to guide communication with superiors:

1. *Plan a strategy.* Understand the individual and the context of your appeal.

2. *Determine why the superior should listen.* Connect your appeal to something important to your boss.

3. *Tailor the argument to the supervisor's style and characteristics.* Will he or she respond more favorably to statistics or a story? Adapt your evidence to his or her needs.

4. *Assess the supervisor's technical knowledge.* Do not assume his or her knowledge base, know it.

5. *Hone your communications skills.* Be clear and articulate in your appeals.

Communication must always be adapted to audience knowledge, expectations, values, and beliefs. Keys to successful communication to subordinates in the organization are openness and support. Empathic listening is critical to the success of many relationships. Subordinates commonly criticize their superiors for withholding information. They need and want to know information that impacts their work. Thus, effective supervisors pass along information to subordinates and provide them with opportunities for input in discussions that impact workplace behavior and decision making. Supportiveness in communication includes showing concern for the relationships and demonstrating respect for individuals while promoting accomplishment of tasks. Both empathic listening and genuine support from supervisors enhance employee motivation in the workplace. These communication strategies also empower subordinates by building confidence and trust, as you can see in the box Communication and Career Links: Key Principles for Successful Organizational Relationships.

Communication and Career Links

Key Principles for Successful Organizational Relationships

A few years ago, a young man stormed into one of our offices without an appointment and demanded, "There are no seats left in the sections of the basic course that fit my schedule. You have to enroll me in the 12:30 p.m. Tuesday/Thursday section right now because I'm a senior, and I can't graduate unless I take this stupid course." His attitude, demeanor, and communication strategy was, to say the least, ineffective. Not surprisingly, he found that his approach failed to get him what he needed and actually hindered him.

In response, one of your authors said, in a direct but courteous manner, "Before you say more, allow me to help you. First, in the 'stupid course' in which you need to enroll, we teach principles of communication that will help you should you encounter a similar circumstance like this again in your life. However, if you think about it, you probably already know about some of these principles. So, if you'd like to go out of my office, come in again, and use what you think might be a more appropriate communication approach, I'll act as though our first encounter didn't occur. What do you say?" Sheepishly, the young man went out, knocked at the door, and this time significantly adjusted his approach; he introduced himself, softened his tone, explained what he wanted, and received the help he needed. This story illustrates an important principle: *You can more easily get what you need from others when you communicate in a kind, polite, and direct manner that affirms the other person's humanity.* This is true in both college and work contexts. Consider these key principles that can help guide your communication choices when working with others in organizations:

1. **Work on developing a trusting relationship with others.** People are the most important resource in organizations. Trusting relationships between and among people are the glue that holds an organization together. When

you have built trust with others, you can more easily approach them and ask for assistance or offer explanations. For example, if you have developed an honest relationship with your professor, when you tell her that you missed class because you were not feeling well, she is more likely to believe you without the need for any outside confirmation. When your immediate supervisor trusts you because you have proven that you can accomplish assignments in a timely manner with excellent results, you will get even more challenging opportunities and perhaps, eventually, a promotion.

2. **Treat everyone, regardless of rank in the organization, with respect.** Very often students (and faculty too) forget that staff and other support personnel at colleges and universities are essential to the function of the organization. They often have information power (i.e., they know what you need to know) or can help you gain access to a person, place, or equipment you need. Practice genuine, common courtesy in your dealings with everyone since they may literally hold the key to what you need now or later. You can, of course, "be nice to get what you want," but this will probably backfire at some point, because if you are not authentically respectful to everyone, you may at some point "forget to put on your kind face" and unwittingly offend someone.

3. **When disagreements or difficulties arise, respond, don't react.** What will you do if you disagree with the grade you received on a project? Many students tend to complain to others in the class, or, in some cases, appeal the situation to someone else, without ever discussing the issue with their teacher. These are reactive responses that seek retribution, not a resolution. This can escalate the spiral of conflict with your professor who, in most instances, has more organizational power than you. However, if you respond by first approaching your professor in a kind, direct manner and asking questions to clarify the reason for your grade, you open possibilities for dialogue that will solve, rather than exacerbate, problems. Even if you are not satisfied with the result, you may uncover important insights that will help you in completing the next assignment with greater success. Response, rather than reaction, has equal application in the workplace. Undoubtedly, you will encounter coworkers or supervisors with whom you disagree; however, how you handle these differences will impact your satisfaction with your job, the climate of the workplace, and possibly your future with the organization.

4. **Don't be afraid to say you're sorry or take responsibility.** It is never easy to apologize. None of us enjoy being wrong. It is equally difficult to take responsibility to correct what we have done wrong. Given that we are all human and make mistakes or have bad days, relationships in organizations are likely to become strained at some point; we must be willing to make apologies and accept responsibility for doing the right thing, even if it's difficult. This is not just true for students and employees; it is also true for professors or supervisors. James Autry (2001) tells of a time in his career when he was in conflict with his immediate supervisor who micromanaged his department. Autry felt that his creativity and energy were being squelched, so he decided to accept an attractive offer from another company. Upon hearing of his resignation, the CEO of the company, who was traveling in another city, called him and asked him to delay his decision until they could talk. When the CEO returned, he apologized to Autry, explained that he had hoped the situation with Autry's supervisor would resolve itself, and promised to fix the situation if Autry would stay. Autry explains, "To make the story short, I stayed. I didn't stay for more money or power or position. I stayed because I believed the CEO. I had always believed in him as a visionary leader, but it was at that moment that I got the measure of him as an honest, authentic human being—one willing to admit mistakes who did not allow his sense of position or his ego to prevent him from apologizing to someone lower in the hierarchy" (p. 11).

Peer communication provides social support and builds morale.

Communication with Peers

Horizontal or peer communication provides social support to individuals and builds employee morale. We have discussed effective communication in work teams and its benefits in terms of decision making and relationship maintenance. Peer communication also entails talking across departments or units and with customers or suppliers. Today, focus on customer service is essential to business success. Opportunities for feedback between units in the organization and between the organization and its customers, coupled with rapid response to that feedback, can increase organizational effectiveness and success.

Ultimately, individuals at any level of the organization must understand the complexity of its relationships and expectations. Communication that is clear, constant, and supportive within the variety of relational contexts enhances individual, team, and organizational effectiveness.

Using Networks and Channels Effectively

Effective organizational communication is dependent upon the appropriate use of networks and channels of communication within the organization. Who talks to whom? Why? How? When? Where? These were some of the questions we posed in Chapter 1 during our analysis of communication situations, including those within organizations. A network links organizational members either formally or informally and describes how information travels throughout the organization. Some formal networks are used to disseminate critical information to all employees while other networks are more informal and provide information on issues of socialization.

formal networks used most commonly when information is communicated up or down

informal networks used most commonly when information is communicated between peers

Formal networks, or channels, are used most commonly when information is communicated either up (reporting the results of a particular job) or down (giving orders or advising on policy adaptation). **Informal networks** or channels are used most commonly among peers at similar levels of the organization although sometimes the grapevine (a common name for the most pervasive informal organizational channel) is used by many individuals at all levels. The grapevine can be a positive communication channel, because it is one of the fastest ways to disseminate information. Individual members may use the grapevine to confirm information that comes from more formal channels. It assists members in interpreting and understanding information. However, the grapevine can also become a negative channel if organizational members use it as a substitute for more formal channels, such as trying to find out about critical policy or personnel changes when formal channels are lacking in information. As a result, if formal channels do not provide adequate information or allow individuals to interpret information accurately, the informal grapevine rumors replace reliable information.

Communicating Outside the Organization

Many of you will find jobs where you will be dealing with individuals outside the organization, such as customers, clients, suppliers, legislators, community leaders, and others. Managers today recognize that in order to ensure continued profit in the constantly changing marketplace, effective communication between the organization and its customers and other organizations is essential. Businesses must develop and nurture long-term relationships with numerous external audiences. This is not simply a matter of economics; it is also a product of expectations. Organizations are expected to accept and enact proactive social responsibility in their communities and in the broader global marketplace.

Organizational theorist Matthew Seeger (1997) suggests that organizations have four primary responsibilities to audiences both within and outside the organization: philanthropic, environmental, product, and employee. Philanthropic efforts include donations of time and money to local, regional, or national charities, including arts and cultural programs. Environmental responsibility concerns the organization's impact on environmental resources. Product responsibility addresses product safety and conscientious use of materials in product development and production. Finally, employee responsibility includes efforts to provide a safe and motivating workplace. In the past, a common organizational philosophy was, "Let the buyer beware!" Today, however, the reverse may be true. Let the organization beware if its products and services do not conform to customer (and other audience) expectations of social, environment, or product responsibility. Organizations, therefore, are not just about doing business but about building relationships through service and support. This is true of the "business of higher education" as well as more traditional business endeavors. The box Computer Links: Communicating Social Responsibility through a Website explains how organizations are using their websites as one of the most important channels for communicating about the ways the organization conducts itself responsibly.

Computer Links

Communicating Social Responsibility through a Website

One of the most common communication channels used by organizations today is a website. In this way, an organization can communicate to multiple stakeholders in a cost-effective way. Millions of businesses today rely on their website to reach audiences across the world as well as in their own backyard. With the proliferation of websites, consumers need tools to evaluate the credibility, honesty, and ethicality of the information disseminated by organizations. Internet technology has made the communication of ethical values and behavior both more efficient and more complex in our diverse and fast-paced society. Organizations have the ability to communicate more quickly to larger numbers of stakeholders, and they can take advantage of advances in technology to make this communication more focused to meet the needs and expectations of those stakeholders.

As you think about the type of organization you would like to eventually work for, what critical questions do you have about the organization's culture, decision making, and social responsibility? Can you use the typology developed by Seeger to help you identify an organization you would like to work for?

Try this test. Identify an organization where you might like to work and find its website. Using Seeger's four categories, attempt to locate information on the website about philanthropic, environmental, product, and employee responsibility. Does the website address how the organization donates time and money to local, regional, or national charities, including arts and cultural efforts? Does the website discuss use of environmental resources? Does it cover the organization's responsibility to reduce the consumption of nonrenewable resources? Does the website discuss issues of product safety and of responsible use of materials in product development and production? Finally, does it identify its efforts to provide a safe and motivating workplace?

Even if all the categories do not have the same importance to you in terms of a satisfying job, looking at an organizational website and asking these questions can assist you in finding the job with the right "fit." Using Seeger's categories and asking good questions can help you make a more informed decision regarding the job/workplace that's right for you.

CHALLENGES IN CONTEMPORARY ORGANIZATIONS

Today's worker faces numerous challenges in the workplace. Historically workers could count on lifetime employment if they did a good job, but today that guarantee is gone. Communication in the workplace thus takes on greater importance as workers attempt to negotiate their jobs in an uncertain climate. Greater misunderstanding between and among supervisors and subordinates complicates that negotiation. The more misunderstanding occurs within an organization, the more workers are likely to feel fear and distrust, and the less likely they may be to communicate with others.

The Diverse Organization

The workforce today looks dramatically different from that of twenty years ago. Cultural, racial, and gender diversity have never been so pronounced. For example, the number of workers over fifty-five is growing. Additionally, census data tell us that the fastest-growing ethnic population in the United States is Hispanic. As a result, the white, male-dominated workforce of yesterday is being replaced by organizations filled with individuals who look, think, and act in radically different ways.

Organizations at the turn of the twentieth century and through WWI and WWII were predominantly manufacturing based. Today, the manufacturing sector is decreasing while the service industry is exploding. Another change is workers' levels of education are much higher than ever before in history. This educated workforce demands not only pay and benefits commensurate with their levels of training and experience but also employment opportunities that are satisfying and motivating. One way to motivate workers is including them in communication and decision-making processes.

Today's educated workers also demand a more equitable balance between work and home life. Individuals want to balance their job requirements with their family's needs. In the past, all employees were expected to work the same hours, get the same benefits, and develop the same sense of loyalty to the organization. Work was work, and employers expected no intrusions from personal or family issues. Today, however, issues of child care, elder care, and other responsibilities impact employees' lives. Organizations must also consider the number of workers with substance abuse or emotional problems. Increasingly, contemporary employers must develop counseling services to assist employees with substance abuse problems, family struggles, mental health issues, legal problems, child and parent care, or other personal issues.

Organizations that respond to these employees' needs with appropriate policies and benefits and who communicate with them in caring and sensitive ways will remain competitive in today's marketplace. Flexibility and adaptability, hallmarks of systems theory, must become the norm for contemporary organizations. Employees, too, must be flexible and adaptable to the diversity of individuals, values, and communication styles of their customers, superiors, coworkers, subordinates, and others.

Personal Relationships in Organizations

Because today's workforce demands more satisfying personal relationships at work, organizations must also adapt to these new expectations. Workers today spend more than forty hours a week on the job; thus, the opportunity for enhanced social and personal relationships with coworkers is increased. Long-term relationships, both on and off the job, have the greatest potential for success when the partners are matched in such things as level of education, interests, and activities. Today we are just as likely to find these matches in our workplace as out of it.

Organizational theorists Dillard and Miller (1988) suggest that the motivation underlying romantic relationships in organizations is complex, as it involves love and ego. Employees motivated by love are looking for long-term companionship and partnership. Those motivated by ego are looking for sexual excitement and adventure. The consequences of these romantic relationships can, according to Dillard and Miller, provide improved work performance. However, negative perceptions of other employees can create problems for romantic partners. For example, if the romantic relationship ends, coworkers may continue assuming the relationship has negatively impacted the parties involved. Moving from the impersonal to the personal and to the romantic stage of a relationship with a coworker may be highly satisfying, but it could also backfire and have negative consequences both for the individuals and the organization.

Romantic relationships are not the only types of personal relationships that we might develop through our work, however. The potential for developing deep and long-lasting friendships also exists. Sharing the trials and tribulations as well as the joys and successes of our everyday work experiences with close friends adds an additional level of satisfaction to our work experience.

Motivation in Diverse Organizations

The diverse workforce consists of individuals who seek motivating and satisfying employment. But this diversity also means there is no "one-size-fits-all" motivational approach. As a result, organizations must recognize and adopt a variety of approaches to motivating workers. While communication is the common denominator in all types of motivation, the best motivational device or strategy will fail if its message and timing are not matched to individual and organizational needs. Organizational managers must seek out information from employees about what is motivating to them. Likewise, employees must be willing to communicate their needs and expectations to their supervisors. Kreps (1991) defines **motivation** as "the degree to which an individual is personally committed to expending effort in the accomplishment of a specified activity or goal" (p. 154). Eisenberg and Goodall (1997) suggest that communication can function in two ways to motivate: Managers can provide information and feedback about employee tasks, goals, and performance, and they can communicate encouragement, empathy, and concern.

Schutz (1958) suggests there are two levels of motivators important to individuals. The first level is primarily economic and includes such things as pay, benefits, and vacations. The second level is more subjective and includes motivators

motivation the degree to which an individual is personally committed to expending effort in the accomplishment of a specified activity or goal

like inclusion in decision making and opportunities for input into policies, procedures, and products. These are motivating to us as workers because we feel a sense of ownership of our jobs, a sense of pride in our individual accomplishments, and a sense of being respected by others for our knowledge and expertise. Each of us wants to engage in work that offers us personal satisfaction and professional opportunity.

The key to motivating employees, then, is to develop opportunities for collective decision making and risk taking. Effective organizational communication also requires developing multiple channels for information to flow through the organization and creating communication situations that encourage negotiation among participants.

UNDERSTANDING AND AVOIDING SEXUAL HARASSMENT

As we noted earlier, an organization creates and maintains its unique culture. However, internal and external audiences demand that the culture be based on responsibility and sensitivity to issues of gender, race, ethnicity, age, and sexual orientation. Effective and ethical organizations establish cultures of equal opportunity and provide workplaces free of discriminatory actions. For example, one area of prohibited discrimination is **sexual harassment**. Sexually harassing behavior humiliates people. While women are more commonly victims of sexual harassment, sexually hostile environmental harassment may be targeted at any individual in the organization.

According to the Equal Employment Opportunity Commission, harassment on the basis of sex violates Title VII of the Civil Rights Act of 1964. The act defines sexual harassment as unwelcome sexual advances, requests for sexual favors, and other verbal or physical conduct of a sexual nature. Sexual harassment occurs when

1. submission to such conduct is made, either explicitly or implicitly, a term or condition of an individual's employment;

2. submission to or rejection of such conduct is used as the basis for employment decisions affecting an individual; or

3. such conduct has the purpose or effect of unreasonably interfering with an individual's work performance or creating an intimidating, hostile, or offensive working environment.

Situations 1 and 2 are often referred to as "quid pro quo" sexual harassment and usually occur in relationships where there is an obvious power difference between the parties (such as supervisor to subordinate or faculty to student). Situation 3 is often referred to as "hostile environment" sexual harassment and more commonly occurs between coworkers or between students. Sexual harassment may be physical (such as unwanted touching, hugging, kissing, patting, pinching), verbal (i.e., referring to a woman as a "babe," "girl," or "honey"; discussing sexual topics or telling sexual jokes; asking personal questions of a sexual nature; or making sexual comments about a person's clothing or anatomy), or nonverbal (i.e., such as looking a person up and down, staring at someone for a prolonged time, or making sexually suggestive gestures with hands or through body movements).

It is the organization's responsibility to prevent sexual harassment by developing policies and training that educate employees about appropriate behavior and that provide them with opportunities to report harassment. Organizations should investigate these reports promptly and confidentially and should not retaliate against employees who report unacceptable behavior. Responding to this issue through education, training, and communication helps to sustain healthy interpersonal relationships among employees and can benefit the organization in numerous ways. When we work in supportive and caring organizational climates, we are motivated to be productive and creative in our professional responsibilities.

sexual harassment unwelcome sexual advances, requests for sexual favors, and other verbal or physical conduct of a sexual nature

TECHNOLOGY IN ORGANIZATIONS

*R*egardless of the type of culture developed in the organization or the nature of the relationships among employees, some form of communication technology must be utilized. While face-to-face communication is still important in today's organization, advanced technology has made messaging faster, made access to and processing of information much easier, and made communication with others across geographical distances much more accessible. Some technology has made the office virtually obsolete. Computer, video, and teleconferencing capabilities allow us to reach others wherever we are and whenever we want. The Internet allows us to access information from any library in the world with a few clicks of a mouse. Organizations may use computer-assisted technology to send images and voices across time and space or use computer-assisted decision-aiding technology such as databases or programs that provide information to decision makers. For example, Ganga and Lerner (2004) report that in 2001, 15 percent of employed people, almost 20 million workers, worked at least one full day a week at home. Of these, 3.4 million workers had a formal arrangement with their employers that allowed them to work at home. For the most part, these arrangements were possible because of increased technology.

The effects of this technology on contemporary organizations are significant. In order to acquire and keep a good job and to remain competitive, you must understand and develop expertise in many types of communication technology. For the organization to remain competitive, it means that training must be ongoing to meet changing technology.

Technological advancements also provide opportunities for organizations to monitor and improve employee productivity. Computerized monitoring of employees is the norm in businesses today. However, managers must recognize that abuse of individual rights and privacy (also possible because of changing technology) negatively impacts corporate culture. Employee–employer rights issues are complex and continue to cause concern for employees and employers alike. As an individual beginning your career or updating your skills for a career change, you need to know how, why, and when your behavior at work will be monitored. To counter the impact of technology that monitors your behavior, be up-to-date on the latest advances in technology and use it wisely so as not to jeopardize your job or your unit's productivity.

EFFECTIVE ORGANIZATIONAL COMMUNICATION BEYOND COLLEGE

*F*irst impressions often have the most impact on whether or not a personal relationship will blossom or wither, or in the case of your professional life, whether or not you will be offered a position. All of the communication skills we have discussed so far in this text will assist you in making the best impression when you interview for the job/career you have been preparing for in college. But the interview itself is not the first step in the job-search process. Before you interview, you should first research the type of organization you want to work for and learn what the business needs and expects of its employees. Therefore, one of the first steps in your research is to develop an understanding of the qualities or skills necessary for work in a particular organization. Second, you must know how to prepare the required employment materials that will assist you in getting that job.

The Job Search Process

One of the best places to begin your research is the Internet. A host of websites provides information on every aspect of the job-search process. You can learn how to

The ability to keep up-to-date on technology in your workplace will enhance career success.

write and post a résumé, write cover letters, find job opportunities, prepare for interviews, determine commonly asked questions, and get advice on interview attire. Most companies offer a wealth of information through their websites about who they are and what they do. Many of these websites even have links aimed at potential employees. In fact, many organizations guide you through the steps for submitting an application, posting a résumé and cover letter, and requesting more information on the company.

In this section, we provide information that will assist you on a job interview, but first we discuss the types of skills most employers look for in potential employees. Despite advances and changes in technology within organizations, employers still seek candidates who can show they have effective and flexible interpersonal communication skills. As we said earlier, flexibility is critical to effective interpersonal communication in diverse and multicultural organizations. The ability to speak intelligently and assertively with colleagues, superiors, and subordinates is vital. Working effectively in groups and managing conflict in problem-solving teams are equally critical.

Key skills employers expect from workers today include self-motivation, assertiveness, ambition, as well as cultural sensitivity and understanding. Once you have developed your skills in these critical areas, you are ready to find your ideal job. After you have identified the job you want, investigated what the organization expects of you, and written and submitted your résumé and cover letter, you may be called for an interview. Remember that the résumé and cover letter may get you an interview, but the interview itself will be what lands you the job.

The résumé briefly describes your educational, employment, professional, and extracurricular experiences. Critical information that you must provide in the résumé includes education (college and/or graduate school); work history (both paid and volunteer); professional or academic organizational experience (fraternity, sorority, political, or professional); and awards, scholarships, military experience, and references (names, titles, work addresses, phone, and e-mail). The résumé must be well organized, neat, and error free. A general rule is to keep the résumé to one or two pages. Use keywords and action verbs throughout the résumé to describe critical skills you have developed through your wide range of experiences. Once you have written a first draft, proof it for errors. Then have someone in your college or university career center evaluate it and offer constructive advice. You might also ask a trusted professor or mentor to assess it as well.

A cover letter should accompany your résumé unless you are hand delivering the résumé to the person conducting the interview. Simply type "cover letter guidelines" into any search engine to find many suggestions and examples.

However, as a general guideline, your cover letter should be no more than one page long, follow a simple business letter format, and include three paragraphs. The first paragraph identifies the job in which you are interested and how you heard about the position. The second paragraph is what some call the "sell paragraph." Here you explain how your skills, experience, and background specifically relate to the company and its position. This paragraph should demonstrate that you have done your homework about the company and have a clear sense of how you can benefit the organization. The third paragraph should explain how you intend to follow up on the letter and should indicate that your résumé is enclosed. Like your résumé, the cover letter should be clean, correct, and concise. If you provide employers with a well-done cover letter and résumé, you will be well on your way to being contacted for a job interview.

Interviewing

Before arriving for your interview, you should have conducted thorough research on the company or firm. Know some of its history, its products or services, its various offices or plants, its economic health in the past few years, and its goals and objectives. You should also know something about its employee benefits and work issues like training, promotion, and performance expectations. Again, this information can be obtained from company websites, from staff members already employed there, or from library and specialized publications that report on the status of companies worldwide. Reference books like *Dun and Bradstreet's*, *Moody's*, or *Standard and Poor's* list virtually all businesses, their products, locations, and other valuable information. Doing the appropriate homework will help you understand the organization and how you can mesh with its missions and objectives. Furthermore, you will be well prepared to answer and pose questions during the interview process.

Types of Interviews

So, you know what employers expect, you have prepared a strong résumé, and you've researched your company. Now you're ready for the interview. But what type of interview? One type of interview is the **information-gathering interview**. For example, you may have done this type of interview when preparing a paper in one of your classes. Individuals doing survey research interview patrons in their local mall. Journalists do this type of interview when preparing for a story. In an information-gathering interview, you may have opportunities to meet professionals working in a job you might like to have someday and ask them questions. A key to effective information gathering is knowing the person you will interview and to prepare a set of specific questions in advance. Prepare open-ended questions that call for explanation rather than closed-ended questions that require simply yes or no or one-word answers. Also, prepare follow-up questions to make sure you get all the information you need, but be prepared to deviate from your list if important information surfaces during the interview. Visit www.quintcareers.com/information_interview.html for help with drafting suitable and useful questions for the information-gathering interview.

information-gathering interview an interview in which an individual speaks to professionals working in a job he or she might like to pursue

Remember that the person or persons you interview are taking valuable time from their work to speak with you. Be courteous, attentive, and sensitive to both their verbal and nonverbal communication, and be flexible so that you can respond to their needs during the interview. Show up on time, dress appropriately, and use the interviewees' time appropriately. Take good notes, listen attentively, express your thanks, and send a follow-up thank-you letter.

If you are ready for an **employment-selection interview**, then be prepared to sell yourself and your qualifications. This means that you must be able to explain, in

employment-selection interview an interview in which an individual sells him- or herself and his or her qualifications for a job

detail, how you can be an asset to the organization. The most common types of questions that will be asked focus on what you can bring to the job, how you have prepared for the job's responsibilities, and why the employer should hire you over other candidates. You will probably be asked to identify your strengths and weaknesses for the job as well as your goals for the next five years. Go to www .collegegrad.com/ezine/22toughi.shtml for help answering interview questions. Remember, the first five minutes of the interview are critical in establishing the impression that you are prepared and experienced and, thus, are the best candidates for the position.

How to Be Interviewed

The interviewer will also likely ask if you have any questions regarding the job and the company. Successful applicants respond to questions clearly, directly, and substantively, and they prepare questions that show they are truly interested in working for the company. Ask about the organization's working environment and culture, or inquire about a project that employees are working on. Refer to sources of information you reviewed in preparing for the interview such as the company's website or annual report. Be alert for verbal and nonverbal signals that communicate whether the interviewer is interested in continuing the interview or whether he or she is ready to end the discussion. When you think the interviewer is ready to end the interview, express appreciation for the interviewer's time and interest in your candidacy, shake his or her hand firmly, and tell the interviewer that you are truly interested in this position.

Successful applicants for a job in today's highly competitive market know themselves, express confidence, exhibit a high level of organization prior to and during an interview, and show enthusiasm and interest in the type of work they will be doing. Unsuccessful applicants fail to express themselves clearly, are unrealistic about the type of work they will be doing, are unclear about their future in the organization, or are focused on "selfish" issues like salary, benefits, or vacations.

Avoiding Common Mistakes in the Interview

Perhaps the most common mistake that interviewees make is having unrealistic expectations. These may center on the skills and knowledge the interviewee thinks he or she has, or salary expectations that do not fit the job. Unrealistic expectations also can be related to communication. You may expect an employer or fellow employees to communicate more than they do, or you may believe that your communication is "enough" for others, when they expect more of you. While you may take for granted that your communication style is effective, others may not. In order to avoid unrealistic expectations, engage in practice interviewing. You may be able to practice interviews at your campus Career Center or its equivalent. Practicing for interviews can mean the difference between successfully landing a job or continuing your job search.

Following Up the Interview

After you complete the interview, there are a few things you can and should do to follow up. A thank-you letter can increase the odds of an interviewer remembering you and keeping you high on his or her list of candidates. This also provides you with an opportunity to add any additional information requested by the interviewer. If anyone other than the interviewer was instrumental in helping to arrange the interview, such as a secretary or administrative assistant, send him or her a thank-you letter as well. It is also wise to contact your references if the interviewer has requested letters of recommendation or communicated that he or she will be in contact with them. There is not complete agreement on whether you should call the

Successful applicants in today's competitive job market know themselves and express confidence during an interview.

interviewer after several days to ask about the progress of your application. However, if the interviewer has given you a deadline for a decision with regard to your hire, and the deadline has passed, it is a good idea to call and ask whether your application was successful. This phone call also communicates your continued interest in the job.

Your success in interviewing for and obtaining a position and in working within an organization is dependent upon your experience, knowledge, expectations, abilities, and communication skills. We come to any organization as a person with knowledge and with a predisposition to act in certain ways; however, successful organizational communicators must learn to adapt knowledge and predispositions to the organization's goals and expectations. This means each member must balance individual skill and creativity with the organization's rules and structure. Organizations are most successful when they recognize and provide opportunities for individual creativity within their formal structure. The workforce of today and of tomorrow is increasingly diverse, and within this mix are employees with unique and valuable abilities, values, and communication styles. Valuing this diversity, and providing opportunities for communicating social inclusiveness, enhances the communication competency of individuals and the success of organizations. The box Campus Links: Should I Work While Attending College? can help you make effective decisions about working while you are in school.

 **Campus Links**

Should I Work While Attending College?

Ask yourself the following questions:

- What is your personal experience with working while in college?
- What valuable or helpful lessons have you learned from working while in college?
- What difficulties have you encountered while trying to hold a job and go to college?
- What would you tell an incoming student regarding working while attending college?

According to Orszag, Orszag, and Whitmore (2001), students today are more and more likely to work while in college. Since 1984, the fraction of college students aged sixteen to twenty-four who also work full or part time has increased from 49 to 57 percent. Not only are students more likely to work while attending college today, but they are also more likely to work full time. The share of students working full time while going to school full time has nearly doubled, rising from 5.6 percent in 1985 to 10.4 percent in 2000. They categorize working students into two groups: those who primarily identify themselves as students but who work in order to pay the bills, and those who are first and foremost workers who also take some college classes. Two-thirds of undergraduates who work consider themselves "students who work"; the other third consider themselves "workers who study." In their study, these researchers identify several positive and negative impacts that working

part or full time has on a student's educational experience.

Positive Impacts of Working Part Time

- Part-time student employment may have beneficial effects: for example, an on-campus research position may spark a student's interest in further academic programs or provide important work experience that will improve future labor market prospects.
- Working part time as a student generally appears to replace nonproductive activities, such as watching television and visiting with friends.
- Students who work fewer than ten hours per week have slightly higher GPAs than students who work more than ten hours per week

Negative Impact of Working Full Time

- Full-time employment may impair student performance. For example, 55 percent of those students working thirty-five or more hours per week report that work negatively affects their studies.
- Students working full time also reported the following liabilities: 40 percent report that work limits their class schedule; 36 percent report it reduces their class choices; 30 percent report it limits the number of classes they take; and 26 percent report it limits access to the library.

- Students who work full time are also more likely to drop out of school. For example, available research suggests that there is roughly a 10 percentage point differential in graduation rates between full-time and part-time workers.

In summary, it appears that working part time has positive impacts on student performance, while working a significant number of hours has adverse consequences. It is unclear at what point student employment moves from being beneficial to being counterproductive. Since full-time work appears to have negative effects on student enrollment rates and perhaps also on academic performance, it is, therefore, of particular concern that full-time work among full-time college students has risen sharply over the past fifteen years. For these students, the research suggests that, if possible, it may be prudent to find other ways of financing college so they can complete their degrees, maintain their academic performance levels, and, thereby, reap the long-term benefits of a college education (pp. 1, 2).

EFFECTIVE ORGANIZATIONAL COMMUNICATION IN COLLEGE

*U*p to this point, we have largely focused on organizational communication theory and its application in the work setting. However, organizational communication also directly relates to your higher education experience since, after all, your college or university is an organization. While there are numerous issues that we might consider, let's focus on how communication flows in a college or university and what this means for you as a student.

Increasingly, higher-learning institutions are facing lean economic times. Many states face budget crises, and state legislators are calling for greater accountability from colleges. Likewise, private institutions often face equally difficult economics because the overall economy impacts donations, endowments, and other revenue streams. As a result, many colleges, both public and private, have announced tuition hikes to help defray the burgeoning costs. However, you may not be aware that such intentions even exist unless you listen to the local news or read the school newspaper. The point is this: Many decisions that impact your college experience are made by boards or administrators, and you only learn about the policies after they are instituted. Consequently, although you may have insights or information you would like to add, you do not have the opportunity to voice your concerns. This is, obviously, a communication problem. But how do you solve it? First, you need to understand the flow of communication in your college or university. This means becoming acquainted with who, how, and when decisions are made and what opportunities, if any, you have to speak to decision makers directly or indirectly through student government representation or other intermediaries. In short, if you want to add your voice, you must understand organizational structure and the flow of communication within that structure.

This may be far removed from your everyday interests, so let's consider some additional situations. Let's assume you've seen your advisor and, to your knowledge, have registered for classes for the upcoming semester. However, at the semester's start, you realize you are not registered at all! Where do you go to address this problem? How can you effectively communicate your needs when you find the appropriate contact person? These and similar organizational communication issues are an all-too-real part of college life. To respond, you have to understand organizational structure and how to get help.

To take another example, as teachers, your authors have all had students arrive unexpectedly at our office doors in tears because they thought they were all set to graduate, only to discover that they lacked one course or credit hour. How could this distressing situation occur? How could a student think he or she is ready to graduate and not be? This is a real organizational communication problem that can and does have a disturbing impact on students' lives. However, you can save yourself these heartaches by learning how your college or university's organizational communication system operates and making it work for you. In the end, it's up to you to gather and process all the information necessary to complete your college education. This means you must learn to communicate in the organization of which you are now a part. Consider the information in the box Campus Links: Using Campus Services, which helps outline the organizational nature of colleges and universities. You will, however, need to educate yourself about your institution more specifically and implement the other communication skills you are learning in this textbook in order to navigate and succeed in your college environment.

 **Campus Links**

Using Campus Services

In essence, many colleges are truly mini-communities that offer students an array of services and opportunities. Find out what your school offers by browsing through its phone directory, scrolling through an online copy of the student handbook, or looking at your college or university website. While what you find may differ from one school to the next, many college support services can be found in offices categorized under the following headings: academic outreach; technology support; health, fitness, and safety concerns; personal matters; and financial assistance. Learning to use these organizational resources can enhance and simplify your college experience.

Academic Outreach

Academic outreach services focus on helping students perform well in the classroom or providing students with opportunities to enhance what they've learned in the classroom.

- *Academic advising* often involves interaction with faculty, staff, and peers working together to plan, select, and register for the appropriate courses leading toward one's choice of degree programs.
- *Career advising services* may help students determine what career or field is right for them. It may also provide declared majors with important advice about degree requirements or developments in students' chosen programs or fields of study.
- *Disability services* provides accommodations for students who are qualified under the Americans with Disabilities Act (ADA). Students who qualify for assistance may be provided with test readers, note-takers, recorded textbooks, and the like.
- *International affairs* offers support and assistance to international students attending the college as well as to American students planning to study abroad. This support may be academic (such as planning on-campus workshops on understanding American culture) or

social (as in putting on weekend trips to help students make friends and see local sights).

- *Job placement* may assist students in locating part- and full-time employment as well as internships or cooperative educational opportunities both during college and after graduation. Job placement may also host job fairs, résumé and interviewing workshops, and on-campus interviews.
- *Tutoring centers* provide students with one-on-one or small group tutoring in beginning and upper-division courses. Generally, schools offer tutoring in mathematics, English, foreign language, sciences, and other challenging courses.

Technology Support

While many campuses have on-site computer labs and support staff, much of the learning students do now is from remote locations via the Internet using their own home computers or laptops. As a result, it is important for students to know that technical support and instruction are available and how to access them.

- *Computer labs* are found on most campuses. They may be located in residence halls, classroom facilities, or learning centers. Normally, they have an on-site monitor and are available to all registered students.
- *Help desk* support is provided online or live (via phone) to students who need computer help or online course assistance. As more and more campuses implement technology in the learning environment, an increasing number of students may need to use help desk services.
- *Library or instructional media center* offers students facilities for study or research. Librarians and media specialists are trained to help students at any point in the research process and are familiar with the latest search engines.

Health, Fitness, and Safety Concerns

Like most small communities, colleges also have services to meet the health, fitness, and safety needs of their residents, whether they live on campus or commute.

- *Health center* offers students the services of physicians or nurse practitioners as well as registered or licensed nurses. Health centers may have pharmacists or lab technicians too. While on campus, many students make the school's health center their primary source of health care.

- *Intramural sports* are offered at most campuses to provide students with good exercise and offer them a chance to build friendships with others. Intramural team sports are open to all students interested in some friendly competition and normally are offered at several times throughout the day.

- *Physical education center* or fitness centers offer students workout and training facilities. Many campuses have weight rooms, aerobic equipment, and sports injury or nutrition workshops.

- *University police* protect members of the campus community and enforce the laws and regulations to provide a safe living and learning environment. Campus security officers may also work together with local and regional law enforcement professionals on cases of mutual concern.

Personal Matters

Members of any community, including a campus community, have personal matters that need to be attended to. Many students today are raising children or caring for aging parents, working part or full time while going to school, or struggling with personal or family issues. Because life goes on while students are getting their education, many schools respond with services and opportunities that can positively impact students' lives both inside and outside of the classroom.

- *Campus ministries* offer students an array of denominations and services to meet their spiritual and religious needs. Some campuses have religious organizations on campus while others cooperate with local or regional churches and provide transportation to off-site services.

- *Child care centers* are found on many college campuses today. Indeed, an increasing number of students with young children are returning to college or starting school for the first time. As a result, many campuses provide on-site child care or offer information about other child care providers or preschool facilities in the community.

- *Counseling centers* offer counseling and psychological services that help facilitate students' personal development and enable them to be active members in the campus community. Many schools have psychologists and counselors or staff who provide therapy and workshops for students.

- *Dean of students* is, at most schools, the "one-stop shop" where trained professionals can answer students' questions, respond to students' concerns, or address students' problems. The dean of students office at most campuses has information on all campus services and programs available to students.

- *Residence Life* is responsible for creating a living and learning environment for students staying on campus in residence halls and campus apartments. Residence Life strives to create a positive social and physical climate to foster students' development.

- *Multicultural student centers* provide services and programs to facilitate the personal development, academic success, and retention of underrepresented minority students. In addition to its role in supporting individual students, Multicultural Student Affairs provides educational programming for the campus community to promote cultural diversity and awareness.

- *Student organizations* offer students opportunities to meet others, build skills, network with mentors, or relax with friends. Students may find opportunities with student government, academic clubs and honor societies, Greek fraternities and sororities, media organizations (radio, TV, newspaper, or website), community service clubs, and an array of special-interest groups.

Financial Assistance

Skyrocketing college costs are making it increasingly difficult to pay for an education. Consequently, colleges and universities have professionals on staff to help students find ways to meet the short-term financial challenges of college so they may reap the long-term benefits of their educational investments. Financial aid offices help qualified students identify means of financial support such as grants and scholarships; part-time, on-campus employment; low-interest loans; or special funding sources (i.e., Veterans Administration benefits, BIA tribal grants, or ROTC scholarships for students planning to serve in the military). Normally, students' eligibility for financial assistance is determined when students file a FAFSA, or a Free Application for Federal Student Aid application.

SUMMARY

In the world of work today, structures are changing, organizational decision making is changing, and requirements for employee effectiveness are also changing. As a college student, you need to understand how to negotiate the organizational environment of your institution. More importantly, once you begin your career in the working world, understanding how to develop and maintain effective organizational relationships is vital to your work success. In this chapter, we have identified some essential elements of effective communication in organizational settings:

- "The new knowledge worker" today must possess four key characteristics: college education; analytical thinking; commitment to lifelong learning; and good communication skills.
- Organizations operate as distinct cultures. A culture represents the actions, practices, language, and artifacts of a group.
- A number of symbolic practices make up culture, including language, stories, rites and rituals, and structure.
- The characteristics of organizational systems include wholeness, interdependence, adaptability, and equifinality.
- Effective organizational communication is dependent upon the appropriate use of networks and channels of communication within the organization.
- You are entering an era where the cultural, racial, and gender diversity in organizations has never been so significant.

- Effective and ethical organizations establish cultures of equal opportunity, free of prohibited discriminatory actions.
- While face-to-face communication is still important in today's organization, technological advances have made communication faster, made access to and processing of information much easier, and made communication with others across geographical distances much more accessible.
- The job search process includes steps before, during, and after an interview.
- Organizational communication is important to successfully navigating the college environment.

Questions for Discussion

1. What are the elements of organizational cultures?
2. What are the components of an organizational system?
3. What communication behaviors will best allow you to adapt to the diversity of the modern workplace?
4. What are the essential elements of a good résumé?
5. What must you do to effectively prepare for a job interview?
6. What questions should you be prepared for in the interview?
7. What should you do to follow up after the interview?

EXERCISES

1. Draw a floor plan for your "ideal office." Analyze the symbolic communication in that floor plan. What are you communicating to others about yourself?
2. Interview an individual working in the profession you have chosen. Ask questions about the culture in his or her organization. Ask the individual to list what he or she believes are the most effective organizational communication behaviors.
3. Develop a list of ethical principles and practices for communication in organizations. Under what circum-

stances would you say no to a manager or supervisor who asked you to violate your ethical values and beliefs in accomplishing some project? Under what circumstances would you "blow the whistle" on someone in your organization who violated the law?
4. Develop a list of employee and employer "rights" on the job. What limits should be placed on the rights of employers to monitor employee behavior on the job? Off the job?

KEY TERMS

Organizational culture
Language
Stories and myths
Rites and rituals
Roles
Rules and policies
Environment

Wholeness
Interdependent
Synergy
Openness
Adaptability
Equifinality
Formal networks

Informal networks
Motivation
Sexual harassment
Information-gathering interview
Employment-selection interview

⊚ REFERENCES

Autry, J. A. 2001. *The servant leader: How to build a creative team, develop great morale, and improve bottom-line performance.* Roseville, CA: Prima Publishing.

Berger, C. R., and Calabrese, R. J. 1975. Some explorations in initial interaction and beyond: Toward a developmental theory of interpersonal communication. *Human Communication Theory* 1:99–112.

Dillard, J., and Miller, K. 1988. Intimate relationships in task environments. In *Handbook of personal relationships,* ed., S. Duck, 449–465. New York: John Wiley & Sons.

Drucker, P. 1992. *Managing for the future: The 1990's and beyond.* New York: Truman Talley Books/Dutton.

Eisenberg, E. M., and Goodall, Jr., H. L. 1997. *Organizational communication: Balancing creativity and constraint.* 2nd ed. New York: St. Martin's Press.

Ganga, E., and Lerner, J. 2004, March 28. Working at home. *The Journal News.* Retrieved April 16, 2004, from www.thejournalnews.com/newsroom/032804/k1928wfworkingathom.html.

Katz, D., and Kahn, R. 1966. *The social psychology of organizations.* New York: John Wiley & Sons.

Kreps, G. 1991. *Organizational communication: Theory and practice.* 2nd ed. New York: Longman.

Orszag, J. M., Orszag, P. R., and Whitmore, D. M. 2001. *Learning and earning: Working in college.* Retrieved April 16, 2004, from www.sbgo.com/Papers/Final%20Student%20Workers%20Paper.pdf.

Radtke, J. M. 1998. *Strategic communication for non-profit organizations: Seven steps to creating a successful plan.* Hoboken, NJ: John Wiley & Sons. Retrieved April 13, 2004, from www.tgci.com/magazine/98fall/mission.asp.

Riley, P., and Eisenberg, E. 1991. The ACE model of management. Unpublished working papers. University of Southern California.

Schutz, W. C. 1958. *FIRO: A three dimensional theory of interpersonal behavior.* New York: Holt, Rinehart, & Winston.

Seeger, M. W. 1997. *Ethics and organizational communication.* Cresskill, NJ: Hampton Press.

Shockley-Zalabak, P. 1999. *Fundamentals of organizational communication.* 4th ed. New York: Longman.

CHAPTER 14

Technology and Mass Communication

Definition of Mediated Mass Communication

Characteristics

Convergence
Watchdog Function
Regulation
Ownership
Audience
Feedback
Messages

Effects

On Culture

Social Construction / Cultural Theories
Critical Theories
Cultural Importance

On Individual

Gatekeeping / Bias
Uses and Gratification
Agenda Setting
Attitude Shaping
Behavioral Influences

Being Critically Conscious

Requires Critical Analysis

Message
Channel
Senders
Receivers
Context
Noise
Feedback

Knowledge Checklist

✓ To explain how the mass communication model is similar to and distinct from the basic communication model

✓ To define mass communication and mediated communication

✓ To understand how mass communication shapes culture

✓ To understand how mass communication affects individuals

✓ To become a more critical consumer of mass communication

DEFINITION AND CHARACTERISTICS OF MEDIATED MASS COMMUNICATION

Think over the past week. How many times did you have the radio or television on? Did you watch cable TV? How often did you access your e-mail, enter a chat room, or use instant messaging (IM)? How often did you go on the Net to play games, gather information, or shop? Did you use a DSL ISP (Internet service provider) or dial-up? Did you listen to a CD? How many billboards have you passed while driving? Have you read a magazine, novel, or other reading material? When did you last see a film in a theater or rent a video?

These questions make sense to you, even though they have quite a bit of jargon. The fact that you understand this specialized language indicates the pervasiveness of mass communication in our culture, to say nothing of our frequent use of it.

This pervasiveness of mediated communication in our culture and throughout the world provides us opportunities to see, hear, think, and do things that people prior to the 1950s never dreamed of. We can "travel" to far away places through the Internet or the Discovery Channel. We can "chat" with people from every corner of the globe with a click of a mouse or the touch of a button. The media at our disposal provide opportunities to expand our knowledge and understanding of the world faster and more comprehensively than ever before. Understanding the unique characteristics of mass communication helps us reflect upon its impact on our lives and learn about its influence so that we can be more astute consumers and users of these media. Read the box Computer and Communication Links: Are You Computer Savvy? and see how prepared you are for the technology you will use in your career.

Computer and Communication Links

Are You Computer Savvy?

Effective communication using computer technology is now a requirement for completing your education and launching your career. While you may interview well, deliver successful presentations, or work well in teams, you must also add computer literacy to your communication repertoire. Consider the following excerpt from *Educating the 21st Century Citizen*, a white paper published with the Education Solutions Group at the Microsoft Corporation:

Lacking 21st century skills, individuals are hampered trying to access online employment offerings or submit a job application online, reducing their employment options. They may miss the cost savings of Internet purchasing and banking online, putting more of their income into services than into sustenance or savings. They may be unaware of the convenience of filing their income tax digitally and checking their credit rating online, reducing access to a timely refund or the ability to preserve their purchasing profile. They may also miss the opportunity to access online learning after hours to attain further education, limiting their ability to advance in their job because of their work schedule. Without appropriate education, citizens lack knowledge and skills to use the tools of our time, and as a consequence suffer by exclusion. (Retrieved July 10, 2006, from www.microsoft.com/Education/MSITAcademy/ ITAPCCTI.mspx)

But it's not just access to technology that is important in creating a digitally inclusive world. Of even greater importance is acquisition of "digital literacy"— the knowledge and skills necessary to use these technologies and the ability to adapt to the rapid pace of their change, which is the hallmark of their ongoing development. The understanding of how technologies work, now and in the future, provides opportunities to succeed in the workplace and participate in society.

Many colleges and universities now require students to master "information technology literacy" as a part of their general education or graduation requirements. For example, here is a list of "literacy" components from Indiana State University's IT literacy requirement:

General Computing Concepts

Internet Concepts

Word-Processing Concepts

Presentation Concepts

Spreadsheet Concepts

Database Concepts

How would you rate your literacy in each of these areas? Possessing and using these basic skills is an essential element in your communication profile in a technologically sophisticated era.

Mediated Mass Communication Defined

Folkerts and Lacy (2001) distinguish between a mass medium, mass communication, and mediated communication. A **mass medium** refers to a channel that carries a message to many receivers. **Mass communication** refers to sharing information with a large audience either at a given time or across an extended time frame. An institution, such as the news media or other organization, distributes the information. Newspapers, magazines, books, film, television, radio, recordings, and the like are all channels for mass communication. The Internet, direct-mail advertising, and telemarketing are considered by some scholars to be mass communication as well, but there is some argument over this. **Mediated communication**, according to Folkerts and Lacy, requires a technological channel to complete the communication process; "Individuals may share messages using an intermediate device or mechanism, perhaps to overcome distances or obstacles or to reach a large number of other individuals" (p. 26). Therefore, when we speak of mediated mass communication, we are usually focusing on communication that relies on technology but that can also reach one or more people at the same time. E-mail, cable TV, cell phones, DVDs, and more conventional forms of mass communication such as newspapers, radio, and printed books fit within this broad definition.

mass medium a channel that carries a message to many receivers

mass communication sharing information with a large audience at a given time or across an extended time frame

mediated communication communication that requires a technological channel to complete the communication process

Characteristics of Mediated Mass Communication

What follows are the seven primary characteristics of mediated mass communication: media convergence, watchdog function, regulation, ownership, audience, feedback, and messages.

In today's world, we take technology for granted.

Media Convergence

According to Folkerts and Lacy (2001), in every generation, there are old media and new media. "Today, we use the term **new media** to refer to media forms and media content that are created and shaped by changes in technology. Therefore, the Internet became one of the new media of the twentieth century. However, the term *new media* also is used to refer to changes in content. For example, news as presented on MTV is a new form of media content. As new media evolve, old ones change forms" (p. 5). As new technology replaces old, media forms and technologies come together; this is known as **media convergence**. Now, for example, we can access major newspapers online or read an e-book. While you may still use media in the old form (i.e., reading the *Chicago Tribune* in its paper form), you are more likely to use media in a new form (i.e., downloading travel directions from Tampa, Florida, to St. Louis, Missouri, from MapQuest). *Convergence* simply means "coming together," and when applied to mass media, it refers to blending technology and content in new and unique ways.

For anyone under the age of thirty, the world has always had the Internet, satellite television, cable access, conference calling, cell phones, and an array of technology that those who are a little older may still try to navigate. The bottom line is that we take our technology for granted. We want information immediately; we want entertainment at the touch of a button. For children today, the impact on their lives is even more significant, as we discuss in the box Cultural Links: Children's Access to Computers and the Internet.

new media media forms and content that are created and shaped by changes in technology

media convergence media forms and technologies coming together as new technology replaces old

◎ Cultural Links

Children's Access to Computers and the Internet

While the Internet is pervasive and available in our society, not all ethnic/cultural groups have equal access to this technology. Consider the following informational facts from the 2000 Census (www.census.gov):

Access

- More children have access to a computer or use the Internet at home than ever before.

- Nearly two-thirds (65 percent) of all children three to seventeen years lived in a household with a computer in 2000, up from 55 percent in 1998.
- Thirty percent of all children used the Internet at home in 2000, compared with just 19 percent in 1998.

Internet Use

- Although girls were as likely as boys to use the Internet at home, children's Internet use varied with age.
- Only 7 percent of the youngest children, those three to five years, used the Internet at home.
- Among children six to eleven years, 25 percent used the Internet at home, and 48 percent, nearly half, of children twelve to seventeen years used the Internet at home.

Racial Differences

- White non-Hispanic children are more likely to have home computer access or use the Internet than are black or Hispanic children.
- Among children three to seventeen years, 77 percent of white non-Hispanics and 72 percent of Asians and Pacific Islanders lived in households with computers, while only 43 percent of black children and 37 percent of Hispanic children did so.
- While 38 percent of white non-Hispanic children and 35 percent of Asian and Pacific Islander children used the Internet at home, just 15 percent of black children and 13 percent of Hispanic children did.

What are the implications of the inequality of access/use among different ethnic and cultural groups in the United States? What does this information suggest about privilege, ethnicity, and class in the United States? In what ways, if any, does this difference matter to cultural harmony?

Computer Use at School and at Home

- School is a major influence on children's access to computers. More school-age children use computers at school than have access to them at home.
- Nine out of ten school-age children had access to a computer somewhere, however.
- Ten percent of children had no access to a computer in any locale.
- The net result of the effect schools have in giving computer access across income, racial, and ethnic groups is a leveling of the computer access that children of different groups have compared to what they would have had if home were the only place available for them to use computers.

Does the fact that students have access to computers at school mean that equality of access has occurred? Can you identify a place in your community, other than schools, where children would be able to use computers or the Internet?

Watchdog Function   The "watchdog" function of media refers to the responsibility of the press to act as guardians of the public interest. The press are sometimes referred to as the fourth branch of government because they are responsible for guarding citizens' rights to have access to information and activity that impacts their lives. The press, therefore, constantly report about government activities, the lives of "important" persons, and the activities of business: each of these provides newsworthy information to the public so that we can make informed decisions about our lives.

Regulation   Like other types of communication, mass communication involves senders, receivers, messages, channels, noise, context, and feedback. Unlike the senders in other types of communication, senders of mass communication, with the exception of communication on the Internet or political speech, are highly regulated. This **regulation** covers content both prior to and after distribution. For example, the Federal Trade Commission (FTC) regulates commercial advertising. The FTC enforces regulation that controls what may be communicated about a commercial product or service in order to protect consumers from false claims that are misleading. Regulation also controls messages deemed obscene or indecent, limits access to crime scenes or courtrooms during trials involving juveniles, and protects owners of copyrighted works from use without their permission. While this second characteristic is paralleled by legal constraints on speech, as is seen, for instance, in libel or slander, the degree of regulation in mass mediated communication is much higher and even more codified or restricted.

regulation controls over content prior to and after its distribution

Ownership   Another distinction between the mass communication process and communication in other contexts is ownership and how it impacts the content and form of mass or mediated communication. Mass communication is big business. Because of the competition for viewers, readers, and consumers, smaller companies are being swallowed up by larger media conglomerates; consequently, the ownership of many traditional media is concentrated in the hands of very few owners. Today, media conglomerates dominate. Conglomerates are collections of businesses under one ownership, such as those involving newspapers, radio stations, television stations, cable companies, filmmaking companies, and magazine publishers. In 1993, for example, fewer than twenty corporations had majority control of the newspaper, magazine, TV, book, and movie industries (Cohen & Solomon 1993, p. A11). Today, the numbers are significantly smaller. Consider, for example, a conglomerate such as TimeWarner, which owns a cable TV business and an Internet service provider (AOL) while also playing a major role in the movie and print industries. Because such conglomerates are expected to produce huge profits, some critics of this concentrated ownership suggest that we now have a potential threat of a monopoly on information "by self-interested outside corporations that have no commitment to the journalistic imperative and spirit" (Day 2003, p. 247). This profit-motive ownership worries critics because the economic incentive to make high profits for stockholders may override an incentive to monitor government activities and provide comprehensive information to the public. Media conglomerates may be inclined to shirk their "watchdog" commitments to free press in favor of more lucrative financial ventures.

Audience   The nature of the audience constitutes yet another characteristic of mass mediated communication. The audience for a mass or mediated channel can be larger, heterogeneous, diverse, and geographically separated, or it can be highly specialized, homogeneous, and geographically close. So, for example, people from across the country can attend a professional workshop by dialing a toll-free telephone number while also logging on to a protected website. By blending these two channels, participants can share in a conference call where they can offer observations and ask questions while viewing video clips or PowerPoint® slides on their computer screens. Mass and mediated communication, therefore, allow opportunities to send messages to an almost unlimited potential audience.

On the other hand, new technology allows companies and other senders the opportunity to pinpoint targeted audiences through, for example, direct mail or e-mail advertising. Have you ever wondered how you got on a mailing list for information about a group, activity, or product you didn't want? Any time you make a purchase or inquire about a product or service, your name is sold to one group by another group or by one company to another company. In other words, you are a targeted consumer. At the same time, when you subscribe to a free e-mail service or register a product you purchased online, you are probably asked to answer questions

Technology and Job Hunting

Technology has made searching for a job considerably easier than in the past. There are many sites such as monster.com, yahoo.com, and careerbuilder.com that provide job-posting and searching services. Additionally, there are a growing number of online sites dedicated to finding jobs in particular fields of employment, geographic locations, or particular companies or organizations. However, using these electronic tools requires some insight, knowledge, and awareness of communication. Here are some websites that you may find useful in starting your electronic job hunt:

- www.rileyguide.com/jobsrch.html: This site explains how to use the Internet to search for a job.
- www.quintcareers.com/maximizing_net_job_search.html: This site offers specific strategies for job searching using Internet sources and provides free articles discussing a variety of issues related to electronic job hunts.

- www.collegegrad.com/forum/internet.shtml: This site specializes in helping recent college graduates find jobs by answering specific questions and offering advice.
- www.jobhuntersbible.com/intro/intro.shtml: This site offers advice and assistance in finding a job using the Internet.
- www.mnwfc.org: This site offers Internet job-search strategies sponsored by the Minnesota Workforce Center. This is but one example of state-sponsored job-search sites. If you are interested in a specific geographic area, you can easily limit your search by focusing on such areas either in the search terms you select or in using the search engines at job search sites.

about you and your preferences. This information helps marketers send you messages that will more likely interest you. Of course, you can also use search engines or other information-gathering services to find products, people, or services you are interested in. In this instance, you help marketers, companies, or others find you. Technology enhances your access not just to products and services, but also to potential employers, as we discuss in the box Career Links: Technology and Job Hunting.

Feedback   Perhaps the biggest difference between mass communication and, for example, interpersonal communication, involves feedback. In some mass communication channels, feedback is often delayed or nonexistent. For instance, one of your author's grandmothers used to talk back to the TV as though the sender of the message could hear her complaints or praise. Perhaps you, too, plead with your computer, attempting to coax it into doing your bidding. While this monologue may relieve some immediate tension, you know that the computer will not respond to your verbal coaxing. On the other hand, some new technology offers us opportunities to provide feedback that were nonexistent even a decade ago. For example, you can engage in mediated conversation through IM or chat rooms. Additionally, you can use your computer to make toll-free long-distance calls around the world and speak into a microphone or use a Web cam to interact with your caller. Do you have or know someone who has a Palm Pilot? With this device, you can check e-mail, send messages, surf the Net, buy and sell stock, give your opinion of a political candidate's speech all in the palm of your hand. In another example, we have colleagues who use Palm Pilots to share syllabi, assignments, and other information with their students. So, the first day of class, students don't get a printed syllabus but are beamed the syllabus by the instructors using their Palm Pilots.

Messages   In contrast to the large, commercial conglomerates that control vast information, many websites are developed by individuals or groups with no economic pressures or constraints. This opens the door to a vast array of information and messages. This can be helpful (easier access to information about health and illness) or hurtful (websites devoted to white supremacy and hate). You can learn about products and services you didn't even know you wanted. You can find out about people, cultures, activities, history, and things you didn't know. Access to information is virtually unlimited and almost instantaneous. The media and new technologies provide us instant news. You no longer have to wait for traditional journalists to provide you with the news; today, anyone with a camera or access to the Internet can be a reporter, a filmmaker, an actor, a weather announcer, or a trendsetter. Ready accessibility, then, also distinguishes and characterizes mass mediated communication.

EFFECTS OF MASS COMMUNICATION

The pervasiveness and speed with which we have access to our world means that mass and mediated communication shape and define our culture more significantly than ever before in history. In particular, the developing world now has access to the developed world more than ever. Those of us in the developed world also have greater knowledge of the poverty, disaster, and misery of less fortunate individuals around the world. In addition to understanding the strife and suffering in our world, mass and mediated communication give us access to the richness and cultural diversity of the world. This increased access to information causes many to ask what, ultimately, is the impact of media and mass communication on individuals and culture? And in particular, to other cultures across the world? In the box Communication and Cultural Links: Cultural Imperialism we discuss one potential negative impact of increased access to information.

Communication and Cultural Links

Cultural Imperialism

Cultural imperialism is defined as one nation's practice of promoting the culture or language of another—usually a smaller, less affluent nation adopting the practices of a large, economically or militarily powerful nation. Cultural imperialism can take the form of an active, formal policy or a general attitude (Wikipedia 2005). While cultural imperialism is often accomplished through war or other military activity, some critics argue that it can also occur through the mass media. For example, if you travel the world, you will notice that American television is accessible virtually everywhere by satellite. Individuals and governments around the globe have expressed concern regarding the influence of Western cultural products on other local and national cultures, and this concern has become a topic of debate in not only scholarly circles, but also in economic, legal, and legislative arenas.

The pervasiveness of the Internet in particular causes concern. Cultural imperialism can occur when there is an imbalance of information from various sources. For example, if individuals living in underdeveloped countries have access to Western media but not media disseminated by their own country, they are often more influenced by Western lifestyles and consumerism and may lose touch with their own culture.

Do you believe that mass media present a culturally diverse picture of the United States? Of the world? What do you believe are the responsibilities of media in terms of cultural representation?

What responsibility do you have as an individual to seek out and understand cultural diversity?

Media Affects Cultures

Researchers have been trying to answer this question since mass mediated communication became commonplace. Several mass media researchers believe that the pervasiveness of mass communication significantly impacts the development of culture, which is constantly changing.

Social Construction/Cultivation Theories

The **social construction** (or **cultivation**) **theory** of mass communication suggests that what the media shows us is one of the most important elements of our construction and interpretation of our culture. We use mass media as our primary source of information about the world, thus giving it greater power. This information helps us "construct" our perceptions of the world, of appropriate and inappropriate behavior, of who and what we should be. According to media researcher and developer of cultivation theory George Gerbner (1973; 1976) and his colleagues, heavy television viewing influences the values, roles, and worldview that people adopt. For example, if individuals watch a great deal of violence on TV, they believe the world is cruel and scary. Gerbner and his colleagues also suggest that television, especially television violence, impacts children more significantly than adults. Because television is primarily focused on telling stories, "television cultivates from infancy the very predispositions and preferences that used to be acquired from other primary sources" (Gerbner 1976, p. 17) such as children's books, nursery rhymes, and childhood songs and games.

> **social construction (or cultivation) theory** suggests that what the media portrays is one of the most important elements of the construction and interpretation of our culture

For example, after 9/11, President Bush urged the American people not to draw inaccurate conclusions about Muslims living in the United States. The images of the Twin Towers bursting into flame, along with the indictment of al-Qaeda as the perpetrator, created the potential for U.S. citizens to draw unwarranted conclusions about all Muslims or the religion of Islam. In short, media images shape the way we think about our world. This, in turn, creates cultural stereotypes that have the power to influence our perceptions and, subsequently, the tones and tensions in our communities.

Critical Theories

Critical theorists who emerged in the 1920s suggested that the economic structure of a society determines its social structure. They believed that media, primarily mainstream media, portray only those individuals, values, ideas, and interpretations that support the interests and beliefs of the power elite in this country. The elite represent a predominantly male, white perspective. The messages generated by these people are thus hegemonic, or focused on keeping the powerless silent. Communication professor Julia Wood (1994) suggests that one of the ways the media perpetuates this hegemony is by sheer numbers. For example, in the world portrayed on television, white males make up two-thirds of the population; women over the age of thirty-five represent less than 10 percent of the population. However, the portrayal of stereotypical views of our culture are shifting; we now see a much greater diversity of individuals portrayed in television, film, and advertising. People of color, gays and lesbians, and individuals with disabilities are seen with much greater frequency than even ten years ago. But the sheer numbers still do not portray the reality of our multicultural world. In addition to having a powerful effect on culture, media exert profound effects on individuals as well.

Cultural Imperialism

Scholars also note that cultural, media, and technological imperialism (Martin & Nakayama 2001) all play a definitive role in shaping and perpetuating culture. Specifically, Western popular culture, such as music and movies, are circulated worldwide and cause the profit margins of Hollywood filmmakers to soar (Guback 1969). But how does this cultural and economic domination impact the cultures that import Western media? While some cultures invite this influence, others, such as the French Canadians, are concerned that their cultural uniqueness will be eclipsed or subordinated by Western cultural norms, beliefs, and values. As one travels the globe, the influence of Western media is obvious. For example, in Europe there are advertisements for films made in the United States and

Television influences the values, roles, and worldviews individuals adopt.

stores selling various U.S. newspapers, magazines, CDs, DVDs, and videos. Western media, due to its economic power, tends to dominate the globe and, therefore, raises important questions about cultural, media imperialism.

These theoretical perspectives imply that mass and mediated communication may have a powerful influence on the development and evolution of cultures. Yet most scholars suggest that other factors are involved in the mass communication processes that mediate these powerful effects.

Media Affects Individuals

Not only does mediated mass communication affect culture, but it also impacts individuals. In this section, we will consider its uses and gratifications, gatekeeping/media bias, agenda-setting, attitude-shaping, and behavioral influences.

uses and gratifications theory argues that we turn to media to fulfill preexisting needs

Uses and Gratifications   Some researchers suggest a more microscopic approach to understanding the effects of media. The **uses and gratifications theory** argues that we turn to the media to fulfill preexisting needs. We identify a specific medium, film, television show, or CD that provides us a diversion, an emotional release, a fantasy, or a substitute companion. We turn to a specific medium for value reinforcement, sage advice, or unmet needs or expectations.

gatekeeping the process of determining what is newsworthy and important enough to reach an audience

Gatekeeping/Media Bias   **Gatekeeping** refers to the process of determining what is newsworthy and important enough to reach an audience. Some researchers believe this gatekeeping function of the media is its greatest power. Decisions are made every day by newspaper editors and radio or TV station managers about what stories should be covered and in what depth. Are stories about shootings by teenagers more likely to receive news coverage if they occur in a primarily white suburb than if they occur in the inner city? Are reporters more likely to cover fighting in a country that the United States has an economic relationship with as opposed to nations where our interests are purely humanitarian?

Further, decisions are made about where those stories should appear in the newspaper or during the newscast. Should they be on the front page or be buried in a short paragraph next to the obituaries? Should the story run in the first five minutes of the newscast with other breaking news, or should it air at the end of the newscast with the rest of the human-interest stories? The media's gatekeeping impacts the information we receive and, as a result, the interpretation or importance we ascribe to a person, place, or event.

Effects of Mass Communication 315

The gatekeeping phenomenon is considered to be the place where media bias begins. Conservative media critics argue that the media have a liberal bias in their coverage of individuals, events, and issues. Liberal media critics argue that because the concentration of media ownership is primarily in the hands of conservatives, media content and coverage reflect more conservative values. Researchers on both sides of this issue have discovered biased coverage. While debate continues over whether the media are too liberal or too conservative in their coverage, during recent political election campaigns, the media coverage of both the Democrats and the Republicans was negative. Whether systematic bias exists, there seems to be negativity toward politicians. Media coverage, especially television, tends to focus on the sensational, the unique, and the extraordinary instead of on the trials and tribulations of everyday life.

Agenda Setting Individuals who decide what should or should not be reported have enormous control, then, over what we deem to be important in the world. In this way, the **agenda of news** and information is set for us. Our political agenda is set by more coverage of certain candidates or issues than others. Agendas vary between different media. Newspapers often have more time to cover an issue, an event, or a person in more depth than radio or television. Television, more than any other medium, tends to provide us information in sound bites.

agenda of news the ability of media decision makers to influence what media consumers think is important in the world

Attitude Shaping The media's power is even more subtle in the way our attitudes become synchronous with those represented by the media we choose to follow. The media's power to construct culture impacts individual interpretations of that culture. We learn new vocabulary and expand our language through media. We also learn what is considered "normal" in terms of height, weight, shape, hairstyles, skin color, dress, or hobbies. If you look at women's fashion magazines, for example, apparently a size zero is what all women should be aiming for. Or, perhaps, given media images, men are told that they must be tall, dark, muscular, and handsome. For those who do not embody these media-manipulated images, we are constantly comparing ourselves to these norms and finding ourselves falling short of what is expected. The media impacts our self-esteem if we can never live up to the images portrayed as normal and desirable. Television, magazines, or movies become the yardstick by which we measure ourselves. Because we are surrounded every day by what we ought to be, to know, and to believe, our values become *framed* by these expectations. Therefore, media directly shapes our attitudes and expectations about ourselves and others.

The media's power to construct culture impacts individual interpretations of that culture.

Community Links

Mediated Violence

Consider the following scenario: Alicia had been given an assignment to identify an issue or problem in contemporary society. She was to write an essay that summarizes different points of view and that argued for a "solution" to the problem. This past weekend she and some friends rented the movie *Scream*. She is not a fan of violent movies, and after watching *Scream*, found it was excessively violent.

The next day, Alicia looked into the issue of violence in films and its impact on children. As she researched the impact of film violence, she uncovered multiple sides to this issue. On one side are those who believe that censorship of any kind is a violation of the First Amendment. On the other hand, there are legislators who have tried, unsuccessfully, to pass legislation banning excessive violence in film. She has located numerous lawsuits filed by parents alleging that filmmakers and other media owners are guilty of negligence in airing films and television shows. They claim that many of their children copied what they had seen in the media and then committed acts of violence. In most cases, the lawsuits failed to find the media responsible for the violence.

Alicia also located an article that reported on the 1976 Screen Actors Guild antiviolence resolution, which read in part, "While various studies do not lead to absolute conclusions, there is reasonable cause to believe that imitation of violent acts seen on television is a potential danger and examples of this phenomenon are well documented."

"They made this resolution in 1976," Alicia said to her friend Faith, "but it seems to me that since that time, portrayals of violence in television and film have increased dramatically and so have incidents of violent acts committed by kids after watching these shows! Could the television shows and films really be responsible for this violence?"

What role do you believe the media plays, through the portrayal of violence, in the cycle of violence in our society? In your community, have you seen people imitating violence from TV, film, and so on? What other factors play a significant role in this cycle of violence?

Behavioral Influences Once our values are shaped or framed by the expectations we see, our behavior begins to conform to the expectations as well. We begin to make *social comparisons* to the individuals portrayed by the media. We then "model" their behavior or make a commitment *not* to behave certain ways. Perhaps, for example, some of us watch talk shows like *Dr. Phil, Montel Williams,* or *Oprah* in order to compare ourselves to the guests and say, "I'm *not* them!" We join a gym or try one diet after another because we look at a magazine and say, "Why can't *I* be like them?" At the extreme, some individuals, both adults and children, go so far as to copy the behavior they see in the media. This often leads to violence and tragedy. Thus, mass media consumption influences our behavior, sometimes with very negative consequences. One such potential consequence we discuss in the box Community Links: Mediated Violence.

Passivity or *desensitization* to the violence that we see in the media also impacts our behavior. Gerbner studied this phenomenon for more than forty years and demonstrated that desensitivity to violence is one of the most pervasive and powerful behavioral consequences of significant media exposure. The more desensitized we become to violence, the more violence we need to be entertained, as suggested by the burgeoning amount of violence seen on TV. For example, the Parents

Television Council released a final study that looked at the trend of violence on primetime television since 1998. During the first hour of prime time (8:00–9:00 P.M.), violence increased by 41 percent. Violence was up 134 percent during the second hour of prime time (9:00–10:00 P.M.) and 63 percent during the third hour of prime time (10:00–11:00 P.M.; www.parentstv.org/).

In addition to desensitization and passivity, some critics of mediated violence suggest that viewing too much violence encourages individuals to model what they see. Television and film portray an enormous amount of violence. According to the American Psychological Association (APA), by the age of eighteen, children and teens will have seen 16,000 simulated murders and 200,000 acts of violence (www.healthyminds.org/mediaviolence.cfm). The APA has also reported that children and adults who watch a lot of televised violence are more likely to act violently in their everyday lives. These findings remain consistent regardless of level of education, social class, attitudes toward aggression, parental behavior, and sex-role identity.

While this discussion of the media's power is limited, it suggests that we all need to be critical consumers of media. We now turn to some principles to help you become such a consumer.

BEING A CRITICAL CONSUMER OF MEDIA

As we have just discussed, there are many important issues that impact what, when, and how mass communicators report (as news gatherers) or portray (as filmmakers). Once you recognize these issues, you need to develop a set of critical analytical skills that will assist you in becoming more competent in your "consumption" of mass communication. Our discussion of the appropriate skills required to become a competent consumer will focus on each of the critical elements of the mass communication model: messages, channels, senders, receivers, context, feedback, and noise.

Critical Analysis of the Message

One of the skills needed is the ability to determine the degree of ambiguity in the message. Toward this end, we look at the use of language. The more abstract the language used, the more ambiguous the message and the more open it is to interpretation. Also, look at the message and examine the degree of reason or emotion used. Is the message informative or persuasive? Is the argument supported by appeals to our emotion or our intellect, or both? In addition, examine the message for completeness and accuracy. What information has been left out? Is the message one-sided and manipulative? Does the message convey many points of view or just one? In the world today, where we are almost drowning in information, sometimes its sheer quantity is overwhelming. Our ability to interpret the array of mediated messages is dependent upon our skill at assessing elements of the message itself.

Critical Analysis of the Channel

Media theorists McLuhan and Fiore (1967) claimed that "the medium is the message" in mass communication. They meant that the medium or channel influences how the message is interpreted to the degree that the meaning changes with the medium. McLuhan distinguished between "hot" and "cold" media and explained how each impacted the ways individuals interpreted meaning. Messages relayed through print channels (cold) require us to add our own visuals, whereas more visual media like television (hot) do not require us to add to the message. We must develop and expand our own meaning more significantly

The medium or channel of a message influences how the message is interpreted.

with cold media. In other words, we tend to remain passive when receiving messages on television—we let the medium do the work. And the more dependent we become on visual or hot media, the less likely we are to use critical skills in assessing information.

Some media allow for elaboration and extension of information about issues, persons, or events while others do not. Newspapers and other print media, for example, have more space to devote to an article. Television, in contrast, tends to offer us sound bites of information, with little detail or extension. However, print media, because they are delayed, are often out of date before they are published, while television is up-to-the-minute in its coverage. In the almost forty years since McLuhan wrote about the impact of the medium, we now have electronic media that merge elements of hot and cold. The major news media today (i.e., CNN, FOX, ABC, MSNBC, CBS) now have news websites where you can access news and information, complete with video and audio footage. These websites are updated constantly. We also can find much more interpretation of news in the form of news editorials and news analysis programming. As critical consumers of media, we must utilize a variety of mass communication channels to obtain the most comprehensive information base with regard to an issue, person, or event.

Critical Analysis of Senders

Mass media is big business. The media business exists to make a profit. Thus, part of becoming a critical consumer of media is the ability to analyze the bias or source credibility of the mediated messages you receive. To develop this critical skill, look carefully at whether the media source attributes information (facts, inferences, and conclusions) to any other source. If not, should you assume the initial source is providing fact or opinion? What is the basis of their expertise in providing that opinion? Another question needs to focus on the relationship between the source of the message and the issue, person, or event being discussed. *Conflict of interest*, according to Day (2003), "is the term used to describe a clash between professional loyalties and outside interests that undermines the credibility of a moral agent" (p. 209). Most of us expect that the reports we read and hear are objective—that is, untainted by some relationship that would influence the information reported.

Critical Analysis of Receivers and Context

The one element of the communication model that you have the most control over is the receiver. You are it. As a member of the audience to which the mass mediated messages are sent, it is your responsibility to monitor and examine your impressions or interpretations of this communication. You can choose which messages you will attend to and how or if you will respond. One of the most powerful analytical and communication skills you can develop is recognizing when not responding is the best choice. We should not feel pressured into making decisions and acting before we have all the information we need to make good choices. We can walk away. We should also consider our emotional state when receiving these messages. Are we jumping to a conclusive interpretation because we have some emotional stake in the issue or event?

In addition, we should look at several other variables regarding the context or situation in which we receive these messages. For example, interpreting messages under conditions of danger to others or ourselves might encourage us to accept less than complete information. Do we allow the government, for instance, to have greater control of the amount and type of information we receive when our country is dealing with military or terrorist threats? Do we allow others to withhold more information or keep secrets from us when the stakes in a communication situation are high? On the flip side of this scenario, do we allow political candidates to engage in negative political advertising during a campaign because "they all do it"? We need to examine the time and place of the communication and engage in critical analysis of ourselves as receivers in order to become competent consumers of mass mediated messages.

Critical Analysis of Noise and Our Feedback

Noise impacts the communication situation and the meaning we develop for a mediated message. Therefore, we must be aware of the physical, physiological, and psychological noise that interferes with our examination of mass communication. For example, when you choose which television shows to watch, do you try to find those that portray characters who look, act, and believe like you? How often do you make choices about the music you listen to based on the artist and his or her looks? Can you step out of your comfort zone when making choices about what message you will expose yourself to? Exposing yourself to many points of view allows you to analyze and interpret a message more critically.

As we said earlier, in mass communication situations, opportunities for feedback may be limited. That means the critical consumers of mass mediated messages have to work harder to avail themselves of opportunities to provide feedback. Have you ever written a letter to the editor or to your school or local paper? Have you ever called in to a talk show to provide your point of view? Have you ever participated in a product boycott to let a company know you objected to some action it had taken? Despite the delayed nature of this feedback, it does have power.

Keep in mind that most of us interpret silence to mean implicit consent. When you remain silent in the face of some person, issue, or event that is objectionable to you, then you communicate your acceptance of that event. This absence of feedback is also a form of communication, as we suggested at the beginning of this text. Critical and competent consumers of mass communication are willing to provide feedback despite the obstacles. They have the skills to utilize a variety of channels in gathering information, to analyze the credibility and bias of a source of a message, to examine themselves within the context of receiving the message, and to offer appropriate feedback to the senders of the mediated messages.

We need to examine the time and place of communicating and engage in critical analysis of ourselves in order to become competent consumers of mass media.

MASS COMMUNICATION IN COLLEGE AND LIFE

*A*s a student, consider how you use mass communication in your everyday life. You each expose yourselves to particular types of music, movies, and other forms of popular culture. You probably utilize the Internet in your research for class projects. Perhaps you like chat rooms and are developing relationships exclusively online. You may have instructors who utilize a website where they give assignments and have you turn in assignments and chat with fellow classmates or the instructor. You may have classes that invite you on "virtual tours" of the world in the course of studying and understanding other cultures. An instructor may ask you to find and develop e-mail relationships with a person from another culture.

At many college campuses, Web-based registration has replaced the old system of registering for classes by standing in line. Some even go so far as to have a completely "paperless" system of advising and registering. As you can also see in the box Campus Links: Web-Based, Web-Enhanced, or Face-to-Face Courses? you have many choices with regard to the types of classes available to you in today's college or university.

Campus Links

Web-Based, Web-Enhanced, or Face-to-Face Courses?

College courses today take many forms. You might be enrolled in courses that are "Web-enhanced." Instructors might use such technology as WebCt or Blackboard to add a multimedia dimension to the learning experience. Some courses today are offered exclusively via a Web-based format. Students in a Web-based course may never meet any of the other students or the instructor face-to-face. In a Web-based or Web-enhanced class, instructors may do any of the following: offer the syllabus only online, distribute the assignments through the course website, require assignments to be turned in via e-mail, offer opportunities for students to chat with one another through the website, require students to engage in group problem-solving exercises, or offer audio or video instruction on the website.

In order to enhance your success in Web-based courses, you must consider the following:

What is your level of knowledge and experience with computer technology? The more computer-savvy you are, the more successful you may be.

How successful are you at managing time and meeting deadlines? Often Web-based courses are relatively unstructured, and if you are not a good time manager, you may be less successful in this course format.

Why are you taking an online course? Your attitude matters here. If you are taking the course because you are serious about it but want to maximize convenience, you may be more successful than if you simply want to get through the course without making the effort to get to a regular, on-campus class on time.

How willing are you to contact the instructor for the course? Research suggests that students who ask good questions, contact the instructor for clarification on assignments, and so on, are more likely to succeed both online and in class.

How willing are you to engage other students in "interactive" course requirements, such as e-mail, chats, or group discussions? If you simply prefer to enroll in a class but not interact, you are less likely to succeed in the online course.

You have opportunities to get information about campus activities and even controversy through your campus newspaper, radio, or television stations. You can become even more involved in these mass communication channels by working for them. These organizations can provide you with invaluable experience or perhaps internships.

While some types of mass communication, unlike any other communication context we have discussed in this text, encourage receivers to play a passive role in receiving and interpreting the messages, they also allow you to become a more active participant in your community and in the world. As a consumer, you have the responsibility to play an active role in how mass communication impacts you as an individual as well as to become an active participant in our society or culture. O'Hair, Friedrich, Wiemann, and Wiemann (1997) call these responsibilities **mindfulness**. Mindfulness, they suggest, "refers to the withholding of immediate judgment on a message and a search for new categories, that is, new ways to interpret and assign meaning to a message" (p. 494). Being mindful allows you to consider a range of possible options in interpretation, to reserve judgment, and to avoid stereotyping. You have the opportunity to engage in the mindfulness during your college career, and to begin a lifetime of active engagement in the activities and decisions that impact you, by understanding and utilizing the mass communication that surrounds you.

mindfulness the withholding of immediate judgment on a message and a search for new ways to interpret and assign meaning to a message

By engaging the technology that impacts you, you can become a more "mindful" communicator.

SUMMARY

- Mass or mediated communication pervades our society, impacting or constructing culture and affecting individuals in many ways.
- New and old media today converge to provide us with new ways of receiving the important news and information we need to "live" in the world.
- *Mass communication* refers to sharing information with a large audience either at a given time or across an extended time frame.
- Mass communication is often highly regulated.
- Media conglomerates dominate the mass communication context, and the economic incentive for these big businesses concerns those who evaluate the bias and credibility of sources of information.
- Cultivation theorists suggest that our use of mass mediated messages helps us construct our world and influences the values, roles, and worldview that we adopt.
- Critical theorists suggest that the economic structure of society determines its social structure. Therefore, the mainstream media in our society portray the individuals, values, ideas, and interpretations that support the powerful elite.
- Uses and gratification suggests that we use media to fulfill preexisting needs.
- Media act as gatekeepers in determining what constitutes news of importance and, therefore, sets the agenda for what we believe is important to think about.
- The goals of becoming a more critical consumer of mass communication include recognizing the impact media has on our society and on us as individuals as well as developing a set of skills that will allow us to receive and interpret mass mediated messages more critically.
- Becoming a critical consumer means that we increase our awareness of what we see and how we see it, the language and structure of the messages, the impact of various channels used to disseminate messages, and the credibility and bias of the senders of those messages.

Questions for Discussion

1. What are the pros and cons of having a small number of very large media conglomerates in control of the media?
2. *Spam* is a term used to denote the practice of bombarding people with unsolicited advertising through an Internet provider. What are your feelings on spam?
3. What do you think are the most common uses and gratifications people get from their media choices?
4. Do you think the increasing range and sophistication of technology are changing the way we engage in interpersonal relationships? Is the technology allowing us to get closer to each other or pushing us further apart?
5. Discuss the impact of media gatekeeping and agenda-setting. Do you think the major news media are objective in what they cover and how they cover it?
6. Have you ever worked for a company that used some technology to monitor your work? Have you ever had to take a drug test as part of your employment? In your opinion, do you think this an invasion of privacy or a normal part of everyday working life?

EXERCISES

1. Monitor your television-viewing habits for a week and summarize what you watch. Look at the gender, age, and diversity of the characters on your favorite shows. What kind of "bias" do your choices suggest?
2. Find out who owns your local cable company. Is it a part of a large media conglomerate? How extensive are the "holdings" in the conglomerate? Do you think this constitutes a monopoly of the media in your area?
3. If you haven't tried reading an e-book, find one and try it. Share your impressions with a classmate.
4. Choose a popular magazine and identify the ads that you think depict stereotypical or unreasonable expectations for women, men, people of color, or people with disabilities.
5. Identify three new ways you can become a more critical consumer of media. Use them for a month and summarize the results.
6. Search for websites that relate to ethics in mass communication. What issues, events, and people are discussed?

KEY TERMS

Mass medium	Media convergence	Uses and gratifications theory
Mass communication	Regulation	Gatekeeping
Mediated communication	Social construction (or cultivation) theory	Agenda of news
New media		Mindfulness

⊚ REFERENCES

Cohen, J., and Solomon, N. 1993, October, 23. High-tech media mergers: Good business, bad policy. *Seattle Times* A11.

Day, L. A. 2003. *Ethics in media communications: Cases and controversies.* 4th ed. Belmont, CA: Wadsworth.

Folkerts, J., and Lacy, S. 2001. *The media in your life: An introduction to mass communication.* 2nd ed. Boston: Allyn and Bacon.

Gerbner, G., Gross, L. P., and Melody, W. H. 1973. *Communications technology and social policy: Understanding the new "cultural revolution."* New York: Interscience Publication.

Gerbner, G., and Gross, L. P. 1976, April. The scary world of TV's heavy viewer. *Psychology Today* 10:41–89.

Guback, T. 1969. *The international film industry: Western Europe and America since 1945.* Bloomington, IN: Indiana University Press.

Martin, J. K., and Nakayama, T. K. 2001. *Experiencing intercultural communication: An introduction.* Mountain View, CA: Mayfield.

McLuhan, M., and Fiore, Q. 1967. *The medium is the massage: An inventory of effects.* New York: Bantam Books.

Microsoft Corporation. 2007. *Educating the 21st century citizen.* Retrieved May 31, 2007 from http://findarticles.com/p/articles/mi_qa4011/is_200404/ai_n9366427.

O'Hair, D., Friedrich, G. W., Wiemann, J. M., and Wiemann, M. O. 1997. *Competent communication.* 2nd ed. New York: St. Martin's Press.

Wikipedia. 2005. *Cultural imperialism.* Retrieved June 15, 2007, from http://en.wikipedia.org/wiki/Cultural imperialism.

Wood, J. T. 1994. *Gendered lives: Communication, gender, and culture.* Belmont, CA: Wadsworth.

Glossary

abstract complex and open to varied interpretations and understanding

accommodating style characterized by low concern for self and high concern for the other

actual examples examples drawn from real-life events

adaptability the ability to change in response to a rapidly changing global environment

adaptors a wide range of movements intended to hide or "manage" emotions that we do not want to communicate directly

aesthetic needs the highest level of needs; the need to see beauty for its own sake

affect displays the facial movements or expressions that convey emotional meaning; the posture or gesture cues that convey our emotions at any given moment

agenda of news the ability of media decision makers to influence what media consumers think is important in the world

aggressiveness asserting oneself to an extreme without concern for others

aggressive style forcing one's position on others without allowing for their input

ambiguous having multiple meanings; also known as *equivocal*

ambushing occurs when a person listens carefully in order to attack what the speaker says

arbitrary meaning is created in individual persons or through cultural associations

articulation saying the sounds within words clearly

artifacts a person's dress and adornments, which are a reflection of self-image and a means of communicating messages about the wearer

assertiveness ability to communicate feelings honestly and in a straightforward manner

assertive style communicating honestly and clearly explaining one's ideas and beliefs without harming another

associate signify language

attention the first stage of perception; awareness of certain stimuli

attitude a favorable or negative inclination toward a person, place, event, or object

attraction one of the factors that motivates individuals toward intimacy in an interpersonal relationship

attributions meanings assigned to actions

audience perspective considers the listeners' multiple characteristics and the resulting type of audience they comprise

authentic dialogue dialogue characterized by a willingness to become fully involved with the other, a belief in the equality of each participant, and a climate of supportive communication

authoritative nature of language the rules of communication with particular others in certain communication contexts as dictated by language

avoiding a relationship stage in which parties go their separate ways

avoiding style characterized by low concern for self and low concern for the other

beliefs strongly held ideas about the nature of truth

bonding the stage of a relationship that signifies to the outside world a commitment to maintaining intimacy

brain dominance refers to the side of the brain a person is more likely to use, left (logic- and writing-based) or right (visual- and feeling-based)

brainstorming allowing the thought process to flow freely

briefing a short presentation in an organizational setting

categorical designs speech design that deals with topics or categories that relate to a main theme; also known as *topical design*

categorical imperative the obligation to consistently apply a rule, standard, or principle by which we make decisions

cause-effect designs speech design that identifies how a certain set of conditions brings about a particular result

celebratory speeches speeches that celebrate occasions; also known as *ceremonial, epideictic* or *special occasion speeches*

ceremonial speeches speeches that celebrate occasions; also known as *celebratory, epideictic,* or *special occasion speeches*

channel the means by which a message is delivered from the sender to the receiver; the medium by which the message travels

charts and graphs visual aids that help an audience understand *how much* and offer comparisons of part to a whole

chronemics the study of how people use time as a nonverbal communication channel

chronological design speech design that arranges ideas according to time

circumscribing a relationship stage in which the parties' communication with each other is significantly lessened

civility an attitude of respect for other people as unique individuals

climate the degree of cohesiveness among group members, their willingness to communicate with each other, and the tone of that communication

closure filling in the blanks

co-cultures cultures that exist within a more dominant culture

cognitive orientation how a person processes information—visual, auditory, or kinesthetic; also termed *learning style*

cohesion the attraction that group members feel for one another and the degree to which they are willing to work together

collaborating style characterized by high concern for self and high concern for the other

collaboration incorporating assertiveness and cooperation in decision making

collective identity established as a result of how the group balances social and task dimensions

collectivist cultures cultures that emphasize the group, not the individual; value less direct communication and tend to avoid conflict situations

commitment group members' willingness to accomplish a task and develop relationships with each other

communication apprehension (CA) the fear or anxiety associated with either real or anticipated communication with another person(s)

competing style characterized by high concern for self and low concern for the other

complementary relationships relationships based on difference; each person brings characteristics that balance the characteristics of a relational partner

complex incorporating intention, relation, context, and ethics

compromising style characterized by moderate concern for self and moderate concern for the other

confidentiality keeping secrets and confidences when requested

confirming language language that acknowledges and directly supports the contributions of another person

confirming messages messages that value the partner's presence and contributions

conflict the perception of incompatible goals

congruent messages messages in which verbal communication and nonverbal communication match

connotative meaning the meaning of a word as influenced by an individual's personal history or cultural experience

consequentialist approach the idea that good consequences are the measure of decision making

constructive conflict conflict in which the goal is problem solving, not hurting one another

content the information or request in a message

content conflict occurs when people disagree over facts, definitions, implications, solutions, or procedure; also known as *procedural conflict*

context a specific environment that includes a number of situational factors including physical, cultural, linguistic, social, temporal, and personal aspects.

Creative Communication Model contains all the elements of the transactional model, but emphasizes communication as a creative process and a uniquely human activity

cultivation theory suggests that what the media portrays is one of the most important elements in the construction and interpretation of our culture; also known as *social construction theory*

cultural shock a relatively short-term feeling of disorientation or discomfort due to the unfamiliarity of surroundings and the lack of familiar cues in the environment

culture the values and beliefs shared by group members

dating assigning specific time periods to perceptions in order to emphasize that perceptions can shift over time

decoder the person who interprets the message; the receiver

defensive listening the practice of attributing criticism, hostility, or attacks to the comments of others even when they are not intended

defensive climate a climate in which partners feel threatened and seek to protect themselves from attack

degree of ethical quality an alternative to simplistically labeling words or deeds as ethical or unethical; each situation should be assessed individually

denotative meaning the objective, agreed-upon definition of a word

dependent relationships relationships in which the partners rely so much on one another that their identities are enmeshed with one another

destructive conflict conflict in which communication escalates, and hurting one another becomes the goal

developmental approach includes three levels of rules—cultural, sociological, and psychological—that tell us how to communicate with others

dialectics tension or opposition between interacting forces or elements

dialogic civility a set of communication behaviors that include understanding the importance of public dialogue, the need for respect for one another, the extension of a sense of grace to one another, and the commitment to keep the conversation going

dialogue communication *with* each other, not *to* each other; the foundation of effective, competent, and ethical communication

differentiating a relationship stage that occurs when one or more of the parties withholds or retreats from intimacy

direct quotations word-for-word repetition of what someone has said

disconfirming language language that evaluates or judges the contributions of others

disconfirming messages messages that deny the value of a relational partner by refusing to acknowledge his or her presence and communication

discrimination unfair treatment of a given group of people based on prejudice

disfluencies the fillers that some individuals add within their conversations, e.g., *um, uh, you know*

dominating occurs when others consistently refocus attention on themselves, even if they must interrupt others to do so; also termed *monopolizing* or *stage hogging*; one partner does not allow the other to speak

doublespeak language deliberately constructed to disguise or distort its actual meaning

drawings visual aids that depict how things work

dyadic communication a relationship context involving two persons (a *dyad*)

dyadic phase the stage in which partners confront one another, talk about the relationships strengths and problems, and try to identify solutions to the problems

ego conflict a conflict in which the issue, problem, or task becomes lost in the fight for position; also known as *power conflict*

emblems communication behaviors that substitute for words

empathy a purposeful attempt to understand another person's perspective

employment-selection interview an interview in which an individual sells himself and his qualifications for a job

encoder the person who creates a message by using a system of symbols the receiver will understand; the sender

enumerated preview arranging the main points of a speech in order, e.g., first, second, third

environment the larger system surrounding an organization that provides resources and utilizes products and services

epideictic speeches speeches that celebrate occasions; also known as *celebratory, ceremonial,* or *special occasion speeches*

equality applying group norms to every member

equifinality recognition that the end production can be produced in a number of ways

equivocal having multiple meanings; also known as *ambiguous*

ethics the right or best way to communicate in a given situation

ethnocentrism the view that one's own culture or group is the center of the universe

ethos a speaker's credibility, based upon the perception of his or her goodwill, trustworthiness, competence, and appropriateness

euphemism language used to soften or be sensitive to another person

evaluate decide on the worth or value of information

evaluative listening also known as *critical listening*; analyzing a message in order to judge its validity, reliability, or usefulness

examples illustrations that help an audience visualize your point

experimenting the stage of a relationship in which individuals begin to look for commonalities

expert testimony the insights of someone who has specialized knowledge or experience and is therefore a recognized authority on a given subject

explicit norms norms that are verbally discussed and agreed upon

extemporaneous speeches planned presentations that are delivered using a key-word outline that helps the speaker deliver his or her prepared comments

eye contact looking at everyone in the audience

facial expressions the ways in which an individual animates his or her face

fact a piece of objective, verifiable information

fairness takes many forms; used in making effective and ethical decisions

feedback a verbal or nonverbal response to communication

fidelity greater clarity; keeping promises and acting faithfully

first impressions conclusions based on an initial meeting

flexibility ability to adapt and alter one's behaviors in order to accommodate changes in a relationship

fluency a smooth flow of speech without frequent stumbles or fillers

formal networks used most commonly when information is communicated up or down

formal time scheduled time; used for appointments with paid professionals such as doctors, lawyers, and psychologists

forming stage the stage in which group members get to know one another and determine how the group process will occur

functional approach identifies two categories of functions that are necessary for effective leadership—*task functions* and *process* (or *relational*) *functions*

functional communication communication that achieves practical ends; also known as *instrumental communication*

gatekeeping the process of determining what is newsworthy and important enough to reach an audience

general purposes (1) entertain, inspire, or celebrate; (2) inform; and (3) persuade

gestures movements of the hands, arms, or sometimes the shoulders, legs, or feet

grave-dressing phase the stage in which each partner must come to terms with his or her perceptions of the relationship, its problems, and how they should remember the relationship

group goals the outcome the whole group seeks to accomplish

groupthink a mode of thinking that occurs when people are deeply involved in a cohesive group and desire for unanimity overrides a realistic appraisal of alternatives

growth groups groups that assist members in learning about themselves and solving personal problems; also known as *therapy groups*

gunnysack adding to the "weight" of avoided conflict

halo effect drawing conclusions about an individual after observing a single factor based on the belief that certain traits, behaviors, and personality characteristics belong together

hate speech speech aimed at attacking or denigrating the status of entire groups—whites, blacks, gays, Jews, homosexuals, etc.

hearing the physical process that allows people to perceive sounds

heterosexism a form of prejudice regarding issues of sexual orientation and the issue of whether a person's attraction to the same or opposite sex is one of choice or not

hidden agenda the unstated personal goals of a selfish group member

high-contact cultures cultures that engage in communication that encourages interaction, physical proximity, large gestures, and warm greetings; e.g., Arab, Latin American, and Mediterranean

high-context culture culture in which more value is placed on indirectness and social harmony, and nonverbal aspects of communication play a significant role; e.g., China, Japan, Korea, Malaysia

honesty and truthfulness the first two principles of ethical communication

human communication negotiating symbolic meaning

hypothetical examples examples created from information the speaker has collected

illustrators communication behaviors that accompany words to add vividness or power to them

immediacy behaviors such as direct eye contact, smiling, facing the other person directly, and using vocal variety

implicit norms norms that occur through repetition of behavior that is not questioned

implicit personality theory the idea that people rely on deductions based on a combination of physical characteristics, personality traits, and behaviors to draw conclusions about others

impression management strategies people use to positively influence others towards them; also termed *self-enhancement*

impromptu speeches presentations that are given at a moment's notice, without prior planning or practice

incongruent messages messages in which verbal communication and nonverbal communication do not match

independent relationships relationships in which the partners live separate and disconnected lives

indexing qualifying generalizations when they are applied to specific circumstances

individual goals the motivations of individual group members

individualist cultures cultures that emphasize the importance of individual success; cultures that place more importance on the individual within certain types of relationships; value direct, open communication

individual roles roles that offer group members opportunities to interfere with effective group process

informal networks used most commonly when information is communicated between peers

informal time often spontaneous; used for activities like dropping in on a friend or calling someone just to chat

informational listening listening to discern

information-gathering interview an interview in which an individual speaks to professionals working in a job he or she might like to pursue

informative speeches speeches that instruct or assist the audience in gaining understanding

initiating the stage of a relationship in which the parties attempt to create an impression

instrumental communication communication that achieves practical ends; also known as *functional communication*

integrating the stage of a relationship in which two individuals become a couple

intensifying the stage of a relationship in which individuals begin to disclose in a more personal manner

intentional purposeful

interaction turn-taking that allows each partner to engage a conversation

interactive model emphasizes the role of feedback in human communication; communication flows from the sender to the receiver and back

interdependence mutual influence

interdependent components of a system rely upon one another in order to function properly

interdependent relationships relationships in which the partners rely on one another, but are not so dependent that they cannot make independent decisions when warranted

interpersonal relationships the relationships a person has with others

interpersonal validation the times when someone else offers to help us, expresses interest in us, or supports us

interpret assign meaning to information

intimacy the process of coming to know the other and yourself as a relationship develops

intimate space the zone of comfort only for those with whom a person is most intimate, such as a parent, lover, child, or close friend; about 0 to 18 inches

intrapersonal communication internalizing messages and communicating with yourself about yourself

intrapsychic phase the stage in which an individual explores the costs and benefits of leaving a relationship

jargon a language strategy used by a specific group to create a sense of community among group members

Johari Window a tool for analyzing a person's level of self-disclosure

key-word outline the outline that contains cue words or phrases that help you recall what you have planned and practiced when you actually deliver the speech; also called the *presentation* or *skeletal outline*

kinesics body behaviors including the eyes, face, gestures, and posture

knowledge and understanding needs needs that make individuals curious about the world and about others

labels words used to classify

language the vocabulary that is used to refer to the activity of group members; the level of formality between members of different statuses

lay testimony the views of people who are not, necessarily, experts

leadership the ability to influence others

learning groups groups that focus on increasing the knowledge and skills of their members

learning style how a person processes information—visual, auditory, or kinesthetic

linear model depicts communication as a straight line where communication flows in only one direction—from sender to receiver; also known as the *transmission model*

linguistic determinism the power of language to influence interpretations of the world in a specific culture

listening the mental process that requires a person to focus upon specific sounds in a certain time and place in order to create meaning

love and belonging needs the need for affection, support, approval, and love from friends and family

low-contact cultures cultures that maintain more distances, use smaller gestures, and more formal greetings; e.g., American, German, Scandinavian

low-context culture culture in which individual self-expression is valued, and messages are primarily communicated verbally; e.g., the United States

manuscript speeches speeches in which the speaker reads the presentation word-for-word

maps visual aids that help an audience understand where things occur

mass communication sharing information with a large audience at a given time or across an extended time frame

mass medium a channel that carries a message to many receivers

media convergence media forms and technologies coming together as new technology replaces old

mediated communication communication that requires a technological channel to complete the communication process

memorized speeches presentations that speakers write word-for-word and then memorize

message the content one person seeks to share with another; the topic or substance of communication

message complexity containing complex ideas, numerous details, or new skills

message overload receiving too many messages at the same time, making it difficult to listen

mindful paying attention

mindfulness willingness to create new categories of meaning and understanding in communicating in new situations; the withholding on immediate judgment on a message and a search for new ways to interpret and assign meaning to a message

mindlessness the use of fairly habitual or scripted ways of communicating regardless of the others in the communication experience

monochronic cultures cultures that generally prefer a linear approach to activities; e.g., American, English, Swiss

monotone rarely changing the pitch in one's voice

motivated sequence design speech design that motivates people to act

motivation the reason or *why* of communication

movement encompasses whether the speaker stands still or moves his or her entire body

narratives stories that illustrate a point or idea; usually have a clear introduction, body, and conclusion

new media media forms and content that are created and shaped by changes in technology

noise any interference that occurs as people communicate

nonassertiveness feeling of powerlessness and inability to express feelings honestly and comfortably

nonassertive style suppressing one's own feelings because of shyness, laziness, or fear that other group members will dislike you

nonconsequentialist approach focuses on principles that appear to rights, duties, and promises

norming stage the stage in which group rules roles are developed

norms standards that guide a group

olfactics the influence of smell in human communication

openness the way a system uses feedback to adapt to changes in the larger environment

organizational culture the actions, practices, language, and artifacts of a group

organizational perspective recognizes that speakers may represent an organization and, as a result, may need to be sensitive in choosing a subject

organize creating relationships among stimuli

paralanguage the vocal sounds we make such as pitch, volume, emphasis or other similar sounds; also known as *vocalics*

paraphrase restate a someone's ideas or feelings in your own words

passivity one partner is reticent or unwilling to enter the interaction

perception the process of becoming aware of people, events, or objects and attaching meaning to that awareness

perception checking a process that acknowledges initial perceptions, but also recognizes that there may be multiple explanations for them

performing stage the stage in which group members risk confrontation and resolve conflict or ignore conflict

personal examples examples drawn from the speaker's own experience

personal perspective takes into account an individual's knowledge, attitudes, interests, experiences, and beliefs to help generate speech topics

personal space the second zone of comfort, for family and good friends; about 18 inches to 4 feet

persuasive speeches speeches that stimulate an audience to reaffirm or alter beliefs or encourage the adoption of new behaviors or the continuation of past behaviors

phatic communication small talk

photographs visual aids that show what the speaker is discussing

physiological needs biological needs necessary to sustain life, including air, water, food, sleep, and sex

pitch how high or low a voice is

plagiarism using someone else's ideas without giving them appropriate credit

planning outline a rough collection of ideas and supporting material

pleasurable listening listening for appreciation

polychronic cultures cultures that generally prefer to do multiple things at once and view time as a flexible concept; e.g., Bolivian, African, Samoan

posture overall stance

power conflict a conflict in which the issue, problem, or task becomes lost in the fight for position; also known as *ego conflict*

practical perspective considers the availability of adequate, recent research materials and time limits for the preparation and presentation of a speech

prejudice a definitive negative attitude toward a group

preparation outline the formal, typewritten outline that clearly identifies an introduction, body and conclusion as well as the required portions in each section

presentation outline the outline that contains cue words or phrases that help you recall what you have planned and practiced when you actually deliver the speech; also called the *key-word* or *skeletal outline*

principle of veracity the idea that a negative weight is attached to any lie

pronunciation saying words correctly

problem-solution designs speech design that describes or defines a problem and then offers potential solutions

procedural norms norms that govern how members coordinate tasks

procedural conflict occurs when people disagree over facts, definitions, implications, solutions, or procedure; also known as *content conflict*

process an ongoing activity

proposition of fact a debatable issue that a single piece of objective evidence cannot resolve

proposition of policy advocates a particular response or specific course of action

proposition of value focuses on the worth or value of a particular person, idea, event, or object

problem-solving teams groups that focus on a project external to the group

proxemics the study of the use of space to communicate

pseudo-conflict situation in which the parties are actually in agreement, but perceptions and misunderstanding prevents them from seeing the areas of agreement and compatibility

pseudolistening pretending to listen

public space the widest zone of comfort, for public performances and presentations; 12 feet to the limits of our visibility or hearing

rate how rapidly one speaks

receiver the target or recipient of the message

receiver apprehension the fear of misinterpreting, inadequately processing and/or not being able to adjust psychologically to messages sent by others

reflected appraisal accepting how others define or describe you

refutative design speech design that presents the arguments that oppose the speaker's proposition or claim and show how they are fallacious, inadequate, inconsistent, or deficient

regulation controls over content prior to and after its distribution

rejection messages messages that acknowledge the partner's presence and communication, but do not fully accept or agree with the partner

relational indicative of the relationship between the sender and receiver

relational communication communication that expresses emotions, strengthens bonds with others, or secures a sense of belonging

relational dissolution model identifies the intrapsychic, dyadic, social, and grave-dressing phases of relationship dissolution

relational listening listening to understand, support, and empathize with others

rhetorical sensitivity concern for self, concern for others, and a situational attitude; the ability to adapt to the widest range of communication experiences with skill, considering the most appropriate response based upon a comprehensive understanding of the entire communication experience; the ability to adapt a message to the people, place, and timing of the communication

rigidity inability to adapt and cope with changes that occur in a relationship

rites and rituals practices that symbolize the tools organizational members use to create and maintain culture

roles titles and/or job responsibilities

rules and policies standards by which organizational members make decisions

safety and security needs feeling free from violence and feeling a sense of stability in life

Sapir-Whorf Hypothesis language is the most significant factor in determining what we see in the world and how we think about and evaluate what we see

scripts mental organization patterns that help arrange information and inform behavior

selection the second stage of perception; focusing on specific stimuli

selective listening occurs when listeners focus on parts of a message that appeals to them because they like or dislike the topic at hand

self-actualization needs encompass an individual's drive to be the best that he or she can be

self-concept the relatively stable mental image a person holds of him- or herself

self-disclosure process of purposefully sharing information with others that they would not otherwise know

self-efficacy sense of self

self-esteem the value or worth a person places on him- or herself; an individual's attitude about him- or herself

self-esteem needs the need for confidence or self-worth; they motivate individuals toward success

self-fulfilling prophecies events that are more likely to transpire because someone expects them to

self-presentation the ways in which a person presents some of the more personal aspects of him- or herself

sender the originator of a message

sexism a form of prejudice regarding issues of gender, expectations of what is appropriate female and male behavior, and assertions on gender superiority

significant choice having sufficient information about a situation to make a "good" decision

situational factors group context that influences a leader's style or approach

situational perspective focuses upon the context of a speech in selecting a topic

skeletal outline the outline that contains cue words or phrases that help you recall what you have planned and practiced when you actually deliver the speech; also called the *key-word* or *presentation outline*

small group three or more persons who interact together for a purpose, influence one another over a period of time, operate interdependently, share standards and norms, develop a collective identity, and derive satisfaction from the cohesion and commitment in the group

social anxiety a feeling of apprehension in any social setting in which an individual meets another for the first time

social comparison how a person sees him- or herself in comparison with others

social construction theory suggests that what the media portrays is one of the most important elements on the construction and interpretation of our culture; also known as *cultivation theory*

social dimension the personal relationships among group members

social groups groups that focus primarily on the belonging needs of the participants

social loafing occurs when an individual sits back and allows other group members to pickup the workload

social norms norms that guide the relationships among group members

social penetration model depicts self-disclosure as a process that gradually reveals both breadth and depth of information

social phase the stage in which partners discuss the possibility or actuality of dissolving the relationship with friends and family

social roles roles that help members shape the relationships within the group

social space the third zone of comfort, for impersonal business, classroom interactions, and general interactions; about 4 to 12 feet

sound bites a brief statement taken from an audiotape or videotape and broadcast, especially during a news report

spatial designs speech design that relies on a geographical or spatial relationship

special occasion speeches speeches that celebrate occasions; also known as *celebratory, ceremonial,* or *epideictic speeches*

specific purpose the purpose of a speech in relation to its specific topic

speech of definition an informative speech that helps an audience understand what something means

speech of demonstration an informative speech that shows how something is done using visual aids and movement

speech of description an informative speech that relies on mental pictures created by pictorial language

speech of explanation a speech that explains an idea, concept, or process

speeches of tribute speeches that celebrate a person, a group of people, or an event

speech to actuate a persuasive speech that motivates the audience toward a particular behavior

speech to convince a persuasive speech that challenges the audience to alter widely accepted beliefs

speeches to entertain and inspire celebratory speeches that are general in nature and may occur in a variety of settings

speech to reinforce or stimulate a speech that reinforces the beliefs or behaviors to which the audience already ascribes

stagnating a relationship stage in which communication disappears

state-the-case-and-prove-it speech design in which the speaker sets forth a proposition or claim and then proves it systematically by offering evidence and reason to support the arguments

statistics numeric facts that include such information as percentages, averages, or amounts of money

stereotypes oversimplified categories that people associate individuals with in order to reduce uncertainty about them

stories and myths tales of past successes and failures and of past and present heroes that help socialize new members of an organization

storming stage the stage in which group conflict emerges as members react to norms and rules negatively

structured governed by a set of rules

styles approach identifies three different leadership styles—*autocratic, democratic,* or *laissez-faire*

subject a broad area of knowledge

supportive climate a climate in which partners feel comfortable and secure

symbolic using words, vocal utterances, or body movement to represent a host of referents; representative of a particular thing, idea, concept, or event

symmetrical relationships relationships based on similarity; both individuals share traits, interests, and approaches to communication

synergy collective energy

tables visual aids that summarize information

task dimension the ways groups make decisions and solve problems

task norms norms that focus on how decision making and problem solving occur

task roles roles that assist group members in goal accomplishment

terminating occurs when no significant intervention is attempted at the avoiding stage

territoriality the characteristic of marking one's environment

testimony the words or ideas of another person used to support a speaker's points

text charts a poster, flip chart, chalkboard, or slide that previews or summarizes key ideas

therapy groups groups that assist members in learning about themselves and solving personal problems; also known as *growth groups*

thesis the central idea of a speech

thesis statement a single, declarative sentence that summarizes the essence of a speech

tolerance respect for one another and the belief that every human being has value

topic the specific focus of a speech

topical designs speech design that deals with topics or categories that relate to a main theme; also known as *categorical design*

trait approach presumes that leaders are either born with or cultivate a set of behaviors that guarantee they will assume leadership positions

transactional model depicts communication in which people act simultaneously as senders and receivers

transmission model depicts communication as a straight line where communication flows in only one direction—from sender to receiver; also known as the *linear model*

trigger words words that stimulate a negative emotional reaction in listeners

uses and gratifications theory argues that we turn to media to fulfill pre-existing needs

validation the times when someone else offers to help us, expresses interest in us, or supports us

values deeply held convictions about the undeniable worthiness of a certain ideal

value system guides the development of norms, roles, and structure within a group

vocalics the vocal sounds we make such as pitch, volume, emphasis or other similar sounds; also known as *paralanguage*; the use of the voice to communicate

vocal inflection frequently changing the pitch on one's voice

volume how loudly or softly one speaks

wholeness the unique configuration of the parts in a system

Photo Credits

Index

Bold – definition
Italics – figure
t - table

A

Abstract, **90**
Abstraction ladder, 90
Academic advisor, choosing, 160–161
Academic outreach services, 301
Academic success, 60
Accent, 237–238
Accommodating style, *165*, **166**
Accuracy, 122
Achiever, 51–52
Activity, communication as, 18
Actual example, **219**
Actuate, speech to, **197**
Adaptability, **286**
Adaptive communication, 288
Adaptor, **114**
Adler, Alfred, 275
Adolescent, body image of, 53
Advocacy, 287
Aesthetic needs, *131*, **132**
Affect display, **114**
Agenda of news, **315**
Aggressiveness, **139**
Aggressive style, 269–270
Ambiguous communication, **93**
Ambushing, **74**
American Psychological Association, 317
American system, 286
Animal, communication and, 8
Anxiety
    communication apprehension, 176–177
    social, 135–136
Apathetic audience, 189–190
Appearance, perception of, 70
Arbitrary, **89**
Articulation, **236**
Artifacts, **117**
Ascending order, 206
Asian culture, 109–110
Assertiveness, **139**, 149
Assertive style, 269–270
Assignment, *178*, 179
Assistive technological device, 71
Associate, **91**
Attending stage, 68, *68*

Attention, **44**
Attention-getting device, 207t
Attitude, 95, **187**
Attraction, **129**, 130
Attribution, **56**, 56t
Audience analysis
    characteristics and types of, 184–186, 184t
    for mass communication, 310
    motivation for learning, 187
    stereotyping, 186
    types of, *189*, 189–190
Audience perspective, **183**–184, 183t, 184–187
Authentic dialogue, **147**
Authoritative nature of language, **92**
Autocratic leadership, 263
Autonomy, 32
Avoiding stage, **140**
Avoiding style, *165*, **166**

B

Baby boomer, 199t
Bachelor's degree, income potential, 3
Balance, 206
Barefoot, Betsy, 76
Bar graph, *240*
Becoming a Master Student, 143
Behavior
    attitude influencing, 95
    forbidden, 28
    media influencing, 316–317
    poor listening, 76
    during relationship dissolution, 140–141
Belief
    audience analysis and, **186**–187
    language and, 99
Belongingness, *131*, **132**
Bias
    attribution, 56, 56t
    gender, 97
    of media, 314–315
    in newspaper articles, 103
    in speech preparation, 186
Biological needs, *131*
Blood brothers, 136
Bodily intelligence, 188
Body, of speech, 208
Body, Identity, and Interaction: Interpreting Nonverbal Communication, 123–124
Body language, 108t

Body movement (kinesics)
    for effective speech delivery, **238**
    as nonverbal communication, 113–114
    as symbolic communication, 8
Bok, Sissela
    justifying lies, 35–36
    truthfulness and deception, 30
Bonding, **136**
Brain dominance, **48**
Brainstorming
    model for speech preparation, *178,* 179
    rules of, 271
    for speech subjects and topics, **182–183**
Breathing, proper, 233–235
Bridges, Not Walls, 136
Briefing, **196–197**
Bush, President George, 313
Bypassing, 89

C

Campus. *See* College
Campus Links
    academic advisor, choosing, 160–161
    classroom discussion, 274
    combating hate speech on campus, 104
    doing research, 215
    "I" messages, 143
    lecture as informative speech, 195
    nonverbal communication in dating, 113
    physiological needs and self-care, 131
    recall/cue system of note-taking, 76
    student perception of teacher, 45
    time management, 247
    transitioning, 3–4
    truthfulness and romance, 33
    understanding moral growth, 29
    using campus services, 301
    web-based, web-enhanced, face-to-face courses, 320–321
    working and college, 299–300
Canfield, Allan, PhD, 123–124
Career Links
    costs of poor listening on job, 69
    creating nonsexist environments, 96
    critical skills, 220
    dependence, independence, interdependence, 255–256
    effective communication, 7
    feedback and interpersonal communication in workplace, 150
    gender and nonverbal communication in workplace, 118–119
    job interview as impromptu speech, 232
    public speaking as market strategy, 174
    reducing conflict at work, 164–165
    self-fulfilling prophecy, 51–52
    successful organizational relationships, 288–289
    technology and job hunting, 311
    workplace honesty, 31
Caste system, 47
Casual dating, 113
Categorical design, **213**
Categorical imperative, **36**
Cause-effect design, **213**
Celebratory speech
    descriptors for, 182t
    as general purpose speech, 180
    reframing topic for, 182
    relating topic to, 192
    relevance to college, 199–200
    types of, 193, 194t
Ceremonial language, 108t

Ceremonial speech, 180
Ceremony, building community, 123–124
Challenger, 272
Channel, **10, 70**
    as component of communication, 15, 16t
    critical analysis of, 317–318
    decisions for listening, 76
    time as nonverbal communication, 117
    using effectively, 290
Chart, **239**
Chat room, 10
Children
    computer and Internet access, 308–309
    media influencing, 316–317
    spiritual child, 136–137
    transmission of culture to, 98
Choice, making, 32
Chronemics, **117**
Chronological design, **212**
Circumscribing stage, **140**
Civility, **81, 84**
Clarity, 205, 236
Classroom discussion, 274
Climate, **266**
Closure, **55**
Co-culture, **73**
Cognitive needs, *131*
Cognitive orientation, 48
Cohesion, **258**
Collaborating style, *165,* **166**
Collaboration, 270
Collective energy, **285**
Collective identity, **257**
Collective rationalization, 273
Collectivism, 268
Collectivist culture, **99,** 157–158
College
    classroom discussion, 274
    communication in, 2, 6, 21
    graduation statistics, 3
    groups in, 274–275
    hate speech on campus, 104
    intercultural relationships, 158
    interpersonal dialectics and, 157
    lecture as informative speech, 195
    mass communication and, 320
    mission statement of, 282
    organizational communication in, 300–301
    organizational skills, 227
    Palm Pilot and, 311
    plagiarism penalties, 221
    public speaking and, 198–199, 249
    relational development with professor, 141–142
    relevance of celebratory, informative and persuasive speaking to, 199–200
    rhetorical sensitivity in, 167–168
    service learning, 4–5
    technology support, 301
    transitioning to, 3–4, 5–6
    web-based, web-enhanced, face-to-face courses, 320–321
    working while attending, 299–300
    See also Professor
College language, 103
Columbia, 272
Commitment, **258**
Communication
    adaptive, 288
    animals and, 8
    channels of, 10

Communication (*continued*)
  characteristics of, 18–19
  classroom discussion, 274
  college experience and, 2
  components of, 9–13, 15, 16, 16t
  computer-mediated, 10, 71
  context of, 10
  as creative, 13
  cross-cultural, 120–121
  culture and, 11
  definitions of, 7–9
  dialogic civility, 81
  dialogue as effective, 40
  effective, 7
  ethical principles in, 30–31, 30t
  guidelines for competent, *37*
  international student and, 17–18
  issues for student-learner, 6
  juggling as metaphor for, 17
  language understanding and, 88
  misconceptions of, 20–21
  models of, *16*, 16–17
  motivation and, 13
  noise and, 12
  nonverbal, 8
  within organizations, 280
  with peers, 290
  process of, 10, 18–19
  public speaking as linear, 175
  role after college, 6
  self-perception and, 50–51
  self-talk and, 53–54
  service learning and, 5
  silence and, 34
  superior-subordinate, 287–288
  transitioning and, 4
  as unique human activity, 18
  verbal and nonverbal, 108
  See also Ethical communication; Nonverbal communication;
      Verbal communication
Communication apprehension (CA), **176–177**
Communication competency, 280
Communication Links
  addressing professor, 159
  clarifying terms, 206
  communicating with people with disabilities (PWD), 58–59
  communication apprehension, 176–177
  concentration, 12
  cultural imperialism, 312
  detecting lying, 110–111
  gender label, 94
  group contract, 257–258
  listening, 83
  mentor-professor characteristics, 148
  multiple intelligence theory in public speaking, 188–189
  National Communication Association credo, 27
  proper breathing in public speaking, 233–235
  rhetorical sensitivity, 78
  successful organizational relationships, 288–289
  uncertainty reduction theory, 284
  willingness, 14–15
Communications Decency Act (CDA), 100
Community
  belonging to, 34
  groups in, 274–275
  interpersonal dialectics and, 161–162
  interpersonal relationships and, 146–147
  public speaking, 174–176, 251
  role of ceremony and ritual in building, 123–124

Community Links
  article biases, 103
  community listening session, 81–82
  contribution and reward, 275–276
  interpersonal relationships and community, 146–147
  labs for ongoing practice, 246
  mediated violence, 316
  public speaking and community, 174
  role of ceremony and ritual in building community, 123–124
  service learning, 4–5
  silence, consequences of, 34
  Teaching Tolerance, 162–163
Community listening session, 81–82
Competent communication, 147
Competing style, *165*, **166**
Complementary relationship, **137–138**
Complex communication, **19**
Compromising style, *165*, **167**
Computer. *See* Internet; Technology
Computer etiquette, 38–39
Computer Link
  communicating social responsibility through website, 291–292
  dating and relationship development online, 135
  expanding knowledge of culture, 158
  finding a speech topic, 192
  nonverbal communication on the Internet, 111–112
  online support group, 260
  PowerPoint as visual aid, 243
  self-discovery, 48
  software for speakers, 225
Computer-mediated communication (CMC)
  role of listening, 71, 72
  types of, 10
Concentration, 12–13, 67
Concept map, *226*
Conclusion
  strategies for, 212t
  summary as, 211–212
Confidences, keeping, 31
Confidentiality, 30t, **31**
Confirming language, **102**
Confirming message, **138**
Conflict, **142**
  cause of, 164
  emotions and, 269
  of interest, 318
  reducing at work, 164–165
  in relationship, 163–164, 169
  resolution styles, 269–270
  types of, 163, 165
  value of, 163
Conflict-management style, *165*, 165–167
Congruent message, **108**
Connotative meaning, **90**
Consequentialist approach, **35**
Constructive conflict, **165**
Content, 15
Content conflict, 267, **268**
Context, **10**
  attending to, 101–102
  as component of communication, 15, 16t
  critical analysis of, 319
  effective delivery for differing, 249
  meanings and, 17
Contextual distraction, 76
Contextual relativism, 30
Convergence, 308
Conversation, face-to-face, 71
Convince, speech to, **197**

Country club style, 165
Couple, becoming a, 136
Cover letter, 297
Covert conflict, 142
Covey, Stephen, 255
Creative communication
    human communication as, 13
    meaning and, 18
Creative communication model, **17**, **18**, *18*
Creativity, 271
Credibility, 69
Credo. *See* National Communication Association
Critical analysis, of media, 317–319
Critical listening, 79
Critical theory, 313
Cross-cultural communication, 120
Cultivation theory, **313**
Cultural imperialism, 312, 313–314
Cultural lenses, 144
Cultural Links
    children's access to computers and Internet, 308–309
    communication, 11
    cultural differences among group members, 267–268
    cultural imperialism, 312
    culture and evidence, 215
    dialects and accents, 237–238
    influence of culture on perception, 57
    intercultural relationships on campus, 158
    intercultural romantic relationships, 145
    nonverbal communication between Asian and Western cultures, 109
    organizational culture and missions statements, 281–282
    rhetorical traditions, 185
    silence as Responding, 66–67
    transmission of culture to children, 98
    values, understanding different, 28
Cultural mindset, 122
Cultural rules, 128
Cultural symbol, 283
Culture
    collectivist and individualist, **99**
    communication and, 11
    differences in group members, 267–268
    evidence and, 215
    expanding knowledge of, 158
    in group, **264**
    impacting perception, 56–57
    interpersonal dialectics and, 157
    language shaping, 92
    low- and high-context, 144
    media affecting, 313
    mediated mass communication and, 312
    nonverbal communication and, 120
    of an organization, 281
    in relationship, 144–145
    shaping perception, 99
    stereotypical views of, 313
    timing of group activities, 268
    transmission to children, 98
Culture shock, **17**
Cybersegration, **10**
Cyberspace, 38

D

Dating, **59**
    cross-cultural, 145
    nonverbal communication and, 113
    online, 135
Deaf, assistive technological device for, 71
Deception, 30–31

Decision making
    beliefs and values, 26
    effective, 32
    good consequence as measure of, 35
    groupthink and, 272
    reflective-thinking approach, 270–271
Decoder, **9**, 16t
Defensive climate, **266**
Defensive listening, **74**
Defensive relational atmosphere, **138**
Definition, speech of, **196**
Degree of ethical quality, **36**
Democratic leadership, 263
Demographics, 184, 186
Demonstration, speech of, **196**
Denotative meaning, **90**
Dependence, 255–256
Dependent relationship, **138**
Descending order, 205
Description, speech of, **196**
Descriptive phrase, 8
Design, speech, 212–214
Destructive conflict, **163**
Developmental approach, **128**
Dialect, 237–238
Dialectics, **137–139**
    in college, 157
    family and, 155–156
    friendships and, 156–157
Dialogue, 40, 147
Dialogue civility, **81**
Differentiating stage, **140**
Digital divide, 10
Direct eye contact, 120
Direct quotation, **218**
Disability, 58–59
Disconfirming language, **102**
Disconfirming message, **138**
Discrimination, **47**
Discussion, classroom, 274
Disfluency, 115, **116**
Disorganization, fighting, 247
Dissenter, direct pressure on, 273
Dissolution, 139–140
Dissolution model, *134*, **140–141**
Distraction, 67
Divergent thinker, 271
Diversity, of organization, 292
Dominating, 74–75
Domination, 139
Doublespeak, **93**
Drawing, **240**
Drucker, Peter, 280
Dualism, 30
Dyadic communication, **128**
Dyadic phase, **141**

E

Eating disorder, 53
Economic justice, 35
Economic motivator, 293–294
Educating the 21st Century Citizen, 306–307
Education
    communication apprehension, 177
    computer technology requirements, 306–307
    liberal, 161–162
    public speaking, 173–175
    web-based, web-enhanced, face-to-face courses, 320–321
    See also College

Ego conflict, 267, **269**
Egotistic approach, 35
Ellis, David, 143
E-mail
    as computer-mediated communication, 10
    netiquette, 38
Emblem, **114**
Emoticon, 111–112
Emotion
    communication expressing, 13
    conflict and, 269
Empathy, **60**, **77**, 80–81
Employment
    college and working, 299–300
    communication skills, importance of, 6, 7
    critical skills needs for, 220
    interviewing, 297–299
    job search process, 295–296
    technology and, 311
    See also Workplace
Employment-selection interview, **297–298**
Encoder, **9**
English, learning difficulties, 17
English as second language (ESL), 237
Entertain, speech to, **193**
Enumerated preview, **208**
Environment
    creating nonsexist, 96
    organizational system, **284**
Epideictic speech, **180**
Equality, **265**
Equifinality, **287**
Equivocal, **93**
Ethical communication
    choices for, 20
    competence and, 147
    goals of studying, 37
    National Communication Association credo, 27
    sources of guidelines, 27
    truth and lying, 26
    understanding, 25
Ethical growth, 30
Ethical nonverbal communication, 121
Ethical principles, 30–31, 30t
Ethical quality, degree of, **36**
Ethics, **19**
    romance and, 33
    study of, 25
Ethnicity, 184–185
Ethnocentricism, **99**
Ethos, **69**
Euphemism, **93**
Evaluating, **46**
Evaluating stage, 68, *68*
Evaluative listening, **79**
Evidence
    culture and, 215
    evaluative listening and, 79
Example, **218**
Existential intelligence, 189
Experience, framing perception, 46–47
Experimenting stage, **136**
Expert testimony, **218**
Explanation
    for communication apprehension, 177
    speech for, **193**
Explicit norm, **256**
Expressed struggle, 163
Extemporaneous speech, **232**

External distraction, 67
External noise, 12
Eye contact
    gendered, 120
    for speech delivery, **238**

F
Face-to-face communication, 10
Face-to-face conversation, 71
Face-to-face course, 320–321
Facial delivery, 238
Facial expression, **238**
Facial movement, 9
Fact, **217**
Fairness, 30t, **32**
Faithfulness, 31
Family
    beliefs and values of, 27
    interpersonal dialectics and, 155–156
    learned behavior, 28
    types of, 155
Family label, 136
Feedback
    as component of communication, 9–10, 16t
    critical analysis of, 319
    mass communication and, 311
    role of, 17
    in workplace, 150
Feelings
    communication of, 9
    expression of, 111
    "I" messages, 143
    suppressing, 156
Feminism, 97
Fidelity, **9**, 30t, **31**
Filler, **115**
Financial assistance, 302–303
First impression, **56**, 136
First They Came for the Jews, 34–35
First-year student, transition stages, 3
Flaming, 38–39
Flexibility, **139**
Forgetfulness, 82
Forgiveness
    netiquette, 39
    in relationship, 33
Formal network, **290**
Formal time, **118**
Forming stage, **264**
Friendly audience, 189, *189*
Friendship
    bonding and, 136
    concept of, 130
    hierarchy of, 96
    interpersonal dialectics and, 156–157
    within organizations, 293
Frown, communicating feelings with, 9
Functional approach, **263**
Functional communication, **13**

G
Gardner, Howard, 188–189
Gardner, John, 76
Gasp, 8
Gatekeeping, 314–315
Gender
    of audience for speech, 184
    culture in relationships, 144–145

in group, 264–265
sex and, 96
Gender bias, 97
Gendered eye contact, 120
Gendered fashion, 119
Gendered language, 96
Gendered nonverbal communication, 118
Gendered space, 119
Gendered touch, 119–120
Gender label, 95
General purpose, **180**, 192
Generational differences, understanding, 199t
Generation Next, 199t
Generation X, 199t
Gerbner, George, 313, 316–317
Gesture, 9, **238**
Goal, **259**
Grapevine, 290–291
Graph, **239**
Grave-dressing phase, **141**
Grimace, communicating feelings with, 9
Group
    characteristics of, 254
    cohesion and commitment, 258
    collective identity, 257
    in college, community and career,
        274–275
    communication process within, 276
    conflicts within, 168–169
    cultural differences, 267–268
    culture and evidence desired, 215
    effectiveness of, 257
    goals of, 259
    individuals versus, 260–261
    interdependence, 255
    leadership in, **262**–263
    making quality decisions, 270
    managing conflict, 266–267
    mutual influence, 255
    norms of, 256
    online support, 260
    power within, 263, 268
    purpose of, 255, 258
    reflective-thinking approach, 270–271
    roles in, 261–262
    size of, 254
    as speech audience, 185–186
    stages of development, 263–264
    stereotyping, 185
    timing of activities, 268
    types of, 259–260
Group contract, 257–258
Group culture, 264–265
Groupthink, **272**–273
Growth, moral, 29
Growth group, 259–**260**
Gunnysack, **166**–167

H
Hall zone, 117
Halo effect, **55**
Hammarskjold, Dag, 26
Handwritten letter, 10
Haptics (touch), 115
Hate speech, **100**–101, 104
Hearing
    as physical process, **67**
    as stage in listening, 68, 68
Heterosexism, **96**

High-contact culture, **120**
High-context culture, **144**
High school graduate
    income potential, 3
    transitioning to college, 5
Hofstede, Geert, 157
Homesickness, 3
Honesty
    conflict and, 142
    as ethical principle, 30–32, 30t
    in workplace, 31
How, 15, 16t
Human beings, value of, 34, 39
Human Communication. *See* Communication
Human touch, 10
Hypothetical example, **219**

I
Illustrator, **114**
Immediacy, **122**
Impersonal relationship, 128
Implicit consent, 34, 319
Implicit norm, **256**
Implicit personality theory, **55**
Impoverished style, 165
Impression, first, **56**
Impression management, 55
Impromptu speech, **231**, 232
Income potential, 3
Incongruent message, **108**
Incorporation stage, 4
Indecent speech, 100
Independence, 256
Independent relationship, **138**
Indexing, **59**
Individual
    groups versus, 260–261
    media affecting, 314–315
Individualism, 268
Individualist culture, **99**, 157
Individual relativism, 30
Individual role, **261**
Inflection, 236
Influence, group, 255
Informal network, **290**
Informal time, **118**
Informational listening, 75, 83
Information-gathering interview, **297**
Information technology, 280
Informative speech, **180**
    descriptors for, 182, 182t
    lecture as, 195
    persuasive speech compared to, 181t
    relating topic to, 192
    relevance to college, 199–200
    types of, 193, 195
Ingham, Harry, 54
Initiating stage, **134**
Innate communication, 109
Inspire, speech to, **193**
Instant messaging (IM), 10
Instrumental communication, **13**
Integration stage, 4, **136**
Intelligence
    types of, 188–189
    using big words to show, 205
Intensifying stage, **136**
Intentional communication, **19**

Interaction, 112, **139**
Interactive model, **17**
Interconnected individuals, 163
Intercultural relationship, in college, 158
Interdependence, **255**, *256*, **285**
Interdependent relationship, **138**
Internal distraction, 67
Internal noise, 12–13
International student, communication difficulties, 17–18
Internet
    as 21st century media, 308
    children and, 308–309
    communicating social responsibility, 291–292
    cultural imperialism and, 312
    lurkers on, 71
    as medium for communication, 100
    nonverbal communication and, 111–112
    support groups online, 260
    See also Netiquette
Interpersonal bond, 136
Interpersonal communication
    in college, 147–148
    competence and ethics, 146
    dialectics, 137, *137*
    feedback in workplace, 150
    importance of, 4
    rhetorical sensitivity in college, 167–168
Interpersonal dialectics
    in college, 157
    community and, 161–162
    family and, 155–156
    friendships and, 156–157
Interpersonal intelligence, 188
Interpersonal needs, Schultz's theory of, 133
Interpersonal relationship, **128**
    community and, 146–147
    conflict management in, 163
    expectations of, 130
Interpersonal validation, **84**
Interpret, **46**
Inter-role conflict, 168
Interview
    following up, 298
    successful, 298–299
    types of, 297
Intimacy
    conflict and, 142–143
    key concept of, 129
    need fulfillment and, 130
    relationship development and, 134, *134*
    See also Relationship
Intimate space, **117**
Intrapersonal communication, 50, 54
Intrapersonal intelligence, 189
Intrapsychic phase, **141**
Introduction, presentation, 207–208
Involved dating, 113
Invulnerability, illusion of, 272

J
Jaksa, James, 37
Janis, Irving R., 272
Jargon, **102**
Jensen, Dr. J. Vernon, 25
Jewler, A. Jerome, 76
Jews, First They Came for, 34–35
Job interview, as impromptu speech, 232
Johannesen, Richard, 25
Johari Window, 54, *54*

Juggling, 17
Justification process, 35–36

K
Kant, Immanuel, 36
Kaplan, R. B., 185
Key-word outline, 232
Kinesics (body movement), 109, 113–114
Knowledge needs, **132**

L
Label, **93**
    family, 136
    gender, 95
    power of, 96
Laissez-faire leadership, 263
Language
    addressing leaders, **282**
    authoritative nature of, 92
    clarifying meaning, 95
    classifying people, 93
    college, 103
    competent and ethical use of, 101
    confirming and disconfirming, **102**
    confusing meaning, 93
    creating meaning, 92
    culture and, 98
    developing rules for, 237–238
    as direct and implicit, 99
    gender bias in, 97
    gendered, 96
    nonsexist, 98
    of an organization, 281
    power of, 91–92
    shaping culture, 92
    structure of, 89
    symbolism, 88–89
    understanding, 88
    values and belief development and, 99
Lay testimony, **218**
Leadership, in groups, 262–263
Learning
    distractions to, 5
    service, 4–5
Learning group, **259**
Learning style, **48**
    as four-stage cycle, 187
    types of, 49t
Lebacqz, Karen, 40
Lecture, 195
Letter, handwritten, 10
Liberal education, 161–162
Life, 21
Linear communication, 175
Linear model, **16**, *16*, 17
Line graph, *241*
Linguistic determinism, **98**
Listening
    on campus, 83–84
    channel-based problems, 70
    community session, 81–82
    context-based problems, 73
    cultural environment influencing, 73
    encouragement and, 77
    as expression of selflessness, 72
    gender-based problems, 73–74
    importance of, 6
    improving habits of, 74
    on job, 69, 75

lurkers and, 71
as mental process, **67**
message-based problems, 72
poor behaviors of, 74, 76
problems in, 68
receiver-based problems, 72–73
reluctance in, 66
rewards of, 80
role in college, 84
role in learning, 82–83
role in text-based CMC, 71
sender-based problems, 69–70
types of, 75
Listening model, *68*
Listserv, 10
Logical intelligence, 188
Love needs, *131*, **132**
Low-contact culture, **120**
Low-context culture, **144**
Luft, Jo, 54
Lurker, as listener, 71
Lying
  detecting, 110–111
  ethics and, 26
  in workplace, 31

M

Maintenance role, 261
Manager, types of, 52
Managerial grid, *165*
Manuscript speech, **232**
Map
  concept, *226*
  as visual aid, **240**
Marriage, bonding and, 136
Maslow, Abraham, 130
Maslow's hierarchy of needs, 130, *131*, 131–133
Mass communication, **307**
  college and, 320
  cultural diversity and, 312
  effects of, 312
  feedback of, 319
  individuals affected by, 314–315
  regulation of, 310
  social construction/cultivation theory, 313
Mass medium, **307**
Materials, supporting
  evaluation of, 216
  finding, 214–215
  types of, 216–219
  using effectively, 219–220
Mature learner, transitioning to college, 5
McCauliffe, Christa, 272
Meaning
  creation of, 9
  creative communication and, 18
  denotative and connotative, **90**
  language clarifying, 95
  language confusing, 93
  language creating, 92
  triangle of, 89, *90*
Media
  bias of, 314–315
  critical consumer of, 317
  culture and, 313
  individuals affected by, 314–315
  violence and, 316–317
  visual or hot, 318
  See also Mass communication

Media convergence, **308**
Mediated mass communication, **307**
  characteristics of, 307
  cultural diversity and, 312
Mediated violence, 316–317
Memorized speech, **232**
Men
  communication skills, 265
  fashion and, 119
  gendered language and, 96
  nonverbal communication behavior, 118
Mentor-professor, 148
Merton, Robert K., 51
Message
  characteristics of, 138
  as component of communication, 9–10, 16t
  congruent and incongruent, **108**
  critical analysis of, 317
  sending and receiving, 17
  understanding, 75
  vocal and nonvocal, 108
  websites and, 311–312
Message complexity, **72**
Message overload, **72**
Metacommunication, 92
Middle-of-the-road style, *165*
Millenials, 199t
Mindful, **67**
Mindfulness, **101**, 121–122, **321**
Mindguard, emergence of, 273
Mindlessness, **101**
Miscommunication, symbols, 9
Misleading, 31
Mispronunciation, 236, 237t
Mission statement, 281–282
Monochronic culture, **120**
Monopolizing, **74**–75
Monotone, **236**
Moral growth
  stages of, 30
  understanding, 29
Morality, belief in, 272
Moral theory
  consequentialist approach, 35–36
  nonconsequentialist approach, 36
Motivated sequence design, **213**, 213t
Motivation
  communication and, **13**–14
  as component of communication, 15, 16t
  improving within group, 271
  within organizations, 293
Motivator, in workplace, 293–294
Motley, Dr. Michael T., 176
Movement, body, **238**
Multiple intelligence theory, 188–189
Multitasking, 71
Multi-user dungeon (MUD), 39
Musical intelligence, 188
My Big Fat Greek Wedding, 145
Myth, **282**

N

Narrative story, **219**
National Center for Education Statistics, 3
National Communication Association (NCA)
  credo of, 27
  tolerance, 39–40
National Issues Forum, 146

Naturalistic intelligence, 189
Need fulfillment, 130
Needs, Maslow's hierarchy of, 130, *131*
Netiquette, 38–39
Network, **290**
Neutral audience, *189*, 189–190
New media, **308**
News, agenda of, **315**
Newspaper, 315, 318
Nilsen, Thomas, 25
Noise
    as communication interference, 12
    as component of communication, 16t
    critical analysis of, 319
Nonassertiveness, **139**
Nonassertive style, **269–270**
Nonconsequentialist approach, 36
Nonsexist environment, 96
Nonsexist language, 98
Nonverbal communication
    body movement (kinesics), 113
    in college, 122–123
    competent and ethical, 121
    culture and, 120
    defining, 108t
    functions of, 110, 111–112
    fundamentals of, 109
    gendered, 118
    in groups, 267–268
    Internet and, 111–112
    paralanguage, 8, 108t, 115–116
    physical characteristics, 114–115
    regulating interaction, 112
    as symbolic, 8, 9
    touch (haptics), 115
    understanding, 108
    in workplace, 118
Nonvocal message, 108, 108t
Norm
    categories of, 257
    types of, **256**
Norming stage, **264**
Note taking, recall/cue system of, 75, 76

O
Olfactics, **115**, 120
Online support group, 260
Openness, **285–286**
Opposed audience, *189*
Oral communication, 6
Orderly, 206
Organization, 83
    challenges within, 292
    in college, **45**
    communication, importance of, 280
    communication contexts in, 287
    communication outside of, 291
    diversity, 292
    importance of skills in, 227
    motivation within, 293
    patterns for informative speech, 212–212
    patterns for persuasive speech, 213–214
    personal relationships within, 293
    principles for effective, 204–205
    sexual harassment, 294
    technology in, 295
Organizational culture
    of group, **281**
    mission statement of, 281–282

Organizational perspective, **191**
Organizational relationships, successful, 288–289
Organizational structure, 283
Organize, **45**
Orientation, cognitive, 48
Outcomes of Education report, 3
Outline
    alternatives to, 225
    concept map, 226
    format sheet, 222–223
    key-word, 232
    model for speech preparation, *178*, 179
    planning, **221**
    preparation, **222**, *223–225*
    tree, *226*, 227
Overt conflict, 142

P
Pain, of relationship dissolution, 139–140
Palm Pilot, 311
Paralanguage, 8, 108t, 115–116
Parallelism, 206
Paraphrase, **77**
Parents Television Council, 316–317
Passivity, **139**
Pattern
    for informative speech, 212–213
    for persuasive speech, 213–214
Peer, communication with, 290
People in Quandaries, 59
People with disabilities (PWD), 58–59
Perception
    academic success and, 60
    adjusting, 59
    cognitive orientation, 48
    cultural influence on, 57
    culture shaping, 99
    improving, 57
    influences on, 55
    of others, 55
    prior experience, 46–47
    process of, **44**
    selectivity, 47–48
    of self, *50–51*
    stereotyping, 47
    of teacher, 45
Perception checking, **59**
Perceptual error, 57–58
Performing stage, **264**
Perry, William G., Jr., 30
Personal example, **218**
Personal inventory form, 190
Personal perspective, **189**
Personal space
    culture and communication, 109
    Hall zones of, 117
    nonverbal communication and culture, 120–121
Persuasive speech, **180**
    descriptors for, 182, 182t
    informative speech compared to, 181t
    relating topic to, 192
    relevance to college, 199–200
    types according to proposition, 197–198
    types according to purpose, 196–197
Phatic communication, **136**
Philanthropic feedback, 286
Photograph, **240**
Physical ability level, of audience, 185
Physiological needs, 130–131, *131*

Pie chart, 239, *240*
Pitch, **116**, 236
Plagiarism, **221**
Planning outline, **221**
Pleasurable listening, 75
Policy, **283**
Polychronic culture, **120**
Posture, **238**
Power
    within groups, 263, 268
    hierarchy of, 96
    of media, 315
Power conflict, **269**
PowerPoint, 241, 242, 243
Practical ends, 13
Practicality, 206
Practical perspective, **191**
Practice, speech preparation, *178*, 179
Prejudice, **47**
    cause of, 94
    heterosexism as, 96
Preparation outline, **222**, *223–225*
Presentation
    attention-getting devices, 207t
    concept map, *226*
    conclusion of, 211–212
    introduction, 207–208
    main points of, 208–209
    model for speech preparation, *178*, 179
    organization of, 212–214
    practice for effectiveness, 245
    preparation for, 244
    proper breathing for, 233–235
    to the public, 251
    reading word-for-word, 232
    supporting materials for, 214, 216–220
    transitions in, 210, 210t, 211t
    using voice effectively, 233
    in workplace, 250
    See also Outline; Visual aids
Principle, consistently applying, 36
Principle of veracity, **35**
Pritchard, Michael, 37
Privacy, netiquette for, 39
Problem-centered approach, 161
Problem-solution design, **213**
Problem-solving group, **260**
Procedural conflict, **268**
Procedural norm, **257**
Procrastination, combating, 247
Produce or perish style, 165
Professor
    cultural guidelines for addressing, 159
    mentor-professor characteristics, 148
    relationship with, 141–142
Promise, keeping, 31
Pronunciation, **236**, 237t
Proposition of fact, **197**
Proposition of policy, **198**
Proposition of value, **198**
Proxemics, 109, **116**
Pseudo-conflict, **163**, 267
Pseudolistening, **74**
Psychological rules, 129
Public Conversations Project, 146
Public Dialogue Consortium, 146
Publicity
    concept of, 35
    public speaking for, 174
Public space, **117**

Public speaking
    audience analysis and, 186
    college and, 198–199, 249
    community and, 175–176
    dialects and accents, 237
    for differing contexts, 249
    for general purposes, 180
    model for speech preparation, *178*
    multiple intelligence theory, 188–189
    practice for effectiveness, 245
    preparation for, 244
    process of, 178–180
    proper breathing for, 233–235
    software for, 225
    for specific purposes, 181–182
    studying, 173–175
    in workplace, 250
Purge list, 13
Purpose
    model for speech preparation, 179
Purpose, of speech, *178*

R
Racism, 94
Rate, **235–236**
Rationalization
    collective, 273
    for communication apprehension, 177
Reasoning, evaluative listening and, 79
Recall/cue system of note-taking, 75, 76
Receiver
    as component of communication, **9–10**, 15, 16t
    critical analysis of, 319
    of mass communication, 321
Receiver apprehension, **73**
Reception, monitoring, 76
Reciprocal relationship, **50**
Referent, 8
Reflected appraisal, **53**
Reflective-thinking approach, 270–271
Refutative design, **214**
Regulation, mass communication, 310
Reification, 89
Reinforce, speech to, **197**
Rejection message, **138**
Relational communication, 13, **19–20**
Relational dialectics, *137*, 137–139
Relational listening, 75, 77
Relationship
    attraction in, 129
    conflict in, 163–164, 169
    developing online, 135
    dialectics, *137*, 137–139
    dissolution, stages of, 139–140
    dissolution model, *134*, 140–141
    forgiveness in, 33
    gender and culture in, 144–145
    honesty in, 143
    "I" messages
    impersonal vs. interpersonal, 128
    importance of communication, 6
    intercultural romantic, 145
    within organizations, 293
    with professors, 141–142
    reality of, 155
    spiritual child, 136–137
    stages of development, *134*, 134–136
    types of, 138
Relativism, 30

Relaxation, for communication apprehension, 177
Religious background, 28
Remembering stage, 68, *68*
Reno v. ACLU, 100
Research
    model for speech preparation, *178*, *179*
    for speech preparation, 215–216
Resident advisor (RA), 104
Resident director (RD), 104
Resolution, styles of, 269–270
Respect, mindfulness, 121–122
"Respect for the word", 26
Responding
    silence as, 66–67
    as stage in listening, 68, *68*
Resume, **296**
Rhetorical sensitivity, 77–78
    in college, **167–168**
    employing, **102**
Rhetorical Sensitivity Scale (RHETSEN), 78
Rigidity, **139**
Rite, **282**
Ritual
    of organization, **282**
    role in building community, 123–124
Role, organizational, 283
Romance
    intercultural, 145
    within organizations, 293
    truthfulness and, 33
Rule
    consistently applying, 36
    of organization, **283**

S
Safety needs, **131**, *131*
Salesperson, types of, 51–52
Sapir, Edward, 92
Sapir-Whorf hypothesis, **92**
Schroeder, Dr. Charles, 249
Schutz's theory of interpersonal needs, 133
Scripts, **46**
Secret, keeping, 31
Security needs, **131**, *131*
Selecting stage, 68, *68*
Selection, **44**
Selective listening, **74**
Selectivity, 47–48
Self-actualization, *131*, **133**
Self-care, 131
Self-censorship, **273**
Self-concept, **50**, 53, 135–136
Self-determination, 32
Self-disclosure, **54**, 156
Self-discovery, 48
Self-efficacy, **53**
Self-enhancement, 55
Self-esteem, **50–51**
    anxiety and, 135–136
    increasing, 53
    needs for, *131*, **132**
Self-expression, 144
Self-fulfilling prophecy, 51
Self-image, 117
Self-perception
    academic success and, 60
    body image, 53
    communication and, 50–51
    development of, 53
Self-presentation, 121

Self-respect, 51
Self-talk, 53–54
Sender, 9–10, 15, 16t
Sensory information, 45
Sentence structure, 89
Separation stage, 3
September 11, 286, 313
Service learning, 4–5, 275
Seven Habits of Highly Effective People, 255
Sex
    of audience for speech, 184
    gender and, 96
Sexism, **96**
Sexual harassment, 95, 294
Shea, Virginia, 38
Shockley-Zalabak, Pamela, 280
Significant choice, 30t, **32**
Sign language, 108t
Silence
    consequences of, 34
    as implicit consent, 319
    language conquering, 91
    as responding, 66–67
Simple conflict, 267
Simplicity, 206
Situational factor, **263**
Situational perspective, **189**
Skills, for employment, 220
Small group, **254**
Smile, communicating feelings with, 9
Social anxiety, **135–136**
Social comparison, **53**, **136**
Social construction theory, **313**
Social dimension, **258**, 266
Social group, **260**
Social institution, 35
Social justice, 35
Social norm, **257**
Social penetration model, 54
Social phase, **141**
Social responsibility, 291–292
Social role, **261**
Social space, 109, **117**, 268
Sociological rules, 128
Software, for speakers, 225
Sound bite, 70–71, 318
Source, citing, 221
Source, evaluative listening and, 79
Southern Poverty Law Center, 162
Space
    cultural differences in groups, 268
    cultures and communication, 109
    Hall zones of, 117
Spatial design, **212**
Spatial zone, 117
Speaking skills
    importance for employment, 6
    in public life, 7
Special occasion speech, 180
Specific purpose
    descriptors for statements of, 182t
    relating topic to, 192
    of speech, **181**
Speech
    analyzing audience, 184t
    attention-getting devices, 207t
    audience perspective, 183–184
    avoiding bias, 186
    burden of, 180
    college and, 198–199

concept map, *226*
conclusion of, 211–212
delivery methods, 231–233
dialects and accents, 237
for differing contexts, 249
hate and indecent, 100
introduction, 207–208
main points of, 208–209
organization of, 204–205, 212–214
perception based on, 70
practice for effectiveness, 245
preparation for, 173–175, *178*, 244
proper breathing for, 233–235
to the public, 251
reading word-for-word, 232
relating topic to purpose, 192
selecting a topic for, 191–192
service learning, 5
software for, 225
subject of, 182
transitions in, 210, 210t, 211t
types of, 180
using voice effectively, 233
in workplace, 250
See also Outline; Visual aids
Speech of definition, **196**
Speech of demonstration, **196**
Speech of description, **196**
Speech of explanation, **193**
Speech of tribute, **193**
Speech to actuate, **197**
Speech to convince, **197**
Speech to entertain and inspire, **193**
Speech to reinforce or stimulate, **197**
Spiritual child, 136–137
Stage hogging, 74–75
Stagnating stage, **140**
Standard, consistently applying, 36
State-the-case-and-prove-it design, **214**
Statistics, **218**
Stereotyping, 47, **94**
  audience analysis and, 186
  communication behavior of others, 121–122
  culture and, 313
  "out group" members, 273
  power of, 95
Stewart, John, 88, 136
Stimulate, speech to, **197**
Stimuli
  awareness of, 44
  organization of, 45
Storming stage, **264**
Story, **282**
Structure, organizational, 283
Structured, 89
Student-learner
  communication and, 2, 4, 6
  quitting college, 3
Student-learning approach, 161
Study circle, 146
Studying, 12–13
Styles approach, **263**
Subject, **182**
  brainstorming for speech, 182–183
  model for speech preparation, 179
  perspectives for considering, 183, 183t, 190–191
  relating topic to purpose, 192
  selecting a topic, 191–192
  See also Audience analysis

Subjective motivator, 293–294
Superior-subordinate communication, 287–288
Support group, online, 260
Supporting materials
  evaluation of, 216
  finding, 214–215
  types of, 216–219
  using effectively, 219–220
Supportive climate, **138**, **266**
Supportive relational atmosphere, **138**
Symbol
  creating messages using, 16t
  cultural, 283
  meanings of, 9
  vocal and nonvocal, 108, 108t
Symbolic, **88**
  communication as, 9
  gender impacting listening, 8
Symbolism, 88–89
Symmetrical relationship, **138**
Synergy, **285**
Syntax, 89
System, 284, 287

T

Table, **239**
Tactile communication, 119–120
Talking 9-5, 118
Tannen, Deborah
  communication between men and women, 265
  gendered language, 96
  gender impacting listening, 73
  Talking 9-5, 118
Task dimension, **258**
Task norm, **257**
Task role, **261**
Teaching Tolerance, 162–163
Team style, 165
Technology
  in 21st century, 308
  in college, 301
  human touch, loss of, 10
  job hunting and, 311
  in organizations, 295
  requirements for, 306–307
  web-based, web-enhanced, face-to-face courses, 320–321
Telecommunication, 280
Telegraph, 10
Telephone, 10
Television, 313
Terminating stage, **140**
Territoriality, **116**, 119
Testimony, **218**
Text chart, **239**
Therapy group, 259–**260**
Thesis, *178*
  model for speech preparation, 179
Thesis statement, 192–193
Thinking, divergent, 271
Thomas, W. I., 51
Thoughtlessness, 121–122
Throughput, **285**
Time
  formal and informal, **118**
  as nonverbal communication channel, 117
Time continuum, 120
Time management, 247

Time orientation, 117–118
Tinto, Dr. Vincent, 3
Tolerance, **39**
Tone, of voice, 236
Topic
    model for speech preparation, *178*, 179
    relating to purpose, 192
    selection of, **191**–192
Topical design, **213**
Touch (haptics)
    gendered, 119–120
    human, loss of, 10
    as method of communication, 115
Trait approach, **262**
Transactional model, *16*, **17**
Transition
    in speech, 210, 210t
    stages of, 3–4
    types of, 211t
Transmission model, **16**, *16*
Tree outline, *226*, 227
Tribal language, 108t
Tribute, speech of, **193**
Trigger word, **72**
Trust, in friendship
    in friendship, 156–157
Truth, 26
Truthfulness
    as ethical principle, **30**–32, 30t
    romance and, 33
Tuning in, 66–67
Turn-taking, 17, 71

U
Unanimity, illusion of, 273
Uncertainty reduction theory (URT), 284
Understanding
    relational listening and, 77
    as reward of listening, 80
    as stage in listening, 68, *68*
Unintentional communication, **19**
University. *See* College
University system, 285
Unsupportive audience, *189*, 189–190
Uses and gratification theory, **314**
Utilitarian, 35
Utterance, vocal, 8

V
Validation, interpersonal, **84**
Value, of human beings, 34, 39
Values
    audience analysis and, **186**–187
    of generations, 199t
    in group, 264–265
    language and, 99
    understanding different, 28
Value system, **265**
Veracity, principle of, **35**
Verbal communication
    in groups, 267–268
    nonverbal communication modifying, 110
    nonverbal communication versus, 108, 108t
Verbal intelligence, 188
Verbal symbol, 108
Video conferencing, 10
Violence, mediated, 316–317
Visual aid
    guidelines for using, 241–242

    integrating with delivery, 242
    model for speech preparation, *178*, 179
    types of, 239–241
Visual intelligence, 188
Visualization, for communication apprehension, 177
Vocalics, 8, **115**
Vocal inflection, **236**
Vocalization, 115
Vocal message, 108, 108t
Vocal utterance, 8
Volume, **235**

W
Watchdog, 309, 310
Web-based course, 320–321
Web-enhanced course, 320–321
Website
    accessing information and messages, 311–312
    communicating social responsibility, 291–292
    news media and, 318
Western culture, 109–110
Western media, 312, 313–314
What, 15, 16t
When, 15, 16t
Where, 15, 16t
Who, 15, 16t
Wholeness, of system, **285**
Whorf, Benjamin Lee, 92
Why, 15, 16t
Willingness to communicate (WTC), 14–15
Women
    communication between, 114
    communication skills, 265
    fashion and, 119
    gendered language and, 96
    income potential, 3
    nonverbal communication behavior, 118
Wood, Julia, 313
Words
    bypassing, 89
    language and, 88
    mispronunciation of, 236, 237t
    pronunciation of, 236
    trigger, **72**
    understanding meaning of, 90
Word symbol, 108t
Work life, 283
Workplace
    feedback and interpersonal communication in, 150
    gender and nonverbal communication in, 118–119
    groups in, 274–275
    honesty in, 31
    listening, importance of, 69
    motivators in, 293–294
    perception and, 60
    reducing conflicts, 164–165
    sexual harassment, 294
    speaking skills, 250
    stereotyping in, 47
    See also Employment
Writing skills, 6

Y
You Just Don't Understand: Women and Men in Conversation, 73–74
Your College Experience: Strategies for Success, 76

Z
Zone of comfort, 117